What readers said about the *Shadowmagic* series:

'If Percy Jackson were to be hurled across dimensions into Middle Earth, you might hope to see a story like this one evolve'

MARK ROBSON

'I hate fantasy books and over the years have used all the magic at my disposal to avoid them (i.e. not buying them when I'm in a bookshop) but this has redressed the balance because it's very readable, absorbing and FUNNY'

JO BRAND

'Why can't all fantasy writers have John Lenahan's knack for story-telling and adventure?'

PODIOBOOKS.COM

'I would only have expected the best from the man who did the voice of the toaster in *Red Dwarf* and he does not disappoint'

JENNIFER LAW

'Lord of the Rings in miniature, couldn't put the book down'

CHRIS STEER-KEMP

'This book has everything, tension, suspense, magical creatures, tele-pathic trees, love and a very strong storyline'

MR N BARDELL

'As a long time fantasy fan, it's a pleasure to discover a new author. Conor, the hero of the story, is a breath of fresh air – a modern teen-ager dealing with ancient Gaelic customs and behaviour. The support-ing cast are well crafted and the writing sharp and witty'

JULES

'Lures you into reading the next chapter, and the next one, and so on until, breathless, you have reached the final page, and you have a very readable, very enjoyable and very magical tale indeed'

PHANTOM ZONE

'Once I picked this up, I just couldn't put it down again and finished it in one afternoon. It is a fast paced, well characterised, hugely enjoyable read. *Shadowmagic* is very funny but the dry, tongue-in-cheek humour doesn't undermine the rest of the story. Though I sniggered all the way through the book, I did cry not long before the end'   Y MARTIN

'*Shadowmagic* has you gripped from the first page. John's wild imagination and powerful story line, threaded through with the sort of humour that makes him such a wonderful comedian, makes for a great book. I bought 6 and all who read it (aged from 10–55) were hooked'   YVONNE

'Fun and action-packed, it takes the "fish out of water" fantasy trope and turns it on its ear, giving us a protagonist that isn't an idiot and knows full well he's out of his depth'   WWW.DUNGEONEERING.NET

'I've just finished this after reading it in one sitting – well I stopped to make tea. I downloaded it for my son initially, but really enjoyed it myself. Well written, funny but moving too'   GILLIAN

'I would recommend this book to everyone, it's a proper old fashioned fantasy for both kids and adults to enjoy'   SARAH LINEHAN

'Completely, refreshingly, original. John Lenahan brought this amazing world to life; every molecule of it was filled with amazing vitality. I want to visit it over and over again. Loved it'

NUR KHADIJAH AHMAD

'A novel with hints of modern-day-meets-Middle-Earth gives a very satisfying read. An excellent baddie, who would do just about anything, and a cast of characters with secrets and loyalties that can shock and surprise. Lots of Machiavellian plotting and a hero with a modern sense of humour give this tale an engaging up to date feel. The story left me wanting more'   P BAILEY

'An amazing fantasy story for 12–120-year-olds to enjoy'   NATASHA

THE
SHADOWMAGIC
TRILOGY

Shadowmagic

Prince of Hazel and Oak

Sons of Macha

THE
SHADOWMAGIC
TRILOGY

JOHN LENAHAN

The Friday Project
An imprint of HarperCollins*Publishers*
77–85 Fulham Palace Road,
Hammersmith, London W6 8JB
www.harpercollins.co.uk

This collected edition first published in
Great Britain by The Friday Project in 2014

SHADOWMAGIC first published in 2008
PRINCE OF HAZEL AND OAK first published in 2011
SONS OF MACHA first published in 2013

Copyright © John Lenahan 2014

1

John Lenahan asserts the moral right to be
identified as the author of this work

A catalogue record for this book is
available from the British Library

ISBN: 978-0-00-756990-8

Printed and bound in Great Britain by
Clays Ltd, St Ives plc

MIX
Paper from
responsible sources
FSC
www.fsc.org
FSC® C007454

FSC™ is a non-profit international organisation established to promote
the responsible management of the world's forests. Products carrying the
FSC label are independently certified to assure consumers that they come
from forests that are managed to meet the social, economic and
ecological needs of present and future generations,
and other controlled sources.

Find out more about HarperCollins and the environment at
www.harpercollins.co.uk/green

CONTENTS

SHADOWMAGIC

For Finbar, of whom I am exceptionally proud

ONE

AUNT NIEVE

'How come you never told me I had an aunt?' That was the first thing I said. I know, my first question should have been, 'Are you alright, Dad?' He didn't look alright. The light was awful, but I could see blood on the side of his face. I'm amazed I didn't say, '*What* is that smell?' because it sure stank in there. I'm not talking about a whiffy locker room smell, but the kind of stench that can make it possible to see your breakfast a second time around. Or most obviously I guess I should have asked, 'Where are we?' or, 'Why are we chained to a wall?' But instead, the first question I asked when I regained consciousness was about genealogy.

'Well, Conor,' Dad croaked, not even looking at me, 'the first time you met her, she tried to kill you.'

She had, too.

I was sitting in the living room watching crappy morning television. I was dressed, shaved and ready to go. You had to be with my father. It wasn't unusual for me to run out of the house two minutes behind him and find that he had left without me.

'Are you ready?' he called from the bedroom – in almost Modern Greek.

That was a good sign. It was a simple matter to gauge my father's moods – the older the language, the worse his frame of mind. Greek wasn't too bad. I shouted back, in the same language, 'Born ready!' I had learned a long time ago that I had to speak in *the language of the day*, or else he would ignore me completely.

He came out of his bedroom in a white shirt with a tie hanging around his neck. 'Could you do this for me?'

'Sure,' I said.

Tie tying was one of the very few things that Pop found impossible to do with just one hand. Most of the time I didn't think of Dad as having a handicap at all – I know a lot of two-handed men much less dexterous than him, and anyway, I was happy to do him a favour. I was just about to hit him up for a bit of cash, so that tonight I could take Sally to a nice restaurant, as opposed to the usual crummy pizza joint.

'What's with the tie?' I asked.

'The dean wants me to smarten up a bit. There is some *famous* ancient languages professor visiting who wants to talk about my theories of pronunciation. As if I don't have anything better to do than babysit some idiot.'

That question was a mistake on my part. He said that last sentence in Ancient Gaelic. That was the language he used when he was annoyed or really meant business – it was almost as if it was his mother tongue. I'm not talking about Gaelic, the language of the Irish, I'm talking about Ancient Gaelic, a language found only on crumbling parchments and in my house.

'Aw c'mon, Pop,' I said as chirpily as I could, 'maybe this professor is a beautiful *she* idiot, and I can finally have a mom.'

He gave me a dirty look, but not one of his more serious ones, and tucked the bottom of his tie into his shirt.

I plopped myself down on the sofa. I could hear Dad humming some prehistoric Celtic ditty as he brushed his teeth in the bathroom. A fight broke out on the television show I was half-heartedly watching: two women were pulling each other's hair and the studio audience was chanting the presenter's name.

'Turn that damn television off,' he shouted, 'or I'll put a crossbow bolt through it!'

I quickly switched off the TV – coming from Dad this was not an idle threat. He owned a crossbow – as well as a quarterstaff, a mace and all sorts of archaic weaponry. If it was old, he had it. Hell, he even made me practise sword fighting with him every week before he gave me my spending money.

This gives you an idea of what life was like with my father – the mad, one-handed, ancient languages professor Olson O'Neil. People said that he lived in the past, but it was worse than that – it was like he was *from* the past. It was cool when I was a kid, but now that I was older, I increasingly thought it was weird – sad, even.

That Dad embarrassed me from time to time wasn't really the problem. Now that I was starting to get a few whiskers on my chin, what really got me down was that he seemed disappointed in me all of the time and I couldn't figure out why. I was doing well at high school. In a week I would graduate, OK, not at the top of my class, but pretty up there. I had never really been in trouble. My girlfriend didn't have pink hair and studs through her nose, or eyebrows, or even her bellybutton. Dad liked Sally. It seemed as if he wanted me to be something – but he wouldn't, or couldn't, tell me what.

A knock came on the front door that was so loud, it made me jump to my feet. Now, weird is what my life is these days, but here is where all the weirdness began.

We live in a converted barn outside of town with a regular-sized front door that is cut into two huge barn doors. When my father answers a knock, he always peers through a tiny hatch to check who's out there. I, on the other hand, like to undo the bolts and throw open the two big doors. It shocks visitors and it has the added effect of annoying Dad. I don't do that any more.

I dramatically swung open the two doors and found myself face to face with two of the biggest, sweatiest horses I had ever seen. Riding them was a man in full King Arthur-type armour and a woman in a hooded cloak. With hindsight I wish I had said something clever like, 'The stables are around the back,' but to be honest, I was too gobsmacked to speak.

When the woman pulled back her hood, she took my breath away. She was astonishingly beautiful, with a wild mane of amber hair. She seemed to be about five or ten years older than me – twenty-five, twenty-seven maybe, except something about her made her seem older than that.

'Is this the home of Oisin?' she asked.

'There is an Olson here, Olson O'Neil,' I stammered.

She considered this for a second and took a step into the room – or, I should say, her horse did. I had to back away to stop from being trampled.

'Who are you?' I demanded.

She looked around the room and her eyes stopped on an oak fighting stick that was mounted on the wall. A look of satisfaction crossed her face. 'I am his sister,' she said.

I started to say, 'Yeah, right,' and then two things struck me. One was that she was speaking in Ancient Gaelic – I was so stunned by the appearance of those two that I hadn't noticed it before. The second was her eyes – she had Dad's eyes, and nobody had dark peepers like my father.

'Dad!' I called out. 'There's a woman out here who says she's your sister.'

That is when all hell broke loose. Dad came charging out of the bathroom screaming at the top of his lungs, with toothpaste foaming out of his mouth like a rabid animal. He grabbed the war axe off the mantel, which I always assumed was there just for decoration, and hurled it at his sister. She pulled her head back just in time to avoid getting a quick nose job, but her companion wasn't so lucky. The flat side of the axe hit him square on the shoulder and knocked him from his saddle. The rider desperately tried to stay on his mount. The horse made a horrible sound as he pulled a handful of hair out of its mane, but it was no good. He hit the ground with a crash of metal and then, as if being attacked in my living room by equestrians wasn't surprise enough – he disappeared – he just vanished! One second I was watching the Tin Man falling through the air, arms and legs flailing in all directions, and the next second he was gone – poof! In the space where he should have been, was a pile of rusted metal in a swirl of dust.

Dad shouted, 'Conor, watch out!' I looked up just in time to see a spear leaving my aunt's hand – and it was heading directly for my chest.

Then everything seemed to go into slow motion. I remember looking into my aunt's eyes and seeing what almost looked like pain in them, and I remember turning to my father and seeing the utter defeat on his face. But what I remember the most was the amazing tingling sensation that I felt all over my body. An amber glow seemed to cloud my vision, then I noticed the glow cover me from head to toe and then encircle the spear, just as it made contact with my chest. The spear hit me, I fell over from the force of it, but it didn't hurt. For a second I thought, *That's what it must be like when you receive a mortal wound – no pain.* Then I saw the spear lying next to me. I felt my chest and I was fine.

Dad sat me up. 'Are you OK?' he asked.

I wish I had a picture of my face at that point – I could feel the stupid grin I had pasted on it. A horn blew – Dad and I looked up in time to see my would-be assassin galloping away from the door.

'Can you stand?' Dad asked.

I remember answering him by saying, 'That was very strange.' I was kind of out of it.

'Conor,' he said, helping me to my feet, 'we have to get out of here.'

But it was too late. Two more riders, this time in black armour and on black horses, burst into the room. Tables and chairs went flying in all directions. Dad grabbed my hand and we tried to run out the back, but before we could take more than a couple of steps I saw, and heard, a black leather whip wrap around my father's neck. I tried to shout but my voice was strangled by the searing pain of another whip wrapping around my own throat.

The next thing I remembered, I was chained to a dungeon wall talking to my father about the family tree.

'What's her name?'

'Nieve,' Dad said, without looking at me.

I was about to ask, 'Why does she want to kill us?' when I felt something crawl across my ankle. It was a rat – no, I take that back – it was the mother of all rats. I'd seen smaller dogs. I screamed and tried to kick it away. It moved just out of reach and stared at me like it owned the place. Just what I needed, a super-rat with an attitude.

'Where the hell are we?' I yelled.

'We are in The Land,' Dad said in a faraway voice.

'The Land? What land?'

'The Land, Conor – Tir na Nog.'

'Tir na Nog? What,' I said sarcastically, 'the place full of Pixies and Leprechauns?'

'There are no Pixies here, but yes.'

'Dad. Quit messing around. What is going on?'

He turned and looked me straight in the eyes, and then with his *I'm only going to tell you this once* voice he said, 'We are in The Land. The place that the ancient Celts called Tir na Nog – The Land of Eternal Youth. I was born here.'

I began to get angry. I was in pain, we were definitely in trouble, and Dad was treating me like a kid, making up some cock-and-bull story to keep me happy. I was just about to tell him what I thought of him, but then I thought about the guy who fell off his horse. 'Did you see that guy disappear?'

'He didn't disappear,' Dad said, and I could tell he was struggling to make this so I could understand. 'He just grew old – quickly.'

'Come again?'

'When someone from The Land steps foot in the Real World, they instantly become the age that they would be there. That soldier was probably a couple of thousand years old.'

'What!'

'He was an immortal. Everyone from The Land is an immortal.'

I looked deep into his eyes, waiting for the twinkle that lets me know he's messing with me. When it didn't come, I felt my chest tighten.

'My God, you're not screwing around, are you?'

He shook his head – a slow no.

'So what,' I said half jokingly, 'like, you're an immortal?'

'No,' he said, turning away, 'I gave that up when I came to the Real World.'

I shook my head to clear the cobwebs, which was a mistake, because I almost passed out with the pain. When my vision cleared, Dad was staring at me with a look of total sincerity.

'So you *used* to be an immortal?' I asked.

'Yes.'

At that point I should have come to the obvious conclusion that this was all just a dream, except for the fact that dreaming isn't something I had ever done. Famously, among my friends and classmates at least, I had never had a dream. I had an idea what they were like from TV shows and movies but it was not something I had ever experienced. People always said, 'Oh, you must dream, you just don't remember it,' but I don't think so. When I put my head down, I wake up in the same place and I don't go anywhere in-between. And anyway, I knew this was real – there was something in the air, other than the stench, that felt more real than anything I had ever known.

I was silent for a long while and then I asked, 'Do I have any other relatives I should know about?'

The answer came, not from my father, but from a shadowy figure standing in the doorway on the far side of the room.

'You have an uncle,' he said.

TWO

UNCLE CIALTIE

The instant he emerged from the shadows, I knew he was my uncle alright. He looked like an old high-school photo of my father, before the grey hair and the extra twenty pounds. He had that *evil twin* appearance about him, like one of those crappy TV movies where the same actor plays the part of the nice *and* the wicked brother. He even had the black goatee and a sinister sneer.

Don't get the impression that this was a comical moment. Even chained against a wall, I tried to take an involuntary step back – this guy was scary. But the person who scared me the most at that moment wasn't my uncle, it was my father.

'Cialtie,' he said, with more malice than I had ever heard from anybody – let alone Dad.

'Brother Oisin,' Cialtie dripped, 'you look, what is that word? Oh yes – old.'

'Where is Finn?'

'You mean our father? I thought he was with you. Last time I saw him he was riding into the Real World looking for you. His horse didn't look very healthy though.'

'You murdered him.'

'Oh no,' Cialtie replied with false innocence, 'I wouldn't hurt Father. I merely stabbed the horse,' and then he smiled. It was my first experience of Uncle Cialtie's smile, and it made my stomach churn.

'I'll kill you,' Dad hissed.

'No, I think you will find that that is what I am going to do to you. But first I am going to kill your boy here, and you know the best part? After that I'll be considered a hero – a saviour even.'

'Why would killing me make him a saviour?' I said, finding my voice.

Cialtie addressed me directly, for the first time, instantly making me wish I hadn't asked the question. 'Hasn't Daddy told you anything?' Cialtie scolded. 'Tsk, tsk, Oisin, you really have neglected his education. Haven't you told him of the prophecy?'

'What prophecy?'

'I didn't think this would ever happen,' Dad said without looking at me. 'We were never supposed to come back.'

'What prophecy?'

'You are *the son of the one-handed prince*,' quoted Cialtie, 'a very dangerous young man. It's true, it was foreseen by a very gifted oracle.'

'Who,' my father said, 'you murdered.'

'Water under the bridge, Oisin. You really must learn to let bygones be bygones. You see, your daddy here carelessly lost his hand – which I still have upstairs, you know, it's one of my favourite possessions – so that meant that having a baby was a no-no, but as always Oisin thought he knew best and it looks like it's going to take his big brother to sort things out.'

'You are using my hand,' Dad hissed, 'to keep the throne.'

'Oh yes,' replied Cialtie, 'I find it works just as well in the Chamber of Runes without the rest of you. Better, in fact – because your mouth isn't attached to it. That Shadowwitch you used to run around with did a really good job of preserving it.'

I could see the blood vessels in Dad's temple stand out as he strained against his chains. My temples must have been throbbing too. I didn't have a clue what was going on. Some oracle predicted that I had to die? Cialtie was using Dad's hand? And what throne?

'I would love to stand here and reminisce all day,' said Cialtie, 'but I have a nephew to kill. Now, your father's runehand has come in so useful these last few years, I thought I might as well have yours too. The start of a collection, maybe?' He reached into his cloak and took out an ornate golden box. Inside was an imprint of a hand.

'I'm going to cut off your hand,' Cialtie continued, 'preserve it with proper magic, not that Shadowmagic stuff she used on your dad's mitt, and then you bleed to death and die. Your dad gets to watch and everybody is happy.'

I used to think that anger was a bad thing, but now I realise that in times of extreme stress and fear, anger can be the emotion that focuses your mind and gets you through. Did I hate my uncle? You bet. And the idea of killing him was the only thing that kept me from whimpering like a damp puppy. I held on to that thought as he came at me.

Cialtie paused. 'You know, I just had a thought. Is it not ironic that the day you become an immortal is the day you die?'

'If I'm an immortal, how are you going to kill me?'

Cialtie laughed, a sickening laugh that deliberately went on too long. 'Oh my. I never thought I would see the day when I would meet a son of Duir who was so thick. Immortality, my boy, may save you from illness and getting old, but it won't save you from this.' He drew his sword and swung at my wrist.

Then it happened again. The world seemed to slow down and a golden – no – an *amber* glow encircled Cialtie's sword and me. I felt the pressure of the blade on my wrist but it didn't hurt, and more importantly, it didn't cut. Cialtie flew into a rage – he began hacking and stabbing at me. I didn't even try to dodge it – the amber glow seemed to protect me. Finally he threw the sword across the room in a rage.

'This is Shadowmagic,' he hissed. 'That witch's doing, I'll wager. Well, I have a sorceress of my own.' He turned to leave – then looked back. 'You have a reprieve, nephew. I suggest that you and Daddy say your goodbyes. Just don't take too long,' and then he was gone, leaving me shaking, half from fear and half from anger.

'I'm sorry, Conor,' Dad finally said.

'How come you never told me?'

Dad laughed. 'What was I supposed to say? "*Son, you are old enough now for me to tell you that I am the heir to the throne of a magical kingdom ...*" You think I'm loony enough as it is. I can imagine what you would have said to that.'

'So, you're the heir to a throne?'

Dad thought for a second, and took a deep breath that looked like it hurt. 'My father – your grandfather – was the lord of this castle. His name was Finn and he held Duir – the Oak Rune. He was the king, if you like, of Tir na Nog.'

I was struggling to make sense of all of this. My head was spinning. 'You're a prince?'

'Yes.'

'The one-handed prince?'

He nodded.

'So why did Cialtie say I was dangerous?'

'Ona,' Dad said, 'made a prediction.'

'Who is this Ona?'

'She was my father's Runecaster.' When I looked puzzled he said, 'Like a fortune teller.'

'And what did she say exactly?' I could tell that the question pained him but I was angry. Some old bat throwing stones around was causing me a lot of trouble.

'She said, "*The son of the one-handed prince must die, lest he be the ruin of Tir na Nog.*"'

'That's ridiculous! You don't believe this crap, do you?'

Dad lowered his head, and when he spoke I could hardly hear him. 'Ona was never wrong.'

'So let me get this straight. You lose your hand in a gardening accident and then everybody wants me dead!' As soon as I said it I realised how ridiculous it sounded. 'You didn't lose your hand in a lawnmower, did you?'

'No.'

'Are you going to tell me about it?'

'That is a long story,' I heard a woman's voice say. It sounded as if it was coming from inside the wall to my right. 'And if you want to get out of here,' she said as she appeared right before my eyes, 'we will have to save it for later.'

You could have knocked me down with a feather. If I thought my aunt was stunning, this was the most beautiful woman I had ever seen. Dark, tall, with a straight black ponytail plaited to her waist and wearing – check this out – animal skins. She seemed to just step through the wall.

She worked fast. She placed what looked like honey in the locks that shackled our wrists and Dad's neck. Then she dropped to one knee, lowered her head, mumbled something and the irons fell away. I can't tell you how good it felt. If you have ever taken off a thirty-pound backpack after a twenty-mile hike, you have the beginnings of an idea. Dad and I stood up.

'Quickly!' she said, and walked straight through the wall.

Before Dad could follow I put my hand on his shoulder. 'Who's the babe in the skins?'

'That's no way to talk about your mother,' he said, and followed her through the wall.

THREE
MOM

I stood there as if rooted to the spot. *I don't have a mother. My mother is dead. My father told me so.* Emotions swirled around me like a leafy breeze. I was five years old. I remembered the pain in my chest, the taste of my tears. I remembered the look on my father's face as I stared up to him from my bed.

'Is Mom in heaven?' I sobbed.

'I'm not sure I believe in heaven,' a younger version of Dad replied. 'The ancient Celts believed in a place called Tir na Nog, where people never grow old. I think that's where your mother is.' He held me until the tears slowed and my sobs were replaced by sleep. Was this the only time my father had ever told me the truth?

'Conor?'

I looked up and saw her standing there. 'Are you my mother?' I said in a voice I hadn't used in fifteen years.

'Yes,' she said, and I knew it was true. I looked into that feminine mirror of my own face, complete with the tears, and I could hardly stand it. I know it contravened all eighteen-year-old cool behaviour but I couldn't help myself. I threw my arms around her.

She held me tight and stroked the back of my head.

'Conor, oh my Conor,' she said.

I could have stayed in those arms for days, for months, for the rest of my life. She gently pushed me back by the shoulders, and in a motherly voice I so long had yearned for, said, 'Conor?' When I didn't reply I heard the other motherly voice, the one that says, *I'm your mother and you had better listen to me or else*. She shook me and said again, 'Conor!'

That got my attention.

'We don't have time for this. We must leave here.'

Still in a daze, I wiped my eyes and nodded.

Mom gestured to our right. 'This way.'

That was when I heard *his* voice at the door.

'You!' shouted Cialtie.

That snapped me right out of it. I looked to the door and saw my uncle standing there with some tall, spindly, pale woman. She was dressed in hanging black lace with dark, dark eyes, black lips and a skunk-like streak in the front of her jet-black hair.

I lost it – I flipped out. 'Leave me alone!' I screamed so forcefully that spit flew out of my mouth. Neither of them was prepared for a fight. They expected to find us chained to the wall. I loved the look on Cialtie's face as he reached for his sword and realised that he had thrown it across the room after he had failed to cut off my hand. It was lying on the floor to my left. We both looked at it at the same time. Cialtie went for the sword, but I went for Cialtie. Some people would think I was brave, but bravery had nothing to do with it. I was plain loco. All of the day's craziness, the pain, the revelations, the emotions – I had just had enough! I hit Cialtie with a picture-perfect American football tackle. My shoulder caught him square in the solar plexus and smashed him into the wall. I actually heard all of the air fly out of his lungs and I knew he wasn't getting up in a hurry. Out of the corner of my eye I saw the goth woman smash into the wall with a shower of golden light from something my mother did. I reached down and picked up the sword. It was so much lighter than it looked. The pommel fitted in my hand as if it was made for me. I started to raise it, fully intending to bring it down on my uncle's head, when two guards ran into the room. As they reached for their weapons my mother grabbed me by the collar and threw me at the wall.

Passing through a wall is a scary thing. I instinctively threw my hands in front of me but they went right through. When my face reached the stones every cell in my body said, *This is going to hurt!* – and then pop – I was on the other side. Technically speaking I hadn't gone through a wall, I had gone through an illusion of a wall. The real wall was in front of me with a big hole chiselled in it. I could see daylight through the opening and Dad beckoning me through. My mother appeared next to me and lobbed an amber ball behind her. I heard screams of, 'My eyes!' and then I crawled through. Dad was on the other side standing next to three enormous horses but I hardly noticed him. My eyes were filled with my first look at Tir na Nog – The Land.

Imagine spending all of your life in a world of black and white and finally seeing in colour … No, that's not right. Imagine never being able to smell and then walking into a bakery, or being sealed in a bubble and feeling a touch of a hand for the first time. Even that doesn't explain it. Try to imagine that you have another sense, one that you feel in your soul. A sense that activates every nerve in your body. Imagine a view that makes you feel like you could live forever – and you can. That's what I was looking at now.

Ahead of me I looked down onto a vista of magnificent oak trees. Trees that if you hugged, might just hug you back. Trees that you could call family without irony. Trees that if you were to chop one down, it would mark you as a murderer to the end of your days. To the left, rolling fields started as foothills and culminated in blue, snow-capped mountains that seemed to touch the sky. To my right the trees changed to beech, but not the thin spindly trees I was used to; spectacular white-barked beeches with the girth and height of California redwoods. When I finally tore my eyes away, I saw that my father too was lost in that panorama, and his eyes were as wet as mine.

'Come on, boys,' my mother said as she came through the wall, 'tearful reunions and sightseeing will have to wait for later.'

'What about Cialtie?' I asked.

'He didn't seem to be breathing all that well,' she said with a smile. A smile of approval from my mother – I can't tell you how good that felt.

'Nice sword,' Dad said.

'Yeah, my Uncle Cialtie gave it to me.'

Dad smiled. 'I always liked that sword.'

'You recognise it?'

'I should,' he said, as he swung himself up onto a horse. 'It used to be mine.'

'Come, Conor,' my mother said as she jumped into a saddle, 'he will be back with reinforcements in a minute. Mount up.'

'I can't ride that thing!'

'Surely you know how to ride,' she said.

'Nope.'

She gave my father a stern look. 'You didn't teach him to ride? You, of all people, didn't teach your own son to ride?'

'I taught him to speak the tongue,' he explained, 'and I taught him swordplay.'

'But not ride,' she said, in a tone that made me realise she was not a woman to be trifled with. 'Typical.' She kicked her steed and galloped directly at me. Next thing I knew she grabbed me by the collar and hoisted me into the saddle in front of her.

'Hold on tight and be careful with that sword.'

She took two amber balls out of her pouch and hurled them over the top of the wall above us. 'Cover your eyes!' she said. Even at this distance and with my forearm over my eyes, I saw the flash and could imagine how painful it must have been up close. To the sound of more screams, we galloped off towards the beech forest.

Considering that this was my first getaway, I thought it went pretty smoothly. I got spooked by a couple of arrows that zinged past us, but by and large we just rode away. I sat in front of my mother as we galloped and imagined I was an infant and she was behind me in my pushchair.

'What is your name?' I asked.

'Deirdre,' she whispered.

We entered the beech forest. Every time I spoke she shushed me, like I was speaking in a library, but when the trees thinned out, Mom answered a couple of my questions. She told me that she had been planning this jailbreak for a long time. She and some people she called the Fili had been secretly tunnelling through that wall at night for weeks. Each morning she would cast some kind of magic to conceal it.

I asked her how she could have known that we were going to be there. In a conspiratorial tone of voice, she told me that she cast Shadowrunes. When I asked her why we were whispering she answered, 'Because beech trees are very indiscreet.'

Other than that we rode in silence for about an hour. The beeches gave way to flowering ash trees. Fine yellow flowers covered the ground and marked our hoof prints like snow.

Dad pulled up beside us. He looked very tired. 'Castle Nuin is near. Can we get sanctuary there?'

'I'm afraid when the lords find out about Conor,' Mom said, 'we won't have friends anywhere.'

Dad nodded in resignation.

'We don't have much further to ride. I have a boat up ahead. If we can make it to the Fililands we will be safe.'

We travelled for another fifteen minutes or so until we came to a river. Dad dismounted and splashed his face with the water. 'River Lugar,' he sighed, 'I thought I would never see you again.' He looked up at my mother. 'Nor did I think I would ever see you again, Deirdre.'

'Come, Oisin.' Her voice cracked a little as she spoke. 'We don't have time for this. The boat is just a little way downstream.'

The boat was a canvas-stretched canoe. Dad called it a carrack. It was hidden under some ash branches. Mom returned the branches to underneath a nearby tree, then placed her hand on the trunk and said, 'Thank you.' Maybe it was a trick of the light but I could have sworn the tree bowed to her – just a little.

The boat was lined with straw mats and was big enough for Dad and me to lie down next to each other. Mom sat in the back and told us to rest. We had drifted downstream for maybe thirty seconds before I was out cold.

Let me tell you, the dreams in Tir na Nog are worth the price of admission. Even though I had nothing to compare it with, I can't imagine that people in the Real World have dreams anything like I had in that boat.

I dreamt my father was teaching a lecture at the front of a classroom and I raised my hand in answer to a question. He drew a sword and sliced it off! My hand landed on my desk where it seemed to be encased in amber glass, like a huge paperweight. When I looked back, my father was now my uncle and he was laughing at me, saying, 'No glow now.'

The classroom became a room in a high tower; my mother and my aunt were clenched in a fight to the death. Mom's pouch was open and amber balls were falling to the floor in slow motion. Each time one hit the ground there was a blinding flash, and after each flash the scene in front of me changed. One moment the two women were fighting, the next, they were embracing, like two sisters sharing a secret. Fighting – embracing – fighting – embracing – the scene kept changing until the flashes came so frequently that I could see nothing but bright light.

The last image I saw before I awoke was Sally. She was waiting for me outside the cinema. She waited so long that her legs became tree roots and burrowed into the ground. Her arms turned to boughs and sprouted leaves. At the last second before she turned entirely into a tree, she saw me. She tried to say, 'Where are you?' but the wood engulfed her in mid-sentence.

I awoke from my first dream with such a jolt that I instantly stood up, which was a mistake. I was still in the boat. Even though it was beached, it tipped over. I fell smack down in the shoreline as the boat flipped over painfully on the back of my legs. I quickly struggled out from under it and desperately searched for Sally (or the tree that had become Sally) before I came to my senses. I collapsed on the ground and rubbed the back of my calves. *So that's what a dream is like.* I couldn't decide if I wanted to close my eyes and continue it, or never fall asleep again.

A tug on my collar made me realise that something was hanging around my neck. Attached to the end of a leather strap was a beautiful gold ornament. It was shaped like a tiny tornado with leaves spinning in it. As I marvelled at the intricacies of my new jewellery, the smell of food and a campfire hit me. My nose went up like a batter who had just hit a fly ball. It was a smell I was powerless not to follow.

At least this day was starting better than the previous one. Yesterday I awoke to the nightmare of finding myself chained to a wall by a lunatic uncle who was determined to give me a new nickname – *Lefty*. Today I walked into the dream-come-true of my father and my mother sitting around a campfire. They were holding hands (well, hand) and deep in conversation when I came around a huge weeping willow. They broke off when they saw me.

'Good morning,' my father said.

'Good morning,' I replied, not really looking at him. My eyes were glued to my mother. At a glance I would have thought she was my age until I looked into her eyes. I was starting to learn that here, in Tir na Nog, it wasn't grey hair or a wrinkled face that betrayed someone's age, like in the Real World – it was the eyes.

'Good morning,' I said.

She stood up. It was an awkward moment, like we were meeting for the first time. She was nervous.

'Good morning, Conor.'

I wrapped my arms around her. I had a lifetime of mothering to make up for. Her return hug told me she felt the same.

'I could get very used to this,' I said, trying unsuccessfully to stop the dam from breaking behind my eyes.

'And I too.' She wept.

Dad left us for a respectable amount of time before he interrupted. 'Cup of tea, Conor?'

I wiped my eyes and saw Dad grinning from ear to ear, holding a steaming cup in his hand. 'Thanks,' I said as I took a seat next to him. 'I think I just had a dream.'

'Yeah, me too. Intense, isn't it?' he said.

'Are all dreams like that?'

'I don't know. Like you, I never had a dream in the Real World. This being your first one, it must have … What's that phrase you use? *Freaked you out.*'

'Freaked you out?' Mom said.

'You'll get used to it,' Dad replied.

I have had a lot of breakfasts in my day, but let me tell you, if all breakfasts were like this, I would never sleep late again. The tea was made from willow bark. It didn't taste good as much as it felt good. Mom said that it would ease the strains and bruises of the previous day. It wasn't until the willow tea started to do its work that I realised just how much pain I had been in: my neck from the whip, my arms and wrists from being clapped in chains, my back from the horse ride and my head from – just plain shock. Blessed relief came as each part of my body stopped hurting, like the peace you get when a neighbour finally stops drilling on the adjacent wall.

'Found this around my neck,' I said.

Dad reached inside his shirt and produced an identical necklace. 'Me too. It's one of your mother's specialities. It's a *rothlú* amulet.'

'Thank you,' I said, 'it's beautiful.'

'It's not for show,' she replied, 'it's for protection.'

'I don't think I need any protection around here. Every time I get attacked, I seem to be surrounded by some gold force field.'

'You have been lucky,' she said. 'I placed that spell on you when you were born, but it only protects you from attacks from your relatives.'

'Like a spear from Aunt Nieve,' I said, 'or Uncle Cialtie's sword.'

'If Cialtie had gotten someone else to cut your hand off …' she said.

'Then Dad and I would be bookends.'

'Yes. Also,' she said, 'it only works for one battle with each relative.'

'So next time Aunt Nieve decides to make a Conor kebab – I'm on my own?'

'What's a kebab?' Mom asked.

'That's right,' Dad said, 'that's what the *rothlú* amulet is for.'

'What's it do?'

'It's only to be used in an emergency,' Mom said. 'All you have to do is place your hand over the amulet and say "*Rothlú*". Then you're somewhere else.'

'Like on the edge of a cliff,' Dad said, 'or a snake pit.'

'There are no snakes in The Land,' Mom retorted. 'Oisin here is not a fan of this spell.'

'It's dangerous, Conor, you can end up anywhere and it hurts like hell. Did she mention that?'

Mom nodded reluctantly. 'But it may save your life. Make sure you do not use it unless you really need it.'

'Is this that Shadowmagic I've been hearing about?'

They both seemed to jump a little bit when I mentioned Shadowmagic, like I'd blurted out the plans of a surprise party in front of the birthday girl.

'No,' Mom said. 'This uses gold. It's Truemagic.'

My fifty next questions were stopped dead by the next course. I had never had roast rabbit before but I can tell you right now, I'm never going to be able to watch a Bugs Bunny cartoon again without salivating. Breakfast finished with an apple each. I thought it was a bit of an anticlimax but Dad took his apple like it was a gift from God. He held it in his hand like a priest holding a chalice, and when he bit it, a moan escaped from his throat that was almost embarrassing. I looked at my apple anew. It looked ordinary enough but when I bit it – I'll be damned if the same moan didn't involuntarily pour out of me. What a piece of fruit! It hit you everywhere and all at once. This was real food, not the fake stuff that I had been wasting my time eating all my life. This is all I will ever need – this is the stuff that makes you live forever. This was forbidden fruit!

'Wow,' I garbled with my mouth full, 'I feel like Popeye after his first can of spinach.'

Dad thought that was funny. Mom looked confused.

'Come,' Mom said, 'we cannot stay here any longer – I would like to reach the Fililands before tomorrow night.'

Dad packed up the mugs and the water skin. Mom placed the bones and the apple cores on the burning wood and then placed her hands *in* the flames. The fire died down and then went out. The charred wood and earth seemed to melt into the ground until only a dark circle remained.

As he left, my father placed his hand on the trunk of the willow we were under and said, 'Thank you.' My mother did the same.

When I started to walk to the boat, my mother said, 'Are you not going to thank the tree for his shelter and wood?'

Feeling a bit stupid, I went up to the tree and placed my hands on its bark and said, 'Thank you.'

I swear the tree said, '*You are welcome.*' Not with words – it felt like it spoke directly into my head. I will never make fun of a tree-hugger again.

I got back to the boat to see Dad rooting through the supplies. He found a belt with a sword in a leather scabbard. Without any of the clumsiness that you would expect from a one-handed man, he withdrew the sword from its case and replaced it with the one I had taken from Cialtie.

'You're taking your sword back?'

'Actually, I think you should have it,' he said.

He handed me the belt and I buckled it on. He reached for the hilt and withdrew the sword, holding the perfectly mirrored blade between us. It made for a strange optical illusion. I saw one half of my own face reflected in the blade, while the other half of the face I saw was my father's weathered countenance.

'This is a weapon of old,' he said with gravity, 'it belonged to your grandfather Finn of Duir. It is the Sword of Duir. It was given to me and stolen by my brother. He was foolish to lose it.' He turned the sword horizontal, breaking the half-father, half-son illusion I had been staring into. 'I want you to have it.'

'Are you sure?' I said as I took the blade.

'Yes, I'm sure. To be honest, I would be glad not to have it hanging around my waist – reminding me.'

'Reminding you of what?'

'That's the sword that chopped my hand off.'

FOUR
THE YEWLANDS

I was so stunned I couldn't speak. Not until we were well under way and I had gotten the knack of paddling did I blurt out, 'You lost your hand in a sword fight?'

'I find it hard to believe,' Mother said, 'that you never told your son how you lost your hand.'

'Dad told me that he lost it in a lawnmower.'

'What is a lawnmower?' she asked.

'It's a machine that they use in the Real World to keep the grass short,' Dad said.

'What is wrong with sheep?'

Dad and I smiled.

'OK, Pop, tell how you lost your hand – the truth, this time.'

'I refuse to let you tell that story while we are in a boat,' Mom said, 'and we are approaching Ioho – we should not be talking in the Yewlands.'

'Why not?' I asked.

'Because it disturbs the trees and you do not want to disturb a yew tree.'

Under normal circumstances, I would have thought about calling a shrink and booking her into a rubber room, but I had just had a little chat with a tree myself. 'What could a yew tree do? Drop some leaves on us?'

She gave me a look that made me feel like a toddler who had just been caught with his hand in a cookie jar. It was going to take a while to get used to this mother and son stuff.

'Yew trees are old. The oldest trees in Tir na Nog. We of The Land think we are immortal, but to the yew we are but a spark. To answer your question, if you wake a yew, it will judge your worth. If it finds you lacking – you will die.'

'What will it do, step on me?' I said, and got that same icy stare as before.

'It will offer you its berries, which are poisonous,' she said, in a tone that warned me that her patience was thinning, 'and you will be power-less to resist.'

'I find that hard to believe.'

'Please, Conor,' she said, 'do not put it to the test today.'

I didn't have to ask if we were in the Yewlands, I knew it when we got there. Heck, I knew it *before* we got there. We rounded a bend in the river and ahead I saw two huge boulders on opposite sides of the bank. On top of them were the most awesome trees I had seen yet. They weren't as big as the oaks, but these were definitely the elders – the great-great-grandfathers of all of the trees and probably everything else in creation. The roots of the yews engulfed the rocks like arthritic hands clutching a ball. It seemed as if these two trees had just slithered up onto their perches to observe our approach. It made the hairs stand up on the back of my neck. Past the guard trees we entered a thick forest that stretched as far as the eye could see. A dense canopy turned the world into a dark green twilight, and there was no light at the end of *this* tunnel.

The first corpse was just inside the forest. Within ten minutes I must have seen fifteen of them. On both sides of the bank, human remains in various states of decay adorned the base of one tree or another. Some of them were clean, bone-white – others were still in their clothes. Many of them had quivers with arrows on their back. All of them were looking up, open-mouthed, as if to say, 'No!' or maybe, 'Thy will be done.'

Mom's warning about not speaking in the Yewlands proved to be unnecessary. I wasn't going to say a word. Never have I felt so humbled and insignificant as I did in the presence of those sleeping giants. I didn't want them to know I was there, and I definitely didn't want them to judge me. If they bid me to eat their berries, or throw myself off a cliff for that matter, I would do as they commanded, just to make them happy. Like a dog to a master – or a man to a god.

We spent most of that day silent, in an emerald dusk. It was slow going: each paddle was done with care so as to not make any splashing sounds. The frequency of the corpses diminished, but still from time to time a skyward-facing skull, encased in moss, would be just visible. As we came around a bend my mother's breath quickened. Ahead was a moss-covered altar surrounded by a semicircle of what must be the oldest of these primordial trees. The bases of the trees were littered with women's corpses. Each tree was surrounded with five or six sets of bones, some bleached white, some in white robes, a couple still with long, flowing hair, and all were in the same position. They were embracing a tree trunk, as if for dear life – which I suppose they were. I noticed that my mother didn't look.

When, in the distance, I saw a clear white light at the end of the forest, I let out a tiny yelp of joy that I instantly regretted. My parents shot me a disapproving look. Luckily the trees took no notice.

The fresh air and sunshine made me feel like I had been rescued from a premature grave. I waited until the Yewlands were out of sight before I dared to speak.

'Well, that was fun,' I said, trying to sound cooler than I felt. 'Who were all those dead people?'

'Archers mostly,' Dad replied.

'Why archers?'

'The best bows are made from yew; if you want to be a master archer, you have to ask a yew tree for wood.'

'And those were the guys that didn't make the grade?'

He nodded.

'Have you ever been judged by a yew?'

'Not me, I was never much of an archer. Good thing too – one-handed archers are traditionally not very good.'

'I have,' my mother said, in a faraway voice that sent a shiver down my spine. 'I have been judged by a yew. Next to giving up my son, it was the hardest thing I have ever done.'

I thought that maybe she wasn't going to say anything more – her face told me it was a memory that was painful to remember. I waited – she took a deep breath and went on. 'The place you saw with the altar is called the Sorceress' Glade. Like archers with their bows, a true sorceress must translate a spell onto a yew branch.'

'What, like a magic wand?'

'If you like.'

'And you were judged?'

In reply she reached into her pouch and produced a plain-looking stick, carved with linear symbols.

'What does it do?'

'It gives me power over the thorns,' she said.

'Huh?'

'You will understand when we reach the Fililands.'

We were floating by fragrant fields of heather, inhabited by sheep, rabbits and deer. I even saw a black bear fishing on a bank. It was like a 3-D Disney film. I almost expected the bear to wave.

'How did you become a sorceress?'

'Her father,' Dad said, 'wanted to make a superwoman.'

'My father wanted his daughter to be educated,' Mom corrected. 'He hired twelve tutors to teach me in the arts, philosophies, combat and magic. I loved all my tutors, almost as much as I loved my father for providing them for me. Of all my studies, it was at magic that I excelled. Against my father's wishes, I made the pilgrimage to the Sorceress' Glade with my tutor, my mentor, my friend.' Mom fell silent and sadness invaded her face.

'It was Nieve,' Dad said.

'Nieve? My Aunt Nieve? The one who tried to pierce my sternum with a javelin?'

'I am sure she took no joy from that task,' Mom said. 'Nieve has a very strong sense of duty.'

'Could you give her a call and maybe we could sit down and talk about this?'

'Nieve and I have not spoken to one another for a long time,' she said.

'Because of me?'

'No, before that, when I left her guidance to study Shadowmagic.'

Shadowmagic – there was that word again. Every time someone mentioned it, they sounded like they were selling a stolen watch in an alley.

'What is the deal with this Shadowmagic stuff?'

'Magic is never without cost,' she said. 'Like wood is to a fire, gold is to magic. Gold is the power that is made by the earth. In order to cast a spell you need to spend gold. The greater the spell, the more gold you need. That is what they call, here in The Land, *Truemagic*. Gold is not the only power in the world, it is just the easiest to find and use. There is power in the air and the water, that is too difficult to control, and then there is another power – the power of nature that can be found in the trees. Harnessing this power is the force behind Shadowmagic. It is not as powerful, but it can do things that Truemagic cannot.'

'So what does Nieve have against it?'

'Shadowmagic is illegal,' Father said.

'Why?'

'Ages ago,' Mom explained, 'in the early reign of Finn, there was a Fili sorceress named Maeve. Maeve detected power in amber stones and devised a way to use amber to power magic. Since amber is only petrified tree sap, she started to use fresh sap, the blood of trees, to power her magic. She became very powerful and that power drove her mad. She decimated an entire forest and used its energy to raise a huge army. Maeve and her army laid siege to Castle Duir. No one knows what happened – it is believed that in the midst of the battle, Maeve cast a mammoth spell that catastrophically failed. Maeve and all of the Fili army were killed. Afterwards, Finn outlawed Shadowmagic and decreed that Maeve's name should never be uttered again. The Fili were so decimated it was thought they were extinct.'

'You found them, I take it?'

'Yes. Maeve's daughter Fand lives.'

'And she taught you Shadowmagic?'

'She was reluctant at first. She was deeply ashamed of her mother, of
the wars and death and the forest she destroyed, but deep down she
knew that it was her mother that was wrong, not her magic. Together,
we found and read Maeve's notes to try and find out what happened. It
was the killing of trees that corrupted her soul. We found trees that
agreed to allow us to tap them for sap, and we swore never to kill a tree.
We revived the art of Shadowmagic and found that it was good. Just as
valid as Truemagic. After all, the yew wand is an integral part of
Truemagic but at its heart, it is actually Shadowmagic.'

'Did you ever try to convince Nieve?'

'Oh yes. When I returned from the Fililands I told her about it. She
was shocked and appalled that I would do such a thing. As I mentioned
before she has a strong sense of duty, but she agreed to discuss it again.'

'And what happened?'

'We never had that talk.'

'Why not?'

'I was banished,' Mom said.

'Banished?'

'Yup,' Dad said, 'your mother here is an outlaw. A regular Ma Barker.'

'Who banished you?'

'Finn,' she said.

'Finn, my grandfather? Why?'

'Your mother performed a very public display of Shadowmagic in
front of almost every Runelord in The Land. My father had no choice.'

'He should have had me executed,' she said.

'What happened?'

'That is part of the tale of how your father lost his hand. Not only is
it a long-overdue story – it is a long one as well. I know a shelter up
ahead. We can camp for the night and you can hear the tale properly
over food and a fire.'

Food and fire, now that was a good idea. After paddling all day and
the stress of the Yewlands, I was overdue for a break.

The meadows of heather gave way to fields of tremendously tall
holly trees. We pulled the boat ashore and stashed it under a bush.
(Mother of course asked the holly for permission.) We walked a faint
path until we saw a stone hut with a thatched roof.

'This is a lovely Gerard hut,' Mom said.

'Is Gerard home?'

'I shouldn't think so.' Dad laughed. 'Gerard is an old Runelord who likes to travel. He built a bunch of these huts so he wouldn't have to sleep out-of-doors.'

'Well,' I said, 'it looks cosy.'

'They usually are,' my father said, opening the door.

I had heard the sound of a crossbow firing before, but I had never heard the sound of an arrow piercing flesh. In the old cowboy movies, the sound of an arrow entering a body was always a clean *thwap* – in reality, the sound is a pop, followed by a hideous squelch. Dad spun completely around like a top and hit the ground hard on his back – a crossbow bolt was sticking out of his chest.

FIVE
ROTHLÚ

When I saw the air gurgling out of the wound in my father's chest, I dropped to my knees and screamed, 'Dad!' This turned out to be a lucky choice – if I had remained standing the second arrow would have got me right between the eyes. As it was, it still gave my hair its first centre parting. Dad had opened the door to an ambush.

'Don't move,' I heard a woman's voice order.

I looked up expecting a second attack, but instead I saw a deadly scene frozen in time. Aunt Nieve was standing in the doorway, and behind her were two soldiers with empty crossbows. My mother and my aunt were face to face, eyes locked – Mom was holding an amber ball while Nieve was holding a gold sphere made of wire.

'Make one move towards him and we all die,' Mom said.

'If the boy dies then my duty is done,' Nieve replied. 'If we die with him – so be it.'

'If I set off this Shadowcharm then all will die *except* the boy,' Mom said. 'You have seen the protection I have given him already. Your *duty* will fail and you will be dead.'

They stared at each other for a time.

'You should be with me in this,' hissed Nieve.

'You want me to stab my own son in the *neck*?' My mother said *neck* with such vehemence that it made me jump. 'We all realise that if Conor wasn't around we would all be safe.' She spoke in such a strange voice that it made me think she wasn't talking to Nieve – she was talking to *me*. 'You don't expect me to risk his *neck* just to make us *safe*.'

The amulet! She was talking about the *rothlú* amulet around my neck. I reached up, slowly wiped my lips and casually let my hand drop to the gold charm hanging around my neck. I wrapped my little finger around it.

'Do you really think you and Dad would be safe if I was gone?' I said to my mother.

'Listen to him,' Nieve said, 'the boy is beginning to understand.'

'I hope he does understand,' Mom said, talking to me, while never taking her eyes off Nieve. 'Yes, it would be safer for all if you were gone.'

I looked down at my father, who nodded to me with his eyes. I did understand. Mom wanted me to escape with the amulet and defuse this situation, so that maybe Dad could get some help.

'You know, Aunt Nieve,' I said, 'all of my life I wished I had an aunt that would send me an unexpected birthday present, like other kids. Instead I got one that tries to kill me every time we meet. Well, I want you to know that I am taking you off my Christmas card list. Oh, and by the way – *rothlú!*'

A *rothlú* spell kicks in fast but I did have a split second to see Nieve's expression before all went black. It was so satisfying that it was almost worth the pain.

Pain! Did I mention pain? Man, did I hurt. I didn't hurt all over, like with a killer hangover – it was more like every little bit of me hurt. My lips hurt, my earlobes hurt, my toes hurt, my hair hurt and I don't even want to talk about my groin. It felt as if every tiny fragment of me was torn apart and then quickly reassembled. For all I know that's what actually happened.

I was lying on my side in a foetal position. I must have been unconscious all night because I could feel the hot sun on my eyelids, but there was no way I was going to open my eyes, let alone move – I knew it was going to hurt too much. I think I would have stayed like that for a day or twelve, if I hadn't been disturbed by a tug on my foot. Normally, a tug like that would have had me alert in a flash, but I was so out of it that I only managed to crack one eye open, a slit. The light sent a pain into my head that made me want to moan, but I was sure that moaning would have hurt too. When I finally could focus, I saw a disgusting leather sandal on the ground next to my face and a pair of hands fumbling with a shoelace as they tried to pull one of my Nikes off.

I heard a voice say, 'Not bad,' and then I felt a tug on my other foot. He was stealing my shoes. Some twerp was nicking my sneakers! Concussion or no concussion, I wasn't going to stand for this. You can whip me, shoot me, kidnap me or try to kill me, but there is no way I was going to let my Nikes go without a fight. I jumped to my feet, and in one swift movement drew my sword. I caught the thief completely off guard. First, he was utterly engrossed with my shoelaces and second, I think he presumed I was dead. I must have looked dead – I certainly felt it.

I found myself standing over him with my sword pointed at his chest. He was a young man in both face *and* in his eyes. His hair was the remarkable thing – it was jet-black with a pure white tuft in the front. He was surprised to see me standing over him, and to be honest, so was I. Then the world began to spin – I had gotten up *way* too fast. I was going to faint.

As I swooned, I blurted out, 'Were you stealing my shoes?' Then I lost my balance. I stumbled forward, the tip of my blade inadvertently moving towards his chest. He understandably thought I was going to kill him. I tried to pull my sword away. I tried to keep my balance. I thought I was going to be sick. That's when I saw his sword. Even if I had been alert I don't think I could have parried it. With the quickest of flicks, he cocked his right wrist and a short blade travelled like lightning out of his sleeve. In one instantaneous motion he caught the pommel in his hand and stabbed me in the chest.

The amber glow engulfed the two of us the microsecond before his blade touched my chest. I realise now that life is made up not of days, or hours, or even seconds, but moments. One tiny moment follows another. One moment I saw the blade about to enter my heart – the next I was impossibly balanced on the tip of a razor-sharp sword, protected by my mother's wonderful amber force field.

I had just met another member of the family.

SIX

FERGAL

I stood there at a forty-degree angle with the shoe thief's blade holding me up, and I started to chuckle. I couldn't help it. I was losing it. I held my arms straight out at my sides and laughed. Not a *that's a funny joke* sort of a laugh but a crazy laugh, the kind of maniacal sound that comes out of Dr Frankenstein just before he screams, 'It's alive!'

Through the golden glow, I could see that my opponent was confused. He pushed at my chest a couple of times, trying to figure out why I wasn't perforated. Every jab just made me laugh louder. Finally, I rolled off the point of his sword and fell to the ground, in hysterics. He stood up fast, leaned over me and actually poked a couple of times. Each prod made the glow return and I howled, tears pouring from my eyes. I saw the thief take off my Nikes and carefully pick up his sandals. I could tell he was a bit freaked, ready to run.

I tried to compose myself. 'Wait,' I croaked, as I struggled to sit up. He started to back away. 'No, wait,' I repeated as I wiped my eyes on my sleeve, 'I won't hurt you – look.' I threw my sword away and held up my hands. 'Sit down for a second.'

He stopped, still wary. 'I'm not looking for any trouble,' he said. 'Honest to the gods, I thought you were dead. Well, not dead but I didn't think you were going to last long.'

'I believe you. Sit down.'

He sat a respectable distance away. I rubbed my eyes with my palms, trying to make them focus. The specific pain of before was becoming one giant all-over pain – an improvement but not much.

'I think we have gotten off on the wrong foot.'

He stood up and started to back away. 'I told you I was sorry for the shoe thing.'

'No, no, relax,' I said, palms forward. 'I mean, I don't think we should be fighting. I'm sorry I pulled a sword on you but I have had a really rough couple of days. Can we start over?' I stood up and extended my hand. 'My name is Conor.'

He looked me square in the eyes for a time and then slowly an amazing smile took over his whole face. It was so infectious that I couldn't help turning up the corners of my own mouth in reply. He cocked his wrist and his sword disappeared instantly up his sleeve. He stepped right up and shook my hand enthusiastically (which hurt) and said, 'They call me Fergal. Pleased to meet you, Conor.'

'The pleasure is all mine, Fergal.'

'So tell, Conor,' Fergal said like we were old mates, 'what the hell were you doing lying in a ditch?'

'That's a long story. You wouldn't have a couple of aspirin and a glass of water, before I start, would you?'

'Don't know what that first thing is but there is a lovely wee stream just over there if you're thirsty. Follow me.'

We put our shoes on, I picked up my sword and we climbed up out of the ravine. My legs howled in pain, as if I had just run a marathon with a sumo wrestler on my back. When we reached the top I saw that we were in the middle of rolling farmland. Fields of waving grain, periodically interrupted by the odd tree, stretched as far as the eye could see.

'Where are we?' I asked.

'The fields of Muhn. The Castle Muhn vineyards start not far – just over that rise.'

My vision was clearing. I looked in the direction of Fergal's finger and saw rolling hills in the distance. Fergal's definition of not far was quite different from my own.

'Oh, I get it,' Fergal said, way too loud for my liking, 'you were at a shindig at Castle Muhn last night – weren't you?'

I almost said, *I wish*, but then it occurred to me that everyone who knew who I was had tried to kill me. 'Maybe,' I said, thinking that lying might be a sensible idea.

'Well, that explains it.' Fergal laughed. 'You wouldn't be the first guy to be found hung over in a ditch after a party at Castle Muhn.' He slapped me on the back. It felt like I was hit with a sledgehammer.

The water made me wonder if I had been drinking sawdust all of my life. It was cool and crystal clear. It hit the back of my throat and made me feel like I would never be thirsty again. That's one of the best things about The Land, it forces you to appreciate the simple things in life: fresh water, fragrant air, magnificent views, and not being dead. All of my problems and pressing engagements in the Real World were fading in my mind, except for that nagging image of Sally, still waiting outside the movie theatre.

'I thought the big party was at moon bright,' Fergal said. 'Oh no! I haven't missed it, have I? I could have sworn it was tomorrow night.'

'No. You're alright. It was an unofficial thing last night,' I lied, 'tomorrow's the big night.'

'Phew. I would have been well upset if I'd missed it,' he said, slapping me on the back again. I had to figure out how to break him out of that habit. 'So what are you doing then, Conor me friend? Are you on your way home or are you coming back for a bit of the *hair of the dog*?'

What to do? I knew that I should keep a low profile, especially when the motto around here seemed to be – *to know Conor is to kill Conor*. But what could I do on my own? I had to find my mother and father again. But where were they and how could I find them without telling people who I was? And a party! Why not? After all I'd probably get murdered by an in-law before the week was out – so why not party? This Fergal seemed like a nice guy and he *was* family (which may or may not be a good thing). If I hung around with him maybe I could come up with a plan before someone figured out who I was.

'What the hell,' I said. 'One more night of partying can't kill me.'

'Well, maybe you should go easier tomorrow, you look awful rough.'

'Thanks for the advice,' I said, and together we set off for a party at Castle Muhn.

'That was a clever bit of magic you pulled back there,' Fergal said.

'Yes, I liked it at the time.'

'It's a snap spell, isn't it?'

'A snap spell?'

'Hey, sorry,' Fergal said, raising his hands. 'I shouldn't be prying into another man's magic.'

'No, it's OK,' I said, 'I just never heard of a snap spell.'

'A snap spell is one that happens by itself. You don't have to cast it or pay for it or anything – it just happens. Kings put them on their jewels and such to stop them from getting nicked. I never saw a proper one before – till now.'

'I guess it is a snap spell then.'

'Where'd you get it?'

What should I say to that? The problem with lying is that it gets you into trouble. I learned that painful lesson last year. I was dating a girl named Dottie when I met Sally. I told Dottie I was going out to dinner with my father when I was really taking Sally to the movies. The next day I saw Dottie and she said, 'What did you have for dinner, popcorn?' Man, was I busted.

The other problem with lying is you have to remember what you said, and since it seemed like I was going to be doing a lot of lying in the near future, I decided to tell the truth as much as I could.

Fergal noticed my hesitancy. 'Hey, mate, you don't have to tell me nothing. I talk too much and ask too many questions. Just tell me to shut up, that's what all my friends do.'

'No, it's alright. My protection spell was a gift from my mother.'

'Phew. Nice gift. Must have cost her weight in gold.'

'Don't know. Never asked.'

'Well, I'm glad she gave it to you. I never stabbed anybody before, it would have been a shame for you to be the first. There's something about you, I don't know what it is but it seems like we are old friends already, or should be. You know what I mean?' Then he slapped me on the back – again.

'I do,' I said, and meant it. We were definitely related. Fergal didn't know what this feeling was, but I did, my mother's spell confirmed it – we were kin. I slapped Fergal on the back, hard, so he would know what it felt like. It hurt my hand.

'That sword of yours appeared like it was magic,' I said.

'What, this little thing?' he clicked his wrist and the long knife popped into his hand with frightening speed. 'My Banshee blade.'

'You're a Banshee?' I blurted.

'No,' he said sarcastically. 'What gave it away? Was it the bit of white hair? Or was it the bit of white hair?'

'I think it must have been the bit of white hair.' I smiled and replied as casually as I could. Banshees have a tuft of white hair. I stored that piece of information away.

'So how do you get it to pop out so fast?'

'Ah well, that's the magic part. Here, let me show you.' He stopped and took off his shirt. His right arm was strapped with leather in three places. Entwined in the straps was a gold wire that seemed to be on some sort of pulley system. The wire was attached to the blade, so as to propel it in and out of his sleeve. 'The magic is in the gold wire,' he said. 'It cost me a packet. When I need the blade, I do this motion and this half of the wire straightens and expands – poof – instant sword. The spell doesn't use much gold. The wire's supposed to work for years.'

'Cool.'

'No, it doesn't get hot or anything.'

'I mean, nice.'

'Oh, I could set you up with a guy to make you one if you like. It isn't cheap though.'

'I am afraid I'm a bit broke at the moment.'

'Me too. You and I have got so much in common,' he said with another slap.

As we followed the stream Fergal waxed on about the intricacies of Banshee blade manufacture but I didn't take much in. His voice was increasingly drowned out by the bass drum solo that began playing in my head. After I don't know how long (by which time the pounding in my head had graduated into a full-blown marching band), Fergal turned to me and said, 'You haven't been listening to a word I've said, have you?'

'Huh? Oh, sure I have.'

Fergal looked me in the eyes and I had a scary moment when I thought he was going to quiz me. Then he broke into an ear-to-ear smile and said, 'I like you, Conor, it usually takes friends ages to learn to ignore my babbling – you figured it out right away.' He went to slap me on the back but then stopped when he saw me flinch. 'You know, you look awful rough. We're in no hurry; how 'bout we make camp here?'

We found the remnants of an old campfire under a tall, broadleaved tree that had roots creeping into the stream. Fergal said it should be OK to camp under an alder this far away from the Fearnlands. I wanted to ask him what that meant but I had a feeling asking too many questions would arouse suspicion, and anyway I was too tired. Fergal took some kindling out of his bag and piled it within the ring of stones.

'You wouldn't have a decent fire-coin, would you? Mine's practically silver.'

'No. I've lost everything except my sword,' I said, which was pretty much the truth.

Fergal produced a half-dollar-sized disc out of his pocket and placed it beneath the little bits of wood.

'I think this thing has one more fire in it.'

He mumbled under his breath, there was a faint glow and then smoke appeared under the wood. He blew it into a small flame. 'Keep an eye on this and I'll beg for some wood.'

Fergal climbed the alder as I lay on my side and blew on the tiny flame. Just this was enough to make me feel light-headed. I was still in pretty bad shape after that damn *rothlú* thing. Whether I fell asleep or passed out I don't know, but the next thing I remember, Fergal was shaking me awake and handing me a stick with a fish on it that he had just cooked on a roaring fire.

'Is there anything else I can do for you, Prince Conor?' For a second I thought he had figured out who I was. I sat bolt upright expecting his Banshee blade to fly out of his sleeve, but then he smiled and said, 'You're a fat lot of good around here. Next time I'm nursing a hangover, you wait on me.'

'Deal,' I said with a nervous laugh, and took the fish. 'Thanks.'

We ate in silence. I'm not a big fan of food that can stare at me but I was too hungry to complain. I apologised to the trout's face and wolfed the rest of it down.

After dinner Fergal put a couple of logs on the fire and said that even though he would love to talk all night, he was beat. He touched the alder, put his pack under his head and closed his eyes. My short nap had done little to ease my overall body pain. I put my head on the ground and moaned. Just before I went out, I thought I saw some strange movement in the branches above. I sat up and had a good look but then decided I was just spooking myself.

I dreamt I was back in the Real World in a super-posh shoe store where I didn't even have to put the shoes on myself. Sales clerks actually knelt down and placed all kinds of really cool footwear directly on my feet.

Dawn, as it always does, came too early. I find that going to sleep under the stars is lovely but waking up outside is a drag. It leaves me itchy, damp and with terminal bed hair. It wasn't until I stood that I realised my shoes were missing. Well, that explained the theme of my dream. I walked over to the still-sleeping Fergal and lightly kicked him with my bare foot. He shot straight up.

'What?' he sputtered.

'Ha ha, Fergal, very funny. What did you do with my shoes?'

'What are you talking about?' he said, getting his bearings.

'My shoes, I don't know how you did it without waking me up but I want my shoes back.'

'I don't have your shoes,' he said, confused.

'Quit mucking around, Fergal, I had them on when I went to sleep.'

'I'm telling you I don't have your … uh-oh.' Fergal jerked his hand a couple of times and then pulled his tunic over his head. 'Damn it,' he said, 'damn it, damn it, damn it!'

'What? What is it?'

'My Banshee blade is gone – and the wire too.'

'What do you mean gone?'

'Robbed, we were robbed last night.'

Oh, just great, I thought, *now I'm going to have to walk in this godfor-saken land barefoot*. Then I had a terrible thought. Slowly I reached down to my waist and felt for my scabbard – the Sword of Duir was gone.

SEVEN

BROWNIES

'They took my sword. Oh my God, my father is going to kill me.'

Fergal went over to the alder and placed his hand on the bark, then kicked it. A rain of branches showered down that made us run out from under its cover.

'Fergal, what the hell is going on?'

'We got rumbled by the alder last night.'

'Are you telling me the tree mugged us?'

'Don't be stupid.'

'Then who could take my shoes and your wire from under your shirt without waking us up?'

'Brownies, damn them.'

'Whos-ies?'

'Brownies – who else?'

'You mean like girl scouts?'

'Why do you think they were girls?' Fergal said, confused.

'Never mind. I have to get that sword back. It is very important.'

'Well, that's not going to be easy. Brownies weigh nothing and are famously difficult to track.'

We looked around at the dew-covered grass and then at each other. We were both wearing the same ear-to-ear grin. You see, Brownies are usually difficult to track – except when one of them is wearing Nikes.

Whoever stole my shoes must have had tiny feet because he dragged them along the ground, trying to keep my size elevens from falling off. The tracks led into the stream but were easy to pick up on the other side. Fergal dashed under the tree and grabbed a couple of branches that we could use as weapons. He shouted a sarcastic, 'Thanks,' as the alder tried to rain more wood down on him.

We followed the trail across some wide, open fields that led to rolling hills. The trees were thin and the ground pretty spongy but periodically my bare feet made contact with a rock or a twig that made me yelp. I wasn't sure how long I would be able to keep up this pace, but saying that, I felt a lot better than I did yesterday.

Every time I wanted to ask Fergal if we could rest, I remembered the Sword of Duir – I had to get it back. I had a vision of meeting up with Dad and him saying, 'Let me get this straight, I give you a sword that has been in our family for *thousands* of years and you lose it – in a day!' I really wanted to avoid that conversation. After about an hour of jogging we rounded a small hill. I lost the trail but Fergal laid his head on the ground and pointed to a small cliff face about a quarter-mile to our right.

'If we are lucky, they are camping in those rocks,' Fergal said.

'What makes you think they made camp?'

'Look, my Nanny Breithe always got mad at me when I talked badly about any race but the truth of it is, Brownies are cocky and stupid. They think they are so stealthy that they are untrackable, but look at these idiots. Not one of them bothered to look behind them to check if they were leaving a trail. My guess is that they were up all night watching us, so I'm hoping they are camping in those rocks.'

'And if you're wrong?'

'Then you're going to have to buy a new pair of those fancy shoes of yours. Where did you get them anyway?'

'Scranton,' I said without thinking.

'Scranton? Never heard of it.'

'Yeah.' I laughed. 'A lot of people say that.'

The way was a bit harder here and Fergal shushed me every time a pebble underfoot made me bark. When we reached the foot of the knoll Fergal and I took a minute to rub the small stems and leaves off the branches we were carrying so as to fashion them into staffs. They weren't the best weapons in the world but they would have to do.

Climbing the rocks would have been a cinch if I'd had anything on my feet, but barefoot it was flipping difficult. What was harder than the actual climbing was trying not to curse every time I stepped on some jagged edge. My poor tootsies were taking a beating. If I got through this without getting stabbed by my own sword, I was going to throttle whoever took my Nikes. Fergal reached the summit before me. He peeped over and instantly ducked down, placing his index finger over his lips and indicating that our light-fingered quarry was just over the rise. I pressed up next to him.

'There's only two of them,' he whispered. 'We need a plan.'

'Have you ever done this before?'

'Done what?'

'Attacked two armed men with sticks?'

'No, but I'm looking forward to it.' He smiled.

His smile was so infectious I said, 'OK, what's the plan?'

'One of us should circle around behind them, and when he is in position the other one makes a frontal attack from here. The one of us that comes from the rear should be able to take them out before the one who attacks from here gets sliced up too much.'

'As much as I don't fancy the idea of getting "sliced up too much", you have to go around the back – my feet are killing me.'

'OK, take a quick look and you'll see the gap in the back. I'll be coming from there.'

I was nervous until I stuck my nose over the ledge. They looked like a couple of teenage street urchins. They had black matted hair and wore tight dark green clothes stretched over bodies so skinny they would have made a supermodel look chunky. Between them was a campfire that had a dome of gold wire over it. The smoke rising from the fire seemed to disappear when it hit the wire. The two swords and Fergal's pack were lying behind them on the ground. When the larger guy got up to tend the fire I saw that the smaller one had my shoes on the ground between his legs. He had removed the laces from one of them and then to my horror I realised he was about to cut the tongue out of the sneaker. That's when I kind of forgot where I was. I stood up and yelled, 'Hey!' vaulted over the ledge and slid down to two very surprised Brownies.

'What is the matter with you?' I shouted.

The little guy just froze. The bigger one grabbed the Sword of Duir and pointed it at me. What confused him was that I just ignored him. I walked over to the little guy and grabbed the shoe – I was mad.

'What's the matter with you? If you are going to steal my Nikes the least you could do is give them a little respect. What the hell are you cutting them for?'

The bigger guy poked me in the back with my sword. I turned to him and said, 'I'll deal with you in a second.' I looked around – Fergal was nowhere to be seen.

I turned back to junior. 'I'm talking to you. Why the hell were you cutting up my sneakers?' He seemed too terrified to speak. I towered over him. 'Well?'

'My, my feet got sweaty in them,' he stammered.

'Oh, so after sweating in my shoes you decided to cut them up.' I think I would have slapped him if the big guy hadn't just then given me a good jab in the ribs that demanded my attention.

'If you take one more step towards my brother,' the bigger one said, 'I'm going to run you through.'

I turned. He had striking pale blue eyes that, unlike his brother, had no fear in them. He was holding my sword to my chest but I remained calm.

'That is my sword,' I pointed out, 'and in about three seconds I'm going to take it back.'

'And how are you going to do that?' His voice betrayed a tiny loss of confidence.

'I'm going to pick it off the ground after my friend Fergal clocks you in the head with a tree branch.'

He went down like a house of cards. I quickly turned to little brother, who was still frozen like a rabbit in headlights. I picked up my sword and pointed to the soles of my feet.

'Look at my tootsies! Do you see how dirty they are? I should make you lick them clean.'

I took a step towards him and he started to shake. I instantly felt sorry for him – this kid was way out of his league. I crouched down.

'Hey, little guy, relax, we're not going to hurt you.' I turned to Fergal. 'We're not going to hurt them – right?'

'Well, I'm not going to hurt anybody,' Fergal said as he began to tie up big brother, 'but you seem a bit worked up about your footwear.'

'Well, I like these shoes.'

'I've noticed.'

I turned back to the boy. 'OK, it's decided, no one is going to hurt you. What's your name?'

'My brother said I'm not supposed to tell you my name even if you torture me.'

'Wow, you guys are a real bunch of desperados. Mind if I call you Jesse?'

'I, I guess.'

Fergal finished hogtying the brother and came over.

'Fergal, meet Jesse.'

Fergal leaned over the boy. 'What kind of a name is Jesse?'

I tapped him on the shoulder and said, 'I made it up but I think he likes it – just go with it.'

'OK, hi, Jesse. What are you two doing so far from the Fearnlands?'

'My brother said there would be easy pickings out here but we haven't seen anybody for ages. I wanted to go home – only he made me keep going. He said Father would let him take his scrúdú early if we came back with quality acquisitions. I, I didn't mean to hurt your shoes, honest. What are you going to do to us?'

'Scrúdú?'

'It's the manhood test,' he said, then the poor kid turned ghastly white. 'Oh gods, I shouldn't have told you that.'

So that was it – a story as old as time, big brother with delusions of manhood, roped little bro into doing something incredibly stupid.

I picked up a canteen from the ground, walked over to big bro and poured some water on his head. He spluttered awake and tried to get up. When he realised he was hogtied he looked at Fergal and me. His bravado from earlier had vanished.

'Good morning, Frank,' I said.

'What is Frank?' he said.

'You are. Since your little brother over there has informed me that we won't know your real names until after we torture you, I decided to call you Frank and him Jesse until then.'

'My name is Demne and my brother is Codna.'

I turned to Jesse/Codna, who now had his mouth wide open in amazement. 'Well, Jesse, it looks like your brother isn't much for torture.'

I turned back to the big bro. 'You know, Demne, I like Frank better. You don't mind if I call you Frank, do you?'

'No, sir.'

'Good. OK, Frank, here's what we are going to do. First, we are going to take our *acquisitions* back. You don't have any problems with that, do you, Frank?'

'No, sir.'

'You know, I really am starting to like your attitude, Frank. Next I'm going to borrow your shoes and let you have the opportunity, like I had, to climb barefoot over those rocks.' I crouched down and took Frank's sandals off his feet, picked up Jesse's from the ground and threw them over the stone ridge as far as I could. 'We are going to leave you now, but before we do, you are going to promise me that the next time you have a harebrained idea, you are not going to drag your brother into it. Right?'

'Yes, sir.'

'Good. Fergal, do you have anything to add?'

Fergal had reattached his Banshee blade and was now examining the gold wire dome he had taken from its position over the fire. Smoke was now floating freely in the air. 'Now that you mention it, Conor, I was thinking of taking this interesting thing as payment for our troubles.'

Frank tried to stand when Fergal said this, and fell on his side. 'Please don't take our father's smokescreen. He'll kill us if we lose it.'

I grabbed Frank by the arm and pulled him back up into a sitting position. 'So let me guess, Dad doesn't know you took it?'

He shook his head – a pathetic no. I took the smokescreen from Fergal and placed it on Frank's head like a skullcap.

'Jesse, can I give you a little piece of information that will help you for the rest of your life?'

Jesse just stared at me and then slowly nodded yes.

'Your big brother is an idiot.'

He nodded to me again.

As we walked to the rim of the knoll Fergal said, 'I would really have liked that smokescreen.'

'Yeah,' I said, 'but I know what it's like to get in trouble with your dad and I didn't have the heart to do that to them.'

I gave them one last look before I climbed back down. Jesse was still sitting stock still.

I called to him. 'Jesse, you can untie your brother any time you want but if I were you I would make him suffer for a little while longer.'

He looked up to me and then gave me the tiniest of smiles and then waved.

'Behave, you two,' I shouted as I jumped down the rock face.

Our encounter with the outlaws had put us behind schedule for the party. Fergal set a jogging pace that made me wish I had tortured those two a little bit.

'So I said we need a plan,' Fergal said to me as he ran alongside, 'and you said "OK". Do you remember that?'

'I do.'

'And then we made a plan. Do you remember that too?'

I nodded, conserving my breath.

'Good, now here is the point I'm getting to. I don't know how they do things in Skwinton.'

'Scranton,' I corrected.

'OK, Scranton, but where I come from, after you make a plan you don't just up and jump over a wall screaming.'

'Well, it worked, didn't it?'

'Yes, Conor, but remember, some of us don't have a priceless snap spell to come to our rescue.'

I almost told him that my mom's protection spell didn't have anything to do with it, since it works solely on relatives and only once, but then I thought, *He doesn't need to know all that and I'm a bit out of breath anyway*, so all I said was, 'Yeah, sorry.'

'Do not worry about it,' he said, slapping me on the back, almost precipitating a full-speed jogging wreck – somehow I kept my footing.

Fergal seemed to think that running at this pace for a couple of hours was an OK thing to do. It wasn't easy but amazingly I kept up. Usually any sport more strenuous than bowling pushes me over the edge. Maybe those annoying callisthenics that Dad used to make me do before and after sword fighting lessons were paying off. After a while I started to enjoy it. I got a glimpse of the high that joggers say they get from running. I took in the magnificent scenery as my body set a cadence that echoed in my brain. I think I was about to slip into a perfect Zen-like state when Fergal slapped me on the back again and snapped me out of it.

'Hey, you hungry? There's an apple tree over there.'

Hungry? Now that I thought about it, I was starving! I saw the tree and ran straight towards it. The apples looked even better than the one that my mother had given me. I know I go on and on about the trees in The Land, but I can't emphasise enough how magnificent they are. Never in my life had I ever seen a fruit tree so bountiful. Directly above my head was an apple bigger than my fist. I stared at it for a moment and marvelled at how my face reflected in its mirror-like red skin. I bent my knees and jumped to grab it.

That's when the bus hit me.

EIGHT

ARAF

OK, it wasn't a bus, but it sure felt like one. One moment I was in mid-jump with an apple in my hand, the next moment I was hit – hard in the shoulder and went flying ass over teacups through the air. Luckily I landed in a pile of thick barley that was pretty soft.

Fergal was at my side in a second. 'Are you mad?'

'Did you get the licence number of that truck?' I groaned.

'Are you OK?'

'Give me a second to check my bones to see which of them *aren't* broken.'

'For the gods' sake, haven't you ever picked an apple before? Wait here and I'll talk to her.'

'Talk to who?'

I sat up and found that I was a considerable distance from where I had been moments before. Fergal slowly approached the apple tree and placed his hands on the trunk. He mumbled a few things, pointed to me and then jogged back.

'She said she won't hit you again. She wants to talk to you. If I was you I'd start with an apology.'

The tree hit me? The tree hit me! Of course it did. If I had to thank a willow tree for its shade, I must certainly have had to ask permission before picking an apple. I just wished I could learn something in this place without it being so painful.

I stood up. I wasn't hurt as bad as I should have been. The blow was so unexpected that I didn't have time to tense up. Still, I had one hell of a dead arm. I walked warily towards the tree. I had spent a lifetime with trees. I always knew they were living things but I never really treated them like they were living in the same world as me. Again, The Land was forcing me to re-examine my perceptions. I placed my hand on the trunk.

A conversation with a tree is not like communicating with anyone or anything else. It's not a dialogue, it's more of a meeting of the minds. Even though I spoke out loud it was not necessary – words are not the medium of communication.

I didn't have to worry about convincing the apple tree that I was sorry, she knew as soon as I touched her and I knew I was forgiven – the sensation of it washed over me. She was happy I was not seriously hurt – she had never hit anyone so hard before. I learned that it was not uncommon for her to give a child a little smack, just to teach a lesson, but she had never had a poacher as old as me and let loose a good one. She told me (felt me?) that Fergal and I could each have a couple of apples with her blessing. The only part of the conversation that was almost in words, was when I thanked her and said goodbye. I could have sworn she said, 'Good luck, little prince.'

We sat under the apple tree's shade and ate and drank water from Fergal's canteen. Who'd have thought that an apple and some water could make such a superb meal? It was so satisfying I felt as though I could live on these two things alone. I have since found out that many people in The Land do just that.

'You still look pretty wrecked, Conor. The castle's only an hour or so away and we don't want to be too early. Why don't you have a snooze? I promise I won't steal your shoes.'

'I won't argue with that,' I said as I put my head on the soft grass. Before I dozed off I raised my hand behind me and touched the apple tree. I asked her if she minded me resting here a little bit. She told me she would look after me as I slept. Next thing I knew, I was dreaming again.

* * *

I dreamt I was a child, maybe five years old. I was walking between my parents, holding their hands as we passed under huge yew trees. These yews were not menacing like the ones on the river. The trees moved out of our way and bowed to us as we passed. An arrow sailed through the air and hit my father in the shoulder. I was upset but my father told me not to be silly and pulled the arrow from his flesh, like he was dusting dandruff off his suit. Mom rubbed the wound and it healed.

We sat together under a tree. Mom pointed and I looked up. I saw that the yew we were sitting under was now an apple tree. I turned to ask my mother if I could have an apple but she and my father were gone. Next, the apple tree raised itself up on huge roots, pushing itself free from the ground and kicked me! I rolled like a ball into the base of another tree and that one kicked me as well. Soon all of the trees had gathered around me having a kick-about, with me as the ball! The funny thing was I liked it. They weren't hurting me, it was fun. After a while I got bored with the game and I laid down under a tree. The tree kept kicking me but I refused to move.

I awoke with a tree root sticking in my back. I am sure it wasn't there when I fell asleep. Fergal was snoring away to my left. I toyed with the idea of stealing his shoes as a joke, but I wasn't sure he wouldn't stab me first and get the joke second. I sat up and rubbed my eyes. That's when I saw him approach.

He was close enough that I could see that he was short, but not slight. He was built like a brick outhouse – not fat, just a solid body with a head sitting directly on the shoulders. I got the impression that if I ran at him with all of my might I would just bounce off. Maybe that's where they got the word *bouncer* from – 'cause that's exactly what he looked like. If you got rid of the leather toga he was wearing and put him in a tuxedo, you could imagine him standing in the doorway of any night club. He was walking directly towards us.

I stood and said, 'Hi.'

He didn't even notice me. In his hand he held a thick wooden stick with a gnarled top and seemed to be heading for Fergal. 'Ah, excuse me,' I said, trying to be polite, 'can I help?'

He walked straight at Fergal and raised his stick. I drew my sword and covered the ground between us. That got his attention at least.

'If you are looking for your neck, I can assure you we don't have it.'

I looked him in the eye but he gave me nothing back. I couldn't read the face at all. I kicked Fergal and said, 'We've got company.'

Fergal opened his eyes to see the Incredible Hulk Junior and myself standing over him with weapons drawn.

He looked at Hulk, then at me. 'For the love of the gods, Conor, haven't you ever met anybody without drawing a sword?'

'A friend of yours?'

Fergal nodded and I lowered my weapon. 'Conor, meet Araf – Araf, meet Conor.'

'Sorry,' I said, offering my hand, 'I've had a rough couple of days.'

'That's what he said when he pulled a sword on me,' Fergal said.

'That's not fair – this time I was defending you.'

Araf shook my hand and almost broke it.

'He was coming at you with a club.'

'It's a *banta* stick,' Fergal said, 'and Araf always wakes me with it.'

'Why?'

'Because once, *and only once*,' Fergal said defensively, glaring at Araf, 'I attacked him with my Banshee blade when he woke me up. I was having a bad dream – and it was a long time ago. Ever since then he always wakes me with a stick.'

'Sounds sensible,' I said, thinking that I was lucky not to steal Fergal's shoes while he slept.

Araf nodded at me in agreement. It was the first true communication between us.

'Come on,' Fergal said, picking himself off the ground, 'we've got a party to go to.'

'Are you coming to the party, Araf?' I asked.

'Are you kidding?' Fergal replied for him. 'Araf here is a party beast!'

As we walked to the party I got Araf's life story – not from Araf, I might add, but from Fergal. I was starting to wonder if Araf could speak at all. Araf and Fergal had grown up together in a place called Castle Ur in the Heatherlands. It was obvious they weren't blood relatives. One look at the two of them told you that they came from different gene pools – hell, different gene oceans. It turned out that both had been raised by the same nanny, who was now dead. When I asked Fergal about his parents he seemed to sidestep the question.

And check this out – Araf is an Imp! I came very close to bursting out laughing and saying, 'Isn't he a bit big for an Imp?' but I kept my mouth shut. The Land was going to throw quite a few surprises at me. If I wanted to look like a native, I would have to take stuff like this in my stride. I couldn't help thinking what a funky couple of days I was having. How many people can say they've been in a sword fight with a Banshee and an Imp and then went off to a party with them?

The landscape changed the closer we got to Castle Muhn. The fields of grain changed into towering vineyards. Ancient trellises of black hawthorn were draped with vines producing grapes in bunches so large I was amazed that they could stay on the vine. Bees the size of hummingbirds roared through the white and pink blossoms. Castle Muhn was not like the imposing fortress of Castle Duir. It was huge – it must have taken up over an acre, with low walls, and I noticed a conspicuous lack of sentries. Actually, with the vineyards around it, it looked more like a sprawling French chateau.

We walked in silence for a while, which I was starting to realise was unusual for Fergal. Things had been so crazy, this was the first moment I had time to collect my thoughts. Jeez, I hoped Dad was alright. He looked bad when I left him but he was definitely alive. I felt guilty going to a party, but something in my mother's voice back there made me think Dad would be OK. And then there was my dream. Was that a vision or just wish-fulfilment? Well, as much as I would like to be able to help him, there was nothing I could do about it. Still, that didn't stop me from worrying.

I decided to look at the big picture. Right. My father is a prince or maybe a king. My mother is an outlaw sorceress, and everyone in this place (that shouldn't even exist) wants to kill me. OK, let's forget the big picture – that was just freaking me out. I needed a plan for the here and now. What should I do? I should get out of here, that's what I should do. I needed to get out of The Land. If the prophecy was right, and everyone around here seemed to take it seriously – deadly seriously – then my parents' plan was a good one. Let me live a long and happy life in the Real World and when I reach a ripe old age, I pass away in my bed. The son of the one-handed prince will die, and Tir na Nog will be saved. Good plan – I liked it. But how do I get back to the Real World? There had to be a way, after all my father and I had done it. The answer was Mom. She was the one that sent us in the first place. If I could find my mother, I could get out of here. OK, I had a plan – find my mother. Where? How? She said she was going to the Fililands, so now all I had to do was find out how to get there. I chuckled to myself – the fact of the matter was that I was lost and scared and the only plan I could come up with was – *I want my mommy!* – real mature.

The approach to the outer wall of the castle was strange – eerie, in fact. The gate was wide open but there were no guards, no anybody. I could just about hear music coming from within but there was no one outside or inside the doorway as far as I could tell.

'I'm not an expert on castles,' I said, 'but aren't you supposed to, like, guard them?'

'Gerard doesn't need guards, he's got a mountain of gold,' Fergal said. 'This place is crawling with snap spells. I'm sure if you were up to no good, you wouldn't get in here.'

'Gerard?' I said. 'Is this the same guy who built the huts?'

'Of course.'

We were actually inside the castle and still there was nobody around. There was definitely something going on. I could hear music but there was no sign of a party. I was startled when huge wooden doors at the end of the hallway opened and half a dozen servants with trays of dirty mugs and plates hurried past us without even a second glance. Music and the smell of food escaped from the room like a caged bird. The sound and the aroma were instantly intoxicating. I had been thinking that maybe going to such a public event was a bad idea, but after I got that nose- and earful – just try to keep me out.

Fergal reached the door first and then jumped when he heard a voice saying, 'Name?'

To the right of the door was an alcove with a split door, the top half open. Behind the door was an old guy – and I mean an ancient old guy. Physically he didn't look that old, but I could see the years in his eyes.

It's amazing how quickly I had gotten used to examining people's eyes. This guy's peepers had been around for a long, long time.

'Name?' he repeated.

'Fergal of Castle Ur.'

'Castle Ur?' the old man questioned. 'You don't look like an Imp to me.'

'He is with me,' Araf said, in a beautiful bass voice.

'My God!' I said. 'He can speak.'

'Ah, Master Araf,' the old guy said, 'it is good to see you again.'

'This is my kinsman, Fergal,' Araf said. 'He is indeed of Castle Ur, and this is Conor of …'

They all three looked to me for an answer – what could I say? 'I am Conor of – the Fililands.'

They all looked at me like I was from another planet (which I guess I was) and then burst into laughter.

'The Fililands!' the old man repeated. 'That's a good one. Try not to eat any babies tonight, will you?'

Fergal and Araf laughed at this. So I did too.

'I promise,' I said.

'Any friends of Master Araf are welcome in Castle Muhn,' said the old man. 'I'll take your weapons now, if you please. That would include the one up your sleeve, Master … Fergal, was it?'

Fergal looked shocked but produced and unhooked his Banshee blade.

'I was hoping to get into a banta match.' Araf spoke again. 'Can I not keep my stick?'

The doorkeeper held out his hand and Araf handed him his banta stick. The old man inspected it and placed it with a bunch of others behind the door. 'There will be sticks provided if you wish to compete. And our sticks,' the old man said with a wry smile, 'have the added advantage of not being hollowed out and filled with lead.'

Araf nodded like a guilty schoolboy.

Fergal and I both handed over our weapons. He filed Fergal's blade away, but looked at mine for quite some time.

'This is an exquisite sword,' the old man said, as he placed it alone in a narrow cupboard. 'Does it have a name?'

'Does what have a name?' I asked.

'Your sword – a weapon as superb as this should have a name.'

'Oh, of course – I – I call it,' I announced, '*the Lawnmower*!"

NINE

ESSA

S ince my first experience of a castle was inside a sewer-scented dungeon, I was expecting the other side of the door to be filled with disgusting barbarians in bearskins. I imagined them chomping on huge legs of animal flesh as they slapped the backsides of passing serving wenches, their greasy chins glistening in dim torch-light. How wrong can a boy be?

This place was spectacularly elegant. We were no longer strictly in the castle but in the Great Vineyard, a football-pitch-sized courtyard adorned with fountains and huge black and white marble statues. The statues were like oversized chess pieces strewn about in a haphazard manner – some upright, others on their side. It was as if the gods had just dumped out a giant chess set before they set up for a game. Roofing the courtyard was a black trellis that supported grapevines with fruit as big as plums. What was left of the day's light filtered through the leaves, giving the room a majestic green hue.

Remembering the incident with the apple, the first thing I did was place my hand on a vine and ask nicely if I could have a grape. '*NO YOU MAY NOT!*' The answer came back so clear it made my head hurt. These were proud plants.

Fergal whacked me on the back. 'You weren't thinking about pluck-ing a grape from the Great Vineyard, were you?'

'Who, me?' I lied. 'I wouldn't be that stupid.'

'Come on, let's try Gerard's new vintage.'

The party was in full swing. The music was infectious. It instantly lifted me into a party mood and made my walk resemble a little dance. It reminded me of Irish traditional music – but not quite. I was starting to think that there must have been some cultural exchange between my world and this one, because so much of The Land was *almost* familiar. The couple of hundred guests were standing around with mugs or sitting at wooden tables. I noticed that no two tables were of the same wood and each one would have made an antique dealer drool.

It seemed that all were welcome here. The guests' clothes ranged from farmers' rags to elegant flowing gowns, and everyone was mixing. I was expecting to get that *we don't like strangers around here* stare but everyone was smiling and nodding, especially to Araf. We got to the bar and Fergal ordered 'three of the new stuff'. While we were waiting for our wine, Fergal noticed he was standing next to someone he knew and slapped him on the back. He was a tall, lean man with very straight, shoulder-length blond hair. I could see by his expression that he liked being slapped on the back almost as much as I did.

'Esus! How the hell are ya?'

'Ah, Fergal, this must be your first celebration at Castle Muhn.'

'It is indeed.'

'And good evening, Master Araf,' the tall man said.

Araf bowed.

'Esus,' Fergal said, 'I would like you to meet Conor. Conor, Esus.'

'Good evening,' I said, bowing in the same manner as Araf.

The tall man bowed back, but only slightly.

'Esus,' Fergal explained, 'is the Elf that takes care of the trees around Castle Ur.'

'You're an Elf?' I blurted before I could stop myself.

'I have that distinction – yes.'

'Well,' I said, trying to recover my composure, 'some of my best friends are Elves.'

'Oh yes,' Esus said, 'who?'

What a stupid thing to say. What was I going to do now? This was the first person I had met in The Land that I hadn't tried to stab – I was starting to miss my old method of greeting people.

'Ah ... Legolas. Do you know him?'

'No,' said Esus. 'What clan is he in?'

'I don't know,' I said. 'Hey, when I said best friends, I really meant acquaintances.'

The awkward moment was saved by the arrival of our wine. Fergal and even Araf got very excited.

'Ah, my first taste of the new vintage. To Gerard and his vines,' Fergal toasted, and we all clinked our mugs.

I'm not a real big fan of wine. Oh, I'll have the odd glass at a posh dinner, but by and large I'd rather have a beer any day of the week; but this was wine I would sell my soul for. It was the nectar of the gods. I had an image of Bacchus, the Roman wine god, waltzing in and throwing a barrel of this stuff over his shoulder.

I don't know why I was so surprised that this was the finest wine I had tasted, as everything I had tried in The Land had been the best thing I had ever seen or smelt or tasted – but surprised I was. 'Wow! This is awesome!' I shouted, so loud that everyone around the bar turned to look.

'It's alright,' Esus said, dropping his voice to a whispered, 'I think Gerard is skimping on the gold a bit this year – but so is everyone.'

'You mean there is better wine than this?' I said, between slurps.

That was a mistake. Esus went into a litany of vintages, giving detailed descriptions of each year's colour, flavour and bouquet. He was a wine bore. I spotted it instantly and didn't even try to keep up. While I pretended to listen to him, I contemplated meeting my first Elf. He didn't look like an Elf. Here I was in a room full of Elves, Imps, Banshees and God knows what else and everyone looked so – normal. To be honest I was a bit disappointed. In the back of my mind I wanted this party to be like the Cantina scene in *Star Wars*, but it seems that the difference between an Elf and a Banshee is like the difference between a Norwegian and an Italian. Sure, you could tell the difference, but underneath they were all pretty much the same.

The sun had almost set, and the light shining through the vine trellis was waning. Just as I thought, *We could use a little light in here*, as if on cue about twenty of the waiting staff entered the room each holding a small pyramid of glowing gold wire balls. A handsome and distinguished man, also holding five glowing wire balls, strode into the centre of the room. The golden glow from his hands was brighter than all of the others – it illuminated his purple velvet outfit and his silver beard, and twinkled in ancient but still-mischievous eyes. He looked like a king out of a pack of cards. The crowd parted and applauded as he made his way to a small dais in the centre of the room.

Fergal nudged my side. 'Look, it's Gerard.'

Gerard tried to raise his hand to quiet the crowd and almost dropped the balls he was holding. He laughed heartily at this, as did everyone. We all quietened down to hear.

'My good friends,' he boomed, and I instantly knew he meant it – he loved these people and they loved him. 'Welcome to Muhn. Every year I am amazed and humbled that so many of you would travel so far just to sample my newest vintage.'

Someone shouted, 'Wouldn't miss it for the world!' and the assemblage replied with a, 'Hear, hear!'

'Thank you,' Gerard continued. 'I am especially heartened that so many of you have come for this harvest. I know how difficult a time you have had this year.'

The crowd mumbled. I heard Esus whisper, 'That's a first.'

'What is?' I asked.

'Gerard never makes political statements like that.'

'But as you know,' Gerard continued, 'Castle Muhn is no place for talk like that – even by me. Anyone heard grumbling tonight will be tossed out of my highest window' – this brought laughter and cheers – 'for tonight is a celebration!'

At that, he threw the five glowing balls he was holding up into the air and began to juggle. All of the servants threw theirs, and all at once the air was full of cascading, glowing wire orbs. The jugglers then began to pass the balls among themselves. Guests everywhere were ducking as glowing missiles just missed their heads. Now I have done a bit of juggling in my day and I can tell you – these were no ordinary juggling balls. The jugglers weren't even breaking a sweat. They never dropped one or hit anybody and if you watched closely, you could see sometimes the balls waited until the juggler was ready before they fell back to earth.

Someone shouted, 'Hup,' and all of the jugglers threw their remaining balls high in the air, where they just kept on going! The balls intertwined themselves with the vine trellis and then glowed even brighter. They bathed the room in golden light. The applause, the hoots and hollering were deafening. The music kicked in and the party truly began.

Fergal slapped me on the back and said, 'We need some food!'

Food! Every time I heard that, I thought, *What a good idea.* We weaved our way through vines of people until we came upon what looked like a five-acre buffet table. I have never seen so much food. Who was it all for? It made me worry that the busload of three-headed Giants and Trolls hadn't arrived yet. I found a plate and just piled it on. I took a little bit of everything – if the apples were anything to go by, this was going to be the best meal of my life. I stopped when the food on my plate started to resemble the Leaning Tower of Pisa. One more crumb and I would have had a spilled food disaster of horrific proportions.

I looked up to find that I had lost my friends. I searched around a bit but I couldn't see them. I couldn't risk weaving through the crowd looking for them with this overflowing plate, so I sat down alone in a nearby chair. My intention was to try to eat the top off my food mountain until it was transportable. The food was so good, my moaning drew stares. I chomped in ecstasy as I spied on the other guests. I was starting to figure stuff out. Banshees and Elves were mostly tall, with Banshees being dark while the Elves were fair. Imps were shorter and, as a rule, built like bowling pins, including the women. There were others that looked like they could have been TV presenters and still more that I couldn't put into any category I knew yet. I was also starting to gauge how old people were without seeing their eyes. A sense of seniority poured out of some like an aura. The way they talked and walked, or just held themselves, made it easy to separate the young ones from the elders.

A large dance started up. It looked like fun, but unbelievably complicated. It seemed as if the dance was designed for the room. Partners held hands and then danced around the statues in circles of eight, then sixteen, or more if a statue was on its side, and then as if they all had a secret radio in their ears, they made a huge undulating circle around the room before somehow finding their partners again. It was lucky they were immortals because it probably took a couple of hundred years to learn it.

The monument of food on my lap had vanished. My stomach was full and the wine had pleasantly gone to my head. I was just about to dance my way through the room and search for my newfound friends when I was overcome by an awful pang of guilt. I slumped in my chair and thought, *What right do I have to celebrate? My father is lying wounded somewhere, maybe even dead. I may never get back to my life in the Real World and even if I do it will be in tatters. I'll most likely flunk out of high school and Sally will never speak to me again.* All of a sudden I felt out of place and alone – just a little boy who had lost his mother. That's when I heard a woman's voice behind me.

'My father says that Castle Muhn does not have enough magic to solve all your problems – just enough to allow you to leave them outside the front door.'

I turned and almost fell in love. She was casually rolling one of those glowing juggling balls over her fingers and from hand to hand, making the light waltz around her face and sparkle in young, dark eyes. She wore a purple velvet dress and her curly black hair cascaded onto her bare shoulders. I know I should be ashamed of myself, but at that second, my parents, Sally, my life – all shot straight out of my head. I was filled with the vision before me.

'It seems by your face,' she said, 'that you have smuggled your problems in with you.'

'Not any more,' I said. 'They're gone, out-a-here.'

She smiled and my heart pounded.

'I couldn't help noticing the strange runes on your tunic.'

I looked down and laughed. I was amazed that no one had mentioned it before. I was wearing my New York Yankees sweatshirt.

'These are special runes where I come from, they mean I'm cool.'

She reached out and touched them. 'They don't feel cool.'

'My name is Conor.'

'I am pleased to meet you, Conor. I am Essa.'

We bowed to each other without losing eye contact.

'I am sure we have never met, Conor. What house are you from?'

'I came with Araf,' I said, sidestepping the question.

'Araf!' she screamed and jumped up and down. 'Is he here? Where?'

'I don't know, I've lost him.'

'Well, we must find him.'

She grabbed my hand and pulled me into the party. She was moving fast and I was being thrown into fellow guests and upsetting mugs, but there was no way I was going to let go of that hand. We found Fergal and Araf with a bunch of others sitting on a horizontal black pawn. Essa released my hand and launched herself at Araf, who caught her and returned the hug. It was the first time in my life I wished I was an Imp.

'Why didn't you tell me you were coming?' she said.

Araf shrugged.

'And you must be Fergal. Araf has told me so much about you.'

I couldn't help wondering when Araf did all this talking. A servant brought us fresh mugs of wine. Fergal looked as if he'd had plenty already. Essa whispered into the servant's ear.

'Your father throws a hell of a party,' Fergal slurred.

'He does, doesn't he? Here's to Dad!' Essa said, raising her mug in a toast.

'Your father is Gerard?' I asked.

'The one and only.'

'Well, I'll drink to that.'

The waiter returned, carrying two banta sticks that he handed to Essa. She took both sticks and threw one to Araf. The assembled crowd *ooh*ed at the challenge. Araf caught the stick but didn't look interested. Another servant arrived with headgear and protective clothing. Essa put on leather gloves, a heavy leather jacket that almost came down to her knees and a protective headpiece – a white helmet with a thin gold wire mesh covering the face.

Despite the heckling of the crowd, Araf refused to stand up. Fergal came up behind him and put a helmet on his head – but still he sat there.

'I, Essa of Muhn, challenge you, Araf of Ur, to single banta combat.'

She struck a stance similar to an *en garde* position in fencing – right foot forward with knees bent. She looked magnificent. In her right hand she held the banta in the middle. The weapon had a knot of wood at one end which she pointed directly at Araf. If this was a proper and formal challenge, Araf showed no sign of partaking. He just sat there.

A smile crossed Essa's face. She spun the banta in her hand like a baton twirler and in a flash covered the distance between her and Araf. She brought the smaller end of her stick down on his head and then bounced backwards, retaking her defensive stance – her stick across her chest with the left hand stretched forward for balance. I had never seen anything so graceful. She obviously knew what she was doing.

The audience loved it. The group erupted when the thud came from Araf's helmet. Someone shouted, 'One to Essa.'

Essa waited in her defensive pose but it was unnecessary. Araf wasn't playing. He sat there like an old dog ignoring a rambunctious puppy. This didn't seem to bother her. She launched herself into a spinning, swirling attack that hit Araf on the right shoulder. If it hurt, and it sure looked like it did, Araf didn't show it. The crowd, that was getting larger by the minute, howled with delight.

'Two to nought for Essa!' Fergal shouted.

'How high does the score go?'

'Essa challenged him to a formal match,' Fergal said. 'Each landed blow is one point and a knock-down is five. The first to eleven is the winner.'

Essa attacked again. This attack was a mirror image of the previous one. This time she landed her stick on Araf's left shoulder.

'Well, it looks like Araf is going to lose this one,' I said.

'I don't think so,' Fergal said.

'Why not?'

'Because he never has.'

'Never has what?'

'He has never lost. Araf is the undefeated banta fighting champion of all of The Land.'

'Well, at the moment,' I said, 'Essa looks pretty good.'

Fergal smiled. 'Keep watching.'

Essa backed away and then launched into a new and bolder attack. She came at Araf and then leaped over his head! I once saw a deer on a country road jump over a tall fence – Essa had the same majestic poise. In mid-air she connected with two blows on the side of Araf's helmet and landed behind him with two more points under her belt. The crowd applauded. Araf didn't even turn around.

Essa walked around Araf and stood directly in front of him. She crouched down and looked into his eyes and smiled. There might have been a flicker of a smile from Araf in reply. With the big end of her stick she tapped Araf's faceplate. The wire mesh glowed for a second. There was obviously some magic protecting the face. The entire audience shouted, 'FIVE.' She tapped again. 'SIX,' again, 'SEVEN, EIGHT, NINE.'

On the blow that should have been 'TEN', Araf moved his head quickly to the left, Essa was thrown off balance and Araf poked his stick between her feet and tripped her. She went down fast. The audience booed but in good humour. Essa had been cocky – she had that coming. She rolled quickly to her feet. Araf slowly stood.

Now things were getting interesting. The crowd was buzzing. Essa backed away and the partygoers gave them room. A giant people-edged arena formed, with everyone watching. Essa backed into the middle of the room and retook her defensive posture. Araf walked towards her and stopped two stick-lengths away and bowed. Even though the score was nine-to-five, he was indicating that *now*, the duel had truly begun. Essa nodded in reply.

Araf took a stance. Not the graceful Tai Chi-like posture of Essa, but a flat-footed straight-on stance. He held his banta across his chest with both hands, like the staff fights in old Robin Hood movies. This was a battle between style and brawn.

Essa mounted a twirling attack to the head. Araf parried it and brought the bottom end of his stick up for a counter-attack. Essa spun and dodged it – just. The two of them were feeling each other out. Essa tried a lower attack but this failed. Araf's parry was so strong that she momentarily lost her balance, allowing Araf to get her with a counter-blow to her side that made me wince.

'SIX,' came a cry from the crowd.

The combatants stared at each other for a minute and then Araf initiated his first offensive attack. For a big guy, he moved fast. There was no twirling or pirouettes, just a direct attack – wide, quick, sweeping blows from alternating sides. Essa had no difficulty with the speed but she didn't have the strength to block the blows without a step backwards. She gave ground with every parry and was running out of room. I expected her to start swinging around in a circle but she continued straight back, each block pushing her closer into a corner. Just when I thought it was all over for her, she bent her knees and dived, head first over Araf's head! With the poise of an Olympic high diver, she jumped Araf's banta stick and then planted her own stick on top of Araf's shoulder, pole-vaulting and somersaulting behind him.

The crowd went wild. 'TEN,' they screamed in unison.

Six to ten – if Essa could land one more blow, she would win. I heard someone yell, 'Who is the student and who is the master now?'

So that was it, Essa had studied under Araf. This was a student-teacher grudge match. The light-heartedness that marked the beginning of the duel was gone. Araf clumped into his stance – Essa flowed into hers. We waited to see who would initiate the next attack. The only sound was Essa's breathing.

Araf broke the calm. With an unexpected twirl of his banta stick he came at Essa with a series of angled-down swings that blurred into a continuous figure of eight. It looked as if Essa had just stepped in front of a taxiing airplane. I could see in her eyes that the master had not taught the student everything. Initially she didn't even try to parry. She backed away, attempting to decipher the rhythm of the attack. Before she ran out of space, she experimented with parries that succeeded in slowing down the attack – but only a bit. For a second time she tried her flipping pole-vaulting manoeuvre – she should never have attempted it twice. Araf dodged her stick, turned and made contact with her calf in mid-air. She landed on one foot, not enough to keep her balance. She hit the floor skidding. The only thing hurt was her pride. A five-point knockdown – she had lost.

Araf helped her to her feet, then stood in front of her and formally bowed – Essa hit him over the head with her stick. The crowd erupted in laughter. The fighters took off their masks and Essa planted a huge kiss on Araf's cheek. For the second time today I wished I was an Imp.

Essa hung on Araf's arm as they returned. Fergal added his slap to all of the others that Araf had received on his back as he travelled through the crowd.

'Thank you for upholding the honour of the House of Ur,' Fergal slurred. He was past tipsy and well nigh on to very drunk.

'That was very impressive,' I said to Essa.

'I would have been more impressive if I had won.'

'I was rooting for you.'

She smiled. It was very nice.

'You should have a fight, Conor,' Fergal said as he stumbled into me. 'You would kick ass around here with that snap spell you are wearing.'

'You are *wearing* a snap spell?' someone said behind me.

I turned to answer when out of the corner of my eye I saw Fergal grab Essa's banta stick.

'It's an amazing spell – watch this!' he said as he swung. I remember the look of surprise on everyone's faces as the stick hit my skull. Then everything went black.

The first thing I remember thinking as I came to was, *Is this my third concussion this week or my fourth?* In my whole life, I had never even been dizzy – now it seemed I couldn't go a day without being knocked cold. I was disappointed that you don't actually see stars and tweeting birds, like in cartoons, but I can assure you that you get great big bumps.

I felt a cold compress being applied to my forehead, and when I opened my eyes I saw that my nurse was Essa.

'I've died, haven't I?' I said.

'I don't think so.' She looked worried.

'No, I must be dead because you're an angel.' OK, it was a bit corny but I was quite proud of coming up with a line that good so soon after multiple concussions.

'I think you must be feeling better,' she said, and took the cold compress off my forehead.

I sat up. I had a pain in my head that I hadn't experienced since my last blow to the head – earlier that day I think. I winced.

'You wouldn't have any of that willow tea around, would you?'

'Here, drink this.' She handed me a tiny glass with no more than two thimblefuls of brown liquid.

'Is that all I get?'

'Believe me, that is all you need. It's my father's special tonic. It will make you feel better.'

I downed it in one. Had I been facing a mirror, I would have seen steam shooting out of my ears. I sat bolt upright in bed and croaked, 'WOW!'

Essa laughed. 'You'll be better now,' and stood to go.

I was instantly better but I didn't want to let her go. I grabbed the wet cloth and put it in her hand. 'Don't go, I think I'm going to faint,' I said, trying to look as ill as I could and lying back down on the bed.

'What makes me think that you are not being sincere?' She smiled.

'Oh, the pain!' I said and I pulled her hand, to make her place the cloth on my forehead. She lost her balance and pretty much fell on top of me. She laughed a little bit and didn't immediately get up. Her face was only inches away, her lips were so close I could feel her breath. I stared straight into her eyes, those magnificent dark eyes and then … her father came in.

Essa sat bolt upright. I think she moved even faster than she did during her banta fight with Araf. 'I think he is feeling better, Father.'

I sat up.

'That, I can see. Leave us, daughter, will you.'

Essa gave me a glance. She looked worried, and to be honest I didn't like Gerard's tone either.

Before she left Gerard said, 'May I borrow your pendant for a little while?'

This seemed to shock her. She removed a finger-sized crystal that was hanging from a plain gold chain around her neck and handed it to her father. She gave me one last apprehensive look and left.

Gerard took a step closer to the bed, drew a sword and pointed it an inch from my throat.

'Honest, sir,' I said, 'I didn't even kiss her.'

TEN

GERARD

'Do you recognise the sword at your throat?' Gerard asked. With extreme effort I released my attention from the point and glanced down the mirror-like blade to the pommel. 'It's mine.'

Gerard held Essa's necklace in his left hand. The crystal that hung from it was embedded with flecks of gold. 'This is an Owith glass,' he said, 'it will darken if you lie. If I were you, I would tell the truth. Did you steal this sword?'

Now that was a tricky question. I sort of stole it from Cialtie, but Dad said it was his. 'My father gave it to me.'

The crystal flickered but remained clear.

'Is Conor your real name?'

'No,' I said, just to see what would happen.

Essa's necklace instantly went dark. This truth crystal was the real thing. I felt the point of my blade at my throat.

'I suggest you try that again. Is Conor your real name?'

'Yes.'

'And who is your father?'

'I can't tell you that.'

'Why not?'

'Because you will kill me if I do.'

'Well then, Conor, you have a dilemma, because I'm going to kill you if you don't.'

'What do you have against me?'

'This blade, that you casually checked in at my door, is the Sword of Duir. Did you know that?'

'Yes,' I said. The crystal remained clear.

'The only way you could possess this blade, is if you stole it. I am a very tolerant man, but I cannot abide a thief.'

'I told you, my father gave it to me.'

'The crystal bears you out – so the thief must be your father.'

I felt my anger rise. 'My father is no thief – the sword was his to give.'

'Are you claiming to be the son of Cialtie?'

'Cialtie?' I spat, and before I could stop myself, 'I am the son of Oisin of Duir.'

Gerard looked at the crystal and stepped back. 'Stand up,' he ordered.

I did as I was told. I wasn't as shaky on my feet as I should have been. That little drink had really done its stuff.

Gerard kept the sword pointed to my chest and looked at me as if anew. How could I have been so stupid? I just blurted out who I was and now he was going to do his duty and kill me.

'My gods! You *are* of Duir,' he roared. 'I don't know how I missed it before. Oisin's son – you are Oisin's son!' He raised the sword and came at me, fast.

There was nowhere to run, I was finished. I placed my hands in front of my chest and closed my eyes.

He wrapped his huge arms around me and gave me a hug that would have put an anaconda to shame. 'Oisin has a son!' He laughed – a hearty laugh that shook the room. He put both hands on my shoulders and looked at me from arm's length.

I opened one eye. 'Don't you want to kill me?'

'Why in The Land would I want to do that?'

'Everyone else around here does – the son of the one-handed prince thing.'

'Oh my, that *is* an old prophecy – one of Ona's, is it not?'

I nodded.

Gerard laughed. 'I can't tell you how many times some sorceress told me that my next harvest would fail or be the finest vintage – bah! I don't have much faith in soothsayers. The good ones (like Ona, may she rest in piece) don't lie – but that doesn't mean that what they say is the truth. Anyway, it takes an awful lot for me to kill someone, and I'm certainly not going to kill a young man as fine as you because of something an old witch said thousands of years ago. Oisin's son!' He hugged me again, this time lifting me off the ground.

'Tell me, Conor, where have you been hiding all of these years?'

I wondered for a second if I should make something up, but I just couldn't help trusting this man. I sat down on the bed and told Gerard the whole tale – it just poured out. Gerard pulled up a chair and I went through it all: my life in the Real World, the death threats, the revelations, the emotions, the journeys, the fights, the meetings – the concussions. I wasn't only telling Gerard, I was telling myself too. I had been living moment to moment, just trying to stay alive. Now that I had put it all together I realised it was a hell of a story. I ended by saying, 'So I have to find my mother. I think she is in a place called the Fililands, but Fergal says they don't exist. Can you help me?'

'Oisin and Deirdre have a son,' Gerard mused. 'This,' he said, breaking out of his reverie, 'is the finest news I have heard in a long, long time. Are you thirsty, Conor?'

'You wouldn't have a beer, would you?'

Gerard roared with laughter at this. 'In all of The Land I am the only man who could answer that question with a "yes".' He put his arm around me and waltzed me out of the room. We walked down a corridor that overlooked the courtyard. Through imperfect glass windows I could see another banta fight in progress. The party was still in full swing. At the top of an immense staircase Gerard bellowed, and several servants appeared.

'Bring ale and food to the library,' he ordered. 'After that, we are not to be disturbed.'

We continued and then turned down a corridor with numerous small alcoves cut into the walls. In each was a carved wooden statue. Some were model castles, some were miniature thrones, most were busts of men and women. All were of different wood. Gerard stopped at a bust of a handsome man with a full beard carved in red wood.

'This is your grandfather.'

'Finn?' I asked.

'No. This is your other grandfather, on your mother's side, Liam – the last lord of the House of Cull. He was a good man.' Sadness invaded Gerard's face and for a moment he looked old. 'He was my friend.'

We arrived at the library at the same time as our food and drink. I was expecting an impressive chamber with bookshelves towering to the sky, but instead I found a smallish, comfortable room with just a few books, a wine rack, a desk, some overstuffed chairs and a deerskin sofa.

'I'm not much of a reader,' Gerard said, guessing my thoughts. 'If you wanted to see a great library you should have seen your grandfather's. It was a huge affair with a courtyard in the centre where he grew the Tree of Knowledge.'

'The Tree of Knowledge?' I asked.

'Yes – I told you. He held the Rune of Cull.'

I must have looked confused.

'Oh gods, I forget you don't know about all of this. Right, Liam, your grandfather, was Lord of the Cull – the Hazellands. He sat in the Hazelwood Throne and was the custodian of the Hall of Knowledge. The best and the brightest from all The Land were welcome to study in his library, and before they left, they were allowed a hazelnut from the Tree of Knowledge. The fruit of the Tree of Knowledge ensured they would remember all that they had learned. It was a wonderful place.'

'You talk like it's no longer there.'

'It's not,' he said, the heaviness returning to his face, 'it's all ruin. The Land lost the Hall, and I lost a friend – and my only son.'

'Your son?'

'My son was studying at the Hall, in fact he was one of your mother's tutors.'

'What happened?'

'No one knows. Something, an army or a force, attacked Cull, and there was little defence. It was unthinkable that anyone would want to attack the Hall of Knowledge. Why would you defend against the unthinkable? Your mother and your Aunt Nieve were on some sort of sorceress' quest. They were the ones who found the Hall and the Tree destroyed, and all of the students and tutors dead.'

'I'm sorry.'

'As am I, but I have learned not to dwell on it. Although I will always remember, my mourning days are done. I do not want it to consume me like it almost consumed your mother.'

'My mother?'

'Yes, until I spoke to you today I had not heard of her since her banishment. You see, it is believed that the need for vengeance drove her to learn Shadowmagic. I think she thought it would allow her to discover who, or what, destroyed Cull. From what you say, it would seem she still does not know. Maybe like me, she has put the matter to rest. I hope so.'

I took a sip of my beer. It was dark, a bit sudsy and too warm but it was drinkable. 'Not bad,' I said.

'Thank you. I learned how to make ale in Ireland but I have never gotten it to catch on over here.'

'Ireland? You mean like the Ireland from my world?'

'Yes, long ago. I made a trip to the Real World the year before my Choosing. I travelled with my cousin, Cullen.'

'Cullen? Cu-cullen,' I said, using the Celtic prefix that literally means hound but is used to mean hero or king, 'the Irish warrior?'

Gerard laughed so hard at that he spat out his beer. 'A warrior!' he howled. 'Where did you hear that?'

'Irish mythology is full of stories of the great warrior King Cucullen, his great battles and how he slew entire armies single-handedly – but this was thousands of years ago.'

Gerard was still chuckling. 'Yes, I guess that would be about right. I went to the Real World with Cullen but I didn't return with him. He just loved those Irish women and they loved him. You see, Cullen was a wonderful storyteller and like all good storytellers, he never let the truth get in the way of a good tale. Those Irish folks back then just couldn't get enough of his stories and his music. Gods, when he played the flute it was like a spell, he could make you dance one moment and weep the next. I can imagine him telling a few tall tales about himself.'

'Did he never return?'

'Oh, he did, but he was never happy here. He was a fool, always wanting more than he had – a good man but a fool nonetheless. He used to take little holidays to the Real World on horseback – he never returned from the last one.'

'What happened to him?'

'Probably the same thing that happened to the poor guard that came to your home with Nieve.'

'You think Cucullen fell off his horse and got old quick?'

'There were rumours that he forgot and got off by himself. He never was the sharpest arrow in the quiver.'

'So if your foot touches the ground in the Real World and you become the age you would be in The Land, then how come my father didn't dust-it? I get the impression that he has a few hundred years under his belt.'

'That is a question for him and your mother – as are most of the other questions I can almost hear flicking through your mind. Before I send you to bed, Conor of Duir, I shall answer one more question – it is the first question you asked of me. You asked if I could help you find the Fililands. The answer is yes. Many people think the Fililands are a myth, a story to scare children, but they are real. Long ago the Fililands were sealed off by your grandfather, Finn, but since then a new frontier has opened. I think you may be able to enter the Fililands through the Reedlands.'

'The Reedlands?'

'The Reedlands came into being when your Uncle Cialtie chose the Reed Rune.'

'I thought I heard Cialtie say he held the Duir Rune?'

'He does now. But his first rune was the Reed Rune. After your father and then your grandfather went missing, he repeated the Choosing and chose the Duir Rune. People thought it was strange but he does hold the rune now.'

'What happened to the Reedlands?'

'Cialtie explored them, renounced them and left them to fallow. They lie just past the Hazellands and I suspect they border the Fililands. If I am right, the border will not be sealed there. You should be able to enter the Fililands from the Reedlands.'

'Can you take me there?'

'Me?' Gerard laughed. 'Good gods! The last thing you need is me giving you directions. No, I know someone who could get you there. Sleep tonight and tomorrow I shall see if I can persuade my guide to accompany you.'

'Thank you, Lord Gerard.'

'No, thank you, Conor.'

'For what?'

'For being the son of Cull and Duir. For a long time I have feared for the future of both of those houses – less now.' We stood and he put his arm around my shoulder as we walked to the door.

'Did you really like the beer?' he asked.

'To be honest, sir, I would like it a little lighter and colder – oh, and fizzier.'

He opened the door. A servant was waiting. Gerard instructed him to escort me to the tower and to give me a shot of poteen to help me sleep. As Gerard closed the door I heard him mumbling to himself, 'Lighter and fizzier – hmm.'

The tower turned out to be a very comfortable room with a bed big enough for a football team. It wasn't until I saw the sheets that I realised how exhausted I was – I wasn't going to need the poteen. I undressed and got under the covers, and the servant put a small glass of clear liquid on the bedside table. Sleep was seconds away when I remembered something that Cialtie had said to my father. He said the last time he saw Finn he was on horseback on the way to the Real World and that he had stabbed the horse! He killed him, he killed his own father. He killed my grandfather. Rage enveloped me, my blood boiled and my thoughts turned to revenge. Sleep was no longer an option. I sat up in bed and fantasised about the different ways I would kill Cialtie. My hand shook as I grabbed the glass and thoughtlessly knocked back the poteen. Instantly, Cialtie didn't seem like such a bad guy after all. I laid back and put my hands behind my head. I thought, *Why make such a fuss out of everything?* I started to count my blessings. I was asleep before I got very far.

*   *   *

I awoke to a slap in my face – considering the dream I was having, I deserved it. But this slap in the face wasn't from Essa in dreamland, it was real. I opened my eyes to see a fully dressed Fergal passed out next to me in the bed. He had rolled over and backhanded me in the face. I threw his arm over to his side, only to have it come back and whack me a second time. I made a mental note never to sleep with Fergal again and got out of bed.

A servant was waiting in the hallway. He showed me to a bathroom kitted out with a steaming Olympic-sized sunken bathtub. Ah, life's simple pleasures. I had a feeling I had better enjoy it while I could – the trip to the Fililands didn't sound like it was going to be a Sunday afternoon stroll.

When I got out of the bath I noticed that my clothes had been replaced with linen underwear and a soft leather shirt and trousers. Well – when in Rome.

Breakfast was busy. Obviously many of the partygoers had stayed the night, or more probably hadn't gone to bed at all. I saw Araf sitting with Essa, and joined them.

'Good morning,' I said.

Araf nodded.

Essa said, 'Good morning, sir.'

'Sir? What happened to Conor? *Sir* is my dad.'

'Good morning – Conor, I have to go now,' she said and left.

I turned to Araf. 'What was that about?'

He shrugged.

If I hadn't just taken a bath I would have sniffed my armpits – she acted like I had just cleaned out the elephant stables.

'Have I done something to upset her?'

Araf shrugged again.

'You know, you're a real pleasure to chat with, Araf – and by the way my head is fine. Thank you for asking.'

This got a nod.

We ate in silence. I had a billion questions but I knew trying to strike up a conversation with Araf would be like trying to build the pyramids on my own. I was almost finished when a servant informed me that I was wanted in the armoury.

I followed him to a different wing of the castle until we arrived at a gymnasium-sized, glass-roofed room. Hanging on racks around the chamber was an impressive collection of weapons: swords, bows, crossbows and an entire wall of banta sticks. In the centre of the room stood the same old man who had taken our weapons from us when we first arrived at the party. He was holding my sword belt. He motioned me over.

'You are Conor?'

'Yes,' I said.

'This is your sword?'

'Yes.'

'Put it on.'

I fastened it around my waist.

'So, Conor of Duir – son of the one-handed Prince Oisin – BE AT GUARD!' He drew his sword and assumed an attacking stance.

I raised my hands. 'Hey, I'm not going to fight you.'

'Pity,' he said, 'I so dislike stabbing an unarmed man. Oh well – so be it.'

He drove the point of his sword directly at my heart.

ELEVEN

THE DAHY

I jumped to the left, just in time to stop myself from being pierced. 'Hey! Let's talk about this.'

'I'm not here to talk,' the old guy said. 'If I were you, I would draw my sword, or duck.'

He came at me with a high backhanded cut to the head. Not only did I duck, I hit the floor and rolled to my left. I quickly got back on my feet in a crouch.

'The roll was good,' my attacker informed me, 'but the position is not.'

I took a quick glance around me and saw what he meant. I had boxed myself into a corner.

'Since you like to talk so much,' the old man said, 'I will tell you one more thing. I am going to come at you with a forehand mid-cut. It will be too low to duck and too high to jump. The only defence is to draw and parry, or run and bleed.'

I only took a microsecond to realise he was right. He cocked his sword way back and then came at me with both blade and body. I drew my sword, deflected the attack with a low parry and retreated to the middle of the room.

Our chatting phase was obviously over. He instantly attacked me with a series of sweeping and powerful cuts, alternating high and low.

I blocked and back-pedalled. To be honest, I was terrified. For as long as I could remember my father trained me in sword fighting, and I had also won a few local fencing tournaments, but this was the real thing. The swords were steel and the points were sharp. One sloppy parry and I was dead! Then my father's words came back to me – '*In a real sword fight, son, all thoughts of winning and losing must be suppressed. Keep one eye on his eyes and the other on his blade. Be aware of your surroundings, block and counter until your opponent tires.*'

I used to laugh at him when he said stuff like that. 'When will I ever be in a real sword fight,' I'd say, 'and for that matter, when were you ever in a real fight?' *I take it all back now, Pop – if I live through this.*

I forced my father's advice into my head and the fight attained a rhythm. In fact it became familiar. This old guy's forearm attack was very similar to my father's favourite assault. My father would start a major attack with a flurry of forearm cuts, then change into a reverse grip, like he was holding an ice pick, then follow through with an elbow to the chin. He called the move a Dahy Special. Sure enough, that's exactly what this guy did! I knew from experience that the sword in this manoeuvre was less dangerous than the elbow. I parried the sword hard, forcing his arm to straighten, and then ducked the elbow. I sent the old guy off balance and then started a counter-attack of my own. I came at him with a series of low cuts. I like swinging up – it's unsettling for an opponent. It leaves my face exposed, but I'm pretty good at bobbing and weaving. The sword felt good in my hand, like an extension of my arm. The old guy parried the cuts with grace, but I could see that I had him working. He parried my last cut and countered with a high downward thrust that caught me by surprise. By the time I blocked it, I was down on one knee. We locked swords – pommel to pommel. I racked my brain for a means of escaping – I knew that as soon as our swords disengaged I was very vulnerable. The sweat was streaming into my eyes and my arm was starting to shake. I couldn't keep this up for much longer.

'That's enough!' came a shout from the door.

The old man pulled back and Gerard entered the room. I dropped my guard, sat on my feet, and breathed a huge sigh of relief.

'How is he?' Gerard said.

'Not too bad,' the old guy said, 'his left side is weak but his footwork is good. Nothing that cannot be fixed.'

'Wait a minute,' I said, 'this was a test?'

'It was indeed,' Gerard said. 'I wanted to make sure if I was going to risk my best guide, that you could at least take care of yourself. Dahy here is my master-at-arms.'

'Dahy! You taught my father.'

'Yes, I did. And may I say, my student taught you well, but not well enough.' He addressed Gerard. 'In two days I can get him to a minimum preparedness.'

'Conor, you are under Dahy's tutelage now, so work hard. You shall leave for the Fililands in three days' time,' Gerard said, and left us alone.

'Now, Conor,' Dahy said, with a gleam in his eye that I wasn't sure I liked, 'we begin.'

The next two days were the hardest of my life. Dahy drilled me like an SAS sergeant gone berserk. We worked on swordplay, archery and banta stick fighting. My biggest difficulty was my left hand. I had always fought with my non-sword hand empty but Dahy taught me a method of using the sword in my right hand and a banta stick in my left. It made my head spin and my muscles scream. Luckily I found a supply of willow tea that helped me make it through the days, and some poteen to help me through the nights.

At mealtimes, I met a handful of people who had still not gone home from the party. Discussions of politics were outlawed in the castle, but when Gerard was out of earshot I learned that my Uncle Cialtie was universally hated. It seemed that Castle Duir sat on The Land's only gold mine. My grandfather Finn used to allocate a stipend of gold to each of the lords. The gold was used to fuel necessary magic. As of late, Cialtie had refused gold to most of the families and cut back considerably to the rest. The question was – what was he was doing with all of that gold? No one seemed to know.

I only saw Essa twice. Once I caught her watching Dahy and me from the viewing box above the armoury. I looked up and smiled.

Dahy hit me painfully in the shoulder with a stick, and by the time I looked back, she was gone. The second time was at lunch on my second day of training. I spotted her sitting at a table and sat down next to her. She immediately stood up to leave. I grabbed her wrist so I could talk to her – big mistake. The next thing I knew, I was face down in my lunch with my arm twisted painfully up my back and her forearm pushing my head into a bowl of salad.

'Don't ever grab me again,' she hissed in my ear.

'What is your major malfunction?' I spluttered.

She pulled my head back by the hair. 'What did you say?'

I wasn't sure if she hadn't understood the phrase, or if the face full of greens had screwed up my diction, so I rephrased. 'What have I done to make you act like this?'

She put her mouth close to my ear and whispered, 'I know who you are.'

'Who told?'

'My father.'

'Man, he's telling everybody.'

'Just me and Dahy.'

'So let me guess,' I said, wincing from the pressure that was still on my arm, 'unlike your father, you're a prophecy fan and you want me dead?'

'That's right.'

'Then go ahead.'

'My father has forbidden it.'

'Then let me go.'

She let go and walked away. I picked lettuce out of my nose with as much dignity as I could muster. 'Oh yeah,' I called after her, 'well, that tunic makes your bum look big.' It was a stupid thing to say. She didn't look back, but it did make her stop for a second before she continued off.

The afternoon light was disappearing on my second day of training when I received a message to meet with Gerard in his library.

Before I left, Dahy said, 'I have a gift for you.' He handed me a banta stick with copper bark and a pale knob.

'Do you recognise the wood?' he asked.

'I don't, it's too light for oak.'

'It is hazelwood. Light enough to be used for walking, but strong enough for a fight. It was given to me by your grandfather Liam. I want you to have it.'

I looked at the lacquered finish. It almost looked like the skin of a snake.

'Did you know him – my grandfather?'

'Yes, he was a good and wise man.' He chuckled to himself. 'He was also stubborn and careless. For ages I tried to get him to set up a garrison in the Hazellands, but he would not hear of it. "*The House of the Tree of Knowledge is a place of learning, not war*," he would say. Well, I was right but there is no comfort in that.' He sighed. 'I know he would have wanted you to have the stick. Now go, Conor, Gerard is waiting.'

'Thank you, Master Dahy,' I said, and I bowed my lowest ever bow.

I was surprised to find Fergal and Araf sitting with Gerard in the library. I had not seen Fergal since he had woken me up with a backhand. I had seen Araf around, but as usual we didn't gossip much.

'Sit down, Conor,' Gerard said. I did and almost disappeared into an overstuffed chair. 'It seems that the fates have thrown you and Fergal together. Not only did you meet by chance on the road, but your future paths also seem to be linked. Fergal here would like to meet Deirdre too.'

'Why?' I said, a little shocked.

Gerard replied for him. 'Fergal's motivations are his own, as are yours. I know why both of you seek an audience with Deirdre, and I can assure each of you that the other's reasons are noble. If you wish to tell the other, that is up to you. For now, I need to ask you, Conor – will you accept Fergal as your travelling companion?'

It didn't take long for me to decide. 'As long as he promises not to stab me, or hit me with sticks, or steal my shoes, or sleep with me – then I'm fine.'

Fergal's smile matched my own. He stood up and then, seeing me struggle, helped me out of my chair. We shook on it with both hands and then he slapped me on the back.

'And you have to stop slapping me on the back.'

'OK,' he said, and then he did it again.

'Araf has agreed to accompany you.'

'As our guide?'

'No, Araf does not know the Eastlands. I am having difficulty procuring you the proper guide – but I will. You will leave the day after tomorrow.'

'How will we travel?' I asked.

'I will provide horses,' Gerard said.

'Oh – I can't ride.'

'What!' Fergal and Gerard said in unison.

'It's not my fault. They didn't have horses in … where I grew up.'

'Right,' Gerard said, 'you have a day to learn to ride. Araf, will you teach him?'

Araf nodded.

I looked at Araf. 'In order to teach me, you might actually have to speak, are you prepared for that?'

He gave me one of his hallmark blank stares.

'This calls for a special toast.' Gerard climbed the ladder to the top of his wine rack and found a bottle. He blew the dust off and placed it in a gold bucket. As he went to the cabinet to get glasses, the cork slowly rose out of the bottle by itself. He poured us each a glass of the blood-red wine.

'This is a very special vintage. I pressed these grapes when Essa's mother was pregnant with her. I have saved most of it for her wedding, but I steal a bottle now and again for special occasions.' Gerard raised his glass. 'To your success and a safe journey.'

We drank. Man, was it good. Even if Essa looked like Porky Pig I would have considered marrying her, just so I could have another glass of that wine. As things stood, she wouldn't even talk to me – so I guessed that marriage was a long shot.

That night I dreamt that Sally and Essa had a banta fight. They both kept looking at me – wanting me to root for one or the other. The problem was I couldn't decide who I wanted to win. It finally made both girls so mad, they stopped fighting each other and came at me ...

I was shaken awake in the darkness. When my eyes adjusted I saw that it was Essa.

'I was just dreaming about you.'

'Get up,' she said. 'We have to go.'

'We? Go? Where?'

'We leave for the Fililands – now.'

'You are coming with us?'

'I'm your guide.'

'Cool, but I thought we were leaving tomorrow.'

'Change of plans,' Essa said. 'We leave now.'

'Why?'

'Because Cialtie and his Banshee witch are on the way. They will be here for breakfast.'

That popped me wide awake and out of bed. I threw on some clothes. 'Does he know I'm here?'

'I'll go and ask him, shall I?'

'Hey, unnecessary sarcasm. Are you going to be mean to me this entire trip?'

'We'll see.'

I grabbed my sword and hazel stick. 'Seriously, do you have any idea what Cialtie is doing here?'

'I think he is coming to see me,' Essa said.

'Why you?'

'Rumour has it, he is going to ask me to be his bride.'

'Yuck!' I said. 'We gotta get out of here.'

TWELVE

ACORN

A raf and Fergal were waiting for us in the hallway. We followed Essa down a narrow stairway that was concealed behind a tapestry. With every step the smell of horses became stronger. A short passageway led to a bale of hay that we pushed aside, and we found ourselves in the stables.

Gerard and Dahy were almost finished saddling the horses. Let me tell you – the horses in The Land are just huge! I had no idea how I would even get up on one of those guys, let alone ride it. The thought terrified me.

Gerard bid Fergal and Araf goodbye and then gave me a hug so he could whisper in my ear. 'When you see your mother and father, tell them they are welcome here. Take care of yourself, son of Duir, and take care of my daughter.'

'Yes, sir, and thank you.'

Dahy presented me with a knife. 'It is a throwing dagger,' Dahy said. 'The gold tip assures that it hits its target. Only use it as a last resort. Remember, when you throw a weapon, your enemy can pick it up and throw it back. It's bad form to be killed by your own knife.'

That was Dahy's idea of a joke. I smiled, bowed and stashed the knife in my sock.

'OK,' I said, 'how do you get up onto one of these monsters?'

Essa broke off from her goodbye embrace with her father and said, 'You don't know how to ride? I don't believe it!'

'Maybe I should have a T-shirt with *I CAN'T RIDE* printed on it. That way it won't come as a shock to everyone that finds out around here.' Araf pointed to a horse to my left. 'Is this one mine?'

He nodded. I examined the magnificent stallion. He was light grey with a wild white mane. As I craned my head back I wondered if I would actually be able to make it *all* the way up to the saddle.

'Don't you have any ponies? I rode a pony once at a birthday party.'

Araf interlaced his fingers together to give me a step up. I put my foot in his cupped hands and he hoisted me up over his head. I had an inkling that Araf was strong but I didn't realise just how strong. He damn near threw me over the beast without the slightest hint of effort! I arrived on top of my horse and unceremoniously hung onto its neck until I got some semblance of cool.

'Does he have a name?'

'Acorn,' Gerard replied, and smiled at me. '*From a tiny acorn grows a mighty oak*. He belonged to my son. Acorn here wandered back from the Hazellands after it was destroyed. He is the only thing to have made it out of there alive.'

I patted the enormous neck in front of me. 'Well, Acorn, you and me are going to be pals – right?'

Acorn turned his head and gave me a look with a plum-sized black eye that I unmistakably read as – '*We'll see*.'

A servant appeared and informed us that Cialtie's entourage would be arriving at first light – in about half an hour. Gerard and Dahy pushed aside a wall of hay bales, revealing a back door.

'Do you have any advice on riding this thing?'

'Hold on,' Araf said, and started through the door.

Acorn seemed happy to follow the other horses, which was fine with me. I leaned down and whispered in his ear, 'You just follow those guys and we'll be OK.'

He gave me a snort, as if to say, '*Don't tell me my business*.'

Even though the doorway was massive, I still had to duck as I went through. My confidence level was low. I couldn't help thinking what a long drop it was going to be *when* I fell off this monster. The back exit of the stables led almost directly into a path cut through a field of towering grain. We didn't have to hurry – the vegetation hid us completely. Just when I thought this horse riding lark wasn't too bad, the horses broke into a trot. Never in my life have I ever been bounced around so much. I figured another ten minutes of this would ensure that I never had an heir.

'Is riding supposed to be this uncomfortable?' I asked Araf with a jiggling voice that came out higher than normal.

'Stand up in your stirrups every three gaits,' he said.

I did, and what a difference it made. I got into the rhythm of the strides and started feeling like a rider.

We rode silently in single file for about an hour. I was behind Fergal, Essa was in the lead and Araf brought up the rear. The sun was fully up when we cleared the field. We entered a vast open meadow dotted with two-hundred-foot spire-like poplar trees. The land was green and rolling, a vast emerald carpet scattered with massive poplar exclamation marks. Essa gave what I now know is a hand signal and all of the horses broke into a canter – including Acorn. I grabbed the reins for support and Acorn ground to a halt, pitching me over his head. I flew butt over noggin and landed on the grass – still holding the reins. Luckily the grass was as soft as a gymnastics mat and I hurt nothing. It was probably the first time that I learned a lesson in The Land without pain. An upside-down Acorn gave me a look of pity. The company turned around and rode back.

'Don't say anything, Araf,' I said, 'let me guess. If you pull the reins the horse stops, right?'

'Everyone knows that!' Fergal said.

'Including me – now,' I said, slowly standing.

After two tries at remounting Acorn I said, 'Why don't these things come with ladders?'

Araf dismounted and helped me up. Essa warned me this time and we all broke into a canter. Compared to trotting, cantering is a breeze. My back and arms fell into rhythm with Acorn. I was so delighted with myself I let out a '*YEE-HA!*' I think a few trees gave me a dirty look. Fergal wanted to know why I shouted. I told him that it was the kind of thing that cowboys did.

'Are they boys that look like cows or cows that look like boys?' he asked.

'Never mind, just try it – it feels good.'

He let out a pretty good '*YEE-HA!*' for a beginner.

Essa pulled up next to us. 'If you insist on letting the entire land know where you are, I'll be leaving now.'

Fergal and I looked at each other like naughty schoolboys. When she was out of earshot we both let loose with a very quiet '*yee-ha*' in defiance.

The sun was low in the sky by the time Essa decided to stop. 'We'll make camp here,' she said. 'Araf and I will double-check the maps and get some food ready. Fergal, you tend the horses. Conor, go *ask* for firewood.'

Everyone dismounted except me. 'I can't move,' I said.

Fergal laughed and Essa told me to stop acting the fool, but I really couldn't move. I hurt in places I didn't even know I had places. We had ridden *all* day. I was exhausted. After the poplar meadow, all that I really remember of the ride was not stopping for lunch. We begged apples from a particularly unpleasant apple tree (a crab apple maybe) and ate them on horseback. Fergal complained all afternoon. I joined him, but after a while I was so tired, it was painful even to speak. The countryside was a blur after that.

I looked around to find that everyone had left. 'I'm not kidding,' I moaned, 'I really can't get off of this thing.' I flopped forward and dropped my arms around Acorn's neck. 'You wouldn't do me a favour by any chance,' I whispered in his ear, 'you wouldn't mind crouching down so I could roll off?'

It was meant to be a joke but Acorn did just that! He dropped to his front knees, then his back and then laid his belly on the ground. My stirrups almost touched the ground. With a monumental effort, I hoisted my leg over and flopped face first in the grass. I lifted my head and looked at my new best friend. 'Thank you, Acorn. I owe you one.' He stood up and went to find his fellow horses.

My legs were killing me. All of the hairs on the inside of my thighs had been rubbed out of my skin, which was turning the colour of a

Caribbean sunset. After taking my trousers down for a look, I didn't have the strength to pull them back on. I flopped on my back and instantly fell into a dreamless sleep. It was in this unseemly position that the rest of the group found me – asleep on my back with my trousers at my ankles. Fergal told me later that he tried to wake me up but I just babbled. I didn't open my eyes until it was dark and the smell of food hit me.

Dinner was beans around a fire. Essa ate, then walked off by herself. Araf handed me a cup of much-needed willow tea. 'If I could get some of this tea back to the Real World,' I said, 'I could make a fortune.'

'The Real World?' Fergal said. 'You're from the Real World?'

Me and my big mouth. 'Yes, I am.'

'So that's why you say so many stupid things.'

'I don't say stupid things.'

'You do,' Fergal said, flashing a smile that seemed to light up the place. 'Is that why you want to see Deirdre, to help you get back?'

'That's part of it. I really can't tell you the rest – sorry.'

'That's OK. Can you tell me about the Real World? What's it like?'

'Some of it is like here, only not as vivid. Compared to The Land, the Real World seems to have a thin veil of grey over everything.'

'Sounds awful.'

'Sometimes it is – but it's my home, or at least was – and no one ever tried to kill me there.'

'I didn't try to kill you!' Fergal protested.

'I didn't mean you.'

'Who else has tried to kill you?'

'It's a long list.'

'Conor,' Araf said, and I jumped. The guy is so quiet, you forget that he is there. 'If you have enemies, your travelling companions should know about it.'

He had a point. 'OK, two people have tried to kill me – Cialtie and Nieve.'

'Cialtie and Nieve,' Araf repeated, 'this is not good. Why do they want to kill you?'

I searched for a lie to keep them happy but couldn't do it – I had to trust these guys. I just hoped they weren't big prophecy fans. 'Because Deirdre is my mother.'

For the first time, probably in history, Araf looked startled. 'Who is your father?'

Before I could answer we heard the whinny of horses and a cry for help – it was Essa. I grabbed my stick and leaped to my feet. We found her with her banta stick drawn, standing between the horses and four wild boars. I had never seen a live boar before but I am certain that the ones in the Real World are nowhere near as big as these boys. They had Essa surrounded and looked mean. I was shocked to see Fergal and Araf walk up to them like they were puppies. One turned and charged at Fergal, four hundred pounds of flesh pushing two enormous tusks, hurtling towards him, and he just stood there, like a rabbit caught in headlights. I dived and pushed him out of the way, almost getting clobbered myself.

'What is the matter with you?' I screamed as we both clambered to our feet.

'What's the matter with me? What's the matter with the boar?'

We circled over to Essa.

'I have never seen anything like this,' she said. 'Something is very wrong with these animals.'

'What do you normally do when a boar attacks?' I whispered.

'Boars don't usually attack,' she said. 'This is a very bad sign.'

'Shoo!' Araf said, waving his hands and walking towards the biggest one of them. 'Go home!'

I was a bit jealous that Araf was having a longer conversation with this pig than he had ever had with me. Suddenly the boar charged him. Amazingly Araf stood his ground and with the reflexes of a cat, grabbed the boar's tusks and twisted. The two of them rolled once and came up on their feet. Araf skidded backwards then found footing on a tree root and held fast. I have never seen such a display of strength.

As I marvelled, the boar that had attacked Fergal charged back for a second shot at him. Fergal legged it into the night. I would have helped him but the remaining two animals simultaneously came at Essa and me. Now I understood why Fergal had frozen. Forget horror movies, if you really want a fright that will soil your trousers, then stand in front of a charging boar. It's amazing how fast your mind can work when you are about to be gored. The first thing I hoped was that I was somehow related to the charging swine, then I remembered an old history lesson that mentioned how people in medieval Europe used to hunt boar. They would plant the end of a sharp stick in the ground and wait for the animal to charge. If they got it right, the boar impaled itself – if not, the hunter was the one that got run through.

This animal was almost on me. I dropped to one knee, planted the base of my stick in the ground, aimed the knob of my staff just below the neck and ducked my head. I got lucky. If I hadn't hit directly in the centre of its chest the stick would have glanced off and I would be singing soprano in the boys' choir. Amazingly my aim was true and that sucker was actually launched over my head! Its back hoof clipped me on the forehead as it went over, but other than that I was unharmed. My hazel stick bent but it held and pole-vaulted a very surprised creature sideways into a tree. It ran off, squealing into the night like a frightened piglet.

I didn't have time to gloat – Essa was in trouble. She had lost her stick and was down on her side, and her attacker was preparing for a killer charge. There was no way I was going to cover the distance between us in time to help. I reached into my sock and threw Dahy's dagger just as the boar began to move. I swear that knife swerved with the movement of the animal and stabbed it in the neck – right up to the hilt. It literally stopped it dead.

Essa had been winded by her own staff as she tried to block the first charge, but she hadn't been gored. Araf's opponent just gave up and ran away – smart animal. Fergal returned with a flaming branch from the fire that he had used to frighten his pursuer away.

Essa got slowly to her feet and looked at the dead animal. 'You shouldn't have killed it,' she said.

'Excuse me, didn't you mean to say, "*Thank you, Conor, for saving my life*"?'

'We don't kill animals in The Land without their permission.'

'I didn't see the boar asking you if you wanted to be turned into a pegboard!'

'Nevertheless, you shouldn't have killed it.' She placed her hands on the dead hulk and mumbled a prayer.

'I can't believe this. I thought you might at least be grateful enough to maybe not want me dead.'

'She wants you dead too?' Fergal said. 'What is going on?'

It was moment of truth time.

'My father is Oisin – OK?'

'You are the son of the one-handed prince?' Araf said.

'Yes, I am.'

Araf raised his banta stick and came at me.

THIRTEEN

THE HAZELLANDS

This was an attack I was not going to survive. I had seen Araf's banta stick prowess and I had seen his strength and agility with the boar – plus I was unarmed. I dropped to my knees and covered my head. I felt the swish of his lead-filled stick as it travelled close to my head, and then I heard a crack and a squeal of a boar behind me. I opened my eyes, without taking my hands off my head, looked around and saw an unconscious boar.

'Good one, Araf!' Fergal yelled. 'I didn't even see him coming.'

'This is a bad sign,' Essa said. 'The Pookas need to be informed of this.'

'Pookas?'

'Pookas are the animal tenders in The Land. They are having a hard time at the moment. Cialtie has stopped their gold allowance completely. They must have abandoned the Eastlands. We should get back to the fire.'

'So, none of you is going to kill me?' I called after them, still on my knees with my arms covering my head.

'Not me,' Fergal said.

'Maybe later,' Essa said.

'How about you, Araf?' I asked, standing.

'I'm just a farmer,' he said. 'I don't kill people.'

* * *

After the animal attack Essa decided we should keep a guard. My trouser-less sleep, the boar fight and a near-death experience had left me wide awake. I volunteered to take first watch.

My three companions went out like cheap light bulbs. I was relieved to see that that I wasn't the only one who was tired after a long day of riding. I threw a piece of wood on the fire and softly said, 'Thank you,' to whichever tree gave it to us. It was the first time in The Land that I had been outside at night and not been unconscious. I studied the stars. It unnerved me to see a night sky so unfamiliar. The air above me was packed with stars that seemed close enough to throw a rock at. There was no moon but the night didn't need one – the starlight cast a shadowless glow on everything that made the forest seem incandescent. Other than Fergal's flopping in his sleep, all was perfectly still.

It was nice to be out of the closet – so to speak. I'm not a very good liar and it felt right to be honest – I liked these people. OK, it would be nice if Fergal talked less and Araf talked more – but those were not big problems. I really liked Fergal. Underneath the laddish exterior I knew he had heart. Araf, on the other hand, was a tough nut to crack. I was beginning to realise that although he was the most taciturn man I had ever met, when he did say something, it was important. I had no problem placing my life in their hands.

Essa was my real dilemma. She was just the most wonderful girl I had ever met, but she was so hostile. If she had been like this when I first met her, I don't think it would have bothered me so much. A beautiful woman who turns out to be a jerk, loses her beauty in my eyes, but Essa and I got along great at first. These days I flinched every time she scratched her nose. I watched the firelight dance on her face. No matter how cold she had been to me lately, I couldn't help thinking how lovely she was. I don't think I fell asleep looking at her but I kind of got hypnotised. I let the fire get low and didn't snap out of it until Essa shot open her eyes.

'What are you looking at?'

'I was just thinking how nice you are – when you're asleep.'

'You have almost let the fire out. Did you close your eyes?'

'No. But I will now. It's your watch.' I put my head down. It stung where the boar hoof had clipped my forehead, and I winced.

Essa picked up a twig, set fire to the end and brought it towards my face for light. 'Let me clean that wound for you, it looks nasty.'

'No thanks,' I said, 'I prefer not to be nursed by people who want me dead.'

I rolled over but sleep wouldn't come. She was trying to be nice and I was mad at myself for being stubborn. I stewed over how I could have dealt with that better. Soon the stillness of the night and the crackle of the fire lulled me. Then I heard it. It might have been a dream but I don't think so – just before I fell asleep I could have sworn I hear Essa whisper, 'Thank you, Conor, for saving me from the boar.'

I awoke to the smell of bacon. *Ah, it was all a dream*, I thought to myself, *I'm back home in my bedroom and Dad is cooking me breakfast*, but instead of a face full of cotton I opened my eyes to a face full of grass. Araf had butchered the boar I had killed and was cooking ham steaks over the fire. Essa was not to be seen and Fergal was still asleep.

'Good morning,' I said, not expecting an answer and not getting one. I stood up and went over to Fergal and shook him on the shoulder to wake him. His Banshee blade popped out of his sleeve and stabbed the air in the exact place where my nose had been seconds before. I jumped back and grabbed my banta stick.

'For crying out loud!' I screamed. 'You almost killed me with that thing.'

'What are you talking about?' Fergal said as he got up. Then he saw his blade was out. He cocked his wrist quickly and it disappeared up his sleeve. 'I did it again, didn't I?'

Araf nodded.

'That's it!' I said. 'From now on I wake you with a stick too.'

Essa returned. 'What is all the noise?'

'You have heard of sleepwalking? Well, Fergal was sleep-stabbing.'

'What?'

'Never mind. Just be careful if you have to wake him up.'

*   *   *

We broke camp. I washed the dried blood off my head wound. It hurt like hell. I should have let Essa do it last night. I climbed into Acorn's saddle unaided. I was quite proud of myself, even if no one seemed to notice. The inside of my legs howled in protest at the prospect of another day on horseback but it didn't hurt as much as I expected.

The landscape was green and rolling, sprinkled with the odd tree here and there. The day was warm and pleasant. The Land was in the height of summer. It made me wonder how spectacular the autumn must be.

Since it seemed we weren't being followed, we rode in pairs and talked freely. Essa had lightened up – a bit. She told me we were not taking the most direct route to the Reedlands, so as to avoid castles and villages. We would be travelling all day in the Eastlands – the so-called No-rune Lands – and tonight we would camp on the edge of the Hazellands.

'The Hazellands?' I said. 'You mean my mother's home?'

'Yes. The shortest path is through Castle Cull.'

'Castle Cull? You mean the Hall of Knowledge?'

'Yes.'

'Wasn't it destroyed?'

'It was, my father told me to avoid it, but I want to see ...'

'Where your brother died.'

Her head snapped around and she had a fierce look in her eyes. 'How do you know that?'

'Your father told me. I'm sorry – it must be awful to lose a brother.'

Her face softened. 'He left to study at Cull when I was very young. He sent me a letter every week telling me all the gossip from the Hall of Knowledge. I so desperately wanted to study there when I grew up. He used to write quite a bit about your mother, he was very fond of her.'

'Does anyone know what happened?'

'No. Your grandfather Finn called a meeting of the Runelords. Ona was going to try to find out who (or what) destroyed Cull, but the night before the runecasting she died in her sleep.'

'My father accused Cialtie of killing Ona.'

'What did Cialtie say?'

'He didn't deny it.'

'The more I hear about this uncle of yours – the less I like him.'

'Well, I certainly took an instant dislike to him.'

'I'll leave it up to you, Conor, should we go to the Hall of Knowledge and see for ourselves?'

'I think we should.'

She smiled. A weak smile, but a smile nonetheless, the first one I had seen on her face since the party.

Fergal yelled, 'Cherries!' and broke into a gallop.

Araf and Essa kicked into a gallop and Acorn followed suit, and I almost fell off his back. Once I got used to the terrifying speed I found that galloping was the smoothest ride of all. Acorn seemed to almost float in the air as I pumped my arms in rhythm to his bouncing head. Ahead, the others had stopped in front of an orchard of cherry trees. Acorn stopped next to them and I nearly went over his head again. (The riding part, I was getting good at – it was the stopping, turning and starting I was having trouble with.) Fergal reached up, picked a fruit and popped it in his mouth.

'You didn't ask permission,' I said.

'You don't have to with cherries,' Fergal mumbled, and then spat out a pip. 'Cherries are the friendliest trees in The Land. They love getting picked. It's like you are doing them a favour.'

As we walked our horses through the grove, the trees lowered their branches to us, and we picked and ate to our hearts' content. Some trees even dropped cherries on me. They were delicious. Araf filled his hat and I stuffed as many in my saddlebag as I could fit. The feeling of welcome among these trees was overwhelming, and when we left I could sense that they wanted us to take even more.

That night around the campfire Fergal told me why he wanted to see Deirdre. 'I want to find out who I am,' he said. 'I was raised by a woman called Breithe – she was Araf's nanny. As you can see I am not an Imp. Breithe knew who my real parents were, she promised to tell me all when I reached Rune-age. She died before she could tell me.'

'How did she die?'

'She went out foraging for mushrooms and ate a poisonous one. A lifetime of mushroom picking – I can't imagine how she could have made such a mistake. She was a good woman.'

'I'm sorry for you both,' I said.

Araf nodded.

'So that is why I want to see Deirdre,' Fergal concluded. 'I hope she can use her magic to tell me who I am and where I came from.'

'I hope so too,' I said.

Essa took the first watch. I was asleep the moment my head hit the ground.

I dreamt I was in a rainstorm but it wasn't raining water, it was raining cherries. I put my arms out to my side and leant my head back and caught cherry after cherry in my mouth. I looked and saw Fergal doing the same. Scores of cherries were pouring into his mouth, and as he tried to chew them the dark red juice poured out of his mouth. I awoke with that image in my eyes.

Essa woke me – it was my watch. She had just closed her eyes when I saw a light approach. It was erratic, like someone running with a candle. As it got closer I saw that no one was holding it; an incredibly bright light just floated in the air and it was coming directly for us. I shook Essa and pointed.

She sat up alert and then laughed. 'Conor, haven't you ever seen a firefly before?'

'Not like that. That's a flying sixty-watt light bulb.'

'I don't know what you are talking about but it's just a firefly. Look.' She closed her eyes and whispered, '*Lampróg*.' It flew straight to her and lit her face.

'I used to do this when I was a little girl.' The firefly flew into her cupped hands, she whispered to it and it fluttered into her hair and sat there like a magic jewel.

'Good night, Conor.' She put her head down and closed her eyes. The firefly stayed in place and illuminated the side of her face.

'You must have been a lovely little girl,' I said.

She didn't open her eyes but she smiled and said, 'I was.'

The firefly stayed there until her breathing became regular and then flew off, I imagined, to find a proper little girl.

* * *

The next morning, we had travelled for less than an hour when we reached the border of the Hazellands. You could actually see it on the ground. One step was green and alive, the next was brown and dead. Acorn was hesitant to cross the line. We travelled in silence and saw nothing alive. I had seen drought-stricken land before, but this was worse – it was as if the life force of the place was gone and nothing had the will to survive.

Araf was in front. He crested a hill, stopped and dismounted. Actually to say he dismounted is being generous, he almost fell out of his saddle. He stared at the landscape ahead of him and dropped to his knees. I crested the hill and saw what he had seen. A huge field as far as the eye could see was blackened with ash and burnt crops.

'Oh my gods,' I heard from behind me. It was Fergal. 'Is that the Field?'

Araf nodded without looking up.

'What is so special about this field?' I asked.

'They studied everything at the Hall,' Fergal explained, 'even farming. This was a special garden where the Imp students would try new things. It was supposed to be beautiful. Araf lost a cousin here.'

I dismounted and put my hand on Araf's shoulder. 'Sorry,' I said. It didn't seem enough but he placed his hand on mine in thanks.

This was the true beginning of the desecration of the Hazellands. Before, everything was just dead; here as I got closer to the Hall, I could see the deliberate destruction. Hazel bushes were torched, and worst of all, we saw an apple tree cut down and left to rot. It made me feel ill. As the top of the Hall started to come into view, Acorn got very jittery. He sidestepped, whinnied and stopped unexpectedly. I got the impression that Acorn had memories of this place and they were not pleasant ones. I toyed with the idea of getting down and walking. I wish I had. Just as I crested a rise and received my first full view of the ruins of the Hall of Knowledge, we startled a flock of ravens. For hours the Hazellands had been completely lifeless, and this explosion of squawking and beating wings was too much for Acorn – he bolted.

I didn't think anything could be scarier than standing in front of a charging boar – I was wrong. Acorn was breaking all known horsey speed limits and I was powerless to stop or even influence the beast.

I was flying past some outbuildings of the Castle when I heard Fergal come up on my left yelling. Boy, we were moving fast. He reached over to grab my reins, but he didn't make it. He never saw what happened – I did. As we galloped between two burnt-out buildings, I saw a thick rope pop up and stretch across our path. It was too low to duck. I only had time to think, *This is going to hurt*. It did.

FOURTEEN
LORCAN

I awoke tied to a pillar inside a roofless ruin of a room. This waking up in bondage and pain was getting old real fast. Fergal was tied to the next pillar over. His chin was on his chest and his eyes were closed.

'Fergal,' I said in a loud whisper. He popped his head up.

'Conor! You're awake. Are you OK? What the hell happened?'

'I'm alright, at least as alright as I can be in this godforsaken place. The last thing I remember, we got clotheslined.'

'That explains why I hurt so much.'

'Hey, do you have your Banshee blade?'

'No, they must have taken it.'

'Where are the others?' I asked.

'I haven't seen them.'

'Have you seen anybody?'

'When I came to, some short guy was tying you up. He was a Leprechaun, I think.'

'A Leprechaun? You mean a little guy with a beard and a green suit?' I chuckled to myself and then started laughing.

'I don't think he was wearing green,' Fergal said. That only made me laugh louder. 'Conor, are you OK?'

I thought about this question for a moment, and all of the humour left me. 'No, I am not OK!' I spat. 'I had a perfectly good life. It may not have been exciting or important, but it was a good life. No one hit me, or made me ride horses, or knocked me off horses, or wanted me dead, or made me sleep outside at night or … or … ANYTHING! The only thing I had to do was homework – which I will never complain about again for as long as I live. Which is probably about five more minutes, because everybody wants me DEAD!' I was babbling now. 'HEY, WHY DON'T YOU JUST GET IN HERE AND FINISH ME OFF!' I screamed.

'Quiet, Conor.'

'Why? What difference does it make? It's not like they don't know we are in here – they tied us up, for God's sake. And who are *they* anyway? WHO ARE YOU? GET YOUR BUTTS IN HERE AND UNTIE ME!'

Well, whoever *they* were, it got their attention. A very short man with a beard came into view from behind me. It was disappointing that he didn't have a green outfit and a pointed hat, because if he did he would have been the spitting image of one of Snow White's dwarfs. He was followed by a bulkier guy who had to be an Imp.

'Is this the Leprechaun you told me about?' I asked Fergal.

He nodded yes.

'Hello, Mr Leprechaun,' I said. 'Top of the morning to you. For my first wish I'd like a chocolate sundae with a cherry on …'

'Silence!' the little beardy guy shouted.

'OK,' I said, 'how about I cut to my favourite wish – I'd like: me untied, you boiling in oil and don't forget to leave me that pot of gold.'

The Imp handed Beardy Guy my sword. 'Is this yours?'

'It looks like it's yours now. You know – finders keepers.'

He crouched close and placed the edge of the sword at my throat. 'I'll ask you again.' I could smell his breath and it wasn't pleasant. 'Where did you get this sword?'

I looked him in the eye and said, 'Do it. Cut my throat. Get it over with. I'm tired of being tied up and threatened. Just kill me and then – LEAVE ME ALONE!'

I actually scared him when I shouted. It made him jump up and back off. He turned to Fergal and pointed my sword at him. 'Who are you?'

'I am Fergal of Ur.'

'Ur! Well, what do you know,' he said sarcastically to the bigger guy, 'a fellow Imp.' He put the blade to his throat. 'Start speaking the truth, Banshee, or you won't be able to speak at all.'

'Leave him alone,' I said. I was just about to say it again, when I heard a voice behind me say the same thing.

'Leave him alone!'

I didn't recognise the voice right away because I actually hadn't heard it that much.

'Who are you?' the Leprechaun said. His question was answered by his Imp partner.

'Prince Araf!'

Sure enough it was Old Chatty himself. He strode in, followed by Essa and a horde of confused Imps.

'Untie my companions,' he demanded.

The Imp made a move to do just that but the Leprechaun stopped him.

'Hey, Leprechaun guy,' I said. 'Don't make Araf repeat himself, he's not fond of saying things the first time.'

Araf and Beardy stared at each other for a while. It was a struggle as fierce as any sword fight. At last Beardy gave in and nodded to his Imp, who untied us.

We stood and joined Araf and Essa. I whispered to Fergal, '*Prince* Araf?'

'Yeah, Araf is the heir to the throne of Ur. Didn't he tell you that?'

'He babbles on so, I guess I just missed it.'

I approached the Leprechaun. 'Can I have my sword back, please?'

He reluctantly handed it to me and said, 'I would still like to know who you are and where you got this.'

'The business of my companions,' Araf stated, 'is of no concern to you. What is of concern to *me*, is who you are and why so many of my kinsmen are here.'

The stare-down started again. Finally the Leprechaun said, 'Lord Araf, if I may speak with you alone?'

'Anything you wish to say, you may say in front of my comrades.'

This provoked another staring contest. At this rate we were going to be here all day. 'Very well. May I invite you all to join me in my headquarters for tea?'

Araf nodded.

'You wouldn't have any of that willow stuff, would you?' I asked.

It wasn't until I got outside that I realised where we were – in the ruins of the Hall of Knowledge. The first thing I saw was a lone standing wall with a beautiful yellow and blue stained-glass window in it. The window depicted a woman sitting in the middle of a willowy tree. Amid all of the destruction it was amazing that the glass had survived.

As we walked, Imps and Leprechauns peeked around corners tying to get a glimpse of the strangers. Beardy's headquarters had obviously once been part of the Great Library. Gerard had told me that the Library was a circular room surrounding a courtyard. What was left of it made my blood boil. I don't even like it when someone folds down the corner of a cheap paperback – here, heaped around the room, were towers of partly burnt books and piles of scorched manuscript pieces. The bookshelves that were still intact were blackened with soot. Who could do this to a library?

Essa spoke first. 'You are trying to save some of the manuscripts, I see.'

'That was not our intention,' Beardy said, 'but none of us could stand to see it like this, so I have delegated a handful of people to try to make as much order of the books as they can.'

'What is your intention here?' Araf asked.

Beardy straightened and thought for a moment. I recognised the look. I'm sure I had worn it quite a bit recently – it was the look of someone who was deciding whether to tell the truth or not.

'I am Lorcan.'

'Lorcan the Leprechaun?' I blurted out and laughed. Lorcan and the others gave me a dirty look and I instantly apologised.

'I am Lorcan, I was chief engineer in the mines of Duir. Three years ago I asked Lord Cialtie what he was doing with all of the gold, now that he had stopped the allowance to most of the Runelords. For an answer he imprisoned my wife in his tower and told me that the next time I had the audacity to ask questions, she would die. Over the next two years I smuggled gold out to the Runelords that had been cut off, and planned a rescue of my wife. I had not seen her for months, and when I finally gained access to the tower, she was not there. I learned that my wife had been killed a month before, defending a fellow prisoner. No one had told me.' He paused and then forced himself on. 'I knew that Cialtie would find out I had been there, so I escaped. Ever since I have been organising this secret fighting force. We call ourselves the Army of the Red Hand. Our goal is to dethrone Cialtie.'

'If your army is a secret one,' I said, 'then why are you telling us?'

'Out of respect for Prince Araf I will not lie to you, and also because you will not be allowed to leave here until we have mounted our attack.'

'What?' Araf shouted.

'I am sorry, my lord, this must be,' Lorcan said, as the room filled with scores of armed guards – none of them, I noticed, were Imps.

We drew our weapons but it didn't look good – even if we hacked our way out of this room there was an army outside.

'Put down your weapons,' Lorcan said, 'your detainment will not be long. Our attack begins soon.'

The way I looked at it, putting down weapons was a good idea. If these guys wanted to stuff Cialtie, I wasn't going to get in their way. I lowered my sword and looked at Araf. He reached into his shirt and came up with a wooden whistle. He blew two shrill notes on it that were so high I thought they were going to pierce my eardrums. The effect was instantaneous: at once there was a tremendous commotion outside the room, and every entrance was flooded with confused Imps brandishing weapons. Araf dropped his staff and held his hands up in a calming gesture. I found myself standing in the middle of a room packed full of confused and agitated Imps and Leprechauns all pointing swords. As usual in situations like this, I laughed.

An important-looking Imp pushed through the crowd. 'Prince Araf, what is amiss?'

Araf glanced at Lorcan. 'Nothing is amiss, my kinsman. Master Lorcan and I were talking about the loyalty of the Impmen and I provided a demonstration – well done. Now, with Master Lorcan's leave, you may all go back to your posts – Imps *and* Leprechauns.'

All eyes turned to Lorcan, who kept his gaze firmly fixed on Araf. We were in for another one of their famous stare-downs. As usual Araf won. Lorcan nodded and once again it was just Beardy and us.

Araf stepped up to the Leprechaun – there was so much tension in the air, you could swim in it. Araf spoke first. 'I have no desire to create a mutiny in your ranks, Lorcan. I understand your need for secrecy and I am not unsympathetic to your ultimate goal, but we must not be detained.' Before Lorcan could speak, Araf continued. 'Let me introduce to you a member of my company. This,' he said, pointing to his left, 'is Essa of Muhn.'

Lorcan looked very surprised. He bowed and said, 'Princess.'

Essa barely nodded back. It was a nice moment.

'By your lady's leave,' Araf said to Essa, 'would you show Lorcan what is around your neck?'

Essa pulled out the finger-length crystal that her father had used on me.

'Do you recognise this?' Araf asked.

Surprising Lorcan seemed to be becoming a pastime of ours. 'Is that an Owith glass?' he stammered.

'It is,' Essa answered. 'I believe the queen of the Leprechauns holds the other one.'

'She does. I have seen it.'

'Then you know what it can do?' Araf asked.

'It catches lies.'

'Essa, would you be willing to give Lorcan a demonstration?'

Essa took off the necklace and held it towards Lorcan. 'What is your name?' she asked.

'Lorcan of Duir.' The glass remained clear.

'This time,' Essa said, 'I want you to lie. What is your name?'

'I am – Finn of Duir,' Lorcan said. The crystal instantly went black.

'Why we are here and where we are going,' Araf said, 'we cannot tell you, but with Essa's leave, I propose that you may use the glass to swear us to secrecy. The glass will show if we intend to break our vow.'

Lorcan agreed. We all, in turn, swore to keep secret our knowledge of the Army of the Red Hand and their plan to attack Castle Duir. The glass remained clear. Lorcan returned the necklace and thanked Essa.

I broke the awkward silence. 'Hey, what about that cup of tea you promised?'

By the time dinner was served we were all pals – comrades in arms. Lorcan explained that he really wasn't ready for an invasion but he had to hurry it because of the meeting of the Runelords.

'What meeting?' Araf asked.

'Cialtie has called a meeting of the lords for a Runecasting. We suspect he is going to try to find out where we are hiding. We need to attack soon if we want surprise on our side.'

'Who is performing the Runecasting?' Essa asked.

'Cialtie said it will be Nieve, but according to our sources Nieve has been missing for days. We can't confirm this.'

Essa and I looked at each other but said nothing.

'How long before you attack?' Araf asked.

'I have sent word to all of my reserves to meet here by the end of the week – after that, as soon as we are ready. Some lords are on our side and are trying to delay the meeting.'

'Too long have the Imps and the Impwives watched our crops wither and our children suffer for the want of gold,' Araf said. 'I do not know Cialtie's motives for hoarding so much gold. I only know that I do not trust him. We will leave in the morning. I cannot speak for my companions, but I will try to return to join you before you move out.' He stood and extended his hand. Lorcan took it.

'I stand with my kinsman,' Fergal said.

Essa and I stood. 'I am ruled by my father and do not know his mind on this matter, but I wish you success,' Essa said.

'My future is just too crazy to promise I'll be back in time,' I said, 'but kick a bit of Cialtie butt for me – will ya?'

Araf and Fergal went outside to address the Imp troops. Essa asked Lorcan if we could see the courtyard where the Tree of Knowledge once stood. It wasn't far. The room we were in was adjacent to the courtyard – it was one of the few rooms that had remained whole. The courtyard was strewn with rubble from walls that had been pulled down. The ground was charred like the bottom of a giant campfire – it smelt like an old campfire as well. Essa walked to the middle and scrabbled in the black dust until she found a charred root.

'This was the Tree of Knowledge,' she said in a faraway voice. 'I sat in it once when I was young.'

'You sat in it?' I asked.

'Yes, it was a hazel tree. It didn't have a thick trunk like an oak, it had hundreds of thinner branches coming out of the ground. Over the ages the branches were trained and bent into a living chair. On the day a student left the Hall of Knowledge, he or she would sit in the tree for a leaving ceremony. The student would receive and eat a hazelnut from the tree. It would ensure that the student would never forget what was learned here.'

'Wow, it sounds like a heck of a tree.'

She looked me in the eyes – hers were wet. 'Your grandfather died trying to defend it – so did my brother.'

Her eyelids could hold back the tears no longer. I reached for her and she collapsed in my arms, shaking with sobs. I cried a bit too. Together we mourned a grandfather I had never known and a brother that she would always remember with the emotions of a little girl.

I don't know how long we knelt there. Being brave only postpones the inevitable – sooner or later you have to mourn your dead with all of your being, and that was what Essa was finally doing. When her sobs subsided, I picked up my staff and used it as support to help us both to our feet. The hazel staff slid into the ground like it was sand and then stuck there. Essa stumbled. I let go of the stick and held her with both arms. She leaned on me until we cleared the courtyard, then she stopped, wiped her eyes and put on her brave face before we joined the others. I forgot all about my staff.

Essa was fine the next morning. We exchanged knowing glances at breakfast. After that, nothing was said. We packed our horses. Acorn had gotten used to the place and was his old self again. Lorcan rode with us to the end of the castle's lands. As we said our goodbyes, I remembered that I had left my staff in the courtyard. Lorcan gave me his blackthorn banta and promised to look after my hazel stick until I returned.

Before he rode off, Lorcan said, 'The Reedlands are more treacherous now than ever before.'

'Who said we are going to the Reedlands?' Araf said.

'There is nothing else in the direction you go. It is a bad place. This land may be dead, but that place is foul. The last two scouts I sent there have not returned. Be careful.'

I was looking forward to getting out of the Hazellands. I needed to see something growing again. I promised myself that I would hug the next living plant I saw. It was a promise I did not keep. If I had hugged the first living plant I saw – it probably would have killed me.

FIFTEEN
THE REEDLANDS

I could see the border of the Fililands a mile away. The sight of green in the distance made us all quicken our pace. I couldn't wait to be among living, breathing plants again. I fantasised about galloping straight into the forest. Thank God I didn't. As we approached I saw that the woods were sealed off by a tall, dark hedge. Huge blackthorn trees stretched for as far as the eye could see, and these weren't the kind of thorns that gave you inconvenient scratches – one look at the forearm-length, needle-sharp thorns was enough to make me realise we were not getting into the forest from here. I remembered once seeing razor-wire on top of a fence at an airport. It was barbed wire with razorblades stuck in it. It was the nastiest barrier I had ever seen – not any more.

'My gods!' Fergal said. 'Don't tell me we're going in here.'

'That is where we are going,' Essa said, 'but not through there.'

'Is this the Fililands?'

'Yes, Ona sealed it off with the blackthorns after the Fili war.'

'Do we have to go around? Can't we hack our way through?' I said.

'You would be dead before your sword touched them. They can fire those thorns.'

'How about if I asked nicely?'

'Go ahead,' she said, with a knowing smile I didn't like.

I dismounted. I had gotten pretty good at getting on and off Acorn – I wasn't Robin Hood or anything but I didn't look like a giraffe on an escalator any more. As I approached the blackthorns I could hear the wood creaking as they pointed their *very* sharp thorns at me. I instantly felt this was a bad idea. I found one place where I could reach through the thorns and touch a branch. Before I could say a thing a command shot straight into my brain. '*You have until the count of ten to back off and go away!*' the plant told me.

'But my mom is in there.' As soon as I said that I realised how pathetic it sounded.

'*Five.*'

'But …'

'*Three … two …*'

I backed off fast. This bush was not one for negotiation. I looked up and saw my three companions smiling at me. I straightened my shirt and regained a little composure. 'He said that he would let me through but not you guys, so I thought I might as well stay with the group.'

'How nice of you,' Essa said.

We travelled north along the thorn wall. On the other side of the spikes we could hear sounds of life – birds chirping and an occasional running deer. When a breeze came from the east, we were blessed with fresh, plant-cleansed air that was scented with wildflowers. It made me hate this living barbed-wire fence even more.

I fell in next to Fergal, who was quieter than usual. I asked him what was bothering him.

'It's the way Lorcan said *Banshee* – hell, it's the way everyone feels about Banshees, like we're scum.'

'Why is that?'

'Oh, I don't know. I was raised by Imps, remember? I guess it's because people are afraid of us. Banshees are the undertakers in The Land and nobody likes death. More than that it seems they can sense death approach, so every time someone sees a Banshee they think they are going to die.'

'Can you do that?'

'Sometimes I think I can, but I never learned all of that Banshee magic stuff.'

'I can see how that would make you guys a bit spooky.'

'It's also what makes us – them, such good warriors. Banshee armies can sense if an enemy will die, they almost know if they will win a battle before it begins.'

'So Banshees are warriors?'

'That's their primary role, to defend the western shore from invasion.'

'Men of war always make people nervous in peacetime,' I said.

'I guess.'

'Well, I like you, Fergal, no matter what anybody says.'

That brought a smile that seemed to bring him out of his funk. He babbled on for the rest of the afternoon. I almost regretted cheering him up.

We camped that night still in the Hazellands. We were all exhausted. We had been teased all day with the promise of life but were doomed to be stuck in this land of death. Tomorrow we would reach the Getal – the Reedlands – no matter how bad it was there, it had to be better than this. We went to sleep without much chat, in the hopes of a better tomorrow.

I dreamt I crested a hill and saw an army of Banshees. When they spotted me they all pointed, as if to say, *You soon will die*. I ran to escape but every place I turned blackthorn trees sprouted and blocked my path. Eventually I was encased by a blackthorn cage, surrounded by screaming Banshees. The huge thorns closed in on me. I awoke with a scream in my throat.

We smelt the Reedlands before we saw them. Just one whiff of the sulphur and decay dashed any hopes of our landscape getting better. Our only consolation was that we were just going to nip the Reedlands. The plan was to enter it just enough to find an opening to the Fililands, but this was not to be. When we got to the border, all we found was swamp. Murky water choked with black vegetation that bubbled with a smell so bad it put rotten eggs to shame. It was like a disease. You could see in places where it had started encroaching upon the Hazellands. There was no way *we* could walk in that stuff, let alone the horses, so we followed the unholy border west in hopes of finding some sort of a path. This meant that inevitably we would have to trek through a large part of this foul place.

After fifteen minutes the swamp gave way to reed-covered bogs. It was still too soft to travel through but it was an improvement – at least it smelt a bit better. Ten minutes later Essa called a stop.

'What is it?' I asked.

'Someone has been here,' she said, in a low voice that made me look over my shoulder.

She pointed to tracks that I could hardly make out. We followed them until they turned into the Reedlands. The footing was dry and solid where the trail led.

'We enter here,' Essa said. 'Be careful – I don't think we will be alone in there.'

The life in the Reedlands made me miss the desolation of the Hazellands. If this was life – it was a corruption of it. Plants of tan and black grew in odd shapes without the symmetry that nature usually provides. The Land had struck me as being so wholesome – this place was the opposite. It was just plain wrong.

Instinctively we travelled as quietly as we could. We didn't want to meet anyone that would choose to live in a place like this, and I didn't like the look of the vegetation – I didn't trust it. A snake slithered quickly across my path. I grabbed on tight to the pommel of my saddle. I don't know much about riding but I had watched a lot of cowboy movies and I knew that horses freak when they see a snake. Surprisingly, Acorn took no notice, but everyone else did.

'What was that?' came a girly cry from Araf that made me laugh.

'What's the matter,' I said, 'haven't you ever seen a snake before?'

'That's impossible,' Essa said, 'there are no snakes in The Land.'

'Well, it looks to me like there are now.'

'I don't like this place,' Fergal said.

I was just about to make some sarcastic quip to Fergal about the obviousness of his statement, but then I saw his face – this place was really stressing him out.

'None of us does, Fergal,' I said. 'We'll be out of here soon.' I hoped that wasn't a lie.

The path here was easier to follow and obviously well used. Fergal took the lead, anxious to have this stretch over with. He was a good three lengths ahead of us when he reached a stretch of the path that was black instead of brown. As soon as his horse's foot touched it, the black surface seemed to lift off the ground. The path had been covered with flies. Fergal was instantly surrounded by a swarm of black insects. He flailed his arms and kicked his horse into a gallop, trying to outrun them.

We sped after him. It was a terrifying sight. Fergal tried to keep his mount in control while swatting uselessly at his own personal black cloud. It must have been maddening. The sound of incessant buzzing from those oversized bugs was loud from behind – where Fergal was it must have been deafening.

The road ahead forked – we needed to go right if we wanted to get to the border of the Fililands, but Fergal in his panic kept going straight. We followed, not daring to shout. Fergal's breakneck speed was finally working – the swarm was diminishing. The flies couldn't keep up. When his vision cleared, Fergal slowed to a halt. I was quite impressed by the fact that during the whole ordeal, he had never shouted out. It didn't make any difference though – they had seen us.

Fergal and the rest of us were in plain view of a major camp of Banshees. A handful of them were standing around a small fire in front of about fifty tents. They were obviously surprised that the four of us would just gallop into view, but their confusion didn't last long. One of them let loose a scream and, not unlike the flies, the camp suddenly came alive. Hundreds of black-haired Banshees poured out of their tents. All of them armed, many with bows.

'I'm not an expert or anything,' I said as calmly as I could, 'but I think we should – get the hell out of here.'

'Good plan,' Fergal said, and we took off like four mice in a cathouse.

Luckily they were on foot, or we would have been dead meat. As it was, they covered a lot of ground for guys that had just gotten out of bed. We pulled ahead of them, but not as much as I would have liked – these guys were quick as well as handy with the old bows and arrows. I have never been shot at with a gun but I think I would prefer it to being the target of an archer. This was the third time this week some-one had fired an arrow at me and I knew it was going to produce night-mares. At least with a gun you can't see the bullet come at you – arrows you see all the way until they either hit you or miss. It only takes a second but it's the most frightening second in your life. The other prob-lem is that the relief you feel when one misses you is short-lived, because there are usually more arrows following. After seeing three shafts over my shoulder just narrowly miss me as I galloped at full speed, I turned my attention straight ahead and waited for one to plant itself in my back.

We got to the fork where Fergal had taken the wrong route, and went left. The Banshees were out of bow range and falling behind but we could see that they were not giving up. They let loose an ominous yell when we took the left fork.

Essa slowed down. 'This path seems to be going in the right direc-tion. If we can get into the Fililands, we can lose them in the forest.'

'If?' I said. 'Can we get a bit more positive here?'

'I can't be sure that there is no blackthorn fence bordering the Reedlands,' she said, 'it's just a guess.'

'At the moment it's very important that you are right.'

Our pursuers were out of sight but we could still hear them scream periodically. On either side of the path was a deep, foul-smelling swamp – there was no turning off this road. If the path ended in black-thorns – we were done for. I remembered the Banshees' yell when we took this route and wondered if they knew something that we didn't. We rode in silence, straining our eyes and trying not to let the others see how scared we were.

We rounded a hill and saw it. The path led straight into – a wall of blackthorns.

'This is not a good thing,' I said.

Araf and Essa sped ahead, Fergal and I followed.

'You won't be too bad with that snap spell protecting you,' Fergal said.

'It only works with relatives,' I said, without thinking.

'What?'

Me and my big mouth – ah, what the hell, we'd probably be dead soon anyway. 'My mother told me that my protective spell only works with relatives. So, Fergal, I guess that means you and I are related somehow. I'm sorry I didn't tell you before but I wanted to talk to my parents about it.'

'So you and I are blood relatives?'

'I think so.'

'Like cousins?'

'Maybe.'

'I never had a cousin,' he said.

'Me neither.'

'I'd like it, Conor, if you really were my cousin,' he said, flashing me one of his famous Fergal smiles.

'Me too.'

The closer we got, the worse it looked. These thorns were more menacing that the ones bordering the Hazellands. Araf and Essa had dismounted by the time we caught up.

'This is not a good thing,' I repeated.

'There are only two options,' Araf said. 'We try to make it through the swamp or we stand and fight.'

Fergal got down and went to the edge of the path. It was definitely not a pretty swamp. The water was black, and choked with unhealthy-looking white roots and reeds, pale imitations of real vegetation. Fergal took a rope out of his pack, tied it around his waist and handed the other end to me.

'This is not a good thing,' he said and smiled.

'I'll keep a good hold on this end – cousin.'

He didn't hesitate, he just jumped right in. I thought it was the bravest thing I had ever seen. I had an instant vision of him disappearing under the black ooze and never being seen again, but the water only came up to his waist. The stench that wafted up from the disturbed water almost made me retch – how Fergal didn't lose his lunch I will never know.

'The footing on the bottom seems pretty solid,' he shouted. 'If you can stand the smell I think it might work.'

So my choice was: fight to almost certain death, or go in *there*. It smelt so bad I was still leaning towards *stand and fight* when my mind was made up for me. All of the vines and roots in the water were converging on Fergal.

'Fergal, get out!' I yelled.

I didn't have to ask him twice, I think he could sense that something was wrong. He got to the bank before the vegetation took hold. The vines that had been creeping up on him seemed to realise that he was trying to escape. They wrapped around him with the speed of a striking snake. He was dragged back into the water with such force, I was almost pulled from my saddle. Araf and Essa ran to the edge of the swamp. Fergal went under. I wrapped the rope around the pommel of my saddle and told Acorn to pull. Sometimes Acorn could give me a hard time, but when the chips were down, I had no better friend. Acorn pulled and Fergal broke the surface with his Banshee blade in hand. He hacked and scrambled onto the road, spluttering, sore and stinky – but unharmed. I jumped off Acorn.

'Are you alright?'

He nodded, trying to get back his breath.

'I thought I lost you there,' I said and hugged him. Boy, did he stink.

Araf and Essa started digging a shallow gutter. For a moment I wondered if it was our graves. They ripped buttons off their clothes and threw them into the trench.

'Do either of you have any gold?' Essa asked.

'No,' I said, 'my mother gave me an amulet but I used it.'

'I have some,' Fergal said, getting to his feet.

He took off his shirt and removed the gold wire that held his Banshee blade in place and handed it to Essa. Her eyes lit up.

'Perfect!' she exclaimed, and kissed Fergal on the cheek. From the look on her face you could tell that she instantly regretted it. Other than not dying, getting Fergal into a bath was our top priority.

Essa and Araf stretched the gold wire along the trench along with the gold buttons. Essa dropped to one knee and incanted a spell that caused the gold to glow and then hum. She stood up, sighed and then she and Araf covered the gold over with earth.

'This should take care of the arrows for a time,' she said.

'And then what?' I said, and instantly regretted it. We weren't going to make it through this. 'There has to be a way through these blackthorns,' I said, drawing my sword.

Araf was on me in a second. I am always amazed at how fast that Imp can move. He took the sword out of my hand. 'Don't,' he said, 'you would not last a heartbeat.'

'Well, at least let me talk to them.'

'Go ahead, but it will do no good.'

I've mentioned before, communicating with a tree is a wonderful experience – most trees, that is. A conversation with a blackthorn is like trying to talk your way past a junkyard dog. It's just no good. The spikes bore down on me as I touched a branch.

'*You have to the count of ten before I run you through!*' The voice of the tree exploded in my head.

'*Ten!*'

'You have got to let us in!' I pleaded.

'*Nine!*'

'I'll buy you some plant food.'

'*Eight!*'

'We're gonna die out here!'

'*Seven, six ...*'

'I have to see Deirdre!'

'*Five, four ...*'

'She's my mother!'

For a second I could have sworn the countdown stopped – then ...

'*Three, two ...*'

I backed off. I didn't want to find out what happened after *One*. I have no doubt that that tree would have enjoyed perforating me.

I turned back to the others, expecting to see them busying themselves with some sort of plan, but they were just standing there.

'The thorns won't let us pass,' I said. 'What do we do now?'

After a long pause, Araf said, 'Surrender.'

'What!'

'We wait behind the arrow shield. When the Banshees come in sight, we drop our weapons and put up our hands.'

'They didn't look like the prisoner-taking type,' I said. 'What if they attack?'

There was another pause. This time no one said anything.

We stood in a line. Our eyes fixed on the rising path before us. I have always hated waiting. Even if it was for something unpleasant like getting a tooth drilled, I prefer to do it and get it over with. That was not the way I felt now. I had a feeling that getting it over with would be the end of me. I wanted these moments to last forever – and they did. Our pursuers were not hurrying to catch us, they knew there was no place for us to go. I thought about my parents: a mother that I had only briefly known, and a father that I was only now truly starting to understand. If only I could see them again. I had so many questions to ask, so much to say.

I think Fergal must have seen my despair. He leaned into me and said, 'If you get killed, can I have your shoes?' And then he flashed me a Fergal smile.

Well, that was it. I tried to keep a straight face but I matched Fergal's smile and then my shoulders shook and before we knew it, Fergal and I were bent over in hysterics. Araf kept his eyes straight but even he was laughing.

Essa was not amused. 'Stop it. We have no time for this,' she said.

'This is exactly what we have time for,' I said, while trying to get my composure back. 'Laughing is as good a way as any to spend your last minutes. How would you prefer to spend yours?'

She looked at me. Our eyes locked and her pupils dilated. At that moment I read her mind and knew the answer to my question. I grabbed her by the shoulders and planted on her the kind of kiss you see in old black and white movies. As usual with women, my mind reading was all wrong. She pushed me back and swung. Not a slap, like in the movies, a left hook that decked me!

I looked up from the ground to see Essa standing over me with her banta stick high in her hand and her eyes raging. 'We are *not* going to die!'

I looked past her and saw the Banshees crest the hill. 'Tell them that.'

SIXTEEN

BIG HAIR

The Banshees approached slowly. They knew they had us cornered but I think they weren't sure if we had any long-range weapons. The four of us stood shoulder to shoulder, watching their approach. The closer they got, the less I liked the look of them – it was a motley crew. I doubted any of them had ever signed the Geneva Convention on prisoners of war – as they got closer, I doubted any of them could sign their name. A wild-haired Banshee in the front raised his hand and they all grumbled to a stop. They were close enough now that they could see us clearly. Araf undid his sword belt and dropped it and his staff to the ground. He held his empty hands out in a peaceful gesture. We all did the same.

The Banshee with big hair seemed to be in charge. He saw our surrender and bowed to us formally. He then turned to his troops and barked something. A group of twenty archers jogged to the front and nocked arrows in their bows. Hair Guy turned to us, smiled, and yelled, 'Fire!'

A wall of arrows came straight at us. I didn't move a muscle. Partly because Essa said we would be safe behind the shield, but mostly because when a couple of dozen arrows are coming at you, there is no place to run.

The afternoon's light highlighted the chief Banshee's hair – it grew straight out of his head, like too much cotton candy. I remembered a pencil I owned when I was a kid. It had a troll doll with hair like that sitting on the top of it. If you rubbed the pencil in between your hands the troll would spin and its hair would shoot straight out. I wished I had a pencil big enough to impale him on. Under that mop of white-streaked black hair I could see the glee in the Banshee's face. All of this and more went through my mind as the flock of arrows came at me. It felt like an eternity before the missiles hit the shield wall. Just two arm lengths in front of my face, the arrows burst into flames. For a second I thought I was going to be engulfed in fire, then the flames instantly dissipated. I shot a look at Essa who was breathing a sigh of relief. It made me think she wasn't quite as confident in her wall as she said.

The joy of not being killed by arrows was short-lived. The Banshee archers put away their bows, drew their swords and casually came for us. There was no need to hurry. They had us. I felt like I was in a scene in a cheap movie and I was some helpless girl in a dark alley surrounded by a vicious gang (I always wondered what those girls were doing wandering in dodgy alleys so late at night), but there was no superhero in a leotard to save us, this was the real deal. These guys were coming to kill us.

I know it's a cliché but my life flashed before my eyes and it annoyed me because it was so dull. The most exciting time of my life had been in the last week – before that, the biggest thrill I had ever had was in a bicycle accident in the sixth grade. I was actually more annoyed than scared. I was annoyed that I wouldn't see my father again. I had a life-time of my father making no sense and I was finally understanding him. Sally would never know what happened to me and I would never know whatever happened to her. Maybe she hadn't even missed me. And I wanted to see my mother again. Finding a mom after all these years was the most wonderful thing that had ever happened to me – one more hug would have been nice.

Bad-Hair-Day Banshee stopped his troops about twenty-five feet away. He smiled at me and I smiled back.

Fergal leaned in to me and whispered through his teeth, 'If I go, I'm taking him with me.'

'I was just thinking the same thing,' I replied.

Bad-Hair Banshee ordered his troops to split and come at us from the left and the right. At first I thought it was a tactical move, then I realised that they probably thought that our arrow wall would burn them as well. Well, I wasn't going to tell them their mistake, it was better than a frontal attack – not much, but you take what comfort you can get in a situation like this. Araf and Essa squared off to meet the attack from the left, Fergal and I turned to face the right. I looked at Fergal and he was grinning from ear to ear, we both were. We were definitely related.

When Hair Guy pointed behind us, no one looked. We weren't stupid enough to fall for that old trick. So I jumped when I heard, from the rear, my mother's voice shouting my name. She may not have been there for me when I was a little kid but she sure was making up for lost time now. There she was, in all of her animal-skinned splendour, yew wand in her hand, standing next to a V-shaped gap in the blackthorn wall.

The Banshees were almost on us. I grabbed Fergal by the collar and called to the others. As soon as we jumped through, Deirdre raised her wand and invoked something to close the thorns behind us. Seven Banshees dived through the gap before it closed with a sickening scream on the eighth. Araf, as usual, was ready for action. He instantly knocked out the Banshee that went for Deirdre. I didn't have time to thank him because one came for me.

If I close my eyes I can still see his face, I can still picture the stripes embroidered on his tunic and can still see the eyes – young eyes. I can remember everything about him – he was the first man I ever killed. I didn't want to. As soon as the fight began, I knew I was a much better swordsman. After a couple of parries, I saw that he had almost no defensive skill. One counter-strike would have drawn blood, so I tried the Dahy manoeuvre in hopes of knocking him out with my elbow. He parried the feint just as he should have, but when I went in with the elbow I lost my footing and went down. My opponent was not as gracious as me – he came at me with a *coup de grâce*, and I had only one option. From the ground, I beat the point of his sword to the outside and planted my blade in his chest. I will always remember the shock on his face. I'm sure that when he woke up that morning this was not the way he imagined his day would end.

I stood up and saw the second one coming at me and did nothing. I was in such a daze about actually killing someone that I just stared with almost amusement as this screaming Banshee ran at me with an axe cocked over his head. I probably would have just watched him until he split my head open, but that didn't happen. Like it was in a dream, I saw a shadow step in front of me and the flash of a blade. The next thing I knew, I was casually watching the Banshee run past me – minus its upper arms and a head. I turned to look at my saviour and said, 'Thanks, Dad.'

One of Big Hair's troops on the other side was stupid enough to take a swipe at the blackthorns with a sword. The air filled with flying thorns and screams. The Banshees backed off – fast. Araf, Essa, Fergal and I were miraculously unharmed. Four of the seven attackers that had followed us in were dead, three were unconscious. Deirdre used her wand again and the thorns opened enough for Araf to throw the dead and unconscious Banshees through.

I watched all of this as if in a trance. I was a bumbling idiot. It felt as if my mind had left my body and I was floating above it all, watching with an uncaring attachment. Basically my mind snapped – that's it – no more thinking. I had been seconds away from my death and then I had caused the death of another. I reached inside and switched my head to the *OFF* position. I recalled a T-shirt I once saw that read, *Don't bother me, I can't cope.* That was me. I wished I was wearing it.

Mom and Dad seemed to understand, or maybe they were just patronising me. Either way, they spoke to me in calming tones and got me up onto Acorn. Acorn treated me nice too. He nuzzled up to me before I got on – maybe he wasn't being nice, maybe he just wanted to check if I was the same guy. I sure didn't feel like the same guy.

The Fili forest was dense and dark green. My parents rode on either side of me, stopping branches from swiping my face. I don't know how long we travelled like this and I didn't care. I was in La-la land – completely mindless. I have no memories of riding into the Fili village, all I remember was Mother taking me into a hut and putting me to bed. I slept and didn't even dream.

*   *   *

I awoke the next morning with all of my wits intact. I guess that was a good thing but I couldn't help remembering how nice not-thinking had been. That way I didn't have to see the face of the Banshee I killed in my mind's eye and I didn't have to relive the sensation of my sword piercing his chest. I lay in bed wrestling with the memories. *I had no choice*, I said to myself. *He was about to kill me. I didn't want to do it. It wasn't my fault.* I had convinced my head that I had done no wrong, but my conscience would take time to heal and I knew it would always leave a scar.

Mom woke me up. She sat on the edge of my round bed in a round room and pushed the hair back across my forehead. It was like she had been doing it all of my life – I guess in both of our imaginations, she had. 'Are you up for some breakfast?'

'Yes,' I said. 'I'm OK. Sorry about yesterday. I didn't mean to scare you.'

She smiled and held out her hand. 'Come.'

The reason I didn't remember entering the Fili village is probably because I hadn't seen it in the first place. The door of the cottage opened into what first appeared to be an empty wood. When the door closed behind me, I turned and couldn't see a door. I couldn't even find the cottage until I stopped and looked closely. The huts had been built in and among the trees. They were small and round with bark for outside walls. The trees had grown over them, providing roofs that almost made them invisible to a casual glance. I wouldn't be surprised if someone walked straight through these woods without ever even noticing a hut, just a sensation that something was strange. As we walked I got the feeling that we were being watched, but saw no one.

Deirdre touched a tree and surprisingly a door opened in it. 'You'll get used to it,' she said. 'After a while you see everything and wonder how it fooled you in the first place.'

'It's not just camouflage, there is magic working here, too – isn't there?'

'Of course,' she said.

Inside was a long table. Fergal, Araf, Essa, my father and a woman I didn't recognise were already there, having breakfast.

Dad jumped up and put his arm on my shoulder. 'How are you this morning?'

'I'm fine.'

He looked me deep in the eyes, to see if I was telling the truth. I smiled at him. He laughed and gave me a hug.

'What about you?' I asked when he released me. 'Last time we were together you had an arrow sticking out of your chest.'

'Oh yes, I did, didn't I?' He waved his arms around. 'I'm fine now. There is nothing like Fili nursing. The best medical magic in The Land.'

Araf coughed.

'Except maybe Impwife magic,' he said quickly, and winked at me.

'What happened? Nieve was about ready to kill both of you.'

'There is plenty of time for catching up,' Mom said. 'Sit down and have something to eat, and I want you to meet someone.'

My companions stared at me like I was a Martian. 'I'm fine, guys,' I said, 'I just got a little freaked out yesterday.'

'Conor,' Mom said, 'I would like to introduce you to Fand – queen of the Fili.'

I stood and bowed. 'Your highness.'

She smiled. 'Fand will do. We don't have very much protocol in the Fililands.'

I sat. 'You are Maeve's daughter, are you not?'

'I am, but we do not use her name here.'

'Because of what she did?'

'Yes.'

'Those who forget history are doomed to repeat it,' I said, remembering an old quote.

'You sound like your mother,' Fand said.

'I take that as a compliment.'

'You should.'

Breakfast was fruit and dried meats and some sort of tea that woke me right up.

'I imagine you have met my travelling companions,' I said to my parents.

'Essa and I had a lot to talk about,' Mom said. 'I knew her brother well.'

'And Araf's father and I go way back,' Dad said.

'Have you been properly introduced to Cousin Fergal?'

'Cousin Fergal?' Mom looked surprised.

'Haven't you told them yet?'

'No,' Fergal said, 'I was waiting for you.'

'OK then, Mom, you know that protection spell you put on me – the one that only works on relatives?'

'Yes.'

'Well, it worked when Fergal tried to stab me.'

Mom shot an angry glance at Fergal. 'Why were you trying to stab my son?'

'Whoa, Mom! It's alright, it was an accident.'

She looked me in the eyes, then dropped her shoulders and asked Fergal, 'Who are your parents?'

'That's just it. I don't know. I was hoping you could tell me.'

Fergal told Deirdre the story of his upbringing. When he finished, Mom said, 'Well, I don't know of any Banshees in my line. Yours?'

Dad shook his head.

'I'd like to find out myself,' Mom said. 'Perhaps I could perform a Shadowcasting.'

'I'd be interested in seeing that,' said a voice close to my back.

I turned to see Aunt Nieve standing behind me – a knife in her hand.

SEVENTEEN
THE DRUID TABLE

I leaped to my feet and reached for my sword, as did my companions, but none of us had our weapons with us. Fergal cocked his arm a couple of times trying to bring out a nonexistent Banshee blade. I grabbed a fork from the table and brandished it as menacingly as one can with tableware. Essa and Araf were the only sensible ones – when they realised they had no banta sticks, they each ripped a leg off the table. As food and plates crashed to my feet, I slipped on some fruit and fell backwards onto the semi-legless table.

Nieve smiled and took a step forward. Araf, Essa and Fergal came to my defence, standing between me and my evil aunt. Fergal was holding a silver serving tray in front of him as a shield.

Dad and Mom quickly came between us.

'Whoa!' Dad said, putting his hand up in front of him. He was smiling a little. 'Nieve is on our side.'

'What? What do you mean – *our side*? This is the woman who tried to kill me with a spear and she shot you with an arrow, Dad. Remember?'

'It's true,' Mom said, 'Nieve is a friend.'

I stood up, still brandishing my fork. 'The last time we were all together you two were trying to kill each other.'

'Yes,' Mom said, 'but after you escaped, we nursed your father's wound together and then we talked. We hadn't talked since my banishment. We had a lot to say.'

Araf and Essa lowered their table legs but I was unconvinced. I continued to wield my cutlery.

Mom went on. 'I was consumed with the want of revenge. Truemagic could not tell me who had destroyed my home, so I sought out the Fili and the secret of Shadowmagic. That's when I met Fand. Together, we learned that Shadowmagic was not evil – it was like any other power. The evil came from the person who wielded it. She taught me the wisdom of the Fili and it changed me. I have never used Shadowmagic to find out who killed my father and my tutors. The hate would corrupt me and the magic.'

'What does this have to do with her?' I said, pointing my fork at Nieve.

It was Nieve's turn to speak. Her voice was soft. It surprised me. I had never heard it without venom. 'I am an old woman and thought myself wiser than I really was. I was set in my ways. When your mother learned forbidden lore and produced the son of the one-handed prince – I thought it was my duty to stop her. I now see it was wrong to blame Shadowmagic for the Fili war – it was Maeve who was to blame.'

I looked over to Fand. She lowered her eyes.

'What about the *son of the one-handed prince* stuff?' I said.

'Ona's divinations should not be ignored,' Nieve replied, 'but your mother has convinced me that there are other paths than the one I have been travelling.'

'You mean the *kill Conor* path?' I said.

'Yes,' she said, and sounded sincere.

'I was never a big fan of that road.'

Nieve smiled. 'Nor was I, Conor. You will never know how much it pained me.'

'So how come you are coming at me with a knife?'

She glanced down at her hand and looked surprised to see she was actually holding a knife. 'Oh, I was just in the kitchen. I came in to see if I could slice some bread for anyone.'

Dad cracked up at this. 'Are you going to lower your fork, son, or are you going to eat your aunt?'

I looked at the pathetic weapon in my hand and smiled. 'So we start over?'

'I would like that,' Nieve said.

'OK. Hi, I'm Conor – Oisin and Deirdre's kid.' I extended my hand.

'I am very happy to meet you, Conor. I am Nieve, your father's older sister and your aunt.'

She shook my hand and smiled. You know, when Nieve smiles she doesn't look so scary at all. Saying that, I wasn't ready to hug her.

'Can I have my table legs back?' came a quiet voice on the other side of the room. It was Fand.

'Oh gods,' Araf said, 'I am sorry.' Araf lifted the table with one hand and tried to put the leg back – without much success.

'Do not worry, Araf. The Druid Table has been broken before. In years to come I will point out the repairs and tell how the lord of the Imps tore off the leg to protect his friend.'

'The Druid Table?' I said.

'Most of the Fili were killed in the war,' Dad said. 'The few survivors hid in this forest. The rest became mortals and travelled to the Real World. Irish history remembers them as the Druids.'

'I remember you telling me about the Druids when I was young, you told me no one knew where they came from.'

'I lied. I knew.'

'You lied about a lot of things, didn't you, Dad.'

'I did, and I am sorry.'

'So are you finally going to tell me the truth about how you lost your hand?'

'Ah, that's a great story!' Fergal yelped. 'You see, Oisin and Cialtie were having a …'

'You know how my dad lost his hand?'

'Of course, everybody knows that story.'

'Why didn't you tell me?'

'You never asked. I can't believe you haven't heard it. You see, Oisin and Cialtie …'

Araf placed a hand on Fergal's shoulder. 'Perhaps Lord Oisin should tell his own tale.'

'Oh yeah – sorry.'

'You two go for a walk,' Mom said. 'You have much to talk about and we have much to do here, if I am to cast Shadowrunes tonight.'

'Come, son, and I will tell of things I have long wished I could tell.'

Dad and I walked outside in the dark shade of beautiful trees adorned with clusters of red berries.

'What trees are these?' I asked.

'Rowan. The Fililands are the Rowanlands. Maeve used to hold the Luis Rune,' Dad explained. 'The berries are poisonous but the Fili manage to somehow make jam out of it. I think I saw you have some this morning.'

'I did. It was nice.'

'The Fili are a clever people; my father was wrong in punishing them all. My mother asked him to be lenient but he was so appalled by the war – he ruled with his heart and not with his head.'

'Your mother?' I said, suddenly wondering why I had never even thought to ask before.

Dad closed his eyes for a second.

An evil thought entered my mind. 'Did Cialtie kill her too?'

'No, after I was born she went over the water on a sorceress' quest. She never returned. Finn had Ona perform a Runecasting to find her – but to no avail. She must have died.'

'Who was she?'

'My mother – your grandmother – was a sorceress. Her yew wand held the power of the horses. I never knew her. It was said that she raised the finest horses in The Land. Her name was Macha. There is a town in Ireland called Emain Macha.'

'*Emain* means *twin*, doesn't it?'

'That's right. Cullen – or should I say Cu-cullen – named it during one of his tall tale sessions, I believe. He was referring to Cialtie and me.'

'You and Cialtie are twins? I thought he said he was your older brother.'

'He is, but everyone called us twins because there is only a year between us. Immortals don't have very many children – otherwise the place would be overrun. It is very rare for someone to have two children so close together. So we were called *Emain Macha* – Macha's Twins.'

'But Cialtie is the oldest and heir to the throne?'

'Heirs are not decided by nepotism in The Land. Runelords are made at their Runechoosing.'

'I keep hearing about this Runechoosing. What is it?'

'When a young man or woman comes of age they prepare a small disc of oak and place it on a piece of gold. They then carry the oak and gold through the three antechambers of the Hall of Runes. At each doorway a muirbhrúcht is passed.'

'*Muirbhrúcht?* I don't know that word.'

'It literally means *tidal wave* but most people who have performed the Choosing say it's more like a riptide but in the air all around you. What it is, is incredibly difficult, both mentally and physically. A Chooser may give up after the first antechambers; after that stopping means death. The rune becomes hot in your hand after each muirbhrúcht. The gold melts into the oak. When, or if, you pass through the final barrier, you may turn over the piece of oak in your hand. Upon it, engraved in gold, will be a rune. Some runes are major runes – these are for Runelords. Others are minor runes – these are for heirs. Only after a Runelord has left or died may the holders of the minor runes retake their Choosing to see who is to be the Runelord.'

'What rune do you hold?'

Dad held up his stump. 'One cannot choose a rune without a rune-hand. I have never attempted the Choosing.'

'Cialtie has, hasn't he?'

'Yes. Everyone expected him to choose one of the Duir Runes but he chose a Virgin Rune.'

'A Virgin Rune?'

'Yes, a Virgin Rune is one that has never been chosen before. It had been so long since a new rune appeared that most of us thought it was myth, but then it happened. Cialtie chose Getal – the Reed Rune. A week later, word arrived that the Reedlands had appeared east of the Hazellands. Then we knew that the legends of the Origins were true.'

'Hold on,' I said, 'let me get this straight. Cialtie chose a new rune and poof, some land appeared out of nowhere?'

'Out of the sea,' Dad corrected. 'The Land is an island.'

'Right, so the Reedlands appeared out of the sea – and this never happened before?'

'Not since the beginnings.'

'And when was that?'

Dad smiled at me like I was a kid again. 'That – was before time. Sit down, son, and I'll tell you of our ancestors.'

We had walked to the edge of the forest – before us was Ona's blackthorn wall. Beyond that was the blackened Hazellands. Dad placed his hand on a fallen rowan tree and asked its permission to use it. He sat on the tree and I sat cross-legged at his feet.

'Ériu was the first, she is the mother of The Land and is considered a god among many – especially the Leprechauns. My father believed that she was his great-great-great-grandmother. When she came, The Land was a tiny island. Some think she found the oak trees here – others say she brought an acorn with her. Either way, she was the first lord of Duir. Together with the Leprechauns, she built the first House of Duir and excavated the mines.'

'Where did the Leprechauns come from?'

'Who knows? They believe that Ériu made them. That is why they are so loyal to the House of Duir. Anyway, Ériu was a great sorceress. Your mother believes she may have possessed Shadowmagic, but most of her skills were with Truemagic, powered by the gold in the mines.

'She sent for her sisters: Banbha and Fódla. Together they created the Chamber of Runes. Banbha chose the Iodhadh Rune and created the Yewlands. Fódla chose the Quert Rune, and her Choosing created the Orchardlands.'

'Where did the Imps and the Banshees come from?'

'When a Virgin Land is created by a Choosing, it is said that often it appears with full-grown trees, but sometimes it appears with people. The Imps supposedly appeared with the Orchardlands. Later, an Imp attempted the Choosing and chose the Ur Rune for the first time, creating the Heatherlands (or the Implands as we call them). That would be one of your friend Araf's ancestors.

'The Banshees are different. They believe they were sent for from the Otherworld by Banbha, to protect our shores.'

'Is this all true?'

'I don't know,' he replied. 'When I was young, I thought all this was just myth and legend. When the Reedlands appeared, I started to think again.'

As I sat at his feet and listened to him, I realised that I had not only missed a mother in my life, but also a father who could tell the truth. The years of holding back were lifting off his shoulders. He looked younger as he told me things that he had been aching to tell before. I was just about to hear the story of how he got his hand chopped off (and it was easy to guess who did it), when we heard the pathetic yelp of a wounded animal.

Dad and I ran to the blackthorns. It was a wolf – a big wolf. It was manically trying to dig under the blackthorn wall, but the blackthorns were having none of it. The thorns had wrapped themselves around the wolf's head. There was fresh blood where a thorn had pierced the side of its ear but that wasn't its only wound. A black arrow stuck out of the wolf's hindquarters. The whole of its back end was caked with dried blood. The beast made a sickening yelp as the thorns pressed harder. Dad spoke to the blackthorns and they reluctantly loosened their grip.

Dad called to the wolf and said, 'It is alright, I'll help you.' I was shocked when the wolf looked him straight in the eye like he understood. Then the animal collapsed on the ground and if I hadn't seen it myself, I wouldn't have believed it – he changed into a man.

'Get your mother.'

Mom was already on her way when she met me on the road. The blackthorns had told her.

When we arrived back with Dad, she used her wand to part the thorns and we carried him in.

'What was that?' I asked, still a bit stunned.

'He's a Pooka,' Dad said. 'They can change into animals.'

'Oh, right,' I said.

Fand and another Fili woman arrived and tended his wounds. They gave him water (which woke him up) and a tonic (that put him to sleep) and carried him back to the village.

The story of how Dad became a lefty had to wait.

Later, back at the village when things had calmed down a bit, Araf, Fergal, Essa, Mom, Aunt Nieve, Dad and I had a late lunch. The food was a vegetarian's dream. It made me think I would buy a pair of sandals, listen to folk music and forgo hamburger joints forever. The others had been collecting tree sap all morning in preparation for a Shadowcasting after nightfall, and they were almost ready Fand popped in and informed us that her Pooka patient hadn't regained consciousness.

Fergal interrupted the chomping. 'So, Conor, what did you think of the story of how Prince Oisin lost his hand?'

'I didn't hear it,' I said. 'We were interrupted by a rabid Pooka.'

'Oisin,' Mother said, 'it is time you told your son the tale.'

'Now?' Dad said.

Deirdre nodded.

EIGHTEEN

THE RACE OF THE
TWINS OF MACHA

D
ad planted his elbows on the table and wearily rubbed his
eyes. It made me realise that these were probably not the
most pleasant memories to retell. He pushed away his lunch
plate, slapped his palm on the table and began.

'Ona made many predictions,' my father said. 'We all know about the
son of the ...' He lifted his handless arm and pointed to it. 'But there was
another prediction that only my father knew. Ona predicted that, *The
first of Finn's sons to perform the Runechoosing would attain the throne.*

'Now, at a very young age, I realised that my brother was a horrid
child that would grow up to be an evil man. Finn, like any parent, was
slow to see this but by the time my brother reached Rune-age, even my
father knew that he did not want Cialtie to hold the throne.

'Cialtie attained Rune-age a year before me, but Father forbade him
to take his Choosing until I was of age as well. Finn told him that he
would hold a huge pageant to celebrate The Land's first double
Choosing. This infuriated my brother. He left the castle and did not
return for almost a year.

'After he left, my father revealed to me Ona's prediction and his wish
for me to take my Runechoosing first. We concocted a plan. I pretended

to take up fishing as a hobby – in fact, I spent most of my time on Loch Duir, not fishing but – practising rowing.

'A fortnight before my birthday, Cialtie returned with a group of Banshees. He claimed that Banshees were not treated well in The Land and that these men and women should stay in the castle to promote understanding among the races. Even then, it looked to me as if they were at least bodyguards – and at worst, the beginning of a private army.

'Father organised a huge celebration, in honour of the two princes of Duir coming of age. The centrepiece of the event was the *Sruth de Emain Macha* – the Race of the Twins of Macha – a boat race across Loch Duir. Cialtie and I would race the length of the lake, starting at the far shore, and the first to place his runehand on the Castle Beach would be the first to Runechoose.

'The Runelords and the people of The Land looked at the race as good fun – innocent sibling rivalry, but my father, Ona and I knew the truth – it was a race for the crown.

'On the morning of the contest, my brother and I left early and rode to the far shore. With each of us there rode a second. I brought Eth, the son of my father's master goldsmith. He was my best friend, the brother that Cialtie was not. Eth knew my brother's treachery as well as I, and his job was to look out for the dirty tricks that we both knew were coming – Cialtie, as usual, was a step ahead of us. He brought with him a Banshee sorceress named Mná – she was beautiful. All the way to the starting point Mná chatted and flirted with Eth, and by the time we reached the farthest shore, Eth was besotted with the Banshee sorceress – as a security guard he was useless.

'Cialtie only spoke to me once during the journey. He rode up next to me and said, "This boat race is not as innocent as it seems, is it, brother?" He is the only man who can make the word *brother* sound like a threat.

'"I don't know what you mean," I replied, as calmly as I could.

'"I think you do. I think this little contest is very important indeed."

'"What makes you say that?"

'"The way you and Father are acting – you are both such bad liars."

'"No one, brother Cialtie, is as good at that as you."

'He smiled, like it was a compliment. "I don't know what you are up to but I am sure that winning this race is very important. Am I right?"

'He looked me in the eyes – I held his stare without wavering.

'"No matter," he said, "even if this is a bit of frivolity, I can see in your eyes that you want to win. That is reason enough to beat you." He laughed that disgusting Cialtie laugh and galloped ahead.'

'There was a pavilion and a small entourage waiting for us at the starting point. After a short breakfast we entered our boats. Mná actually gave Eth a kiss for luck. When their lips parted, he looked like someone had clubbed him over the head. Even I laughed. You see, I was so confident in my rowing superiority that I let my guard down. No one saw Cialtie put the shell under the seat of his boat.

'The sergeant-at-arms dropped a small gold amulet into a tube that set off a spectacular golden flare. The race was on!

'Cialtie was always stronger than me and he seemed to have grown stronger in the time since he had been away, but his rowing technique was awful. I had spent months experimenting with length of stroke and the depth of the oars in the water, and had built up my back muscles – I was by far the better rower. The race was mine, but I didn't want to pull too far ahead. I needed to make it look at least a little close – besides, it was fun. I was a short way ahead of him, effortlessly gliding through the water, watching him strain with sloppy rowing. I was cocky and overconfident – I let him get closer just so he could see that I was hardly even trying.

'I even allowed my mind to wander. I thought about Deirdre. I had first met her at one of Gerard's parties. She made quite an impression on me and I on her.'

Dad flashed Deirdre a smile across the table that she returned.

'I was distressed, like everyone, when I heard that her home had been destroyed, but what really worried me was the news that she had vanished. I persuaded Ona to perform a mini rune reading that hinted to Deirdre's whereabouts in the Fililands. I told everyone I was going on an extended fishing trip and set out to find her.

'The thorns almost killed me before I could finally convince them to give a message to Deirdre. She brought me into the Fililands and … well, we fell in love. I persuaded her to end her self-inflicted exile. I started to row a bit harder knowing she was waiting for me at the Castle Beach.

'When I saw Cialtie put the gold earplugs in, it didn't even ring any alarm bells. I actually slowed down to see what he was doing. It wasn't until he produced the conch shell and pulled the amulet from around his neck that I realised I was in trouble. I rowed away from him with all of my strength – but it was too late. He dropped the amulet into the shell, shouted "*Gream!*" and threw. I dived to block but the shell ricocheted around the bottom of the boat. Before I could get to it – I heard the scream.

'I know now that the spell he dropped in the shell – it was a Banshee pain scream. I thought it was only a legend but Cialtie was always a master of old lore. He has since made many a myth become a reality. Legend has it that in the War of the Others, the Banshees developed a scream that gave the enemy's men – *the pain of childbirth*. I thank the gods for making me a man and I shall forever look on mothers with admiration. Never again do I want to feel such pain. Not even the arrow in my chest compared to the debilitating agony that hit me in that boat. I doubled up, clutching my knees. I was in too much pain even to scream. Cialtie sped ahead.

'Through closed eyes I envisioned how the future would unfold. I saw Cialtie winning the race. I saw my father and Deirdre's disappointment. I saw Cialtie holding the Oak Rune. I saw Cialtie holding the Sword of Duir. I saw Cialtie sitting on the Oak Throne, and I saw Cialtie with a queen by his side – it was Deirdre!

'That was more than I could bear. I let loose a howl and opened my eyes. The shell was lying on the bottom of the boat, right next to my face. With an effort I know I will never be able to duplicate, I took my hands from my knees, grabbed the shell and hurled it with all of my might. I only threw it about a foot but that was enough – as the shell sank, the scream and the pain subsided. When I finally sat up, I saw that I was in the middle of the lake and Cialtie had an impossible lead.

'I retook my oars and began to row but without heart, for Cialtie's lead was too big. Cialtie will win – *Cialtie will be king* – that thought, like a lightning bolt, shot through my body. "No!" I screamed and I pulled at my oars with all of my strength. The pain of my attack racked my body but I pushed it away. I melded my mind and my body into one. With every stroke, I recalled the indecencies my brother had committed – it fuelled my arms and my back with superhuman strength. The front end of my boat rose up with the speed, and the wake behind me looked as if it came from a galleon ship with fifty oarsmen.

'I was spurred on not only by the desire to stop my brother, but by anger. I was angry with myself. It was my own fault that I was in that position. I should never have let Cialtie get so close. I only did it so I could gloat. It was pride that defeated me. I realised how foolish I had been and that pushed me even more. I had been so confident of winning the race that I had even taken the Sword of Duir with me. I had disguised its hilt that morning with leather straps so no one would recognise it. You see, in my mind I was already king. I thought I had won the race before it had even begun – it had cost me dearly.

'Even these thoughts left me as I became a mindless rowing machine. I forgot I was even in a race. *Rowing stops Cialtie, Rowing stops Cialtie*, ran through my mind like a Fili mantra. I didn't even know that I had caught up to my brother until I heard him sneer, "Too little, too late, brother."

'That snapped me out of it. I heard the roar of the watching crowd. I looked to my left and saw the tip of my boat was almost even with Cialtie's stern, but when I looked fully around I saw that my brother was right, we were almost at the Castle Beach and I was a full length behind.

'I have found that important moments in life either happen so fast you don't even remember them, or so slow that each second seems like a lifetime. I remember what happened next as if I was swimming in honey.

'Cialtie's boat grounded first. He jumped into the knee-deep water and began the thirty-second run to the beach. My boat grounded just as he hit the water. There was no way I could beat him. As I have said, the next few seconds seemed like hours, and although it seemed as if I had plenty of time to think through what I did next – in retrospect, I wasn't thinking at all. I remembered that the winner of the race was the brother that first placed his runehand on the Castle Beach. I lowered my runehand on the seat of the boat, drew the Sword of Duir with my left hand and without even a second thought – I cut off my hand. I didn't even wait for the pain to register, I dropped the sword and hurled my severed runehand to the shore. The throw pitched me out of the boat, but before I hit the water I saw my hand sail past Cialtie's astonished face. It landed on the beach, to the silence of a stunned crowd. I had won, my runehand had been the first to touch the Castle shore. *I had won* – that was the last thing that went through my mind as I splashed unconscious into the reddening water.'

NINETEEN

THE CASTLE BEACH

Y ou did it to yourself?' I almost shouted. 'You cut off your own hand?'

'Yes,' Father said.

'But didn't you realise that you couldn't take the Choosing without a right hand, or that you would become the one-handed prince?'

'No.'

The look on my father's face made me realise how insensitive my questions were. Of course he realised these things – now.

'At the moment I raised the sword,' Dad confessed, 'the only thought that went through my mind was winning – or more to the point, beating Cialtie. All thoughts of Runechoosing, or prophecies, or even the pain, were superseded by the desire to win. It was foolish.' I could see in his eyes, he had paid dearly for that impulsive act.

'It was courageous, Lord Oisin,' said a voice. It was Araf. I had almost forgotten that the others were there.

Dad gave him a soft smile. 'Thank you, Araf. You Imps and Leprechauns are a romantic bunch. You have always considered my moment of madness as courageous. It wasn't, it was stupidity.'

'Is that why Lorcan's army is called the Army of the Red Hand?' I blurted, without thinking.

Mom, Dad and Aunt Nieve simultaneously shouted, 'What?' Araf and Essa gave me a very dirty look. I had made a solemn vow to keep Lorcan's army secret.

Fergal tried to change the subject. 'It must have created quite a commotion at the finish line when you threw your hand to shore.'

Dad ignored him and looked directly at me. 'What did you just say?'

'Me?' I squirmed. 'I didn't say anything.'

'You did,' Dad said, 'you said something about Lorcan and an army.'

'No, I didn't,' I interrupted. 'I do have a few secrets that I have kept from you, Father. Most of them, like what happened at the party I had in the house when I was sixteen and you were out of town, I keep so I will not get into trouble – others I keep because I swore an oath on the House of Duir. There are things it is not in my power to tell.'

I wanted to tell him all, especially now that he was finally telling me the truth, but I had sworn an oath. Dad looked me deep in the eyes and I saw that he understood.

'You had a party in the house when I was out of town?'

I smiled.

'Seriously,' Fergal said, 'I want to know what happened after you threw your hand to shore – there must have been pandemonium.' He looked like a little boy being told a bedtime story.

'I wouldn't know,' Dad said, 'I was unconscious at the time.'

'I was there,' Mom said. 'I wouldn't say, Fergal, that it caused a commotion, at least not at first. Everyone was stunned into silence. You have to realise that only a handful of us knew how important this race was – most people thought it was harmless family fun. No one could understand what made Oisin do such a desperate thing. Lord Finn and I dived into the lake and carried Oisin to shore. He was bleeding terribly. Finn tore off a strip of his robe and tied a tourniquet around the wrist, but the bleeding would not stop. I thought he was going to die. I had some tree sap hidden in my satchel, I used it on the wound and incanted a Shadowspell. I heard Ona and Nieve gasp, "Shadowmagic!"

'Lord Finn looked at me and asked if this was really Shadowmagic. I told him it was and saw the conflict in his face. I had just saved his favourite son, but I had also just performed an act that was punishable by death. Since the damage was already done, I picked up Oisin's hand, and using Shadowmagic again, I preserved it in amber sap.

'Finn came close and whispered in my ear, "Do you have a place to go?" I nodded. He said, "Go there and never come back."

'There were tears in his eyes when Lord Finn stepped back and announced to all that I was banished, and my name was to be purged from our minds, and my memory was to be purged from our hearts. That was the last I saw of anyone from The Land, other than Oisin and the Fili, until the Shadowrunes told me to rescue you and your father from Cialtie's dungeon.'

'How could he do that to you?' I said. 'Finn sounds as bad as Cialtie.'

'Do not judge your grandfather harshly,' Mom said, in that motherly tone that made me a bit ashamed of myself. 'He should have had me executed on the spot. I am sure many thought he was wrong to let me live. You must remember how much pain Maeve and her Shadowmagic had caused. It is hard to be a good man and a great king. Your grandfather Finn was a great king.'

'So you came back here?' I said.

'Banishment was not really that much of a hardship for me. I came back here to live among the Fili. I had found peace here. The only hardship was that Oisin was not with me.'

'I didn't find out about all of this for two days,' Dad said. 'After the boat race, Ona gave me a tonic that made me sleep.'

'Who broke the news to you?' I asked.

That question sent a shiver down my father's back. 'When I awoke, I was in bed being nursed by Cialtie.'

'Cialtie! What was he doing there?'

'Oh, I'm sure he put on that sickening Cialtie charm, and convinced the nurse that he should look after his poor brother for a while.' Dad's face hardened. 'When I opened my eyes, my first sight was his glaring countenance.

'"Well, well, little brother, what were you thinking?" Cialtie asked me.

'I was terrified,' Dad admitted. 'I tried to shout but my throat was so dry, I could hardly make a sound.

"'Shhhh, don't exert yourself, little brother, you have been through an ordeal. What I can't figure out is, what were you, Daddy and that witch Ona concocting that made winning that race so important? Or was it that you just hate me so much that beating me was worth losing your hand?'"

Dad's voice faltered. 'All of the realities of what I had done crashed down on me like a wall of stone. I could hardly breathe.

"'Oh my gods," Cialtie said, smiling, "you didn't think about this before, did you? It's just occurring to you," and then he laughed. "Well, let me sum it up for you – without a runehand you can never take the Choosing and without a Choosing you can never be king, and because you are *a one-handed prince*, you can never have an heir. If I didn't know better, I would have thought you did this as a present for me."

'When I finally found a whispering voice, I said, "Where is Father?"

"'Oh, Father dear is off talking to the other lords, trying to explain why he didn't have Deirdre killed."

'I tried to sit up and failed.

"'Oh, I forgot," Cialtie said, "you have been out of it for the last two days. How can I break this to you? Deirdre is gone. You'll never guess – that little vixen is a Shadowwitch."

'I panicked,' Dad said, 'I couldn't breathe.

"'Oh my, little brother, I can see that you already knew. Shame on you. You see, she performed a little Shadowmagic show with your wrist and hand. You should have seen it. It was quite a demonstration. I thought our big sister Nieve was going to pee herself. I expected Daddy to chop her head off right then and there but instead he just banished her. He is as weedy as you."

'I gathered up all of my strength and took a swing at him. I would have connected, too – if there had been a fist attached to my wrist. Cialtie thought this was so funny, he cackled loud enough to alert the nurse. He explained to her that he was overcome with joy, seeing that his brother was going to recover, and danced out of the room.

'Eth arrived just after Cialtie left. He was beside himself with grief. He blamed himself for what happened to me. It wasn't his fault. I am sure he was enchanted by that Banshee witch Mná, but I was tired and angry. I shouted at him. I told him he was weak, that this was all his fault and that I never wanted to see him again. He left the castle that day. I never had the chance to tell him I didn't mean it.

'In one day I had lost my love, my best friend, my hand and had given my crown to the most evil man in The Land. If I had had the strength – I would have killed myself then and there.'

Dad stopped talking, looked down and wiped his eyes. How could I have lived with a man all of my life and never really known him? I stood up and put my arms around him.

Mom picked up the story. 'After Cialtie's Choosing (where he surprisingly chose the Reed Rune), Oisin came to find me here in the Fililands. By then I was very pregnant with you, Conor. Even the Fili were concerned when they saw that I was carrying the child of the one-handed prince. We consulted the Shadowrunes and came up with a plan. Your father and you would give up your immortality, just like the Fili Druids had done, and then, after a full mortal life, the son of the one-handed prince would die a natural death in the Real World. It was the best we could do for you, Conor. I performed the spell that sent the two of you to the Real World – it was the worst day of my life.'

This lunch was starting to turn into a blubber-fest. I let go of Dad and hugged Mom, and when I could finally speak again I asked, 'Why didn't you come with us?'

'The Shadowrunes forbade it,' she said.

'These Shadowrunes,' I asked, 'are they really as clear as all that? All of the fortune-telling I have seen in my life was always so vague that it could be interpreted as anything.'

Before Mom could answer, a voice startled me from behind. 'Why don't you see for yourself?' It was Fand. She was standing in the door-way – I was surprised to see that it had grown dark outside. 'The Shadowcasting is ready.'

Mom stood. 'Well, let us see if the Shadowrunes can tell us of Master Fergal's lineage.'

TWENTY

THE SHADOWCASTING

We walked among the rowan trees in fading light. It would soon be pitch dark, not that that would bother our escorts – the Fili seemed to be as much a part of these woods as the trees themselves. Fergal walked like a man in a trance. I caught up to him.

'Are you cool about this?' I asked.

Fergal gave me a strange look. 'I'm a little cool, but it's pleasant out.'

'Sorry, that's not what I meant.' I laughed. 'Are you worried about finding out about your parents?'

'Oh, ah no … well, yes … oh, I don't know what I think,' he said, 'I just have to know. All my life I have been fantasising about having parents – I feel like I won't be whole until I find out. Do you understand?'

'If anyone understands, my friend, it's me.' I stopped him, gave him a hug and whispered in his ear. 'No matter what happens, Fergal, I'm there for you.'

'And I for you, Conor,' he replied, and slapped me on the back. I gave him a dirty look for the slap, and he returned it with a twinkling smile.

We arrived in a glade surrounded by a ring of very old rowan trees. Light was provided by glowing pinecones in glass holders. The golden glow showed the seriousness on everyone's faces. It made me want to crack a joke, but I decided against it. Maybe I was growing up a bit, or maybe I was just chicken.

Mom sat cross-legged on the ground next to two large bowls. We all sat around her.

'Before we begin,' she announced, 'we must state our intentions. Shadowmagic, like any power, can be corrupted. Only by keeping our motives pure can sins, like those done in the past, be avoided. This sap,' she said, pointing to a bronze bowl full of the stuff, 'was given freely by trees who knew what it was for. We thank them.'

The Fili in the circle thanked the trees aloud and then so did we. Mom continued.

'Fergal of Ur, come sit by me.'

Fergal stood up, flashed a forced Fergal-ish smile to Araf and me, and sat next to Deirdre.

'Do you, Fergal of Ur, come to this Shadowcasting freely?'

'I do,' Fergal replied.

'Why do you seek this Shadowcasting?'

'I want to know who my parents are.'

'Do you seek this knowledge out of malice or revenge?'

'I just want to know,' Fergal said, his eyes sparkling in the Shadowlight.

'Very well,' she said, 'I shall instruct the runes to tell us of your life as it has affected others. This may be painful to watch and difficult to share. Are you still willing?'

Fergal thought for a bit, then answered with resolve. 'I am.'

'We shall begin.'

Mom waved her hand and the pinecone lights dimmed. She took a pebble-sized dollop of sap and rubbed it between her palms. She spoke in a language I didn't understand – Ogham, the oldest tongue – the language of the trees. She pressed her ball of sap between her hands and spoke the Ogham word, '*Beith*.'

Mom looked to me for recognition. When she saw none she translated.

'*Beith* – birch.'

She opened her hand, revealing a glowing amber disc, and when she turned it over it was engraved with a rune – the Birch Rune. She carefully placed it on the ground between her and Fergal. She rolled and pressed another bit of sap between her palms.

'*Luis* – rowan.'

A second glowing rune was placed next to the birch one. The next word she spoke I did recognise.

'*Cull* – hazel.'

The Hazel Rune, my mother's rune. The real one was destroyed – here was its shadow. Mom made a point of showing it to me before she placed it with the rest. She continued to produce runes for a long time.

'*Fearn* – alder.
Saille – willow.
Nuin – hawthorn.
Duir – oak.
Tinne – holly.
Quert – apple.
Muhn – vine.
Ur – heather.
Nion – ash.
Gort – ivy.
Getal – reed.
Straif – blackthorn.
Ruis – elder.
Ailm – silver fir.
Onn – gorse.
Eadth – poplar.
Iodhadh – yew.'

Each rune was placed in a specific order. When she was finished, I couldn't help thinking how it reminded me of an old chemistry class. There were empty spaces for runes not yet discovered, just like in the Periodic Table of Elements.

She rubbed one last ball of sap between her palms and told Fergal to extend his hands. In Ogham and then in the common tongue, she said, 'Fergal of Ur, this is your last chance to back away. Is it your wish to go on?'

Fergal instantly said, 'Yes.' I would have been disappointed with him if he hadn't, especially when I could see in my mother's face how much effort it had taken for her to make all of the Shadowrunes.

She placed the ball of sap into Fergal's palm and then pressed his hands together. 'The rune you make, Fergal, will be blank. Only a Choosing in the Hall of Choosing can give you your proper rune, but your Shadowrune will complete the casting.'

Fergal opened his hands like a book. Deirdre took his rune and placed it in the centre of the pattern – then it began.

The runes began to glow and then to flame. Not a candlelight flame, but a soft, almost invisible flame like the fire on a gas stove. The flames rolled along the ground between the runes. In some cases the runes repelled the fire, other runes absorbed the flames. After a few minutes, it was clear to see that some runes were joined with others by fire. Mom picked up the flaming runes and rearranged them, so that the runes joined by fire were together. The fire obviously did not burn – this was Shadowfire, not the real thing. When she had finished, Mom had five Shadow-bonfires before her. She sat cross-legged in front of them, her face fixed in concentration, her hands, still burning with Shadowfire, outstretched at her sides. Fergal sat opposite her, unmoving. They were both bathed in the same amber glow. Looking at them, I couldn't help thinking how different they were from each other – opposites, in fact. Still, these two opposites were locked eye to eye, both bent on the same goal. It sent a chill down my spine.

Mom waved a hand over a group of flaming runes and its fire increased as the others subsided. The flames grew higher until forms appeared. I began to make out a face and was surprised when I realised it was mine! The vision cleared and I found myself looking into a fiery 3-D movie of Fergal's life. Around the edge the apparition was a golden blur, but at the heart it was crystal clear. The images ran fast and made no sound, but I heard what was happening in my … soul. Like a conversation with a tree – it surpassed language. It was pure under-standing. We watched the whole story of Fergal and my meeting: the shoe theft, the comedy of him knocking me out, the terror of the boar attacks and the courage of our stand against the Banshees in the Reedlands. More than just seeing, I was understanding Fergal, from

Fergal's point of view. I had already decided that he was a good man – not perfect, but worthy of my trust. Now the Shadowmagic confirmed it. Fergal was a true free spirit. I saw that living for him was a joy, and that malice was a waste of his time. I realised then that I loved him – how could I not?

The images of Fergal and me dimmed as Mom brought up the fire in another set of runes. Visions formed before us of a young (and very cute) Fergal practising sword and banta stick fighting with Araf. Fergal did OK with his swordplay, but never even came close to winning the stick fights.

Another collection of runes showed Fergal turning down a kiss from a pretty young Imp girl. Not because he didn't like her, but because he didn't want her to get teased for kissing a Banshee. It nearly broke my heart.

Another runefire showed Fergal with his nanny – Breithe. Blissful images of walks in the woods, baths, kisses and being tucked into bed made my heart ache. Fergal may not have known his real parents, but he had the kind of motherly love that I always dreamt about.

Finally, Deirdre calmed all of the fires except one. This was it, this was the runefire that had the answer. The other fires sputtered and went out as the last group of runes roared with an amber inferno a third higher than the rest. We all leaned in, trying to make sense of the forms. As the vision cleared we saw Breithe! She was washing her hands in a tent. Could that be it? Was Breithe Fergal's mother? No, Breithe walked to a bed where a heavily pregnant woman screamed in labour. Wild, jet-black hair with a white streak covered her face – she was a Banshee – this was Fergal's mother. It was the moment of his birth. Breithe was the midwife, but who was the mother?

The contractions stopped. The Banshee mother fell back into the bed, her face still obscured. Breithe said, 'It's almost over, Mná dear,' and pushed the hair away from the mother's face. Mná! Dad had just mentioned that name – she was Cialtie's Banshee sorceress. The one who had bewitched Eth and had made the screaming shell for Cialtie in the race. That's when the realisation shot through my mind like a lightning bolt – if his mother is Mná, then his father must be … then he walked into the vision, Fergal's father – Cialtie.

A gasp went through the group. Why didn't I see this coming? Mná looked up and saw that Cialtie had entered. She pushed her hair back in an attempt to look better and smiled at him. 'Is it done?' she asked.

Cialtie smiled broadly. 'It is done.'

'Now you are king?'

'Soon.'

Mná smiled. 'And I shall be your queen.'

Cialtie's smile vanished. 'I don't think so.'

Mná sat up, confused.

'You don't think I could have a Banshee for a queen, do you?' Cialtie said *Banshee* like it was a profanity. 'What would people say?'

Mná went to attack him but was struck by another set of contractions. She fell back onto the bed, screaming. Breithe came up behind Cialtie and told him that he should leave and not upset the girl. Cialtie answered her with a backhanded punch that sent her across the tent, unconscious on the floor.

'You have been very helpful,' Cialtie said to Mná, 'but I'm afraid your usefulness has run out.'

I don't know if Mná was screaming from the pain of labour or because she saw the sword – either way, the screaming stopped abruptly when Cialtie chopped her head off.

Fergal freaked. He screamed, 'No!' and tried to stand.

Mom reached through the fire and grabbed him by the collar. 'It is dangerous to leave before we are done.' Her voice meant business.

'Please,' Fergal cried. His face was soaked with tears. 'Don't make me watch this.'

'I don't want to see any more either, Fergal, but we must. The Shadowmagic would crush us if we broke the casting. We are almost finished.'

I wasn't sure if I was allowed or not, but I had to go to him. I got up and sat next to Fergal and put my arm around him. Araf did the same on the other side and Essa held him from behind. Sobs racked Fergal as, together, we watched to the end.

In the vision we saw Cialtie pick up an oil lamp and walk to the entrance of the tent, then without emotion he smashed the lamp on the ground. He turned and exited, leaving the tent aflame. Breithe came to before the flames reached her. I wish I had met her – she must have been a remarkable woman. When she saw what had happened to Mná, she allowed herself only a second of horror – then she pulled a knife from her sock, jumped on the bed to avoid the flames, and went to work. Breithe performed a Caesarean section. She made a careful incision in Mná's midriff and gently removed Fergal from his dead mother's body. Just as swiftly, she tied off the umbilical cord, cut through the side of the tent and escaped into the night – leaving the evidence of Fergal's birth to burn behind her.

'It is done,' Deirdre said, her shoulders slumping with exhaustion.

Fergal collapsed, shaking, on Araf's lap. He was beyond weeping, he was, as the Irish say, *keening*. A soft, constant wail came from his throat. There was nothing to say. What could I say? I remembered a friend who was adopted who had hired a detective to find her real mother. She told me that all of her life she had dreamt that her real parents were some sort of aristocracy and she was really a princess. She told me how much it hurt when she found that her mother was just a poor, uneducated woman who had tried to forget her. I saw how much pain that caused her; I couldn't imagine what Fergal was going through.

Fand left to prepare a sleeping draught. We got Fergal to his feet and by the time we arrived at our room he was amazingly calm. Araf and I offered to help him get ready for bed, but he shooed us away. He said he wanted to just lie and think, and he promised he would take the sleeping draught in a little while.

Outside, a voice came out of the dark. 'How is he?' It was Essa.

'Who knows? I'm freaked out after seeing that stuff,' I said. 'Fergal won't get over this in a hurry.'

Essa nodded. 'I too won't be able to sleep. Would you like to walk for a bit?'

'Go on,' Araf said, 'I will keep watch here until Fergal sleeps.'

The night had gotten so dark, walking was actually dangerous. The first thing I did was trip over a small boulder.

'Are you alright?' Essa said, with a tone that sounded like real concern.

'Ow, I hurt my leg, but hey, I only need it for walking.'

'Let me have a look,' she said as she crouched down.

'How are you going to look? If there was any light around here I wouldn't have smashed into the damn rock.'

Essa turned her palms face up in front of her and closed her eyes and whispered, '*Lampróg.*'

A light twinkled in the distance and came at us, and as it got closer I actually had to shield my eyes. It was one of those nuclear-powered fireflies. Another came from behind me. They landed on Essa's fingers as she looked at my bruised shin. 'It's only a little bump, you baby.'

'Hey, you're the one that's making the big deal out of it. I just said *I hurt my leg.* You're the one who went all Florence Nightingale on me.'

'Florence who?'

'Never mind, why don't we just sit here for a while.'

She sat opposite me, cross-legged. A firefly landed on each knee, she whispered to them and they dimmed.

'Can you teach me the firefly trick, or is it a chick thing?'

'I don't know what a *chick thing* is but you have to be a bit of a sorcerer to do it. Since Deirdre is your mother, I think you could be taught.'

She smiled at me, her face bathed in firefly light. She was beautiful and I desperately wanted to kiss her, but the last time I kissed her – she decked me.

Like she was reading my mind, she said, 'I'm sorry I hit you back there in the Reedlands.'

'Don't worry about it. It was a learning experience. Next time I'm in a life-or-death situation with a beautiful woman – I'll ask before I kiss her.'

'I didn't hit you because of the kiss. I hit you because you sounded like you were giving up.'

'So you liked the kiss then?'

'I didn't say that,' she said, smiling a Mona Lisa-like smile that I couldn't quite read.

I returned her smile with a swashbuckling grin. 'Let me put it this way – if I were to kiss you now, would you punch my lights out again?'

'I'm not sure, that is just the chance you will have to take.'

I looked deep into her eyes. I had to make sure I was reading this right. The girl packed a serious punch and I had had enough concussions for a week – hell, for a lifetime. I held her gaze and her eyes gave it away. She wasn't looking for a fight. I was sure of it. At least, I think I was. If I got this wrong, I decided I was going to become a monk.

I leaned in and so did she. There is nothing like a first kiss. When I was a kid I remembered complaining about how slow the first kiss scenes in the movies were – now I know that that's exactly what they are like. Seconds take forever and the anticipation is exquisite.

So what was that first kiss with Essa like? I didn't find out. Araf came bounding up to us, shouting our names in the dark. We were both on our feet in a second.

'Araf, what is it?'

'Fergal's gone,' he said, 'and he has taken your sword.'

TWENTY-ONE
AUNT NIEVE

'Where could he have gone?' Essa asked.

Araf shrugged.

'I know where he's gone,' I said. 'He's going to kill Cialtie.'

'That's madness!' Essa said.

'I don't think Fergal is thinking all that straight at the moment.'

'I'll head south,' Araf said. 'He might try to get out the way we came in. May I borrow a firefly?'

Essa mumbled. One of her fireflies danced into Araf's hand and he was off.

'I'll talk to the Fili and see if they can help,' Essa said, and ran off, leaving me alone and in pitch darkness.

'Hey!' I shouted into the black. I couldn't see a thing and I had no idea where I was, so I did something I had always wished I could do. I shouted – 'MOM!'

Deirdre was there within the minute. 'Are you alright?'

'I'm lost and can't see a damn thing.'

Deirdre spoke quickly to a nearby tree and picked up a pinecone. She smeared it with a bit of sap and ignited it. When she handed it to me I was half expecting to be burnt, but the Shadowfire felt of nothing.

'Fergal is missing and he took my sword. I think he is trying to get to Castle Duir.'

'Oh my gods! He will never get past the blackthorns.'

'Will they hurt him?'

'They will kill him if he tries to cut through.'

'You have got to stop them.'

Mom whipped out her wand and touched it to the ground. A small plant pushed through the grass. Mom touched it with a finger. After what seemed like an eternity, she stood.

'He's this way,' she said, pointing west.

'Is he OK?'

'I don't know. He is contained. We had better hurry.'

We found him in the same area where Dad and I found the Pooka. Unlike the Pooka, Fergal wasn't on the other side of the blackthorns, but then again he wasn't on this side either. He was *in* the thorn wall. He had tried to climb the thorns at the same time that Deirdre had spoken to them. Instead of stabbing him, the thorns encircled him. He was off the ground and trussed up like a smoked ham in an Italian supermarket. It must have hurt like hell. The only thing he could move was his head. And let me tell you – he was not happy about it. He was beyond words, thrashing his head, cursing and ranting with sounds that were before language, like a high-pitched mad dog. His mouth was foaming to match.

Mom took some sap out of her satchel and spoke to a nearby tree, then threw the sap into the air. The top of the tree exploded into flame and light – Shadowfire.

'Fand will be here in a few minutes,' she said.

'Can you let him out?'

'I think we should wait till he calms down. Fand will have something.'

'Can I climb up to him without the thorns perforating me?'

Mom placed her hands on the thorn wall and said, 'Go ahead.'

The spikes turned away from me as I climbed. Fergal was still raving when I reached his eye level. He noticed me and his head whipped in my direction – there was murder in his eyes. Mom was right – if we had let him go, I think he would have attacked us. His mind had snapped.

Fand and some other Fili appeared out of the darkness. They had run without any lights – amazing. Upon seeing Fergal, Fand put away the vial she was holding and took out some greenish sap. She lifted the cuff of Fergal's trousers and rubbed the stuff on his skin. Fergal snarled at her but then started to relax. Mom released him enough for me to get a hold of his shirt and lower him down to the throng of waiting Fili hands. Fergal winced but didn't fight. I jumped down, and the black-thorns creaked back to their original position. Fand sat Fergal up. She was just about to give him something that would knock him out when he opened his eyes and saw me.

'Conor?' he said. The mad dog that had taken over his face was gone. He was Fergal again, without the smile.

'I'm here, Fergal.'

'He's my father,' he said. His voiced quivered and his eyes welled with tears.

'Yes,' I said. What else could I say? *It's OK, Fergal, don't worry about it?* That would be a lie. One thing this was not – was OK.

'Oh, Conor.' He sounded like he was five years old. 'He killed my mother.'

I put my arms around him. His head shook on my shoulder with silent sobs, his warm tears fell down my neck. I don't know how long we stayed like this but when I looked up, everyone else was there: Essa, Araf and my father. Dad leaned down and stroked Fergal's hair.

'Nephew,' he said. Fergal looked up, confused. Dad smiled at him. 'That's right, I am your uncle.' He wiped some of the tears from Fergal's cheek. 'Listen to me, Fergal, I know what it is like to lose all and I know despair, but I promise you – it will get a little better every day. I know you feel as if you can't go on, but it will be better tomorrow and the next day. The pain will never go, but it will get easier. You can do it. You are a son of Duir.'

I saw hope enter Fergal's eyes. I loved and admired my father at that moment more than I ever had.

Then Fergal's eyes went dark again. 'What about Cialtie?' he hissed.

'He will be dealt with soon,' Dad said, 'but we must not seek revenge. Revenge is an evil motive that corrupts the soul.' Dad grabbed Fergal under his arm and helped him to his feet. He looked his nephew in the eyes, and then looked at me. 'We shall seek justice.'

Fergal wanted to walk back to the village but Fand wouldn't hear of it. He didn't fight. He drank what she gave him and the Fili carried him unconscious on a stretcher. I was a bit jealous – I could have used a lift myself.

I didn't fall asleep as fast as I thought I would. One reason was the lump I was sleeping on – I had stashed the Lawnmower under my mattress. I didn't think Fergal would run off, but if he did, I didn't want to lose my sword again. The other reason I didn't drop off was because I was afraid to. This was my first undrugged night in the Fililands, I could sense the power in the place and I had a feeling the dreams here were going to be intense – I was right.

This dream was big. It was a full-blown battle. I watched from the ramparts as Castle Duir was under attack from an army made up of not just Leprechauns and Imps but all manner of beings. The odd thing was that the soldiers around me weren't even looking at the invading army. At first I thought they couldn't see them, but then I realised that they just didn't see this attack as a threat. They knew something I did not.

Cialtie showed up with a big red button, like you would see in a crappy movie about a nuclear war. He smiled as he pressed it. I tried to stop him but like all good nightmares, I was moving in slow motion. I reached the edge of the wall in time to see a golden shockwave hit the first group of attackers. To my horror I knew them all: first was my mother and then my father, followed by everyone I had ever known, even Sally was there looking at her watch wondering why I was late for the movie. I saw the flesh being torn from their bones. I was forced to watch the pain and horror of every person I had known and loved, die – die slowly. The guards on the tower didn't even notice what was happening. Cialtie walked away, whistling. The guards only noticed me when I tried to attack my uncle. They grabbed me and threw me over the wall. I awoke screaming on the floor.

*   *   *

Dad was the only person up in the breakfast room. He looked me in the eyes and said, 'Dreams?'

'Yeah,' I replied, 'intense.'

'Me too. When I left The Land I missed the dreams terribly, but I forgot what the nightmares were like.'

We swapped dreams. His was much more vague than mine but we suspected they were both similar. Dad thought we should talk to Nieve about it.

'How can you trust her?' I asked. 'She tried to kill me – twice!'

'That's one of the reasons I know I *can* trust her.'

'Huh?'

'Look, Nieve is my sister and I love her. I know it caused her much pain to try to kill you, but she did it for the good of The Land. She places duty above all else.'

'So why isn't she stabbing me in the back as we speak?'

'Your mother and I have a plan, and the Shadowrunes have told us it might work.'

'I thought Aunt Nieve didn't believe in this Shadowmagic stuff.'

'She's coming around.'

'So, Pop, what's the plan?'

'Cialtie is using my hand, that's how he got the Duir Rune.'

'What, you think he carried your hand through the Choosing?'

'More probably he got someone else to do it, but yes, he practically admitted it when we were in the dungeon, remember?'

It took me a second to think back that far. 'I do.'

'Well, that proves my hand is still working, and your mother thinks she can reattach it.' He flashed a cheeky grin worthy of Fergal's uncle.

'You're joking.'

'No, she definitely thinks it can be done and so does Nieve. There are just a few difficulties.'

'Like what?'

'We have to break into Castle Duir, find my old hand and perform an unauthorised Choosing ceremony in the Hall of Runes.'

'That doesn't sound easy.'

'It is not.'

'How are you going to do it?'

'That I haven't figured out yet, but we have time.'

'Can we take Cialtie out at the same time?'

'Getting in and out of the castle and reattaching my hand will be hard enough without adding assassination to the plan. One thing at a time, Conor. If I get my hand back, the Runelords will follow me. Then we deal with my brother.' He looked away, trying to contain his hate. Despite what he said to Fergal, revenge was an emotion he was struggling with too.

Fand came to the door and said, 'Our Pooka guest is awake.'

'Will he live?' Dad asked.

'No,' Fand replied. I could feel the compassion and pain in her voice. 'He has asked to see Deirdre.'

'Deirdre?' Dad said in surprise.

'Yes, she is on her way.'

She led us to the room of healing. The Pooka we had brought through the blackthorn wall was propped up in bed. The last time I had seen him he had been covered with blood – the Fili had cleaned him up but he looked bad. His skin had no colour and his lips were blue. Fand was right, he wasn't going to last very long. Mom arrived right behind us.

'Do you recognise him?' Dad asked.

'No. Poor thing.'

Mom went to the Pooka's side and held his hand. What life there was left in him sparkled in his eyes when he saw her. 'Are you Deirdre the Shadowwitch?' he said in a high, pathetic voice.

I thought for a second that Mom was going to be insulted by that question, but she simply replied, 'I am.'

'I was sent by Lorcan.' I could hardly hear him. He was using every ounce of his strength to speak, maybe even his last ounce of strength. 'We need your help.'

His voice became so faint that Mom had to lean in and turn her ear to his mouth. From the expression on her face I could tell it wasn't good news. She took a tiny piece of gold out of her pocket and placed it in the Pooka's mouth. He instantly changed into a wolf again. Mom stepped back – so did I, and I was on the other side of the room. He let loose a mournful howl and died – then changed back into a man.

'What did he say?' Dad asked.

Mom covered the Pooka with a sheet, and faced us. 'He said Cialtie is going to kill us all.'

TWENTY-TWO

THE ARMY OF THE RED HAND

'Before he died,' Deirdre began, 'the Pooka told me that Cialtie had the power to destroy all of The Land.' We were back in the breakfast room. Everyone was there except Fergal, who was still asleep.

'Do you believe him?' Essa asked.

'I do. He also said that Lorcan needed my help, immediately. But I don't know where Lorcan is or how I can help.'

Araf, Essa and I looked at each other, but Dad looked at me with one of those Dad looks. I was going to have to break my solemn vow. I opened my mouth and waited for the lightning bolt to hit me. 'Lorcan has an army of Leprechauns and Imps,' I said, with resignation in my voice. 'They call themselves the Army of the Red Hand and they're in the Hazellands. They are planning to attack Cialtie. Just don't tell Lorcan the Leprechaun I told you. I don't want that guy mad at me, he's mean when he's angry.'

'I don't think he will mind you telling,' Dad said, holding up his handless arm, 'after all, he named his army after me.' Dad stood and put on his serious face. 'It has begun. I knew it would, I had just not expected it to be so soon. I fear we are going to war with Castle Duir. Deirdre and I shall leave to join Lorcan's army immediately. This fight is ours and I will not force anyone to come. If you choose to go home, I will not think any less of you.'

Fand was first to speak. 'Neither I nor the Fili will go into battle with you. The memory of the last battle of Castle Duir is still with us. However, I support you. Remember, the freedom of the Fililands is yours. There is always refuge here for you.'

Dad bowed low – the bow of a king to a queen.

'I am with you,' Araf said, standing. 'This battle is not only yours. I would have joined my fellow Imps even if you had not returned.'

'I am with you, and so is my father,' Essa said as she got to her feet.

'You can speak for Gerard?' Mom asked.

'I can. At this moment he is making his way to meet with Lorcan.'

'How do you know this?' Mom asked, her eyes narrowing a bit.

Essa reached in her satchel and produced a sheet of gold framed in dark wood. It looked like an old school slate to me. Everyone else gasped in awe.

'Is that an *Emain* slate?' Araf asked with awe in his voice.

'It is. My father has its twin.'

'What's so special about this?' I said, picking it up and casually looking at it.

My father snatched the slate from my hand and gave me a look like I had just scribbled on the wall with a crayon.

'That is probably the most expensive item you have ever held. I imagine it took a roomful of gold to set the spell onto this slate.' Dad placed it gingerly back in front of Essa.

'Sooorry. What does it do?'

'Whatever is written on this slate appears on its twin slate, no matter where it is.'

'Cool, like magic email.'

Everyone as usual looked confused. Dad rolled his eyes but nodded yes.

'Gerard seems to have all of the cool stuff,' I said. 'Your dad is like a Tir-na-Nogian James Bond.'

'Who?' Essa said.

That was one of the many times I wished I was back in the Real World, just so people would get my jokes.

'Essa, would you send a message to your father for me?' Dad asked. Essa nodded yes.

Dad turned to his sister. 'Nieve – sister, are you with us?'

Nieve was looking down at the table. When she looked up I could swear she was close to tears. 'I remember you both as babies. I played with you and Cialtie when you were infants. Now you want me to choose between brothers and go to war with my home.' She paused. 'The decision is difficult but I have made difficult decisions before. Choosing to attack you, Conor, was the hardest, and now it seems it may not have been the right thing to do.' She stared at her hands for a moment and then slapped them on the table. 'I can no longer blindly follow the prophecies of the past. I must be guided by my heart and mind. Cialtie must be stopped.' She stood. 'I am with you, Lord Oisin.'

Dad's eyes were shining when he bowed to her.

'Well,' I said, 'I think I'm just gonna stay here and work on my tan.' Everyone looked at me, completely stunned.

'Hey, I'm kidding, for crying out loud. Of course I am in. Mom, Pop, I'm sticking with you.'

'Thank you all,' Dad said. 'May the gods be with us. We leave at dusk.'

'Great,' came a voice from the doorway. It was Fergal. 'Where are we going?'

We waited until it was pitch black before we left the Fililands. The arrow that we found in the Pooka was a Banshee arrow and we didn't want to tangle with those guys again. The only light came from the tiniest sliver of a moon. Sorley, our Fili guide, led the way. I swear the Fili can see in the dark. The horses had ribbons in their tails that Fand said were visible in the dark only to horses' eyes. It must have worked. Acorn was perfectly happy to follow behind Essa's horse.

We didn't stop until the sun came up. I was beginning to realise that here in The Land I was capable of feats of stamina that would have been impossible back in the Real World. Still, I welcomed the break. It was the first time I had a chance to talk to Fergal since our journey began. Mom, Dad and I had all spoken with him before we left, and we were surprised at how sane he seemed. We all agreed it was probably an act and that deep down he was a seething mess. There was talk of leaving him with the Fili but Dad said he had as much right to see this through as the rest of us. Fergal promised he would do as he was told. By the time we left, his smile was almost convincing.

He was sitting on a rock eating a packed lunch the Fili had made for us.

'How you doing, cuz?' I said.

'I wish people would stop asking me that.'

'It's a rule – when someone freaks out like you did yesterday, you have to ask him how he is. So how are you?'

'I'm alright.'

I looked at him.

'I really am,' he said. 'OK, when I start thinking about it I feel myself tensing up and going crazy, but then I take a few deep breaths and clear my mind, like the Imps taught me to do, then I can go on.'

'I was worried about you. I thought you were going to do something stupid.'

'Me?' he said, flashing me a Fergal smile. 'I never do anything stupid, except when I wake up and stab people – but you don't even have to worry about that – look.' He pointed to his Banshee blade in a scabbard on his belt. 'I tried to get some more gold wire so I could replace my blade in my sleeve, but the Fili don't do that kind of magic. I hate having my sword at my waist but at least I won't kill you next time you wake me up.'

We didn't rest long. Dad wanted to make the Hall of Knowledge before dark. We quickened our pace. Acorn was a star. I could sense he didn't like being back in the Hazellands but he trudged on like a trooper. At one point he let loose a whinny when I started to fall asleep in the saddle. The hours on horseback, the sun, the fresh air and Acorn's rhythm lulled me into a bit of a hypnotised state.

* * *

Late in the day, we entered the outskirts of the Hall of Knowledge's grounds. Sorley, our guide, was in the lead when we reached a small hill. He turned when he reached the top of the rise. I think he meant to shout a warning, but all he managed was a grunt as he fell from his saddle. He had an arrow sticking out of his chest. That woke me up.

It was Big Hair and about ten other Banshees. It must have been a scouting party. We had practically stepped on them. I think we surprised them just as much as they did us, but that didn't stop them from instantly going on the offensive. I tried to turn Acorn to get some space between us and the screaming attackers, but as I tried I saw something fly through the air, and Acorn fell over – hard. I got my foot out of the stirrup in time and hit the ground rolling.

'You hurt my horse!' I screamed. 'You son of a …' The first Banshee came at me and I ducked and rolled. When I got to my feet he came at me, holding his sword like a baseball bat. His whole left side was wide open. It was so obvious I thought that maybe it was a trick, so I decided to parry the blade instead of attacking his weak spot. I was right – the handle of the Banshee's sword had a dagger sticking out of it. If I had attacked on his left, he would have stabbed me. Instead, I planted my back foot and put all of my weight behind my sword. He was so shocked that I had not gone for his weak side that he was completely unprepared for the impact. The Lawnmower pushed his blade back so hard, that *his own sword* sliced his neck right up to the bone! That's the problem with tricky sword manoeuvres, the first time they don't work – they can kill you.

I didn't have time to marvel at the fact that I had just semi-decapitated a guy with a parry, there was a lot more fighting going on. I looked around – everyone seemed to be doing OK. I almost felt sorry for the guys who were attacking Nieve and Deirdre. I saw one Banshee take a swing at Nieve and bounce off her like he had hit a stone wall. Araf and Essa were using sticks against swords, but the way they used sticks meant that the swords weren't doing very well. Dad was in a fight with two men. I was about to go and help him when I saw the Banshee with the big hair coming up behind Fergal.

'Hey, you!' I shouted as I ran to intercept. 'Yeah, you with the bad perm!' He probably didn't know what a perm was but he understood the tone and knew it wasn't a compliment.

He turned. The smirk on his face meant he recognised me. Well, I remembered him too. This guy didn't make the mistake the last guy made. No mad advances, no tricks, he just pointed his sword and walked towards me. Up till now, the Banshees I had fought hadn't impressed me. Big Hair was the exception – his swordsmanship was good. The two of us cut and parried half a dozen times, trying to size each other up. I was very impressed with his speed. His thrusts were so fast that I had trouble seeing them coming. This was a problem. Dad had taught me to cut and parry until my opponent tired, but I had a feeling his speed would get me before he flagged. I looked for a flaw in his technique and I found it. His attacks were fast but he hesitated a microsecond afterwards to see if he connected. On his next attack I shouted, 'Ouch!' even though he missed me. When he looked, I came at him with a quick jab to his shoulder. He saw it coming and twisted out of the way, but lost his footing and went down. I had no moral qualms about attacking this guy on the ground but I didn't get the chance. He rolled backwards and was on his feet in a flash. I was going to have to work for this one.

And then he did it – the oldest trick in the book. His left hand slid down to the butt of his sword pommel. I thought maybe he had a dagger stashed in there, but when his hand came away seemingly empty, I thought nothing of it. That was a big mistake. He closed the distance between us, brought his sword up, as if to attack – and threw something in my eyes with his left hand. I found out later it was sand that had been soaked in lime juice. It felt like he had thrown pins in my eyes. I was completely blinded. I tried to open them, so I could defend myself, but my eyelids would not obey. I was as good as a dead man. I swung my sword wildly in front of me, while back-pedalling; amazingly the attack failed to come. The bastard was toying with me. I calmed myself and listened. Maybe if I could hear where he was I could get in a lucky stab that might catch him off guard.

I listened – nothing. Then I heard a soft footstep to my left. I didn't move. I didn't want him to know I could hear him. He was trying to come up from behind me. It was terrifying. I knew I had to wait until he was in striking distance, but I also knew I could get a blade between my ribs at any second. I waited for one more footfall and I made my move. I spun and sliced into the space I was sure he occupied. My sword hit steel, was parried up and then something hit my hand and I lost my grip. My sword went flying. I was blind and disarmed. I might as well have been naked too. I toyed with the idea of running but I knew that would do no good.

The last time I thought I was going to die, my life flashed before my eyes. I always have hated reruns on TV, so this time I just raised my arms and said, 'Do your worst.'

TWENTY-THREE

THE RETURN OF THE HAZELLANDS

'I never do my worst,' said a familiar voice. 'I always do my best.' I knew that voice. It definitely was not Big Hair. 'Master Dahy?' I asked into the darkness.

'You were doing well until you let him throw sand in your eyes,' Dahy said.

'Where is the Banshee?'

'He is quite dead,' Dahy stated. 'I hated to interfere – but I lost my temper when he used sand. I threw a knife into his neck.'

'Thanks,' I said. My knees started to buckle as relief washed over me. I sat down hard. 'How are the others?'

'They are all fine, don't worry. Let us take a look at those eyes.'

He left me and came back with a water skin to rinse out my peepers. They stung like crazy but I was relieved to find that I could see again. I was afraid the Banshee had blinded me for life.

By the time I could use my sore eyes properly, all of the fighting was finished. The ground was littered with dead Banshees. Mom and Nieve were tending Sorley, and no one else seemed to be harmed. I was relieved to see Acorn on his feet. Essa was examining his front legs.

'Is Acorn OK?'

'I don't think anything is broken,' she said. 'He was tripped by some sort of rock and rope weapon. You should not ride him for a while.'

'You've got the rest of the week off, old friend,' I said as I stroked his nose.

He snorted a reply, as if to say, '*Don't worry about me.*' What a great horse.

A shout came from Dahy. 'Deirdre, I think you should look at this!'

Something in his voice made us all gather around. In his hand he held a leather cord with a small gold amulet hanging from it.

'I found this around the neck of that Banshee with all the hair. It looks like the one that your father used to wear.'

He held it up and showed it to my mother. She gasped and placed her hand over her mouth. Her eyes instantly watered up. 'I made that for him when I was a little girl,' Mom said.

A voice behind me spoke with so much venom that I didn't recognise it. 'Now we know who destroyed the Hall of Knowledge.'

I turned – it was Essa. You could almost feel the heat from the fire in her eyes.

I always wondered what it would be like to be a celebrity walking into a movie première and having hundreds of people pushing, just to get a glimpse of me. Now I know – it's quite nice. Gerard and Dahy had arrived the night before and had told Lorcan all about us. The news that the one-handed prince, Oisin of the Red Hand, was about to arrive at the camp apparently sent the whole place buzzing. Imps and Leprechauns lined our route and saluted as we passed – even me. Luckily Imps and Leprechauns don't believe in prophecies much.

Lorcan and Gerard were waiting for us outside of Lorcan's headquarters in the ruins of the Hall of Knowledge. Lorcan obviously wanted to greet the returning prince of Duir with pomp and ceremony, but Gerard spoiled that idea. As soon as we came into view, Gerard started laughing that infectious laugh of his. Essa broke ranks and ran into her father's arms. Lorcan was about to salute my father when Gerard stepped forward and took Dad by the shoulders.

'My gods, Oisin, what has the Real World done to you?' Gerard's voice was without his usual mirth.

'It has made me older, Lord Gerard,' Dad said.

Gerard smiled. 'Has it made you wiser?'

'That is what we are here to find out.'

Gerard nodded in agreement, then gave Dad a big hug. 'Welcome home, Oisin.'

Lorcan tried once more to introduce himself but Gerard thwarted him again. He grabbed Fergal and me by the neck and then gave us a hug that almost banged our heads together. 'Well, well, Deirdre, these two young things found you after all.'

'They did indeed,' Mom answered, 'and I am very glad that they found you too. Thank you for looking after them – Lord Gerard.'

Gerard laughed. 'Ah, they are good boys,' he said as he tightened his uncomfortable hug. 'Give them a hundred years and they will make good men.'

We rubbed our sore necks as he approached Mom. 'Deirdre, you have been too long away. Why did you never contact me?'

'I did not want to get you into trouble,' Mom answered.

'From now on, let me be the judge of the trouble I get into,' Gerard said. He took Mom's face in his huge hands and kissed her on the forehead.

'Speaking of trouble, I think we should get a drink and make some plans.' Gerard grabbed Mom and Dad by the arms and whisked them into the Hall. Everyone followed except Lorcan, who was still standing to attention. I seemed to be the only person who noticed how uncomfortable he was.

'Would you like me to introduce you to my dad?' I asked him after everyone else had gone.

'Yes I would, Prince Conor,' he replied very stiffly.

Well, well, I thought, *it's* Prince Conor *now*.

'Should I tell him that you knocked me out and tied me up?'

'I would appreciate it if you did not,' he replied.

I let him stew for a bit and then smiled. 'Come on, Lorcan, we have a war to plan.'

Inside the headquarters it was pandemonium. Gerard was laughing and dishing out drinks and generally being the life of the party that he is famous for.

'Excuse me,' I said, but Gerard took no notice. I looked over to Essa, who gave me a *He's always like this* look. She tapped him on the shoulder and I whispered in his ear. He settled down after that.

'Lord Oisin, Lady Deirdre,' I said in my most regal of voices, 'I present to you Lorcan the Leprechaun' – Lorcan obviously didn't like the title but I couldn't resist it – 'Commander of the Army of the Red Hand.'

'I remember your father, Lorcan,' Dad said. 'Where is he?'

'Dead, my lord. Soon after you left, most of the senior engineers died in a mining accident. Now many of us are suspicious about the cause.'

'I am sorry for the trouble my family has caused you,' Dad said, bowing his head.

'Your family had caused me no harm, my lord, the source of my – *our* – trouble is Cialtie,' Lorcan went on. 'I am sorry to interrupt your reunions and I know you must be weary after your travels, but we have little time.'

Lorcan walked up to a large round table in the middle of the room. Everyone circled around it. From a satchel around his waist Lorcan produced a medallion and threw it on the table. It was about the size of a beer mat, made of silver and crafted into the shape of a tree. The branches of the tree flowed into the roots, making a continuous circle. It was beautiful and very stylised. 'This is a template for an amulet,' Lorcan said.

'What?' came the instant response from almost everyone around the table. This seemingly innocuous statement made Mom and Nieve snap their heads around and drop their mouths wide open. It was as if Lorcan had just said, '*I eat babies for breakfast*.'

'Cialtie is making this out of *gold*?' Mom asked.

'He has done it already.'

'How do you know?' Dad asked.

'We have spies in the castle,' Lorcan said. 'Cialtie has set up a secret gold smithy in the east wing.'

'We must stop him before he uses it,' Nieve said.

'I am afraid it is too late. He already has.'

'Where?' Dad demanded. 'When?'

Lorcan turned to a soldier and said, 'Ask Master Brone to join us.' The soldier nodded and left.

'Excuse me,' I interrupted, 'sorry for being a little thick, but I'm new around here. What's so bad about making this thing out of gold?'

Nieve answered me. 'Most of the magic in The Land is fuelled by gold. Most gold is used to make amulets, like the *rothlú* amulet you once wore around your neck. The most important rule when designing an amulet is to make sure the power has a place to go. An amulet must always have a point for the spell to exit from.'

'What if it doesn't? What if it's a circle like this one?'

'Then it explodes.'

'Did you notice,' my father said, 'that you hardly ever see gold finger rings in The Land?'

I hadn't, but when I looked around the room I saw that everyone there was wearing at least one ring but all were made of silver.

'There are very few goldsmiths that can make a ring that won't blow your hand off,' Dad said.

Nieve nodded in agreement. 'An amulet in a circle will explode – an amulet like that one, where all of the power is channelled back to the centre, is …' she searched for a word.

'A bomb,' Dad said.

'Not just a bomb,' Mom said, 'there is no way of knowing how much energy it will build up before it explodes.'

'You mean it's like a magic nuke?'

Nobody knew what that meant except Dad. 'That's about right.'

How bad?' I asked. 'Could it take out a village?'

'It can,' came a weak voice at the door, 'and it has.'

I have seen people who were depressed and down on their luck, but I had never seen a truly broken man before. The man who entered the room was in bad shape.

'This is Brone from the village of More,' Lorcan said.

'I know Brone,' my father said. 'You run the Riverside Inn – I have fished there.'

Brone perked up a bit when he saw Oisin but then the weight of his news pushed back on his shoulders and he looked down. 'It's gone, Lord Oisin, all gone.'

'What is gone, Brone?' Dad asked gently. 'The inn?'

'Everything, my lord.' I didn't think he was going to say anything more, but then he gathered what little strength he had and went on. 'A week ago I was upriver fishing when I heard an awful sound, and then a wave came that threw me out of my boat. A wave came upriver! I never heard of such a thing. My boat was damaged, so I had to walk back to the village, but when I did – it was gone. At first I thought I was lost but I was not – I was home. Not one stone was left on top of another. Everything – everyone, gone.' Brone could speak no more. A soldier caught him before he could fall and led him out of the room.

Dad looked to Lorcan for confirmation. Lorcan nodded *yes*.

'Why would he do this? Why destroy a village as peaceful as More?' Dad said as he sat heavily into a chair.

'I think it was a simply a test,' Lorcan said.

'A test for what?' Dad said, smashing his hand on the table. He looked at Lorcan with daggers in his eyes and then composed himself.

'For this.' Lorcan unrolled a sheet of paper on the table. It was obviously printed plans of Castle Duir, as seen from above. Around the castle was a thick circle in red ink with thinner lines circling under the castle and then back into the outside circle. It was obvious even to me what it was.

'You are saying that Cialtie is going to circle the whole castle with a circular amulet?' Dad asked.

'We think he is almost finished,' Lorcan said.

'That is why he was hoarding all of the gold,' Gerard said, understanding. 'Can you imagine how much gold it must have taken?'

'I saw this in a Shadowcasting, but I didn't know what it was,' Mom said in a faraway voice. 'How could I know? How could I imagine anyone would do such a thing?'

'Let me get this straight,' I said. 'If Cialtie sets this off, he kills any army attacking the castle – right?'

'If Cialtie sets this off,' Nieve replied, 'it could destroy all of The Land and everything in it.'

TWENTY-FOUR
THE EVIL EYE

'Is there any chance of getting another boarburger?' I asked the Imp that was serving food. He replied with the customary blank look I seemed to get from everyone around here when I tossed in a Real World reference.

I was delighted to sink my teeth into some meat. The Fili food was amazing but I was tired of nuts and berries. The Imps had barbecued a couple of dozen boars. They were so good it made me think that McDonald's should have McBoar on the menu. Araf, Fergal and I were chowing down, while most of the others were having high-powered meetings: Essa was off with Nieve, and Mom and Dad were with Gerard. After my second burger I spotted Essa walking among the ruins and excused myself.

I found her standing alone, staring at the stained-glass window of the woman sitting in the hazel tree. She saw me and quickly turned away, wiping her eyes.

'Hey, are you OK?' I said.

'Yes,' she said, putting on a brave face, 'it's just this place. How would you say it? – *It freaks me out.*'

I laughed, and so did she, but it was a bit strained.

'Are you sure that's all?' I asked.

She looked away and didn't answer.

I took her hand in mine and said, 'It will be alright.'

She turned and looked at me, but I still couldn't read her expression. 'So you have become an oracle, have you?'

'I have talents you can't even begin to imagine,' I said, flashing a smile that I learned from Fergal.

And then the strangest thing happened. She threw herself into my arms and kissed me – hard. It wasn't a tender kiss. It wasn't even passionate – it was almost desperate. Then she turned and started to run off, saying, 'I can't do this.'

I grabbed her arm before she could go. When was I going to learn never to grab Essa when she wanted to leave? She did her customary anti-attack manoeuvre – which meant I ended up on the ground, with her holding my arm behind my back in an extremely unnatural position.

'Ow, ow, ow,' was about all I could say.

'We have a battle to prepare for,' she said, letting me go, and stormed off.

'Hey!' I shouted after her. 'You kissed me, remember?'

I sat there, rubbing my arm, and thought about Sally. She may not be as beautiful as Essa, but at least she was less painful.

'Girl trouble?' It was Dad, with a smile on his face, the first smile I had seen him wear since he heard about what Cialtie was doing.

'Are all the women in The Land that fiery?' I asked.

'The good ones are,' he said and helped me up. 'I'm just about to meet with Lorcan. I think you should be with us.'

Lorcan and his generals were standing around the table, looking at the map of Castle Duir. They all came to attention when Father and I entered the room.

'Lorcan, your army is not large enough to breach Castle Duir.'

'It must be, my lord, we have to attack before Cialtie completes his circle of gold.'

'How do you know it is not finished already?'

'We must assume it is not. If it is finished – all is lost.'

'We must assume that the circle *is* complete, but all is not lost. Cialtie thinks his weapon is a secret and therefore has not bothered to guard it sufficiently. Deirdre says that the perimeter of the castle is only patrolled by a single troop of Banshees.'

'That is so.'

'I assume you have some goldsmiths in your ranks.'

'Half of my army are Leprechauns, my Lord, they know how to work gold.'

'Give me ten of your most trusted goldsmiths. Cialtie's ultimate defence may prove to be his downfall. Can your army be ready to march at dawn?'

'It can, my lord.'

'Can you make Castle Duir in two and a half days?'

'We can.'

'Good. Deirdre, Nieve, Conor, Fergal, Essa, Araf and myself shall try to gain entrance to the castle on the morning of the third day. If all goes well, my brother will open Castle Duir for you.'

'And if all doesn't go well?' I said, and instantly regretted it.

'Then,' Dad said with a sigh, 'there won't be anyone left to worry about it.'

That night Gerard opened several barrels of his finest wine.

'Remember when Cialtie came to visit me a little while back?' Gerard said as he tapped another barrel. 'Well, he came in person to complain about the quality of the wine I was sending him.'

'What a jerk,' I said.

'No,' Gerard said, 'he was right to complain. I have been sending him swill for years. This is the good stuff, but I can't let him have it. It shall go to people who deserve it.'

All of the army got at least a cup. It wasn't a celebration, it was more like a ceremony – something solemn.

That night I had another dream. Dad's right hand was on fire. I tried to run to him but I couldn't move. I was forced to watch him burn as I was frozen solid.

*   *   *

Lorcan woke me at dawn. 'Good morning, Lorcan the Leprechaun,' I said, rubbing the sleep out of my eyes.

'I would appreciate it if you stopped calling me that.'

'Sorry, General, what can I do for you?'

'Why did you not tell me you were a prince of oak and hazel?'

'Well, everyone I ever told tried to kill me. Now that I think of it, you tried to kill me without even knowing.'

'I am sorry for that.'

'No probs, you were just doing your job. Speaking of jobs, shouldn't you be leading an army into battle?'

'My army awaits but I must show you something before we leave.'

I dressed quickly and followed him into the ruins of the Hall of Knowledge.

'You left something behind last time you were here.'

'Oh yeah, my banta stick, I almost forgot.'

'Do you remember where you left it?'

I tried to think back that far. Days in The Land seem like lifetimes. 'I think I left it in there.'

We rounded the corner into the courtyard and I saw it. The hazel-wood banta stick that Dahy had given me, and had once belonged to my grandfather Liam – Runelord of the Hazellands. It was exactly where I had left it.

'You cannot take it back.'

'Why not?'

'Take a closer look.'

I had stuck it into the ground in almost the exact place where Essa had found the roots of the Tree of Knowledge. I drew closer and had a good look. Three green shoots with tender leaves had sprouted from the sides of my stick. My grandfather's hazel staff had taken root.

'It looks as if a hazel will once again bloom in the Hall,' Lorcan said behind me. 'A new Tree of Knowledge perhaps?'

I touched it. It was too young to speak, but I could feel the life in it.

Lorcan placed his hand on my shoulder. 'This is a good omen. Good luck, son of hazel and oak. When we next meet, it shall be in your father's house.'

'I'll buy you a beer.'

He smiled and left me alone with the young hazel. 'This is for you,' I said aloud to a grandfather I had never known.

It was strange being on horseback without Acorn beneath me. Lorcan had lent me a mare named Cloud. She was smaller than Acorn and lived up to her name by giving a softer ride, but I refused to get too friendly. It felt like I was having an affair with another horse.

I was relieved to find that our route wouldn't be taking us through the Yewlands – I didn't want to go through that again. Apparently, the only reason we went that way the first time was to make sure no one was following us. I can understand that. There is no way I would take a walk among the yews again, unless my life depended on it. Even then I would have to think about it.

There were nineteen of us in our party. On horseback were: Mom, Dad, Nieve, Essa, Fergal, Araf, me and ten Leprechaun goldsmiths. Gerard and Dahy rode in the front of a wagon pulled by a pair of magnificent workhorses. I thought the horses I had seen here before were big, but these things were colossal! They might as well have been elephants for the size of them. Gerard's wagon was packed with about three dozen massive barrels of wine, but they pulled them as if they were hauling feather pillows.

We kept a leisurely pace. We wanted to arrive at the castle only half a day before Lorcan's army, so we didn't have to press too hard. Nieve and Deirdre spent the first day gabbing on horseback like long-lost sisters. Essa and Fergal were both in introspective moods. I understood it with Fergal but I couldn't figure out what was bothering Essa. The Leprechauns were a bit in awe of us, so they pretty much kept to themselves. I rode abreast with Araf – and you know how chatty he is. Actually, I wasn't in the chattiest of moods myself. I know this sounds crazy (after all I had been through), but for the first time since I had been here – I was nervous. When I first heard Ona's prophecy, I wondered – *How could I possibly destroy the whole land?* – but now it occurred to me, that that might be exactly what I was doing. Cialtie had a weapon that could trash everything, and we were on our way to provoke him. Maybe I was playing right into destiny's hand.

That night around the fire, I put that point to Dad.

'I remember when I was working at the university,' Dad said, 'I used to laugh at the science professors who were so sure that everything could be explained. They were all buffoons except for one of them. His name was Tobias, he was Italian.'

'I remember him. He taught physics, didn't he?'

'That's right. Even though his entire life was dedicated to provable facts, he believed in *the Evil Eye*.'

'The what?'

'*The Evil Eye* – some Italians think that a person with special power can harm you with just a look. Tobias even wore a gold necklace to protect him from it.'

'That sounds like one of Mom's amulets.'

'Exactly. I asked him once how a man of science could be so superstitious and he told me about quantum physics. Apparently there are things going on in the tiniest of matter that just cannot be explained. He told me about an experiment where a scientist made an atom spin in some laboratory and it made another one spin in the opposite direction ten miles away. He couldn't explain it – no one could. He said if the smartest people in the world can't explain something like that – then he was keeping the necklace on. I liked him, he had an open mind.

'One day, he explained the Chaos Theory to me by holding up a piece of paper. He asked, "What would happen if I let go?" I told him that the paper would flutter to the ground, but then he asked me – "*Where will it hit the ground?*" He let the paper go and it landed not far from his feet. He said he could explain mathematically how the air and gravity reacted with the paper and why the paper landed where it did – "*but*," he said, "*no one could ever predict where the paper would land before it was dropped.*"

'That is the essence of the Chaos Theory. We know things *will* happen but until they do, we cannot tell *how* they will happen. I am sure Ona was right – she always was – but we don't know the how, or the when. Just because we have a glimpse of the future does not mean we should run and hide. We must do what must be done. Cialtie must be stopped and I must get my hand and fix the damage my brother has done.'

I looked at the man I had spent my entire life with, and realised just how much I had underestimated him. I remembered a Mark Twain quote: he said something like – '*I left my family at fifteen because my parents were so stupid. When I arrived back home two years later, I was amazed how much they had learned in that time.*'

'I haven't said it in a long time, Dad, but I love you.'

'And I you, son.' He kissed me on the cheek. 'Get some sleep, we have a long day tomorrow.'

We spent the next day riding fields dotted with poplar trees – the Eadthlands. I think the poplars are my favourite trees in The Land. They are solitary, straight and unimaginably high, like huge green rocket ships. I leaned back to try to see the top of one as we rode by and almost fell out of my saddle. I wanted to stop and speak to one of them but Mom said they are not very good conversationalists – their thoughts are too much in the clouds. Apparently the Fili used to converse with them about philosophy, but only if they would climb to the top. If I was to climb that high, the tree had better say something pretty important. I would be angry if I risked life and limb to get to the summit and the only thing the poplar said was, '*I can see your house from here.*'

The other nice thing about the Eadthlands is that the trees are so far apart. It gives you a chance to notice all of the other plants and animals that populate The Land. Rabbits the size of puppies came out of their burrows to watch us go past. I saw a fox with a coat so red and lush I wanted to hug it. The wildflowers were in full bloom. Fields were covered with colours that you just don't get in the Real World. There were reds, yellows and purples the like of which I had only ever seen in a tropical fish tank, and then colours I didn't even have a name for.

Essa rode up beside me and said, 'Stop it.'

'What are you talking about?'

'Stop looking at The Land like you are never going to see it again.'

'That's not what I am doing,' I protested, but she had fallen back already. The thing is, she was right – that is exactly what I was doing. I think everyone was. Even Gerard was quiet. To give you an idea of how nervous we all were, Araf came abreast of me and started a conversation without me even saying anything to him!

'I went to Castle Duir with my father once, when I was a boy,' he said without prompting. I almost fell out of my saddle with shock. 'I remember sneaking off and exploring the castle and getting terribly lost. I ended up in the library. I had never seen so many books before, but being a child, what interested me the most were the weapons. There was a beautiful oak banta stick on the wall. I was climbing on a desk to have a closer look at it when Lord Finn – your grandfather – came in. I must have startled him – he shouted, "What are you doing here?" I was terrified and ran out of the room. He gave chase and caught me at the end of the corridor. I kicked and screamed as he picked me up by my shoulders and held me at arm's length. Then he laughed, that wonderful laugh that your family seems to own, and he gave me a smile – now that I think of it, it was a smile just like the one Fergal has.

'I stopped kicking and Finn said, "You must be young Prince Araf." I only managed a nod. Then he said, "Come with me. I want to show you something." I followed your grandfather down, deep into the castle until we came to a chamber lit with a hundred candles. He told me that the Leprechauns make the candles with wax mixed with gold dust and that they burn for years. Did you know that?'

'No,' I said, smiling. This was an introspective and loquacious Araf that I had never seen before. I liked it.

'I will never forget what he told me. He said, "This is the Chamber of Runes; some day you will undergo the Rite of Choosing here. I suspect, my young Imp, that you will eventually choose the Major Rune of Ur. When you do, you will be a Runelord. Most people think us lucky to become Runelords and they are right – but it is also a responsibility. We do not choose the runes – the runes choose us. To hold a Major Rune means that you give up part of your life to The Land, or even all of your life if The Land demands it."

'When I left, Finn gave me that oak banta stick. It's in my room in Ur Keep. I wish I had it with me now.'

'It will still be there when you return home,' I said.

'I hope so, Conor, but if we fail, and tomorrow we are no more, then at least I know I have done my duty.'

Believe it or not, Araf chattered on for the rest of the day. He talked about his home, banta fighting and the joys of farming. It worked for both of us – Araf talked and talked to allay his nerves, and I concentrated on what he was saying and didn't have time to think about my possible impending doom.

I spoke to Fergal only once in the day. When I pulled up next to him he said, 'If you ask me how I am, I'm going to punch you.'

'How are you?'

He did punch me, on the arm. It made me sad that Fergal and I had just met. We should have grown up together. His punch was like a punch between brothers, not hard enough to do any damage but hard enough that it hurt.

I rubbed my arm and laughed. 'Any time you want to talk, cuz, I'm right here.'

Long before dark, Dad called a halt and made an announcement. 'This is as close to the castle I want to get in daylight. We will leave well before dawn tomorrow. Tonight we can camp at Glen Duir.'

Glen Duir was at the beginning of the Oaklands, and a more picturesque spot is hard to imagine. We camped near a stream nestled in rolling hills. I was helping set up camp when my father tapped me on the shoulder. 'There is a tree I want you to meet,' he said.

TWENTY-FIVE

MOTHER OAK

Dad mentioned Mother Oak once when I was a boy. He caught me carving my name in a tree and was furious. He took my knife from me and said, 'If you had done that to Mother Oak you would be dead now. I would have killed you myself.' It sounded like he meant it too. He was so mad I didn't have the nerve to ask him what he was talking about. Now I know.

We walked upstream for about ten minutes. The way my father said, *Mother Oak*, I was expecting something magnificent. When he stopped at an unremarkable tree and beamed, 'Here she is,' I was a bit disappointed. Mother Oak was pretty much a normal-looking tree. I'm sure I have seen bigger oaks in parks at home. The difference came when you touched her.

Dad went first. He wrapped his arms around her trunk like some hippy tree hugger. I swear the tree hugged him back. A huge canopy of branches covered him over to the point where I couldn't see him any more. When the leaves retreated, he had a goofy look on his face, like a kid who just got offered an ice-cream cone. 'Say hello to Mother Oak,' he said.

I placed my hands on the knurled bark and it hit me like a wave. A feeling of goodness and love swept over me, and into me, and through me, the likes of which I had never known. I am sure I was wearing the same stupid grin that I saw on Dad's face a moment ago.

'*Oh my, my, my*,' came a voice in my head that was as gentle as it was obviously wise. It felt as if I had instantly found the grandmother that I had never known. I hugged her in earnest as she swept her leafy arms over me. Tears involuntarily poured from my eyes. '*There, there*,' she said soothingly, '*oh my, you have had a difficult time lately, haven't you, my child?*'

I had, I realised. In the last week, my life had been turned completely upside-down and I had dealt with it by being brave, but now, in the face of such compassion, all of the fears and the weariness that I had been hiding in every bone, came to the surface. My knees buckled and I wept openly.

I was in such a state I didn't realise what was happening. She caught me and carried me up into her branches and held me like a child that won't go to sleep. I finally got a grip on myself and noticed I was about ten feet off the ground and let loose a little shriek.

Mother Oak laughed. '*Don't worry, I have you, I won't let you fall. Now let me get a look at you. Climb up a little higher.*'

I hadn't climbed a tree in years and realised then just how much I wanted to. Mother Oak placed branches in my path for me to grab, and boosted my footholds.

'*Oh, my dear, I think that is far enough.*'

A tangle of branches congealed behind me and I sat in them. I felt like a newborn baby being admired at arm's length.

'*Oh yes, you definitely are Oisin's seed. There is so much oak in you but also something else – let me guess – hazel. Am I right?*'

'Yes, ma'am,' I said out loud. I still hadn't gotten used to talking to trees without speaking.

She seemed tickled that I called her *ma'am*. I felt her smile. '*Oak and hazel*,' she mused. '*Strength and suppleness, brawn and brain – what a good combination, no wonder Oisin is so proud.*'

I had a question on my mind since I first touched her and I finally found my voice. 'Are you the first tree?'

'*Oh my, what a question. I can't remember that far back, I'm an old woman, you know. I have been here a long time. I imagine all of your fathers and most of your mothers have climbed in my branches. I know I have watched over the children of Duir since the beginning. But am I the oldest? Who can tell?'* She chuckled to herself. *'I feel like the oldest some-times. Picking up a big strapping boy like you was harder than it used to be.'*

'I'm sorry.'

'Don't be. It is a pleasure to meet you, young Conor. I don't like to say it, but not all in your family have such a good heart. It pleases me down to my roots to meet a child of oak as fine as you.'

I stood up and hugged her – I couldn't help myself.

'Will you come and visit me again?'

'If I can,' I said, thinking about the dangers that lay ahead.

'Oh, my poor dear, your trials are not over, are they?'

'No.'

'Do not you worry. Remember you are oak and hazel, you will know when to be strong and when to bend.'

Then she hugged me, a hug of wood and leaves that was softer than any I have ever had from flesh and blood. *'Will you be alright climbing down by yourself? I have had enough bending for a day. I'm an old woman, you know.'*

Dad was asleep when I reached the ground. When I woke him he looked at me and said, 'Well?'

I couldn't even begin to put my feelings into words, so I just said, 'That's a heck of a tree.'

Dad roared with laughter at that. 'That she is, son. That she is.'

On the way back to camp several of our horses galloped past us. 'Where are they going?' I asked.

'Deirdre is sending them home, we don't need them any more.'

Back at the camp Mom was whispering in Cloud's ear. She finished and Cloud galloped off. 'You can talk to horses?' I said, amazed.

She started to answer and then remembered she had a small gold disc on her tongue. She took it out and said, 'One of my tutors was a Pooka.' Then that little shadow of sadness passed in front of her face for a second. The same look she always gets when she is remembering her youth at the Hall of Knowledge.

'You know, Mom,' I said and then paused – I didn't know how to continue. I wanted to tell her how glad I was to have found her and how wonderful and brave and beautiful I thought she was. I wanted to tell her that I loved her. 'I just ...'

'I know, son, me too,' she said and then held me. She was right, we didn't have to speak.

Dahy whipped up a roast rabbit dinner. He only cooked about five of them but they were so big they fed us all. We ate pretty much in silence. After dinner, Dad announced that he and Dahy would finalise the plan tonight. He told us to get some sleep and he would fill us in at breakfast. At the mention of sleep I instantly realised just how tired I was. Two days of riding and the outpouring of emotion with Mother Oak had drained me so much, I hardly had the strength to unfurl my blanket.

At about the same time I put my head down, Fergal came over. He sat next to me, cross-legged. He looked like he wanted to talk but he didn't say anything.

'How you doing?' I said, hoping he wouldn't hit me.

He gave me a weak smile. 'Conor, I want to tell you something.'

I let loose a big sigh and said, 'Fergal, I don't think I can take another emotional scene today. I already had one with my mother and my father and even one with a tree. Look, cousin. I'm glad I met you and I love you too, but we are not going to die tomorrow. Why don't you get some sleep?'

'Yeah, I guess you're right, Conor. Good night,' he said and left.

As soon as my head hit the ground I remembered what I had said to him earlier, about *always being there, if he wanted to talk*. Damn, I can be a jerk sometimes. There was no way I could just go to sleep now, so I dragged myself off the ground and went looking for him. I couldn't find him. He told someone in the camp that he was going for a walk. There was no way I was going to find him in the dark, so I went back to my blanket. When I got there Essa was lying on it.

'I think you will find that that is my blanket,' I said.

'I know,' she said, 'lie with me.'

'Essa,' I said in a whisper, 'your father is just over there.'

'Oh, shut up and lie down, Conor, I just need someone to hold.'

I lay down next to her and she placed her head on my chest. We didn't speak. Her hair tickled my nose but I didn't mind. It was what she needed and to tell the truth, it was what I needed too. Just before I fell asleep I had a scary thought. I imagined Sally standing over us with her arms crossed, saying, 'And just what is going on here?'

That night I had another vivid dream but this one was not about The Land, it was about the Real World. I saw buses and hamburger joints, sweet shops, TV sets, traffic lights, shopping malls, and Sally was everywhere. I didn't see these things in a bad light. I missed them. This was my home – or at least it used to be my home. *Is The Land my home now?* I asked myself. *Do I fit in here? Do I fit in there?* The Real World was all I had known and I loved it. Had I lost it? I didn't want to.

Essa wasn't there when Gerard woke me – thank the gods. I didn't want to have to explain that. It was long before dawn. He handed me a cup of tea that made every cell in my body stand at attention. 'Come and get something to eat, Oisin wants to talk to us.'

There was a big cauldron of porridge on the fire. It was stodgy but it did the trick. I was glad to see Fergal there – he looked OK.

Dad stood up and put on his leadership face. 'The Leprechauns have left already. They are going to try to sabotage the Golden Circle from the outside. The map shows us that there are interconnecting gold lines buried in the courtyard. Essa, Araf and Fergal, it is your job to sever them where they meet by the central well. Deirdre and Nieve, you go to the Chamber of Runes and prepare for my Choosing. Conor, you are with me, we have to find my hand.'

'Where is it?'

'Cialtie has taken Finn's bedroom. It must be in there. Any questions?'

'Yeah,' I said. 'How are we going to get into the castle?'

'You are going to be delivered personally,' said Gerard, 'by the finest winemaker in The Land.'

TWENTY-SIX

BORN READY

Never in my entire life have I ever been so uncomfortable. When Gerard told me that he was going to smuggle us into the castle in empty wine barrels, I thought we would hop in just before we got there. Oh no, Dad insisted that we hide in them for the entire three-hour journey to Castle Duir. He wanted to make sure we were not spotted en route. Which was fair enough, but three hours! The porridge I ate for breakfast was sitting in my stomach like a rock. I had a scary moment when I thought I was going to see it again. I cursed Dahy for cooking it and then I cursed him again for devising a plan that put me in here and allowed him (along with Gerard) to sit comfortably up front. Every bump jarred me like an ice cube in a cock-tail shaker, and with every one of those bumps I knocked my head into the side of the barrel. At one point we went over a rock that was so big I hit my head on the lid, and howled. Fergal was in the barrel next to me. 'Shut up,' he said, 'I'm trying to get some sleep.'

'Sleep!' I shouted over. 'How can you sleep when your head is being bounced around like a pinball?'

'What's a pinball?'

'Never mind.'

'Put the blanket next to your head,' he said, 'then it's not so bad.'

'I don't have a blanket.'

'You are travelling three hours in a barrel and you didn't bring a cushion? I thought you were smart. Didn't you say you went to a place of learning in the Real World?'

'They didn't have any courses on how to sneak into castles,' I said.

'Doesn't sound like a very good school to me. Now will you please keep the groaning down.'

I suffered in silence. I actually started wishing the cart would drive over a huge boulder that would knock me out. Another concussion would have been a small price to pay, if it made the journey quicker.

Gerard had no trouble getting in to the castle. A delivery of the Vinelands' finest was a cause for celebration.

Cialtie met the wagon himself. 'Lord Gerard,' he said. The second I heard that voice all of the hairs stood up on the back of my neck and I stopped breathing. I was instantly terrified, but at the same time I had to overcome the urge to pop out like a deranged jack-in-the-box and chop his head off. 'I hope this shipment,' Cialtie continued, 'is better than the vinegar you sent me last time.'

'I am so sorry, Lord Cialtie, that you found my last batch not to your liking,' Gerard oozed. 'I assure you this is the finest of vintages.'

'I should hope so,' Cialtie said.

I had plenty of reasons for hating my uncle, but the disrespectful way he talked to Gerard made me want to throttle him – after I decapitated him.

'Your daughter is not with you.'

'No, my lord.'

'Why not? You know I wanted to meet her.'

'It is a very busy time in the fermentation cycle. I needed her to supervise the winemaking in my absence. I'm sure she is up to her neck in a barrel of wine as we speak.'

I had to put my hand over my mouth to stop from laughing out loud. You had to love this guy.

'Lord Cialtie,' Gerard said, putting on a serious tone, 'may I ask you why you have an entire army on patrol? Is there something amiss that I should know about?'

'What are you talking about? I have no army on patrol.'

'Oh my,' Gerard said in a fey aristocratic tone that was definitely not him. It made me smile. 'Then I think you should know that there is one on the way.'

'What? How do you know this?'

'Oh, I have a very good Elvish spyglass, they use gold in the optics you know. I saw them yesterday. I'm surprised you haven't noticed. I'd say they were only half a day away.'

Gerard hadn't turned traitor – this was part of the plan. Lorcan and Dad figured that if Cialtie thought he was under attack from the outside, he wouldn't be guarding the inside all that well. It seemed to work.

Cialtie instantly sprang into action, shouting orders. 'Put the wall fortifications on alert,' he yelled, 'and send out a scouting party to find out what he is talking about. Gerard and Dahy, come with me.'

'Of course, my lord, if I can be of any help, but I would ask if Master Dahy could supervise the stowing of the wine. It is a delicate vintage and I wouldn't want to see it bruised.'

'Very well. You two help him,' Cialtie grumbled.

I heard them leave and then the wagon began to move. We travelled a way over cobbled streets. I had a childish urge to sing just so I could hear my voice vibrate. We stopped for the opening of large doors and then turned left. I could tell by the sound that we were inside.

'Close those doors, you idiots! You are letting the cool air out,' I heard Dahy bark – then I heard two bangs, two short grunts, followed by the unmistakable sound of bodies hitting the ground.

Fresh air! The things you take for granted. I stood up, breathing deeply and stretching, while everyone else went to work.

Dahy crawled under the wagon and brought out the weapons. Araf and Fergal went about stealing the two guards' uniforms. The shocking bit was when Mom, Nieve and Essa started tarting themselves up. They unbuttoned their shirts and pushed up their cleavages. Essa and Mom put on skirts with revealing slits in them while Nieve started ripping one in hers.

Essa caught me staring. 'What are you looking at?' she snapped.

'What are you doing?'

'We are blending in,' Mom said, giving me a practice provocative smile. 'Women of, how shall I say, dubious virtue are common in Castle Duir these days.'

'Well,' I said to Essa, 'you look – great.'

She didn't return the compliment with a provocative look. It was more like an evil eye.

'Conor,' Dad said, 'stop gawping at the women and help Dahy and me stow the barrels.'

Dad was being his thorough self. They might not miss the guards, but if someone saw that the wine was still on the wagon, they might know something was up. I promised myself that I would have a word with Gerard about putting his wine in smaller barrels. Man, they were heavy.

When we were finished, Dahy said, 'I will stable the horse and then rejoin Gerard. Good luck.' We hid behind the door as he left.

Mom gave the naked guards a dose of Shadowmagic that would ensure they slept the rest of the day, and then Dad lined us up for an inspection. People like the women, Dad and me were commonplace in the castle, so we wouldn't raise too much suspicion. Fergal looked just like the Banshee guard he had stolen the uniform from, but Araf was a problem. Imps were not very welcome in the castle and the guard uniform could not disguise the mop of sandy hair on his head – he stood out like a sore thumb. That's when Mom pulled out the wig.

To call it a wig was to do an injustice to every hairpiece that was ever made. It was supposed to simulate Banshee hair but in reality it looked like a skunk that had been dead on the freeway for a week. Araf put it on and I lost it. I don't think I ever saw anything so funny in my life. I was laughing so hard that Dad actually slapped me.

'I'm sorry,' I said, struggling to get my composure back, 'I get like this when I'm nervous.'

'Don't,' Dad said in that voice that meant business. A voice I know only too well.

I shot a glance over to Fergal for support, expecting to see his cheesy grin, but he wasn't even smiling. That kind of sobered me up.

'You three have the most difficult job of all,' Dad said to Essa, Araf and Fergal. 'Those gold lines must be severed.'

'We will not fail, my lord,' Araf said. I felt my stomach churn. This was it. They were my friends and they were heading straight into danger. Fergal didn't look at me but Essa and I locked eyes before she left. She smiled but it was a strange little smile. It seemed to mean something, but as usual I couldn't figure out what. They walked out the door like they owned the place. Essa, dressed as a loose woman, arm in arm between two soldiers. Essa even tried a provocative swish of her skirt, but to be honest, she wasn't very good at it. Then it was just family.

Mom gave Dad a passionate embrace. Nieve offered me her hand. 'Come on,' I said, 'you're my aunt for crying out loud.' I gave her a hug that she didn't return very well.

Mom gave me a kiss on the cheek. 'You look after your father.'

'I will. I'll see you in a little while in the Chamber.'

They sashayed out the door and then it was just Dad and me – like old times.

'Are you ready, son?'

'Born ready, Dad.'

My father knew the castle like he was raised there – which of course he was. We made our way up to the north wing by way of the servants' stairs. Dad figured (rightly as it turned out) that it would be empty this time of day. A Leprechaun was sweeping at the other end of a corridor but he didn't see us. We didn't come across anyone else until we got to the floor the bedrooms were on.

Dad stuck his nose into the main corridor and then motioned for me to follow. At the end of the corridor was a T junction with a grand oak door. There was nobody around.

'That's Cialtie's bedroom,' he whispered.

We tiptoed towards it. I wasn't as worried about the sound of my feet as much as I was worried about the sound of my pounding heart. We were about halfway there when a soldier came up from the corridor on the left. Cialtie had a guard posted at his door! If the soldier had been looking our way, he would have seen us. There was an open door next to us – we both ducked into it.

That's when I heard the scream.

TWENTY-SEVEN

AEIN

The scream came from a slight Leprechaun chambermaid. We scared the hell out of her. Dad tackled her onto the bed and covered her mouth. She looked up with wild eyes. Then Dad called her by name. 'Aein, shhh, I won't hurt you. It's me, Oisin.' He showed her his missing hand. Her eyes widened more, which I didn't think was possible.

A voice came from the corridor. 'What's going on in there?'

Dad rolled off the maid, hitting the floor on the far side of the bed. I ducked behind the door, my banta stick ready.

The guard stepped into the doorway. The maid quickly sat up in the bed. 'What's all this noise?' the guard asked.

She shot a quick glance to me behind the door. I didn't know what she was going to do. If she raised the alarm, we were done for. I'm surprised I didn't pass out – I wasn't breathing.

'I, I,' she stammered, 'I saw a mouse.'

I could see the guard through the space in the doorjamb. He let out an exasperated sigh and said, 'Stupid cow.'

'No! Don't go,' she said.

Oh no, I thought, as every muscle in my body tightened to breaking point, *she is going to give us away*.

'No, please come and look.'

'I have got better things to do than catch mice.'

She shot a knowing glance to me and nodded slowly once. 'Please, I think this mouse has *two* heads.'

I smiled at her then. She was on our side. She knew I couldn't get a clear swing at the guard from where I was – she was luring him into the room. I was impressed by her fast thinking. If I was the guard, there was no way I would have missed a chance to see a two-headed mouse.

The guard stepped into the room. I adjusted the grip on my banta stick and clocked him good, square in the temple. I felt the solidness of the contact clear down to my toes. He did a little comedy pirouette and crumpled to the floor. I leaned over him and said, 'That will teach you for calling her a *stupid cow*.'

I closed the door. Dad popped up from behind the bed. 'Thank you, Aein,' he said.

The maid threw her arms around Dad and pressed the side of her face into his chest. 'Oh, Prince Oisin, it really is you.'

Dad stroked her hair.

She stepped back and wiped her eyes. 'Are you going to fight your brother?'

'I'm afraid I am.'

The sweetness vanished out of her – all of a sudden she looked like she was made of granite. 'Good,' she said, almost spitting. 'How can I help?'

Dad's smile covered his face. At that moment he looked a lot like Fergal. 'Do you know where Cialtie keeps my hand?'

'In his room, in that fancy box of his.'

'Of course,' Dad said. He kissed her quickly on the forehead and turned to leave.

'But,' she said, 'he keeps his chamber door locked.' That stopped us both in our tracks, and then we heard a jingle behind us. We turned to see Aein holding a fob of keys in her hand and smiling. 'But I have a key.'

Cialtie's chambers were decorated with dead things. The walls were covered with mounted animal heads and on every surface there were stuffed birds and beasts. I hate this kind of stuff in the Real World – in The Land, it was a sacrilege beyond measure.

The box was in a small alcove. It was a beautiful thing. It must have been made of wood from every tree in The Land, an intricate patch-work, lovingly made from timber of every hue. Dad put it on a table and stared at it. There was a strip of cherry-coloured wood running along the top. Dad slid it to the left about an inch and then moved a darker strip of wood down. He stepped back and sighed.

'What's the problem?' I asked.

'It's a puzzle box. Some Elf lord gave it to Cialtie when we were kids. You have to perform about thirty of these little moves, in the right order, to unlock it.'

'Can you do it?'

'I did it a couple of times, but that was a long time ago. This is going to take hours.'

I picked up my banta stick and came down hard on the lid of the box. It shattered into about twenty pieces. 'My way is quicker.'

'I wish you hadn't done that,' Dad said.

'Why?'

'What happens if Cialtie comes back here and finds his favourite box has turned to kindling?'

'Oh, I hadn't thought of that.'

Dad gave me that Dad look. 'Obviously.'

With his lone hand he gently pushed aside the splintered wood – he was shaking a bit. Underneath was a packet wrapped in a red velvet cloth. He unwrapped it and – there it was. Something I never thought I would see – Dad's right hand. It almost glowed from the yellow Shadowmagic that encased it, like those dragonflies trapped in amber. He picked it up and stared at it. It was a very strange moment. I tried to imagine what I would be thinking, the first time I saw the back of my own hand in twenty years, and I couldn't.

'Is this going to work?' I asked.

'Deirdre thinks so,' Dad said, dreamily.

'Well, that's good enough for me. Come on, let's get out of here.'

We reassembled Cialtie's box as best we could. It looked OK, as long as you didn't touch it – or sneeze.

* * *

We had to get all the way to the other side of the castle in order to get down to the Chamber of Runes. Aein offered to scout ahead for us. Dad told her it was too dangerous, but she insisted. Who says you can't get good help these days? Whenever we came to a corner we couldn't see around, Aein got down on her hands and knees with a scrubbing brush and crawled around the corner pretending she was cleaning. Once we had to wait a couple of minutes for a guard to pass. Another time, the way was too well guarded, so we ended up on the walkway that overlooked the courtyard. It was more exposed than we liked but it was our only choice. It actually wasn't a bad route. There was a lot of activity above us, with the soldiers fortifying the ramparts, but this level was empty.

It also allowed us to get a look at how Essa, Araf and Fergal were doing. They looked OK. Araf had his back to the well. He was hiding it, but if you looked close you could see he was holding a length of rope that was hanging into the well. Fergal was standing guard, so we assumed that Essa was down the well cutting the gold cables. The strange thing was, even though Araf was wearing that ridiculous wig, Fergal was the one that looked out of place. As a Banshee his appearance was perfect, but his body language was so rigid I could feel the tension all the way to where we were.

We came to the south wing and entered a corridor. This part of the castle was old, real old. You could sense it. The end of the corridor sloped around to the left. Aein got down on her hands and knees again and did her cleaning routine. She was gone for what seemed to be an eternity, then appeared back, still on her hands and knees.

'There is a guard in front of the door to the Chamber,' she whispered.

'What did he look like?' Dad asked.

'He is standing at attention.'

'Go up to him and ask him if he wants a glass of water.'

This obviously scared her, but she did it. She came back looking a bit confused. 'He completely ignored me.'

Dad smiled, walked around the corner and right up to the guard. I thought I was going to have a heart attack. What was he doing? I followed. I mean, what else was I going to do? Dad strolled up to the

guard and snapped his fingers in front of his face. The guard didn't
even blink. He just stared straight ahead, like he was in a trance –
which he was.

'One of Nieve's specials,' Dad said. 'She practised it on me once
when I was younger; it's not very pleasant.'

Aein wouldn't go down to the Chamber of Runes. It wasn't that her
bravery was faltering, it was just that it was not her place. She offered
to guard the door and warn us if anyone approached but Dad said that
wouldn't help. 'Can you do one more thing?'

'Anything, Prince Oisin.'

'Make sure there are no Leprechauns in the east wing. It might get
dangerous today.'

'Leprechauns don't go there if they can help it but there might be
some servants. I will only warn the ones I can trust.'

'Don't stay there too long yourself.'

'May the gods protect you, Prince Oisin.' Aein hugged Dad quickly
and left.

Dad opened the door.

The Chamber of Runes was a long way down. The spiral staircase
was lit by huge candles every couple of steps. I remembered what Araf
said about them being able to burn for years. I was glad they were
there, otherwise we would have broken our necks. There were no
windows, but I suspected after a little while that we were well underground.

Halfway down was a landing and an unconscious guard – so far, so
good. I knew we were getting close to the Chamber by the glow. It got
so bright I half expected to walk into a television studio. Mom and
Nieve had heard our approach – they were standing at the bottom
landing, posed, each holding some magical weapon: Nieve's made of
gold and Mom's of amber sap. They lowered them when they saw us.

'Hi, girls, did you miss us?' I said.

Mom flew into Dad's arms. Nieve asked, 'Did you get it?'

'No problem,' I said. 'Dad's got one hand on his wrist, and another
hand in his pocket.'

Nieve gave me a dirty look. It's amazing how quickly the women I
meet learn that expression.

The Chamber wasn't as big as I expected, but it was sure well lit. Araf said there were a hundred candles down here – it was more like a thousand. The walls looked as if they had been there forever, seen it all. It made me want to ask them questions. It gave a new meaning to *talking to a wall*. The chamber had no furnishings except for a stone table. At the opposite end of the room was an archway made of oak, like a proscenium in an old theatre. Beyond that were two more just like it, and at the far end was another stone table exactly like the one in this part of the room. I walked towards the archway.

'Don't go near that!' Nieve warned.

'Why not?'

'That's the First Muirbhrúcht. Trust me, you do not want to cross that by accident.'

I couldn't see anything but I stepped back. I could tell by her voice that she was not kidding.

Dad unwrapped the hand and held it in place. Mom produced a wide golden bangle and opened the clasp. The gold bracelet was a clamp and she used it to secure Dad's hand to his wrist. Dad held his amber hand up to his face. He turned it, staring at the front and back. He had that faraway look in his eyes, like he had in Cialtie's bedroom. It took my breath away. I had always known this man as a one-handed wonder – now I was looking at him whole – the way I had seen him in my dreams.

Mom placed a piece of gold on his amber palm and then a square of oak, a blank rune. He turned to the archways – he was finally going to take his Choosing, something that he had been preparing for all of his life but had thought was denied to him forever.

He took a deep breath and said, 'I'm ready.'

'I'm going with you,' Mom said.

Dad, who was out of practice with his right hand, was so shocked he dropped the gold and the rune. 'You most certainly are not!'

It was Mom's turn to be shocked and she shot back with the same indignation, 'Yes I am!'

Oh my, I thought, *I'm witnessing my first parental argument*. I wondered if I should go upstairs and hide in my bedroom.

'Deirdre,' Dad said, softening his tone a bit, 'you can't take a Choosing, it will disrupt your sorcery.'

'I'm not taking a standard Choosing, I'm going to choose a Shadowrune.' She placed a glob of tree sap in her palm and placed a disc of dark amber over it.

I hadn't seen Dad that shocked since – well, never. I was shocked too. Dad had explained to me how gold was the fuel that powered the creation of a rune – Mom was going to attempt it using tree sap powered by Shadowmagic. I was sure no one had tried that before. Even with my limited understanding of all this stuff, the suggestion terrified me.

'That is the craziest idea I have ever heard,' Dad said.

'It should work, Oisin,' Mom said. 'You and the Duir clan have had the monopoly on magic forever. You think that your gold is the only power there is, but you are wrong, I have proved it. And you might need help in there. What I'm doing may be unknown, but no one has ever tried to do what you are doing, either.' Mom looked fierce. I made a mental note to get into as few arguments with her as possible.

'Nieve,' Dad pleaded, 'help me on this.'

'Deirdre and I have discussed it,' Nieve said. 'I think this has a good chance of working – possibly more of a chance than even you have.'

I heard the words *good chance* and *possibly*, and I didn't like it. I had an awful thought that instead of having only one parent, I was soon to be an orphan.

Mom picked up the gold and the blank rune and replaced them in Dad's hand. Dad attempted one last pleading look, but Mom was not for turning. A look of acceptance washed over his face, and they turned to the archway.

'Wooh, hold on,' I said, as I ran in front of them. 'I, I love you both.'

'You don't have to tell me that, Conor,' Dad said, 'I know.'

'And I, my son,' Mom said, 'will never grow tired of hearing it.'

I didn't want to touch them and break their concentration. I said, 'Good luck,' and got out of the way.

'May the gods be with you,' Nieve called.

Then together, as if they had been rehearsing it all of their lives, they took a step towards the archway.

TWENTY-EIGHT
THE CHOOSING

'They have entered the First Muirbhrúcht,' Nieve said. I couldn't see anything before but I sure could now. A wall of light sprang to life as Mom and Dad hit it. It was like a force field in a science fiction movie, the air filled with tiny particles that glowed every colour of the rainbow and some colours that rainbows hadn't even thought of yet. Mom's black hair flew up and wildly floated about, as if she was underwater and caught in a riptide. It was beautiful and terrifying.

Their progress was painfully slow. It was obvious that this was not easy. At one point, Dad turned his head enough so I could see his face. He looked like he was screaming but I couldn't hear anything. In fact the Chamber was eerily silent. Nieve told me that no sound could penetrate the barriers.

'The first barrier is the easiest,' she explained. 'A Chooser can abandon an attempt and come back after the First Muirbhrúcht and survive – after that, there is no turning back.'

It didn't look easy. I could tell that Mom and Dad were using every ounce of strength they had in order to push forward, but even so I've seen hour hands on a clock move faster. We watched in silence. All the muscles in my body tensed up in sympathy. I looked on helplessly for what seemed like an eternity, and then the wall of light subsided – they made it through and I found myself breathing again. Neither of them turned around or even paused. I could see Dad's leg shake as he put his weight on it, like a weightlifter who had just overexerted himself. He was having a tough time of this.

'Do you think they are going to make it?' I asked.

'I do not know,' Nieve said. 'I *do* know that both of them would rather die than fail.'

The second barrier was a lot brighter than the first.

'The Second Muirbhrúcht is the hardest,' Nieve stated calmly.

Mom and Dad pushed on. I ached to see their faces, to get a sense of how they were doing, but was also glad I couldn't. I don't think I could have stood it.

'Conor, place the Sword of Duir on the table.'

Nieve's request came so out of the blue. I said, 'Huh?'

'The Sword of Duir,' Nieve explained, 'always sits on the stone table when a child of Duir is chosen.'

She said it in such a matter-of-fact voice that I just did as I was told – I figured she knew what she was doing. I placed the sword on the table and turned my attention back to Mom and Dad. I didn't think it was possible but they were moving even slower than the last time.

'Do you have any other weapons?'

'What?' I said, distractedly, not even looking at her. 'Oh, just a knife that Dahy gave me.'

'One of Dahy's throwing blades? Can I see it?'

Oh, for heaven's sake, I thought, *my parents are a second away from killing themselves and you want to admire cutlery*, but then I thought, *OK, if this is how she is dealing with the pressure, who am I to complain?* It didn't even occur to me what she was really doing. She was disarming me.

I reached down in my sock and handed her my knife without even looking. She took the knife and with the reflexes of a cat came up behind me. Her left hand grabbed me by the side of the neck and her right hand brought the blade to my throat. I was so stunned I didn't react right away, but when I did I realised I couldn't move. My neck was killing me. Nieve was wearing a ring with some sort of needle in it, a gold needle, I rightly assumed – I was completely paralysed. I tried to pull away but nothing was moving. I was rigid as a flagpole. I attempted to speak and was surprised that I could.

'What are you doing?'

'Don't try to move, Conor.'

I tried anyway, but the only things that seemed to be working were my eyeballs. I looked down and saw that my own knife was about an inch from my throat. 'Nieve,' I repeated, 'what are you doing?'

'My duty,' she said.

'Hey, I thought we dealt with this already. Dad gets his hand back and I'm no longer one-handed junior.'

'If Oisin succeeds, I will let you go.'

'If he doesn't?' I asked. She didn't answer, but I guess it was a stupid question.

I continued to watch Mom and Dad – I had no choice, it was the way I was facing. The Second Muirbhrúcht was putting on a spectacular display. It was so beautiful and terrifying that I almost forgot I was paralysed and had a murderous relative holding a knife to my throat – almost. I relaxed for a second when I remembered Mom's protection spell, but then I remembered that it only works once – Nieve had tried to kill me already. I had an infantile urge to call out to my parents but they couldn't help me, or even hear me, and I wouldn't have wanted to break their concentration anyway.

We were so engrossed in the fireworks that we didn't hear the footsteps coming down the steps until the last second. Nieve spun me around on one of my tent-pole legs, like a comedian dancing with a department store mannequin. She took the knife from my throat and cocked her hand back in readiness to throw. It was Essa. When Nieve saw who it was, I felt her relax and replace the knife to my throat.

Essa stood still and took in the situation. Her expression turned serious but it wasn't the look of shock that I had expected. 'How is it going?' she said.

'How is it going?' I shouted. 'What do you mean, "*How is it going*"? She is trying to kill me! That's how it's going!'

Essa lowered her eyes in guilt.

'They are almost through the Second Muirbhrúcht,' Nieve replied, calmly.

'You knew about this, didn't you?' I spat at Essa. 'You're part of this!'

'Conor,' she said in a compassionate voice that I had never heard come out of her before, 'if this works, you have nothing to worry about.'

'What if it doesn't work, eh? Maybe you'll allow me to worry about that!'

'Conor …'

'Don't *Conor* me. I'm not surprised that my dear old aunt would pull something like this. She has been trying to kill me ever since we met – but you! I thought we … Aw, never mind …

'Nieve,' I said, trying to turn around, which of course failed, 'if this doesn't work, I want *her* to be the one that sticks the knife into my neck. I don't want someone who loves me doing it!'

Oh boy, I may have been paralysed but I sure got her in the solar plexus with that one. Essa instantly placed her hand over her mouth and then turned her back on me. Right away, I regretted saying it – but I was mad. And what was I supposed to do? Apologise to a girl who was trying to kill me? She finally looked at me again – her face was wet with tears. I don't think I have ever seen a more miserable countenance. Then her eyes widened in sudden alarm. She looked around the chamber and said, 'Where is Fergal?'

'What do you mean, "*Where is Fergal*"?' I said. 'I thought he was with you!'

'Araf sent him down here to tell you that I had found the gold lines and would be done soon.'

'You let Fergal wander around the castle alone! How long ago was that?'

'Ages ago,' she said. Panic took over her face. 'It took longer than I thought to cut the gold lines, and then I wasted time before I discovered that the guard upstairs was petrified.'

'Oh my God,' I said, as the realisation dawned on me, 'I know where he is. He's going to kill Cialtie.'

'Oh my gods,' Essa said, 'oh my gods.'

I was about to tell her to get out there and look for him, when the whole chamber started to rumble. Nieve spun me back around.

'They have entered the Final Muirbhrúcht,' she said.

The overall colour of the third barrier wasn't as bright as the second's, but Mom and Dad's right hands looked like they were spouting out the entire contents of a fireworks factory. The rumble got louder and the floor vibrated beneath our feet. That's why we didn't hear him approach.

TWENTY-NINE
THE TRUTH, A SECOND TIME

'You lied to me!' Fergal shouted as he appeared in the Chamber in a rage. He flew at me with murder in his eyes – it shocked the hell out of me. I instinctively wanted to run, except that I couldn't. For a split second I had a moment of hope in thinking that Nieve would be startled enough to take that damn needle out of my neck, but she was her usual cool self. She didn't even take the knife from my throat. Essa stopped Fergal before he throttled me. She had to use all of her strength.

His arms were flailing and spit was flying out of his mouth. 'You lied to me. You and that witch mother of yours!'

'Fergal, what are you talking about?' I said.

'You're not from the Real World,' he shouted, with so much vehemence that I could feel the force of his breath. '*You* killed my mother. You and that lying family of yours!'

The rumble in the Chamber increased, as if in sympathy with his mood. To say I was baffled doesn't even come close. It was like having a cuddly cocker spaniel that all of a sudden turned into a killer.

'Fergal, what are you talking about? Who told you that?'

'I did,' Cialtie said as he stepped into the chamber. He was flanked by four guards holding crossbows. 'Son,' he said in that dripping voice of his, 'come over here.'

Fergal did as he was told and Cialtie actually put his arm around his shoulders. I wanted to throw up.

'Oh, Fergal,' I said as I put the pieces of this puzzle together, 'you don't believe *him*?'

'Of course he believes me,' Cialtie said as he smiled down at Fergal. 'Sons should always trust their fathers.'

I tried to speak but nothing came out. The guards looked pretty edgy and their crossbows were aimed at our heads, but I hardly even noticed.

'Sister Nieve, I must say I'm surprised to see you with a knife to my young nephew's throat and it looks like you've paralysed him as well. If I didn't know you any better I would think you were on my side.'

Nieve didn't move a muscle.

'Oh, and you must be Princess Essa of Muhn,' Cialtie said, addressing Essa who had backed up next to us. 'I have been longing to meet you. You are even more beautiful than I had heard.'

Essa didn't say anything, she just pulled her banta stick out of her belt and assumed an *en garde* position.

'Ooh, feisty. I like a girl with spirit.'

I wanted to kill him but judging from the sound that came out of Essa's throat, it seemed like I would have to get in line.

The rumble in the chamber abruptly stopped. Cialtie looked past us.

'Well, well, my son told me what Oisin was attempting. I could hardly believe it, but what do you know, it looks like he did it.'

Nieve spun herself around and me with her. Mom and Dad were at the far end of the archways. The pyrotechnics had stopped. I could see them clearly. They were standing on either side of the stone table. Both were looking at Dad's right hand. The gold bangle that had been on Dad's wrist was gone, presumably used up to fuel the magic that made possible the reattachment – because reattached it was! I followed the line of Dad's right arm down and I'll be damned, there was a hand on the end. I gasped as Dad opened his fingers. It worked! In his palm was a rune. He tilted his wrist down and it fell to the table. Mom did the same, and an amber-glowing rune dropped on the stone surface next to Dad's. They were ecstatic, but their ecstasy was short-lived. They looked to us and their faces filled with horror. I felt so sorry for them.

Dad ran towards us but the Third Muirbhrúcht sparked to life and threw him back, like a tennis ball off a racket. I heard Cialtie laugh at that.

Then I felt the needle leave my neck. Nieve whispered in my ear, 'Don't move.' I felt the sensation returning to my body. It took all of my will not to stretch at the relief but I pretended to stay frozen. Nieve turned back around and I spun with her, Dahy's knife still at my throat.

'They will take ages getting out of there,' Cialtie sighed. 'Oh, what a shame, all of that effort and I'm just going to have to cut it off again. I wonder if I can convince Deirdre to preserve it a second time before I kill her.'

'You said you weren't going to kill anybody,' Fergal said.

'Oh my, my,' Cialtie said. 'Fergal, was it? You are as gullible as your mother. She actually thought I was going to make her a queen. Can you imagine – a Banshee queen? You know, I was shocked when I learned that you survived after I lopped her head off, but now that I know you, I'm astonished you have had the wits to live this long.'

There it was – the truth. It was awful watching Fergal learn it the first time – this time it nearly killed me. The realisation of it hit him in waves, like a baby standing hip-deep in the ocean. I could almost read his mind: first came the pain of reliving his mother's murder, next came the shame of being so easily duped, and then came the horror at the realisation that he had betrayed his friends. He wasn't broken, it was more like he was shattered.

Cialtie pushed him and he crashed into me. 'I think you should stand over there with your friends.'

Fergal crumpled to the floor. He hugged my legs and made a noise that I had never heard from a person before, and never wanted to hear again. Tears poured out of his clenched eyelids, and his mouth hung open, saliva spilling out of it. 'I'm sorry,' he whimpered. 'I'm so sorry.'

'Pathetic,' Cialtie said.

Never in my life had I wanted so badly to do two things at once. I wanted to put my arms around my poor cousin and tell him it was OK, and at the same time I wanted to tear Cialtie limb from limb – with my bare hands. I didn't do either. I don't know how I did it, but I stood perfectly still. Cialtie thought I couldn't move. It was the only advantage that we had.

'You know, I suspected you were here, even before my sprog showed up and spilled the beans,' Cialtie said. 'You know what gave you away? It was that rinky-dink army. I've seen bigger circuses. I thought to myself, *What could that tiny gaggle of stumpy people do, other than disturb my sleep?* And then I realised it must be a diversion. Oh well, I'm glad they are here. I'll enjoy seeing them all dead.'

As if I hadn't had enough shocks for a day, Cialtie reached into his pocket and removed a crystal vial that was filled with gold. It wasn't the vial that shocked me, it was what was attached to the top of it – a red button. It was the only Real World-looking thing that I had ever seen in The Land, other than my clothes. I almost craned my neck to get a better look, but I managed to remain perfectly still.

'Ah, nephew, I see you recognise this. I wondered if you would. I had a dream a little while back, it was a good one. You had it too, didn't you? I thought you must have, because in it was the strangest little device that was completely foreign to me. I liked it so much, I had my goldsmiths whip one up. Now all I have to do is push this little red thing and that pesky army will pester me no more.'

'Cialtie,' Nieve said, 'don't do it, you will destroy everything.'

'Oh, sister, I'm disappointed in you. I thought you clever in the ways of magic. I won't destroy *everything* – we will be fine. All of the rest of The Land will be wiped clean, but I never really liked them anyway. Everyone and everything I need is right here inside my Golden Circle. Trust me, The Land will be a better place when I rebuild it in my own image.'

He had his thumb on the button. I didn't know what to do. Even if I surprised him, by being able to move, he was still too far away. I wouldn't be able to stop him from pressing it.

'I'm waiting,' Cialtie said. 'Is this not someone's cue to tell me I'm mad?' He looked around. 'Disappointing.'

That's when Araf burst into the room and all hell broke loose.

THIRTY

A TIME TO BEND

Araf didn't know what was going on. He instinctively went for one of the armed guards first, not my uncle. Cialtie had time to press the button – and he did. The entire chamber lurched to the sound of a huge explosion. Burning candles toppled all over the place and everyone lost their footing.

It worked! Not from Cialtie's point of view, but from ours. The explosion meant that the Leprechaun goldsmiths had done their jobs. Mom had explained to me, that if the Golden Circle went off the way Cialtie wanted it to, we wouldn't hear anything in the castle – but if the Leprechaun goldsmiths succeeded in crafting spikes in a section of the Golden Circle, the explosion would blow out the whole east wall of the castle. It did, and that's what Lorcan's army was waiting for.

All of the guards let loose their crossbow bolts. Two of them were way off the mark, one from a soldier that fell down from the explosion, the other from the guy that Araf had just clocked with his banta stick. Two bolts unfortunately were right on the mark. One came directly at Essa's chest. With skill that must have made Araf and Dahy proud, she actually deflected the bolt with her banta stick – then she performed one of her head-over-heel manoeuvres. That was the last thing her attacker saw.

The other bolt flew straight at my chin. I think The Land has given me two special gifts: one is dreams and the other is the way time seems to slow down in a crisis. I actually saw the bolt spring off the bowstring. I had time to remember what Mother Oak had said to me, '*You are oak and hazel, you will know when to be strong and when to bend.*' It was time to bend. With flexibility that a Russian gymnast couldn't duplicate, I arched my back and watched the bolt sail past my face. Nieve wasn't so lucky. It got her in the shoulder, but not before she could flick my knife at the archer. Her throw was wide of the mark but due to the extraordinary properties of Dahy's golden tip, it honed back on its target like a guided missile. The heartbeat it took for all this to happen was the guard's last. I didn't stop bending, I went right over like an upside-down U. How I stayed on my feet, I will never know. I kept going until I planted my hand on the stone tabletop – right next to the Sword of Duir. In that upside-down world I grabbed the Lawnmower and reversed the process.

When I straightened up, I saw a scene that has haunted my thoughts ever since. Fergal was on his feet. His face was contorted with rage and he was charging Cialtie. As he stepped forward, he cocked his wrist in the gesture that I recognised as the sequence that released his Banshee blade, but the sword wasn't in his sleeve – it was on his belt. He never did get to replace the gold wire.

Cialtie recognised the gesture, too – because he had a Banshee blade of his own. He mirrored Fergal's wrist movements, with the difference that when he did it, a shiny silver sword appeared in his hand.

I screamed, 'No!' and flew at the sword in hopes of deflecting it. I was too late. My slow-motion gift became a curse. I saw the tip of the blade touch Fergal's chest, I saw the threads on the fabric of his shirt part and break, I saw every single millimetre of that cursed weapon enter my cousin's chest and not stop until it reached his heart. My swing was late, Cialtie was too fast. My blade came down a foot behind where I needed it to be. I sliced into Cialtie's right wrist and took his hand clean off. He screamed in pain as blood shot around the room.

Fergal looked down in shock. What he saw was Cialtie's sword sticking out of his chest with his father's hand still wrapped around the pommel. Then he did that most Fergalish thing – he laughed. He pointed to the handle of the sword and said, 'Will you look at that.' He wore a typical Fergal, ear-to-ear grin on his face, as he fell over backwards. Just then Dad burst through the First Muirbhrúcht.

With a force of will that was unprecedented, Dad had pushed back through the three barriers in record time. He came out roaring and, as if he had never missed it, he drew his sword with his right hand and flew at his brother. Dad didn't even see what happened next, but I did. Cialtie saw him coming. With his remaining hand, he quickly reached to his neck, grabbed an amulet and shouted, '*Rothlú!*' Dad connected with nothing but air. He would have smashed into the far wall, if Araf hadn't caught him.

Fergal was still conscious. I dropped down next to him, just as Mom popped through the Muirbhrúcht. She quickly joined me. I pried Cialtie's hand off the pommel and threw it across the room. When I started to remove the sword Mom stopped me. She placed her hands on both sides of Fergal's head and closed her eyes. When she opened them they were filled with tears. She shook her head *no*. It felt like *my* heart was the one that had a sword in it.

'Hey, cousin,' Fergal said, 'why the long face? We've laughed through worse times than this.' The tears came so hard I had to squeeze my eyelids to clear my vision. When I opened them, he was gone. He still had a little smile in the corners of his mouth.

It wasn't me. It was Fergal. Fergal was the one. He was *the son of the one-handed prince*. Fergal was the one who had to be sacrificed in order to save The Land. Oh, Fergal. At that moment I couldn't imagine anything that was worth that price.

THIRTY-ONE
A DECISION

The ensuing battle didn't amount to much. At the moment Cialtie's ring misfired, most of his crack troops were standing on the ramparts of the eastern wall watching Lorcan's army approach. They were killed in the blast. The battalion that had been sent to meet Lorcan legged it back to the castle when they saw the explosion. The Imps and Leprechauns charged after them. During a fierce battle in the courtyard, Dahy killed their captain with a knife throw reportedly from fifty yards away. Without any commanders Cialtie's army surrendered. Maybe their Banshee sixth sense informed them that they had lost.

At sunset most of the mopping up was done. Lorcan ordered all of his troops to muster in the courtyard. Aein gathered the servants there too. Many of them she had saved by telling them to evacuate the east wing. Dad and I climbed to the upper walkway.

At the top of the stairs, he said, 'I'm afraid I'm going to have to ask for the Lawnmower back.'

I handed it to him and together we walked to the edge of the railing. In his right hand he held aloft the Major Rune of Duir, and in the other hand the Sword of Duir. The roar that went out was deafening. After several tries Dad silenced the throng and put his arm around my shoulder.

'People of The Land,' he shouted, 'this is my son of whom I am exceedingly proud – I give you – Conor of Duir!'

The crowd just went crazy. I used to want to be a rock superstar but after that experience, I'll take being the son of the two-handed prince any day.

The week that followed was mad. Reconstruction of the eastern wall started immediately. News of Dad capturing the throne and regaining his hand spread even faster than if they had television around here. Dignitaries poured in every day to meet with Pop.

Mom and Nieve spent most of their time tending to the wounded. Dad would wheel me out periodically to meet Lord Whoosit or Lady What's-her-Name but other than that I really didn't have much to do.

There was a nice moment when Dad sent for me to meet the king of the Brownies and his two sons. I entered from the rear of the throne room, nipped up next to Dad and without looking bowed just like Pop taught me to. When I straightened up I saw a very potbellied Brownie flanked by two open-mouthed youths.

'Frank, Jesse, how the hell are you?'

A look of terror crossed Frank's face as I walked towards him. He pulled his head back from his father's peripheral vision and shook his head. The desperado boys had obviously not told their father about their little walkabout.

'You know my sons?' the Brownie king asked.

I walked up close and looked each of them square in the eyes from about six inches away. I was close enough to see the sweat form on their brows – it was fun.

I backed off. 'I'm sorry, your highness, I don't see very well since my ordeal in the battle, I am mistaken.'

As they left, Jesse glanced back smiling and slipped me a little wave.

'What was that about?' Dad asked.

'I'll tell you later,' I said.

I left the throne room and sent a message to Dahy to have the two Brownie boys' luggage searched by the porters before they left. I found out later they both had a couple of choice souvenirs in their bags.

*   *   *

I got tired of everybody gaping and bowing to me everywhere I went, so I spent most of my time sitting in my room trying to piece Cialtie's wooden box back together and thinking of Fergal. So when I heard that Lorcan was returning to the Hazellands to clear out his old head-quarters, I jumped at the chance to go.

I overslept on the morning we were supposed to leave. I still hadn't gotten used to the luxury of sleeping in clean sheets and in a soft bed. I ran down to the courtyard to see a stern-looking Lorcan and his guard all mounted and waiting for me. I ran into the stables to get Cloud (Acorn was still on the disabled list) – and imagine my delight when I saw Mom saddling up.

'Are you coming?'

'Nieve can handle what is left of the wounded, and more impor-tantly, I have not spent enough time with my son.'

'Cool,' I said.

'Yes, it is pleasant out.'

Araf came in and chose a horse.

'Are you coming too?' I asked.

'Yes,' he replied, with one word more than usual.

Lorcan set a swift pace. I think he was trying to punish me for being late. Cloud seemed to be obeying not only my commands but my thoughts. I'm not sure if it was because she was responding to the glori-ous morning or I was becoming a pretty good equestrian. I'd like to think it was the latter. I didn't imagine it was possible but the place seemed even more alive than before. The air was crisp and clear and the colours of the landscape were more vivid than ever. It was as if Tir na Nog itself knew that the proper order had once again come to The Land.

We camped that night out in the open on the edge of the Eadthlands. Lorcan's guards sang songs and passed around some sort of Leprechaun brew that made me feel shorter. Mom told tales of the Fili and Shadowmagic. You could see how delighted she was that these things were, by the order of the new king, no longer forbidden. The only one who seemed not to be enjoying himself was Araf. I went over to where he was sitting.

'You seem awfully quiet tonight,' I said, 'and when you seem quiet that's saying something.'

'Quiet, yes. That's the problem,' he said, staring into his mug of Leprechaun-shine. 'I often would pray that Fergal would just stop babbling so I could have a chance to think. I never imagined how painful silence could be.'

'Yeah, I miss him too.'

We sat for a while in painful silence before I said, 'You know, I can babble on good as anyone.'

And I did. I told him all about the Real World and my life with Dad. How we lived in Ireland and then England before we came to Scranton, Pennsylvania. I explained: TV and shopping malls, soccer and baseball, hamburger joints and airplanes.

When I had finished he said, 'You have devices that toast bread with a touch of a button and machines that fly? It surely must be a magical place.'

I laughed – then thought – maybe he was right.

I spent the next day riding abreast with Mom. She told me about the history of the Hall of Knowledge, her childhood in the Hazellands and stories of my grandparents. By the time we were ready to camp for our second night, she had just about reached the part where she discovered her home destroyed. The rest of our party sensed the seriousness of our conversation and left us alone.

'It must have been horrible for you,' I said. 'I can't even imagine what it must have been like.'

'To be honest, son, I was so consumed by rage, I do not truly remember much. I knew the Fili were the only ones that could help me with my revenge. As it transpired, they did not help me with revenge – only my rage.'

'Now that you know it was the Banshees from the Reedlands, do you think Cialtie had anything to do with it?'

'I would be lying if I said that thought did not cross my mind. We know he is capable of terrible things, but he has done one thing for which I am truly grateful. He brought you back to me.'

The next day we rode parallel to the blackthorn wall. The thorns pointed at us in respect to Mom as we passed – a creaky vegetable Mexican wave. When we reached the scorched border of the Hazellands, Mom stopped, dismounted and stared into her former home. She looked lost. I dismounted and stood beside her.

'Are you OK, Mom?'

'I have been back here twice,' she said. Her voice betrayed the slightest of trembles. 'The last time was with you. We had pressing business then and I performed a Fili concentration trick on myself so as not to think about it. The time before that was when I found it destroyed.'

'If you want to go back I will ride with you.'

She turned and smiled at me – a pained smile, the same expression I had seen recently in the mirror when I thought of Fergal stealing my shoes.

'Thank you, son, but no. I have delayed this too long. But first there is something I must do. Lorcan!' she called to guards who had been waiting a respectful distance away. 'Bear witness to this.'

Mom stood with her back to the thorns. Lorcan and his men dismounted and stood to attention around her in a semicircle.

Mom drew her yew wand and spoke. 'By order of Oison, Chooser of the Rune of Duir, I forthwith lift the banishment of the Fili and once again grant all of the peoples of The Land the freedom of the Fililands.'

She touched her wand to the blackthorn wall, incanted and stood back. Nothing happened at first – but then began that spooky creaking sound, the sound that usually means the plant is about to kill you. This time the thorns parted, leaving a huge archway large enough for at least four horsemen to ride abreast.

Although they were standing to attention, Lorcan and his men strained their necks to get the first glimpse of the Fililand in a generation – and a generation is a long time around here. The ominous rowan forest was lush and shadowy – the exact opposite of where we were standing. It took a moment for our eyes to adjust to the dark, green leaf-filtered light. A gasp went though the crowd as Fand appeared. Like some TV magician's optical illusion, she seemed to appear right out of a tree trunk. Behind her, dozens of other Fili seemed to fade in from nothing.

Fand stopped at the edge of the archway. She looked at Mom and me and said in that soft voice of hers, 'I have never been outside of the Fililands.'

'Well then,' I said. 'I think it's about time.'

Fand stepped blinking into the sunlight.

Mom turned to me and said, 'Prince Conor …'

'Prince Conor what?'

'As the senior representative of the House of Duir, announce the queen.'

'Oh,' I said, clearing my voice. 'Ladies and gentlemen and Imps and Leprechauns and whoever else – I give you Her Excellent Royal Highness the Queen of the spookiest folks I have ever met – Fand of the Fili. She's a great cook too.'

Lorcan and his men saluted and then cheered. Mom looked at me and shook her head.

'I guess I have to work on this princely stuff.'

'Yes, you do,' Mom said with that disapproving look I cultivate.

Mom and Fand embraced. The soldiers broke ranks to shake hands and feel their first Fili.

We all mounted up. Fand rode with Mom, more for emotional support than for Fand's benefit. A group of Fili jogged along beside us like presidential bodyguards.

The small contingent that Lorcan had left behind had been busy. The stones that had made up the ruined Hall of Knowledge had been stacked as if in preparation for rebuilding. Mom went to work immediately. She helped organise all of the documents that had been found, and insisted, for some reason, that every piece of parchment, no matter how small, should be saved.

That night after dinner I found Fand and Mom in Lorcan's old head-quarters, engrossed with Shadowmagic.

'I hate to bother you, Fand, but can I borrow my mother for a little while?'

'Of course, Conor.'

When Mom looked at my face she asked, 'What is it, Conor?'

'Come with me, I have a surprise for you.'

I led her out of the room past the wall with the stained-glass window and stopped her before we entered the courtyard.

'Dahy gave me a hazelwood banta stick that had belonged to Liam.'

'I remember Father giving that to him. And he gave it to you? That was nice of him.'

'Yes, it was. The first time I was here I left it behind in the courtyard. I'd like you to see it.'

We turned the corner together. I was shocked at how much it had grown. The last time I had seen it, my staff had sprouted tiny green shoots – now it sported full leaves and had grown almost a foot. Mom dropped to her knees and placed her hand on what once was my weapon. She removed her hands and beamed at me – tears sparkled in her eyes.

'Lorcan thinks it may be a new Tree of Knowledge,' I said.

'He is correct – it is. It is a miracle.' She hugged me. 'You, my son, are a miracle.'

'Aw shucks, Ma – it was nothing.'

If not for the nagging feeling that something was missing, that I knew was the absence of Fergal, the following few days were the happiest I spent in The Land. I helped the Imps and Leprechauns shift rock, organised papers with Mom and even did a little gardening with Araf.

The night before we left to return to Castle Duir I asked Mom if she was going to reopen the Hall of Knowledge.

'That is not a task for me,' she said. 'This is no longer my home. My home was destroyed. That is a job for another. You, perhaps?'

'Mom, I'm eighteen years old.'

'Some think youth has a certain kind of wisdom.' Her eyes twinkled and I didn't like it.

'No thanks. One Professor O'Neil in this family is quite enough.'

I was loath to leave this place. Not just because I enjoyed it so much, but because I knew I was now forced to make a decision. During most of the ride back I wrestled with comparisons between the Real World and The Land. When we reached Glen Duir I let everyone ride ahead except for Araf, who insisted on remaining as my royal bodyguard.

'*Oh my, my,*' Mother Oak said to me as she swept me into her limbs. '*You have a difficult decision to make.*'

'Yes,' I said, 'and I don't know what to do.'

'*My poor dear, I can feel the conflict inside you. A choice between the heart and the brain – is it not? Most say one should go with the heart but I have touched many a brain that has regretted that decision.*'

'What should I do?'

'*Oh dear, do not ask me. My advice would be to grow bark and sprout leaves. There is nothing I would love more than to calm your mind but that decision, I am afraid, my son, is yours.*'

I hugged Mother Oak and dreamily mounted Cloud, but I didn't go anywhere. I sat there thinking, long enough to try even Araf's patience.

Finally he asked, 'What do you want to do now?'

'I think,' I said, making up my mind on the spot, 'I want to buy a new pair of sneakers.'

THIRTY-TWO
GOODBYES

We buried Fergal in the family plot, next to his great-grand-father's memorial. Gerard and Dahy sang a lament. There wasn't a dry eye in the house.

When it was finished, I was left alone except for about ten Imps. They lifted a massive flat rock across two upright stones that stood on either side of the grave. It was just like the *dolmens* that the ancient Irish chieftains were buried under. That was my idea. I threw a pebble on top for good luck and said goodbye. On the way back to the castle I got a stone in one of my sandals. It hurt but it made me laugh. I had an image of the ghost of my cousin slipping it in there, for a joke. I had buried Fergal in my Nikes.

Gerard and Dahy were standing next to me when I stood up.

'I don't think my dagger will work in the Real World,' Dahy said, 'but it might come in handy anyway.'

'I won't need it,' I said, 'I've got an even better weapon.' I cocked my wrist and Fergal's Banshee blade, newly equipped with a gold wire, dribbled out of my arm and then I missed it. It hung from my sleeve like a child's mitten. 'I still haven't got the hang of it yet.'

Gerard laughed that hearty laugh of his. 'There is always a beer waiting for you in the House of Muhn, Conor.' He gave me a bear-hug that lifted my feet off the ground. When I got my breath back, he asked, 'Have you spoken to Essa?'

'No,' I said, a little ashamed.

'Speak to her at least.'

I spotted Lorcan outside the castle before I went in. He was supervising the rebuilding of the east wall that had been destroyed by Cialtie's Golden Circle. He had traded in his sword for a straight edge and a hammer. He was an engineer again and looked happy. He climbed down from the scaffolding when he saw me approach.

'I'm sorry I missed the burial, but I need to get this done before the winter sets in,' he said.

'That's OK, I don't even think Fergal would have minded.'

'He was a good man, Conor. I'm sorry.'

'Thanks,' I said.

I shook his hand. As I walked into the castle I shouted, 'Goodbye Lorcan the Leprechaun!'

'Do not call me that!'

I smiled. One of his workers, who must have been listening, yelled, 'Look, it's Lorcan the Leprechaun!' Lorcan shook his fist at him but he didn't look that mad. He wasn't a general any more and that suited him just fine.

Araf was in the courtyard planting flowers.

'I'm leaving today,' I said. 'I can't thank you enough for all you did for me. I'll miss you.'

He nodded and said, 'Goodbye.'

That's all he said. I think I would have been disappointed if he said more.

I hesitated before I knocked on Essa's door. This was going to be difficult. She stood up like a nervous schoolgirl when I came in, and brushed down her dress. She looked fantastic.

'You're leaving today?' she asked.

'Yes.'

'I wish you wouldn't.'

'It's not because of you,' I said. But if I was honest with myself, a lot of it was. I couldn't get over what she had done to me in the Chamber. I just didn't think I could trust her again. 'So I guess this is goodbye.'

She threw herself into my arms. I could feel her warm tears fall down my neck.

'Oh, Conor, I am sorry. I am so sorry about everything.'

'I know,' I said, stroking her hair. 'I know.'

Then we kissed. Not counting that attack kiss in the Hall of Knowledge, or the movie kiss in the Reedlands, this was our first real kiss. It almost made me want to stay.

Mom, Nieve and Dad were waiting for me in the Room of Spells. Mom explained that it was the most magically charged place in the castle and she could get me back to the Real World from there.

Nieve's arm was in a sling. I know it was mean of me, but I hoped it hurt like hell.

'I was wrong,' Nieve said. 'I will never again try to force the hand of fate.'

'Well, I'd certainly be a happier guy if you quit the prophecy-fulfilling business.'

'I'm sorry you are leaving, I'd like to be a proper aunt to you.'

'Well – maybe I'll put you back on my Christmas card list, if you promise to behave.'

'What is a Christmas card?' she asked, as another joke bit the dust. Then she kissed me on the cheek. 'That is what I really wanted to do when I first saw you,' she said, and left me alone with my parents.

Mom was wearing her new rune around her neck. It appeared to be made of amber but it was almost insubstantial. It looked like if you tried to touch it, your hand would pass right through. Engraved in it was a marking that I didn't recognise – no one did.

'Have you figured out what your rune means?'

'No. When things calm down around here, Oisin and I will organise an expedition to see if there is any new land.'

'If it is your land, then I know it will be wonderful.'

Mom hugged me even harder than Essa. 'I only just got you back.'

These women, who were so strong in battle, were killing me with just their tears. 'I know, Mom,' I said, 'but I ...'

She pushed back and wiped her eyes. 'No, no, you don't have to explain. You have to make your own way.' She wasn't the first mother to have to say that. 'Here, I have a present for you.' She picked up a velvet bag and took out two *Emain* slates and handed me one. 'Write to me.'

I looked down at the wood-framed sheet of gold. 'Will it work?'

She smiled – my mother *is* the most beautiful woman in The Land – in any land.

'It is worth a try,' she said.

I embraced her again – I thought my heart was going to break.

My father stood in front of me – all of him, right hand included. That was going to take some getting used to. He looked ten years younger, a picture of vitality in his royal clothes, standing in his castle. For the first time I can remember, he looked like he belonged somewhere.

'You know, you look great, Pop.'

'Deirdre here thinks I have my immortality back. We'll see.'

'What about Cialtie?' I asked.

'We'll find him, and if not, I'm sure he will find us.'

'Maybe he didn't survive.'

'Maybe, but if I know my brother, he probably did.' He put on his concerned father look. 'There is nothing back there for you,' he said. 'This is your home.'

'I think I have to find that out for myself.'

Boy, had things changed, he didn't even try arguing with me. His face softened and he said, 'I guess you're right.'

'Dad, I want to thank you, not just for the recent stuff but for everything.'

'If I had to do it all over again, I wouldn't change a thing. I'm proud of you, son.'

And then we did something that I never thought would happen. We shook hands.

I woke up on the floor of my living room. I was back. I was back in the Real World and it amazed me how fast Real World concerns flooded into my brain. Believe it or not, it was the first time I wondered, *Just what in the heck am I going to tell Sally – or anybody, for that matter?* I pushed those problems aside for a minute and stood up.

The room was completely trashed. The tables and chairs were mostly smashed. There was a horrible odour, which I soon discovered came from a pile of horse dung behind an overturned sofa. I surveyed the disaster area and almost said out loud, 'There's no place like home,' but there wasn't anyone around to hear it, and nobody ever gets my jokes anyway.

THE END

PRINCE OF
HAZEL AND OAK

For the oh so achingly beautiful Nadene

ONE

DETECTIVE FALLON

Detective Fallon seemed to have given up on shouting.
'I've seen people get off by claiming insanity,' he said, sitting back in his chair. 'Conor, you ain't doing it right.'

'So you don't think I'm crazy then?' I asked.

'Oh, I think you're plenty crazy but not insane.'

'Aren't they synonyms?'

'Not in my thesaurus. If you want to get off by reason of insanity you have to be a nutcase all the time, you know, with the drooling and the swatting at imaginary bats. You, on the other hand, kill your father and then act completely normal – except for claiming that Daddy was attacked by Imps and Pixies from Faerieland.'

'Tir na Nog,' I corrected.

'Sorry, from Tir na Nog.'

'And there are no Pixies in Tir na Nog.'

'Look, O'Neil' – Detective Fallon leaned in and I could see he was inches away from returning to shouting mode – 'you've been arrested for murder. They've got a death penalty in this state.'

'I didn't kill my father – honest. If I killed him where's the body? If there is no body there can't be a murder.'

'You've been watching too much TV, O'Neil. You can fry without a body – trust me.'

'So what do you suggest I do?'

Fallon softened back into his good-cop mode. 'Tell the truth.'

'Oh that. I was kinda hoping you had a better suggestion.'

The truth – telling the truth is how I had gotten into this mess in the first place. As soon as I returned to what the Tir na Nogians call 'the Real World', all of the Real World problems crashed in on me like a tidal wave. I've never been very good at lying but what else could I do? Dad's boss had reported him missing and the cops were waiting for me when I returned. They had lots of questions after finding the front door wide open and the living room trashed. I made up a lame excuse about a boisterous party and told them that Dad was on a spontaneous trip with old fishing buddies. The cops accepted that explanation, but as I later found out, they didn't believe it.

Sally was really mad at me. She went on and on about how worried she had been and how thoughtless I was for not getting in touch. The sad thing was I didn't care – not only about Sally but about pretty much everything. What's that old saying? Home is where the heart is. Well, I had left my heart back in The Land.

Even though I missed the actual ceremony, apparently I had gradu-ated high school. I forced myself to show up for enrolment at the University of Scranton but after just one day I knew I couldn't face it. What could a college professor teach me? What did they really know?

All food tasted like cardboard and, even worse, when I slept – I didn't dream. I remembered once telling Fergal that some of the Real World was like The Land but covered in a grey film. Now all of it seemed like that.

And then there was Essa. I knew it was unfair but I couldn't help comparing her with Sally – and Sally didn't match up – how could she? It didn't take a soothsayer to notice my thoughts were elsewhere. Sally finally had enough. She said I had changed, and she was right – we broke up.

I suppose I should have gotten a job but that seemed even more trivial than university, so I spent my time staring at the walls. I couldn't even stomach watching television.

The trouble really started when the electric company turned off the power. I hadn't opened any mail, let alone paid bills, but darkness forced me to do something about it. I had the PIN numbers to Dad's bank accounts (well, he didn't need money any more, with him living on top of a gold mine). I can remember standing in front of the cash machine as Dad's words swirled around in my head, 'There is nothing back there for you.' I hated it when he was right. I punched the buttons and withdrew a wad of cash. I didn't think I could feel any lower – I was wrong.

The police showed up at the house that evening with a search warrant. They had been monitoring Dad's bank accounts, waiting for me to do exactly what I did. Forensic specialists in plastic jumpsuits took samples of the carpet, confiscated my clothes and all of the weird weapons in the house. When they finished, a policeman told me not to leave town, like he was in some old TV cop show.

Word of the police raid spread through the neighbourhood like wildfire. The authorities, it seems, weren't the only ones who thought I had committed patricide. I didn't know what to do. Sally showed up as I was packing in preparation for making a run for it. I decided to tell her the truth. I sat her down and told her everything (playing down the Essa stuff) and amazingly she took it in her stride. She told me that she believed me and wished me luck. Two minutes after leaving the house, she called the cops and told them I was crazy. The only crazy thing I had done was to come back for her.

A uniformed officer and a badge-brandishing Detective Fallon were standing on my front porch when I opened the door with a bag over my shoulder. It was Halloween. The first thing I said to Detective Fallon was, 'Don't you have a policeman's costume?' The first thing he said to me was, 'Conor O'Neil, I have a warrant for your arrest.'

'Here's how I see it, Conor,' Detective Fallon said as he paced around the interrogation room. 'Your father – the mad one-handed ancient language professor – was a strange man. I'm not saying that to make you angry, but I've done some research and you have to admit he was, at least, unusual.'

'You won't get any arguments from me on that one,' I said. 'Pop was the weirdest guy in town.'

'I also heard that he used to make you sword-fight with him just to get your spending money.'

'Strange but true.'

'So one day you just had enough, in the heat of one of your fencing practices—'

'Broadswords,' I interrupted, 'Dad hates fencing.'

'OK, in the heat of one of your broadsword bouts you flipped out and accidentally killed him – then you panicked and buried the body.'

I laughed, 'You don't know how many times I came close to doing just that, but no, that's not what happened.'

'Conor, we found your father's blood on the carpet.'

'He was injured when we were attacked. I didn't do it.'

'And we found traces of blood in a splatter pattern on a leather shirt.'

'That's not Dad's blood.'

'The pathologist disagrees. She said the shirt and the carpet had one of the most unusual DNA patterns that she had ever seen.'

'That's 'cause the blood on the shirt came from one of his relatives.'

'I thought your father was an orphan?'

'So did I!' I said, throwing my hands in the air. 'Look, I've explained all of this. Haven't you been listening?'

Fallon sat down and sighed, 'To be honest with you, no I haven't. As soon as you start going on about hobgoblins and dragons I just glaze over. I figured if I let you ramble on with this cock and bull story you would get it out of your system and we could get down to the facts.'

'Sorry to disappoint you, Detective Fallon …'

'Call me Brendan.'

'Sorry to disappoint you, Detective Fallon,' I repeated, 'but those are the facts.'

'OK, Conor, I'll humour you. Tell me this thing from the top and I promise I'll pay attention.'

So I told him the truth. What else could I do? I knew it wasn't going to help but lying wasn't working either. I told him the whole tale about how Dad and I were abducted and taken to The Land of Eternal Youth

– Tir na Nog – where I found out that Dad was the heir to the throne. Unfortunately, because of an ancient prediction saying that '*The son of the one-handed prince would be the ruin of all The Land,*' everybody wanted me dead, especially the unlawful king – Dad's nasty piece of work brother, Cialtie. With the help of a mother I never knew I had, we escaped Cialtie's dungeon and hooked up with an army that was preparing to forcefully oust my slimy uncle. They had scary information suggesting that Uncle Cialtie had hidden a magical bomb that was threatening to destroy everything. Dad and I and a couple of others snuck into the castle before the attack and disarmed the bomb. Cialtie was dethroned but he got away.

'So,' Fallon said with a quizzical look on his face, 'you saved the world?'

'I had help.'

'And when in all of this did you cut your uncle's hand off?'

'Just after Dad reattached his.'

'I take it all back, Conor, you are insane after all.'

After listening to myself I wondered if he was right. It wasn't the first time, since my return, that I had grappled with my sanity. The only thing that had kept me from going over the edge was the stuff I had brought back with me: my clothes, Fergal's Banshee blade and Mom's present. Many a night I sat and just touched them, wishing they could somehow transport me to The Land. But they weren't with me now, and at that moment I wondered if I had imagined them, too.

I think I would have lost it right then and there if Fallon hadn't unknowingly thrown me a lifeline. He reached into an evidence folder and placed in front of me a paperback book-sized sheet of gold in a wooden frame. 'What is this?' he asked.

I picked it up. 'It's called an *emain* slate,' I said, feeling my throat tighten. 'My mother gave it to me.'

'It's solid gold.'

'I know.'

'We found faint writing on it. What's it for?'

'Anything written on this slate appears on its twin.' I picked up a pen from the table and clicked the ball point back into the chamber, with the blunt end I wrote the contents of my heart. I wrote, '*HELP!*'

'And you are saying your mother has the other one in this land of yours.'

'Yes.'

'So how is she?'

My anger erupted. How dare he be so flippant about this! If I had had a banta stick I would have clocked him in the head for that. But anger gave way to understanding. Firstly, he was trying to get me mad and I wasn't going to play his game, and secondly, he didn't take this seriously, he didn't understand how deep his quip cut.

After spending one day back in the Real World and waking from a dreamless sleep, I realised how much of a mistake returning had been. I had found a mother – my mother – something I had wished for with all of my heart, for all of my life, and as soon as I found her – I left her. How stupid is that? I wrote her every day for a month and spent countless hours wiping the tears out of my eyes just so I could see that the *emain* slate gave me no reply.

I looked Fallon in the eyes and admitted, 'It doesn't work here.'

'Are you sure? Maybe your mother sent you little notes on this thing and told you to kill your father?'

'No. I told you it doesn't work!'

'Look, Conor, I'm just trying to help you. The story about the Leprechauns didn't convince me that you were insane, but getting letters from an imaginary mother just might save you from the chop.'

I thought about that. Maybe he was right, maybe he was my friend and this was good advice. I looked into his kind countenance and almost bought it, but then his eyes gave away the truth.

'You're not trying to help me,' I said. 'I know what you are doing. You are trying to get me to say I did it, so you can get a tick in your little score sheet and go home to your wife and kids and tell them that, "Daddy got a bad guy today", but I am not going to oblige. I did *not* kill my father!' I screamed. 'I love him and I miss him and I … I hate myself …' I broke down and wept.

'Why do you hate yourself, Conor?' Fallon said in a calm voice, like a psychiatrist getting to the crux of a problem. 'You hate yourself because you loved him and you hurt him?'

I picked my head up off my damp arms and looked at him through the blur of my tears. 'No,' I said, 'I hate myself for being so stupid. I hate myself – for leaving him.'

Fallon picked up his notepad and stood up. 'Let's take a break,' he said. 'Maybe you should just sit and think for a while.' I could tell he was disappointed. I'm sure he thought I was about to confess. He unlocked the door, but before he went through he stopped and said, 'Just one thing.'

I looked at him confused.

'I don't have kids. I just got one – a girl. And I promise I won't tell her you're a bad guy. You're not a bad guy, Conor, you're troubled and *in* trouble – but you're not a bad guy.'

That was it. I had hit rock bottom. I dropped my head onto the *emain* slate and closed my eyes not caring if I slept or not. Sleeping brought me no relief; I couldn't even escape into a dream.

I felt the message before I saw it. My cheek was resting on the *emain* slate and a tickling sensation stirred me enough to lift my head and take a look. There underneath my cry for help was a sentence, 'Are you in trouble?'

'Yes!' I screamed. I don't think I had ever been happier in my life. Like a bawling child lost in a shopping mall, I was found, and my mother was going to clutch me to her breast and wipe away my tears. I reached for the pen and realised that Fallon had taken it with him. I frantically searched around the room trying to find something I could etch a reply with but the only thing in the room was me, two chairs and a table. I tried to use my fingernails but I had bitten them down to nothing. I hammered on the door and shouted. After what seemed like ages it opened. Standing there was Detective Fallon and a uniformed cop holding a club.

'Gimme your pen!' I shouted as I jumped up and down.

'Back off, Conor,' he demanded.

'OK, OK,' I said, putting my hands up and doing as I was told, 'just give me a pen.'

The two policemen cautiously entered the room. 'Why do you want a pen?' Fallon asked.

'I just do! Give me your damn pen!'

'I'm not going to give you my pen,' the detective said in pacifying tones, 'until you tell me what you want it for.'

'OK, I did it. I want to confess. Give me your notepad and pen and I'll write a confession.'

'What did you do?'

'What you said I did. Give me your pen and I'll write it all down for you – everything.'

The two policemen looked at each other in amazement. Fallon gave me a sceptical look but he offered out his notepad and pen. I snatched the ballpoint, ran over to the table and turned the slate around to write on it. Fallon grabbed the pen back before I could etch a mark and tried to read the Gaelic sentence aloud. 'Did you write this?' he said.

'Yes, yes I did. See I'm crazy. I'm writing letters to myself in made-up languages. Here I'll show you.' I reached for the slate but he pulled it out of my reach.

We stared at each other, his eyes narrowed with an effort to figure out what was going on. I gazed back wide-eyed and pleading. 'Please,' I said. 'Trust me, this is important.'

He handed me the slate and I wrote on it, 'YES!!!'

I dropped the slate on the table and stared at it. So did Fallon. Just when I thought my eyes were going to burn a hole in the gold surface, letters appeared one by one. 'I WILL BE RIGHT THERE,' it said.

Fallon's eyes shot up to look at me. They were a lot wider than before. 'What just happened here?'

'I got a magic email.'

'What … what does it say?'

'It says, "I will be right there."'

'And what does that mean?'

'It means – my mom's gonna bail me out.'

TWO

JAIL BREAK

'Conor,' Detective Fallon said, 'no one is going to bail you out.'
It was just the two of us again. I had finally calmed down enough for him to dismiss the guard. 'You saw what was written on the slate.'

'I did. How did you do that, some sort of conjuring trick?'

That made me laugh. 'Not a conjuring trick, it's a magic trick – real magic.'

Fallon picked up the *emain* slate and turned it in his hands. 'So what, is there some sort of electric gadget in here?'

'Look at it. It's just a sheet of gold. Come on, you're a detective. What did Sherlock Holmes say? "When you have eliminated the impossible, whatever remains, however improbable, must be the truth." I've been telling you the truth all along. My father is fine and my mother is coming to take me to him.'

'So you imagine she is going to show up and you and she are just going to walk out of here.'

'Ride out of here,' I corrected, 'she'll be on a horse.'

'OK, that's it,' Fallon said, slapping his palms on the table, 'you win, I'll get you the psychologist.'

He stood to leave but I grabbed his wrist. He instinctively balled his other hand into a fist but then relaxed when he saw I wasn't going to attack him – I had something important to say.

'When she comes, Brendan, don't fight her. She is … well, she's not a normal mom.'

Fallon threw off my grip and said, 'Bah!' Just then there was a knock at the door. A young officer poked his head in looking excited. 'What?' Fallon barked.

'There are two women outside on horses,' the officer stuttered. 'You have to see them, they're gorgeous. They want to see the prisoner.'

Fallon whipped his head around and stared at me, the colour draining from his face.

I shrugged. 'That will be my ride.'

I paced around the room for what seemed like an eternity. I don't think I had ever been so excited, it took all of my willpower to stop from jumping up and down shouting, 'Mommy, Mommy, Mommy!' I tried to relax. 'Right, what should I do?' I said, talking to myself. 'Pack.' I looked around the room and laughed, the only thing there was the *emain* slate. I picked it up. I paced some more. 'Come on, come on,' I said out loud.

The door flew open and Fallon came storming in. 'What the hell is going on here?'

'Where is she? What's happening?'

'There are two women outside on huge horses wearing trick-or-treat outfits. The one who spoke said her name was Deirdre and that the other was called Nieve.'

'Nieve! Nieve's here? She's my aunt.'

Fallon was angry. He grabbed my shirt with both hands and pulled me close to his face. 'What are you playing at?'

I tried to be as calm as I could. 'What did you tell them?'

'I told them they had to wait.'

'You didn't …?'

'I did.'

'That probably wasn't a good idea.'

'Why?'

'Well, I don't know my aunt all that well but waiting isn't Mom's strong suit.'

As if on cue a huge explosion shook the room. Fallon let go of me and said, 'Stay here!'

As the door swung behind him I dived across the room and painfully trapped my arm in the doorjamb before it could lock.

The hallway was filled with dust and smoke. Cops were lying unconscious everywhere. In the distance I could hear screams of 'My eyes!' Nieve was casually riding towards me. She had blown out all of the door archways so she didn't even have to duck. Her right hand was held out to her side and two marble-sized balls of gold were orbiting it like atoms around a nucleus. Two policemen appeared out of a room to her left. Without even looking at them, she flicked her wrist and the gold marbles hit them in the chest. They were thrown back into the room with an explosion of light.

She spotted me. 'Conor, are you harmed?'

'No, I'm OK,' I shouted. 'Where's Mom?'

'She is outside preparing a portal. Catch,' she said, throwing me an oak banta stick.

I examined it. 'I prefer hazel.'

She gave me a dirty look but then smiled. 'Come,' she said, holding out her hand.

I started to reach for it when I heard a voice from behind me say, 'Freeze!'

I turned to see Detective Fallon pointing a gun at Nieve. He was obviously freaked.

'Nobody move. Put your hands in the air and get off the horse, lady.'

'Conor,' Nieve said, 'what is that in his hand?'

'It's a weapon, Aunt Nieve.' She went to reach under her cloak.

'I said freeze!'

'Hold on, Nieve,' I said, 'let me talk to him.'

Fallon kept the gun pointed at Nieve but flicked a glance in my direction. He was real edgy.

'Brendan,' I said in my calmest voice, 'this is my Aunt Nieve, my father's sister. She's from Tir na Nog, that's why she is riding a horse. Remember, I told you about that?'

The muscle in Fallon's jaw twitched. I wasn't sure if I was getting through to him.

'I'm going to go with her. Put your gun down and no one will get hurt.'

'What, I'm just supposed to let you walk out of here?' His gun shook as he spoke. 'She killed all of my officers.'

'Conor, why are we talking? What is he saying that is so important?'

'He is upset 'cause you killed his men.'

'They will live,' Nieve said. I could hear the impatience in her voice. 'Conor, we do not have time for this.'

She was right. The longer we stood here the more likely it was that more cops would show up and I was desperate to see my mother. I decided to take Fallon out of the equation.

Unfortunately I was holding my banta stick upside-down so I had to flick the gun out of his hand with the heavy end and then use the light end on his neck. Dahy wouldn't have been very impressed with the blow but it did the job and the detective went down. I grabbed Nieve's hand and she lifted me onto the back of the saddle as if I weighed nothing.

'I never got your Christmas card,' she said as she manoeuvred the horse into the opposite direction.

'Christmas isn't for two months.'

'Well, that explains it.' I wasn't sure if that was a joke or not.

We rode back through what used to be a police station. No one stopped us. The only sounds were a few moans. Daylight poured through what used to be the front door. I shaded my eyes and was rewarded with the sight of my mother. My heart leapt and I involuntarily kicked the back of the horse, the mount lurched and I almost fell off.

'Be careful, Conor!' Nieve said. 'I would prefer not to fall.'

'Of course, sorry.'

Nieve walked her horse next to Mom's. I hugged Mom and she returned it. 'Conor, are you all right?'

'I am now,' I said.

'Deirdre,' Nieve said, 'I do not like this place.'

'How's Dad?' I asked, still holding my mother. I never wanted to let go.

Mom pushed me back. 'Nieve is right. We must get out of here – we can talk when we get home.'

Mom took some sap and a gold disc out of her saddlebag and began to chant as she rubbed them both between her hands. Amber light shot from her fingertips and created a spider web that eventually filled in to produce a large glowing disc.

'Are you ready?' Mom asked.

'Born ready.'

'Everybody stay right where you are!' It was Fallon – with one hand he held his neck, in the other he held a gun.

Nieve and Mom stepped their horses sideways for a look. 'Who is this?' Mom demanded.

'Mom, this is Detective Fallon – Detective Fallon, this is my mother.'

Fallon pointed the gun menacingly. 'Everybody get down, we're all going back inside.'

Mom and Nieve started to reach inside their cloaks. I raised my hand and stopped them. 'No we're not, Brendan, we don't belong here – I don't belong here.'

'I said get down!'

'They can't, Brendan, it would kill them. You see that glowing disc over there, that's a door into another world – The Land. We are going to enter it and we will be gone. If we are not, then you can shoot me.'

'I'm warning you, O'Neil.'

'Brendan, I didn't kill my father, he is right on the other side of that door, you have the wrong man. You said it yourself – I'm not a bad guy. Please – you have to trust me.'

I could almost hear his brain cells working; he lowered his gun and we walked towards the disc. I didn't look back.

We arrived in the Hall of Spells. I expected the journey to be painful (most of this Shadowmagic stuff is) but other than a few spots in front of my vision and an annoying ringing in my ears, I was fine.

I jumped down and gave Mom a proper hug. She returned it quickly but then said, 'I have to go, I will talk to you later.' I didn't like the way she looked; she was still undisputedly the most beautiful woman in the world, but in her eyes I saw a haggard look. She dashed out of the room.

I was a bit taken aback. I turned to Nieve and said, 'Is she all right?'

'She is fine, Conor.'

I let out a sigh of relief and then took in a lungful of air and it hit me, I could feel the vitality seep into every cell. A smile took over my face and I said to myself, 'I'm back.' Then I threw my hands out to my sides and shouted to the roof, 'I'm back!' I startled a stable boy who quickly led the horses away – that's when I saw him. Detective Fallon with dishevelled clothes and hair shooting out in all directions was crouched in the corner and he had a wild glint in his eyes. He looked like one of those girls in a slasher movie that had just witnessed her entire sorority get killed.

'Oh my gods,' I said.

Our eyes locked, it scared me, I had seen that look before. He was wearing the same face that Fergal wore when he went mad and tried to kill Cialtie.

'Brendan?'

At the sound of his name he pulled the gun from between his knees and levelled it at me.

I dropped my banta stick and said, 'Hey, calm down, Brendan, no one is going to hurt you.' I walked slowly towards him, palms up. He aimed the gun at my face, his arm shaking. I wondered if he even knew who he was. 'It's OK, you're safe. Your name is Brendan Fallon, you have a wife and a daughter, it's OK, we'll sort this out.'

At the mention of his family a spark of sanity fluttered in his eyes. He dipped the gun a bit, but then both of us were startled by a voice to the left shouting my name.

'Conor – catch!'

A banta came sailing through the air. As I caught it, time slowed like it always does when I'm in mortal peril. I saw the lights go out in Fallon's eyes and I could actually see the muscles in his fingers as they tightened on the trigger, I could almost hear them. I suspected that guns didn't work in The Land but I didn't want to take that chance. I performed the same manoeuvre as before, except this time I hit the gun with the light end of the stick and rounded on Fallon's head with the heavy end. I hit him way harder than I wanted to – that wasn't my fault, the stick had been thrown by Araf and his stick is filled with lead.

The gun clicked at some point during the fracas but it didn't fire. I was right, they don't work here. Fallon went down like a ton of concrete and I instantly felt real guilty.

I rushed to him – he was out cold. Nieve strolled over and placed her hands on both sides of his head. 'Did I kill him?' I asked.

'He'll live,' she replied and unceremoniously dropped his head back onto the floor.

Two guards arrived and I instructed them to carry him to the infirmary and keep a guard. 'Be nice to him,' I called after them, 'and make sure he gets some of that willow tea when he wakes up, he's going to need it.'

'Can I have my stick back?'

'Araf!' I shouted as I turned. I had almost forgotten he was there. I ran to the Imp and wrapped my arms around him. It was like hugging a refrigerator and I could tell he didn't like it.

'Are you injured?' he asked.

'No, I'm fine.'

He nodded. 'I have to get back to work now,' he said and turned to leave.

'Well, it's great to see you again too,' I called after him. I laughed – this was the strangest of homecomings.

Well, it was just me and Nieve. Not my favourite relative but I didn't care. She stood in the middle of the room wringing her hands; the look on her face wiped the smile off my own.

'Where's Dad?' I asked.

'Conor,' she said, looking down at her hands and then directly into my eyes, 'Oisin is dying.'

THREE

DAD

I followed Nieve through the winding corridors of the west wing.
Dad was in The Lord's Chamber, the same one that Cialtie had
used and where we had found Dad's runehand.

'Prepare yourself,' Nieve warned, 'he does not look good.'

My stomach churned as I opened the door. Mom, Fand and an
Imp-healer were standing around a bed wearing expressions ranging
from puzzlement to grief. I had to cover my mouth to hide the gasp –
he looked awful. My father's skin was ashen grey, paper-like, and his
face was dotted with sores. Most of his hair had fallen out and what was
left was pure white. My first thought was that he was dead already,
that's how bad he looked. I knelt down next to the bed and held his
hand.

'Dad, Dad, it's me, Conor.'

I didn't think he could hear me but then his eyes flickered and
opened. An almost Duir smile lit his face. 'Conor? Conor, are you all
right?' His voice was faint and raspy. 'Deirdre said you were in trouble.'

'I'm fine, Dad.' I didn't know what to say, his famous dark eyes had
lost their shine. I could hardly stand it.

'Good,' he said, 'I was worried about you. So how was your trip
home?'

I laughed, one of those painful laughs that are half a chuckle and half crying. 'It was awful.'

'What happened when you got back?'

'The police arrested me for your murder.'

This brought a huge grin to his face. 'No!'

'Yes,' I laughed through tears.

Dad started to laugh too but his laughter was replaced by a spasm of coughs. He had to close his eyes for a half a minute. When he opened them he squeezed my hand and said, 'I'm glad you're here.'

'Me too.' I held his hand for a while and then said, 'Thanks, Dad.'

'For what?'

'I never realised until I went back, just how much you gave up for me. I don't know how you stood it.'

'Well, when it got really bad, I used to go to your room and watch you sleep, that gave me strength.'

I dropped my head on his chest and wept openly. He stroked my hair. 'I have to rest now,' he said, 'we'll talk later.'

Mom put her hands on my shoulders and guided me out. In the hallway we held onto each other; then she led me into an adjacent room.

A Leprechaun brought in a tray of tea. Mom thanked her and sent her away. As she handed me a cup, I asked, 'What's the matter with him?'

'We're not sure,' she said as she poured herself a cup, 'but we think it is his hand.'

'His runehand? The one he reattached in the Choosing?'

'Yes. The Land has a life force that binds us to it; your father gave that all up when he escaped to the Real World. I thought getting his hand back would restore his immortality – I was wrong, it has done just the opposite. Our best guess is that The Land is confused, it sees your father as two things, a young hand that belongs here and an older man that does not. The Land is choosing his hand.'

'Like a heart transplant patient rejecting a donor organ?'

'I don't know what you mean but *rejecting* is a good word. Oisin's hand is rejecting the rest of him. It is killing him.'

'Isn't there anything you can do?'

'We have tried everything, to no avail, but there is one desperate measure left to us. Just before you arrived Fand and I decided it is our only hope.'

'What?'

We are going to use Shadowmagic to encase all of Oisin in tree sap, just as I did with his hand. It will not cure him but it may give us time.'

'Are you sure it'll work?'

Mom took a long time before answering. 'No,' she said, 'I am not.'

I stood on the ramparts of the east wall. The stones under my feet were new and whiter than the rest of the castle. This was the wall that was blown out when Cialtie's golden circle misfired. Lorcan had done a fine job rebuilding it.

I looked out and took a deep breath, savouring the pollution-free smell of summer's end. At a first glance I thought the forest in front of me was on fire. The oaks were incandescent with the colours of fall. Leaves the size of notepad paper had transformed themselves into reds and yellows and golds that looked as if they were lit from within, like Christmas decorations. I remembered the first time I had seen this vista when it was green, I remembered the strength and joy that it had given me. I felt the strength returning, but the joy was denied to me now.

Below I saw the top of the dolman that Fergal was buried under. 'Oh Fergal,' I said to myself, 'how I could use a friend right now.'

'I'm sorry, Conor,' said a voice from behind me – it was Araf. 'I'm sorry about your father and I'm sorry I was so short with you before. It wasn't my place to be the first to tell you and I'm not very good at hiding my emotions.'

'You surprise me, Araf, I didn't know you had any emotions,' I chided, trying to lighten the mood.

'I have them, Conor, although right now I wish I did not.'

I put my arm over his shoulder and together we looked down at Fergal's grave. 'I still miss him terribly,' he said. 'He was truly my brother – I never had the chance to tell him that.'

'He knew, my friend, he knew.'

A guard showed up and said my mother wanted to see me in The Lord's Chamber. Araf led me down to Dad's room but he didn't come in. When we got to the door he didn't say anything, he simply nodded. I think he must have used up all of his allotted words for the day. Mom, Nieve, Fand and the Imp-healer were standing around Dad's bed; a Shadowfire flickered on a table. I didn't think it was possible but he looked worse than he did only a couple of hours earlier.

'We are almost ready,' Mom said. 'He wants to speak to you.'

I knelt down next to him; he turned to me and I could see the effort it took. 'Conor,' he whispered, 'you must take the Choosing. The Land needs a Lord of Duir.'

'You're the Lord of Duir, Pop.'

'Promise me.'

'I promise.'

He straightened his head and took a deep breath. 'Deirdre,' he said, trying to raise his voice above a whisper, 'I'm ready.'

Mom placed a small gold disc on Dad's tongue. He received it like a Catholic at church, then Mom and Fand each picked up a waxy fist-sized ball of amber sap. They cupped their hands and held it over the Shadowfire; the sap melted leaving them both holding a pool of glowing amber, as if they had scooped water from a stream. Dad's sheets were removed and I gasped to see that the sores on his face covered his entire body. The only part of him that looked healthy was his rune-hand. Its health and vitality only highlighted just how deathly the rest of him looked.

Mom and Fand stood at the foot of the bed incanting in Ogham – the oldest of tongues. As they chanted they let the sap drip onto Dad's toes. It covered his feet, then his ankles and then his legs, like it had a mind of its own. I watched in horror as the amber travelled up his chest. When it reached his neck he closed his eyes, took one last gasp of breath and was completely engulfed.

Mom carried away the remaining sap and let it drip into a bowl. It left no residue on her hands. Then she slowly examined the Shadowmagic shell. When she rolled Dad onto his side to have a look at his back, it shocked me to see him pop up like a marble statue. Fand covered him with a sheet as Mom placed her hands on both sides of his head. After a few minutes she let him go and wiped her nose on her forearm; she looked drained.

'Did it work?' I asked.

'We will know tomorrow,' she said.

I wanted to keep watch over Dad all night but Mom wouldn't let me. Since she missed my rebellious teenage years, I toyed with the idea of making this my first defiant stand against her, but she was right, I was exhausted.

She led me to a room two doors along. 'This is The Prince's Chamber,' she said, 'it once belonged to your father. It is your room now.'

It was huge. A massive bay window and an equally large four-poster bed were draped in purple fabric. *When I get some time*, I thought to myself, *I'm going to have to do some redecorating*. The walls were panelled in hand-carved oak depicting all of the major trees of The Land. I noticed one of the panels was full of chips and holes.

Mom followed my gaze. 'Oisin told me that is where he used to practise throwing Dahy's knives. He got in trouble for that.'

'I promise I won't throw any knives in here, Mom,' I said, but I knew I would.

She wrapped her arms around me. 'I have missed you. I wrote you every day.'

'Me too. How did you finally get the slates to work?'

'It was Samhain.'

'Samhain, I remember that word,' I said. 'When Dad wouldn't let me go out trick-or-treating at Halloween he used to say, "There is no way I am going to let you wander around alone during Samhain." What does that have to do with the *emain* slates?'

'Samhain is when The Land and the Real World are closest. The slate must have started to work simply because it was in range.'

'Well, I'm glad it did. I'm here now, Mom, and I'm not going anywhere.'

She squeezed me tighter then kissed me on the cheek. 'Get some rest.'

'You too, you look like you need it.'

'I will try,' she said and left me alone in my new bedroom.

A chambermaid came in and placed a pitcher of water next to a bowl on the dresser. When she turned I recognised her. It was the

Leprechaun who helped Dad and me sneak into Cialtie's room. 'Aein!' I said, calling her by name.

I surprised her when I hugged her but then she returned it, her arms only making it to my sides.

'How is Lord Oisin?'

'Not good.'

'If he—' She stopped and placed her hand over her mouth as if to push back the words.

'What is it, Aein? You can say anything to me.'

'If … If Lord Oisin should die …' she said and made a little gesture like she was warding off evil spirits, 'will Cialtie come back?'

'Over my dead body.'

Her worried eyes went steely. 'Mine too.' We shared a determined smile. 'If you need anything, you pull that cord.'

'Thank you, Aein.'

'Welcome home, Young Prince.'

My head hit the pillow like I had been hit with Araf's banta stick. In that twilight moment between wakefulness and sleep I felt the impatience of a dream desperate to begin, like a troupe of actors waiting for the opening curtain. 'Here we go!' I mumbled aloud.

I was a bit disappointed with my first dream back. Deep down I had hoped that I would be able to have a conversation with my father, but my dream was a collage of fleeting images. Trees, salmon, horses, knives, castles, bears, mermaids, archers and a myriad of other images zoomed in and out of my sleep. I only had one vision that stayed with me. It was of a young girl I didn't recognise; she was crying, and an older woman that I somehow knew was her grandmother was comforting her.

I had slept later than I meant to. I dressed quickly and jogged to my father's room. Fand was sitting at his feet, cross-legged with her hands folded in her lap, Buddha-like. She turned to me when I entered. 'There is no change, Conor. We will know more after nightfall.' I leaned over and kissed Dad on the forehead; it was like kissing a cue ball, cold and hard. 'Hang in there, Pop,' I whispered.

'Go get something to eat,' Fand said, 'we will find you if there is any change.'

I found the breakfast room all by myself (well, after getting lost for a half an hour). Everywhere I went people pointed at me and whispered to their companions, or, even worse, bowed. No one dared to sit with me at breakfast but that didn't stop them from staring at me. I'm not sure if it was 'cause I was their prince or 'cause the food was so awesome that I moaned while I ate.

A guard approached as I was finishing. I was surprised to see he was a Banshee. I was glad that Dad had chosen not to banish all of the guards that worked for Cialtie.

'Prince Conor,' the guard said, bowing. He was young and I could see he was nervous. I smiled at him. 'The prisoner is getting – difficult.'

'Prisoner? What prisoner?'

'The one who shouts with the strange tongue.'

'Oh my gods,' I said, 'Detective Fallon, I forgot all about him. You'd better take me to him.'

FOUR

PRISONER FALLON

I heard him before I even rounded the corner. When I reached the door two guards, a Banshee and an Imp, snapped to attention.

'Take it easy, guys,' I said. They relaxed but not much.

I jumped when I heard the volume of the shouts on the other side of the door.

'DO YOU KNOW WHO I AM?' Brendan bellowed with a voice that was going hoarse. 'YOU ARE ALL IN BIG TROUBLE! DO YOU HEAR ME?'

I motioned for the door to be opened. The Banshee reached for the handle and the Imp stepped in front of me gripping his banta stick.

'Hold on,' I said, putting my hand on his shoulder. 'That won't be necessary.'

'Are you sure you want to go in there alone?' the Imp asked.

'I'm sure.' Just then a thunderous crash shook the door from the inside. 'Well, maybe you could lend me your stick.'

The Imp stared at me with an *It's your funeral* look and handed me his banta stick. 'Brendan,' I called through the door, 'I'm coming in, don't attack me. OK?'

There was no answer so I braced myself and stuck my nose around the jamb. Detective Fallon was standing in the middle of the room. His shirt tail was half out, his hair stuck out at a wacky forty-five-degree angle. He was panting and covered with sweat. His eyes weren't as crazy as the last time I saw him, but I wasn't about to shake his hand. I closed the door behind me. 'I see you have been busy turning our furniture into toothpicks.'

'Kidnapping is a very serious crime.'

'You can add it to the murder charge if you like, but I didn't do either of them.'

'Where am I?' he said, taking a menacing step towards me.

'Easy, fella,' I said, positioning my stick, 'I don't want to hit you with one of these a third time.'

'A third time?'

'Yes, I hit you once in the neck at the police station and once in the head upstairs.'

'That was you?' he said, rubbing the side of his head where I am sure it hurt.

'Yeah, sorry, I got a little carried away.'

'I don't remember much about the second time,' he said calming down a bit, 'I was ...'

'Freaked out,' I finished for him. 'Don't worry about it, The Land can do that to you – I know. Hey, let's sit down and talk about this nicely.' I looked around the room but there wasn't any place to sit. Not one piece of furniture was any bigger than my forearm. Keeping one eye on Brendan I backed up to the door and opened it a crack. 'Could you get us a couple of chairs?' I glanced back at the devastation of the room. 'Cheap ones.'

Brendan glared at me while I kicked pieces of smashed furnishings into the corner. A guard came in carrying two simple chairs. 'Are these cheap enough for you, Your Highness?'

'They'll be fine,' I said, indicating with a tilt of my head for him to leave.

Brendan examined his chair before he sat in it. I wasn't sure if he didn't trust me or if he was studying it to see how easy it would be to smash. 'What language are you are speaking?'

'Ancient Gaelic. It's the lingo around here.'

'And where is *here*?'

'You're in *The Land*, Brendan. I wasn't lying.'

'You're telling me that I'm in that Never-Never Land you babbled on about?'

'Tir na Nog actually, but now that I think about it, the concept is the same.'

'And who are you – Tinkerbell?'

'Well, I would prefer to think of myself as more of a Peter-like person but we are getting off the subject. You're here now. I don't know how you got here.'

'The last thing I clearly remember is grabbing onto a horse's tail.'

'Ah,' I said. 'That explains it. You were pulled through when my mother opened a door to another world, this world, The Land.'

'I don't believe you.'

'I don't blame you, it even sounds crazy to me and I've done it a couple of times before, but that's the truth of it. It would be easier if you accepted it.'

Brendan rubbed his head in the place where I had clocked him.

'Head hurting?'

He nodded.

'Have you eaten?'

In response he pointed to his left. A tray lay at the foot of a wall surrounded by broken crockery. Above it dripped the remains of a breakfast.

'I'll take that as a *no* then.'

I stood and opened the door a crack and spoke to the guards. 'Could you get me a couple of apples and some willow tea?'

'OK,' Brendan said when I sat down again, 'for the sake of argument, let's say I believe you. When are you going to let me go?'

'I'll talk to my mother about sending you back as soon as things calm down around here.'

'I want to see her now!'

A knock came at the door. I was glad for the excuse to stand up and put a bit of space between us. He was getting agitated again. The guard handed me a tray with two apples, a teapot and a couple of mugs. I placed it on the floor between us and offered Brendan an apple. He stared at it but he didn't take it.

'I'm not trying to poison you, Brendan. Look.' I took a bite out of the apple. It was gorgeous, as good, if not better than I remembered. 'You have got to try this,' I garbled as I wiped juice off my chin. 'It will change your whole outlook.'

Brendan took the already bitten apple from my hand, stared at it for a moment then took a bite. The look on his face made me laugh and almost spit out the chewed apple bits in my mouth. Now I know how I looked like the first time I ate an apple in The Land.

I watched as Brendan, while making the mandatory moans of delight, demolished the piece of fruit. When he finished he threw the core over his shoulder and then slapped himself in the face – hard.

'What are you doing?' I asked.

'I'm waking myself up. I get it now. This is a dream.'

'A dream?'

'Of course. Why didn't I see it before? Two beautiful young women single-handedly demolish a police station, I get kidnapped by extras in a King Arthur movie and I just had an apple that tasted like a five-course meal at the Ritz; of course it's a dream.' He slapped himself again.

'OK, Brendan, if that's what makes you happy then, fine, you believe it. Now, are you going to behave in this dream?'

'Sure, why not? I might as well enjoy myself before I wake up. The shame of it is that I probably won't remember it. I never remember my dreams.' He stood up and stretched and actually looked like he was having fun. 'Can I have the other apple?'

'Sure. Look, if you promise not to turn any furniture into kindling and generally settle down I'll get you a bath and a new room.'

'And more apples?'

'And more apples. Just behave. Oh, and try that willow tea, I think you'll enjoy that too.'

I instructed the guards to get Brendan a bath and a change of clothes and a new room. I told them he shouldn't give them any more trouble but they should keep a close eye on him. They looked sceptical but agreed.

*　*　*

I went back to Dad's room and kept vigil with Mom, Nieve, Fand and the Imp-healer, who I learned was named Bree. Minutes felt like hours, and as every one crawled by I wanted to ask how he was doing, but I knew they didn't know, so I didn't ask. I hate waiting, I always have, but that was the worst. I felt so helpless. Fand recited a healing mantra in Ogham and I asked her to teach it to me. I could feel the healing magic in the words but wondered if it was getting through Dad's amber shell. As the afternoon moved on, we all five chanted it together.

The curtains were drawn so I couldn't tell if night had fallen but Mom and Fand both looked up at each other at the same time, as if they were alerted by some soundless alarm.

Fand removed Dad's sheet as Mom placed a small dollop of amber sap in her palm and held it over the Shadowfire that was burning on a table at the foot of the bed. She dripped the molten sap onto Dad's foot. It was a darker shade of amber than his shell and I watched as it passed through the shell like water in a bowl of oil. The darker sap began to entwine and elongate, wrapping around the leg like a serpent and then continued to thin, until it wrapped his entire body with a fine line just under the surface of his glass-like sarcophagus. Fand placed her hands on either side of Dad's head and incanted in Ogham. The dark lattice-work spiralled and pulsed darker. Mom held Dad by his legs and swung them to the left so his right foot hung out of the bed. Even though I had seen it before, it shocked me to see Dad's whole body move as if he were made of marble. Fand released Dad's head and Mom cupped her hands under the foot. The dark spiral retraced its path and when Mom pulled her hands back, in her palm was the dark sap.

Mom held the sap over the Shadowfire and Fand, on the other side of the table, placed her hands under hers. Together they chanted words that sounded so strange I wondered how their tongues could make them. The sap dripped through their fingers and onto the Shadowfire. An image formed as they withdrew and as the vision cleared I saw it was my father, standing before me, upright, naked. His body was whole except for his right hand – it was in its proper place but detached from him by a few inches. The two Shadowwitches placed their hands into the vision and caressed Dad's shadow-form. Mom had her back to me but I could see Fand's face. Tears formed in her eyes – I didn't know what that meant. A cry escaped from Mom's throat and the two women reached for each other, breaking the vision, and embraced, both openly weeping.

'What?' I said, not knowing if I should speak but I couldn't take it any longer.

Mom turned and wiped the tears from her eyes but kept her hands over her mouth as she tried to compose herself. Finally she dropped her hands and crossed them on her chest. 'It worked,' she said.

It wasn't until it was all over that Mom allowed her fatigue and strain to show. Nieve and I had to help her walk to her chamber where she permitted herself to truly rest for the first time in a long while. I went back to check on Dad. Fand was still there, clearing up.

'Does he dream?'

'I do not know,' she replied.

'What happens now?'

'Now we have time to find a cure.'

'How long can he stay like this?'

Her answer should have comforted me but instead it sent a chill down my spine. 'For ever,' she said.

I checked on Dad before I went down to breakfast. The sound of Fand saying 'For ever' echoed in my brain and I wondered if this was the way I would start my day for the rest of my life. I was shocked by a transformed Brendan when I arrived at the food hall. He was smiling, cleaned up and wearing a leather shirt and trousers that surprisingly suited him. He was trying to communicate with an attractive red-headed woman who, when I arrived, stood, bowed and quickly departed.

'Aw, you scared her away,' Brendan said. 'I was doing quite well there. I already found out her name was Faggy Two.'

When he said that, I started to laugh.

'What's so funny?'

I then laughed so hard I had to sit down and cover my face until I could get some semblance of composure. It wasn't just what he had said that made me laugh, it was the tension of the last couple of days bubbling to the surface. 'I'm sorry, Brendan,' I said, wiping my eyes, 'I don't think you were doing as well as you thought, fágfaidh tú is Gaelic for *Go away*.'

'Oh.'

'And what are you doing trying to pick up women? You're a married man.'

'First of all, this is my dream, remember? A man can't get into trouble for having an affair when he's asleep, and secondly, I'm not a married man.'

'You told me you had a wife and a daughter.'

'No, *you* said I have a wife and a daughter. I only said I have a daughter.' His mood dropped a bit. 'I'm a widower.'

'Oh, I'm sorry.'

'Me too. Hey, what do you think of my new threads?' he asked quickly, obviously trying to change the subject.

'You look like a native,' I said and meant it. 'You're even growing a beard I see.'

'No, Frick wouldn't let me have a razor.'

'Frick?'

Brendan pointed to the Imp and the Banshee guards that I had assigned to keep an eye on him. 'I call them Frick and Frack.'

I waved to the guards who were standing by the entrance of the room; they gave me an official nod. I could tell this was not their favourite detail. 'Which one is Frick?'

'I don't know. I keep getting them mixed up.'

Breakfast arrived and Brendan ate like there was no tomorrow. Except for the chopping and moans neither of us spoke until our plates were clean. When we had finished Brendan said, 'The food in this dream is just fantastic, half the time I can't wait to wake up but for the other half I hope it will continue until the next meal.'

'Brendan, you have to stop thinking like that. I know it makes you feel better, but this is real.'

Nieve entered the dining hall. Brendan jumped to his feet and backed off. She sat down across from me and said, 'How is our guest?'

Warily, Brendan sat next to me, as if for protection, and pointed to Nieve. 'That's the witch that trashed my police station!'

'What did he say?' Nieve asked.

'Oh, he said good morning, it's nice to see you again,' I lied.

Nieve gave me a sceptical look.

'This is my dream and I don't want her in it!' he shouted, pointing his finger inches from her face.

'Careful, Brendan,' I warned.

'What is he saying?' Nieve asked again, but then said, 'Oh, this is ridiculous. Tell him to place his head on the table.'

It took a lot of convincing, but I finally got Brendan to place the side of his face flat down on the table. Nieve took a small piece of gold out of her satchel and rubbed it between her hands while incanting.

Brendan looked up with a wild panicky expression in his uppermost eye. 'Is this going to hurt?'

'He wants to know if this is going to hurt,' I translated.

'Yes, I suspect it will,' Nieve said calmly.

'No,' I told Brendan, 'you'll be fine.'

Nieve opened her palms and dripped the molten gold into Brendan's ear. He shot up, grabbed his ear, overturning the bench he was sitting on, and danced around the room howling in pain. I was glad no one other than me spoke English. The curse words coming out of his mouth would have made a prison inmate blush. He picked up a silver tray, sending half a dozen wine glasses crashing to the floor, and tried to use it as a mirror to view his ear. At his insistence I inspected the lughole and assured him that it looked OK – which it did – and finally got him sitting down again.

'What the hell did she do to me?'

'Now stick out your tongue,' Nieve demanded.

'No way, lady! I'm not letting you near me ever again.'

I looked at Nieve and she smiled at me. 'Brendan,' I said in Gaelic, 'can you understand me?'

'Of course I can understand you. You keep that crazy woman away from me.'

'Brendan, I'm talking to you in ancient Gaelic. Are you sure you can understand me?'

'Huh?'

'It seems that Nieve has given you a two-second lesson in the common tongue. You just learned a new language.'

'That's impossible.'

'Impossible things happen here every day.'

'Now, Brendan,' Nieve said, 'stick out your tongue and I will complete the process, then we will no longer need to speak through Conor. Personally I don't trust him as a reliable interpreter.'

Brendan clenched his mouth shut and shook his head no, like a baby that won't eat his dinner. It took even more of an effort to convince him the second time. I tried everything, including agreeing with him that it didn't matter 'cause it was all really a dream. It wasn't until I threatened to never feed him again that he gave in.

'Come on,' I said, 'stop being such a baby.'

'It hurt, damn it. You do it.'

I rolled my eyes at him but to be honest it wasn't something I wanted to experience.

'Ask her if it will hurt as much as the last time – ask her exactly that.'

I translated and Nieve said, 'No.'

Brendan watched with crossed eyes as the molten gold hit his tongue. He not only flipped over the chair but the table as well. He hopped around the dining hall screaming bloody murder and this time everyone in the room heard exactly what he was saying. Most of them left in order to get some distance between them and the madman.

'God almighty!' Brendan screamed from behind his hand in perfect Gaelic. 'You said it wouldn't hurt as much!'

'No,' Nieve replied in her usual calm manner. 'You asked if it would hurt as much as the last time and I said, *no*. I knew it would hurt more.'

Nieve gave me a rueful smile; I was starting to realise she had a wickedly subversive sense of humour.

'Now that I can converse with you,' Nieve said, 'I realise I do not want to. If you will excuse me.'

Nieve left. I asked a servant to bring Brendan a glass of Gerard's finest wine. It was a bit early but I figured he would appreciate it. He did. After one sip he downed the glass in one.

'Are you OK?' I asked.

'To be honest, Conor, I'm not sure. This dream is way too real for my liking.'

'I keep telling you – it's not a dream.'

'All right then, as much as I don't relish meeting another member of your family, how about that introduction to your father you promised me.'

'I don't think I ever promised you that.'

'As good as – well?'

'OK,' I said, 'come with me.'

FIVE

FAND

The closer we got to Dad's room the more worried Frick and Frack looked. They obviously thought Brendan was a nutcase and that letting him loose in the west wing was a bad idea. They were shocked when I told them that Brendan could enter Dad's room without them.

The first thing we noticed was that the curtains in The Lord's Chamber were closed but the room was bright with the light of about thirty candles.

'You must have a hell of a candle bill,' Brendan quipped.

'These are Leprechaun candles. They last for years.'

'Of course they do, silly me.'

As we entered the room we saw a woman sitting cross-legged on a stool at the foot of the bed. Her head was covered with an intricate gold-flecked veil that played weird tricks with the candlelight. Her arms were outstretched at her sides and she was chanting in Ogham. I couldn't see her face but I knew from the voice who it was. She stopped chanting when we entered the room.

'I'm sorry, I didn't mean to disturb you.'

'I am a difficult woman to disturb, Prince Conor,' Fand said without moving, 'it is I who will be disturbing you. Shall I leave?'

'No, please go on; Dad can use all the help he can get.'

Fand continued her chanting in a voice so low we could hardly hear. I motioned for Brendan to come closer to the bed and I pulled the sheet back from Dad's chest revealing his right arm and his attached runehand.

'What did you do to him?' Brendan said in an accusing tone.

'Oh give it up, Brendan, I didn't do anything to him,' I said, trying to whisper. I explained about Dad's hand being reattached during the Choosing ceremony in the Chamber of Runes and how Mom and Fand sealed him in this amber shell to stop his hand from killing him.

'So he's in some kind of magical suspended animation?'

'That's about right,' I said as quietly as I could, hoping Brendan would follow suit.

He didn't; he started to chuckle and then laugh out loud. 'Oh boy!' he said with no intention of being remotely quiet. 'I'm going to quit the police force when I wake up. I think I'm going to write science fiction movies.'

'Brendan, could you keep your voice down.'

'Why? I'm proud of myself. Who'd have thought I had such a vivid imagination? Or maybe I should write detective novels. I'll call my first one, *The Strange Case of the Father Who Was Turned into a Paperweight*.' He rapped his knuckles on Dad's solid forehead.

I grabbed his wrist and said, 'Don't do that.'

'Don't do what – this?' He thumped on Dad's forehead again like he was knocking on a door.

That's when I hit him. It was more of a forceful push than a punch but I knew it hurt. Brendan staggered back and held his chest.

'You want a piece of me, O'Neil?' he shouted. 'All right then, let's do it. Can you fight without a stick? Come on, man-to-man.'

I know I shouldn't have done it, there in my father's sick room, but I raised my dukes and squared up to him. I was sick and tired of his *I can do anything in a dream* attitude.

We were about a nanosecond away from going for each other's throats when Fand broke the atmosphere of blood lust. 'I stated before that I was a difficult woman to disturb,' she said in a voice that reminded us that she was a queen, 'but you two have succeeded.'

Brendan and I both turned and pretty much stood at attention as she lifted the veil from her head. Brendan let loose a gasp, and said, 'Oh my God.'

Fand stood and walked towards him. 'You are the traveller from the Real World?'

'Yes, ma'am,' he replied respectfully.

'You look as though you have seen a ghost.'

'Not a ghost, ma'am; for a moment I thought you were my mother.'

'Your mother?'

'Yes, you look remarkably like her, here I'll show you.' Brendan reached for his back pocket then remembered he was wearing new clothes and rummaged around in the pouch of his tunic until he produced an old leather wallet. 'I have a picture of her with my daughter.' Brendan pulled bits of paper out of his wallet looking increasingly confused. He went through everything a second time and then held a blank piece of paper in his hands repeatedly looking at its front and back. 'I don't understand it.'

'What's the matter?' I asked.

'Well, this is the photograph. Look, I wrote the date on the back, but the picture is – gone.'

I took the photo from him and it was indeed blank, not even the ghost of an image remained. 'I think I know what happened,' I said. 'Real World technology often doesn't work here. Electric watches and guns don't work, so I imagine photography doesn't either.'

'You mean I'm stuck in this dream without a picture of my own daughter?'

'Dream?' Fand said.

'Brendan here thinks this is all a long dream and that any second he is going to wake up in his bed.'

'I see. Well, maybe you are right, Brendan. Who can tell what is real and what is illusion? This may be a realm inside a dream but that is not what you think, is it? You think you are still back in the Real World and soon you shall awake – is that not so?'

Brendan nodded but I could see his resolve weakening.

'I am sorry, Brendan, as seductive as that thought must seem – it is not so. It is true you are in a different world but there is only one reality. What was your vocation in the Real World?'

'I was … I am … a detective.'

Fand looked confused. Brendan tried a couple of times to describe his job using words like 'perpetrator' and 'arrest'. Finally he changed his wording to 'I find evildoers and punish them.'

Fand nodded. 'You seek the truth?'

Brendan thought for a bit and then smiled. 'I suppose I do.'

'Like a Druid.'

'Now you not only look like my mother but you sound like her.'

'Oh, how so?'

'That's just the kind of voodoo crap my mother used to spout.'

'Conor has taught me the meaning of "crap" but what is voodoo?'

'OK, not voodoo, but she was always brewing herbs into potions to ward off colds or a rash or evil spirits, and when she wasn't doing that she was dancing naked around a fire or hugging a tree.'

'It sounds as if I would like her,' Fand said.

'Maybe you would. I don't get along with her very well.'

Fand answered that statement with a knowing smile – she had experience with a difficult mother; her mother had been responsible for the near extinction of her entire race.

'Let me see the … What did you call it – photo?'

Brendan handed her the blank piece of paper that once held the image of his daughter and mother. Fand took a glop of tree sap out of a silk bag that was hanging around her waist and walked over to the dresser at the far side of the room. She closed her hand over the sap, placed her fist into the bowl of Shadowfire and chanted under her breath. She then removed her hand and dripped sap onto the front of the paper, where the photo had been. Immediately the sap hardened into a thin film, not unlike the emulsion on a glossy photo. Then Fand dropped it into the Shadowfire.

'Hey,' Brendan shouted as he reached to retrieve his photo.

Fand grabbed his wrist and said, 'Wait.'

It was obvious from Brandon's face that her strength had surprised him.

When nothing happened, Fand asked, 'Has your daughter or mother ever touched this – photo?'

Brendan thought for a moment and replied, 'I don't think so.'

Fand retrieved the blank photo and held it in her palm above the Shadowfire. 'May I touch you?' she asked.

Brendan looked to me for advice. I shrugged; I had no idea what was going on.

'I guess,' he said.

Fand laid her palm across the side of Brandon's face and the Shadowfire jumped to life. An image appeared in the flame. It sent a chill down my spine. The last time I saw anything like this was when my mother performed a Shadowcasting for Fergal – not the most pleasant of memories. This image was of a woman in her late sixties. She was handsome with a strong face and long grey hair tied back in a braided ponytail. She cradled a weeping child of around six in her arms. Brendan pulled away from Fand's hand and the image vanished.

'That's not the photo. The photo is of my mother and daughter when my daughter was an infant.'

'Interesting,' Fand said, smiling. 'Strange things can happen during Samhain. I think, Brandon, what we have just seen is your mother and daughter as they are in the Real World now.'

'I have to get back.' The colour dropped out of Brendan's face like a water cooler emptying. The realisation of his predicament hit him – this was real. 'I have to get home – now!' He walked to the door and then realised he didn't know where to go. 'How do I get back?' His voice was panicky.

'You must speak to Deirdre,' Fand said. 'I know not how you came.'

SIX

MOM

Getting Brendan an audience with my mother wasn't easy. Once Dad had stabilised, Fand had ordered Mom to rest. She agreed and slept but as soon as she woke up she threw herself into the task of queening Castle Duir. It took me a couple of days to get the cop in to see her.

Mom stared hard at the detective when he walked into the room. 'I remember you,' she said with narrowing eyes. 'You are the man that imprisoned my son. You pointed a weapon at me. Conor, what is he doing here?'

'I need to get back,' Brendan said.

Mom shot him a spectacularly dirty look and said, 'You will speak when spoken to.'

Wow, even I took an involuntary step back. I had forgotten how menacing Mom can be when she is in her bear cub guarding mode. She turned her back on Brendan and took a step towards me. 'Now, Conor, what is he doing here?'

Brendan said, 'You don't understand,' and then did that really foolish thing. He grabbed her wrist.

I guess I should have warned Brendan about touching a woman in The Land when she doesn't want or expect it. I had learned that lesson the hard way with Essa but it didn't even come close to how hard

Brandon's lesson was with my mother. In a matter of nanoseconds she turned her wrist, broke the detective's grasp, grabbed his arm, placed her foot in his stomach, and then vaulted him clear over her head. Brendan sailed a good seven feet in the air before luckily hitting the back of a sofa. If the manoeuvre had been in any other direction he would have hit a wall. I ran over and righted the couch and then helped the dazed Brendan into it.

'Sit here and don't say a word,' I said.

Brendan's reply was a predictable, 'Owww.'

I approached my mother slowly. She was still in an attack stance and was breathing heavily.

'Someone should teach him not to do that.'

'I think you just did, Mom – and very impressively too, I might add. Let's all take a deep breath and calm down a little.'

Mom unclenched her fists. I took a seat and motioned for her to do the same. As she sat, she kept an eye on Brendan.

'Relax, Mom, I'm sure he won't try anything again. Will you, Brendan?'

'Owww,' Brendan repeated.

Mom finally turned to me. I smiled at her but she wasn't quite ready to return it. 'You still haven't told me what he is doing here.'

It's not like she had given me much of a chance but I decided to keep that comment to myself – enough feathers had been ruffled already. 'Brendan followed us through that portal you made.'

'That's impossible.'

'Why do you say that?'

'The portal was designed for the three of us and our horses – part of that spell was Truemagic, it should have killed someone from the Real World.'

'Well, I hate to disagree with you on a point of magic but there he is.'

'Strange things happen during Samhain,' Mom mumbled under her breath as she approached Brendan. 'Why did you incarcerate my son?'

Brendan didn't answer but the question succeeded in stopping him from saying, 'Oww, oww, oww,' over and over again.

'Mom, he was just doing his job.'

Mom gave me a sharp look and said, 'I am speaking to him.'

'He's right, ma'am,' Brendan said with a mixture of respect and fear. 'I was just doing my job.'

'And what job is that?'

'I'm a policeman,' he said but when he realised she didn't understand he sighed, 'I catch and punish evildoers.'

'And what evil could this sweet boy have done?'

'I thought he had killed his father.'

'And why would you have thought that?'

'Well, the house was trashed, his father was missing and he was spending his money.'

'Money?' Mom asked, turning to me.

'Like gold,' I said.

'I thought people in the Real World didn't use magic. What would they want with gold?'

I hadn't thought of that before but now wasn't the time to explain micro-economics to my mother. So I said, 'We just kinda like it 'cause it's shiny.'

'Did my son not explain to you about his father?'

'Yes, ma'am, he did but I didn't believe him.'

'Do you believe him now?'

Brendan paused for a moment and said, 'Yes, ma'am, I do. That is why I wanted to speak to you. I must return home.'

'How exactly did you get here?'

'I don't remember much, I was a bit out of it, but I remember grabbing onto a horse's tail and then I remember Conor clubbing me over the head. The next thing I know I was here.'

'You grabbed onto the horse?'

'Yes, ma'am.'

Mom walked back into the centre of the room, thinking. 'I see. Well, Mr ...'

'Fallon, Brendan Fallon.'

'Well, Brendan, I see how you have arrived here but I still do not know how you survived the journey.'

'Well, I'm here and I need to return. The Fand woman said you could get me back.'

'I am sure I can, see me next Samhain.'

'And when is that?'

'In a wee bit less than a year.'

'A year!' Brendan was on his feet. 'I can't wait a year.'

'Why so long?' I asked.

'If I had known you were here earlier then things would be different but sending a mortal back now when the Real World and The Land are apart would be too dangerous – if it was two days ago, then maybe.'

'I've been trying to see you for a week!' Brendan said, raising his voice, which, by the look on my mother's face, wasn't appreciated.

I was about to intervene but then I saw my mother's countenance soften. 'I am sorry for your predicament but I only learned of your existence today. I have been quite preoccupied.'

'Is there no other way?' I asked.

'The only way to safely return him is to use the same piece of gold that I used to bring him here, but I no longer have it.'

'Where is it?' I asked.

'It's in your father's mouth.'

'Oh,' I said.

'What?' Brendan said.

'I placed the gold disc that I used to open the portal in Oisin's mouth so he would not suffocate while we encased him in Shadowmagic,' Mom said.

'So open him up and get the disc,' Brendan demanded.

'That would be far too dangerous,' Mom said. 'We were fortunate that the process worked the first time. I will not unnecessarily endanger the Lord of Duir a second time.'

'Unnecessarily,' Brendan shouted, 'you are going to maroon me in this god-forsaken place, while my loony-tune mother pollutes my daughter's brain with a caravan full of hippy tree-hugging crap?'

'If the girl's grandmother is teaching your daughter to hug trees, then I suspect she is in good hands.' Mom sat back at her desk and took up a pen. 'I'm sorry but that is my final word on the subject.'

I wouldn't say Brendan is a stupid man, but on occasion he is a slow learner. He grabbed Mom's hand and started to say, 'You don't—'

Because Mom was sitting this time she flipped him with her shoulder instead of her foot. On the plus side, Brendan didn't travel as fast or as far as before. On the minus side, he didn't make it to the couch. He took a long time getting up.

I put Brendan to bed with some poteen. I was pretty sure he wouldn't retangle with Mom. Still, for his own safety, I reposted Frick and Frack outside the door. Brendan didn't realise that those two judo throws were Mom's idea of restraint. If he tried something like that again, I wouldn't be surprised if she killed him.

I went back to my room and stared at the chipped wood panelling wishing Dahy was here so I could borrow a throwing knife. Actually I wished anybody was there. I had spent ages longing to return to The Land and now that I was here I was miserable and lonely. Dad was sealed in another world. Mom was preoccupied with castle duties and when she wasn't, she was sitting up all night with Fand in their Shadowmagic laboratory. Araf is a great friend on an adventure but for just hanging out, he can actually make me feel more alone than when I'm alone. And, of course, everything I saw in The Land reminded me of Fergal. Man, I missed him. And every time I was low and alone I would inevitably replay the moment Cialtie stuck a knife in his chest, and in every rerun I could do nothing to stop it.

And where the hell was Essa? No one could tell me where she was. Ah Essa – when I wasn't replaying Fergal's demise I was replaying my farewell with her. I may not have been able to save my cousin but I sure as hell could have handled my last moments with Essa better. I could have forgiven her – I should have forgiven her – I should have stayed with her. Instead I went back to Sally. I wonder if I could possibly have been more of an idiot. I went to sleep and dreamt of all of the stupid things I had done in my life. It was a very long night.

I had just gotten to about the age of twelve, where I broke my arm in a bouncy castle accident, when Mom woke me up very excited. I popped up quickly, holding my elbow. She had a wild-eyed look, like a student who had studied all night and drunk thirty cups of coffee. Over her shoulder hung a satchel.

'Conor, you must see this!' she said as she bounded off the bed and grabbed a book off the bookshelf. 'I think Fand and I have finally done it.'

'Done what?' I asked with a morning voice that made me sound as if I had been gargling with ground glass.

She opened the book, tore out half of a page from the middle and handed it to me. I was still dopey from sleep and stared at the piece of paper wondering what the hell she wanted me to do with it. Then she handed me a gold brooch with an amber stone set in.

'Clip it onto the piece of paper,' she said, bouncing on her toes like a kid showing off a new toy. 'Go on.'

I looked at the brooch. It was about the size of a half dollar with a spring in the back that allowed it to move like a bulldog clip. I pinched it open and clipped it onto the piece of paper. The paper started to glow with an amber light, then so did my hand where I was touching it. An all too familiar tingling sensation began in my fingers. It felt exactly like when I was under attack from a relative, and Mom's protective spell had just kicked in. I dropped the paper and clip and jumped straight up looking around my room for the source of the attack. There was none. When I realised I wasn't glowing any more I looked down on my bed and there attached to Mom's new brooch was a shining translucent book. I picked it up. It tingled in my hand but it felt real. On the cover I could faintly make out the title. It was the same as the book that Mom had just ripped the page from. In my hands it seemed to weigh the same as a regular book and when I opened it, the clear pages turned just like paper.

'What ... what is it?' I asked.

'For want of a better word it is a Shadowbook. It's a hybrid of Truemagic and Shadowmagic. The paper, in a way, *remembers* the rest of the book.'

I turned the Shadowpages. It was strange still being able to see my fingers through what felt like a solid thing. As I moved the book around in the light I saw faint glimmerings on the pages but nothing legible.

'It's a shame you can't read it, though.'

'Ah ha!' Mom exclaimed. 'Here is the cold part.'

'The cold part?'

'Is not that what you say?'

I laughed, 'You mean the *cool* part.'

'Right, the cool part.' She opened her satchel and took out a clip-board-sized sheet of gold and laid it on the bed. When she placed the Shadowbook on top of it, the words appeared almost as if the book was real.

'Wow, Mom, that is very cold.'

It wasn't until her face lit up with pride that I realised that one of the things I missed most during this trip to The Land was my mother's smile.

She gave me a hug and then quickly picked up her things and hurried to the door. 'It shouldn't take too long for Fand and me to make a few more clips. I imagine we could leave the day after tomorrow.'

'Leave for where?'

'The Hazellands. We are going to find a cure for your father in the Hall of Knowledge.'

SEVEN

THE ARMOURY

I listened for the sound of smashing furniture as I approached Brendan's room. Frick (or was it Frack) said that he had been eerily silent. I stuck my head around the door and found Brendan in bed staring at the ceiling.

'Are you OK?'

'I'm still here, aren't I?'

'As far as I can tell, yes.'

'Then I'm not all right.'

'So you're just going to sulk?'

'What else is there to do?' he said. 'I'm stuck here for at least a year. God knows what my life, my career and my little girl will be like in a year's time. I'm under house arrest, followed around by two dolts who keep staring at me like they expect horns to grow out of my head. And I can't even read a book 'cause everything is written in some ancient language that, although I can magically speak it and understand it, I can't read it. And before you offer – there is no way I'm going to let that aunt of yours do that molten gold thing to my eyes.'

'I'm sorry, Brendan, but this isn't my fault and there is nothing I can do.'

'Yeah, I know. I've been lying here thinking about it all morning – it's my fault.'

'Well, I wouldn't say that. How about we say it's nobody's fault?'

'No,' Brendan sighed. 'It's my fault. It started when I arrested an innocent man. Don't get me wrong, I had pretty good reason but, in the end, I arrested a man for a crime that not only had he not committed – it was a crime that never even happened. No good can ever come from something that starts like that. So as much as I would like to blame you – this is mostly my fault.'

'Well, if you insist,' I said, 'but don't beat yourself up too much – it could have happened to anyone.'

'Thanks,' he said, finally looking at me. 'So this is really … real then?'

'I'm afraid so.'

'And I have been acting like a serious jerk?'

'That too, I'm afraid, is true.'

Brendan placed his hand over his face in embarrassment. 'Oh my God, I rapped on your father's forehead like it was a door. Oh, I am so sorry, Conor.'

'Yeah, that was pretty bad.'

'Oh and the furniture and the … I really am sorry, Conor,' he said, sitting up. 'But in my defence, I did think I was going to wake up at any moment.'

'Fair enough, apology accepted.' I held out my hand. 'Shall we start over?'

'I'd like that,' he said, shaking it.

I had come in to tell him that I was leaving for a few days but instead I said, 'How about a road trip?'

That piqued his interest. 'To where?'

'The Hazellands.'

'Isn't that where the Leprechaun army is stationed?'

'Oh my gods, you were listening to me.'

'I'm a man of my word, Conor. I didn't believe or care about your story the first time you babbled it but the second time I promised I would listen and I did. Since Fand convinced me I wasn't dreaming, I've been going over your adventure in my head. Did all of that stuff really happen?'

'Yes,' I said, chuckling. 'Don't feel bad about not believing me. I sometimes have trouble believing it myself. But to answer your question, no, the Leprechaun army was disbanded and I don't know what's there now.'

'Who else is coming?' Brendan said, hopping up and dressing. 'Is that what's-her-name that trashed my police station and burned my ear coming?'

'You mean Aunt Nieve? I don't know.'

'How about the woman who throws me across the room with regularity?'

'Yes, I'm sure Mom is coming.'

'Who else?'

'Araf probably.'

'Who's he?'

'He's the guy who threw me the stick when I hit you on the head.'

'The first time you hit me or the second time?'

'The second time – gosh, you have been having a rough time lately, but The Land's like that in the beginning. It'll get better. Can I buy you some lunch?'

'You're getting to know me, Conor. My wife used to do the same thing. Whenever she saw me getting down she would only have to feed me and I was happy again.'

'Well then, let's get the chef to whip up something special. And if you like I'll teach you how to read Gaelic – since you can speak it, it shouldn't be too hard.'

After Dad regained the throne, in what is now called the *Troid e Emain Macha*, or The Battle of the Twins of Macha, I had a lot of time on my hands and I spent most of it exploring Castle Duir. I even revisited the dungeon and issued my one and only executive order to have the cells cleaned out. I still feel sorry for whoever got that job. The only place that I never got to see was the armoury. After the battle, Dad still couldn't be sure if there were any of Cialtie's loyal followers still lurking around incognito, so he decided to seal off the weapons room until security could be normalised.

So that made this trip to the armoury my first one. Brendan and I hiked to the north wing, sailed past three sets of ten-hutting armed guards and found ourselves in front of a set of huge oak doors inlaid with a fine gold latticework.

Light flooded the hallway as we pushed our way in. Like Gerard's armoury, this was a glass-roofed gymnasium, but size-wise it made the winemaker's weapons room seem like a walk-in closet. Racks upon racks contained carefully stacked weapons: swords, axes, maces and rows and rows of banta sticks. Tournament practice areas were marked off on the floor and the entire far length of the room was an impossibly long archery range that could accommodate eight archers abreast, each with their own targets. At the far end there was a huge contraption that looked like it might be a catapult.

'Wow,' I said.

The sound of Brendan's and my footsteps echoed in the huge space. Surprisingly there was no one around.

Brendan whispered like he was in a church. 'Where is everyone?'

'Probably off pillaging.'

'Damn,' Brendan said, 'you mean it's pillaging season and no one told me?'

I smiled and shouted a tentative, 'Hello?'

'So,' Brendan said in a normal tone, now that it looked like we were alone in there, 'where do they keep the AK-47s?'

'I'm afraid if you want a long-range weapon, Brendan, it'll have to be one of those.'

Brendan turned to where I had pointed; the entire wall was covered with both long and short bows mounted neatly in rows. They were all unstrung with their strings hanging slack from the top notch. There were hundreds of them.

'Ah,' Brendan said, 'you may laugh, but I was a pretty good archer in my youth. My mother made me take lessons.' Brendan walked over to the wall and reached up to take down a medium-sized bow.

I never heard the twang of the bow that fired the arrow at him, I didn't even see it while it was in the air, I only heard the thwap of the arrow hitting its target and Brendan's yelp as he realised his arm was pinned to the wall.

The arrow had tacked Brendan's shirtsleeve to the wall, missing his skin by inches. I hit the ground, rolled to my left, upsetting a stand of bantas, and came up crouching with a stick in each hand. I poked my nose over the now-empty banta stick holder to see Brendan reaching to extract the arrow that stuck him to the wall. As his hand crossed his body another arrow pinned that sleeve as well. This time clothing wasn't the only thing it pierced – he howled in pain.

'I'm hit!'

EIGHT

SPIDEOG

I ducked back down and reviewed my situation. The only thing I deduced was that I was in trouble and Brendan was screwed. What did Dahy tell me? 'When in doubt, stay still and listen.' So I did, but I couldn't hear anything except Brendan's heavy breathing.

'Brendan,' I said in a loud whisper, 'can you see anything?'

'Straight back at the other end of the room I saw a flash of something green.' He strained his neck for a better look. 'Nothing now.'

'Are you OK?'

'I think so.'

'Keep watching. I'm coming to get you.'

I peered around the corner of the weapons stand and was just about to make a dash for Brendan when I heard a footfall behind me. I whirled to see a hooded man in a bright green tunic and brown leather leggings. In one hand he held a bow and in the other an arrow. I instantly attacked with both sticks – one high and one low. Like he was reading my mind he twisted his body vertical and kicked his foot at my fingers where I was holding the low banta. The stick flew out of my hand. My other weapon he blocked with the string of his bow. No one had ever done that to me before. My stick sprang back so far I completely lost form. My whole left side was exposed and my opponent didn't hesitate in exploiting that fact. I'm not quite sure what he did next but I think it was a swipe to the kidneys with the bow and a kick to the back of the legs with his foot, maybe both feet. Whatever – I went down like a hippo on ice.

After bouncing my forehead off the deck I came to a stop with the green goblin kneeling on the backs of my arms and something very pointy sticking into the rear of my neck. My left cheek was pressed against the floor. Out of the corner of my right eye I could just make out an open-mouthed Brendan trying to escape his feathered clothespins. The sharp pain in my neck stopped and an arrow sizzled through the air, planting itself about two inches from Brendan's nose.

'Do not move, Druid,' greeny shouted.

Brendan may not have answered but he certainly obeyed.

The pain in my neck resumed, forcing me to the conclusion that he had a cocked arrow pointing at the back of my collar. Even though he didn't tell *me* not to move, I decided that not moving was a good idea.

'I've been waiting for you, Druid,' the green guy said as he pushed the point of the arrow hard into my neck.

'Hey, buddy,' I said, 'you got the wrong guys. We're not Druids.'

'Do not insult me. There are still people in The Land who can recognise a Fili and I am one of them.'

'The Fili have been exonerated. Haven't you heard?'

'The ones who own those bows will never be exonerated,' he said.

This guy definitely had the drop on me and I figured it was only a matter of time before he garrotted me so I made, what turned out to be, a futile attempt to buck him off my back. It only resulted in my head getting bounced off the floor one more time.

'Relax, Druid. I do not wish to hurt you before the Lord of Duir has a chance to question you.'

Up till then I figured, like I always do when somebody attacks me out of the blue, that this was probably some sort of assassin hired by Cialtie. Now I realised that this idiot worked here.

'The Lord of Duir is incapacitated. Does that mean you will now take commands from his prince?'

The pressure from the arrowhead slacked. 'Yes.'

'Then I, Conor of Duir, command you to – get your butt off of me!'

It's amazing what a royal title can do in the right situation. Greeny hopped directly off me. I groaned erect as fast as my not-quite broken limbs would allow.

My attacker's hood was back. I was a bit surprised to see wrinkles around the piercing green eyes. This guy had been around for longer than probably anyone I had yet met in The Land. He wore a waxed moustache and a meticulously trimmed goatee that pointed directly to the bow and arrow that he still had levelled at my chest.

'Lower your weapon,' I said, trying very hard to sound like my father.

'Yes, my lord,' he said as he released the tension on his bow.

'Who are you and why have you attacked my royal personage?'

As I have mentioned before, I'm not a big fan of all the regal bowing and curtseying people do around the castle but after a guy kicks you in the back of the legs, the sight of him grovelling is very satisfying.

'I am Spideog, Master-at-Arms of Castle Duir. I am sorry, Your Highness.'

Behind me I heard Brendan trying to extricate himself. Greeny pulled back his bowstring and fired another arrow that planted itself about an inch from the previous one. I think if this guy wanted to, he could shoot fleas off a dog at fifty paces.

'Conor, tell him to stop doing that,' Brendan shouted.

'Hey, stop doing that,' I said.

Spideog had already notched another arrow from the quiver on his back. 'Instruct the Druid to leave the yew bows alone.'

'OK, first of all, he's not a Druid and secondly we didn't know they were yew. Brendan!' I yelled over my shoulder. 'Don't touch the bows.'

'If he stops shooting at me I'll put my hands in my pockets and not touch another thing all day. Now will somebody unpin me? I feel like a wanted poster.'

'You heard the man,' I said to Spideog still using my dad voice. 'Put your weapon away and help him down.'

The arrows were embedded so far into the wood that we had to snap them to unpin the detective. Brendan rolled up his left sleeve and examined the cut that the second arrow had inflicted. It wasn't much more than a bad scratch but that didn't stop Brendan from being very mad.

'Why you son of a—' He took a swing at the archer's nose.

Without any seemingly quick movements, Spideog casually brought up his left hand, connecting the back of his palm with the side of Brendan's advancing fist, and pushed the punch off target. His hand sailed harmlessly past Spideog's ear and Brendan stumbled forward. Confused at what had just happened but still just as mad, Brendan took another swing to precisely the same effect.

'Lord Conor, instruct your companion to stop attacking me.'

'Stop attacking him, Brendan.'

He didn't listen. I once heard that the definition of insanity is when you do the same things over and over but expect different results. Well, Brendan did the same thing and he did get a different result. This time Spideog's hand parry was accompanied by a kick that dropped Brendan about as quickly as I had been earlier. It ended with Spideog kneeling on Brendan's back and holding his wrist in what looked like a very painful position. The archer gave me a pleading look.

'Brendan, are you going to knock it off?'

'Yes,' he groaned into the floor.

Spideog let go. I was expecting Brendan to get up furious, instead he came up wide-eyed and said, 'How did you do that?'

'Simple,' greeny said, bouncing on his toes, 'your attack was sloppy and I – well – I am very good.'

Brendan rubbed his sore shoulder and amazingly smiled. 'Can you teach me that?'

'Why, I would be delighted. First stand with your feet in a stance just wider than your shoulders, then—'

'Ah, excuse me. Remember me, Prince of Duir?'

'Oh yes, Your Highness. I will teach you as well,' Spideog said. 'You obviously need some combat training. Take today for instance. You were standing in an armoury with all manner of weapons and shields and when you came under attack from an arrow, you chose a stick. Who in The Land taught you defence?'

'My father and Master Dahy,' I announced defensively.

'Dahy, of course – sticks and elbows. I'm surprised any of you are still alive.'

'Now hold on a minute,' I said, straightening up. 'I'll not have you badmouthing Master Dahy. Why, I ought to—'

'Easy, Conor,' Brendan said, coming between us. 'You don't want to take a swing at him, I tried that, it doesn't work. Anyway didn't we come in here for a reason?'

'Yes,' I said, giving Spideog one last dirty look. 'Mom said the Sword of Duir is here.'

'It is, my lord,' the green man replied. 'The Lawnmower is right over there.'

'What did you call it?'

'The Lawnmower. Your father had it renamed when he returned it to the armoury.'

Sure enough there she was, in the middle of the weapon racks in a gold-flecked clear crystal case – the family blade. At the base was a silver plaque that read, 'Lawnmower – the Sword of Duir'. I couldn't help but laugh.

'Lawnmower?' Brendan asked, confused.

'It's a long story.'

'If I may ask, my lord, what is a lawnmower?'

'What did my father tell you?'

'Lord Oisin and I do not … eh … chat.'

'I can't imagine why not,' I said sarcastically, 'but to answer your question, it's a machine used to keep grass short.'

'What is wrong with sheep?'

Spideog removed an acorn-shaped gold medallion from around his neck and slid it into a slot at the base of the display. The gold embedded in the glass glowed, a seam appeared in the front panel and then it opened on invisible hinges like tiny church doors. I reached in and grabbed the Sword of Duir. It always surprises me how light and contoured to my hand the Lawnmower is. It felt like an extension of my arm. I once let Araf hold it and was amazed when he complained how uncomfortable the handle was. I mentioned what he said to Dad and he said, 'It's a Duir thing – the blade knows a Child of Oak.'

'OK, now that we are all pals,' Brendan said, 'how come you attacked me when I reached for the bow?'

'I did not attack you,' Spideog corrected, 'if I had attacked you, you would be dead. I merely stopped you.'

'OK, why did you *stop* me then?'

'He stopped you, Brendan,' I answered, 'because that bow is not yours.'

'I wasn't gonna steal it.'

'Yew wood is special around here,' I said. 'Only a master archer can use a yew bow and if you want one you have to get the wood yourself. Only a person who has been deemed worthy by the tree can use that bow.'

'Deemed worthy by a tree?'

'It's complicated, I'll explain later.'

'Oh, now I see,' Spideog exclaimed, 'you must be the voyager from the Real World.'

'I am,' Brendan replied.

'Ah. I pay little attention to the gossip of the castle but I now remember hearing of you.' Spideog turned to me. 'If I may, my lord, all that you say is true but that is not why I fired on the voyager. The reason I stopped him was because he looks uncannily like a Fili.'

'Why would you attack a Fili?' I asked.

'These bows belonged to Maeve's Druid archers from the Fili war.'

'Oh my gods,' I said, 'these are from the soldiers who were killed when Maeve's massive Shadowspell backfired.'

'That is correct.'

'But why were they not buried with the dead?'

'Who said they are dead?'

'Ah – everybody.'

'I was there, Prince, I saw no bodies.'

'What?'

'Everyone presumes the Fili died when Maeve performed her foul witchcraft but I saw no dead. I saw an amber wave, I saw the Fili scream and writhe in pain but then they vanished. Behind them they left their clothes and weapons, in fact all of their earthly possessions – but no bodies.'

'No body, no murder,' Brendan mumbled.

'Gosh,' I said, 'where have I heard that before?'

'Most think I'm mad,' said Spideog, 'but I live here in the armoury and guard against their return.'

'He *is* a bit mad,' Mom said later that night when I told her about my adventure in the armoury. (I left out the part where Spideog aimed an arrow at my neck. You know how Mom gets when somebody tries to hurt me.) 'But there is no better fighter in The Land. He has even bested Dahy. While Cialtie was on the Oak Throne he lived deep in the Yewlands and reportedly waged a pretty effective one-man resistance war against Cialtie's Banshee patrols.'

'Apparently Dad doesn't like him.'

'Oh, he drives your father crazy. To be honest, that's one of the things I like best about Spideog,' Mom said with a mischievous grin that quickly changed into the frown that she seemed to always be wearing these days.

'And he keeps that armoury so tidy.'

NINE
MOTHER OAK

I didn't see much of Brendan for the next couple of days. He spent almost all of his time in the armoury with Spideog and I spent most of that time sitting with Dad. Mom said maybe he could hear us, so I read him stories from books I found in the library. Even if he couldn't hear, it was good for me. Many of the tales were about Duir so it helped me bone up on family history and it also improved my ancient Gaelic reading skills. Mom said we were going to be doing a lot of research when we got to the Hazellands.

I read a chronicle of the Fili war. Fand's mother Maeve really did lose it. She not only decimated much of the Rowan forest but took out a lot of alder trees as well – another reason why the Brownies shun everybody in The Land. I read nursery rhymes about not killing animals because they might be Pookas, not sleeping under alders and a story about a bunch of guys who sailed away from The Land and got old. I even tried to decipher Elven poetry. I needed a dictionary for that.

As I sat by his bed conjugating a verb I started to laugh. 'Gosh, Pop,' I said aloud, 'I probably shouldn't do this in front of you. The shock of me doing language homework, on my own, could kill you.' I stared through the amber to see if I could detect the slightest of smiles. I thought I saw something move but maybe that was just the water welling up in my eyes.

When I wasn't with Dad I spent the rest of my time in my room throwing a knife I found in the armoury. If this knife had once had a gold tip it was now well worn off. Let me tell you, without Dahy's magic points, these suckers are hard to throw.

Aein came in while I was practising my knife-play. She gave me a dirty look and said, 'Like father like son,' then informed me that my mother and her entourage would leave at dawn. I went looking for Brendan to tell him. I found him in the armoury practising archery with Spideog. They already knew – Spideog was heading up the Queen's guard.

Every time I go on a trip in this place the person who plans it says, 'We leave at dawn.' What is it with that? Why doesn't someone say, 'Let's leave ten-ish,' or 'Whenever you get up will be fine.' No. Dawn it always is. And leaving at dawn means just that, so you have to get up at least an hour before dawn! I'm not very good before noon, so getting up before dawn means the majority of my day is useless.

Brendan was awake and ready when I got to his room.

'You're late,' he said.

'So shoot me. Oh wait, you already tried that.' I'm not only useless in the morning, I can also be a bit testy.

'I was going to make my way to the stables by myself but I didn't want your mother to ju-jitsu me into a wall when she saw me. What did she say when you told her I was coming?'

'Eh – I haven't quite told her yet.'

'Oh great.'

'You see, my motto is it's always easier to apologise than it is to ask permission.'

'That's a fine philosophy if it's not *you* flying butt over noggin in the air.'

'Fair point,' I said. 'I'll protect you – just don't touch her.'

'The thought of you protecting me fills me with *so* much confidence,' Brendan said sarcastically. 'Don't worry. My hands won't go near your momma.'

*   *   *

As is usual for these crack-of-dawn riding parties, everyone was pretty much saddled up and ready to go by the time I arrived. Being a royal personage means that most people don't give me any verbal grief for tardiness but that doesn't stop the dirty looks.

Mom of course is the exception to that rule. She was just about to chew my head off for being late when she saw Brendan.

'What is he doing here?'

'Chill, Mom, he's with me.'

'I most certainly will not chill, whatever that means – I will not have him coming with us.'

I took a deep breath and said, 'I am a prince of Duir and this man is under my protection. He travels with me.'

Mom and I stared into each other's eyes. I had never stood up to my mother and I was pretty sure pulling a royal card on her wasn't going to work. We glared at each other for about five seconds – the longest five seconds of my life – before she said, 'Very well. Hurry up, you have made us late.'

When I started breathing again and my heart rate dropped down to a manageable rhythm, I was addressed by a Leprechaun I remembered from the ruined stables in the Hall of Knowledge.

'Greetings, Lord Conor. It is good to see you again. When Lady Deirdre told me you needed your horse I was not sure which one she meant, so I saddled both.'

A stable-hand led out two sights for sore eyes. 'Acorn! Cloud!' I yelled. I didn't know which one to hug first and I certainly didn't want to insult one over the other. A woman scorned is trouble but a jealous horse can pitch you into a ravine. I patted both snouts simultaneously. Since Cloud is the easier ride, I suspected that she was the less sensitive of the two – I gave her to Brendan.

We rode through the courtyard past a small throng of bowers and wavers and up to the main oak gates of Duir. While reading to Dad during the previous few days, I had read that Maeve had promised to reduce them to kindling. That would have been a hell of a trick. The two gates were over two storeys high and almost as wide. When closed they displayed a huge carving of an oak tree. On each leaf of the tree, inlaid in gold, were all the runes of the lands comprising Tir na Nog.

The largest rune was the major Oak Rune; next to it was a carving of what was then hanging from my waist – the Lawnmower – the Sword of Duir. As the team of horses pulled open the gates, the depth of these monsters became apparent. The gates were as thick as I was tall. I promised myself that after I woke Dad up I would ask him where they came from.

A small battalion fronted by Spideog and Araf awaited us on the other side of the gates. As we approached they saluted and parted. Araf slipped in next to me.

'Hey, Imp buddy, I didn't know you were coming.'

'A prince of the House of Duir must always travel with a bodyguard. It was one of your father's first rules.'

'Do you mean every time I leave home I'm stuck with you?' I said with a smile. Araf didn't answer me. He doesn't usually answer straight questions. There's no hope he'd answer a rhetorical one.

I promised myself I wouldn't go on and on like I usually do about how beautiful The Land is, but I just gotta say that fall in The Land is awesome. I'm not using the word 'awesome' the way a mall-rat would describe a slush drink; when I say awesome I mean it. The scenery in the Forest of Duir actually inspired awe and not just with Brendan and me. Most of our troop rode with wide eyes and mouths open and the majority of them were probably over a thousand years old. I suspect you could never get tired of this scenery no matter how many times you had seen it.

If you were to hold your hands out in front of you palm up, like you were begging, one of these leaves would cover both of your hands completely. The major colour of the foliage was 'inferno' orange. The leaves were almost incandescent and gave off a glow in the sunlight that made all our complexions look like we had been caught in an explosion at a fake-tan factory. The reds and yellows and greens were there to provide dazzling counterpoint. Periodically you would see a bold tree that was solely in red or another just in yellow. The colours were everywhere, even underfoot, gently rustling under our horses' hooves.

The air, scented with the perfume of fallen leaves, was cool and crisp – you felt like it could almost cut you – and it was crystal clear, like the way the world looks after you clean a pair of dirty sunglasses. I can honestly say I have never experienced a more invigorating morning. Sorry about the gushing – I promise I won't mention spring.

We rode in silence letting our eyes and sighs do all the talking. About an hour before noon we entered Glen Duir and Mom dropped back to talk to me.

'Oisin said Mother Oak was asking after you the last time he spoke to her. Would you like to stop for a quick chat?'

'Yes please,' I said as an involuntary smile took over my face. I kicked into a gallop with Araf close on my tail. I crested the hill and saw the old lady dressed in her fall best. Her leaves were mostly yellows and light browns like a comfortable patchwork quilt. I dismounted before Acorn came to a stop, ran up to her and wrapped my arms around her trunk.

'*Oh my,*' came that lovely voice in my head, '*who is this in such a rush?*'

'It's me, Mother Oak – Conor.'

'*Oh my, my, the Prince of Hazel and Oak; I have been worried about you.*'

'I'm fine.'

'*Oh, but your father is not,*' she said, reading my thoughts. '*Climb up higher and tell me all about it.*'

I climbed a bit and she brought branches in behind me to rest against. I told her about what had happened to Dad, and what Mom and Fand had done.

'*Oh, I had feared as much. I knew something was wrong with your father the last time he came to visit with me. But try not to worry yourself too much, my dear, your mother is a very clever witch. If anyone can find a cure it will be her.*'

I knew that already but Mother Oak has a way of turning knowledge into belief. I hugged her again.

'I have to go,' I said, 'the others are waiting for me.'

'*Take good care of yourself, Conor. Come and see me in the spring.*'

'I will.' I started to leave and then added, 'By the way your foliage looks beautiful.'

'*Do you really think so?*' she asked. '*The fashion among the other trees these days just seems a bit gaudy to me.*'

'Well, I think you look elegant.'

I hugged her one more time and I know it sounds impossible for a tree but I think she blushed.

I walked over the knoll. It always takes me some time to clear my head after talking to a tree. I saw a small group standing around someone on the ground. As I got closer I saw it was Brendan unconscious on his back.

'What happened?' I asked the throng.

'I don't know,' a guard said. 'Ask him.'

Spideog crested the knoll with a bucket of water in his hand. Ignoring my questions, he poured the whole thing onto Brendan's face. The detective popped up spluttering, tried to stand and then dropped back down holding his head.

'Has someone hit me with a stick again?' Brendan asked.

'Did you hit him with a stick?' I asked Spideog.

'No,' he said, 'a rock.'

'Why?'

'I would like to have a word with you in private, if I may.'

Spideog and I walked out of earshot and he said, 'Our friend Brendan was about to shoot a tree with an arrow. I was too far away to stop him so I threw a rock. It was either that or place an arrow in him.'

'Thank you, Spideog; he didn't know what he was doing.'

'I have spent many a year in the Real World, Prince Conor, and I know how mortals treat trees but there are others here who might not be so understanding. Remember he is under your protection. Make sure he does not do it again.'

We walked back. Brendan was on his feet.

'You have to stop your friends from hitting me in the head with sticks.'

'It was a rock.'

'OK,' he said. 'You have to stop your friends hitting me with sticks and rocks.'

'You promised you would keep your hands in your pockets. What were you doing when Spideog threw the rock at you?'

'Spideog hit me? What for?'

'What were you doing?'

'I got bored waiting for you so I notched an arrow and was about to do a bit of archery practice.'

'And what were you aiming at?'

Brendan pointed to a young oak. His misfired arrow was about ten yards behind it.

'Come with me,' I said, grabbing him by the arm and leading him to Mother Oak.

'Hug that tree,' I demanded.

'What?'

'Hug that tree.'

'I'm not going to hug a tree.'

'Hug that tree or I will have you dragged back to Castle Duir in chains and you can stare at Frick and Frack for the next year.'

He looked at me and then tilted his head. 'You mean it, don't you?'

'Yes.'

'If I didn't know better, I'd say my mother put you up to this.'

'Hug!'

Brendan approached the tree and with an *if it will make you happy* attitude, wrapped his arms around Mother Oak. His smirk disappeared in an instant. I wish I could have heard Mother Oak's side of the conversation 'cause all I heard from Brendan was 'Yes, ma'am' and 'No, ma'am.' His conversation finished with, 'It won't happen again, ma'am.' Then he let go of the tree and staggered.

I caught him by the arm. 'Steady, Detective.'

He tried looking me in the eyes but wasn't focusing well. 'I'm still concussed, aren't I?'

'I'm pretty sure you're not.'

'Yeah,' he said, regaining his balance, 'I was afraid of that.'

I waited for him to say something else but he just stood there. Finally I asked, 'So what did you think of Mother Oak?'

'That's a heck of a tree.'

I laughed. 'That's what I said when I first met her.'

A group of soldiers had galloped ahead and had started cooking so that dinner was ready to be served almost as soon as we made camp. Other

soldiers pitched tents for Mom and me. As I have said I'm not a big fan
of the royal treatment I get around here but after a hard day of riding
– well, it would be rude of me to complain about a meal and a clean
bed.

Brendan wolfed down his supper and then disappeared. I had a
silent meal with Araf and then decided to hit the hay in the luxury of
my own royal tent. As I approached it I heard a strange noise coming
from inside. I unsheathed the Lawnmower and pushed open the flap
only to find Brendan snoring in my bed. No amount of shaking and
then kicking could get him to move so I grabbed a blanket and slept
out under the stars on a lumpy piece of ground next to Araf. I fell
asleep thinking of ways to strangle Brendan as he slept.

I was having a dream about Essa talking to an invisible man when I
was awoken by a ruckus at the edge of the camp. I saw Mom heading
towards the commotion. Araf and I followed. At the perimeter of the
paddock we found Mom tending a wounded soldier. Next to him was
a dead wolf with an arrow through its chest.

Mom stood up and walked over to the wolf. 'Who shot the beast?'
she demanded.

'I did,' came a response from the shadows. It was Spideog.

'Explain yourself.'

'It was a last resort, Lady Deirdre. I arrived as the wolves were
harassing the horses. The guards were shooing them away when they
attacked. This man went down and lost his banta stick. I only fired
when the wolf went for him on the ground. I had no choice.'

Mom looked at the wounded guard, who nodded in agreement.
Mom placed her hand on the neck of the wolf and then began to run
both her hands over the animal. She paused for what seemed to be the
longest time, turning her head from one side to another, and then
suddenly reached into her boot and pulled out a knife. She cut a long
incision deep into the creature's abdomen and reached inside. When
her bloody hand emerged she held a short wire necklace with a small
flat gold disc attached. She held it up and displayed it to Spideog. The
look on both of their faces made me feel very afraid.

TEN
THE ATHRÚ

I didn't get a chance to talk to Mom until we were back on the road the next day. I slid Acorn up next to her and asked, 'What was that thing you pulled out of the wolf last night? It looked like it really spooked you.'

'Yes, I was certainly freaked up.'

'Out.'

'Damn, I thought I had that one right,' she said with a smile. 'No matter. The necklace I pulled out of the wolf was an *athrú*.'

'An athrú?'

'Do you remember the Pooka that died when you were first in the Fililands?'

'How could I forget.'

'Do you remember the piece of gold I placed in his mouth before he died?'

'I do, it scared the hell out of me. You put the disc in his mouth, then he changed into a wolf, howled, died and changed back.'

'Well, the disc I put in his mouth was his athrú – a Pooka amulet. The Pooka wear them around their necks, it helps them change. The wire it hangs from expands and contracts so it doesn't fall off during the metamorphosis.'

'Like Banshee blade wire?'

'Exactly,' Mom said. 'The wolf that Spideog killed had an athrú in its stomach.'

'That wolf was a Pooka?'

'No, if it had been a Pooka it would have changed into a man when it died.'

'So where did the wolf get the amulet?'

'I can only conclude that that animal ate a Pooka but that just does not make sense.'

'Why not?'

'The Pookas are very secretive with their lore but I know a small bit.'

'You once told me that one of your tutors in the Hazellands was a Pooka.'

'Well remembered, son; yes, she was. She told me some things she probably should not have. One thing she taught me was that each athrú has a marking for each creature. The athrú I found in the wolf was marked Gearr. It was worn by a Pooka that could change into a hare.'

'So a crazy wolf accidentally wolfs down a Pooka hare. That sounds plausible to me.'

'But it is not,' Mom said, looking perturbed. 'Pookas have an almost telepathic control over animals, and the Pookas that change into small creatures always change back when threatened.'

'So what's the answer?'

'I do not know, my son. I do know that no Pooka has come to Castle Duir since your father took the throne and you said you were attacked by boar in the summer.'

'So you think there is something wrong in Pookaville?'

Mom gave me her quizzical look, 'How do you come up with these words?'

The Land's fall colour spectacular continued throughout the day. Brendan, it turned out, was quite the equestrian. It made me regret letting him ride Cloud. Don't get me wrong, Acorn is a great horse and the best mount a man can have when the chips are down, but Cloud is a much easier ride, like having power steering in a car.

Our second night's camp was uneventful. I kept an eye on Brendan at dinner and followed him when he left early. As he approached my tent I said, 'That would be my tent.'

'Oh,' he said, 'I thought it was for guests.'

'Yeah, right. It's mine and if you steal it again, I'm going to tell my mother.'

'Oh,' Brendan said, 'I guess I'll find somewhere else.'

Sometimes it's handy having a warrior queen for a mother.

Acorn got jittery when we crossed the border into the Hazellands but it wasn't as bad as the last time. Mom rode up next to me and spoke into my horse's ear and settled him down. I think another reason why Acorn calmed down was because the Hazellands were starting to look a lot better. The first time I was here it seemed as if the life had been sucked out of it – now it felt as if the place was on the mend. Like fresh new skin growing on a bad wound. Fallen trees had been cut for wood and charred branches had been cleared away. As we climbed a small hill I remembered where we were. The top of the rise was the spot where Araf had first laid eyes on the destruction of the Field – the Imp garden where Araf had lost so many kinsmen. The last time he had seen the Field it had been trashed so badly he nearly fell out of his saddle. This time he crested the hill and said, 'Will you look at that.'

It is so rare for Araf to spontaneously make any noise that it always startles me when he does. I pulled up next to him and saw what he saw. What was once a scorched and blackened patch of land had been cleared and tilled. A team of Imps were planting trees and tending gardens. Araf looked on like a dog sighting a bird in a bush.

'Master Spideog!' I called.

Spideog rode next to us, taking in the wide-eyed Araf and the Field.

'Master Spideog,' I said, 'I wonder if Prince Araf might be able to be released from his bodyguard duties for a few hours.'

Araf looked at me like a boy getting permission from his mother to go swimming on a hot day.

'I think we can spare his stick for the rest of the afternoon,' Spideog said. 'Prince Araf, you are relieved.'

A rare ear-to-ear smile erupted on the Imp's face as he reached for the whistle hanging around his neck. He simultaneously kicked his mount into a gallop and blew. All of the Imps in the distance immediately stopped what they were doing and then began to cheer as they saw their prince speeding towards them. We watched as a mob of Imps practically dragged him from his horse. How anybody can get excited about spending an afternoon covered in dirt is beyond me but I knew Araf was now as happy as a pig in muck.

As we got closer to the outbuildings it became obvious how much work had been done. All of the rubble had been cleared away or stacked for later repair. Several of the smaller buildings had been rebuilt and then there was the landscaping. Those Imp guys sure can plant stuff. Hedges, young trees and flowerbeds were everywhere.

As we approached what looked like a guard house, Spideog kicked his horse and sped ahead. Just before he cleared the building, he notched an arrow in his bow and performed a magnificent full speed dismount. He hit the ground running using his horse for cover, then pulled his bow to full length and let his mount go on. He stood stock still, menacingly aiming a deadly arrow at something or someone that I couldn't see. I drew my sword and looked to Mom but she seemed more annoyed than concerned. She kicked her horse into a canter and I followed. Mom casually went behind Spideog – I on the other hand peeked around the building. Standing there with a crossbow pointed directly at Spideog's head was Master Dahy.

'*Boys*,' Mom said in a reproachful tone.

'Tell this old man to drop his weapon. His clumsy reconnaissance has been exposed,' Spideog said.

'First of all,' Dahy replied, 'I am younger than you.'

'In age maybe, but not in spirit.'

'Boys,' Mom said again. This time she sounded impatient.

'Secondly,' Dahy continued, ignoring the interruption, 'I have a Brownie crossbow aimed at your head. I'll drop you before you can even let go of that string.'

'Would you like to put that to the test, *Old Man*?'

Mom dismounted and walked between the two Masters. No matter how much they wanted to kill each other (and it sure looked like they did) their duty kicked in as soon as the Queen of Duir stepped into the line of fire. They immediately lowered their weapons.

'Now that is better,' Mom said in an overly calm tone. 'I'm going to return to my mount. I shall assume you two will not again raise your weapons to each other after I leave.' When she got no response, she said, 'Master Spideog?'

'Yes, my lady,' Spideog said, replacing his arrow in his quiver.

'Master Dahy?'

'Of course, Lady Deirdre,' Dahy replied, removing the bolt from his crossbow.

I don't know how many years those two had between them, probably thousands, but at that moment they sounded like eight-year-olds.

'Master Spidcog, you are with me,' Mom commanded. 'Master Dahy, I have royal bodyguard duty for you. He is over there hiding behind that wall – I think you may have met.'

I stuck my nose around the building and waved.

'Conor!' Dahy said as he approached and placed his arms on my shoulders. 'When did you get back?'

'About a week ago; I would have thought someone would have told you.'

'News is slow around here. I don't have an *emain* slate. The Leprechaun who made them was killed when Cialtie blew out the east wing. The new ones don't work very well. I've had to rely on couriers. Tell me, how is your father?'

We mounted up and I told him what Mom and Fand had done to Dad and about Mom's magic Shadowbook paperclip. He took it all in without surprise like I was telling him the latest football scores. I guess if you're as old as Dahy and have lived all of that time with witches and oracles, it's easy to take news like this in your stride.

'So you are going to be with us for a while then?' Dahy asked.

'As long as it takes.'

'Good, I can use you.'

'Use me for what?' I asked suspiciously.

We passed one of the Hall's outbuildings; I recognised it as the one where Lorcan clothes-lined me so long ago. Just past that we rounded a bend and I saw a large group of soldiers standing around a pair of duelling banta fighters in full protective gear.

'You finally got your security force for the Hall of Knowledge,' I said.

'Yes,' Dahy replied, 'I imagine even your grandfather wouldn't have minded, given the circumstances. I wanted a more ecumenical group but they are mostly Imps, Leprechauns and Faeries.'

'Faeries?'

'Of course. There are a few Banshees but I couldn't get any Elves or Brownies to join and nobody has spotted a Pooka in ages. This lot are all very green. I could use your help to train them.'

I was just about to ask what a Faerie looked like when the banta stick duel captured my attention. The one guy wasn't doing very well. Every time he mounted an attack his opponent seemed to know in advance exactly where it was going to come from. His opponent's parries and counter-attacks were minimal and effective to the point of perfection. But what really caught my attention was the posture and footwork. There was only one person that moved like that and it made my heart race even before she took off her head protector and shook her wavy black hair over her shoulders like a model in a shampoo commercial. Essa turned and our eyes locked. She was definitely surprised to see me but, as usual with that girl, I wasn't sure if she was happy about it or not.

All eyes turned to Dahy and me as we approached. Essa's duelling partner took off his headpiece and for a moment I was hit with déjà vu. As he revealed his black hair with a white tuft in the front, I momentarily thought it was Fergal but then the Banshee's sharp facial lines and broad chin broke the illusion.

'Attention, Soldiers of the Red Hand,' Dahy shouted.

The group snapped to attention. I smiled. Dahy had held onto the same name as the army that last occupied the Hazellands.

'I give you Conor, Prince of Duir!'

Everybody dropped to one knee and bowed their heads, except, I noticed, Essa and her Banshee-duelling partner.

I dismounted. 'Hi, folks. Look, I'm gonna be around here for a while so you don't have to do that – OK?'

'As you were,' Dahy ordered and everybody relaxed as a buzz went through the crowd.

Essa gave a loud theatrical cough and thankfully the hundreds of eyes left me and turned to her. 'If our regal visitor doesn't mind, shall we continue with our training?'

Her troops straightened up and quieted down. She was more beautiful than I had even remembered. What kind of idiot was I, leaving a woman like this behind? She finished by staring at me with a question on her face and I realised she actually wanted *me* to answer her question.

'No, no,' I stammered, 'by all means continue.'

She seemed to smile at me but only from one side of her mouth. 'We have been working all day on banta fighting. Excellent for helping improve footwork and winning competitions, but in battle you are most likely to be attacked with a sword. What happens if you only have a banta stick to defend yourself with?'

I came very close to shouting out, 'You're screwed,' but two things stopped me: one was that I had seen Essa fight sword with stick and she was damn good at it; secondly, I instinctively felt that undermining Essa in front of her students would be a bad idea.

'Our new guest, Prince Conor,' Essa continued, 'fancies himself as quite the swordsman. Your Highness,' she said with just enough sarcasm that only I heard it, 'would you like to help me with this demonstration?'

'How about we nip off and spend a little alone time,' is what I really wanted to say. Instead I answered, 'Sure.'

I walked to the midst of about a hundred young eager eyes. Essa and I squared off in the centre and slowly circled each other. For the first time a proper smile crossed her face. Gods, she was stunning. I drew my sword and her smile vanished. She backed into the crowd and threw her banta stick to a soldier and took a training stick from another. She returned back to the centre.

'Conor is wielding a very good sword indeed. Does anyone recognise it?' A few hands went up. 'It is the Sword of Duir.'

A murmur shot through the group. Men and women strained to get a look at the Lawnmower as I held it aloft.

'The difficulty with fighting a sword, especially one as good as this one, is that you must not make direct contact. When wood meets steel head on – it is usually wood that loses.'

Essa was holding her stick straight out in a pre-duel position with her head turned to face her pupils. I swung the Lawnmower high and sliced about a foot off the top of her banta stick. It was like knife through butter. The crowd laughed. Essa turned and even though she had a smile on her face for the crowd, her eyes had a look I didn't like. She inspected the stick and then threw it into the audience. A replacement sailed back immediately. Dahy stepped into the circle holding a dulled training sword. I reluctantly swapped the Lawnmower for it.

'Thank you, Prince Conor, for that demonstration,' she said as she refaced her class. It was probably a good thing Dahy changed my sword 'cause I'm sure I would have done the same thing again. I think stuff like that a second time is even funnier than the first but some people don't agree and I knew Essa was definitely one of them. 'A sword is obviously the stronger weapon,' she continued, 'but it is inferior in length. You must use your superior reach to set the rhythm and tempo of the fight – directing the battle to your terms.'

She faced me directly and stood at attention, so I did too. We both bowed at the waist with our eyes locked. Our faces were inches away – I whispered, 'Miss me?'

She stood erect, assumed a fighting stance and said, '*En garde.*'

I raised my sword, adjusted my footing and asked, 'Is that a yes, or a no?'

ELEVEN

ESSA

Essa and I circled to the right. This time, as she addressed her class, she never took her eyes off me.

'You will probably have almost double the reach of anyone wielding a sword. If your opponent sets up too close …' Essa nodded, inviting me closer, 'then give him a reminder that you are carrying a long stick.' With the quickest of clicks she tapped my blade out of its position and poked me hard in the chest with her stick.

'Hey!' I shouted, stepping back and rubbing my chest. 'You told me to step in.'

'And if your opponent is stupid enough to do what you tell him to do – make sure to take advantage of that.'

The crowd laughed. I forced a smile onto my face and stopped rubbing the place she had hit me – even though it still really hurt.

'Once you have set the proper fighting distance, your opponent will be forced to attack your stick, not you.'

I could see her point but I wasn't going to play her game and I certainly didn't want to stand there and swipe at a stick. I decided to make my first attack a deep body swipe – the kind of advance that would be dangerous to ignore. I bounced backwards and forwards on my toes, made a short backhand fake that brought her stick out of position and then lunged with a full cut to the body. Without seeming to move her legs at all, Essa instantly backed out of reach. I had forgotten just how fast that girl moved. Her stick lightly engaged with the leading edge of my moving sword, circled around it and then pushed it away. By the time I got control my arm was way across my body and my weapon was nowhere near where it should have been. Essa slid one hand to the middle of her stick and swung the base of her banta into my kidney. It dropped me to one knee.

'Usually I would not have counter-attacked so soon in a match. As you all should know, the golden rule is to parry and retreat until you can ascertain your opponent's favourite attack. I have an advantage with the Prince – I already know his favourite attack.' Essa came over to where I was still on one knee. As she helped me to my feet she whispered, 'Miss me?'

I was still wondering if I would ever be able again to pass water with that kidney when she flowed back into her *en garde* position and asked, 'Ready?'

I held up my hand for a time-out and stepped in close to her. 'Do you think maybe I should have some protective clothing?'

'Aw come on, Conor, it's only a stick. You've got a great big sword.'

'You … you could poke my eye out.'

'I promise I won't hit you in the head – even though it is such a large target.'

I tried to remember some old saying about a woman scorned but I didn't have time. She started circling again, this time to my left and she was doing that figure of eight spinning thing with her banta that I had seen Araf do – it made me feel a bit woozy. I decided that maybe Essa's students shouldn't be the only ones paying attention to her tutorial, so I attacked the stick. I just stuck my blade into the twirling thing and she flipped it into a counter-attack. Fortunately I was ready for it and brought my sword up into a high backhanded parry. When she saw the steel coming she checked her swing and bounced back in to her home position.

'Well done, Princess,' came a shout from one of the people in the crowd.

I took a couple more swipes at the stick and every time pretty much the same thing happened. She would make light contact and attempt to counter but would then pull back at the last second, to avoid her wood being damaged by my steel. Essa's bravado, the bruises on my chest and side, her cheering peanut gallery and the fact that she was the third best stick fighter I had ever seen had initially made me feel like I was the underdog but I was starting to remember that I had a sword. I had the better weapon.

I took another swipe at her banta but this time when she attempted her counter-attack I stepped in and took a full power cut at her weapon. My sword made hard contact with the top of her stick. If I had been using the Lawnmower I would have sliced that bit clean off – this dulled thing stuck halfway into the wood. As Essa pulled back I felt the tug and quickly twisted my pommel. I heard the crack as about ten inches of her stick spun into the air.

Essa backed and circled. The same voice from the crowd called out, 'Not to worry, Princess.' As Essa inspected her weapon I stole a quick glance to see who the cheerleader was. It was the Banshee she had been sparring with earlier.

While she was readjusting to the new length of her stick, I moved in a step and began my trademarked low sword attack. That's where I keep my blade low and then swipe upward using my natural agility to bob and weave my head out of the way. I should note that every fighting teacher has told me that this is a very bad idea but it usually unnerves an opponent the first time they see it and I'm pretty sure I never did it when Essa was around. It worked too. She backed up fast but before she ran out of room, she took a full baseball swing to my head that made me hit the ground with a roll.

'Hey,' I shouted as I jumped back to my feet, 'you promised not to hit me in the head.'

'If you're just going to hang your face out there, I can't resist taking a pop at it.'

'Good one, Essa,' the Banshee shouted.

The crowd was getting pretty worked up and from the sounds of it, I wasn't the hometown team. It's dangerous when emotions creep into a practice fight and at that moment I wanted to kill the girl of my dreams. From the look in her eyes *my love* wanted to do the same thing. I should have called it off right then and there – instead I modified my attack.

While protecting my face, I succeeded in backing Essa into her cheering section. Just as she was about to run out of room – she did it. I knew she would. I knew she couldn't resist showing off for her pupils. She launched herself straight up and over my head and attempted to grind her banta into my shoulder as she pole-vaulted over me – but I was ready for it. When she was directly over my head, I dropped to the ground. Her stick made contact with nothing but air. The self-satisfied smile on her face vanished as she realised she didn't have enough leverage to complete her somersault. She instantly went from a graceful gymnast to a flailing circus clown and landed hard on her back.

I stood up and turned to the silenced audience. 'I know some of my opponent's favourite attacks too.' My line didn't do as well as when Essa used it. I think it was safe to say they didn't like me too much.

After rolling over onto all fours and taking a few quick breaths Essa stood and the look on her face made me realise I had gone too far. I lowered my sword and was about to call a stop when that damn Banshee shouted, 'You're not going to let him get away with that are you, Princess?'

Essa dropped right back into fighting mode and came at me with a series of short fast swings that got me back-pedalling. I didn't want this fight any more. I didn't mean to humiliate her in front of her students. I just wanted to sit with her and ask her how she was and tell her how much I had missed her but that stick just kept on coming. One swipe came so close to my nose I smelled the sap in the timber. I finally parried a cut hard and my sword once again stuck into the wood. As she tried to pull it free I stepped in. She was forced close. I don't think I had ever seen her this mad before – and I had seen Essa plenty mad.

'Come on, Princess – you can take this Faerie.'

'Who,' I asked Essa, her face inches from mine, 'is the Banshee with the big mouth?'

Essa grunted and with all of her strength threw me back, disengaging our weapons. 'That,' she said, while assuming a very menacing crouch, 'would be my fiancé.'

'What?' I stood straight up and dropped my guard. I looked directly into her eyes to see if she was serious. That's probably why I didn't spot the stick before it connected with my head.

*   *   *

In movies people wake up from a concussion and then feel their head like the pain comes as a surprise. That's not how it works. The pain comes way before you open your eyes and if you have had as much experience with involuntary unconsciousness as I have, you delay opening them for as long as possible, 'cause that's when the second wave of hurt arrives.

So as I lay there the first thing I noticed was the pain. Then I worked on the basics: who was I? – Conor O'Neil. Good, if you don't know that one you're in trouble. Where was I? – Scranton? No – Tir na Nog. How did I end up out cold and flat on my back? Essa. Essa hit me – she said she wouldn't but she did. I had been looking for Essa. Where did I find her? The Hazellands. And she wasn't as happy to see me as I thought she would be. In fact she seemed downright mad at me.

I felt a cold compress land on my forehead. The blessed cold ratcheted the pain level down a couple of notches.

Well, she couldn't be that mad at me, I thought, *if she was willing to nurse me. She must be feeling bad for hitting me in the head.*

I reached up and placed my hand on hers. So why did she hit me? It was an accident – I had dropped my guard. Why did I do that?

I shot straight up in bed and shouted, 'You're engaged!'

'No I am not,' said the startled and still blurry face in front of me.

TWELVE
THE TURLOW

The aforementioned second wave of pain hit me like a well-swung mace. I closed my eyes and lay back down. The pain was lessened only by the revelation that Essa wasn't engaged. I squeezed her hand and she returned the gesture. This time I slowly opened my eyes but as the world became less fuzzy Essa got increasingly uglier. When I came properly to my senses I found myself holding hands with Araf.

'Who told you I was engaged?' the Imp demanded.

I quickly retrieved my hand. 'Essa?' I croaked.

'Essa told you I was engaged?'

'No, Essa is engaged,' I said.

'I know Essa is engaged but why is she going around telling people I am engaged? I'm a Prince of Ur. A rumour like that can cause a lot of trouble.'

My head hurt too much for this kind of confusion. 'No one said you were engaged.'

'You said I was engaged.'

'I didn't mean you, I thought you were Essa.'

'You think I look like Essa?' Araf looked concerned. 'I'll go get a healer.'

I dropped my head back on the pillow and covered my eyes. 'Maybe you should get a healer – I need something for my head.'

'There is something on your bedside table there.'

I sat up and knocked back the thimbleful of liquid from a silver shot-glass. I'm sure my face went as red as the inside of a thermometer and, as it returned to normal colour, my headache subsided. When I could breathe again I said, 'You knew that Essa was engaged?'

'Well yes, everyone knows that. Gerard announced it about three weeks ago. He sent all of the Runelords a cask of special wine – it was a lovely red. The bouquet had the slightest hint of—'

'Why didn't you tell me?' I interrupted.

'You didn't ask. I assumed, since you left, that you had no interest in Essa.'

'Well, you assumed wrong,' I said, as I slowly sat up and put my feet on the floor.

'But wasn't Essa interested in you by the end of your last visit?'

'She was.'

'And you left her?'

'Yes,' I said, feeling the pain in my head starting to return.

'That is not a good thing,' the Imp said in an ominous tone.

'Why?'

'I have known Essa a long time, my friend – she is not the forgiving type.'

Mom apparently had administered first aid and chewed out Essa for trying to take my head off. You know how she gets when someone attacks her little bear cub. She also had given me some sort of meds that knocked me out for the whole night – so I was surprised when sunshine blinded me as I opened the door. Morning in the Hazellands was a busy place. Imps and Leprechauns were clearing away rubble and rebuilding walls, while others were drilling or practising archery with Spideog.

I've started to realise that Araf only gets chatty when he is nervous or really happy. This morning he was still euphoric about his time with his fellow farmer Imps in the Field, so I pretended to be interested and asked him about his day digging in dirt. That kept him talking until we got our food and found a quiet table in the canteen.

'So who is he?'

'Who?'

'You know who, the Banshee who is engaged to Essa.'

'He is Turlow,' Araf said.

'So who is he then?'

'He's Turlow.'

'What does that mean?'

'He is The Turlow?'

'Araf, it doesn't matter how many different articles you use before saying Turlow, it doesn't explain anything.'

'Have you never heard the story about Ériu and her sisters?'

A spark flickered in my deep memory. Dad told me something about this when we were in the Rowan forest but there was so much going on and so much to remember. 'Remind me.'

Araf sighed like I was a schoolboy who hadn't done his homework. 'Ériu was the first. She discovered The Land. She either found or created the first oak and maybe did the same for the Leprechauns. Then she sent for her two sisters Banbha and Fódla. Fódla,' Araf said as he touched his forehead in a semi-religious gesture, 'created or found the Imps and the Orchardlands.'

'What does this have to do with The Turlow?'

'Banbha was different from her sisters – darker. She created or, depending on what you believe, found the Yewlands. Then she travelled to the Otherworld, killed the Banshee King and convinced his son, Turlow, to come with her to defend Tir na Nog's shores. That is how the Banshees came to The Land.'

'Are you saying that this guy is *that* Turlow?'

'No, Turlow is the name passed down from father to son. This Turlow is said to be the direct descendant of the original Turlow. He is The Turlow. It is his name and his title.'

'So am I supposed to be impressed?'

'It is very impressive.'

'Did you hear him keep calling Essa "Princess"?'

'Essa is a princess,' Araf said, looking confused.

'Yeah, but it's the way he said it. And now that I think of it, he called me a Faerie.'

A little buzz started on the other side of the room which caused me to turn. Mom and Dahy had just entered and were making a beeline to our table.

Araf stood, so I did too. Mom gave me a hug and asked after my head.

'I'm fine thanks.'

'Are you sure?' She held my face in both of her hands and looked deep into my eyes.

'I'm sure, Mom.'

'Good, because we have work to do.'

The next couple of days were exhausting. The Land is a magnificent and beautiful place but it is seldom restful. I spent my time equally between rebuilding walls, training new recruits in sword-fighting and, most taxing of all, deciphering and filing old manuscripts, read with Mom's magic paperclip.

I tried to convince Mom that there were probably, hell definitely, a million people more qualified to sort through ancient Gaelic books than me but she said, 'If the gods will give us a way to cure your father, then I am betting on you finding it.'

There were only two of Mom's amber reader thingies, so ten of us rotated in twenty-four-hour shifts. It meant that I did four hours reading every twenty hours, resulting in my stint getting four hours later every day. My first couple of shifts were mostly spent trying to get my written Gaelic back up to speed. Dad had made me learn how to read, write and conjugate ancient Gaelic but it wasn't the language I read my comic books in and the stuff I was reading could hardly be called page-turners. My first thrilling manuscript was a contract and shipping manifest between the Elves and the Vinelands. It took me all of the four hours to figure out that it was a barter agreement where the Elves would provide wood for barrels and Fingal (who was Essa's grandfather) would pay in wine. From the amount of wine it seemed to me that the timber industry is a pretty lucrative business. I guess it's hard work when you have to ask permission from the trees if you want to cut them down. I had an image of an elf kneeling in front of a tree with an axe, saying, 'Please, I'm desperate for a drink?'

When I finally figured out that the piece of parchment I was studying didn't contain anything that would help us with Dad's condition I would place it in an envelope and label it so that in the future it could be transcribed into a new book. Not a job I will be volunteering for.

It wasn't just the grammar that was proving taxing but the actual reading of a manuscript required immense concentration. The paper-clip thingy sensed the page you were looking at as long as you were focused, but if you were reading, say, a scintillating essay on seed germination and you happened to let your mind wander, the page you were reading would fade into all of the other pages in the book, producing thousands of words on one page. Since there was no way to find your way back to the page you were reading, you would have to go back to the beginning.

After my first session I staggered back to my tent and blissfully closed the eyes that I had been afraid to even blink for the last four hours. Not even the blinding headache could keep me from falling asleep, but I didn't nap long. Dahy woke me and, despite my protests, dragged me out to the training fields and put me in charge of teaching sword-fighting to a group of helpless recruits. As soon as the old man was out of sight I told my charges to take the rest of the day off and I crawled back to bed. The next day Dahy warned me that if I did that again I would be cleaning latrines and I had a suspicion that he meant it.

My second reading session started promisingly enough when I found what I thought was going to be an interesting essay on banta stick manufacture. After I don't know how many pages, I figured out it could have easily been condensed to this one sentence without losing anything: 'Get some good wood and make a stick out of it.' By the end, my head hurt worse than when Essa hit me with one of those sticks.

I periodically saw Essa but we didn't speak to one another. I was desperate for some alone time with her but I was so busy, and when I wasn't busy, I was exhausted. When I did see her she was always with The Turlow. The closest I got was an uncomfortable lunch where the royal couple sat behind me at a table just within hearing distance. I couldn't make out much but every time I heard him say 'Princess' I felt like returning my lunch back onto my plate.

After about a week's worth of reading sessions I was starting to believe that 99 per cent of the books that were in the old library were about farming. I ploughed through endless manuscripts explaining crop rotation, plough manufacture, planting timetables and even one about delineating soil types by taste. I filed that under the heading of 'Eating Dirt'. I got mildly excited when I found a scrap entitled 'Leprechaun Genealogy' but it was literally just a list of names. I filed that as 'A Short History of Short People'.

I started screening my reading material so as to keep my sanity. I'm sure Araf would find a paper on 'Planting Row Orientation According to Crop and Season' fascinating but it just made me want to hold my breath and bang my head against the floor. When no one was looking I scanned my new manuscripts for key terms. I'd clip the reader on a sliver of paper and if I saw any words like: *seed*, or *soil*, or *yield*, I would slip the piece under the bottom of the pile. I prayed to the gods that I wouldn't still be doing this by the time we got down to that fragment again.

The reading eventually got easier, partly because I got better at it but mostly because Mom invented a Shadowbookmark that held your page if your mind wandered. But it was the sword-fight teaching that became the highlight of my day. In the beginning my students were pretty much in awe of me, even after seeing me get popped in the temple by Essa. They all wanted to know about the Battle of the Twins of Macha and how I chopped Cialtie's hand off and the Army of the Red Hand and what the Real World was like. I spent a lot of the first couple of days just talking to them, especially when Dahy wasn't around, but then I really started to get into teaching. A lot of these kids were just bad, so I had to reach back into my memories to the basics that Dad had taught me when I was a kid. Back when I thought it was really cool being taught sword-fighting, as opposed to when I was a teenager and I thought Dad was a borderline lunatic. I found that the nice thing about teaching is that it makes you realise that a lot of the stuff you think you do by instinct and without thinking, is actually a well-honed skill. Dishing out all of this stuff to eager students, who were improving, made me appreciate my father even more and it gave me strength when I had to go back to the reading sessions.

I was usually so tired at night that I didn't have the energy to kick Brendan out of my tent – so we became roommates. He spent most of his days under the tutelage of Spideog. When no one else but me could hear, he made fun of his master's *mystical ravings*, but he listened and adopted every drop of archery advice he was given. When he wasn't talking about arrows and trajectories or how sore his arms and fingers were, he quizzed me on our progress towards finding a cure for Oisin. He never talked about his daughter. I suspected that the reason he had thrown himself so fully into training was to give himself something else to think about.

Mom gently kicked me awake at four in the morning. It was my shift in the reading room. Since Mom had the stint before me we saw each other every day at changeover. We didn't say much. I didn't ask her if she found anything 'cause I knew if she did, she would tell me. She looked tired as she handed me an envelope that had my handwriting on it. Inside it was a fragment of a document I had read the morning before about the cross-pollination of grape plants. I had entitled it, 'Everything will be Vine in the Morning'.

'Is that a joke?' she asked.

'Well, it was supposed to be but obviously it didn't work on you.'

She gave me that patronising mother look.

'Sorry, Mom, I'm just trying to keep my sanity in there.'

'I know, son,' she said as she cupped my cheek in her palm. 'Just have a little thought of the poor people who are going to have to sort this paperwork out after us.'

'OK,' I said, kissing her on the cheek, 'get some rest, you look beat.'

It was still dark when Mom and I got outside. The November air stung my cheeks as I walked her back to her tent. She promised me she would sleep and not sit up all night working and worrying. Then I turned and took a deep cold breath and steeled myself for an early morning adventure in dull literature. It was as bad as being back at school – worse actually; I didn't have Sally's notes to borrow here. As I groped in the dark towards the always lit reading room, a flicker of light caught my eye. As I got closer I saw it was the unmistakable glow of *Lampróg* light. My heart skipped a beat as I saw the only girl I know that travels with a firefly. As she heard me approach she cupped the bug in her hand but when she recognised me, she opened her fingers and bathed her face in light. Wow, Essa is beautiful in any light but she really is made for firefly light.

'What are you doing up?' she said, breaking the magical moment that was obviously playing out only in my head.

'I'm off to do my shift in the reading room. What are you doing up? Is the Turd-low snoring?'

'It's Turlow,' she said, 'and you only have to call him The Turlow at official functions.'

'Like your wedding?'

'Well, yes.'

'So are you really going to spend a lifetime with a snorer? You would think with all of the magic healing stuff around here they could cure that and you wouldn't have to be roaming around all night.'

'I'm not awake because of him. I'm not sleeping with him *and he's not a snorer*.' She was getting more flustered with every word.

'Why not? Oh no, is he diseased? These royal weddings are so treacherous.'

Essa threw both of her hands into the air. 'Why did you have to come back?' she hissed and stormed off, leaving her firefly fluttering around confused. I whispered, '*Lampróg*,' and it tentatively came and sat in the palm of my hand as quietly, in the darkness, I answered Essa's question, 'I came back for you.'

I bounced into the reading room with the echo of Essa saying 'I'm not sleeping with him' rolling around in my head. It wasn't until I placed the first piece of parchment into the Shadowreader that my spirits dipped. The Shadowbook was a collection of Leprechaun poetry. I had to stick it back in the pile – there was no way I was going to sift through poetry at this hour of the morning. The next piece caught my eye 'cause it was short and it had two names I recognised on it. It was a letter from Spideog to Dahy describing the last battle of Maeve's army in the Fili war.

Apparently the forces of the House of Duir were seriously getting their butts kicked by Maeve and the Fili. The Shadowmagic stuff was completely unknown to them and they found it impossible to defend against. After Maeve issued an ultimatum to Finn, which he refused, the Fili regrouped into one giant battalion with Maeve in the centre. Using several barrels of tree sap, the Fili queen conjured up some sort of spell. Everyone watching could feel the power of it building in the air and then, with a large flash of light that seemed to implode without a sound, the Fili were gone.

I always thought the Fili were killed but they just vanished. They left behind their clothes, weapons and every other earthly possession, but the Fili themselves had just disappeared. Spideog finished by writing, 'It was a blessing for The Land, my friend, but a personal disappointment for me. I would have liked to have taken a few Fili down before I died in battle.'

I could see now why my grandfather Finn had forbidden Shadowmagic – it had caused much hardship. Now, ironically, it was the only thing keeping my father alive.

The next slip of paper grabbed my attention; it was a thesis on sword parries and counter-attacks. I knew I would find it interesting and possibly very useful for my students but it wasn't going to get Dad healthy so I just skimmed it and stuffed it into an envelope. I wondered when I would have the leisure time to come back later and read it properly. With a little over an hour to go I found something else. I was pretty sure it had nothing in it that would help Dad but there was no way I was going to skip it. It was entitled: 'Banbha and The Turlow'.

THIRTEEN

THE GREY ONES

This manuscript was old and it certainly wasn't easy to decipher. I admit I started reading it just to get some dirt on Essa's Turdlow boy but I soon forgot all of that when I got into the meat of it. It was the story of the end of the first millennium, when the three sisters ruled The Land. The original Turlow went to Banbha and demanded to be allowed to return to the Otherworld. Banbha told him that leaving was impossible. She warned that the further any of them sailed from The Land, the faster they would age and die. The price of immortality, Banbha told Turlow, was that he and his kinsmen must remain in The Land.

Turlow refused to believe her and set sail for his long-lost homeland. But as he sailed away he and the members of his crew felt the effects of ageing in their bones. Their skin creased and when their hair began to grey, they turned back, daring to go no further. Turlow and his group, now called 'the Grey Ones', still did not give up searching for a way to leave Tir na Nog. A sorcerer atop Mount Cas told them of a creature called *tughe tine* whose blood could renew their youth and allow them to leave unharmed. Even though the sorcerer told them that getting this blood would be an extremely perilous undertaking, they swore that they would find it.

When Banbha heard of their quest she and her guard set out to stop them. Neither Banbha or her guard, nor Turlow and the Grey Ones were ever seen again.

I scoured my dictionaries and allowing for slight changes in spelling I translated *tughe tine* into 'red eel'.

I had been at this manuscript for well over my allotted time. Twice I told the Imp scholar who was scheduled for the slot after me to go away and have a cup of tea. When she came back a third time I could see she was just itching to get stuck into more gardening tips but I told her that I was keeping the Shadowreader and went in search of Mom.

I found her in the canteen sitting with Spideog. When she saw me holding a manuscript she stood. 'What have you found?'

I handed her the manuscript and gave them a brief summary of what I had discovered. It occurred to me that I might be telling a tale that everyone except me knew by heart but judging by the expressions on both of their faces, I was surprising them a bit.

When I had finished Mom said, 'I always suspected that my father had secret manuscripts that he only allowed certain people to see. I remember Banshees coming to the Hall and my father being very secretive with them. This story is amazing.'

'So you have never heard this before?'

'Well, I have heard of "the Grey Ones" of course but I assumed that that was just an old tale to warn us about going too far out in boats. I never heard that they were Banshees that wanted to leave. And there has never been an explanation as to why Banbha left.'

'How about this *tughe tine*?'

'I have never heard of it. Have you, Spideog?'

'No, my lady.'

'But if we could get some of this eel blood then it might reset Dad and the hand will stop killing him.'

'It's a very old manuscript and it doesn't even say if red eels exist. This is an exceptional find, my son, but I wouldn't get too excited.'

'What about this Mount Cas? We can at least check if this sorcerer guy is still there.'

'Conor, this was the first millennium, there will be no sorcerer there now.'

'Actually, my lady, that may not be entirely true.' Mom and I both snapped to attention as the old archer continued. 'The last time I saw Cialtie was not long after Oisin disappeared. I was travelling cross-country and at the base of Mount Cas I saw someone coming down from the mountain. I set camp and waited for the traveller, hoping to swap a meal for information about this mountain that I had never explored. As he approached I was very surprised indeed to find that it was Cialtie. The Prince accepted my hospitality but gave away little of what he was doing on the mountain except that he had been visiting a very old Oracle. A year later I travelled up Mount Cas in search of this man. About two thirds of the way up I found a house, made entirely out of yew wood, built into the mountainside. I knocked at the entrance but was told by a voice on the other side of the door that only those who are worthy receive an audience there. I left and never returned.'

'We should go,' I said, standing.

'Hold on, Conor,' Mom said. 'Let us stop and think about this.'

'What's to think about, Mom? We have been ploughing through these scraps of paper night and day for almost two weeks and what have we found – zip. This is our first good lead. Let me look into it. I'm going crazy around here. Please,' I said, sounding like a ten-year-old asking if he can go to the park by himself.

'It may be too late,' Spideog said.

'What do you mean?'

'Winter is close here but it may already have arrived on the mountain. The pass may be impassable.'

'Then we have to go now,' I said, getting to my feet. 'Mom, you said yourself that maybe the gods want me to find a cure for Dad, well maybe they wanted me to read this manuscript. Look, Mom, I don't want to defy you but I gotta talk to this Oracle guy.'

She stood and I braced myself. It's never a good idea to get into a conflict with my mother. She hugged me and said, 'Promise me you won't do anything foolish.'

'Who, me?' I said, flashing a House of Duir smile.

'And dress warm.'

*   *   *

Araf, Brendan, Spideog and I set off at dawn. It was freezing out but I didn't complain. I was excited to be doing something other than just reading. Brendan and I spent all of the previous night trying to borrow warm clothes off my students. I felt sorry for a few who gave us wool underwear. Tomorrow they would find out from Dahy that I didn't have the authority to give them vacation. I may have looked like I got dressed in total darkness but I was toasty. I tried to dissuade Brendan from coming, on the count that it might be too dangerous, but he insisted. 'I'll be right by your side,' he said. I was a touched by his loyalty until he continued, 'I go where Master Spideog goes.'

Dahy saw us off. Before I mounted Acorn he whispered in my ear, 'If you get into trouble, trust Spideog. He is arrogant and annoying and he talks nonsense and I really do not like him – but he is a good man under pressure.' He gave me a leg-up. As he guided my foot into the stirrup he lifted my trouser cuff and strapped a leather sheath, containing one of his knives, to my leg. Then he pulled down the cuff, patted my leg and winked at me. I saluted the Master with a nod of the head.

Araf and I wanted to bring half a dozen soldiers to help pitch tents and cook and maybe set up a base camp but Spideog said we had to travel light and fast. 'If we beat the snows it will only be by days,' he said, 'and it will be a good thing for you two princes to go without your handservants for a while.' Dahy was right – he was annoying.

We travelled hard and while the sun was in the sky we took no breaks. On the morning of the third day we saw the peak of Mount Cas. It looked close but it took two more days to get to its foothills. On the fifth day we found a field and set up a base camp where we left the horses to graze. After that we went on foot. It took a day to reach the base of the main peak and then another day of circling the mountain to find the trail up. The days were cold and the nights freezing but there was no imminent threat of snow. The night before we started our ascent Spideog disappeared and came back with a couple of pheasants that he had convinced to give up breathing so we could eat. There was little talk over dinner. Araf and Brendan turned in early but something in the old archer's eyes made me think that he was troubled, so I just sat with him by the fire and matched his silence. Finally he blurted out, 'I want to know why.'

I waited for him to say more but when he didn't, I asked, 'Why what?'

He didn't look at me; he just kept staring into the fire. 'Why I was unworthy.'

'Who says you are unworthy?'

He pointed up the mountain. 'The Oracle. The last time I was here he told me that I was unworthy. I didn't ask him why, I just accepted it. This time I want to know.'

'Well, I think it's probably 'cause he's nuts and has been breathing thin air for too long. One thing you are not is unworthy. Even Dahy respects you.'

He looked at me. 'How do you know that?'

'He told me.'

That brought a crooked smile to Spideog's face. 'It must have pained him to tell you that.'

I laughed. 'I think it did.' I stirred the fire with a stick and felt the extra warmth on my face. 'I found a letter of yours in the library.'

'Oh yes?'

'Yeah, it was a letter you wrote to Dahy after the Fili war.'

'Really? Oh, I think I remember someone collating material for some sort of an archive. Good gods, that was so many years ago.'

'It seemed to me that you and Dahy were friends.'

After a sigh he said, 'We were. More than just friends, we were comrades in arms.'

'What happened?'

'What else? A girl. I thought he stole her from me. He thought I stole her from him. In the end we fought. She said that she loved each of us equally and it was tearing her apart. She left us both and I disappeared into the Real World. Dahy always said he wasn't mad about the girl, he claimed he was really mad about me leaving my duties but that is a false memory on his part. It was the girl. I needed to get away from him but more importantly I needed to find some peace of mind. I went to the Real World which was a pretty barbaric place back then. I didn't discover what I was looking for until I travelled east. In Asia I found that *the answer lies within*, and as a bonus I learned their way of fighting. It was exciting and it changed my life. Everyone thinks that fighting is about brawn but in the east I learned that success in a battle comes from thinking.'

'Dahy says that you know.'

'I'm not surprised; Master Dahy is the most natural fighter I have ever known. He didn't have to study to be as good as he is.'

'It sounds to me that you two still like each other.'

'Maybe.'

'What happened to the girl?'

'She found another, a man better than both of us.'

'Well, I think you are both great men,' I said, standing. It was time for bed. 'It sounds to me that this two-timing woman screwed up a great friendship.'

Spideog rose, his face grimaced in the firelight. 'You really shouldn't speak that way about your grandmother.'

FOURTEEN

THE YEW HOUSE

Spideog would say no more that night. I went to bed trying to remember what Dad had told me about his mother. It wasn't much. He once told me that she left on a sorceress quest when he was still a baby and had never returned, but that was all I could recall. It was well into the next day, after the camp was packed and we were hiking up the trail, that I got a chance to speak to Spideog in private. It turned out that the love of his and Dahy's lives was indeed my grandmother, Macha the Sorceress Queen, the Horse Whisperer, Mother of the Twins of Macha – Dad and Cialtie.

'By the time I had come back from the Real World she had married Finn,' Spideog said.

'How did you deal with that?'

'I had found peace in Asia. She was my queen and Finn was my king – I re-entered into the service of the House of Duir.'

'But you never took a wife after her.'

'No,' he said. There was so much emotion in that one word I didn't have the heart to ask him any more.

The path up got steeper and narrower. By midday I was exhausted and ready to stop but Spideog was not a 'stopping for lunch' kind of guy. He was a 'one foot in front of the other' kind of guy. We walked into the night until we found a place where the trail widened enough to make camp. It was cold and windy but dry and we all went out like candles in a hurricane.

The trail got ledge-like on the morning of the second day. Around one bend a small stream had frozen where it crossed the path. It was nothing too dangerous but Spideog lashed us together with ropes. He said one can never be too careful and it would be disastrous if he lost one of the two princes, to which Brendan replied, 'What am I, chopped liver?' We camped well before dusk on the second day. I would like to think it was because Spideog's muscles were howling with the altitude and the cold as much as mine, but it was probably because we came onto a place that was wide enough for all of us to sleep safely.

It was not a comfortable night. The thin air meant that even though we had stopped climbing my legs still ached. We made a small fire to brew willow tea but we didn't have enough wood to build one for warmth. The wind whistled around so that we almost had to shout at each other.

I sat next to Brendan with my back against the mountain and said, 'Are you enjoying our vacation?'

He did a strange thing then, he turned completely away from me and presented his other ear and said, 'Say that again.'

So I did. 'Are you enjoying our vacation?'

He sat back down and asked me to say it again so I said it a third time.

'Well I'll be damned,' he said.

'What?'

'About five years ago I went to the rifle range to test some experimental ammunition. The officer in the firing stall next to me was a quick draw. I thought he was finished so I took off my ear protectors just as his gun misfired. I have only had about 20 per cent hearing in this ear ever since.'

'Sorry to hear that,' I said, wincing at my accidental pun.

'Don't be. The weird thing is, I can hear perfectly now. This place is astounding. If I wasn't so worried about my daughter and the junk my lunatic mother must be filling her head with, I'd think I was in paradise. I'm climbing a mountain without even breaking a sweat. Back home I could hardly walk up three flights of stairs without wheezing.

And my accuracy with a bow and arrow is almost better than with a gun. This place is amazing.'

'As I recall, I told you that a long time ago.'

'Well, I'm starting to believe you, Conor.'

After half an hour of walking on the third day of the climb, we spotted the Yew House above us. Five hours later and after completing almost two circumnavigations, the sun was high in the sky and I was actually working up a good sweat despite the cold. We came to a sharp bend in the path that was covered by another one of those frozen fords and Spideog once again made us rope-up and don crampons and ice picks. I remembered laughing at the old guy when he made us pack all of this stuff, but not now. The wet ice in the noonday sun would have been impossibly treacherous to traverse without crampons.

Spideog, in the lead, had just rounded the corner when his rope went slack. Then Brendan, in front of me, disappeared around the bend, stopped and said, 'Oh my.' Rounding the bend myself I saw what had stopped my fellow mountaineers. Standing on the path just past the ice floe were two tall thin men dressed in tight woolly brown tunics and trousers – Brownies. They stood there with one fist on their hip. They would have looked just like an illustration in an old copy of *Peter Pan*, if it wasn't for the cocked crossbows in their other hands.

Spideog spoke first. 'Greetings. We come to speak with the Master of the Yew House.'

The Brownies just stood there and grinned. I didn't like it. Neither did Spideog. He raised his voice and repeated himself. Still we got nothing from the skinny guys in brown.

Spideog planted his pick into the ice and unslung his bow from his back. He didn't notch an arrow in it but I've seen the master archer load a bow and it doesn't take him but a second. Brendan planted his pick into the floe, mirroring his tutor. I guess I could have just stood there but the others were slamming their picks into the ice, so I did too.

The crack started immediately. It moved like lightning from the point where my pick pierced the ice, to where Brendan's was planted, to past Spideog's feet. Then the rumble began as the entire ice sheet began to slide. I thought the whole mountain was about to collapse. Brendan went straight down on his nose. I managed to keep one crampon on the ice but had to go down on one knee. Spideog kept his footing and yelled, 'Run.'

I dug in my spikes and passed Brendan as he was trying to stand up. Spideog ran straight towards the Brownies, whom I expected at any second to shoot us but instead they just stood there looking bemused. I reached hard ice-free ground not long after the old guy. We both grabbed the rope attached to Brendan and dragged him to safety. I was just about to switch grips to the rope that went from me to Araf when I was pulled sideways off my feet and back onto the ice. As my head smacked onto the cold floor I saw the terrifying image of the Imp prince sliding off the side of the mountain. Araf let out a squeal like a little girl while I dug all ten of my fingernails into the frozen water desperately trying to get any purchase on the sliding ice.

The rope around my waist pushed all of the air out of my lungs as it pulled tight. Brendan and Spideog were on the hard ground and had a good hold of my rope but the pull from Araf's weight was almost cutting me in half. The ice sheet slid past me and rained down on my poor bodyguard. I could feel the impact of every block of ice as it smashed into the Imp, who grunted with every blow. I just hoped his rope would hold.

When the frozen waterfall finished the only bit of ice left on the trail was below me. I rolled to my left and planted my heels into the hard stone.

'Araf,' I yelled, 'are you all right?'

There was no answer for two long seconds then I heard him say, 'I would appreciate it, Conor, if you could pull me up from here.'

Apparently Araf's mother had told him to always be polite even when he was hanging off a fatal precipice attached to a bit of string.

After getting him on solid ground, Araf gave me an uncharacteristic emotional hug that made us both fall over. The two Brownies stared down at us with strange grins.

'Thanks for the help, boys,' I said. 'We couldn't have done it without you.'

That seemed to bemuse them and I made a mental note to leave sarcasm out of any future Brownie communications.

'Now,' I said, getting to my feet, 'I'd like to see this Oracle of yours.'

'Yes,' the taller of the two said, 'but will he want to see you?'

The Yew House was the most un-Tir na Nogian thing I had seen in The Land. The all-wood façade and shuttered windows made it look like some Malibu beach house you would see on a TV show about the rich and famous. The Brownies wordlessly escorted us onto the porch then told us to wait. Unlike a Californian beach house the porch didn't have any furniture so we sat on the steps. Ages later the Brownies re-emerged and one announced that only 'the Son of Duir' might enter.

I was tired and I had recently almost fallen off a cliff and these guys were starting to tick me off, so I didn't even stand up. I just said, 'Nope.'

The Brownie looked beyond confused. 'I do not understand,' he said.

'Either we all go in or we leave,' I said, standing.

Poor Brownie guy, he looked so befuddled I had an image of his head popping off his shoulders and a bunch of spring works and cogs shooting out of his neck. 'Only the Son of Duir,' he repeated.

'So be it; let's go, guys.' I turned and started down the mountain. My companions just stared at me.

'Are we playing a bit of poker here?' Brendan asked, in English.

'Of course,' I replied in the same language, 'you think I'm gonna hump all the way up this hill and not get any answers? Let's just see how much he wants to see me.'

Brendan nodded and put his arm on Spideog's and Araf's shoulders and said, 'All right, let's go.' The boys started to object, there is obviously no Texas Hold-em in The Land. Brendan pushed them off the porch, 'You heard the boss, come on.'

'Wait,' came a squeaky sound out of the Brownie, 'wait here.'

He scurried into the Yew House. I sat on the bottom step suppressing the impulse of making them chase us down the trail.

* * *

Ten minutes later I was still trying to explain to Araf the subtleties of bluffing.

'You mean lying,' he said.

'It's not lying, it's saying an untruth in order to make your opponent give in to you,' I expounded.

'It still sounds like lying.'

'Well, I think we should try a little poker, Araf. I bet you would be quite good at it.'

'I don't lie.'

'It's not lying, it's bluffing!'

Our Brownie messenger came onto the porch, saving Araf and me from going around that circle again. Now that he had new instructions he looked much more composed. 'You may all enter but only the Son of Duir may speak.'

I felt like saying no deal again and sending him back inside but it was getting cold. 'Is that all right with you guys?'

Brendan spoke in English again. 'If I want to say something once I get in there – who's gonna stop me?'

'My thoughts exactly,' I said. 'Spideog, are you OK with this?'

The archer nodded but I could see he didn't like it.

'Araf, do you think you can manage not talking for a while?' I smiled at him but he gave nothing back. You can always count on Araf.

I nodded to the Brownie, who looked very relieved that he didn't have to face his master again with a problem. He motioned for us to follow and pushed open the double doors. Two other Brownies were waiting inside the entrance of a surprisingly long hallway. They fell into step on either side of us. The Yew House it seems was just a front; the dwelling was carved directly into the mountain. As we walked, our footsteps echoed in the lengthy and increasingly dark corridor.

Brendan leaned over my shoulder and said, 'Well, Dorothy, what are *you* going to ask the wizard for?'

A large carving of Eioho, the Yew Rune, marked the end of the stone hallway. To the right a couple of Brownies opened two wooden doors and gestured for us to enter; they didn't follow and closed the doors behind us. It took a minute for my eyes to adjust to the light. The high vaulted ceiling had glass discs inset into the stone which put out as much light as any electric fixture in the Real World. The light bounced dramatically off the black seamless polished marble floors that I assumed to be the stone the mountain was made of. The walls were panelled with yew wood. Mom had told me about how difficult it was for her to earn the tiny wand she received from a yew tree – it made me wonder what kind of power the builder of this house must have. As my eyes adjusted I saw the Oracle in the centre of the room. He was seated in a huge chair, or I guess I should call it a throne, made from the severed trunk of a yew tree – its roots spread out at the bottom like the appendages of a starfish. The discs from the ceiling spewed tight beams of light all around but not directly on him. He wore plain black robes that rippled in the cool breeze. His face was illuminated from the reflection off the black marble. It gave the same appearance as when a boy scout puts a flashlight under his chin to tell a spooky story around a campfire. The room went on for a distance that I could not make out. No one spoke for ages.

I'm not good with uncomfortable silences, so I broke it. 'Nice digs you got here.'

'The Son of the One-Handed Prince,' he said in a whispery voice that seemed as if it was unused to speaking. 'I have heard about you.'

'What did you hear?'

'I have heard that you are impertinent.'

'Yeah, I get that a lot. Have you heard anything good about me?' There was no reply so I continued. 'By the way, I'm no longer the Son of the One-Handed Prince.'

'Are you saying Ona was wrong?'

'No, Ona's prophecy was spot on but it wasn't about me. It was about Fergal of Ur – Cialtie's son.'

'Cialtie has no son.'

For the first time I saw a movement in the back of the room. It was hard to see in this light but it looked like there was a hooded figure towards the back of it.

'Well, if that's what he told you – he lied. I was there when Cialtie met his son, I was there when he killed him and I was definitely there when my uncle lost his hand.'

The Oracle leaned forward on his throne. The change in light allowed me to see him more clearly. He was old. Not decrepit old but at least young grandfather old, with lines on his face and silver hair that blew in the wind, like a singer in a Bollywood music video. For The Land this guy looked ancient. He also looked scarily crazy. He leaned back into the gloom and said, 'You came all of this way to bring me this news?'

'No,' I said. 'I know that you helped Cialtie retake his Choosing with my father's hand.'

This startled the old guy. 'He told you that?'

'No,' I said quickly, sensing that it was a bad idea to get this guy agitated. 'I did the math. Spideog saw Cialtie coming down from this mountain just before he retook his Choosing. Since no one in The Land knows how he did this, it stands to reason that you advised him.'

A smile came to his face that in the light sent a shiver down my spine. 'So you came to prove that you are clever as well as impertinent?'

'No, sir, I came to ask if you would help my father.'

'Why has he not come himself?'

'He's dying. His new hand and his body are in conflict. It is killing him.'

'Your trip is wasted then, Conor of Duir. I would have no idea how to save him from such a singular malady – no one in The Land would.'

'I'm not looking for a cure, sir, only directions.'

'Directions?' He looked confused but interested. 'Directions to where?'

'To where I can find the blood of a *tughe tine*.'

You would think that a wise old oracle would have a better poker face, but when he heard this he definitely twitched before he regained his composure. 'I'm sorry you wasted a trip but I know nothing of the place of which you speak.'

'I think you do.'

'You have charm, young prince, that has allowed me to forgive your impertinence but my patience is running thin.'

'The first Turlow came to you for the same advice. You told the Grey Ones how to find it.'

The Oracle threw his head back and laughed. As he did I noticed the hooded person, who had been lurking in the shadows the entire time, running out of the back of the room.

'You climbed all of this way to quote a nursery rhyme intended to keep children out of the sea? I am weary. Leave.'

'No,' came a voice from behind me. It was Brendan.

'You were instructed not to speak, Druid,' the Oracle hissed in a way that made me think that maybe we all should calm down.

'I'm not a Druid, I'm a policeman.'

'And what is a policeman?'

'I am – a seeker of truth and I don't believe you when you say you don't—'

It was just a flick of the Oracle's wrist but Brendan went over like he had been slugged by a heavyweight. Spideog pulled his bow off his shoulder and was just reaching for an arrow when his bowstring snapped and sliced a gash in his face. Then his bow exploded as he was thrown twenty yards into the air before backsliding along the polished floor into the wall.

A loud gale of wind whipped around the room. Araf and I looked at each other and wordlessly decided to get the hell out of there. It's a good thing Araf doesn't speak often 'cause I had a gut feeling that the next guy that lipped off to the Oracle was going to have his head exploded.

The Imp hoisted the unconscious Brendan on his shoulder and we both backed out of the room. 'Sorry to bother you,' I shouted as complacently as I could, 'and thanks for your help. We gotta be going now.' When I got to Spideog, I unceremoniously grabbed him by the sleeve and dragged him out. We pushed through the exit expecting to be clobbered at any minute. As the doors slammed shut I could have sworn I heard laughter coming from within. The Oracle was definitely off my Christmas card list.

The Brownies on the other side of the doors were beside themselves with terror. They buzzed around, high stepping like little kids in need of a pee.

'What did you say to him?' one asked. I ignored him while I loosened Spideog's neckerchief.

Brendan croaked, 'What happened?' and Araf gently placed him back on his feet.

'I'll explain later. Right now I think we should get out of here.'

I held my ear against Spideog's mouth – he was still breathing. 'Araf, can we swap invalids?' I went over and steadied Brendan while Araf hoisted the old archer on his shoulder like he was a sack of ping-pong balls. Spideog grunted, which I took as a good sign.

The long corridor was longer on the way out. Brownies flitted around telling us to hurry while constantly looking over their shoulders, which was as annoying as it sounds. Brendan got steadier on his feet as we went and was almost walking under his own steam by the time we reached the doors to the outside. It had begun to snow. Araf gently placed Spideog on the porch and the Brownies freaked.

'No, no, you must go. Go now,' the tallest one of them shrieked at us and picked up one of the packs that we had left outside the doors and threw it down the steps. When he reached for my pack I kinda lost it and grabbed him by the throat and pinned him against the wall.

'We have an injured man here. We will go when we are ready.'

The other Brownies didn't come to their comrade's aid but huddled together shrieking. The guy I had by the neck didn't struggle; he just looked at me with puppy-dog eyes and said, 'Please go.'

It was then that I saw that all of their earlier bravado was just that. Talk about bluffing. These guys lived under the servitude of a nasty piece of work who they were terrified of. I let the Brownie go and said, 'Sorry, we'll be as quick as we can.'

'Araf,' I said, 'these guys are annoying but they are also right. Can we move him?'

'He is still unconscious, but I agree. I think we should at least put a wee bit of this mountain between us and this place.'

Brendan tried to pick up a pack and almost fell over, so I assembled all four packs comically on my back while Araf rehoisted Spideog.

Halfway down the trail I looked back. About six Brownies were standing on the porch. They were a pathetic bunch. 'Come with us,' I mimed to them, not daring to shout. The five at the back rocked on their legs uncomfortably. The tall guy at the front just shook his head, no, and with a sad smile waved goodbye.

As I was turning back, I saw out of the corner of my eye an upstairs shutter open and the flash of a hooded black-robed figure throwing something. Even if I hadn't had four packs on my back, I don't think I could have stopped the knife from hitting Brendan square between the shoulder blades.

FIFTEEN

BROKEN BOW

Brendan went down from the force of the impact as the knife bounced off his back. The blade was still in its sheath. I jumped recklessly towards the edge of the cliff trying to catch it before it went over but the knife spun off into the void. The weight of the packs on my back meant that I almost followed it.

I slithered back from the edge and went to Brendan, who groaned, 'Son of a …'

'Are you OK?'

'What the hell hit me?'

I didn't feel like explaining – I just wanted to get out of there, so I said, 'One of those Brownies must have thrown something.'

'Well, it hurt. Would I be overreacting if I shot one with an arrow?'

'Yes.'

'Even if it was just in the leg?'

'Yes. Come on, we have to get out of here.'

I tried to help him to his feet but with four packs on my back there wasn't that much I could do. We skirted around the corner and found Araf waiting for us with Spideog still out cold on his shoulder. Even though the ice sheet that had almost killed us earlier was mostly not there any more, Araf suggested we rope-up, and I agreed with him. As the snow started to come down harder and the wind picked up, I fantasised about starting a Real World/Land smuggling operation. The first thing I would import was thermal underwear.

We made it all the way around the mountain. I called a halt just before we came to the part of the path where we could be seen by the Yew House above. Araf didn't argue with me. I was exhausted walking with the packs and Araf must have been shattered carrying a man on his shoulder. I got a fire going with some kindling I found in Spideog's bag, brewed up some willow tea and got some into the injured archer. It did the trick.

'Where is my bow?'

'Take it easy, Spideog. Don't try to talk.'

The old guy grabbed my shoulder and opened his eyes. 'My bow, where is it?'

'Rest,' I said.

'Tell him,' Brendan said.

'You tell him.'

'I was out cold. If you know what happened to his bow then tell him.'

'My bow,' Spideog said, trying to get to his feet, 'I must go back for it.'

'Wooh, big guy, you are in no fit shape to go anywhere. Your bow is gone. The Oracle trashed it.'

'What do you mean trashed it? You mean he took it.'

'No, sir, it's trashed, destroyed. He waved his hand and it exploded into splinters.'

'That is not possible,' he said, grabbing me by my coat. 'You lie.'

Araf reached over and gently took his hand from my lapel. 'It is true, Master. I saw it with my own eyes. This fell from your clothing when I first put you down.' Araf handed him a splintered piece of yew wood.

He took it and began to cry. 'It is true,' he moaned, 'I am not worthy.'

It was hard to watch a man so strong look so defeated. I rummaged through the bags until I found the flask of poteen that my mother had given me before we left and administered some to the unresisting archer. Brendan held him until he slipped back into unconsciousness.

Araf and I debated how long we should rest. I thought it would be a good idea to wait until dark before we entered the part of the path that exposed us to attack from the Yew House above, but Araf thought we should get going before the snow got so bad that we all just slipped off the side of the mountain. I agreed with him when I realised I could no longer feel my toes.

I didn't even bother to look up when we were in sight of the Yew House. I figured it wouldn't take much to take us out and if it came, I didn't really want to see it coming. Despite our fears, we passed unmolested. We donned crampons when we reached the ice ford we had crossed earlier. The snow on the other side was starting to drift so we tried keeping our crampons on but there wasn't enough snow for that. Crampons are great on ice and packed snow but on solid rock they just make your footing worse. Saying that, when we took them off we still slipped all over the place. After Brendan went down and almost slipped off the side, we all put a single crampon on one foot. We marched through the night limping like the winning team at a shin-kicking competition.

Three quarters of the way down the mountain the snow turned to rain. Wool and rain are not a good mix. It made me feel sorry for sheep. We found a wide and almost sheltered part of the path and camped for what remained of the night. The tea and stale rations did nothing to lift our mood. I had a feeling only a hot bath and a dry change of clothes could do that for me and I wasn't sure if Spideog would ever recover.

Spideog mumbled in his sleep at first but then like the rest of us settled down until awakened by a damp dawn. Brendan shook me awake from what was becoming a recurring dream of Essa holding hands with an invisible man. What did that dream mean? Was the invisible man supposed to be me?

The fog was so bad that dawn was almost unnoticeable; the view seemed as if we were looking at a white sheet. It was damp cold and the squelching noise my trousers made as I got up cemented my misery.

Spideog was up and on his feet. He walked like a man in a trance. Without a word he began to break camp so we followed suit and then trekked after him down the mountain.

'Has he said anything?' I whispered to Brendan.

'Not a word,' he replied behind his hand. 'He just got up and got going. Are you going to say anything to him?'

'I'm not going to talk to him – you talk to him.'

'I'm not talking to him.'

We both looked to Araf.

'I don't say anything to anybody,' the Imp mumbled. 'I am not starting now.'

We followed the silent archer down the mountain. For a guy who had just been pulverised by an evil warlock he set a pretty crisp pace.

You would think that going downhill would be easier than uphill and you would be right, but not by as much as you would think. My calf muscles screamed with the effort it took to stop me from becoming a runaway teen.

It was nightfall by the time we reached the base of the mountain. I suggested to Spideog that he should get some rest, but he looked at me like I had just stomped on his puppy and disappeared into the forest. By the time he had returned with wood and a rabbit, Araf had the beginnings of a fire going. Brendan and I put up a very flimsy lean-to to keep off the rain. Together we ate in silence, none of us daring to speak for fear of being killed by the archer's evil eye. When he finished eating and started to set up a bedroll I bravely said, 'Thank you, Spideog, the meal was lovely.'

He didn't even acknowledge my presence.

Brendan, Araf and I sat around the fire staring at each other for a while. Each waited for the other to speak but none of us wanted to break the vow of silence that the old man seemed to have imposed on the group. We bedded down. Ah, there is nothing like sliding between two wet blankets, in your wet clothes, as the rain leaks onto your head.

Spideog seemed to be as broken as his bow. As the old song says, you don't know what you got till it's gone, and losing the courage and the sureness of our leader was unnerving – scary. I lay there and mixed all of my troubles together, letting them roll down the mountain of my mind like a giant snowball: I was cold and wet, my father was dying and this trip was a complete failure and then there was Essa. I had been trying to avoid thinking about her. I had been trying to cover over my hurt with bravado, but hurt I was. She didn't wait for me. She didn't wait for me.

'Why would she?' replied Araf, who was lying next to me.

'What?'

'You are talking about Essa, yes?'

'Oh, sorry, Araf, I didn't realise I was speaking out loud.'

'Oh dear, that's not a good sign.'

'Do you know him?' I asked.

'Who?'

'The Banshee she's marrying.'

'Of course,' the Imp replied, 'He is The Turlow.'

'Is he a good guy?'

'What is a "good guy", Conor? You are speaking in a Real World tongue – also not a good sign.'

'Sorry,' I said. 'Is he a good man?'

'The few dealings I have had with him have been favourable. Many like him. Some do not, but that is the price you pay when you are a leader.'

'Everybody likes you, Araf,' I said as I playfully kicked him in the back.

'Ah well, I *am* special.'

No matter how low I was I had to laugh at that. Araf cracks so few jokes that ignoring one would be a crime.

'Well, I don't like him.'

'And why do you think that is?' inquired Araf. 'Could it be you don't like him because Essa does?'

'No, that's not why. Well, it's not entirely why. I don't like the way he talks to her. It makes me want to throw up. And he called me a Faerie.'

'What is wrong with that?'

'Well, how would you like it if he called you a Faerie?'

'I would think it strange considering I am an Imp, but why would you object?'

'Are you calling me a Faerie?'

'Why wouldn't I?' Araf said, sounding a bit confused.

'Because I'm not a Faerie.'

'Yes you are, Conor. Surely you knew that? I am an Imp, Turlow is a Banshee and you, Essa, Gerard and Spideog are Faeries.'

'No.'

'Yes.'

'That's just great – a perfect ending to a perfect day.'

I dropped my head back onto my soggy pillow and thought, *well at least I couldn't get much lower* – but then I had another thought.

'Araf,' I called out into the damp dark, 'would I be correct in assuming that I am the Prince of All the Faeries?'

'Of course.'

'Great,' I said, as my head sloshed on my pillow, 'just great.'

Acorn woke me with a head butt and a snort just before dawn. The previous night I had asked Araf where the horses were and he said, 'They will be here.' He was so casual about it I believed him and, sure enough, there they were. I got up – there is no point in staying in a bed when it's cold and damp. Spideog was up too. He had rekindled the fire and was going through the packs.

'I am only taking the bare necessities,' he said without greeting me. 'You three will have plenty of supplies for the rest of the journey.'

'What do you mean you three?'

'I must face the yews,' Spideog said.

'You're leaving us?' I said, loud enough to disturb the others.

He ignored me and continued to pack.

'How will we get back?'

'Travel that way,' he said, pointing, 'and stop when you see oak trees.'

Brendan came up and crouched down next to Spideog. 'Master,' he said, 'I'll go with you.'

'No,' he said in a tone that made it clear that this was not up for discussion.

Still Brendan persisted. 'You can't go alone.'

'I said NO!' the old man shouted, then calmed himself. 'Your party needs an archer.'

Brendan stood and chuckled. 'These two? Araf and Conor will be fine on their own. You are the one I am worried about. You are still weak from your fight. I can help you.'

Spideog stood, turned and with the speed of a striking snake grabbed the detective by his lapels. He had a mad look in his eyes. 'I'm going to face the yews. Do you not understand? I'm going to be judged. I'm going to be judged – again. I'm going to tell the yews that I lost my bow. They are … they are going to kill me.' He let go of Brendan and turned his back on all of us, his head bowed.

'Do not go,' Araf said.

'That would be like asking you not to dig in the ground, Imp. I am an archer, I am Spideog the Archer. To be without a bow would be like being a bear without claws.'

He picked up his pack and set off without looking back.

I ran in front of him. 'Wait a second, you can't go to the Yewlands unarmed.' I reached into my sock and presented him with my knife.

He stared at it and said, 'Do you really think Dahy would want me to have his knife?'

'I know he would.'

As he took it Brendan shouted, 'Master Spideog!'

With a sigh he turned. Brendan was standing at attention. 'You, sir, are the most worthy man I have ever met. Let no man – or tree – tell you otherwise,' and then he saluted.

Spideog stood stock still like he had been slapped, then nodded and turned.

We watched as he faded into the morning mist. When at last he disappeared I said, 'Anybody know the way home?'

SIXTEEN
THE GREEN KNIFE

After getting our butts handed to us good by Mr Yew House we had no other choice but to go home with our tails between our legs. We didn't talk much on the way back. The rain had given way to a wet fog. What my father would have called 'a little mist in the air'. If I had been driving a car I would have had to turn on the windscreen wipers every couple of minutes. We rode in silence while I fantasised about being in a limo with the heat turned up full.

We skirted around Mount Cas hoping to see a familiar landmark. Losing a guide is not a comforting thing. It's only after the guide is gone that you realise you should have paid more attention during the outbound journey. The other problem was how quickly winter had set in. During the trip out, The Land was still vibrant with the colours of fall, but in just the short time that we had been on the mountain everything seemed to have turned brown and grey. Araf remembered that we had approached the mountain perpendicular to a sheer cliff face. Brendan and I said we remembered that too but I think the cop was faking it – I know I was.

I did remember the cliffs when we got to them but I wasn't as confident as Araf when we turned right. I looked to Brendan for confirmation but he just shrugged. That made it official – Araf had become the new guide. I took one last glance behind me – trying to calm the growing fear that I would soon be spending forty days and forty nights lost in a wet/ frozen wilderness – when I saw a speck of green. I would have missed it if it had been summer but among the decomposing colours of winter something stood out. I walked Acorn back to the bottom of the cliff and dismounted. It was the sheathed knife that had hit Brendan in the back.

As soon as I picked it up I saw that it was a beautiful thing. The handle was made of green glass with a spiral of gold wire embedded in it. I untied the leather strap that attached the sheath to the hand-guard and studied the blade. It looked like one of Dahy's throwing blades complete with the golden tip. When I replaced the cover I noticed a piece of paper stuffed inside and fished it out. The message, written in haste on a crumpled piece of parchment, read, 'The changelings have the answers you seek.' It was not signed.

I stowed the dagger under my coat, remounted and hurried to catch up with Araf and Brendan. I tried to tell Araf about the knife but he was trying to concentrate on the path home and told me to shut up.

I said, 'If you are going to be like that, I'm not going to show you the neat thing I found.'

How he ignored me after that I don't know but he did. So Acorn and I fell in behind him and spent the rest of the day concentrating on being cold and wet.

That night I went for firewood. It's easy getting wood in the winter. In the summer the trees are chatty and want to know why you are in their forest and where you are going but in the winter they are groggy and just want you to leave them alone. They pretty much say the tree equivalent of, 'Yeah, yeah, just take some wood and stop bothering me.'

When I mentioned this to Brendan he loped off into the dark and came back with a ton of logs. He heaped my modest little blaze into a full-blown bonfire. Then he made tepees out of lean branches and shocked Araf and me by stripping off.

The very naked Brendan placed all of his clothes and his bedding on the tepees to dry and shouted, 'I am sick and tired of being wet and cold,' then he started jumping up and down like a lunatic.

Araf and I watched – keeping our gaze as high as possible – as our companion enthusiastically lost his marbles. He danced and chanted, and before long Araf and I were mesmerised and laughing.

'You got to try this, it's great,' Brendan said as he dashed stark naked into the frozen night. Araf and I were just about to go and find him when he returned shivering and blue. He threw a stack of thin branches at us and recommenced his dance – dangerously close to the fire.

Araf stood up, made a tripod of branches and took off his overcoat.

'You're not gonna join him?' I said.

'I too am very tired of being wet,' the Imp replied.

I sat in terror as I watched a naked Brendan teach an equally naked Araf how to prance around a fire like a Native American chief. When I could watch no longer I decided to go to bed but when I stretched out my damp sleeping roll I thought, *aw, what the hell*. I wouldn't have believed it if I hadn't done it myself but I got to tell you – if you ever get a chance to dance naked around a bonfire in the middle of the winter with a cop and an Imp – don't knock it until you've tried it. Once you get started you just have to keep going. Spinning is important, 'cause one side is burning while the other side is freezing. After a while the whole world goes away and only the dance and the fire remain. We kept going late into the night and then collapsed into our sleeping rolls and slept like babies – like dry, warm babies.

The next day there was no mention of the night before, but we were certainly happier travellers. For years wise men have searched for the meaning of life; they should ask me because I found it – it's dry clothes. Now that I was unmiserable in the saddle, I was free to admire the stark beauty of The Land in winter. Many of the trees in Tir na Nog are so lush that seeing any distance is impossible but now only spooky skeletal frameworks of trees broke my view to the horizon. It was beautiful but also unsettling and made me wish all the more for a roof and a fire.

There was no fire dancing that night. If someone had suggested it I would have been up for it but I guess too much naked fire dancing is a bit weird. After a trout supper, I finally got to tell my companions about the knife.

'You are telling me those Brownies didn't throw a rock at me,' Brendan said. 'They threw a knife? You should have let me shoot them.'

'It was a sheathed knife and it wasn't the Brownies.'

'Then who threw it?' Araf asked.

'When we were in the room with the Oracle,' I said, 'do you remember a hooded figure in the shadows?'

'To be honest, Conor,' Brendan said, 'I don't remember much of my time in there. I got clocked pretty good.'

'I saw him,' Araf said.

'Well, I got a quick glance at the person who threw the knife and he was wearing a black hood. I think it was the same guy.'

'But why would someone throw a sheathed knife?' Araf asked.

'It was an envelope. I found this inside.' I took out the message and handed it around.

'What is a changeling?' Brendan asked.

'I don't know. Araf?'

'It's a very old term. When I was young and growing up in the Heatherlands my nanny Breithe used to use the name changeling when she told stories about the Pookas. They are beings that can change into animal form at will.'

'Yeah, I saw one do it once,' I said. 'OK then – where can I find a Pooka?'

'That might prove difficult,' Araf said. 'No one has seen a Pooka since before the Battle of the Twins of Macha. Your father was about to set up an expedition to the Pinelands just before he became ill.'

'Well, then it looks like I'll have to go there. Where is it?'

'I would have no idea how to get to the Pinelands,' Araf said.

'I bet my mother would know. She had a Pooka tutor.'

'She might. She is the only one ever to be schooled by a Pooka. They are a very secretive race. How your grandfather Liam persuaded the Pookas to provide a teacher for his daughter I have no idea.'

'Then let's get back to the Hall of Knowledge and ask her. Araf, are you certain we are going the right way?'

'Certain is a very strong word, Conor.'

'Well, that fills me with confidence,' Brendan said.

'Hey, look on the bright side,' I said, 'we may get so lost we find the Pinelands by accident.'

*   *   *

Araf was being unduly modest. Without one wrong step we reached the edge of the Hazellands two days later. It was just starting to get dark when we reached the outer structures of the Hall of Knowledge. Just past the first outbuilding, two Imp sentries jumped from out of nowhere with their crossbows cocked. I was tired and cold and hungry but, worst of all, I smelled really bad.

'The only way,' I said with a large outlet of air, 'you guys are going to stop me from getting a cup of willow tea is to shoot me.'

'Stand down, Imps,' is all Araf had to say and they lowered their weapons.

'Prince Araf and Prince Conor,' the sentry said, doing a bowing thing, 'Lady Deirdre and Lady Nieve have instructed us to keep a watch out for you.'

'Lady Nieve is here?'

'Yes, sirs; she arrived yesterday.'

'Go back to your posts.'

The soldiers snapped-to and double-timed it back to their hiding places.

We cantered into camp. I wanted to gallop – I really needed a bath.

The bath was obviously going to have to wait. Mom was waiting for us outside the library and she wasn't in a hospitable mood. She rudely dismissed Araf and Brendan in a very queen-like fashion. I was jealous – I would have loved to have been dismissed.

'Did you learn anything?' she asked even before I entered the room. 'Where is Spideog?'

'Hi, Mom, I'm fine, knackered but fine – oh yes I'd love a cup,' I said in one breath, as I kissed Mom.

'Hello, Auntie,' I said, planting a kiss on her cheek as I passed.

I collapsed on a sofa. The two of them stood in front of me like I was in trouble. I expected them to accuse me of nicking mead out of the pantry.

'What?'

'Oisin is getting worse,' Nieve said as Mom looked away.

I didn't jump up or shout – I just dropped my head in my hand and rubbed my eyes. Of course Dad was getting worse. Nothing, and I mean nothing, had gone right since I had gotten back to The Land – I should have expected this. I clamped my molars together to stop a flow of tears. 'Fand said he could stay like that for ever.'

'We thought he could. No one has ever frozen a person in Shadowmagic before.'

'How bad is he?'

Mom came over and hugged me. 'Not too bad,' she said. 'It is very slow. It took Fand this long to notice anything at all but it means that our time is not infinite. We need to find a cure.'

'Have you found anything in the *Shadowbooks* since I've been away?'

Mom shook her head, an exhausted *No*. 'What have you learned?'

I told Mom the whole story of our *welcome* at the Yew House, and the loss of Spideog. I left out the part about almost slipping off the edge of a cliff to our deaths so as not to unduly worry her. Finally I showed her the knife and the message that was within it.

Mom examined the knife in silence for a long time and then handed it to Nieve. Finally Mom straightened up and with the same queenly conviction that she had shown my companions earlier, said, 'You leave for the Pinelands tomorrow.'

I instantly changed from a son to a loyal subject. I stood, said, 'Yes, ma'am,' then hugged her.

On the way out the door Nieve pointed out that I could use a bath.

SEVENTEEN
POP-HEAD

When I first came to The Land the dreams completely freaked me out, which was understandable. I never had a dream until I came to Tir na Nog. When I found out that dreams often gave me glimpses into the future I thought they were cool, but since I have discovered that a lot of dreams are just jumbled images of stuff that's rattling around in my noggin, they're starting to really annoy me. That night I dreamt about the usual stuff: Dad encased in amber, Essa walking with the invisible man, and of course the perennial favourite of Fergal with a Banshee blade sticking out of his chest. But then there were others that I couldn't begin to figure out. One was of a bear that then turned into a fox that then turned into an eagle. And then there was a rowboat that rowed itself to the shore where Cialtie was waiting for it. What the heck was that all about? The other problem is that sometimes the dreams get so intense that I wake up less rested than when I went to bed.

As if the dreams weren't exhausting enough, Mom woke me before dawn. 'Get up,' she said, shaking me, 'get up now if you want time for breakfast before you leave for the Pinelands.'

'Oh no,' I said, shaking the visions out of my head, 'I haven't had a bath yet.'

'There is no time for that,' she said, turning to go. 'Your party is preparing to leave now.'

I got up with only my blanket wrapped around me and ran to the bath house just in time to see Brendan leaving damp and happy. He was still steaming.

'Good morning, Conor,' he said, rubbing his hair with a towel. 'Man, I can't tell you how good a hot bath feels.'

I pushed past him. The Leprechaun that runs the bath house spotted me and said, 'Oh, I didn't know there was going to be anyone else this morning. I'll have some more hot water in an hour.'

I ran back to my tent and got dressed. I was going to have my breakfast and then a bath and there was no power in The Land that was going to stop me.

Brendan was the only person in the canteen that I recognised. I got some food and sat down next to him.

'How come you had a bath so early this morning?'

'Araf, your mother and molten gold lady—'

'Auntie Nieve.'

'Yeah her. They had a meeting last night. After the meeting Araf told me that you were going to the Pinelands this morning. So I got up early to be ready.'

'Why didn't you tell me?'

'You were asleep. What was I supposed to do, wake you up and tell you to have a bath?'

'YES.'

'OK,' the cop said, taking out an imaginary notepad and pen, 'let me just note that down for next time.'

'Do you know what is going on?'

'No, your mother still doesn't seem to like me that much. I tried to go to the meeting with Araf but she wouldn't let me in.'

Mom appeared just as I was finishing breakfast.

'Come, Conor.'

'Sorry, Mom, I'm off to have a bath.'

'This is more important.'

'I beg to differ,' I said but followed her anyway.

Brendan fell into step next to me. When Mom gave him a dirty look I said, 'How many times do I have to tell you that he is with me?'

She backed down and I wondered if I had picked the wrong battle to win with my mother. I'd ditch Brendan in a second if it meant I could soak under some warm suds.

Araf and Nieve were mounted up when I got to the corral. 'Have you ever been on time?' Nieve asked.

'On time? On time for what?'

Brendan brought out Acorn and Cloud and handed me Acorn's reins. He was saddled and packed with full supplies.

Mom slid the strap of a full satchel on my shoulder.

'You looked so tired last night I had my men pack some warm clothes for you while I let you sleep.'

'Mom, it's not sleep I needed – it's a bath.'

'You should have thought of that earlier,' said a voice using a familiar tone. There behind me was Essa, dressed, mounted and ready to go. 'If you think we are going to wait while you lounge under hot water – you have another thought coming.'

I turned back to Mom. 'Essa?'

'Essa is your guide.'

'I thought you were coming.'

'I'm needed here. I'm still not convinced any good will come of this expedition. I'm staying and continuing the research. Also, I do not wish to stray too far from Castle Duir, in case … well, just in case.'

'OK, but Essa?'

'Essa has journeyed to the Pinelands before. She is one of the few people who ever has. You are lucky to have her.'

I looked at my party mounted up and waiting for me and nodded.

'Be careful, it is wild in the Pinelands at the best of times,' Mom said. 'No one has returned from that part of The Land in a long time – I have no idea what conditions are like.'

Mom handed me a muslin-wrapped parcel. 'Rhiannon is Queen of the Pookas – or at least she was the last time anyone was there. Give her this.'

'What is it?'

'It is the first of the hazelnuts from your new Tree of Knowledge. My father sent a regular supply of hazelnuts to the Pinelands. My Pooka tutor once told me that that was the reason Queen Rhiannon agreed to send her to teach me. Remember, son, never look at an amorphous Pooka in the eye – it can antagonise their animal self. And always look a Pooka directly in the eyes when they change back.'

'Why?'

'Because they will be naked.'

'Oh yeah.'

I hugged her.

'Go,' she said, pushing me away. 'You are losing sunlight.'

As I walked towards Acorn I felt a slap on my back. I turned to see Turlow dressed in shiny black leather. He put his arm around me.

'Ah, Faerie prince, I'm looking forward to getting acquainted with you on this adventure.'

'You're coming with us?'

'I travel with my betrothed,' he said.

'Great,' I said with as much enthusiasm as I could muster – which wasn't much.

Just before I mounted up, Turlow looked over his shoulder and placed his face close to mine. In a conspiratorial whisper he said, 'I don't want to embarrass you in front of the others, Conor. But from one royal to another, I'd like to give you a piece of advice.'

'What's that?'

'Well, my friend,' he said, 'you could really use a bath.'

People always complain about winter but not me. I like winter or, I should say, I used to. What I used to like about winter was the indoor stuff: the crackling warm fires, hearty soups and stews, and cosy quilts. This travelling around outside on horseback in the winter is for the birds. I take that back – even the birds have enough sense to fly someplace warm in the winter. Saying that, if I had to be outside this time of year it might as well have been on a day like this one. It was glorious – sharp, cold, with bright sunshine pouring from an indigo-blue sky. Mom had packed me a fox fur hat and mittens that kept my ears and fingers toasty warm. If only I had a pair of cool Rayban sunglasses I would have been perfectly contented to be out in the elements.

This was not a Sunday afternoon jaunt to visit Mother Oak – we had serious distance to cover. Essa set a near brutal pace that meant leisurely chats on horseback were out. Not that a private chat with Essa would have been possible anyway. The Turd-low stuck to her side like a duckling to its mother. Even during the infrequent short rests, he was attached to her like a burr. It made me think that she really must like him, 'cause if I crowded Essa that much I'd probably be bleeding before not very long.

On the first night I went to bed immediately after dinner. I said I was tired but the truth of it was that I just couldn't stand to watch the two of them snuggled up together in the firelight.

I awoke the next morning and thought I had gone blind overnight. Fog had crept in that was so thick I literally couldn't see my hand in front of my face. When The Land does weather, it doesn't do it in halves. It made me hope that we would avoid snow on this trip. At breakfast I spoke to Brendan and asked him to strike up a conversation with Turlow sometime during the day so I could have a chat with Essa. He said he would and added that he would also pass a note to her in the playground, if I wanted him to.

The morning ride was so slow that we might as well have been walking. It wasn't until an hour before noon that the fog lifted enough so that we could at least canter without braining ourselves on trees. Turlow dropped back and said that Essa wanted to talk to me. It looked like Brendan wouldn't have to make forced small talk after all.

When I pulled up next to Essa she said, 'So what do you want to talk to me about?'

'I thought you wanted to talk to me?'

'Turlow told me that you asked Brendan to distract him so you could talk to me in private.'

'Oh, he heard that, did he?'

'That is what he told me. So what is so important?'

'Nothing's important, I just wanted to … you know, talk.'

'About what?'

'I don't know; maybe about how come you got engaged in like three months?'

'That's what you wanted to talk about?'

It wasn't – well, it was, but it was stupid to use it as an opening conversational gambit but since I started, I just ploughed on. 'It's as good a topic as any.'

'And I have to justify my actions to you – why?' she said in a tone that made me realise that we were probably going down a conversational cul-de-sac.

'You don't have to justify anything. I just think it's strange that you went all bridal so soon after my departure.'

'Let me get this straight – you think that my getting engaged is because I couldn't have you?'

'Well, I wouldn't put it like that but …'

'Don't even think about finishing that sentence,' she hissed. 'You are the most arrogant, pop-headed imbecile I have ever met.'

'Pop-headed?'

'Do you have anything else to discuss?'

'Yeah, what does pop-headed mean?'

She made that exasperated Essa noise that she frequently makes just before she pummels you. 'You are dismissed,' she said.

Now I wasn't really into continuing this stupid argument, or getting pummelled for that matter, but I was not about to be sent away like a lackey. Thinking about it, I wouldn't even be that rude to a lackey – and I don't even know what a lackey is.

'Dismissed! You are dismissing me? Oh thank you, Your Royal Highness, for the privilege of your company. If there is anything else your Sire-ship requires don't hesitate to order your Turd-low to sneak in and overhear it.'

I pulled the reins on Acorn and let Her Ladyship pull ahead. Turlow passed me on the left and said, 'That did not sound very good.'

I spotted a glimpse of a smirk on his face as he caught up with his fiancée.

Araf came abreast. 'That didn't sound very good,' he said.

Araf, it seemed, had learned how to make unnecessary comments. I have only myself to blame 'cause I think he learned that from me. I let him go by and dropped into step with Brendan.

'That didn't sound very good,' Brendan said.

'That seems to be the consensus. Could you really hear us all the way back here?'

'Let's just say if you two ever get married, I don't want to live next door.'

'Don't worry, there is not much chance of that.'

'Conor, can I give you a piece of constructive advice?'

'Go ahead,' I sighed.

'Stop being such a jerk.'

'That's constructive advice?' I asked.

'Well maybe not – but it *is* advice.'

'So I'm the jerk? What about her? She was the one that tore my head off.'

'And you did nothing to provoke her?'

'No. Well, OK yes, but she overreacted and what about Turd-low creeping around in the dark listening in on our conversations.'

'It wasn't dark, it was in that pea-soup fog, remember? And he told me that he was just sitting next to us doing some Banshee meditation and *we* disturbed him.'

'And you believe him?'

'Conor, I can see why you don't like him but I hate to tell you this – he seems like a nice guy.'

'Well, you thought I was a murderer, so forgive me if I don't trust your judgement.'

Brendan just shrugged. He wasn't looking for a fight and it made me realise I didn't need another one either, so I changed the subject.

'Speaking of difficult women, where is my aunt?'

'She's a gone out a-huntin'.'

'Hunting? My Aunt Nieve?'

'She thought it was strange that we weren't seeing any animals the closer we got to these Pinelands. So she nipped off to look for some. Ever since she mentioned it, I've noticed that I haven't seen a lot of living things around here for a while. Have you?'

'I haven't been looking,' I replied. 'I've been too busy wooing Essa.'

'Right, how's that going?'

'You know, Brendan, I liked you better when you were a mean cop. This sarcastic Brendan is annoying.'

'Nieve doesn't think I'm annoying. In fact this morning she said I was quite funny.'

'You had a conversation with Nieve? I thought you were scared of her?'

'Oh, I'm still plenty scared of her but you can't deny that she is quite beautiful.'

'Yes, I noticed that when I first saw her, but it went away.'

'When you found out she was your aunt?'

'No, when she tried to kill me. I find I lose that loving feeling with women that try to kill me.'

'Didn't Essa try to kill you?'

I didn't have a good answer for that, so I ignored it.

EIGHTEEN

THE PINELANDS

T he next couple of days were clear but icy cold. In the morning, frost covered our tents, which meant getting out of my cosy sleeping roll was almost impossible. Essa continued to set a pace bordering on the maniacal. In short, the entire trip was extremely not fun – but it seemed I was the only one who thought so. The princess and the Banshee lovebirds were as sickly as ever. Brendan and Nieve were getting along so well I could have sworn I heard my aunt actually giggle. That left me and Araf, and when he did talk, it was about the native flora or what a nice guy he thought Turlow was. I decided that my only course of action was to pout.

Either this group was a bunch of insensitive louts (which I am not discounting) or I wasn't doing it right. A proper pout should influence the mood of the entire group making them all almost as miserable as the poutee but my travelling companions seemed to be un-bring-down-able. If I complained about the cold they would say, 'Yes, but look at the blue skies.' If I sighed heavily and went to bed immediately after dinner they would just say, 'Good night.' I figured they would notice if I went off my food but as soon as chow was placed in front of me – I ate it. You have to be really committed to call a hunger-strike pout.

Actually one person noticed my sulk – Turlow. He slipped in next to me and said, 'You don't seem to be enjoying our little jaunt, Master Faerie.'

'I'm having a grand time,' I answered without looking at him.

'I don't believe you. How can you not be in high spirits when you are in the company of Essa of Muhn? Oh, but you're not really in her company that much, are you? Shame, I'm having a lovely time.'

'You done?' I asked.

'Funny,' he said as he kicked his horse and sped back to the front, 'I was going to ask you the same thing.'

A couple of days later the mood of the group turned, but I suspect that it had a lot less to do with my pouting than it had to do with us reaching the edge of the Pinelands.

Like many of the lands in Tir na Nog, you know you're in the Pinelands when you get there. It starts with rolling hills filled with – can you guess? – pine trees. Actually the trees are silver fir – *ailm* in the ancient language of Ogham. If you think that a hill filled with pine trees would give the place a nice Christmassy feel, you'd be wrong. These pines were scraggy and downright menacing. Like weird old men with long bedraggled beards who, if you talked to them, would probably say, 'We don't cotton onto strangers around here,' and when you got back to your car your girlfriend would be missing. These trees grew high and hunched over like they wanted to block out as much light as possible. The ground between the trees was a spongy carpet of brown pine needles in which nothing grew.

The trail grew steeper and the pace slower. It was tiring. You would think that since I was on horseback it wouldn't make any difference whether I was going uphill or down, but Acorn and I had a bond that made me feel some of his effort. All the good riders experienced the same thing, so I guess I was getting pretty good at this riding stuff. We also travelled slower 'cause none of us wanted to make too much noise in this place. If we could have gotten our horses to tiptoe, we would have.

After a couple of wordless hours inclining the Pinelands, Brendan rode up close to me and in a low voice said, 'This is going to sound very clichéd but I—'

'You feel like someone is watching you?' I interrupted.

He nodded.

'Yeah, me too. I thought something was shadowing us over to the left but maybe it's just these damn trees.' I said 'damn' wordlessly so the trees couldn't hear me.

We decided that we were better safe than sorry (or dead) so we kept watch. I looked right while Brendan tried to observe left. (Until our necks got sore and we traded sides.) The shapes that this forest made were so different than any nature we had seen before it really spooked us. We were like scared cub scouts by nightfall.

Essa built a tiny fire with the kindling from her pack. It was enough to make some tea and provided just enough light to pitch our tents by. No one complained because the person that did knew that they would have to be the one to ask one of the scary trees for wood. Brendan and I thought we should keep a watch and since we were the only ones that suggested it – we got to do it.

'I'm going to go out on a limb and say, I don't really like the Pinelands,' I said.

'I'm with you on that one, Mr O'Neil. Miserable, ain't it?' Brendan said, trying to warm his hands on the pathetic fire. 'For the first time in a long while I'm glad my daughter isn't with me.'

'You don't talk about her much.'

'I think about her all of the time, that's enough.'

'What's her name?'

'Ruby.'

'Ruby, that's a nice name.'

'You think? I like it now, I can't imagine her having any other name but when my wife suggested it I thought it sounded like the name of the local good-time girl.'

'It's also the name of a precious gem.'

Brendan smiled a sad smile of a homesick man. 'That's my pet name for her – Gem.'

I wanted to ask him more about his family but it was too cold and too dark.

'Screw this,' I said, standing. 'What is the point of keeping watch if it's so dark that you can't even see anything coming?' I turned to the woods. 'And I'm freezing my butt off.'

'You going to bed?' Brendan asked.

'No, I'm gonna get some firewood.'

'From where? You're not going to talk to those trees, are you?'

'What are they going to do, kill me?'

'Didn't you tell me that there are trees in The Land that can?'

He had a point, but I ignored him. If this stupid quest was going to force me to be out of doors in the middle of the winter I was going to have a roaring fire, damn it. I walked up to the nearest pine, which wasn't very close. We had chosen a campsite in one of the few clearings we had found. The closer I got to the trees the worse this idea got. My courage slipped out of me with every step. The faint light from our poor excuse for a campfire cast creepy shadows. I started to think, *do I really need to be any warmer? I'll just throw another blanket over me.* I stopped under the huge gnarled tree. A cold sweat ran down my armpit and then a shiver shook me from ear to knee. *What am I,* I asked myself, *am I a man or a mouse?* I knew I didn't have any cheese with me so I closed my eyes and touched my hand to the rough bark.

When you first touch most trees in The Land it's like a brain-scan. You don't tell them anything, they just zap into your cranium and take any information they need. I squeezed my eyes closed and waited. Nothing. I opened one eye and quietly said, 'Hello?'

'*Are you a Pooka?*'

That question shot into my head but instead of it sounding (or should I say feeling) like a nasty old hillbilly, I got the impression of a scared kid.

I tried to reply just by thinking – still nothing. *Hello*, I thought, then out loud I said, 'Anybody in there?'

'*Are you a Pooka?*' the tree asked again. His voice sounded frantic, laced with childish overexcitement.

'No, I'm ...' I sighed and admitted, 'I'm a Faerie.'

'*Do you know where the Pookas are?*'

'No, we are looking for them ourselves.'

'*Oh, when you see them could you tell them ...*'

I don't remember anything after that for a while. Brendan said I shot straight back about three feet and was out cold for about five minutes. At first he thought I was dead. When I came to I had a huge throbbing headache and couldn't really make sense of anything for a while. Brendan helped me over to the fire, gave me some willow tea and put me into my tent. In my dreams, I was a pinball going from pine tree to pine tree. Every time I was just ready to stop, a pine would whack me and I would bounce around the forest until I stopped at another, then I would get whacked again. I wouldn't call my night ... refreshing.

I awoke to the smell and sound of a roaring fire. Everyone was up. Essa and Nieve were in the distance with their arms around trees. Brendan handed me a cup of tea.

'Where'd you get the firewood?' I asked.

'From the pines. They are very nice once you get to know them.'

'Or until they attack you with some sort of brain-exploding beam.'

'No one tried to explode your brain. It's just that M over there' – Brendan pointed to the tree I had chatted with last night – 'has been way behind on his emailing. He got overexcited.'

'M?'

'Well, I can't pronounce his name – I think it starts with an M so that's what I call him. He likes it. He never had a nickname before. Nice kid.'

'What are you talking about?'

'OK, here is what M and L over there' – he pointed to a big old tree – 'and Nieve have told me. Trees communicate with one another in The Land. Like when you told me not to talk around the beech trees because they gossip and I thought you were bonkers?'

'Yeah.'

'So when you enter a wood, the whole forest knows about it 'cause they talk to each other.'

'Brendan, you're not telling me anything I didn't know.'

'Yes, but that's the point. Pine trees can't talk to each other. And nobody knew it, except the Pookas.'

'So why did M attack me?'

'He didn't attack you – he just got carried away. The Pookas carry messages from one tree to another. L, that old tree over there, told me that they do it without even thinking. Apparently Pookas just walk through the forest touching trees, picking up and dropping messages as they go. They're like tree postal workers.'

'So where are they?'

'Well, L over there thinks he has seen a couple of Pookas in their animal forms but they haven't spoken to him and he hasn't seen one in human form since the middle of the summer. Poor M is just a kid. He hasn't been able to send a message to any of his gang in ages. When he talked to you he got excited and loaded about five months' worth of notes into your head. It was equivalent to having a hundred pound mailbag dropped on your noggin. He told me to tell you he was sorry.'

'So where are the Pookas?'

'That's what Nieve and Essa are trying to find out. It's slow going. Every time you talk to a tree they beg you to pass a message on for them. It's hard to say no.'

That day's journey was slow going. I had no intention of touching a pine again, but Essa, Araf, Brendan and Nieve had all promised a tree they would pass along a couple of messages. Turlow and I would go a couple of hundred yards and then wait while our companions zigzagged all over the forest. I got so bored with waiting, I actually struck up a conversation with the girlfriend-stealing Banshee.

'How come you're not playing Postman Plank?'

'I, Prince Faerie, am not an admirer of wood.'

'You don't like wood?'

'Oh, I like it fine in a chair or a fire but I don't like trees.'

'How can anybody not like trees?' I asked incredulously. 'Have you ever spoken to an oak or an apple?'

'I do not speak with trees.'

'Why not?'

'If you must know, I do not like the way their roots reach in to my thinking. My mind is my own.'

'Sounds like you have something to hide. A copy of *Naughty Elves Monthly* in the bottom of your sock drawer, maybe?' He gave me that Turd-low look that translates to 'I'll not dignify that with an answer.'

'Well, I wouldn't worry about talking to these guys,' I said. 'They're as thick as two planks. Get it? Planks – pine trees?' I waited. 'You wouldn't laugh at my jokes even if they were funny.'

'When it happens, Faerie, I will let you know.'

Not long after that Brendan rode up and said, 'That's it. I quit.'

'What, no more neighbourhood postman for you? You will have to hand back those snazzy Bermuda shorts.'

'Every tree wants me to send a message to ten others.' He scratched his head with both hands. 'It's just not possible. The sooner we find the Pookas the better these trees will be.'

'Poor guys, it sounds like they really miss the Pookas. They're *pining* for them.'

Brendan gave me a look not unlike the one Turlow had given me moments before and kicked ahead.

'Oh, come on,' I called after him, 'that was a good one.'

NINETEEN

HAWATHIEE

That night most of the Tir-na-Nogian Postal Workers Union Local No.1 went to bed early – exhausted. Just Brendan and I were left to tend the roaring fire.

'Do you still think we need to keep watch?' Brendan asked. 'We have been prancing around these woods all day, I don't think there is anybody in here.'

'Me neither but I'm keeping watch just in case one of the postmen goes berserk and shoots us all.'

Brendan laughed. It was good that there was at least one person who got my Real World jokes, even if he didn't always laugh at them. He pulled out a couple of tin mugs then uncorked a bottle with his teeth and poured us both a drink.

'To your father,' Brendan said, holding his mug high. 'Long live the King.'

'Hear, hear,' I said and drank. 'Heeeeyooow,' I gasped as the firewater travelled down my throat, into my chest and then exploded out of my toes. 'Where did you get this stuff?'

'I was really in the mood for a drink so I kind-of found it ... in Essa's bag.'

'A thieving policeman – you should be ashamed.'

'I am,' he said. 'Would you like some more?'

'Yes please. How did you know it was there?'

'Her father makes the stuff, so I just deduced.'

'You know, Brendan, when you are not charging me with murder, you are quite the detective.' I raised my glass. 'To your little Gem,' I toasted.

He nodded and stretched a pained smile across his face. 'To Ruby.'

We drank and he looked at his mug for a while.

'What's she like?'

'Ruby?' He laughed. 'She's seven going on thirty-five. Ever since her mom died she has taken it unto herself to be the grand bossy woman of the house. When she's home you'd hardly even know she's blind.'

'She's blind?'

'Yeah, she lost her sight in the same accident that killed my wife.'

'What happened?'

After a deep breath Brendan said, 'My wife liked to speed around on those back roads. Do you know Cobb Creek? It's not that far from your place.'

'I do. It's nice up there. Is that where you live?'

'Yes, my mother found the spot with her voodoo divining rods. She said there were ley-lines or some such thing there. My wife used to like my mother's craziness. I didn't care about energy lines; I just liked it because it is beautiful. Anyway, my wife was driving in her little red sports car with the top down, when, right outside our house, a horse ran in front of the car. We were having a conservatory built at the same time and the car slammed sideways into the truck carrying panes of glass. My wife was killed and Ruby lost her vision to flying shards.' He stopped and took another drink.

'My gods,' I said and put my hand on his shoulder. 'I'm so sorry.'

'Yeah, me too,' and then with a forced smile he said, 'More booze?'

'I think so,' I replied, offering my cup. 'How long ago was this?'

'About two and a half years.'

'Whose horse was it?'

'We never found out. It was injured pretty badly; my partner arrived about the same time as the ambulance and put it down. I was crazy mad and checked every farm and stable in a thirty-mile radius – no one said that they had lost a horse and I could never trace the markings on the saddle.'

'The horse was saddled?'

'Yes.'

'But there was no rider?'

'No,' Brendan shook his head. 'Well, if you ask Ruby about it she says otherwise.'

'What does she say?'

'You have to realise she was just five. She claims the horse had a rider dressed in black and that they appeared out of nowhere. She says it's the last thing she ever saw.'

The next day everybody gave up trying to carry messages for the trees. We just weren't up to it. The Pookas must have some special microchip in their heads 'cause we found the task impossible.

The path grew steeper but the mood was lighter. We no longer looked at each tree as a potential assassin. We saw them as they were, lost lonely souls who had been abandoned by their pastor. Oh, and I wasn't sulking any more.

The previous night's chat with Brendan rolled around in my noggin all morning and it sparked off memories that in turn ignited unanswered questions. As I watched my aunt riding in front of me I remembered the first time I had seen her. The memories were vivid and unsettling: Dad going berserk, throwing his axe at her head and knocking her guard off his saddle. The guard hitting the ground and instantly turning into a thousand-year-old swirl of dust. Nieve throwing a spear at me and then high-tailing it out of there and letting Cialtie's henchmen, all dressed in black, knock us out and chain us up in Dungeon Duir.

I cantered up alongside my aunt. 'Nieve, can I ask you a question?'

'I'm sure you can, Conor, because you just did.'

'Right,' I said a bit nervously. Nieve had an uncanny ability to instantly put me ill at ease. I wondered if she did it to everyone and I also wondered if she did it on purpose. 'Do you promise you won't get mad at me?'

'No,' came her immediate reply.

'OoooK, how about – do you promise you won't hurt me?'

She thought about that for a moment and said, 'No.'

'Oh well, never mind then.' I dropped back and waited for her curiosity to get the better of her.

And I waited – and waited.

About an hour later I pulled up next to her and said, 'OK, I know you are secretly dying to know – so here's my question: how come you helped Cialtie find me in the Real World?'

She quickly reached her left hand into her cloak and with her right hand she reached for the short knife on her belt.

I looked around to see if anyone else was watching us – they weren't. When I looked back Nieve had already cut the apple in her hand and handed half to me. There was a wicked twinkle in her eyes.

I took the apple half. 'You like messing with me, don't you?'

'If I understand the meaning of *messing with you*, then yes, but don't get too flattered.' She leaned towards me and in a conspiratorial whisper she said, 'I like *messing* with everybody.'

We rode and ate in silence for a little while. Nieve sported a little smile. I felt privileged that she shared that small secret with me. I felt like a nephew.

Finally she said, 'I didn't help Cialtie.'

'Well, you showed up at my doorstep and the next thing I knew I had chains for jewellery.'

'Do you not remember that I left when I heard Cialtie's men approach?'

'Yes. Why did you do that?'

'Because I was afraid of them. I did not wish to be unseated from my horse. I'm quite fond of my looks, Conor; I would rather not look my age.'

'So how did they find us?'

'They followed me. Remember the soldier that was with me?'

'The guy that fell off his horse and then dusted it?'

'*Dusted it* – that is an apt way of putting it. Yes, him; I found out later that he was one of Cialtie's spies.'

'I feel less sorry for him now,' I said.

'That is what I said when I found out.'

'So how did *you* find us?'

'I'm a very good sorceress you know,' she said without a smile. It was no brag – just fact. 'I found a war axe that was made at the same time as your father's axe was made. The gold inlay in the handle came from the same vein and gave off the same …' she searched for the words, 'magic resonance. It was not easy to track but as I said, I am very good.'

'OK, now I see the how, but can I ask you one more question? Why? Why then? I mean, I was going to die in the Real World some day. What was your hurry?'

'I wanted to kill you before Cialtie did.'

That was an answer I wasn't expecting. 'Isn't that taking sibling rivalry a bit too far?'

'I was satisfied with your father's solution. I was happy to see you die in the Real World but when I learned that Cialtie was using the Hall of Spells to send forays into the Real World looking for you, I had to kill you first.'

'Why?'

'I was afraid that Cialtie would make a big spectacle of killing you. Maybe even a public execution. I couldn't have that. I wanted to kill you privately and cleanly.'

'Gee, thanks – I think.' I smiled at her but she did not return it.

'I took no joy in that task,' she said.

'I know,' I said. I put my hand on her arm, and then I changed the subject. 'So Cialtie sent riders to look for me and Dad even before last summer?'

'My information is that he was looking for years.'

'Where did you get your information from?'

Nieve smiled. 'Cialtie is not the only one with spies.'

That night I put it to Brendan that maybe his daughter really did see a rider dressed in black and that maybe they really did appear out of nowhere, but he got angry with me for even suggesting such nonsense and wouldn't speak about it.

Later I was awoken by rustling in the forest. Something *was* moving out there and it was something big. The fire was almost out so I walked up to a nearby tree to ask for wood.

An ancient voice appeared in my head. '*You are not Pooka.*'

'No, sir,' I said aloud. 'We seek the Pooka.'

'*There is Pooka in the forest tonight,*' he said.

'Have you spoken to them?'

'*The Pooka no longer speak to me – I am alone.*'

I felt so sorry for the old guy. I said, 'I can take a message to a tree for you. Just don't give me more than one – I can't handle it.' I shut my eyes expecting an onslaught of messages but none came.

'*What good is one message? The Pooka have renounced us, we are alone.*'

I heard the familiar creaking of the tree sucking the moisture out of some of its limbs. I said, 'Thank you, sir,' and backed off before he cracked off his branches and dropped them to the ground. I stoked the fire and kept watch. I continued to hear something moving in the gloomy dark but never saw anything.

That changed the next morning. Something was in the woods, on both sides of us, and whatever is was, it was tracking us. At noon Araf said he saw a wolf. About an hour later I saw one too. Like seeing a shark's dorsal fin in the water, seeing a wolf running low in a forest will make your heart go pitter-pat.

The higher we got in the Pinelands, the more the trees thinned and we got a better look at our escorts. It was a pack about ten strong. They shadowed us with military precision – four on each side and two slipping close in at our rear. If we turned in our saddles to look, the two that followed would slip back into the trees and wait patiently until our eyes turned ahead when they would slink back into position. It was unnerving. Essa said she thought the Pooka headquarters was over the rise. I bit my tongue before saying, 'You think?' This crowd was too tense for teasing and I knew from experience that annoying a stressed Essa was a dangerous thing.

The closer we got to the summit the bolder the wolves got. They moved in closer and no longer attempted to conceal themselves among the few remaining trees. These guys were big – Great-Dane sized – but they looked thin and just a little bit mangy. If you caught their eye it gave you a feeling that they were unpredictable – capable of anything.

Our mounts definitely didn't like them. Horses, I have learned, are travelling machines. They focus on the minutiae of the terrain ahead and because of that almost never put a foot wrong. What they don't do well is worry about what is behind them. It pulls their focus. Acorn periodically tried to look behind and every time he did I looked as well. A couple of times I almost fell off.

An explosion of gold light erupted behind me that nearly made me jump out of my skin. The wolves yelped and I saw one dart into the forest with his fur shooting straight out in all directions. Brendan notched an arrow.

'Put away your bow, archer. They are Pookas.'

'What did you do?' I asked my aunt.

'I didn't harm anyone but they were getting a bit too close for my horse's liking. Now they have a better idea of who they are dealing with.'

The wolves gave us a wider berth but it didn't last. They slipped in closer, zigzagging behind us, sometimes so close that our horses tried to kick them. Not the kind of thing you want your mount to do unexpectedly.

Essa pointed to a rock formation not too far off to the left. 'That is where I was greeted by Queen Rhiannon the last time I was here.'

Nieve blasted the Pineland wolves again. Any sane creatures would have scampered away with their tails between their legs but I wasn't too sure that these creatures were sane.

Now that we were closer to the rock wall I still couldn't decide if it was Pooka-made or natural. The wall looked like it could have been a long fault line that had collapsed in an earthquake. In the middle was an archway. Our plan of riding through the opening and fending off the wolves there was dashed when we saw that thick pine branches blocked the entrance from the other side.

'Nieve,' Essa shouted from horseback, 'can you move those trees?'

'That depends on the trees,' Nieve shouted back. 'I may need your help.'

'Everyone,' Essa shouted, trying to sound like a seasoned commander but there was a slight quiver in her voice that betrayed a fear that I think we all shared. 'Dismount quickly and protect the horses while Nieve and I clear the gateway.'

Turlow moved first, he performed a very impressive dismount while in full canter. In midair, even before his feet hit the ground, his Banshee blade rocketed out of his sleeve. It surprised the lead pack wolf to the point that he stumbled as he slowed. Acorn was barely walking when I dismounted, still I almost fell over. We fanned out and put our nervous snorting horses behind us. The wolves fanned too and paced sideways snarling – looking for a weakness in our defences. I couldn't help thinking that they were looking at me more than the others.

'Tell me again why I can't shoot one of them?' Brendan shouted.

'Because they are Hawathiee,' Araf said.

Now there was a word I hadn't heard before. 'Hawa what?' I asked, never taking my eyes off my junkyard dog.

'We are all Hawathiee: Faeries, Imps, Leprechauns, Fili, Elves, Brownies and Pooka. We are children of the trees. We do not kill each other.'

'You know I've read some of your history,' I said, 'and that's not exactly true.'

'Well,' Araf replied a bit sheepishly, 'we are not supposed to kill each other.'

'Notice he didn't mention Banshees in his little list,' Turlow said.

One of the wolves made a faint attack at Araf which it instantly abandoned. The rest of the pack quickly ran sideways and swopped positions.

'I do not think that *now* is the time to debate that, Turlow,' Araf said.

Turlow's reply was almost too soft to hear. 'That's what they always say.'

I really didn't like the look of the slobber that was drooling off the lips of one of the wolves in front of me. He had a look of desperation about him and his patience was growing thin.

'How's the tree pruning going back there, girls?' I shouted without turning around.

'The trees are alive but they will not speak to us,' Nieve called back. 'I do not wish to hurt them.'

'Well, something or someone is going to get hurt real soon,' Brendan said, 'and I would prefer it not to be me.'

Turlow broke the calm. With a well and proper Banshee scream, he lashed out at the two beasts that were facing him. They initially stood the charge with bared fangs but as he grew closer and louder they scampered away like poodles being reprimanded by a maid with a broom.

When I looked back to the wolves that were dogging me, I was surprised to see that they had crept in to almost a lunge-length away. I swung the Lawnmower and let loose a scream that sounded weedy compared to Turlow's. The wolves backed off and then, as one, they all turned and ran away.

I smiled at Araf. 'Well, I guess I showed them who's boss.'

Araf didn't look at me. He seemed to look above me. 'I can only guess at what *boss* means,' he said, 'but I am guessing that the boss is not you.'

I turned. That's when I saw the bears.

TWENTY

TUAN

There were two of them. Kodiak-looking fellows about twenty feet high – or so it seemed at the time. To call them bears would be doing them an injustice, like calling a couple of sabre-toothed tigers kitty-cats. They were actually hairy mountains with teeth and claws. They loped towards us on all fours but as soon as they made eye contact, they stopped and reared up on their hind legs. I mentioned before that the sight of wolves in the forest made my heart skip a beat – well, the sight of these guys at full height produced a code-red cardiac arrest.

They dropped back to all fours and slowly came towards us. They didn't look menacing exactly – I think I could have coped with that – their expression was far more terrifying. They looked hungry.

I heard the creak of Brendan's bow as he pulled his weapon back to full tension. 'These guys I can shoot, right?'

'NO,' came a shout from Essa and Araf.

Brendan turned to Araf. 'Why not?'

'It will only make them mad,' the Imp replied.

'Girls,' I shouted behind me, 'you better hack through those trees.'

'No, Conor,' Essa hissed back.

'You either hack the trees or I have to hack a super bear and I have a suspicion that the bear is going to hack back.'

'We did not come here to kill trees and Pookas,' Essa said.

'Well, I didn't come here to get a good look at my lower intestines either. Make a decision or these bears are going to make one for us.'

A screech tore my wide and terrified eyes away from the approaching colossi. I looked up and saw what at first looked like a falcon, but as I watched the feathers on his wings began to be absorbed into what began to look like arms. The sharp beak disappeared into his widening face; talons extended and became long lean legs. He was fully human when he hit the ground. I'd like to say it was a stunning and graceful manoeuvre but that would be a lie. What I saw was a bird that, in midair, turned into a very naked man that then awkwardly slammed face down into the earth. I'm pretty sure even the bears thought it looked painful.

As he lay there moaning, one of us really should have asked him if he was all right, but, like the bears, we were frozen in shock. By the time he got up, the bears had seen enough and were moving again. He stood and shouted, 'BE GONE.'

Now, I don't know about you but if a naked man fell from the sky and then, in all of his dingly-dangly naked glory, stood in front of me and shouted, 'BE GONE,' then I would probably go. But these Pookas/ bears, like the wolves, were not in their right minds – they kept coming. I didn't know what to do. Part of me wanted to step in front of this obviously deranged Pooka and save him from almost certain disembowelment. Of course the other part of me was delighted to have anything between me and the two mountains of slobber, fangs and claws that were heading my way.

'Hey,' I called to him. When he ignored me I tried again. 'Excuse me, naked Pooka guy. Can we help in any way?'

He turned to look at me; one side of his face was covered with dirt and grass stains. 'Stand back,' he commanded. Then he reached his hand to his neck, dropped his head to his chest and went down onto one knee. It looked like he was praying and I hoped it was a short prayer because the bears were almost on him. I heard Brendan's bow creak. I couldn't stand to watch. Just as I was about to turn away, he stood up – then he kept standing up. His feet thinned at the bottom, then his backside grew a tail and widened to the size of a downtown bus. His head grew a rack of flat antlers that must have been as wide as the bears were tall. He grew dark brown short hair all over his body. When the transformation was done, we all stood open-mouthed. It was one of the most impressive things I had seen to date. Standing between us and certain death was what I now know was a prehistoric Celtic deer. Imagine a moose the size of a large elephant and you've got the idea. He dropped his antler-adorned head, scratched in the earth with his hind legs and charged.

The bears didn't give it a second thought. They scrabbled out of there fast. Mr Moose gave a short chase then changed back into a naked man before collapsing onto the frozen earth.

Brendan and I ran up to him. 'Are you all right?' I asked.

He replied with moans that then became words. 'Aahh ... leave ... this ... mountain.'

Araf ran up with a blanket and placed it over him. Without looking up he angrily pushed it off. 'Leave this mountain.'

I placed the blanket back over him. 'Really, you're going to freeze out here. Can we—'

He scrambled to his feet with a speed that surprised me. Apart from a gold disc that hung on a wire around his neck, and the mud and dirt, he was still very naked. He spotted Essa and Nieve still working on the trees that blocked the gateway. 'Get away from there!' he tried to scream but his voice was tired and thin. They looked but continued. He threw his head back, almost falling over. 'LEAVE THIS MOUNTAIN!' he shouted. He staggered as he brought his head down, his eyes still closed. I took a step forward to catch him if he fell. He opened his eyes. I think he expected us to be gone, instead of standing around staring at him. A look of mad anger took over his face. He dropped to his knees and grabbed the medallion around his neck. Brendan, Turlow, Araf and I all took an involuntary step back.

Black fur sprouted from every pore, his nose blackened and broadened. The teeth changed just before the snout formed, giving us a good look at the fangs. We took another step back. As his height increased he tried to stand. That's when the transformation stalled then stopped altogether. His eyes blinked rapidly and he shrank quickly into naked Pooka guy again as he fell face first unconscious into Araf's waiting arms.

Araf carried him over to the gate where Essa and Nieve had started a small fire and were brewing tea. Essa wrapped him in more blankets while Nieve placed her hands on his temples.

When she released his head she said, 'He is exhausted and starving.'

'Was he changing into a bear?' Essa asked.

'I think so,' Araf said.

'And he flew in as a bird,' Turlow said. 'Did you see that?'

'Very strange,' Essa said. Everyone, except Brendan and me, nodded in agreement.

'Look, everyone, changing into mooses,' Brendan said, 'is mighty strange for me but you people are talking like that's not strange enough.'

Essa answered him. 'Pookas spend decades, centuries, studying how to change into their chosen animal. I have never heard of a Pooka that could change into more than one. This must be some sort of master Pooka.'

'Have you had any joy with the trees?' Turlow asked.

'No, we cannot pass without hurting the trees,' Nieve said.

'Then we must hurt the trees,' Turlow said. 'I will do it.'

'Slow down, honey,' Essa said. 'We have a local here. When he wakes he may help us through.'

'Or he might turn into a wolverine and rip our throats out,' I said. 'And did I just hear you call him "honey"?' I said that last bit loudly. I shouldn't have but I was a bit stunned. The only thing I could ever imagine Essa calling honey is that yellow stuff that bees make.

'What is wrong with calling my fiancé "honey"?' Essa said with that customary fire in her eyes but also with, maybe, just a touch of embarrassment.

'Yes, Faerie, what is wrong with that?' her Banshee added.

I was racking my brains for a suitable quip that would stop me from getting clocked by Essa or stabbed by the Turd-low when I was saved by a moan from the Pooka. We all looked at him.

His head was resting on Nieve's lap. He had a mop of sandy blond hair sitting on top of an almost boyish face. As we watched, he opened his eyes; they were piercing blue. Usually it's the eyes here in The Land that give away how old a person is, but this Pooka's eyes confused me. I instantly thought he was very young but then I got a fleeting impression of very old age. After that his peepers were just unreadable. Nieve brushed a piece of grass off of his cheek and smiled at him. It was nice to see such tenderness from my aunt – I certainly hadn't seen that before.

The Pooka didn't get up and when he spoke he was hoarse and hard to hear. 'You must leave.' He closed his eyes again and I wondered if he had passed out, but then he opened them and looked at each of us. 'I can't protect you,' he said.

Nieve sat him up and Essa got some willow tea into him.

'I could have sworn I had some poteen with me,' Essa said. Brendan gave me a furtive guilty glance.

A little bit more of the spark of life returned to our shapeshifter with every sip of willow tea. Araf gave him some food and he gobbled it down. With a boyishly guilty look, Brendan produced the almost-finished bottle of poteen and handed it to Essa, who gave him such a dirty look I was sure glad I wasn't him. A shot of Gerard's special moonshine brought all the colour back to our patient's cheeks and maybe a little extra. He sat with us around the fire wrapped in about four blankets.

'We do not seek your protection,' Essa said, breaking the silence. 'We seek Queen Rhiannon.'

Pooka guy made a snorting, laughing sound that I didn't like and said, 'Queen Rhiannon is indisposed.'

'None the less, we must see her.'

'You cannot.'

'We have come a long way and will see the Queen with or without your help,' Essa said.

He threw off his blankets and stood up. Our friendly fireside guest once again became very angry naked Pooka guy – which was disconcerting, 'cause we were pretty close and seated. 'You can't see her. YOU MUST LEAVE.' His face became repossessed – he reached for his neck.

'Woah, woah, woah, Pooka guy,' I said, as I grabbed his wrist before his hand made it to his medallion. 'I don't know you very well but I don't think you are up for one of your quick changes. And anyway, there are six of us and we are all pretty handy. You'd have to turn into a T-Rex to stop us.'

He stood there, unmoving. I wasn't sure if I was getting through to him.

'It's OK, really,' I said, 'we're like a royal honour guard here. Me and Araf are princes, those two are princesses and Turlow here is like a king.' Brendan coughed. 'Oh yeah, he's a cop.'

The Pooka placed his face in his hands. From behind his palms he said, 'You cannot see her. No one can see her.'

'I have even brought gifts, look.' I took out the muslin parcel, untied it and displayed the six hazelnuts.

The look on the Pooka's face was like that of a man lost in the desert for a week being offered a glass of ice water. 'Where did you get them?' he almost whispered.

'From the Tree of Knowledge.'

'You lie, the Tree was destroyed.'

'This is from the new tree. Essa and I planted it ourselves from my grandfather's hazel wood.'

The Pooka stared hard at my face. 'You are Liam's son?'

'I'm his grandson, Conor.'

'I will take them to her,' the Pooka said.

I pulled the hazelnuts out of his reach. 'No, this is a royal gift from Queen Deirdre of Duir to Queen Rhiannon of Ailm. I was instructed to present it to Her Highness in person or not at all.'

'Lady Deirdre has been found?'

'Ages ago,' I said.

'I sent a runner to find her. He never returned.'

'Was he a curly-haired guy who changed into a wolf?'

The Pooka nodded yes.

'He found her but I have bad news, he's dead.'

Sadness mixed with resignation crossed the Pooka's face.

'I'm sorry. Look, is there any way we can have this conversation while you wear clothes? You're making me cold just looking at you.'

He took the blanket I offered and wrapped it around himself. I filled him in on all the major news of The Land: Mom and Dad's and my return, Cialtie getting booted out of Castle Duir and the rebuilding of the Hazellands.

'So you are Deirdre's son. My sister was your mother's tutor – she was very fond of her.' He didn't have to say any more. The look on his face told me that she must have died when the Hall of Knowledge was attacked. 'My name is Tuan. I will take you, Prince Conor, to see Queen Rhiannon.'

He stood and placed his hands on the thick branches that blocked the stone portal, mumbled something in a language I didn't recognise and the trees creaked up and away. 'Quickly,' Tuan said, 'before the larger animals come back.'

We grabbed our horses and led them through. As the trees were bowing back down into position, I spotted the pack of wolves eyeing us from among some far trees. They didn't look happy.

Inside the wall, small animals, horses and sheep wandered freely. After I unsaddled Acorn I expected him to join the local horses for a frolic but he and the others grazed uneasily close by. Tuan said that the others in my party could make camp where they were and offered to take me alone to see Queen Rhiannon.

'I walk with Prince Conor,' Araf said.

'No.' Tuan was adamant. 'Conor alone may see the Queen.'

Turlow stood. 'What is to stop you as soon as you are out of our sight from changing into a bear and taking Conor's nuts?'

I hoped he was talking about hazelnuts but either way he had a point. 'Yeah, what assurance do I have that you won't go all hairy and fangy?'

'You have my word as a Child of Ailm, but if that is not enough then here.' He reached for the wire that held the medallion around his neck and it expanded at his touch. He slipped it over his head and dropped the gold disc into my hand.

I looked to my travelling companions, wordlessly asking them, 'Should I trust him?' Tuan stepped away and allowed us to confer.

Amazingly Araf spoke first. 'We have come a long way. I do not like leaving you on your own, and if you are hurt I shall have to hide from your mother for the rest of my days, but I think you should go.'

Nieve and Essa both agreed.

'I think he is exhausted and desperate which makes him unpredictable,' Brendan said, 'but I think he is one of the good guys.'

'You thought I was a murderer.'

'Yes, but if you remember I also said that you were not a bad man.'

Turlow was the sole dissenter. 'We have his changing medallion. We can force him to take us to the Queen without risk.' He looked around for support. 'Oh, don't look at me like that. This is a desperate place and we have been attacked three times today. Desperate times require desperate measures.'

I don't know what the others thought but I was glad of Turlow's opinion. It's good to have at least one person on the team that errs on the side of caution.

'Tuan,' I called, 'let's go meet the Queen.' Then I surprised everybody by handing him back his medallion. 'If you eat me, make sure you let Essa watch – she'd like that.'

I turned back to the group and said, 'If I'm not back in two days …' then realised I didn't know how to end that sentence. 'If I'm not back in two days – then I'm dead. You can do what you want.'

'We will be back tomorrow,' Tuan said. 'Do not eat any animals. They are not as they seem.'

Tuan and I walked along the wall until we reached a pile of clothes at the base of a tall pine. Tuan touched the tree and said, 'Thanks.' He put on a pair of very baggy brown trousers, a black shirt, a black seal-skin coat, some leather boots and a rabbit-fur hat. For a guy that changed into animals, he didn't seem averse to wearing dead ones. We walked over a ridge until we could no longer see my companions.

'Now is a good a time to change into a wolf and eat me,' I said.

'I am not that kind of Pooka,' he replied.

'The ones on the other side of the wall were though – weren't they?'

'Those Pooka are … they are lost.'

'What do you mean "lost"?'

I could see he was struggling to come up with an answer. Finally he said, 'It is not in my power to tell you these things. What you may learn is up to the Queen.'

The hill levelled out into a broad plateau that led to a thick forest in the distance.

'Any chance of you changing into a horse and giving me a lift?' I asked, flashing my House of Duir smile. 'Or would that be too demeaning?'

Tuan laughed at that. 'Not demeaning, Prince Conor, just short.'

But when I asked him what he meant, I got the same stonewalling that I got before. I hoped the Queen was more forthcoming.

The sun was fully down by the time we entered the forest but a gibbous moon provided enough light for us to navigate. Not far in, the path became broad and ran parallel to a stream. A while later we came upon small bridges that spanned the stream and led to modest huts. I saw neither a person nor an animal. Finally we came to a series of ponds, each with a tasteful two-storey pine cottage with a porch that hung over the water. They reminded me of really nice country hunting lodges. We must have passed about a dozen pond/house combinations before we came to the last and most impressive house. We entered and Tuan lit several oil lamps. The large room was sparse but elegant. It had that minimalist feng shui chic – like it was inhabited by someone who didn't need earthly things. In the corner was an ornate high-backed chair made from polished white pine.

'Is that the Pine Throne?' I asked.

'It is. This is Queen Rhiannon's home.'

I looked around. 'Where is she?'

Tuan walked outside onto the porch. At intervals along the railings there were torches connected by a string of gold wire. The Pooka touched the gold and mumbled something that made a spark zoom around the wire, igniting the torches around the porch and then around the pond. I now got a good look at the outside of the house. It was nice, really nice but I still wouldn't have taken it to be a royal palace. The light glimmered, mirror-like, off the football-field-sized pond, reflecting the circle of flickering torches.

'There,' Tuan said, pointing to the pond.

I was about to say, 'Where?' when a large fish broke the surface of the pond and then vanished underneath the rippling water.

'There she is,' Tuan said, pointing, 'there is Queen Rhiannon.'

TWENTY-ONE

BARUSH

'The Queen's a fish?' I blurted.

'In her fauna state Queen Rhiannon is *braden* – a salmon.'

'Can I speak to her?'

'May I have one of your hazelnuts?' Tuan tried to look calm but it was a look of calm desperation. I handed him a hazelnut and he cracked it with his teeth. 'Do you have a knife?'

I reached into my sock and handed him the green-handled blade I found at the bottom of Mount Cas. He stared at it for a moment then walked to the edge of the porch and shaved five tiny slivers off the nut, allowing them to drop in the water. The two of us stood shoulder to shoulder shielding our eyes from the bright torchlight. It probably only took a couple of minutes for Queen Fish to swim to the spot under the dock but it seemed like ages – I never was a very patient fisherman. Finally she tentatively swam up to the floating nut shavings. I thought she was going to ignore them but then she snatched at a sliver and swam away. Tuan sighed and returned my knife. In the middle of the pond, a salmon poked its head above the water. As I watched the large fish mouth pulled tight, the eyes drew closer together and then, as her feet touched the bottom, she rose. Queen Rhiannon did not possess the traditional beauty of, say, Essa or my mother but she was striking none the less. Her hair was long and shiny silver, it floated around her in the water just below her neck. The features on her face almost seemed chiselled but it was the eyes that drew your gaze – they were emerald green.

A set of stone steps rose out of the water. Queen Rhiannon walked out of her pond and up onto the porch. I'm so glad those eyes were that compelling – because I didn't want to get caught looking anywhere else. I didn't bow or say anything. I just looked her square in the peepers until Tuan presented her with a robe.

She started to speak and then stopped. It was almost as if she had forgotten how. She tried again. 'How long have I been lost?' she said in a whisper.

'We have a guest,' Tuan said, pointing to me with an open hand. 'This is Conor of Duir. He has brought us hazelnuts.'

I opened the parcel and displayed the five remaining nuts. 'A gift from my mother, Queen Deirdre.'

'Deirdre lives?' she asked, her voice a bit stronger.

'She does, Your Highness and she has been worried about your people.'

'What have you told him?' Rhiannon asked Tuan.

'I have told him nothing but if the choice was mine I would deem Conor *barush*.'

Rhiannon turned and walked back down the stairs into her pond and gently scooped up the four tiny slivers of hazelnut that were floating on the water and handed them to Tuan. 'Arouse the council while I talk to the Son of Hazel.'

Tuan turned and was almost out the door when the Queen called to him. 'Son, how long?'

'Two months. I have missed you, Mother.' Then he turned and left.

'Would you like a cup of tea, Prince Conor?'

'That would be lovely, ma'am.'

As she walked to a door on our left the Queen stumbled – she was unsure on her feet. I grabbed her arm to steady her. She stopped and shook me off, proudly straightening herself, but then she sighed in resignation and held my arm as we walked slowly to the kitchen.

'Deirdre's son,' she mused. 'That would make you Liam's grandson.'

'Yes, ma'am.'

In the kitchen there was a black kettle covered with a mesh of gold wire. Rhiannon lifted it to see if it contained enough water, then placed her index finger on a bit of the gold and hummed. Within seconds steam issued from the spout. She grabbed a handful of small white flower buds from a jar, distributed them between the two cups and poured in the hot water. I don't know what kind of tea it was but it was lovely and it seemed to revitalise the former fish.

We walked through the kitchen into a comfortable sitting room. The tabletops were dusty. Rhiannon apologised for the state of the place. 'I have been ... away,' she said.

'Lost, was the word you used before,' I said as gently as I could.

Queen Rhiannon looked me directly in the eyes for one of those hour-long seconds and then looked vacantly into the distance. 'Lost ... yes, lost is a better word.'

I waited for her to say something else. She was a queen after all, it wasn't like you could just drill her for information. After a while I feared she was getting lost again. I reached into my pocket and opened the parcel and presented her with the five remaining hazelnuts.

She broke the silence. 'Where did the hazel come from?'

I started to tell her how the new Tree of Knowledge came about and it turned into an autobiography. I told her about how I came to The Land, how Dahy gave me a hazel staff that was once owned by my grandfather and how I accidentally planted it at the site of the destroyed tree and it took root.

'And your mother gave you the hazelnuts to give to me?'

'Yes, ma'am.'

'Did she tell you why?'

'No, ma'am.'

'Can you guess?'

I took a deep breath and thought about this. 'I think you became a salmon, then forgot who you were and the hazelnut helped you remember your Pooka self.'

'You are a very good guesser, Prince Conor.'

I smiled like a schoolboy. 'I have not seen a Pooka since entering the Pinelands, except your son. Is that what happened to everyone?'

'Many were lost before me. I suspect that what you ask is what has happened. I confess I do not know – a sad admission for a queen. I must confer with my son and my council.' As if on cue, Tuan showed up with four confused Pookas in bathrobes. They bowed to their queen. 'If you will excuse us, Conor, we have pressing business.'

'Sure,' I said and then added, 'Hey, would anybody mind if I took a bath?'

It's such a drag to put on dirty clothes after a bath but I had no choice. After almost cooking myself in a bathtub that heated water with the same gold wire system that the kettle used, I re-donned my clothes and smelled pretty much the same as before.

When I arrived downstairs Tuan escorted me to a pair of doors that led to the Queen's council room. There were raised voices on the other side that I couldn't quite understand and then I heard the Queen's voice silence them all. Even if I couldn't hear the exact words the meaning was quite clear – the Queen had decided and *that was that*. Tuan gave me an embarrassed look.

'Don't worry about it,' I whispered, 'I've got a pretty tough mom too.'

His smile was interrupted by the opening of the doors. Inside the chamber there were a dozen or so people. Most looked *compos mentis* but a few still had that abandoned-puppy look. Tuan introduced me in that formal royal court manner that I dislike but have gotten used to: 'Queen Rhiannon, honourable council members, I give you Prince Conor of Duir.'

I did all the proper bowing and scraping and was then invited to sit.

'Prince Conor,' Queen Rhiannon spoke, 'we thank you for your gift.'

'Seeing your need, Your Highness, I can assure you that you and your people will have first priority to any fruit of the Tree of Knowledge.' I thought I was being magnanimous and princely but my statement was greeted by what I can only describe as grumbling. I racked my brains to think what I said wrong. 'Of course I can only speak until someone chooses the major Rune of Hazel but I will ensure that the new head of the House of Cull will know of your need.'

Well, if my first statement was a mistake, this was a blunder of Titanic proportions. The entire council was on their feet and shouting. The Queen raised a hand to silence them, to no avail. Their accents were so thick and they were speaking so fast, I couldn't figure out what they were shouting about.

Queen Rhiannon was forced to stand. 'Silence!' she hissed and the council did as they were told. 'Prince Tuan has recommended that Conor be deemed barush.'

'Prince Tuan is not a member of this council,' a robed woman in the front said.

'And you are not Queen,' Rhiannon said with a voice that almost made me drop to my knees and thank the gods that I was not that woman. The Queen regained a bit of her composure but when she spoke again her voice was still as sharp as a razor. 'While you splashed in your pool Tuan ensured you were not bear-food.'

'But tradition, Your Highness ...' the woman said, this time with much more contrition in her voice.

'If I had followed tradition – we would all be lost.'

One of the council members banged the arm of his chair with his fist in a signal of agreement. Others slowly joined him and soon the entire council was banging their chairs, even the chastised woman.

Queen Rhiannon gestured for Tuan to stand next to her. He looked confused.

'Prince Tuan, I, Rhiannon of Ailm, in recognition of your service to the Pinelands, salute you.' She stood and bowed the lowest bow I have ever seen a queen make. When she came back upright there were tears in her eyes. 'I am so very proud of you, my son.'

Tuan's eyes glistened as he embraced his mother and the entire council rose as one and bowed. They stayed that way until Tuan returned the salute.

'Take your place among the council, Prince Tuan.'

Tuan whipped his head towards his mother in disbelief. She nodded to him and the council resumed their chair banging again until the stunned Tuan took his seat.

Queen Rhiannon sat smiling for a while waiting for Tuan to get a grip on himself. For a moment she looked more like a mother than a queen. Finally she said, 'Councillor Tuan.' It took Tuan a micro-second to realise that she was addressing him. 'Earlier you proposed that Prince Conor should be anointed as barush. Do you still feel this way?'

'I do, Your Highness.'

'Do any council members object?' The lady in the front row that made the stink before had a furtive look around but said nothing. 'Very well, Tuan, would you please bring The Elements? It seems my clerk is still grazing somewhere.' I liked this queen. Anybody that can crack a joke at a time like this is my kind of monarch. 'Prince Conor, you have been chosen for the honour of barush. Do you know what this means?'

I hadn't the faintest idea. I assumed it was a good thing but at that moment it occurred to me that barush might mean lunch and they were all going to turn into lions and eat me. 'No, ma'am, I don't.'

'Barush means friend. It is the highest honour we bestow on a non-Pooka. There have been very few – but one was your grandfather Liam.'

Tuan entered pushing a rolling table that had three bowls on it. Queen Rhiannon stood and walked towards me. I began to rise but Rhiannon motioned for me to remain seated. She stood in front of me and asked to see my hands, which she took and turned palm up. 'Barush like all friendship carries no rules or limits. Do you accept?'

'I would be honoured.'

'Then Conor, Son of Hazel and Oak, in the name of the Pookas of The Land' – she placed dirt from one of the bowls onto my hand – 'and of the rivers and lakes' – she splashed water from another bowl onto the dirt in my palm and smeared it into mud. 'And of the sky,' she said, bringing my hands up close to her face and blowing on them. Then she grabbed a handful of salt from the last remaining bowl and mixed it into the water. She stirred it with her hand then dribbled saltwater onto my palms, 'And in the memory of our sisters and brothers lost to the sea – I name you: barush.' She reached inside her robe and produced a coin-sized gold disc attached to a loop of gold wire no bigger than a bracelet. As she reached up the loop of gold wire expanded and she placed the medallion around my neck. Then she pushed my palms together as if in prayer and kissed me on both cheeks. In my ear she whispered, 'Lord Liam would have been very proud.'

With the pomp and circumstance done Queen Rhiannon announced, 'We have been asleep too long – there is work to do.' She instructed some councillors to house the rest of my party and ordered others to whip up some hazelnut potion to try to revive the herbivore Pookas that were inside the wall. The carnivores without, they wisely decided to leave until daylight.

Tuan led me to the guest wing. As we walked I patted him on the back. 'You are a Pooka hero.'

He blushed and looked embarrassed that anyone would even think such a thing. If he had been a cowboy he would have said, 'Aw shucks.'

'Really,' I said, 'you were the only one that didn't get lost and you're the only Pooka anybody has ever heard of that can change into more than one animal. You're like a super-Pooka. We should get you a tee-shirt with a big P painted on the front.'

'You are very kind …' Then Tuan's ears began to stretch and fur-up. He had to turn away and compose himself to stop from transforming into some creature. 'Sorry, Prince Conor, I sometimes change when I get emotional.'

'Don't worry about it and it's just Conor, OK.'

'You are very kind, Conor, but things are not as they seem.'

'Oh yeah, so what am I missing?'

Tuan paused and I thought he was about to tell me. It was obviously something important but then he looked over his shoulder and said, 'I am very busy. I must help round up some lost bunnies.'

'Of course, Councillor Tuan,' I said with a smile. He blushed again – this guy was cute.

'Just Tuan, OK?' he said.

TWENTY-TWO

MORAN

I wandered around my chambers – they were pretty small for royal digs but the bed was soft and there was an en-suite bathroom. I walked out onto the balcony and let the cold air pink up my cheeks as I looked at the pond that a few hours earlier had been the Queen's swimming pool.

'I hope you do not mind this small room,' Queen Rhiannon said, startling me, 'but this room was a favourite of your grandfather's. I thought you might like it too.'

'I do,' I said, bowing my head. 'Thank you.'

Queen Rhiannon leaned against the banister next to me and looked out over her pond. 'I once asked Liam why he liked this room better than the regal rooms and he said it was because here he had a better chance to see me naked.' The Queen smiled. 'He was very cheeky, your grandfather. You have the same twinkle in your eyes.'

'That is very nice to hear, Your Highness.'

The cold and a clatter of teacups made us go back inside. A mousey little servant, that recently may have actually been a mouse, was twitchingly setting up tea, flatbread and dried fruits. When she spilled the Queen's tea, Rhiannon placed her hand on the servant's and said, with a reassuring smile, that she could go. My tea was served by a Queen.

'I thank you again for the hazelnuts, Conor, but since you did not know of our plight before you arrived, I wonder, is there another reason for your visit?'

'Oisin is dying.'

The Queen tilted her head like a confused puppy and said, 'Dying?'

That's when I realised that the concept of a slow death is quite alien to some of the people in The Land. People here either die fast, in battle or by falling out of a poplar tree – or they commit seafaring suicide by sailing out to sea in a boat – but since there is no sickness, a lingering illness followed by death just doesn't happen. So I told her the long tale about how Dad reattached his hand in the Chamber of Runes and how that seems to be killing him and how Mom and Fand encased him in Shadowmagic.

Queen Rhiannon took it all in, wide-eyed. 'For hundreds of years there is nothing new in The Land – I'm lost for a couple of months and all has changed. But I cannot imagine how I can help.'

'I was hoping you could tell me where I can get some *tughe tine* blood.'

I don't think I could have shocked her more if I had slapped her in the face. 'Who told you of *tughe tine*?'

I explained about the manuscript that contained the story of the Grey Ones and their search for the blood of the *tughe tine* and about our strange encounter with the mountaintop Oracle. Finally I told her of the knife and the message that told me that the changelings would have answers.

Queen Rhiannon just sat there with her hand over her mouth and shook her head for a time before she finally said, 'You certainly do not bring dull stories, Prince Conor. So Deirdre has developed a way to bring back lost manuscripts?'

'Yes, ma'am.'

'She is a very clever witch, that mother of yours.' Queen Rhiannon thought again for a time then said, 'The answers to the questions you ask are … not easily given. There were members of the council today who wanted you and your party dead for what you have deduced already. We Pookas think like animals. So many animals live so much in fear that they hide their injuries. They think that if another animal sees their vulnerabilities that they will use it against them. But some-times we think like animals too much. We forget that there are crea-tures that might want to help. If not for you, Conor, and the Faeries – we all would be lost. Your grandfather was the only non-Pooka to know of our dependence on the fruit of the hazel. If more had known then maybe the Tree of Knowledge would have been better defended.'

'Dahy is building a small regiment to protect it now.'

'Dahy lives? That is good news. I think it is time we ended our isola-tion. Do you think he would accept some Pooka recruits?'

'I know he would.'

'Good. Now to answer your question, Conor, I shall tell you of things that even many of my own people do not know. But in the light of recent events maybe more should learn of our history.' She dropped her head and took a deep breath collecting her thoughts.

'The Pooka were the first new race. We believe that only the Faeries, Leprechauns and Brownies are older. In the beginning we were not changelings but we had an affinity with animals. We tended herds for the House of Duir and learned magic from Ériu. Using gold we learned how to speak to the animals.'

'I've seen my mother do that by placing gold in her mouth.'

'Yes, I authorised my daughter to teach her that. As I said, she is a very clever witch. But we Pooka did not stop there. Soon we were using magic to completely empathise with the animals. Cults began – the most prominent were the Marcach and the Fia.'

'Horse and deer?' I said, remembering my father teaching me names of animals in ancient Gaelic when I was a kid.

'Yes. The cults submerged themselves completely in their chosen animals to the point where the first changes began. The Marcach became half horse themselves and the Fia became half deer half Pooka.'

'Centaurs and Fauns,' I said aloud.

'Yes,' Queen Rhiannon said as if being roused out of a daydream, 'I have heard those words used by Pookas that came back from a Real World sojourn. But the half change was dangerous. Marcach and Fia began to lose themselves – they became horses and deer and no one could bring them back. A council was formed and the cults were banned, but they continued in secret.

'One of our kind was named Moran. He was reported to be the wisest of all the Pooka. He studied every creature that was known on the land and in the air, then he left for the sea. There he studied the fish and found the aquatic mind so different to our own that he could safely change into a half fish and not lose his Pooka identity.'

'Wait a minute. Are you talking about mermaids? Like topless girls with fish bottoms?'

It was only a matter of time before Queen Rhiannon gave me the dirty look that every other woman I had known had given me. 'Mertain is what he called them but yes, mermaid is the Real World name. At about the same time another of my ancestors travelled to the Hazellands. Before the Hall of Knowledge existed, wise men and women would gather at the great hazel tree and share ideas. My ancestor tried a hazelnut and it instilled him with such self-knowledge that he attempted a complete change into an animal and was able to return to his Pooka self. He arrived back at the Pinelands at almost the same time Moran did. Both of them drew supporters, each professing the virtues of their discoveries. Soon most were following my ancestor, changing into all manner of beasts using hazel. Moran warned that dependence on hazelnuts was dangerous but he was unheeded. I have not thought of him in a very long time but I must now admit that he may have been right.'

'What happened to Moran?'

'Finally he and his followers left to live permanently in the sea. The Pookas of the Pinelands never heard of them for centuries. Then a half woman/half fish washed up on the shore injured and the Banshees brought her to us. She told us that the Mertain live in the archipelago off the Fearn Peninsula. She named two of the islands – one was Faoilean Island and the other was Tughe Tine Isle.'

'What happened to her?'

'She was escorted to Fearn Point and she swam home. We have not heard from the Mertain since.'

'Do you have a guide that could take me there?'

'The Fearn Peninsula is in the Alderlands. Our peoples have had no contact in a long time but I may be able to help you, but not for several days. I would like to get my kindred unlost before I lose them again.'

'Of course. Thank you, Your Highness.'

She placed her hand on my cheek. 'It is so good to see Liam's seed in this room. Sleep well, Son of Hazel.' Before she left she stopped and turned to me. 'There is one more thing you should know, Conor. The Mertain that washed up on the shore …'

'Yes?'

'She was … old.'

I spent that night dreaming about a mermaid. I don't know if my dreams were a premonition or just the result of talking about them all day, but I can tell you one thing: the mermaid I dreamt about wasn't old.

I awoke in the morning to the sound of splashing. I had one of those surreal moments when I couldn't figure out whether the sound was coming from my dream or from the waking world. I sat up in bed and listened. Just because my grandfather was a peeping tom didn't mean I was going to cop a look at Queen Rhiannon swimming naked – as much as I'd like to. I dressed, walked downstairs and found Essa speaking to the wet-haired, robed Queen, at the entrance to the council room. They stopped when they saw me. The Queen and I swapped morning pleasantries and she left.

'Is everyone all right?' I asked.

'We're fine,' Essa said. 'Brendan has been complaining about not having any meat in a while. He asked a Pooka if he could change into something he called a New York porterhouse so he could eat him. I'm not sure if the poor Pooka was scared or just confused.' Then she smiled and I realised just how much I had missed that smile. 'The Queen seems to like you,' she said.

'Oh, yeah? What did she say about me?'

'She told me that I was with the wrong man.'

'Well, I have to agree with her there. I don't see how you can ignore such good advice from a queen and a prince. Come to think of it I'm sure I could get a king to join the focus group.'

'Turlow is a king,' she replied smugly.

'And here is me thinking that he was just a Turd-low.'

Essa's face got those lines in it that meant that our pleasant conversation was coming to an end. She turned to leave. I reached for her arm and thought better of it.

'Essa,' I called after her and she stopped. 'Seriously, even if we never get together again I still agree with the Queen. He is not the right man for you.'

She gave me that exasperated look, which was safer than her *I'm about to hit you* look. 'And why is that?'

'When you are around him – you … you just don't seem to be you.'

This looked like it threw her for a second. But then she bounced back, 'Maybe this is the real me and you are the one that brings out my worst.'

I shook my head. 'I don't think so.'

For a second I thought she was going to say something else but then she looked at her shoes and left.

TWENTY-THREE
RE-POOKALATION

T he Pinelands quickly became re-Pookalated. It must not take much hazelnut to help a Pooka remember how to stand on two legs 'cause everywhere I went I saw formerly fur-covered people being led back to their homes looking kinda dopey. I spoke to Tuan and he said that when Pookas are *lost* it takes them a while to start thinking like a person again. I saw one woman lick her hand and then wash her cheek like a cat.

Tuan hosted a dinner for us in his modest house. Believe it or not he cooked salmon.

'That's what I just don't get,' Brendan said between mouthfuls. 'You guys in The Land just go up to a bunny or a fish and say, "Could you please die for me?" and they do?'

'We are not as flippant as that,' Araf answered, 'asking for an animal's life is a skill that must be learned, but that is essentially what happens.'

'Why on earth would an animal agree to that?' Brendan asked.

'Because they know they will be born again,' Tuan said as if talking to a five-year-old.

'How do they know that?'

This question stumped Tuan, as if Brendan had asked him, 'How do you know the sun shines?'

'That is what they tell me,' the Pooka said. 'Why would I doubt them?'

It was nice having a boys' night. Tuan had invited the Turd-low but he said he would rather sit alone and wait for his beloved to return from the dinner she was having with Nieve and the Queen. Brendan, who usually sticks up for the Banshee, called him 'hen-pecked'. I, on the other hand, thought maybe Turlow had the right idea. Perhaps if I had paid more attention to Essa I would be doing something other than talking bull with guys and laying the groundwork for a hangover.

Saying that, it was a delightful evening. The food was good and Tuan produced a couple of bottles of some lovely Pooka mead-like stuff that had milk or cream in it. I almost asked if the milk came from regular cows or Pookas that were cows and then decided that I didn't want to know. It was stronger than it tasted and it loosened Tuan's tongue until I asked him how much hazelnut it takes to make a Pooka remember that he has feet instead of paws.

Tuan clammed up and said that was not information that should be discussed outside of the clan.

'Don't worry, Pooka brother,' I told him. 'Remember I'm a barush and Brendan is my closest adviser. Any Pooka secret you tell him or me will go no further than this room.'

'I'm an adviser?' Brendan said. 'When did that happen?'

'And you can tell Araf anything 'cause he never speaks,' I said, patting the Imp on the back. 'Isn't that right, Prince Araf?'

The big guy gave me his hallmark blank stare.

'See.'

'Anyway what's the big secret?' Brendan asked. 'So you need hazel-nuts. Pookas need hazelnuts and cops need donuts.'

'Do donuts come from *do* trees?' Tuan asked.

'Never mind,' I said, 'but Brendan has a point. Why keep it such a secret?'

'Because it is a weakness,' Tuan said, crouching down as if someone was overhearing him. 'If others were to realise our dependence on hazel then they could use it to exploit us.'

'It seems to me that someone already has,' Brendan said in such a matter-of-fact way that everyone looked at him a bit shocked.

'Explain,' Tuan demanded.

'Well, Conor told me that no one knows why the Hall of Knowledge was destroyed. It seems obvious to me that somebody wanted to take the Pookas out of the equation by destroying all the hazel trees. They almost succeeded.'

My gods, I thought, *it was so obvious. Why didn't I see it before?*

Tuan was unconvinced. 'But no one knew about our need for hazelnuts except Conor's grandfather.'

'Are you sure about that?' Brendan asked. 'The one thing I know about secrets is that there is no such thing. Somebody else always knows.'

'Who?' Tuan asked.

'Someone who is a master of ancient lore,' I said in a dreamy voice as I thought out loud. 'Someone who will do anything to get his own way.'

'Oh,' Araf said.

'Who?' Brendan and Tuan asked together.

I had to take a slug of Pooka-shine before I could even say the name. 'Cialtie.'

This kinda killed the happy party mood of the evening but it didn't stifle the discussion. We all eventually agreed that if the Hazellands were destroyed to stop the Pookas from getting hazelnuts, then that meant that the Hall of Knowledge was once again in peril.

'We should inform Dahy,' Araf said.

'Inform him of what?' a woman's voice asked from the doorway. It was Aunt Nieve followed by Essa.

We filled the ladies in on our epiphany. At first they thought it was just drunken ramblings but then they asked more questions. Soon they thought it was a pretty good theory too.

'We should talk about this on our walk,' Nieve said.

'Good idea,' Brendan replied, jumping up to join her.

'You two have a walk planned?' I asked as I gave a questioning glance to Essa. The tilt of her head implied she knew something that I didn't. The walkers just smiled. Brendan came back into the room to pick up his jacket from the floor beside me. As he leaned down I whispered, 'And what's all this then?'

'It's a walk,' he replied with a smile. 'I have a choice between sitting here listening to you whine or a walk in the moonlight with a beautiful woman. Hmm, let me think on that for a second.' He grabbed his jacket and they left.

I turned to Essa. 'So I suppose you are off to join your snuggly Banshee?'

'Actually,' she said, plopping down on the cushion next to me, 'what I could really use is a drink.'

I jumped up and got her a glass. Tuan poured her a measure of Pooka-shine and she downed it in one.

Then she smiled at me and said, 'Can I have another?'

I took this to be a very good sign.

I really could have used a lie-in the next morning, but Tuan got me up to meet with the Queen so I could tell her about our theory of the night before. After that I had to give a briefing to the entire council. A few Pookas got a bit hot under the collar when they found out that Tuan and I were talking freely about hazelnut dependency in front of outsiders, but I told them that my companions had figured it out by themselves and if our theory was correct, then the cat was out of the bag anyway. Then I spent another twenty minutes trying to explain what an 'old expression' was and why a cat was in a bag in the first place.

In the end they came around and decided that there should be a Pooka presence with Dahy's army at the Hall of Knowledge. The Queen pledged a small detail comprising a handful of bear Pooka soldiers, a courier wolf and a Pooka hawk for reconnaissance. Aunt Nieve agreed to escort the Pooka recruits back to the Hazellands.

'I would really like it if you came with us,' I said to my aunt after the meeting, 'and I think Brendan would too,' I said, testing her reaction.

She didn't return my smile, she didn't really look very happy at all. 'I have a duty to your mother and to Duir. I have too long been too far away. Escorting the Pookas needs to be done and Castle Duir should not be left without one of the family.' Then she smiled, took my face in her hands and kissed me on the forehead. 'When I was young I worked on a spell that would allow me to be in two places at one time – I only ever succeeded in giving myself a headache. I wish now I had worked harder. Be careful, nephew. Find a cure for my brother and come back safe. Now I must tell Brendan.'

'Yeah,' I said, 'what's going on with you two?'

She smiled and gave me a very un-Nieve-like girly shrug then practically skipped away.

That night I was invited back into the Queen's sitting room for tea.

'My son Tuan has asked me if he could be your group's guide to the end of the Brownie Peninsula. Is this agreeable with you?'

'Yes, ma'am. I really like Tuan.'

'He is very fond of you, Prince Conor. May the gods take care of you both.'

'I'm sure we will be fine.'

'Well,' she said in a knowing motherly tone, 'just to be sure I am sending a bear with you.'

'If you insist.'

'I do,' she said in a voice that made it clear that I would have been an idiot to discuss the matter further. 'How you will reach Tughe Tine Isle I cannot counsel you on.'

'Don't worry about it. I'm a fly-by-the-seat-of-my-pants kind of guy – we'll figure it out.'

The next few minutes were spent in talking about what my pants had to do with anything.

'I would be happier if the Banshee were not with you,' the Queen said.

'What have you got against Turlow?'

'You suspect that the Banshees from the Reedlands destroyed the Hall of Knowledge, do you not?'

'I do.'

'Then how can you trust a member of that race?'

'A member of your race tried to eat me a couple of days ago. Should I distrust the Pooka? My father told me that Banshees were some of the most loyal guards he had ever known and one of the finest persons I have ever known was a Banshee.'

The Queen raised her hands and I stopped. 'Banshee loyalty is well known, Son of Duir, but in the past too many Banshees have been loyal to your uncle. Can you honestly say that Cialtie will bother Tir na Nog no more?'

I started to say something then shrugged – she had a point.

She reached across and touched my cheek. 'You remind me so much of your grandfather.'

'I didn't peek – honest.'

She smiled at that – a smile that charmed me as much as I'm sure it charmed my grandfather. 'Liam too voiced his opinions passionately but he was more stubborn than you. He refused to let Dahy put soldiers in the Hazellands and that stubbornness eventually killed him. Make sure you do not allow pride to stop you from what you truly think should be.'

I wasn't sure what she was talking about and obviously it showed on my face.

'Let Essa know how you feel.'

'Oh,' I said, leaning back in my chair. 'Well, Essa is … Essa is a difficult woman.'

'The best ones always are. As a matter of fact, that is what your grandfather used to say.' She reached under her chair and produced a plain wooden box. 'Liam gave me this, years ago. I would like you to have it.'

She opened the box. Inside, on a bed of satin, was a throwing blade with a green glass handle inlaid with gold wire. It was identical to the one that contained the message and was thrown at Brendan on Mount Cas. I picked it up and admired it.

'As you can see I have never used it,' she said. 'The tip is still very golden.'

'Do you know where my grandfather got this?'

'Dahy,' she said. 'It was one of two that he made. Liam told me that Master Dahy gave one to him and the other to his true love.'

TWENTY-FOUR

YOGI BEAR

Uncharacteristically, I was the first to arrive for our crack-of-dawn departure. A small dusting of snow swirled in a bitter wind that stung my cheeks. It was flipping freezing. I wondered for a second why I wasn't snuggled up in a warm bed but then the image of my statue-like father pushed that thought away. Nieve's Pooka entourage mounted up. The five bears were on horseback while the wolf and hawk chose to travel in their animal shapes.

Nieve showed up with her arm locked onto Brendan's. She gave him a right proper thirty-second snog and then leapt on her horse. I was about to make a comment but the look on her face made me stop. She didn't need a joke.

The rest of my gang showed up and mounted up. We had all said our goodbyes the night before so the two groups saluted Queen Rhiannon and her council, then we waved to each other and went in separate directions. If I hadn't known better I could have sworn I saw tough-as-old-boots Aunt Nieve wipe a tear as she turned.

Tuan introduced me to our Pooka bear guard. His name was Yarrow.

'Yarrow the Bear?' I said with a laugh. 'Mind if I call you Yogi?'

I then had to explain what a nickname was. Yarrow liked the concept and he also liked the idea of being 'smarter than the average bear' so the name stuck and he became Yogi Bear.

The path to the Alderlands was on the opposite side of the mountain that we had come up. Tuan and Yogi casually touched trees as they passed, picking up messages that were then deposited on other trees. Pookas in animal form were in the forest as well, especially red squirrels jumping from tree to tree reinstating the pine tree telegraph that had been neglected for so long. Normal animals were also slowly repopulating the Pinelands. Queen Rhiannon had sent out a few envoys to persuade the normal animals that the Pookas were no longer bonkers. I didn't see any big creatures like boar or deer but the fast little guys, rabbits and foxes and squirrels, were back. Tuan said they seemed jumpier than normal but I couldn't tell.

We could have made it out of the Pinelands in one day but Tuan and Yogi decided to call an early halt. 'The less time sleeping under an alder tree the better,' Tuan said. I remembered the last time I slept under an alder – everything I owned, including my shoes, was stolen. I wasn't looking forward to spending time in a forest full of them.

'We are going to have to pay tribute to the King of the Brownies,' Tuan said that night around the campfire.

'Can't we avoid Brownie Castle and just get to the island?' I said. 'I hate all that royal bowing and scraping stuff. And I've met the King of the Brownies – I'm not a big fan.'

'As soon as we enter the Alderlands,' Tuan said, 'the trees will inform all of the Brownies that we are there. We cannot avoid Fearn Keep. Do you have anything to give the King for a tribute?'

'Yeah, Mom gave me some gold, mined by Leprechauns from Castle Duir.' I reached into my saddlebag and produced four slim pieces of gold imprinted with the Oak Rune. They were about the size of a candy bar. 'How many of them should I give him?'

Everyone's eyes nearly popped out of their heads. 'One will be more than ample,' Araf said. 'Put them away and don't let any of the alders see that gold or you won't have any to give.'

Admittedly I had never had a good experience with the Brownies but it kind of bothered me how people talked about them. 'You know, guys,' I said, 'I refuse to condemn an entire race just because the first one I met robbed me blind, but it seems to me that everyone hides their wallets when they come up against Brownies. What is it with those guys?'

'Brownies believe that the Faeries of Duir are pretenders to the Oak Throne,' Tuan said.

'Pretenders?'

'Yes, they believe that they are descendants of Banbha and therefore should be the custodians of the gold mines of Duir.'

'Banbha, she is one of the Three Sisters, right? Isn't she the one that sailed away and brought the Banshees to The Land?'

'That is the legend,' Tuan said. 'The Brownies believe that while she was away the other two sisters, Fódla and Ériu, forced a Brownie named Doran to take a Choosing against his will. He chose the Fearn Rune. Alder Island was created and the Brownies were banished to it. The Brownies believe that the reason the Alderlands are so swampy is because Doran's heart was not committed to the Choosing.'

'The Alderlands is an island?'

'It was,' Tuan answered. 'When the Pinelands were formed it was joined with the rest of The Land.'

'I still don't see why they have such a reputation as thieves?'

'Brownies do not like living by the rules of Duir,' Tuan said.

'What rules of Duir?'

'There really is no such thing,' Tuan said quickly as if I might take offence, 'but Duir was the first Land. It has an army and it has all of the gold. There are no official rules but if a throne displeases Duir then life for them could be difficult.'

I looked to Araf for confirmation. He shrugged and nodded yes. 'So Duir doesn't give the Brownies any gold?'

'Your grandfather Finn was very tolerant of the Brownies. After he disappeared Cialtie was very generous to them and since then they have grown bolder.'

'So let me see if I've got this right,' I said. 'They believe they should have all the gold, so they think it's OK to steal it whenever they feel like it.'

Tuan and Yogi looked at each other and nodded. 'That would be an appropriate summation,' Tuan said. 'Even a Brownie wouldn't mind being called a thief. They are taught thievery and stealth as part of their formal education.'

'Well, that would have spiced up high school.'

I had a quick face wash in a bowl of freezing cold water and stumbled in the dark back to my tent. Brendan was already in there. Now that Nieve was gone it seemed I had a roommate again.

'Don't you have a tent of your own?' I asked as I got into my sleeping roll.

'Why should I bother pitching my own tent when yours is so comfy?'

'I'm like a big important prince, you know?'

'Are you really?' Brendan said in the dark. 'I thought that was just a line you used to meet girls.'

'No, it's real. I got a castle, family sword, servants – the whole nine yards.'

'Gosh,' Brendan said, 'you would think with all that stuff that you wouldn't have to share a tent.'

'Yeah,' I said in resignation. 'Speaking of girls, that was quite a show you put on up there in the Pinelands.'

'What show would that be?'

'The thirty-second movie-star goodbye kiss you had with my aunt.'

'Oh, you saw that did you?'

'They saw it from the space shuttle. You realise, Brendan, that my aunt is probably like a thousand years old.'

'She doesn't look a thousand years old.'

'Well, I'm just saying, are you sure you want to get involved with a woman that you might have studied about in ancient history class?'

'Conor?'

'Yes?'

'Shut up.'

'I'm just saying ...'

'Good night, Mr O'Neil.'

'Yeah, good night, Detective Fallon.'

I had almost fallen to sleep when Brendan just had to get the last word in.

'Conor, no offence, but if I was going to ask for relationship advice – I wouldn't ask you.'

I didn't answer him. I just silently nodded in agreement.

The flaps of the tent cracked with the morning frost. Tuan and Yogi weren't happy with the dusting of snow. It made it difficult to choose the right path into the Alderlands. And being on the right path in the Alderlands is important, 'cause if you're not on the path – you're in a swamp.

After about an hour, the Pookas found what seemed to be a solid trail. The only swamps I had ever seen in Tir na Nog were the ones in Cialtie's Reedlands. I was not looking forward to going into another but once inside I was relieved to see that these swamps were much healthier than the foul and unnatural ones in my uncle's patch. Still, it was spooky. Leafless alder trees draped with long catkins lined our path or lived alone on bogie islands. Even though the ground was white with a light snow and the sky was cloudless, the place still seemed to be darker than it should, as if the light was mysteriously being sucked from the place. Small black birds darted through the trees but moved so fast I could never actually see one. Around the edges, the swamps were frozen but in the dark deeper water near the middle, unseen creatures submerged as we passed – their presence only given away by a tiny splash or an ominous plop.

The Pookas decided that someone should talk to a tree and let them know we were here. Araf was chosen, since nobody has any real beefs with the Imps. He placed his hands on a burly alder for a few moments, said, 'Thank you,' and walked back to us.

'She pretended to be surprised,' Araf said, 'but I got the impression that they already knew we were here. I told her we were coming to see the King and she wished us good luck.'

'Was that like an actual "good luck", I asked, 'or a you're gonna need it "good luck"?'

As usual I didn't get an answer from Araf.

Essa pulled back and dropped in next to me later that day. I stifled the sarcastic comment about Turd-low. Call me genius but I was starting to realise that maybe one of the reasons Essa was so feisty was because I wound her up all the time.

'I have to say, Conor, this is not my favourite place.'

'First trip to the Alderlands then?'

She nodded yes. 'I'm not very happy about being here and neither is my father.'

'Your father? How does Gerard know you are here?'

'I have an *emain* slate with me.'

'You do? Why didn't you tell me? I could have used that to see how my father is.'

'I have been keeping track of Oisin's health. It is unchanged. I would have told you if it was otherwise.'

I relaxed a little. 'Mom said that he was getting worse.'

'That has not changed either but it seems the progression is still very slow.'

We rode in silence until finally I broke it. 'So your dad's not a big Brownie fan?'

'Some of my earliest memories are of Father complaining about the Brownies not paying their bills, but I think this is less about the Brownies and more about me being too far from home. He worries about me.'

'Well, I don't blame him. I worry about you too,' I said. 'I worry about you coming up behind me and clubbing me in the head.'

That one got a laugh out of Essa that was loud enough to make Turlow look around and wonder what we were talking about. I hoped he thought we were laughing at him.

'Maybe I should get back,' she said.

I almost replied, 'Oh, we wouldn't want to keep the Turd-low waiting.' But as she pulled ahead what I actually said was, 'Give your father my best.' Who says I *have* to be immature?

The cold air and the rhythm of Acorn beneath should have lulled me into that hypnotic state that makes travelling hours on horseback bearable, but I kept being disturbed by my companions flitting around me. Finally I broke my personal reverie, slid between Tuan and Yogi and asked what was going on.

'We are being tracked,' Tuan said. 'Can you not sense it?'

'Of course,' I lied, 'I was just asking you for confirmation.'

I had a look around. I neither saw nor felt anything. 'Brownies?' I asked.

'That would be a safe assumption.'

'Have you spotted them yet?'

'No, Brownies are very good at not being seen.'

'Why don't you, like, turn into a hawk and see if you can spot them from the air?'

An almost growling sound came from Yogi. The look on his face made me think that he was about to hit me. Tuan didn't look angry but I knew instantly that I had made a major social faux pas. He kept his eyes down as if embarrassed and said, 'That would not work.'

Even though I wasn't sure what for, I apologised and slunk back to Araf. I told him what I had just said and asked what mistake I had made. He didn't know but added how impressed he was that I could make blunders where no one had ever made blunders before.

TWENTY-FIVE
THE ALDERLANDS

I didn't bother looking for our Brownie shadows. If expert trackers like Essa and Araf couldn't spot anything it was pointless for me to try. Also, from my experience of Brownies, it was unlikely we would get an arrow in the back – the real danger was getting robbed in the dark.

I made Brendan pitch the tent that night. I was drafted into begging wood from an alder. I found a not too menacingly sized tree and placed my hands on it.

'*You have slept under an alder before,*' came a strong and unpleasant voice in my head, '*but not in the Alderlands. You and … a Banshee slept under one of the lonely trees. Am I not correct?*'

'How do you know that?' I said. 'That alder was miles away from any other.'

There was almost a smirk in his voice when he replied, '*Perhaps we leave messages on the breeze. But where is that Banshee?*'

'Dead.'

'*Ah,*' his voiced echoed remorselessly in my head. '*He kicked my brother tree.*'

'And for that he deserved to die?'

'*Did he? I do not know what he deserved. I only know that he kicked a tree.*'

'The tree had just robbed him,' I said.

'*Robbed by a tree? How is that possible?*'

'The one who picks the lock on the door is as responsible as the thief that enters the room.'

'*A door made of wood perhaps?*' said the alder.

'Never mind, I refuse to talk in riddles to you.'

'*You started it, Faerie. What do I know of locks and rooms? If you are plain with me then so will I be with you.*'

He was starting to give me a headache so I just asked him for some firewood. The branches above creaked and fell around me. I thanked him, then just before I let go I said, 'Would you tell me if there are robbers watching us now?'

'*I would tell you, young prince,*' he said in a way that slightly reminded me of my Uncle Cialtie, '*but would what I tell you be true?*'

That night we set a watch again. Tuan took the first shift. I sat with him until everyone had gone to bed.

'Tuan, I want to apologise for what I said tod—'

Tuan grabbed my arm and placed his finger to his lips to shush me. He stared up into the tree canopy and then as I watched, his head sprouted feathers and shrank into his collar. I had to almost stand up to see that his head had turned into an owl's head. He leaned back and surveyed the treetops, then the feathers seemed to melt back into his face and his head popped up as before. He rubbed his eyes and said, 'I thought I saw something moving in those trees. Sorry, you were saying?'

When I could speak again I started with, 'That was pretty awesome.' Tuan shrugged. 'Right, what I was saying before you turned your nose into a beak is that I am sorry for breaking Pooka social protocol before when I asked you to turn into a bird. It would be helpful if you could explain what I did wrong so I could avoid that pitfall in the future.'

'You made no error, Conor.'

'Yogi looked like he was going to tear my head off.'

'Yarrow, or should I say Yogi as he is now known, helped raise me. He is very protective.'

'I still don't get it. What did I say to annoy him?'

'He thought you were teasing me.'

When I looked confused Tuan hung his head and collected his thoughts. Finally, without looking up, he said, 'You once called me … what was the word? A super-Pooka. That implies that I am the best of my race, does it not?'

'Well, even my Aunt Nieve said she'd never heard of a Pooka that could change into lots of different animals.'

Tuan shrugged again. 'I am not the best of my people – I am the least.'

'Why would you say that?'

He looked at his feet again, ashamed. 'I cannot hold to an animal form.'

'What do you mean?'

'Just that,' Tuan said. 'I have studied the disciplines of all the animals and I can change into each and every one but only for a few minutes, after that, my Pooka mind always comes to the fore and I lose the form. I change back.'

'But I saw you fly from a tree as a bird.'

'I climbed that tree when I heard the commotion on the other side of the wall. I almost never fly. To be honest, I am afraid of heights, but I needed to get to you and your party in a hurry. I thought I could make it to the ground before I changed back. As you saw, I didn't.'

'But you saved your people.'

'Not out of choice, Conor. I was saved from being lost because I am too stupid to hold onto a fauna form for more than a few moments. It is nothing to be proud of.'

'But who separated the carnivores from the herbivores?'

'That was me. I allowed the bigger animals to chase me through the gate and then locked them outside.' Tuan chuckled to himself. 'Several times it was a very close call.'

'I can't believe you saved an entire race and still call yourself "the least" of them. The council didn't think so – Councillor Tuan.'

'The council only instated me because of my mother. They think I am weak-minded and I do not disagree.'

This poor guy had been living with this shame for so long, his self-esteem was almost gone. I was tempted to give him a hug but instead I punched him on the arm.

'Ow. Why did you do that?'

'Because you're stupid.'

'Oh,' he said, looking at his feet, 'I know that.'

'No, you don't. Let me ask you something? How many creatures can you turn into?'

'I would guess two score.'

'And every time you failed you tried again and learned another animal?'

'Yes, I have been alive for a very long time.'

'A lesser man would have given up long ago. You have shown determination and fortitude beyond any of your people.'

He shrugged again – a habit I was determined to break him of.

'You have to admit it.'

'Well, I guess.'

'You must be the hardest-working member of a race that was saved from extinction because of you. If I ever hear you speak badly about yourself it won't be your arm I punch – it'll be your nose.'

The way he looked at me made me wonder if anyone in his hundreds of years had ever spoken to him this way. A smile started in the corners of his mouth and he whispered, 'OK.'

'OK?' I said louder.

'Yes,' he said, standing.

I started to stand up with him when he popped back down, grabbed my arm and shushed me again. Then he performed his owl head trick. When his head was normal-sized again he leaned in close and whispered, 'Get Yogi. We have company.'

I woke up the bear as casually as I could and then the three of us sat around the fire pretending we weren't being watched. Tuan passed around a bottle filled with water that we swigged as if it was moonshine. Tuan patted Yogi on the back and then dropped his head on his shoulder in what looked like a display of drunken camaraderie. In reality they were making a plan. Yogi got up and staggered to a nearby tree to relieve himself and Tuan laughingly told him to go further away. When he was under the right tree Tuan slapped me on the back and whispered in my ear, 'Are you armed?'

'I have one of Dahy's throwing blades in my sock.'

'Let us hope you have no need to use it.'

As he was speaking his head shrank down into his collar and those downy white feathers sprouted again. He leaned his whole body back (since his neck no longer tilted up and down), pointed to a space in the tree above Yogi and let loose a screech that made my blood run cold. It was like something out of a cheap horror movie. When I looked to see what Yogi was doing, he wasn't there. In his place was a pile of clothes. Yogi, now fully a bear, was climbing with lightning speed. Once in the tree there was a lot of screaming and growling combined with Tuan's screeching and pointing. I couldn't see much and didn't have a clue what was going on. Then I heard the unmistakable sound of a falling, screaming Brownie. Yogi climbed down so fast that I thought he was falling too. Tuan, now normal-headed, and I ran to the crumpled Brownie but just as we reached him, Yogi Bear came towards him roaring and we both backed off. The bear picked up the fallen Brownie and gripped him in what I can only describe as a bear hug.

'Come down,' Tuan shouted to the treetops, 'and I will try to convince my cousin not to eat your friend.'

We waited for a half a minute. 'Oh well,' Tuan said, gesturing to Yogi, 'enjoy your meal.'

The Brownie was comatose with fear; he didn't even whimper as Yogi opened his jaws wide enough to eat him whole.

'I have a crossbow aimed at you all!' a squeaky voice hollered from the dark. The second Brownie it seemed had jumped to another tree and was now shouting to us from the forest to our right.

Tuan stepped slowly away. 'And just how can you have one bolt aimed at all of us?' he shouted into the dark. 'If you shoot me it will not save your friend. If you shoot the bear then you will only succeed in making him angry.'

From the shadows a man, tall even for a Brownie, appeared. I find it so difficult to judge the age of Brownies, they all look like kids to me, but the way this guy carried himself, I suspected that he had been in sticky situations before. He stepped slowly towards us with his crossbow levelled at Tuan. 'Then I choose to shoot you.'

'You could try,' Tuan said with equal coolness, 'but that would not help your companion.'

Yogi roared again. I felt sorry for his poor captive as bear slobber dripped down the side of his face.

'Tell the bear to release him or I drop you,' the Brownie said.

'Put away your weapon and we can talk,' Tuan replied. 'There is no reason why anyone should be injured here.'

The Brownie in Yogi's arms tried to say something but the bear covered his face with his arm. All that came out were a couple of muffled yelps.

The one with the crossbow nervously glanced from Tuan to Yogi but never took his aim from the Pooka prince. 'The one that is soon to be injured is you, Pooka.'

'I really do not think that will be the case,' Tuan said at almost the exact moment that Essa materialised behind the armed Brownie. With an upward flick of her banta stick she hit underneath the crossbow, sending a singing bolt flying into the night sky. A micro-second later, the other end of the stick cracked him on the neck and he went down onto his knees. Araf appeared out of the darkness and hogtied the would-be assassin with a scarf. Brendan, relaxing his grip on his bow, and Turlow, sporting his Banshee blade, also stepped into the campfire light.

Yogi placed his captive in a one-armed headlock and slipped his athrú disc into his mouth. I'm not sure what scared the poor little guy more: being almost eaten by a bear or instantly discovering that he was in a wrestler's hold with a naked guy. Tuan relieved Yogi of his captive while he went back under the tree and put his clothes back on. The two night stalkers were plopped in front of the fire. Araf asked them if they were injured, but they weren't talking.

'Well,' I said, rubbing my hands together, 'it seems we have guests. Tea anyone?' I addressed the Brownies. 'I suspect you two would like willow, yes?'

The tall one glared at me then said, 'The alders will report that you have us captive. You will be surrounded by the King's men in hours.'

'Good,' Brendan said. 'It's about time we received an escort. This guy here, he's Prince Conor of Duir. Him and him are Princes Tuan and Araf of Pine and Heather?' Brendan looked to the princes to check if he got it right; they nodded and smiled. 'And the girl that clocked you in the head, she is Princess Essa from the boozy Vinelands and oh yeah – over there is The Turlow. I'm pretty sure he outranks everybody.'

'And who are you?' the increasingly worried-looking Brownie asked.

'I'm a cop and you, pal – are very busted. Personally I'm surprised that you want the trees to tell. If I had been rumbled in my own back-yard by a bunch of royal hoity-toities and then laid out by a girl, I'd maybe not want my boss to know about it.'

The Brownie started to say something but Brendan interrupted him.

'On the other hand if you call your boss and tell him that you have met the royal entourage and are escorting them to Castle Alderland, then I suspect my fellow travellers would be delighted to have you along.'

Brendan looked around; everyone shrugged and nodded yes.

The tall Brownie was no dummy. It only took him about a second for the truth of what Detective Fallon was saying to sink in. Despite the panic in his eyes his voice was incredibly calm. 'May I speak with the alder, please?'

Araf untied him and he walked quickly over to the tree. Araf released the smaller one too and I handed him a cup of willow tea that he took with appreciation.

When he returned from speaking to the tree, the tall Brownie approached the fire and bowed. 'My name is Dell of the King's guard,' he said formally. 'Welcome to the Alderlands. It is my duty and pleas-ure to escort you to Fearn Keep.'

TWENTY-SIX
DELL AND WHAT'S-HIS-NAME

'S o,' I asked, 'what about that army of Brownies that is supposed to be coming to your rescue?'

'It is not unusual for alder trees to misinterpret the actions of people in The Land,' the Brownie said. 'There is no approaching army.'

You couldn't deny that this guy was smooth.

Dell drank a cup of willow tea with us but wasn't interested in answering our questions. I offered them Brendan's tent. I even volunteered to pitch it for them but they chose to sleep in the trees. Although the chances of being robbed or attacked were slim, now that our stalkers had become our escorts, the thought of sleeping while Brownies looked down didn't fill us with enough security to abandon keeping watch. Tuan was knackered from his birdie-head trick so I offered to take the first shift.

I sat alone in front of the crackling fire and searched the trees to see if I could spot where Dell and his pal were sleeping. I couldn't see anything. I remembered the first time I had been alone at night in The Land, keeping watch by a fire. I remembered how awesome the strange star-filled night sky had been. Now I just stared up and shivered. The black silhouettes of the leafless branches made the starry sky look cracked and broken. On my first trip to The Land everything was new and wonderful but now everything was just cold and miserable. What

had changed – me or The Land? The obvious answer was The Land.
Fergal wasn't in it any more. Tir na Nog in my mind was the place
where my cousin Fergal lived. His loss weighed on me like a stone yoke
around my neck. Even if I was getting used to the weight of it, I always
knew it was there.

And Dad wasn't here. I knew this was the time in my life where I
wanted to figure stuff out by myself but the idea of him not being out
there somewhere, just as a safety net, unnerved me. A world without
Dad – any world without Dad – just didn't seem right. What if he
doesn't make it? I pushed that thought out of my mind.

I was glad Brendan was here. Not just because he got my Real World
jokes but because it felt like he belonged here. But he wasn't gonna stay
long. As soon as Dad got better or come the next Samhain, he'd be out
of here – back to his daughter and his crazy mother.

The most annoying thing was Turlow. I don't care if Brendan and
Araf like him – I just don't *want* to like him. He gets in the way of me
and Essa. There's no law that says I have to like him. Can't I just dislike
someone regardless of whether they are likable or not?

'You look to be a man deep in the midst of a moral dilemma,' said a
voice to my left. It was Turlow. 'Can I be of assistance?'

'Oh no,' I laughed, 'I don't think this moral dilemma is one you can
help me with. What are you doing awake?'

'The thought of Brownies in the trees is not a restful one. Sleep
eludes me.'

'That I can understand,' I agreed.

Considering that this particular Banshee was not my favourite
person, one would be excused for thinking I was annoyed that he
disturbed my solitude, but to be honest I was glad that someone broke
my morose musings.

'Actually, Turlow, there is something I have been meaning to ask you
about.'

'Yes?' Turlow took a seat and I offered him a cup of tea made from
the stuff that Queen Rhiannon had given me. He took a sip and raised
his eyebrows in approval. 'What would you like to know, Conor?'

'You are The Turlow?'

'You have been waiting to ask me that?'

'No, I mean you are like the King of the Banshees – right?'

He frowned at that and took a sip of his tea, collecting his thoughts. 'Actually, Conor, you were right the first time. I am not a king, I am The Turlow.'

'OK, but you're like the head Banshee?' I pressed.

Turlow smiled at this and said, 'I am tempted to repeat myself and say once again that I am The Turlow – for that title is all the definition that is needed by me or my clan – but yes, I suppose you could say I am the head Banshee.'

'And do all Banshees acknowledge this?'

There had been a light-heartedness to our conversation up till then but it disappeared with that question. 'Why do you ask?'

'I was wondering about the Banshees in the Reedlands. You may have heard from Essa that they attacked us and many suspect that they were responsible for the destruction of the Hall of Knowledge. Are they not your subjects?'

'I have no subjects, Conor. Being a Turlow is much more like being a father than a ruler. As it has been since the beginning of time, a father who pushes too hard one day finds that his son chooses to listen no longer. I do not rule, I just am.'

He continued. 'As for the Banshees in the Reedlands, I knew nothing about them or your attack until after your father regained Duir. This is very worrying for me. I have sent parties to find them – most have failed, while others have failed to return. The Reedlands is a treacherous place.'

'But you must know where they came from?'

'I have my suspicions.'

'And they are?'

He started to answer me but then stopped himself and thought for a bit. 'I have not been The Turlow long. During the time of my tenure my clan has been … uneasy. The cause of this uneasiness was your uncle.'

Now there was a surprise. 'Cialtie has been known to have that effect,' I said. 'What did he do?'

'Years ago he travelled to the Banshee shores. No dignitary of the House of Duir had been there in eons. My predecessor the Old Turlow

JOHN LENAHAN

greeted him as befitted a Prince of Oak. Cialtie stayed among us and befriended the younger members of the clan – including, I must admit, myself. He spoke of how lowly regarded the Banshee were in The Land and when no elders were around he spoke of a time when the Banshees would rule at his side.

'When the Old Turlow heard of this, he accused Cialtie of creating unrest. The Old Turlow ordered him to leave. Cialtie, appalled that a Son of Duir should be treated so, left, but with him he took a small group who openly defied the Old Turlow.

'When Cialtie attained the Oak Throne he came back to the Banshee shores. Although the Old Turlow did not like it, he welcomed him as one should the Head of the House of Duir, but when your uncle proclaimed that he wanted the new army of Duir to be made up entirely of Banshees, the Old Turlow said no. "Banshees defend the far shore, they are not mercenaries." Cialtie countered that all of the shores of The Land are the shores of Duir. The Old Turlow put his foot down, but the temptation was too great. Cialtie offered gold and a good life in Castle Duir. Many of my people joined him. The embarrassment of their desertion caused the Old Turlow to sail out to sea in shame. That is the sad truth of how my tenure as The Turlow began.'

'And what did you do?'

'I kept my word to the Old Turlow. I did not meet with Cialtie but I also did not forbid any of my clan from joining his army. After all he did hold the Oak Rune. If the Chamber of Runes deemed him worthy, who was I to disagree? Of course, now, it is easy to see that the Old Turlow had been right. Cialtie did not deserve the throne and too much Banshee blood was needlessly spilled in his name. If I had known then what I know now …' He shook his head. 'That thinking is the path to madness.'

'That still doesn't explain the Reedland Banshees.'

'The causes of war vary but the effects are almost always the same. One effect is that some men of war never tire of the fight. I suspect the Banshees who live in that unholy swamp are of that ilk. That is why I came to help Dahy. If I cannot find my renegades in the Reedlands, at least I can help defend the Hazellands from another attack.'

'So why are you here and not there?'

'Little did I suppose that when I came to the Hazellands that I would meet a royal woman as strong and fair as Princess Essa.'

'Yeah, lucky you,' I said, drinking the last of my now cold tea.

'I am very fortunate indeed. You said, Conor, that you wanted to ask me a question; now I have one that I have always wanted to ask you.'

'Shoot.'

'Once you had her, why in The Land would you have let Essa go?'

I toyed with the idea of grabbing a flaming log from the fire and clocking him with it. I even imagined the spectacular shower of sparks as he went down. Instead I answered his question with a question. 'Do you remember what you asked me at the beginning of this conversation?' When he looked confused I answered for him. 'You asked if you could help me with my moral dilemma. Would you like to know what my dilemma was?'

Turlow shrugged.

'I was debating whether it was OK to like you or not.'

'And what conclusion did you reach?'

'I'd gotten as far as deciding that I don't like you.'

'And you were wondering if that is OK?'

'Basically,' I said.

'I wouldn't worry about it too much, Conor, I don't like you very much either.'

'You don't?' I said enthusiastically. 'That's good to hear.'

Turlow smiled and shook his head. 'You are a strange man, Prince of Oak. Go to your tent, I will take your watch.'

'You don't have to do that.'

'There is no sleep in my near future – go.'

'OK,' I said, 'but don't think this will make me like you any better.'

'Good night, Conor,' Turlow said with that exasperated tone that I usually reserve for my friends and relatives. It didn't sound right coming from him.

I dreamt that night that the two Brownies climbed down from the tree wearing army uniforms. Then uniformed Brownies dropped from every tree, as far as the eye could see. They converged into ranks until a huge Brownie army marched towards me from all directions. Just as they were about to overwhelm me someone pointed to the sky and we all looked up.

I opened my eyes to see Brendan looming over me in the tent. It was still dark outside.

'What's up?' I croaked.

'Nothing,' he whispered. 'Go back to sleep.'

So I did.

Tuan and Yogi offered to share a horse and give Yogi's mount for the Brownies to ride. They declined the offer. I figured that since our guides were on foot that it would be a slow travel day – wrong. These guys were speedy. They moved so fast I felt like an old English fox hunter. It was actually hard to keep up. Mostly because the trails they chose were made for runners, not riders. I spent the whole day getting whipped in the face by alder branches that I suspected enjoyed it.

We broke for lunch and offered food to our guides. They might not be willing to share information with us but they had no problem packing away our food. I guess if you run as fast as a horse for four hours, you are entitled to eat like one. These guys each wolfed down what three of us would have had at a feast. I made sure I didn't reach for any food at the same time as one of them for fear of losing a finger.

I said this to Essa, who I noticed chose to sit next to me at lunch, and she laughed so hard she almost spat out what she was eating. I may not have the Turd-low's good looks or kingly crown but I can make that girl laugh. That's gotta count for something, right?

That afternoon the trail became wider and less whack-a-face but instead of going faster the Brownies slowed down to almost a jog. I couldn't figure out if these guys had burned themselves out on their morning sprint or if they had been running deliberately fast so that our faces were lacerated for the amusement of the alder trees. Araf, who is normally not the suspicious type, had a different take on it. He got the impression that the Brownies were deliberately slowing us down but he couldn't say why.

Late in the afternoon the Brownies halted for 'tea'. Essa forcefully pointed out that we do not halt for tea but even her menacing glare, a look that has withered many a determined man, could not dissuade Dell and his yet unnamed sidekick from plopping themselves down in the frozen dirt and demanding food.

'Don't they feed you in Brownieville?' Brendan asked.

Dell ignored him and the other one's mouth was too full to talk.

Brendan casually pulled me aside during our afternoon tea. 'You had a long chat with Turlow last night.'

'Are you spying on me? I'm surprised I didn't find you waiting up in the tent saying, "And what time do you call this?"'

'I don't have to spy on you, Conor. All I have to do is ask you a question – you're a crappy liar.'

'Thanks ... I think.'

'So what did you two talk about?'

'Well, if you must know, he talked about how my Uncle Cialtie had mucked up his life. I hate to say it but I'm starting to think that maybe Turlow isn't such a bad guy. I mean he's still a pompous jerk but maybe I should cut him a little slack.'

'Maybe,' Brendan said thoughtfully.

'What da ya mean maybe? You told me you liked the guy.'

'I did until he lied to me today.'

'What? Did he say he liked your shirt? Because you are right, that would be a lie.'

After an appropriately dirty look, Brendan said, 'I didn't sleep well last night. Those Brownies bother me.'

'Yeah, I wasn't too pleased with the thought of them up in the trees myself.'

'No, it wasn't that,' Brendan said. He flexed his fingers into and out of a fist. It was the thing he did when he was trying to figure something out. 'It's like when I'm in an interrogation room and there is something I am missing but I don't know what. That's what it's like when the Brownies are around.'

'Well, if you suspect them of stealing something you're probably right. But what's this got to do with Turd-low?'

'I got up last night to relieve myself and saw Turlow talking to that Brownie fellow. When they saw me the Brownie scooted back into the tree – fast – and Turlow looked mighty guilty when he walked back to the fire.'

'What do you think they were talking about?' I asked.

'I don't know. When I mentioned it to Turlow after lunch, he denied it. When I pointed out to him that I saw the two of them together, he suddenly remembered and said that Dell had just come down from the trees to relieve himself and he only passed a casual greeting with him.'

'It sounds like there were a lot of weak bladders roaming around last night. How do you know he's not telling you the truth?'

'I don't really,' he said with a sigh. 'It's just that … something isn't right here and I'm not going to sleep well until I figure it out.'

TWENTY-SEVEN
KING BWIKA

After their afternoon tea, the Brownies resumed the lead – this time at a walk. Yogi once again offered them his mount but they declined and continued like it was a Sunday stroll in the park. At dusk they announced that it was time to break for dinner. Essa freaked out on them but they ignored her and started a fire. When Essa refused to give them any of our food they opened their packs and cooked their own. Everyone else resigned themselves to the Brownies' erratic schedule and dismounted. Finally Essa did too and we began to make camp while the Brownies ate their dinner – which they didn't share.

We were just ready to start cooking our food when Dell said, 'Let's go.'

'Now?' Essa shrieked.

'Of course,' the Brownie said. 'Fearn Keep is just a short way down this path.'

'Then why did we just break for dinner?' Essa asked in a tone that made me step out of her way.

'Because it was dinner time,' the Brownie said, not realising just how close to death he was.

We all walked on foot in pitch blackness for no more than fifteen minutes before we saw the first glimmer of light from Fearn Keep. I'd like to be able to describe what the Brownie castle looked like but I never really got a good look at it from the outside. There were lights in a dozen or so windows over what seemed like a vast structure but other than that nothing was visible. It was like a blackout street in London during the Blitz. As I got closer I saw that many windows were in fact blacked out with dark draperies that were only faintly outlined by the light within. Welcoming it was not.

Sentries popped out of the blackness like answers on a magic 8-ball. We were expected but I didn't get the feeling we were wanted.

Across an old-fashioned drawbridge over what I imagined to be an alligator-filled moat, we entered the castle. Dell and what's-his-name left us without as much as a 'Bye bye'. The sentries escorted us to four sparse rooms.

No one came to greet us that night. Turlow and Essa each took a separate room, forcing Brendan and me to share a bed. Yogi agreed to sleep in bear form on the floor in Tuan's room. I'm glad it wasn't in my room. I'd hate to think what would happen if I woke up in the night and stepped on his paw. We all met before we went to bed and tried to decide if something was amiss or if this was standard Brownie hospitality.

'Our Brownie guides deliberately slowed us down today,' Araf said. 'I believe they didn't want us to see Fearn Keep in the daylight.'

'OK, but why?'

'I didn't say I had all of the answers,' Araf replied.

'What do you think, Turlow?' Brendan asked.

'I too think this greeting is strange but apparently strange is the way of the Brownie. I say we sleep on it and see what the morrow brings.'

Back in the room I asked Brendan what his uber-cop senses deduced from Turlow's answer. 'Either he is a good liar,' he said, 'or he doesn't know anything.'

'So, nothing then.'

Brendan conceded my point with a nod.

I dreamt that night Cialtie was talking to the invisible man. I strained to hear what they were saying but, as in the way of dreams,

I couldn't quite make it out. I awoke wondering what I had done to my ego to make myself the invisible man. I worried that my dream was a prediction and I would soon be face to face with my murdering uncle.

We found breakfast outside our doors – water and a couple of apples. Even though apples in The Land are practically my favourite things to eat, it wasn't like the Brownies knocked themselves out organising a menu.

After our hearty meal, Brendan suggested that we take a stroll outside to test Araf's theory. Sure enough an armed guard at the end of our corridor informed us that we had to wait in our rooms for information about an audience with the King. I said I understood but just wanted a quick nip of fresh air, but apparently nips or strolls were out of the question.

As we walked back to our room Brendan said, 'I'm feeling less like a guest and more like an inmate.'

About a half an hour later Essa came back fuming after an attempt to get past the guards. 'I am going to personally make sure that these people never get a drop of wine from the House of Muhn ever again.' That was a fate she hadn't even bestowed on me – and I'd dumped her.

After a lunch of, you guessed it, apples and water, a guard arrived and informed us that the King would grant us an audience in two hours. Essa was fit to burst. Actually, everybody was pretty peeved, including me. And you know me, I don't like all of the special royal treatment, but these guys were rude on any scale.

Brendan sidled up next to me and whispered in my ear. 'Do you notice that Turlow is taking this in his stride?'

I hadn't, but now that he mentioned it, Turlow didn't look put out at all. Now, I don't know The Turlow very well but he doesn't seem to me to be like the kind of royal who lets a snub slide, but there he was sitting with an 'oh well' look on his face.

Three hours later an honour guard showed up and informed us that the King would see us now. Araf respectfully asked if he could be excused from the audience due to a foot injury that he sustained the day before. It was the first I had heard about it.

'Are you OK, big guy? Why didn't you tell us before?'

'I did not wish to burden the group. It is nothing, Conor. It would simply be uncomfortable for me to stand for a long period. You go ahead.'

I was worried about my Imp buddy. He had never once complained about anything and I'd seen him get hit in the head with rocks. I was about to speak again, when he gave me a slight shake of the head that stopped the words in my throat. He was up to something and now was not the time to find out what.

'You take it easy, pal,' I said, patting him on his rock-like arms. 'Take a load off your feet.'

We were escorted through a series of damp hallways. Even though I wouldn't want to live here, I really liked the look of Fearn Keep. It was like a castle from an old black and white horror film. The walls were made of dark, rough stone built into long, not quite straight, corridors. Torchlight threw dancing shadows through periodic archways, making each corner feel like a place where a vampire might pop out.

We arrived at an open room and were instructed to wait at huge alder wood double doors. On the doors was carved a relief of an alder tree growing on top of a hill that seemed very much like the mound that Castle Duir was built on. A bulky Brownie informed us that we would have to be searched before entering the Hall of the Fearn Throne. Essa by this time was livid and threatened to break any finger that touched her. I pleaded with her to calm down. I pointed out that the last time the Brownies came to Castle Duir I had their luggage searched and this was probably retaliation for that. It took me about five minutes but she finally allowed herself to be frisked. Watching that guy pat her down was one of the tensest moments of my life. Turlow produced and unhooked his Banshee blade and surrendered it without a word. The guard found my throwing blade in my sock. I really had forgotten it was there but the guard didn't look like he believed me. I handed it to him and asked for a receipt. I got a blank stare worthy of Araf.

King Bwika's throne room didn't disappoint. It was as spooky and as overblown as I expected it to be. There were huge tapestries, long rugs, ranks of soldiers in full armour standing at attention and a built-up platform on which the King sat, looking like a fat little kid, in a huge wooden throne. There were no other chairs. On either side of the King stood a dozen or so advisers.

We approached slowly on a long red carpet. Even though I am sure it was designed to be intimidating, I had a hard time not snickering. Long before we reached a comfortable conversational distance the King shouted, 'Prince of Duir.' I looked around to everybody, grimaced and stepped lively to the fore.

When I got to the bottom of the dais I bowed a low one and said, 'My lord, greeting in the name of the House of—'

'You think because you are of Duir you can sneak around my lands at will?'

'Uh, um,' was all I got out. I know it's rare for me but I was at a loss for words. What should I do? I was pretty sure that he shouldn't have been talking to me like that. I wondered if he would respect me if I stood up for myself, or maybe grovelling was the right way to go. I had no problem with grovelling; I really didn't want to be kicked out of the kingdom, or for that matter executed. I really, really didn't want to be executed. I decided to go for a good bow and scrape.

'I meant no disrespect, Your Highness, and had no intention to trespass.' I produced the gold bar. 'See, I have brought you a tribute and have come on a matter of great import.'

The little flash of gold broke his concentration for a second. He motioned to someone on his right and a young man came down the steps to take the gold bar. As he got closer I saw it was the King's youngest son.

'Hi, Jesse,' I said with a smile.

Jesse frowned. He had never told his father about the time that he and his brother had snuck close to the Vinelands and robbed me and Fergal in the night. When I caught up with them and got my stuff back, I gave him and his brother the nicknames Frank and Jesse, in honour of the great American outlaws. He took the gold bar from me, all the while trying to avoid eye contact, and showed it to his father. King Bwika eyed the bar, and casually accepted my gift with a flick of the wrist. Jesse handed it to one of the dozen advisers that were standing in the shadows behind the throne and it disappeared inside his robes.

'That is the second time you have referred to my son as a "Jesse".
What does it mean?'

Wow, this guy had a good memory, better than mine. I racked my
brains for Jesse's real name and then it came to me – Codna. 'The first
time I met your son was in the Hall of the Oak Throne, when my father
bestowed on you the freedom of the Oaklands. I mistook Codna for
someone I had known in the Real World and when we met socially
afterwards I used the name as a small joke.'

'So because your father gave me permission to walk among
the Oaklands, lands that I should rightfully own, and because you
make idiot jokes with my idiot son, this gives you the right to spy on
me?'

I shot a quick glance at Jesse. He looked like he had been slapped. 'I
have no reason to spy on you, Your Highness, I come because my
father is ill.'

'Ill?' he said in a tone that made me realise that illness was a concept
he had never encountered.

'It's like a mortal wound that we cannot see, Your Highness. I need
to find healing magic or he will die.'

This made the Brownie monarch think, which I suspected was
something he didn't do very often. 'Is he cursed?'

'That may be the cause. We need to get to the Isle of the Tughe Tine
that lies off the edge of your land.'

King Bwika threw his head back and laughed. 'What? Are you looking for help from the Grey Ones?'

'I don't know what I will find, Your Highness – I only want to save
my father. For that I will do anything.'

The smile on the Brownie's face vanished in an instant. 'Your father,'
he said, his voice filled with contempt. 'The last time your father was
here … No, I lie – your father was never here. It was your father's
father, Finn. Finn stood and called me "a supercilious toad" and then
spat on the floor, there, before he left. I was a young king then, he was
fortunate. If he had done that today he would have left with a bolt in
his back.'

The more I hear about my grandfather the more I think we all would
have benefited if he had taken a few anger-management classes. I stood

and walked to the place where the King had pointed and dropped to one knee. 'Was it here that my grandfather spat?'

King Bwika stood and walked down the steps of his dais. Towering over me he pointed to a slab of marble floor directly in front of his feet. 'It was there.'

'Then let me spit on the same spot,' I said and I spat. Then I pulled my sleeve over my hand and used my shirt to clean up the spittle. 'So that I may wash away the memory of it. I, Conor of Duir, do humbly apologise for the rudeness of my ancestor.'

I didn't know what else to say, nor, I sensed, did the King. He looked up and scanned the faces in the room, then said, 'Go. My guards will escort you to the ends of the Keep grounds to the Peninsula Trail. There is but only one way to go from there and you must go alone – I cannot spare you a guide. Report to the alder trees daily.'

'Thank you, Your Highness, we shall leave at dawn,' I said, moaning silently to myself.

'You will leave now, before I change my mind, and you will not rest until you are off the Keep grounds.'

He gestured with his hand. The honour guard surrounded us and escorted us quickly from the room.

We found Araf resting on his bed.

'Is your foot up for a hike?'

'Why,' the Imp said, 'are we going on one?'

'The King says we can go, if we go now.'

We began to pack. It didn't take long. It's not like our welcome prompted us to put all of our underwear in drawers. I was almost ready to go when I answered a soft knock at the door.

Standing on the other side was the young prince with a cloth parcel in his hand.

'Jesse,' I said, extending my hand, 'or should I say Prince Codna. It's good to see you again.'

He looked confused and then shook my hand like he had never done it before. 'No, I like Jesse,' he said with a nervous smile. 'My brother and I still call each other Frank and Jesse when we are alone.'

'Are you going to be one of our escorts to the Peninsula Trail?'

'Oh no,' he said with a nervous laugh, like that was a ridiculous notion. 'No, I came because … Well, I stole this from Castle Duir and have been worried that it has been sorely missed by its owner. I would like for you to return it.'

I took the parcel and opened it. Inside was a round piece of brass. 'You stole a doorknob?'

Jesse shrugged. 'Frank got some better stuff but that Dahy man found it and took it back.'

'Well, thanks,' I said, rewrapping the parcel. 'I'm sure there is a door somewhere in my castle that someone is just dying to open. Speaking of Frank, where is he?'

'My brother prepares for war,' he said with a quiver in his voice that made me look at his face. He was almost at the brink of tears.

'Hey, guy,' I said, motioning him over to a set of chairs. 'What's the matter?'

'Demne,' he said, wiping his nose on his sleeve, 'you know – Frank. He's in the Torkc Guards.'

I searched my memory for the meaning of *torkc*. 'Pig Guards?'

Jesse laughed a little at this. 'Boar,' he corrected.

'So what's so bad about that?'

'I never get to see him any more and I'm worried about him. The Torkc are the first to attack in a war.'

'But the Brownies aren't at war with anyone.'

'They're not?' he said, beaming at me. 'Did you sue for peace?'

I didn't answer that right away, I didn't know what he was talking about. Just as I was about to ask, Tuan came to the door flanked by guards saying that the Brownies were insisting that we leave immediately. The guards made Jesse nervous. I told them to give us a sec.

'Thanks for returning the doorknob,' I said. 'Here, I have a present for you.' I reached into my pack and took out the green-handled knife that was thrown at Brendan on Mount Cas. 'Take this and give it to Frank; it's a throwing knife. The gold tip will make sure the blade hits its intended target. Maybe it will keep him safe.' I resheathed it and handed it to Jesse.

He smiled and then hugged me. That Jesse is a cute kid.

TWENTY-EIGHT
FEARN PENINSULA

It was dark outside but I could just make out two Brownies waiting for us at the end of the drawbridge.

'Hi, Dell, miss us?' He didn't answer; he and what's-his-name just turned and jogged into the night.

It was our turn to slow these guys down. There was no way we were going to go full pelt in pitch darkness. Yogi called a halt, dismounted, stripped off and handed his clothes to Tuan. He said he wanted to travel as a bear because his night vision was better. The Brownies came back to yell at us for stopping just as Yogi did his change thing. He towered over them and growled – they shut up. Yogi took the point behind our guides. He growled and snarled almost constantly so we could at least follow the sound. It was difficult going and the further we got from the castle the worse the trail became. Soon we had to take our branch-whipped faces off of our horses and power walk behind Dell and what's-his-name, who constantly told us to hurry up. I decided that when we finally got to where we didn't need the guides any more I would give Yogi permission to eat them.

It was about an hour before dawn when we reached the borders of Fearn Keep and the beginning of the Peninsula Trail. Dell asked Essa, 'What's for breakfast?' and she pulled her banta stick out of her pack. Bravely, I got between them and pointed out to Dell that they might not want to hang out with a hungry bear and a much more dangerous princess.

Dell stared daggers into my eyes and said, 'We will meet again,' then the two of them ran off the way we had come. In the distance I heard Dell yell something that sounded like, 'In Duir.'

Tuan started up a fire while Yogi got dressed. We were all too tired to pitch tents so we just huddled up in front of the flames and napped in blankets for the short time left before dawn. I had one of those sleeps that, although it was probably a couple of hours, seemed like a blink.

The sun was well up at breakfast and nobody was what you could call chirpy. I had been trying to ask Araf about his hurt foot fib ever since we had come back from the throne room but any time I brought it up he would look over his shoulder and soundlessly say, 'Not now.' It wasn't until we were underway for about a half an hour and in a clearing large enough so we couldn't be overheard by the alders, that Araf called a stop.

'I had to be sure we were not being spied on,' the big guy said in a loud whisper. 'While you had an audience with the King, I snuck outside in daylight and saw what the Brownies did not want us to see.'

'And what was that?' The Turlow asked.

'An army,' the Imp replied. 'A large army and they looked to be preparing for war ...'

'But who would the Brownies be at war with?' Essa asked.

'Me,' I said. 'Geez, I can be so stupid sometimes – now Jesse's conversation makes sense. Jesse, you know Codna, Brownie King's youngest son, thought I had come to make peace. The Brownies are going to attack Duir.'

'Or Cull,' Essa said, jumping off of her horse. 'Someone destroyed the Tree of Knowledge once before, maybe they are about to attack the Hazellands? We must warn Dahy.' She opened one saddlebag and looked inside. Then she opened the other and started frantically throwing things on the ground. Finally she unstrapped the bags and dumped the entire contents onto the frozen dirt.

'Damn it, damn it, damn them. They stole it. They stole it. Those little Brownie—'

'Stole what?' Araf said, getting down so he could help her.

'My *emain* slate.'

'You have an *emain* slate?' Tuan said incredulously.

'Not any more!' Essa shouted. 'Those little stinking—'

The rest of us just stood as still as possible while Essa kicked and used language that would have been inappropriate even in a Wild West saloon.

Essa really did need calming down but I had seen the Princess like this before and I wasn't going to go near her. It took someone that didn't know Essa very well to attempt such a foolhardy thing. Tuan walked towards her and pulled down the back of his trousers. I thought he was going to moon her. Then the hair on the back of his head grew *in*, then went coarse, curly and pepper grey in colour. His hands changed to paws as his back went horizontal and straight. His shoes, on what now were his back paws, fell off. Then I saw the reason for the mooning – a long tail, full flowing with long hair, sprouted out of the top of his trousers. Tuan had changed into a fully clothed Tuan-sized dog. An Irish wolfhound or something close to it and it was the funniest thing I had seen in a very long time.

Essa was shocked into silence, then smiled, then laughed, then dropped to one knee and gave doggie-Tuan a big hug around the neck. I would pay lots of money to find out how to do that. Tuan reformed back to his Pooka self during the hug and the two of them fell laughing on the ground.

'I used to do that for my mother when she was upset,' Tuan said, pulling up the back of his trousers.

'Did it always work?' Essa asked, still laughing.

'Never failed,' Tuan said, helping her up.

'Right,' Essa said, straightening her clothes, 'I'm going back to Fearn Keep.'

'Hold on, Princess.' Now that she was calm and it was safe, I dismounted. 'You can't go back there. We only just got out and I'm pretty sure accusing them of stealing and demanding your slate back isn't going to make them say, "Oops sorry, here you go."'

'I must get that slate back,' she said, her voice once again betraying her anxiety. 'Dahy must be warned about the army.'

'Which is probably why they took it,' Brendan said. 'I'm a cop, Essa, trust me, you won't get it back.'

'But I must. I send a message to my father every other day. He will be worried sick about me. And do you know how expensive those things are?'

'Princess, the others are right,' Tuan said. 'I agree that Master Dahy must be informed of what Araf has seen but we cannot go back. We are at the beginning of the Fearn Peninsula. Less than a mile back there is a trail that, if I remember correctly from my last journey in these woods, leads us to the beach. I propose we take it to the sea. From there we can send Yarrow to warn the Hazellands and then the rest of us can follow the coast to Alder Point.'

Everyone looked at Yogi, who said, 'I do not know the way.'

'I will guide you back to the Hall of Knowledge,' Essa said.

'You can't do that, Princess.' Turlow said 'Princess' in that lovey-dovey tone that was enough to make me vomit.

'And why not?' Essa shot back.

Turlow was foolishly about to start an argument with Essa when Araf piped up. And when Araf chooses to speak it's such a surprise that people tend to listen.

'This discussion is not for here. Tuan, will we make the coast before nightfall?'

'Easily, I should think.'

'Let us think on this as we travel and decide at the next camp. Until then, do not speak of this among the alders.'

Turlow looked like he had something to say, but none of us waited to hear it. We turned our horses and remounted.

The rest of the day was in silence not only because the trees were listening but also because the trail was narrow and forced us to ride in single file. By late afternoon the alders thinned out. In the distance the horizon widened and the slight sting of salt could be detected on the breeze. The trees disappeared altogether about a quarter mile from the coast. We trekked over rolling sand dunes covered with long grass until we reached a black sand beach. The warmth of the ocean changed the crisp dry air in to a cold misty one, but the relief from being out from under the spying eyes of the alders meant that no one complained.

'What happened to the trees?' I asked Tuan.

'The alders hate brackish water. They never live near the coast. That is why I proposed we come here. If Yarro – I mean Yogi and Princess Essa hug the coast, there is a chance that they can get out of the Alderlands without the alders knowing.'

'You think she should go with him then?'

'Yarrow is my friend and in a fight I would have no other at my side.' Then Tuan looked over his shoulder and leaned in. 'But he is not the smartest in the clan. Essa, I have learned, is a woman of substance and she is a natural guide. I think together they have a better chance of success.'

We set up camp while Yogi stripped off, bear-ed up and then had a dip in the freezing water. He came out holding a flat ray-like fish the size of a bicycle. I pitched tents while Tuan and Araf fried it up. Araf produced a bottle of Brownie-shine that he had stolen from the stores at Fearn Keep. Everybody knew it was a goodbye party for Essa and Yogi, but no one said it.

I tried to have a little alone time with Essa before I went to bed, but she was deep in conversation with her fiancé. I waved at her, mouthed, 'Good luck,' and promised myself that I would wake up early so as to have a chat with her before she left.

As it turned out she woke me. Long before the dawn she shook me awake to say goodbye.

'What kind of time do you call this?' I asked, rubbing sleep from my eyes.

'Yogi and I thought it might be a good idea to leave before it was light in case any alders could sense this far.'

I got out of bed and walked with her to what was left of the fire. I looked around expecting to see the Banshee.

'Where is Turd-low?' I said, and then mentally kicked myself for starting a fight. But Essa was calm.

'We have said our goodbyes.'

'Goodbyes? I thought he would insist on coming with you.'

'No,' she said dispassionately. I couldn't tell if she was trying to hide emotions or if she didn't really care. 'He tried to persuade me not to go, but when he realised I was not for turning he didn't volunteer to come.'

'If I could, I would go with you.'

She looked me straight in the eyes for one of those hour-long seconds, smiled – then changed the subject.

'Yogi has packed the boat onto Tuan's horse and has taught him how to assemble it. You be careful out there on the ocean.'

'Gosh, it almost sounds like you're worried about me.'

She started to scowl but then gave me a hug. 'I am,' she said.

Yogi appeared with the horses and Essa quickly turned to go, but before she could get away I caught her by the wrist. She tensed up and I instantly let go remembering what a foolish thing that is to do, but she didn't attack and I got to say what I wanted to say.

'Then we will both worry about each other. OK?'

She nodded and mounted up. I watched them disappear into the pre-dawn.

I went back to bed for another hour; when I awoke Brendan was already up. He had a good fire going and was cooking breakfast.

'Have you been up long?' I asked.

'I love the sunrise on a beach. I grew up near a beach,' Brendan said. 'Dawn is a magical time by the sea. That's what my mother always said. She also used to say, "Just because you can't see a skunk doesn't mean that things don't stink."'

'What does that mean?'

'I have no idea,' Brendan said, laughing. 'She used to say all sorts of crazy stuff. I've been thinking about her all morning. Once she woke me up and we trudged to the beach before the sun came up to hunt for driftwood. We built a fire and she told me stories until it was light enough to see. You know what she told me?'

I shook my head, no.

'She told me about a land where people never grow old – she even named it. I've been stretching my memory to remember and I'm pretty sure she called it Tir na Nog. She told me I came from a line of wise men, who were forced to leave.' He stopped and looked away.

'The Fili after the Fili war,' I said out loud as much to myself as to Brendan.

When he turned back his eyes were shining. 'See? That's why I thought this was all a dream at first. I loved those stories when I was young, but when I got older I stopped believing in them. Mom, though, never stopped believing. I started to think that she was stupid and later … crazy. Who's the stupid one now?'

He dropped his head and was silent for a while. I put my arm around his shoulders. Finally he wiped his eyes on his sleeve and stood – shaking off his heavy emotions. 'I'm glad my girl is with her now and I hope Mom is telling her those same stories. I have to get back, Conor. I have to tell them both that it's all true.'

TWENTY-NINE
FIRE DANCING

As we travelled along the coast, a foggy drizzle blew in from the sea. It was cold and damp and very unpleasant but it hid us from prying eyes, and we hoped it hid Essa and Yogi from the alders. Along with being moist and miserable it was also slow going. It was a beach, not a trail and we frequently had to dismount to negotiate boulders, large pieces of flotsam and jetsam or runoff streams. When we came to a good patch of sand we would break into a canter or even a gallop but I could tell Acorn didn't like the sand. It broke my heart to make him stay on the beach. I promised him I would get him some real snazzy oats when we got back to normality.

Dinner that night was what was left of Yogi's ray. Trust me, it was nicer twenty-four hours earlier. The loss of Essa and Yogi had left a hole in the group that no one tried to fill. It was early to bed and the next morning it was early to rise.

The previous day's drizzle whipped itself up into a full-blown storm. I guess I should have been grateful it wasn't snow, but at least then I would have been dry. The near-horizontal rain made me wet in places I didn't even know I had. Equestrianism is no longer fun when your trousers squelch with every bounce. We were all too miserable and frozen to talk. By lunchtime I was practically in a hypothermic coma and would have stayed that way if Brendan hadn't flipped.

We had stopped only long enough to decide to eat lunch on the hoof. Turlow dismounted and opened his saddlebag to get some grub. That's when Brendan lost it. He jumped from his horse and came down hard on poor Turlow's head. The Banshee didn't know what hit him. Turlow jumped to his feet and when he saw Brendan on the ground he assumed that Brendan had fallen on him after being shot by some unseen attacker. He popped out his Banshee blade and turned his back on the policeman, looking for the sniper. Brendan picked himself up and then tackled Turlow from behind like a linebacker in full blown 'roid-rage.

Turlow went face down hard into a sand dune. Brendan jumped on his back and tried to pull his arms, like he was handcuffing him, but by this time Turlow was no longer confused. He wrenched his wrists free and then, like a rodeo bull, he arched his back and pushed his body up on all fours. Brendan sailed three feet into the air. He came down face first with his body at an angle that made me worry he had broken his neck. Turlow was on him in a second. To the Banshee's credit he didn't run him through. Brendan obviously was still not thinking properly; he reached for the Banshee blade with his hand. Turlow pulled the razor-sharp edge out of the way and gave Brendan a swift kick in the side that doubled him up.

'I have been restrained with you, Real Worlder,' Turlow said, pushing his blade at Brendan's side, 'but my restraint is not infinite. Tell me why you attacked me or die.'

I dismounted, ran between them and managed to back Turlow off a bit. 'Brendan, what's gotten into you?'

'He's in league with Cialtie,' Brendan said.

I spun around and my heart jumped into my throat. Turlow stood there with his sword drawn and for a second I thought he was going to attack us both. I reached for the Lawnmower but it wasn't there – it was strapped to Acorn. 'Brendan, what are you talking about? How do you know this?'

Brendan took a step towards Turlow. The Banshee raised his blade menacingly and Brendan stopped.

'Turlow,' I asked, 'what is he talking about?'

'I do not know; your friend has gone mad.'

'All right,' I said, 'let's everybody calm down a bit.' I turned to Brendan. He took a deep breath, dropped his shoulders and nodded. Turlow backed off and reluctantly flicked his Banshee blade back up his sleeve. 'Right, Brendan, explain yourself.'

Brendan composed himself. He straightened his clothes and put on the kind of face I imagine he uses when testifying in court. 'Conor, you told me that you were attacked in the Real World by black riders that were sent by Cialtie.'

'Yes.'

'And your aunt told you that Cialtie had been looking for you for years.'

'That's what she said.'

'My mother bought the farmhouse I live on in the Real World because she thought it was close to ley-lines and portals to an Otherworld. Two years ago my wife was killed in a car accident when she hit a black horse. A couple of days ago, Conor suggested that that horse had a rider and that that rider was sent by Cialtie.'

'If I recall, Brendan, you told me that I was crazy for suggesting that.'

'Well, I have been thinking about it, Conor. It's amazing how living in Faerieland can make one reassess one's opinions.'

'What has this to do with me?' Turlow asked.

'Open his bag,' Brendan said.

'If you think I am going to stand here and let you search my possessions then think again,' Turlow said. I saw his fingers twitch but the Banshee blade didn't reappear.

'Just lift the flap on his saddlebag and look at the marking underneath.'

I slowly backed to Turlow's horse. Man, it was tense. I had a feeling that if I took my eyes off the two of them that they would be at each other's throats in a second. I lifted the flap on the bag and saw what Brendan was talking about. Burned into the leather was a symbol not unlike an Ogham rune but more swirly and stylised. I couldn't read it.

'That is the same marking that was on the saddle of the horse that caused my wife's accident.'

'And from that you have deduced that I am a spy for Conor's luna-tic uncle?' Turlow turned from Brendan and walked over to Tuan, who was still on horseback, and unlatched his saddlebag. He flipped open the flap and sure enough the same symbol was there. 'You idiot,' Turlow said. 'That is the mark of Master Bothy, probably the finest saddler in The Land. That mark may be on a quarter of the saddles in Tir na Nog.'

I looked to Araf; he nodded in agreement. I turned to Brendan and said, 'Oops.'

Turlow was still steamed. He walked right up to Brendan and said, 'To lose a wife must be an awful thing. That has obviously clouded your judgement so I will let this event go unpunished – but touch me again, Real Worlder, and you will see your own blood.'

Brendan didn't waver in his gaze; he looked the Banshee straight in the eyes and said, 'I am sorry.'

Turlow nodded, indicating that he had heard but not necessarily forgiven, and went over to his saddlebag, took out some dried meat and passed it around to everyone, including Brendan.

'And here's me thinking that lunch was going to be dull,' I said, saddling up. 'Come on, let's get out of here.'

We all mounted up except for Brendan who just stood there, staring into space, the rain dripping off of his face. Finally I said, 'Druid, are you coming?'

That broke his reverie and produced a sad smile on his face. 'No, not a Druid, just a cop who should have known better. I'm sorry, everyone.'

That afternoon's journey was silent and tense. I got the feeling that Brendan was kicking himself and that Turlow wanted to join in. The rest of us didn't dare say anything lest we jump-start a bust-up. The ice-cold rain had stopped but a frigid sea breeze made sure we remem-bered how damp we were. Our tongues tasted the salt air and our eyes felt the sting as the sky stayed solid grey as if to match our mood.

I missed Essa. I bet we all did. Hell, we were only without her for one morning before we were at each other's throats. Periodically, I unconsciously looked for her in our group only to be reminded that she was gone. It made me realise that I had spent the entire journey staring at her as we rode. I hoped she was all right.

An hour or so before dusk, as a thick fog crept in from the sea, Tuan announced that we were here.

'Where here?' I asked.

'Here, here,' Tuan replied. 'This is Fearn Point and out there is Red Eel Isle.'

I looked in the direction that the Pooka was pointing. I had trouble seeing the end of his finger let alone an island out to sea.

'Yeah, it looks lovely,' I said. 'I just wish somebody had built a motel here.'

Tuan unpacked the boat that Yogi had brought from the Pinelands. I knew that the Pookas were not known for their nautical skills but this boat was ridiculous. It looked more like a kite than a boat. I knew that it had to be portable but as I examined the skin, which would eventually be stretched over the toothpick frame, I wondered if it would float. I tried to remember if a fortune teller ever predicted that I would end up in a watery grave.

I walked the shore and found a tiny bay on the windward side where the currents had beached tons of driftwood. We were all cold and damp and tempers were frayed. I decided that we didn't need a fire – we needed a bonfire. Brendan pitched tents and Araf and Turlow threw nets into the sea. After chatting to the fish and letting the ones that wanted to live go free, we ended up with a sea bass each.

Araf produced yet another bottle of nicked Brownie-shine. When I asked him how much he stole, Araf said, 'The Brownies were well looked after the last time they came to Ur. I took less than what the Brownie King drank his first night. I don't feel guilty, if that is what you are getting at.'

'Hey, don't look at me – I'm all in favour of shoplifting from Brownies.'

After dinner we felt well fed and watered. Brendan and Turlow sat at opposite sides of my inferno. The flames were so high they couldn't see each other – probably a good thing.

Brendan was in a non-verbal sulk, Tuan was trying to put together a boat in the dark and you know how chatty Araf is, so I was pretty much forced to talk to Turlow or climb into my nice damp sleeping roll.

'You once asked me how I could have let Essa go,' I said, sitting next to him. 'I could now ask you the same thing.'

Turlow didn't look at me, he kept staring into the fire and said, 'Not that it is any of your concern, Faerie, but she did not want me to come with her.'

Well, that was the end of that chat. If I wanted to have friendly banter around this campfire, I really needed to work on my ventriloquist act. I stood up and resigned myself to an early night. It was a shame really. I had hoped to have a little fun the night before I turned myself into fish food.

Before I left him I said, 'Thanks for not stabbing my friend today; he was well out of line.'

'Brendan was lucky,' Turlow said. 'You saved his life today.'

'I saved his life? You stopped yourself before I even got there.'

'I was in a rage, Conor, but I stopped when I spotted you out of the corner of my eye. In that, your friend was lucky.'

'Gosh, I had no idea I had such a calming effect on you.'

Turlow laughed in a way that made me realise I was missing something. 'Do you know about the Banshee affinity with death?'

I did. My cousin Fergal had once told me that Banshees could sense imminent death. 'A little,' I said.

'I was enraged today. Never in my life have I been treated like that. I was fully prepared kill your countryman but then I saw you and I knew that if I killed him – I would have had to kill you too. I was not prepared to do that.'

'Oh,' I said, not really knowing how to reply to a statement like that. 'Well ... ah ... thanks.'

I walked back to my tent spooked with the knowledge that I had recently come so close to being killed. I stuck my nose into my tent and smelled the dampness of everything. When I touched my cold wet blankets, I said out loud, 'Screw this.'

I stumbled back down to the pile of wood by the sea and came back to the fire with an armful of thin branches. I built a little drying frame near the blaze and draped my sleeping roll over it and then I built another for the clothes on my back. Araf spotted me and didn't wait for an invitation. He built his drying rack and joined me stark naked, howling and dancing around the fire like a Red Indian in a Hollywood Western. Turlow looked on in amazement, while Brendan held fast to his funk and refused to join us. I didn't care. I had apparently almost died today and I would probably drown tomorrow, so I was dancing and I wasn't gonna stop. Tuan came back to the fire to ask what all the commotion was about. As I bobbed and weaved I explained the principle of naked dancing/clothes drying. Being a Pooka he had no problem with nudity and was gyrating with us in no time.

The two party-poopers were making it difficult for me to reach that uninhibited mindless state that makes naked fire dancing so much fun. Every time I passed by the moping Brendan or the stern but shocked Turlow, I pleaded with them to join us. It wasn't until Tuan turned into his shaggy wolfhound and barked at Brendan that he finally smiled and before long the only one wearing any threads was the Banshee. I even stopped and risked freezing my thingy off long enough to build a drying rack for Turlow. Finally he broke when we ganged up on him. When you think about it, four naked men jumping up and down in front of someone, while he is sitting, makes for pretty heavy peer pressure. Turlow was unenthusiastic to begin with but then really got into it. He started spinning like a top and then began screaming like … well, like a Banshee.

I still had trouble getting trance-like. Something was tugging on my brain cells that kept pulling my consciousness back to reality. Finally I stopped and checked my laundry. My blankets were still wet but my clothes were dry, so I got dressed and decided to take a walk to clear my head. The others were so lost in dance that they didn't even notice I was gone. I had to walk quite far away before Turlow's howling was distant enough to allow me to think. Something was weighing on me and I wasn't sure what it was. Then it hit me. Essa had said that Turlow hadn't wanted to come with her, but then Turlow told me that Essa didn't want him with her. One of them was lying to me. There were lots of reasons why neither of them would tell me the truth. As Turlow had rightly pointed out it was none of my business. It might mean that their relationship wasn't going as well as it seemed, which from my point of view was good news, but then again maybe it was something else. I had no way of knowing but at least I had figured out what was bothering me. Now that my mental conflict was solved, I turned back to my frolicking companions and decided to give the dangly-dance one more try. As I got closer I saw them bopping in silhouette and I knew something was wrong. I stood stock still, surveyed the area and listened. I couldn't see or hear whatever it was that was making the hair stand up on the back of my neck but something was wrong, something was very wrong. What was it? That's when I saw it; I saw it and my heart jumped in my chest. As I watched my four companions dance around my bonfire, I counted them: one, two, three, four – *five*.

THIRTY

RED

T he four of them were so lost in the fire dance that they didn't notice that there was a strange man bopping along with them. Twice today I hadn't had the Lawnmower on my hip when I wanted it, so I had made sure I brought it with me on this walk. I drew it and advanced slowly. As I got closer I could plainly see that the interloper was without a stitch of clothes, which, on the plus side, meant he was definitely unarmed. I lowered my guard a bit and jogged the last stretch of beach until I stood just outside the moat the dancers had made in the sand. Still none of them noticed me. The stranger was as absorbed in the dancing as the rest of them. His straight red hair flew around like a sixties go-go dancer. If I had seen him clothed and from the back I might have said he was a woman, but in the firelight there was no avoiding his gender. He was dancing behind Tuan and I was struck at how similarly they were built except for the stranger's arms – they would have put a post-spinach Popeye to shame.

I waited until Araf came by and grabbed his arm to pull him out of the circle. Instead he pulled me in. I had forgotten just how solid that guy is and I almost fell into the fire. Anyway, I got his attention. He stood and looked at me confused, like a sleepwalker that just found himself in the hallway of a hotel.

'Look,' I said to him, pointing to the other dancers.

Araf was still out of it and tilted his head like a dog being taught algebra.

'Intruder alert!' I shouted, pointing to the new member of our dance troupe.

He saw him and snapped into action. He leapt over the edge of the fire (something I would never do without clothes on) and grabbed his banta stick. This startled Turlow enough for him to notice that we were not alone. Turlow had the good sense to throw his clothes on. I grabbed a blanket and wrapped it around Brendan. Turlow came up next to us holding his Banshee blade. Tuan was still completely oblivious.

'Who is he?' Turlow asked.

'I don't know. You were dancing with him – you tell me.'

We watched as the stranger and Tuan spun and danced around the dwindling fire. Tuan sailed past us in his own little world, then the stranger, right behind him, turned and gave us a little chest-high wave. On the next pass we grabbed Tuan and made him see who his dance partner was. At first he looked shocked and then he dropped onto all fours and turned into his wolfhound. The stranger kept dancing and spinning like he owned the place. When he came by again wolfhound-Tuan stuck his nose in for a sniff and our visitor stopped and gave him a little pat on the head, like he was casually walking in the park.

'Excuse me,' I started, but the naked stranger just danced away. We all looked at each other. On his next pass I tried again and was again ignored. On the third pass I stepped in front of him. My sword wasn't pointed at him but then again it wasn't in its scabbard – he had to stop and he did.

'Excuse me,' I repeated. 'This is our fire.'

He looked at me. I still couldn't see his eyes in the light and he tilted his head just like Araf had done minutes before and said, 'You own fire. How does that work?'

Now it was my turn to be confused. 'Well … we made the fire.'

'So you think if you make something, then you own it?' He smiled a toothy grin and shook his head. 'I have known many a parent that thought that. They were usually disappointed.' Then he turned and danced around in the other direction.

Tuan returned to Pooka form and the dancer came around again.

'A Pooka that would rather shiver in his skin than stay in his fur.' He pushed past me and we waited for his next lap. 'A Banshee in the company of Hawathiee?' He then put his hand on Araf's head as if to measure him. 'I see an Imp' – he grabbed Araf's hand and looked at it – 'with no dirt under his fingernails?'

He spun off again. This guy was really starting to annoy me. I tried to speak to him when he came around again but he put his hand in front of my face to stop me. I wanted to chop that hand off. I wanted to tell him that I had chopped a hand off before.

He stood inches in front of Brendan and looked him up and down. 'I don't think I have ever seen a Druid look so confused.'

'Who are you?' I demanded.

He finally then gave me the once-over. 'A Faerie. Is it hard for you, Faerie, being so far away from your mountain of gold?'

'Who – are – you?'

'Who am I?' he said indignantly. 'A Banshee and an Imp and a Druid and a Pooka and a Faerie are dancing naked in the Alderlands without a Brownie in sight and you ask – who I am? Whoooo arrrrrre youuuuuu?'

'I am Conor of …'

He dashed into the night and came back roughly dragging the boat that Tuan had almost finished assembling. 'Sailors are we?' Tuan grabbed the boat from him and half of the flimsy frame popped out from the oiled leather skin. 'And where are the sailors sailing to?'

I didn't think that telling him our plans was a good idea but Brendan answered him. 'We are going to Red Eel Isle.'

'And where is that?'

Brendan pointed out to sea.

'Red Eel Isle – is that what you call it?'

'What do you call it?' I asked.

'Why would I call an island? Do you think it would come?'

He cackled and walked over to where our bags were piled together and started looking through them. Turlow ran over and stuck his Banshee blade in his face. 'Leave our possessions alone,' he demanded.

The stranger simply ignored him and continued to look through our stuff. 'Why? If you plan on sailing to Red Eel Island in that boat, you won't be needing your things and it will be easier for me to scavenge them here, than when they are on the bottom of the ocean.'

'Leave our bags alone,' Turlow repeated, poking the scavenger with his Banshee blade.

The stranger stopped. 'No matter, I'll come back and take what I want when you are dead. I'm off home now; I know when I am not welcome. Thank you for the dance.' He stopped with a faraway look and said, 'It has been a long time since I have danced.'

'Where is home?' Araf asked. As I have said, when Araf speaks people listen. Even though our stranger had only just met the taciturn Imp it worked on him too.

He turned and said, 'Red Eel Island. If you had been nicer I would have given you all a trip in my boat.' Then he ran naked into the black night.

I turned to the others. They all had their mouths open. I pointed to the spot in the darkness that our visitor had disappeared into. 'My agent, ladies and gentlemen.' That got a chuckle from Brendan. As I have said, it was good to have him around.

'Who was that?' Brendan asked the night.

'What was that?' Tuan replied.

'Whoever it was, I think we should keep watch tonight,' Turlow said. 'I will take first shift.'

I didn't argue. I got my stuff off my drying rack and within minutes I was inside my warm dry sleeping roll. Brendan followed me. As he got into bed I asked him, 'What did you think of insane guy?'

'Oh,' he said, 'I think he was crazy all right but I wouldn't say he was insane.'

I laughed. 'You said that about me once if I recall.'

'And I was right,' Brendan said. 'I got a feeling that our dancer tonight tried a little too hard to be crazy. Saying that, he did say one thing that I agreed with.'

'What was that?'

'We really are going to drown in that dinghy.'

* * *

I was last up the next morning. Tuan was still working on the boat. Every time he got the skin stretched over part of the frame on one side, the other side would pop out. Araf was off scavenging for driftwood, Brendan was cooking breakfast and Turlow was tending to the horses. I felt a bit guilty doing nothing so I grabbed a brush and joined the Banshee. Since Turlow was brushing Acorn I started working on his horse.

'You know,' I said, 'I don't know your horse's name.'

'Banshees do not name their horses.'

'Why not?'

'It makes it easier in case you have to eat them.'

'Oh, don't listen to him,' I said, covering the mount's ears. 'I won't let him eat you and I'm going to give you a name. I dub thee – Fluffy. There, no one will eat a horse called Fluffy.'

'You are a strange man, Conor of Duir.'

'But loveable, don't ya think?'

Brendan called us to breakfast. Araf was sitting by the fire examining a piece of wood. He didn't seem to notice me when I said good morning.

'You OK, big guy?'

'You,' he said.

'Me? What me?'

He still didn't look up. 'No, you.'

'Who you? Me? Who's on first?'

He finally looked at me with an exasperated face that I usually reserve for my closer relatives. 'The wood,' he said, holding up the branch in his hand. 'It's yew wood.'

'Oh, yew who.' I shrugged. 'So?'

'Most of the wood in that driftwood pile is yew.' Araf handed me the piece that was in his hand. 'And look.'

I saw it right away. I didn't need to be a forensics expert to see that plainly there were axe marks in the bark. 'This ain't wood from the Yewlands I've been in,' I said. 'There is no way you could chop down one of those babies. You'd be dead by the end of the backswing.'

Araf nodded in agreement.

'Could they have come from another island?'

'Conor, today I am going to leave the shores of The Land in a boat. It will be the first time in my life.'

'It will probably be your last – have you seen the boat?'

I got that look again. 'What I mean to say is, I have no idea what is beyond the beaches of Tir na Nog.'

'It is ready,' Tuan said, trudging back to the fire. 'And I am ready for one last meal and then we can go.'

'One *last* meal?' I said. 'I don't like the sound of that.'

'No, no, not one last meal. One meal before we—'

'Drown?'

'Faerie,' Turlow said, addressing me, 'has anyone ever told you that your attempts at humour are often annoying?'

'Yes, often.'

We ate in silence. Fish for breakfast isn't my idea of a perfect last meal but I couldn't see a waffle house anywhere nearby. The morning mist was clearing with a not too chilling offshore breeze. As we ate, a dark shape became visible out to sea – Red Eel Isle. It didn't look too far but I'd had a little experience sailing. Once Dad and I went to the New Jersey shore with a school friend, Dad refused to step into a boat, but I loved it. I remembered that on the water things were usually further away than they looked.

We decided that the less weight we carried on the boat the better. Araf dug a hole in the sand and we wrapped what we weren't going to bring in blankets and buried them in the dune. Tuan placed the athrú that was hanging around his neck into his mouth and whispered to the horses.

'What did you tell them?' I asked.

'I told them to wait here for as long as they could forage and if we don't return then to make their way back to the Pinelands.'

I gave Acorn a rough rub on the nose the way he likes and said, 'You take good care of yourself, ya hear.' I swear he glanced over my shoulder to the boat and then stared at me with eyes that said, 'I'm not the one you should be worried about.'

Araf threw a disc into the fire and it went out fast, like somebody had just put a glass dome over it. Then he reached into the ash and charred wood and dug the fire coin out. I missed the heat of the fire instantly. I looked at the surf rolling onto the beach, the island far out at sea, I felt the cold salty breeze on my face and a shiver ran down my back. I whispered to myself, 'Dad, you'd better appreciate this.'

I'm sure that everyone realised it was a bad idea as soon as we tried to get into the boat. This thing was made for a calm lake – it was not an ocean-going vessel. Tuan kept telling us to make sure we stepped on the big pieces of wood that made up the frame and to, under no circumstances, step on the skin or we'd put our feet through it. If that wasn't unreassuring enough, the boat was as stable as a beach ball – Tuan tipped it trying to get in. We finally figured out that the only way to board the damn thing was in pairs, one on each side to balance out the weight. But when we did that the framework bent so badly that we were sure we were going to break it. Turlow and I were the last in and we had to wade into freezing-cold waist-deep water to get the thing off the sandy bottom. We were only seconds onboard when the first wave hit us. I wasn't ready for it. I bounced around and hit the skin of the boat hard with my fist, but luckily I didn't puncture it. The others grabbed oars and paddled. The 'ship' came with two oars and Araf this morning had fashioned another two out of driftwood.

We survived the next two breakers The surf hadn't looked this rough from shore but now that we were on the water we were really getting tossed around. The fourth wave did us in. The bow raised like it had for the other waves but then it just kept going. It went straight up and tossed us out the stern. I had the tent on my back and when I hit the water it dragged me straight down. The water was so cold it only took a nanosecond to become numb all over – it was like a full body shot of novocaine. I untangled my backpack from my shoulders and then forced my way to the surface. I got my head above water just in time to get creamed by another wave that spun me underwater like I was in a washing machine. Then next time I reached the surface I spotted Brendan and Araf spluttering off to my left.

'Are you OK?' I shouted over to them.

Brendan shouted back, 'I think so.' Araf looked a bit panicky. I had never seen him panicky. I looked around – the boat was upright and seemed to be doing just fine sailing out to the island without us. I couldn't see anybody else.

'Where's Turlow and Tuan?' Just as I said that Turlow surfaced gasping for dear life.

'I lost my saddlebag,' he gulped. He dived down again only to pop up seconds later in even more of a panic. 'I can't see anything. I have to—' A wave came and knocked him over – he resurfaced coughing. Turlow was not a natural swimmer.

Just then a sealion wearing the remains of Tuan's shirt came up underneath Turlow and pushed him towards the shore. I started swimming and it wasn't long before there was sand under my feet. I turned back and saw Brendan was using a lifeguard hold on Araf, dragging him to safety. I waded back in and helped them. Turlow and the now half-naked Tuan were in front of us. The five of us limped back and collapsed shivering on the edge of the surf.

'You just can't beat a day at the beach,' I said while spitting out a mouthful of sand. 'Is everybody all right?'

I didn't hear their reply; what I did hear was a familiar voice shouting, 'Yoo hoo, could you boys use a nice warm fire?'

I looked up. I almost didn't recognise him with his clothes on. There, straight ahead, standing next to our campfire, which was now fully ablaze, was the strange red-headed man from the night before. I can't honestly say I was happy to see him but that fire looked like the nicest thing I had ever seen in my life.

We all dragged ourselves off the sand. My frozen joints moved like door hinges that had been without grease for twenty years. We crouched by the fire trying desperately to get some circulation back into our extremities.

'Thank you for rebuilding our fire,' I said through clattering teeth.

'I knew that you would need it if any of you survived drowning,' he said. 'I wasn't expecting all of you to make it though – I guess I'll have to give your stuff back.' He walked over to the other side of the fire and came back with the blankets and extra clothes that we had buried in the dunes. All of us were too grateful at seeing a dry set of clothes to yell at him. We stripped, dried off and changed clothes while our thief/saviour brewed up some tea.

'What is your name?' Brendan asked.

'Call me Red,' Red said, shaking his hair madly with both hands. 'That is what my friends called me ... back when I had friends. Or maybe you should call me The Red Eel,' he said, doing a snakelike dance.

That perked my interest. 'You're Red Eel?'

'That is the name you gave this island, is it not? I never have heard it called that but since I am the only person that lives out there – I must be Red Eel.'

I should have known better than to get excited by anything that madman said.

'Have you ever seen a red eel?' Araf asked as Red handed him a cup of tea.

'There are eels in the lake but I don't like 'em. Slimy things they are. I cannot say if I ever saw a red one. Why?'

'That's a long story,' I said.

'Well then, why don't you tell me on the way over to the island in my boat?'

'Thanks,' I said, 'but no thanks.'

'Hold on a minute, O'Neil,' Brendan said, holding up his hand to me like a traffic cop. 'You have a boat?'

'It would be pretty strange of me to offer you a ride in my boat if I didn't have one. Do you not think?'

'Everything you do is strange,' I said. 'And one thing's for certain, I'm not getting into a boat with you.'

THIRTY-ONE
THE DIGS

I sat in the back of Red's boat with my arms crossed and refused to speak to anyone all the way to the island. I had fostered a fantasy that I was the leader of this group but when everyone ignored me by waltzing into the strange man's boat, I realised that my leadership qualities only applied to my horse and then probably not even to him. Left with the option of sitting by myself on a cold damp beach or getting a free ride in a sturdy seaworthy vessel, to a destination I had been labouring for weeks to get to, I decided to go but I wasn't going to do it without getting into a really good pout.

The boat was big enough for us and maybe a couple more. There were two large oars set in iron oarlocks. Red ordered Araf and Tuan to man an oar each and the two of them stepped lively to their stations faster than they ever did anything for me. Obviously Red was now the captain. *Well, they'll be sorry,* I thought, *when he makes them row off the end of the world.* The boat cut through the surf like we were sailing on a millpond. When we got out into deeper waters Red ordered the rowers to stop and climbed up to the edge of the bow. From the floor of the boat he picked up two metal rings that were attached to thick ropes. He clanged the rings together, they vibrated in his hands producing an eerie ringing sound, and then he threw them into the water.

'Ooh that tickles,' he said, flexing his fingers and then rubbing his hands together. Then he sat and smiled at us.

None of us spoke. When you are in the middle of the ocean with a leering madman at the helm, silence is definitely the best policy. You literally do not want to rock the boat. Saying that, I was in a bad mood and I'm not very good with uncomfortable silences. I was just about to demand to know what was going on when the ropes in the water went taut, the boat lurched and we started speeding towards the island like we were being pulled by a nuclear submarine.

'How is this happening?' I shouted to Red, but he was oblivious, facing out to sea with his arms spread like he was flying or re-enacting a scene from a movie about a doomed cruise liner.

Tughe Tine Isle loomed before us. It looked like your typical volcanic deserted island. There was a lot of vegetation but no trees. I assumed that the lake Red spoke about was up on the island's plateau.

The ocean air felt warmer the further we got from the shore. About a half an hour out Red turned around and said, 'Can you feel it?'

'Feel what?' Turlow said.

'Can you feel yourself getting older?'

Turlow was on his feet. Araf grabbed onto the side as the boat shook. 'Stop the boat,' Turlow said.

'Why would I do that? We are almost there.'

Turlow flicked his wrist and his Banshee blade flew into his hand with frightening speed. 'Stop the boat now,' he demanded.

'Turlow,' Brendan said, 'what has gotten into you?'

'He is trying to kill us. He is going to turn us into Grey Ones. He is going to take us out to sea and we will all grow old and die.' Turlow took a step towards Red. 'Turn us around.'

'Banshees think that pointy things up their sleeves are the answer to everything,' Red said in his light-hearted manner. Then he turned stone-cold serious. 'Take one more step towards me with that sharp edge, Banshee, and you *will* go back – swimming.'

Turlow and Red stared at each other for a minute, then Turlow flicked his blade back up his sleeve and sat down.

'Good,' Red said, regaining his jovial tone. 'My island will not kill you, Banshee, nor will it turn you grey. Have any of you been to the Real World?'

Brendan and I sheepishly raised our hands.

'You will have to go further than my island to wither and die. The island will age you as fast as you aged in the Real World. Stay for eighty seasons and you will notice the difference.' Red looked out to sea and then quickly turned back to us with concerned eyes. 'You're not going to stay for eighty seasons, are you?'

A wooden dock loomed up ahead as our magical underwater motor died. Red fished the rings out of the water and reordered Araf and Tuan back to rowing duty.

'What was pulling us?' I asked.

Araf gave me a sideways look like he does when I make a Tir na Nogian social faux pas. It's apparently bad manners to ask how someone's magic works. Red didn't seem to mind but that didn't mean he was going to give me a straight answer.

'You were pulled by the past – into the future,' he said.

We followed Red on a narrow path through head-high vegetation. The trail didn't seem to be used much. Periodically it was so overgrown with gorse bushes that they caught and scratched at our clothing and faces.

'Red,' I called out from the back of the parade, 'where is the eel lake?'

He ignored me or maybe he was just lost in his own little world – both were possible. I passed my question up the line to Brendan, who only succeeded in getting Red's attention by tapping him on the shoulder. The message was relayed back to me like we were in a schoolyard playing a game of Chinese whispers.

Over his shoulder Araf said, 'He says we cannot go there today.'

'Why not?' I asked – then shouted to Brendan, 'Ask him why not.'

'Why don't you ask me yourself?' Red shouted back.

I waited then hollered, 'OK, why can't we go there today?'

'Because it is too late and you are almost at The Digs.'

'The whats?' I shouted and got no reply. Red had gone back into his hard-of-hearing mode.

The gorse thinned out and we came to a clearing. In the middle stood a wooden guest house not unlike the ones in the Pinelands.

'Welcome to The Digs. You can stay here the night.'

As we got closer it became obvious that no one had stayed in this place for a long, long time. Vines grew across the porch and there was so much dirt on the windows that Brendan had to wipe the glass with his sleeve to look in. Red opened the door and invited us to enter before him. Inside the only good light was from the window that Brendan had just cleaned. On the floor we left footprints in the quarter inch of dust that reminded me of astronauts on the moon.

'I see your housekeeper is on vacation,' I said, but Red wasn't behind me. I went outside and he wasn't there either. I walked the entire perimeter of the clearing but there was no Red. I went back inside.

'He's gone.'

'Who's gone?' Brendan asked.

'Red's gone, vanished into thin air.'

'Don't be silly,' Brendan said and went outside with everyone else to look for him. They all came back wearing my confused countenance. 'He's gone.'

'Gosh,' I said, 'is he?'

It was dark by the time we got the digs habitable. I just hoped that none of us had dust allergies 'cause if he did, he was going to keep all of us up all night. The stack of wood outside was mostly rotten but there was enough to get a decent fire going. Brendan found a dusty bottle of something. He uncorked it, had a sniff, thought better of it and put it back. The Digs may have been a bit neglected and forlorn but it was good to be inside with a roaring fire for a change.

We spoke into the night mostly about the strangeness of our host, but came to no conclusion except that our host was strange. After a light meal made from our dwindling rations Brendan decided to take a walk and I went with him.

'Are you OK?' I asked him as my breath fogged in the starlit night.

'You sound like I shouldn't be.'

'Well, you did seem pretty mad at yourself yesterday when you wrongly accused Turlow.'

'Oh that. I flew off the handle, for that I am mad at myself. But I'm not wrong about Turlow.'

'I beg your pardon?'

'It took a while but my cop radar tells me he is not to be trusted. I'm sure I was right about him, I just don't have any proof.'

'Your radar once thought I was a murderer.'

'No, it told me that there was something wrong with you, Conor, and I sure wasn't wrong there.'

'So what should I do, tie up Turlow 'cause your bunion is throbbing?'

'I'll figure it out, Conor, I always do. Just … don't turn your back on him.'

That night when I put my head on what I laughingly called my pillow I thought about my chat with the local cop. Part of me wanted to distrust Turlow. If Brendan had dissed King Banshee earlier in our trip I would have joined in but as much as I hated to admit it, I was begrudgingly starting to like the guy. I know I shouldn't put much stock in my nocturnal soothsaying but I had a feeling that if he really was betraying us, I would have dreamt about it. I put those thoughts aside and tried for the first time ever to direct my dreams. I closed my eyes and said to myself over and over again, 'Where are the red eels? Where are the red eels?' I fell asleep with that mantra in my head but it didn't work. The stupid image of Red grinning at me annoyed me not only during the day but in dreamland as well.

The next morning I awoke to see that same grinning face sitting next to a roaring fire inside The Digs. How Red could sneak in and rekindle our fire without waking us worried me. He was wearing a ridiculous outfit made from what looked like snake skin. Imagine a pair of crocodile lederhosen and you get the idea. He had fish cooking between a wire mesh. I expected him to say, 'Guten morgen,' but he just waved when he saw me.

'More fish for breakfast,' I said. 'Yum.'

He offered me a cup of tea and I accepted.

'When can we leave for Eel Lake?'

Apparently his hearing was fine this morning. 'I am waiting for you. I expected everyone to be up and ready to go. It is not an easy hike you know.'

I roused everyone and after a quick brekkie of mackerel and moss tea that surprisingly wasn't as bad as it sounds, we were out the door and heading towards the highlands in the middle of the island.

The trail to Eel Lake was worse than the one to The Digs. The gorse bushes often encroached on the path to a point where it was impossible to pass. Instead of hacking our way through, like I would have done in the Real World, we had to plead with the bushes to back off. It was slow going.

I tapped Red on the shoulder as we walked. I had made sure I was directly behind him so he couldn't ignore me. 'I thought you said you came up here a lot.'

'I do.'

'This doesn't look like a well-used path to me.'

'It's not.'

I waited but Red wasn't in an extrapolating mood. Sometimes it was easier when he ignored me. 'So how do you get up there?' I finally asked.

'I go an easier way.'

'So why aren't we going that way?'

'My way would not be easier for you.'

'Why not?' I asked a couple of times along with some shoulder taps, but Red was just as good at ignoring me when I was directly behind him as he was when I was at the end of the parade.

As the morning progressed the trail became much steeper. Whoever originally designed this route didn't bother with any of that zigzagging to make climbing easier stuff – when the mountain got steep, so did the path. Getting down on all fours became common. Eventually I wouldn't say we were hiking as much as rock climbing. An hour after missing my lunch, we finally took a break on a level shelf about two thirds of the way up. We were all, including Red, uncharacteristically exhausted. I wondered if our lack of stamina was due to being so far away from the immortality mojo of the mainland. It was a thought I kept to myself. We drank from a sparkling clear stream that fed into a small pond. Next to Gerard's wine it was the nicest thing I have ever drunk.

'So tell me, Son of Duir,' Red said, 'what are you going to do with these red eels when you find them?'

'I'm going to use them to cure my father.'

'Cure him? Of what?'

I didn't really want to tell him, but I didn't have the strength to lie so I explained about Dad reattaching his hand and how that same hand was killing him. Red's reaction surprised me. For the first time since I met him he looked truly interested.

'And what makes you think red eels will help?'

'Have you ever heard of the Grey Ones?'

'Oh,' Red said, 'I remember the Grey Ones.'

'I found an old manuscript that told of the Grey Ones' search for the blood of the red eels.'

Red was agitated and on his feet. 'This manuscript said red eels?'

'No, that's the translation into the common tongue. The scroll said they were searching for the blood of *tughe tine*. We came here 'cause a Pooka once called this place Tughe Tine Isle.'

Red placed both of his hands over his mouth to cover his surprise then threw his head back and began to laugh. If anyone else had done this it would have looked like they were losing it but with Red it strangely made him, for the first time, look sane.

'I should have known.' He stood and began to walk down the mountain.

'Wait a minute,' I said, grabbing him by the arm. Still laughing, he spun around like a rag doll. 'What should you have known?'

'I cannot believe I walked halfway up this mountain just so I could find out what you wanted with eels. Thank you for reminding me why I live alone.' He laughed again but then became angry. 'For the love of the gods – has The Land gotten so stupid that the Prince of Duir cannot even translate two simple words?' He grabbed my head with both hands and pulled my face close to his. '*Tine*, my feeble-minded gold miner, does not mean *red* it means *fire* and *tughe* does not mean *eel*. Do you not have scholars in Duir? Have you never heard of the Hall of Knowledge?'

'The Hall of Knowledge is gone.'

'Gone? What do you mean gone?'

'It was destroyed.'

Red grabbed me by my shirt and spun me to the left. I lost my footing and he fell on top of me still pulling my shirt with both fists. 'What have you done?' he said with fire in his eyes.

'I didn't do anything. I lost my grandfather there.'

Red let me go, stood and started back down the path. 'I cannot help you,' he said without turning around.

I chased after him. 'What does it mean? What does *tughe* mean?' I placed my hand on his shoulder. He stopped but didn't face me.

'It means ... *worm*. Now leave my island.' He strode down the path with his arms outstretched, brushing the gorse bushes. As he did, they closed behind him. We couldn't have followed even if we wanted to.

The rest of the gang, mouths open, were on their feet.

'Does anyone know what just happened?' I asked.

THIRTY-TWO
THE INVISIBLE MAN

It took a while before the gorse bushes let us pass. There was little talking on the way back. For the most part we concentrated on not plummeting.

Back at The Digs I volunteered to hike down to the beach and scrounge for driftwood. Tuan agreed to come with me and help persuade some fish to be our main course.

'What do we do now?' Tuan asked as we weaved our way through the gorse. 'Should we start digging for smoking worms?'

'I have no idea what to do.'

'Oh, that's not good. Conor, you are our ideas man.'

I made a guttural sound. It was meant to be a laugh but by the time it made it out of my mouth it was a pitiful grunt of a broken spirit. 'Well, start thinking up your own ideas, 'cause I'm fresh out.'

Tuan wisely didn't say anything else during our walk. I didn't blame him, even I wasn't happy with my own company. What the hell was I doing here? What if Red never comes back? What if this whole thing was a giant goose chase? What if Dad dies while I'm shipwrecked out here and I don't even get a chance to say good-bye?

* * *

My mood was no better back at The Digs in front of a roaring fire. When Brendan sat down next to me he had that look on his face, like he was going to bestow a pearl of wisdom.

Before he could open his mouth I said, 'Shut up.'

'Well, it looks like someone forgot to put on his feathered underwear today.'

'I got them on, Brendan, they're just damp – like everything else in my life. Leave me alone will you.'

'OK, maybe I'll just have a game of checkers with my good buddy Turlow. Where is he anyway?'

It wasn't until the food was ready that we all started asking the same question. We scouted as much of the perimeter as we dared in darkness but The Turlow was gone.

An hour of discussion over a cold dinner couldn't solve the mystery of what had happened to the Banshee. The only constructive product of the conversation was a plan to search for him at first light.

As I stood from the table I said, 'Maybe he's the only one of us with enough sense to abandon this stupid quest.' No one was disappointed when I went to bed.

Later Brendan sat on the edge of my bunk. 'Conor, I know about things being so bleak that it seems easier to give up. I've been there – but now is not the time.'

'I know and you're right,' I said without opening my eyes. It was exactly what I had been lying there thinking for the last hour. 'I'm sorry for my foul mood. Do me a favour, apologise to Tuan for me.'

Brendan nodded.

I made the effort and propped myself up on my elbows. 'I'm not giving up, Brendan. I'm just tired and scratched to hell and cold and … and too tired to even finish this sentence. We've been at this for a long time. I'm going to rest tonight – tomorrow I'll figure out how to save The Land.' I attempted a smile. 'I've done it before you know.'

I dropped my head back on my pillow with that thought on my mind. Sure I saved The Land once before but I had my dad with me then – without him I just didn't have a clue.

'Tomorrow,' I said, not even knowing if Brendan was still there. 'Things will all become clear tomorrow.'

Little did I know how prophetic that sentence would be.

That night was full of fits and starts punctuated by vivid and cryptic dreams. It seemed that the more experienced I became with dreaming the less understandable they were. I had almost given up trying to decipher any meaning in them. That night I dreamt I was in a mayonnaise jar filled with little smoking red-faced worms. I stabbed a tiny red earthworm and he slid away with the Lawnmower. In another dream the invisible man was back. During a phase of amateur psychoanalysis I had decided that the invisible man was me, but in this vision I dreamt that the invisible man was skulking around stealing stuff and I thought maybe it was Red. Red did have a creepy habit of sneaking up on us. I woke in the darkness and listened – nothing. I reached under my bed and strapped on the Sword of Duir then fell back into a fitful sleep. The last dream I had that night would have, under normal circumstances, shot me right out of bed. The invisible man pulled up a chair next to my bunk and stuck something into my shoulder. Then he reached to his collar and removed an amulet from around his neck – instantly he became visible.

When I opened my eyes I knew exactly what had been done to me – I didn't have to wonder. Once you have had one of my Aunt Nieve's paralysing pins stuck in your neck, you don't forget the sensation. This pin wasn't actually in my neck; it was in the top of my shoulder. Otherwise I wouldn't have been able to turn my head when I heard Turlow's voice.

'How do you spell butcher?'

Just like in my dream, Turlow was sitting in a chair next to my bed with his legs crossed as he casually wrote onto an *emain* slate.

'You're the invisible man.'

He looked up from the slate. 'I'm who?'

'You are the invisible man – I dreamt about you.'

'That, Conor, is not possible.'

'No, I did. I dreamt about you but I didn't know it was you. You were invisible. I saw you walking with Essa and talking to Cialtie, but I thought it was me. I didn't see that it was you until you took that amulet off your neck.'

Turlow stopped writing and poked the amulet that was now hanging around the *emain* slate. 'You and your uncle's dream vision is truly remarkable. You are the only ones that have ever seen even the tiniest bit past my *seithe* amulet.'

Seithe, I thought, searching the language database in my head. *Seithe means hide.*

'I suspect all of the dreamers in The Land will spot me now, but I had to use the amulet on the slate 'cause I don't want a reply to come through and erase this message before Red can read it.'

'That's Essa's slate I take it?'

He tilted his head in a gesture of false guilt. 'I always take the opportunity to steal something when I am in the Alderlands. The next time you are there, you should try it. Everyone always suspects a Brownie. But I don't imagine you will be visiting in the Alderlands any time soon – or ever.'

'So Brendan was right, you *are* Cialtie's lackey.'

He stopped his writing and looked sharply up. 'There are no lackeys here. Cialtie rightfully wants back his Oak Throne and I want the Banshees to finally hold the position they deserve in The Land.'

'Yeah, as Cialtie's lackeys.'

I thought for a second that he was going to hit me, but then he laughed. 'I find it very hard to be provoked by a person who can't move from the neck down.'

He had a point. I would have shrugged in agreement if I could have moved my shoulders. It was amazing how calm I was about all of this. Maybe 'cause last night I had already decided that I had failed, this was just the icing on the cake.

'How did you get one of my aunt's paralysing pins?'

'I have a bag full of them. Cialtie stole Nieve's recipe book and he still has a couple of Leprechaun goldsmiths under his protection – so to speak. I've been aching to use one of these on you for ages – if only to shut you up. I didn't know what I was going to do when I lost them and Essa's slate on the bottom of the sea. It took me all night to convince Red to get them for me.'

'How did Red get them?'

'Your uncle is right about you – you're not very clever. You know so little about Red *he* might as well be your invisible man. Now quiet, I have to finish this before he comes back.' Turlow bent back down to the slate and asked, 'How do you spell mortals?'

'What did you tell Red?'

'I just pointed out how you and that traitor Pooka over there destroyed the Tree of Knowledge, marooning all of the Pookas in their fur and then I told Red how you were planning to butcher him, so you could use his blood to bring an army of mortals over from the Real World to take over The Land.'

'Red's blood?'

'Like I said, Conor – there is a lot you don't know about our host.'

'And did he believe you?'

'Well, he hasn't talked to many people in a long time and I do lie particularly well, so yes, he did. And when I show him this letter here that *you* wrote – then I'm fairly sure he'll kill you. It would be better if Red kills you. That way I don't have to lie to Essa when she asks me if I did it – in case she uses that Owith glass she has. I'll tell you what, if she doesn't use that pesky truth crystal, I'll tell her that you died saving my life. Don't say I never did you any favours.'

'I wouldn't want to be you when she finds out.'

'She'll be dead before she finds out – along with everyone else in the Hall of Knowledge. The army of the Banshees and the Brownies will see to that.'

He finished forging the message and said, 'Time to meet Moran.'

'Who's Moran?'

Turlow let out an overly dramatic sigh as he stood up. 'Red is Moran.'

Moran, where had I heard that name? Yes, I remembered, he was the Pooka that left to start the colony of mermaids – the *Mertain*. Queen Rhiannon had said he was maybe the smartest Pooka that ever lived and that he could change into any animal.

'So what – does Red change into a worm?'

'Well well,' Turlow said as he grabbed me by the hair. 'The Faerie can be taught.'

Aunt Nieve's paralysing pin only meant that I couldn't move – it didn't mean that I couldn't feel pain. Turlow dragged me out of bed by my hair and then bumped me like an ironing board over empty bunks. My heels hit the floor hard as I was dragged backwards at a forty-degree angle through The Digs. Just inside the front door I saw Araf, Brendan and Tuan all vertical and propped against the wall. Araf was still curled up like he was asleep. Brendan had his arm outstretched as if to stop an attacker and Tuan looked like a toy soldier who had fallen backwards against the wall while at attention. As I was dragged past, their eyes frantically dashed back and forth in their sockets, but they couldn't speak. Turlow must have pinned them very high on their necks.

'Red is Moran,' I shouted over to Tuan. I saw his eyes widen just before the sunlight blinded me.

My heels slammed painfully into each of the steps that led down from the porch. It hurt like hell but I refused to let the Banshee hear me yelp. He finally propped me precariously up against a tall stump. When he let me go I slid and fell nose first into the hard ground. He didn't even try to catch me. When he propped me up again I spat in his face.

'Ooh,' he said, wiping his cheek with his sleeve, 'I was wondering when you would get a little fight in you.'

'Wouldn't you really like to fight me yourself – man to man? Take this pin out of my shoulder and grab a sword. Only lackeys use lackeys to do their dirty work for them.'

'Conor, I am The Turlow, I do not need to prove my manhood to anyone. I have long ago discovered that it is not the way of winning that matters, just the winning.'

'The ends justify the means.'

'Yes, well put.'

'I can see why you get along with my uncle so well. Tell me, Turlow. Where were you when I cut Cialtie's hand off? Were you in Castle Duir?'

'No, I was in the Reedlands.'

'You're welcome,' I said with a snort.

'For what?'

'I saved your life.'

Turlow shook his head. 'Cialtie told me that you would say something like that.'

'Yeah, 'cause he knew it was true. He tried to kill you.'

Turlow wasn't listening any more. He looked past me – I couldn't turn my head far enough to see what he was looking at. He walked towards me and stuck another one of Aunt Nieve's pins in me. This time in my neck, then he removed the one in my shoulder. I could no longer turn my head and when I tried to speak I found that I no longer could do that either. All I could do was look straight ahead as a strong gust of wind from behind whisked my hair into my face.

'Good morning, Moran,' Turlow said as Red appeared in my peripheral vision.

Red walked around me. All of the previous frippery in his demeanour was now gone. He eyeballed me like a general inspecting his troops.

'What do you have to say for yourself?' Red asked me. When I said nothing he asked, 'Can he speak?'

'He could speak if he chose,' Turlow lied, 'but he knows he is caught. I found him writing this letter to his father – the father that is *supposed* to be encased in glass.' Turlow showed Red the message on the face of the *emain* slate.

'I am sorry for bringing these troubles to your island,' Turlow said, 'but I must go. I must make the tide and I must warn my people of what I have just learned.'

'Of course, Banshee,' Red said, 'and thank you for bringing them to me. I have been away from the treachery of The Land for too long. Where is the Pooka traitor and the others?'

'They are in The Digs – dead. They put up quite a struggle when I found them out. It is a mess in there, I wouldn't go inside.'

'Thank you, Banshee. It is about time I had new digs.'

Red bowed and Turlow returned it, then with the tiniest of smiles to me he turned and jogged to the beach path.

Red crouched down and covered his face with his clenched fists – then he stopped and stood up. 'Have you nothing to say for yourself, tree killer, before I send you and your cohorts to the pyre?'

From Red's point of view I must have looked like the coldest of criminals. I just stood and stared – inside I was screaming.

Red walked up to me. 'Do you not even want another lesson in translation? I told you that *tughe* means worm but worm is an old word. Do you not want to know what worm means in the common tongue? No? Well I'll tell you anyway – no wait, better yet, I'll show you.'

He took off his shirt and then the kilt-like thing he had around his waist. Even though no one could hear it and I couldn't even say it, a wisecrack sprang into my mind along the lines of 'What worm are you talking about?' He dropped down on to one knee and once again placed his balled fists in front of his face in a gesture of intense concentration. I had seen Pooka changes before and it is always impressive but I had never seen anything like this. Not only did it look impressive but it sounded impressive. First he went red – not redhead red but cooked lobster red. Then fist-sized scales clinked into place as he got big. First he got bull big, then elephant big and finally dinosaur big. He raised his head at the same time that his wings fully extended. Of course, I said to myself, worm means – *dragon*.

I think this would have been one of the most magnificent moments in my life if it hadn't been ruined by the realisation that momentarily I would be dead. I could hardly blame Dragon Red, in his eyes all he saw was a cold-hearted expressionless killer. He didn't see my knees knocking 'cause I couldn't move them and he didn't even see me open my mouth in wonder 'cause I was frozen solid. I must have looked like a man prepared to die for his sins.

Dragon Red rocked his huge spiny head back and forth then placed his snout inches from mine. Smoke seeped out from between his fangs, my eyes watered and my nose burned from the smell of brimstone. Then he cocked his head back like a snake getting ready to strike. I saw the hair that was hanging in front of my eyes curl and burn as he sent a fireball the size of a car past me. It was aimed directly at The Digs.

THIRTY-THREE

GRAYSEA

I didn't see the fireball hit but I sure as hell felt it. It felt like I had been clubbed with a refrigerator. The fire passed and surrounded me as I flew through the air like a test dummy at ground zero during an atomic bomb test. The first thing I did was to pat my head to make sure my hair wasn't on fire and then I realised that I could. The blast must have knocked Nieve's pin out of my neck. I turned to see The Digs completely engulfed in flames.

I was instantly on my feet. 'ARAF, BRENDAN,' I screamed. I started running around to the far side of The Digs hoping that the fire was not so fierce on that side. Hoping I could get them out of there.

'TUAN!'

I looked around to get help from Red, to tell him that they were alive in there, but he was nowhere to be seen. At the rear of The Digs, flames were pouring out the back door. I took one step towards it and that's the last thing I remember.

The pain was excruciating. I suspected from the way it was hanging from my hip that I had broken my left leg. My head was bleeding like a stuck pig and there was intense pain in my shoulders where the talons pierced my flesh. But the worst agony came from the sight, hundreds of feet below me, of The Digs completely and totally engulfed in flames. There was no way that Araf, Brendan and Tuan made it out. My friends had been burned alive. I retched and then watched as the contents of my stomach sailed down between my legs, then were dispersed by the wind until they landed in the sea below.

I looked up, a painful and difficult thing to do when you are hung from your shoulders.

'YOU IDIOT!' I shouted at Red. 'YOU KILLED THEM.' I'm sure that with the sound of the rushing wind and considering the substantial distance I was from the huge dragon's head, that Red wasn't ignoring me – he simply couldn't hear – but the memory of Red's games on the island came to mind and made my blood boil. I kicked and screamed some more.

'YOU KILLED THEM AND I'M GOING TO KILL YOU. YOU MURDERER.'

I instinctively reached for the Lawnmower and was shocked to find it hanging at my side. I drew it and slashed at his talon. That got his attention. He screeched and let go of my right shoulder, swinging me to the left. Then he banked sharply right – this swung me up, under his underbelly. The scales there were thinner and a pale yellow-green. I knew I would never get a better chance – I jabbed the Lawnmower as I was propelled up towards Red's belly. The sword found a spot between two scales and it sank almost half its length into the body of the huge beast. Blood spurted out of the wound. Red let go of me and I lost my grip on the Lawnmower. As I fell I saw the huge red dragon flapping away with the Sword of Duir sticking out of his belly.

As I have mentioned before, time usually slows down for me when I'm in mortal peril but I didn't need it in this situation. I was so far up in the air I had a lot of time to assess my dire circumstances. I was plummeting to earth at terminal velocity without the aid of a parachute or even a comedy umbrella. If the fall didn't kill me, I was going to land in the sea about half the way between Red's island and another island behind it. It didn't look like a distance I could swim, even without a broken leg. The major irony was that I was covered with dragon's blood – the blood of the *tughe tine*. The stuff that I had spent so long searching for, the thing that I had travelled so far for and had lost so many friends because of – the blood was all over me, in my hair, on my face, soaked in my clothes and I was about to plunge in the ocean where I would have the privilege of watching it wash away as I drowned.

I stretched my hands out to my sides and used the air current to slowly spin me around. I took in my last look of the beautiful islands on the edge of The Land. Then I shouted, 'I'm sorry, Dad!' and slammed into the water.

'Who is Brendan?'

She was blurry but I could see that she had long blonde hair and was dressed all in white. I know it's corny and clichéd but trust me, if you see someone that looks like that immediately after having an almost certain death experience, you too will think it's an angel and like me – it'll freak you out.

'He is a friend,' I croaked. 'There was … fire. Is he here?'

As she came into focus I saw that she was certainly pretty enough to be an angel. Disappointingly she had no wings but I had a faint image of her floating in the air – or was it … water. Then two things happened that dispelled my illusion of being in heaven. First I tried to get up and was racked with the most enormous wave of pain and secondly my angel giggled. Maybe I could deal with an afterlife that had pain in it but under no circumstances should angels be allowed to giggle.

She lifted my head and put a small glass of liquid to my lips. 'You say the funniest things,' she said as I drank. The liquid was very pleasant, which made me think that it wasn't medicine, but when I tried to speak I realised just how wrong I was. Like with one of Aunt Nieve's paralysing pins, I couldn't move or speak, but unlike my aunt's pins, this was quite pleasant. I drifted off into a dream of heaven filled with giggling angels.

The next time I came to I was mentally in better shape. I was in a cave – a very nice cave. Bottles filled with brightly coloured liquids, as well as unusual scientific instruments and perfectly folded linens, sat on shelves that were carved directly out of sparkling stone walls. Light came from coral-looking glowing things that sat on almost every surface. I touched the one that was on the table next to my bed and I heard it (or felt it in my head) ask me if I wanted it brighter or darker. I asked it to tell me where I was but 'brighter or darker' was about the extent of its vocabulary. I braced myself for the coming pain as I tried to sit up and was delighted to find that I didn't hurt that much, but then I made the mistake of looking under the bed for my clothes – all of the blood rushed to my head and my vision began to darken. Maybe I wasn't in as good a shape as I thought. I pulled myself back, laid my head on the pillow and closed my eyes until the dizziness passed.

I was in this position when my angel zoomed into the room. She was beyond me by the time I opened my eyes. I sat up to watch her golden hair bounce as she knelt down and placed a stack of towels on a low shelf. I was going to say something but instead I just watched her. When she stood she kept her back straight; the way she moved reminded me of a dancer. Finally she turned – and to my forever shame, as she turned – I screamed. She was old – really old. Now don't get me wrong, I don't go around screaming at old people and she wasn't hideous or anything, as a matter of fact she was a very attractive old person. It's just that you get out of the habit of seeing older people in The Land and, also, I wasn't expecting it.

She placed her hands on her hips and said, 'Do I look that scary?'

I started to answer her but I couldn't figure out how to explain why I screamed when I saw her face, so I just said, 'Sorry.' She walked behind me and roughly took my head in her hands. 'What are you …?'

'Shush,' she said and I did. Then she said 'Hmmm,' in a knowing sort of a way that made me want to ask her what was wrong with me but before I could say anything, she left.

I lay there for a long while listening and then dozed off until I heard the old woman saying, 'Faerie, oh Faerie man.'

I opened my eyes and saw the old nurse and her twin – except maybe eighty years younger – my giggling angel.

'I imagine this is the one you were expecting,' the senior nurse said. 'I am sure you will find that she is not as scary as me.'

I looked up with an apologetic gesture but still failed to say anything other than 'Sorry.'

'Pathetic,' she said, shaking her head as she left.

'She *is* a little scary,' giggling angel said and then giggled. 'I do not think she likes you very much, Faerie man.'

'Conor,' I said.

She looked confused and turned her head like a baffled puppy. 'What does Conor mean?'

'It's my name. I am Conor.'

'Oh,' she said, placing her hand up over her face, laughing. 'Oh, I'm very pleased to meet you, Conor,' she said and then did a little curtsey.

'And yours?'

'And my what?' she said, again with that head tilt.

'Your name? What's your name?'

'Oh' – giggle – 'my name is Graysea.'

'It is a pleasure to meet you, Graysea.'

'And it's a pleasure to meet you, Conor.'

'You already said that.'

'Did I? Oops.'

'So tell me, Graysea, where am I and how long have I been here?'

'Oh, so many questions. Which answer do you want first?'

'I don't mind, either.'

'OK,' she said. 'Um … what were the questions again?'

'Let's start with where am I?'

'You're in the Grotto of Health.'

'And where is that?'

That question stymied her for a minute before she came up with, 'In the Grotto of Health.'

'OK, how long have I been here?'

'Ever since I brought you here.'

That was not quite an answer to my question but it was a nugget of information. 'You brought me here?'

'Uh huh.'

'And where did you find me?'

'In the water.'

'And what were you doing in the water?'

'Flying.'

'Don't you mean swimming?'

'I don't think so.'

I took a deep breath and started again. 'So you were *flying* in the water when you just came across me drowning?'

'Oh no, I saw Tughe Tine drop you. That's why I came.'

'You saw the dragon drop me?'

'Oh, everyone did. We don't see Moran very often – usually only once every twenty years at the blood fete.'

'What happens at the blood fete?'

'That's when Moran gives dragon blood to the King so he won't grow old. Don't you know about that?'

'I've heard something about it.'

This seemed to please her. I sat up higher in bed and as I did I winced where my side hurt. Graysea unabashedly pulled back my sheet and asked me where it hurt. I pointed to my side and she told me to 'Scoot over.' Then she sat next to me in the bed, placed her hand on my rib, put her feet up on the bed and crossed her ankles. With her free hand she placed into her mouth a silvery shell that was hanging around her neck by a string of tiny pearls. I watched as her neck thickened, then three slits appeared that began to open and close like a beached fish gasping for air. When I looked down I wasn't that surprised to see that her feet had changed into one fin. Her fingers, now webbed, pressed hard against my rib. That caused a sharp stab of pain that instantly disappeared as Graysea made a deep gasping noise. She reached up and removed the shell from her mouth and by the time I looked at her fin, it was feet again.

'Oh, that one was broken,' she said, getting up and rubbing her own side. 'I'm sorry we missed that.'

I covered myself up and then flexed the rib. It didn't hurt at all. 'How did you do that?'

'I took your hurt and then lost it during The Change. That's what we do here. It took quite a few of us a long time to heal you. What happened?'

'Have you ever seen a hawk swoop down and catch a rabbit?'

Graysea nodded yes, but wrinkled her nose to show that she didn't like it.

'Well, that's what happened to me.'

'You said lots of funny things in your sleep.'

'Like what?'

'Mostly you said "Brendan, Araf and Tuan".'

I wasn't expecting that and her words stabbed me with a pain worse than my broken rib. I tried to push the thought of them being burned alive out of my mind. I knew I would have to deal with the emotions of that loss – but later – I didn't have the strength now. I turned my face away from Graysea and slammed my eyelids closed, willing them not to leak. When I looked back, Graysea was upset.

'Oh, oh what have I done?'

'No, it's OK. They are friends that I have lost. It's not your fault.'

'Oh, no, I'm not supposed to upset patients. Oh, I have to get matron.' She turned and ran out of the room. There was no way to stop her.

A couple of minutes later the older nurse came in and stood at the foot of my bed with her arms crossed. 'Graysea says that you are upset.'

'I think she is more upset than me.'

'What happened? What did you do to her?'

'I didn't do anything. She just mentioned the names I have been speaking in my sleep for the last … How long have I been here?'

'Nine days.'

'Wow, I've been here for nine days?'

'What did you say to her?'

'Oh, nothing, she just said the names of my companions that … they were killed during my … adventure. She took me by surprise and I turned away for a second. Honest, I told her it was OK but she bolted out of the room.'

The matron uncrossed her arms and her countenance softened. 'She is a sensitive little fishy.' She pushed the sheet away from my feet, held both ankles and closed her eyes performing what I presumed was some sort of examination. 'So how did you like your chat with our Graysea?'

'It was … interesting.'

'I bet. I should have warned you about the rule of having a success-ful conversation with her.'

'And what would that be?'

'Don't ask her any questions.'

We both laughed. 'Hey, sorry about screaming when I first saw you. I really—'

She waved her hand and cut me off. 'Don't give it a second thought. If I had seen me when I expected her – I would have screamed too.' She came behind me and held my head with both hands; when I started to talk she shushed me again. 'Actually there are some mornings I want to scream when I look in the mirror.'

'Can I ask you a couple of questions?'

'You can ask.'

'You are mermaids – right?'

'Oh my, that is word I haven't heard in a long while, but yes – I am Mertain.' She pulled my sheet away. 'OK, Faerie, let's see if you can walk.'

'You wouldn't have my clothes around, would you?'

'It's nothing that I have never seen before.'

'Still,' I said, standing with my hands in front of my dangly bits, 'I think you have seen enough for today.'

She said she didn't know where my clothes were, so she gave me a white robe, the same as she and Graysea were wearing. I put some weight on my leg and it felt good. 'It's a little stiff but no pain. It was broken wasn't it?'

'Actually it was dislocated at the hip. What in the sea happened to you?'

'I got pounced on by a dragon.'

'Moran pounced on you?'

I nodded yes.

'Ouch.'

I walked around the room and everything seemed to be OK. I had a twinge in my knee and the matron had me sit while she did her fish trick and then it felt fine.

'Would you mind if I ask you how old you are?'

'Yes.'

'Sorry, I don't want to upset you. I'm just trying to sort some stuff out in my head.'

'And what does my age have to do with your head?'

'Well, I think I'm on one of the islands off Fearn Point.'

'You're under one actually.'

'Under?'

'You're in an underwater cave about half a league under Mertain Isle.'

'That sounds deep.'

'It is. Healing is faster this far down.'

'How did I get here?'

'You will see when you go back up.'

'Which will be when?'

'Soon,' she said. 'I think you are ready to travel and I'll tell them that – once you stop asking me questions. So what does this have to do with my age?'

'Well, I figure you must grow old out here, except for the King …'

'How do you know that?'

'Graysea told me.'

'You got information like that out of our Graysea – I am impressed.' She folded her arms again. 'Go on.'

'I guess I just want to know how fast people age out here. Is it as fast as in the Real World?'

'I do not think so,' the matron said, 'if you must know I am under a thousand.'

'OK, so no then. And let me say you don't look a day over five hundred.'

That got my usual dirty look. 'You are obviously well enough to answer the King's questions. I imagine his school will be here shortly for your ascent.'

'School?'

'Yes, the King's guard.'

'Oh, mermaids, fish – schools. I get it.'

The matron shook her head and left.

THIRTY-FOUR
THE MERTAIN KING

I t took a half an hour before the school came to escort me to the
King. I tried to rest but every time I put my head down I saw
an image of Araf, Tuan and Brendan with wide terrified eyes,
being burned alive. I just didn't have the strength to think about it.
I tried using a Fili mind mantra but eventually I just had to get up.
I spent most of the time before the guards came peeping into all of
the nooks and crannies, searching for my clothes. I didn't find them
so I guess I was doomed to go to see the King in my nightgown,
which I suppose was better than my recurring nightmare of going
naked.

Matron and Graysea walked me to a larger cave containing a beach
and an underground lake. Waiting for me were six humourless macho
thugs – the school. A couple of days previously I would have cracked a
few jokes about them being a bit old for school, but it seemed that
Moran killed my sense of humour along with my friends. In the centre
of the lake was the top of a car-sized submerged brass dome.

'Get in,' the senior guard said.

'How do I get in there?'

'You swim, Faerie,' the matron said. 'Follow Graysea; she will show
you the way.'

'Aren't you coming with us?'

'It is very close quarters in the pressure chamber and I am certain that you would rather have Graysea scrunched in with you than me.'

'I don't know, after the initial shock you're not so bad.'

She scowled at me but it had a smile in it. 'Good luck, Faerie.'

Graysea took my arm and walked into the water. I stuck one toe in and then popped it right back out again. 'It's freezing.'

Graysea giggled, grabbed me by the wrist and said, 'Come on.' That girl was stronger than she looked. I hit the water and my body exploded with cold. I screamed so loud I was sure that the walls of the cave above the water must have collapsed and crashed down on matron like a bad guy's lair in a British super-spy movie. Swimming was out of the question. I struggled to get back to the surface but then Graysea, equipped with her flipper bottom half, zoomed me through the water into the underside of the pressure dome. She placed my shivering hands onto the railings before she was finally forced to push me up the stairs with her shoulder. I was beyond cold and just shy of being cryogenically preserved. I flopped down on a metal deck, dripping wet and rattling my teeth so hard I was sure I was going to crack a molar.

Graysea knelt next to me, looking like she had just stepped out of a garden on a summer's day. 'Dry off,' she said.

'I cccccaaaaan't mmmoove.'

She placed her hand on my robe and it instantly dried itself and me. Then it lengthened and heated up. She tucked the material around my feet and slowly I started to thaw out.

'How did you do that?'

'You can do it too. Your robe is made of kelp. If you are nice to it, it will do what you ask.'

Just as my core temperature was reaching the point where I could talk without sounding like I was riding over cobblestones on a bicycle, the chamber began to move. I looked over the side of the metal platform we were lying on and saw the ocean floor moving horizontally. Periodically a mermaid would zoom past the hole in the floor.

'Aren't they going to close a hatch or something?'

'Why?' Graysea said as we lurched upward.

I looked over the railing and saw the ocean floor disappear at an alarming rate.

'Because I really don't want to—'

I didn't get to finish that quip 'cause that's when the first pressure change hit me. Pain exploded in my ears and Graysea, looking uncomfortably worried, told me to swallow to equalise the pressure. I wanted to tell her that I wasn't an idiot and I had been doing that, but the pain was too intense to allow me to speak. Graysea cuddled up beside me as a spark of pain hit me in the ears, which was so bad I thought I was going to pass out. When I pulled my hand from my head it was covered with blood. Graysea placed her hands on both sides of my head and I felt her flipper flap against my leg. The pain subsided and when I turned to look she was changing back from a fish already. We didn't have much time to talk – the ascent must have happened at a phenomenal speed. In the process I punctured both eardrums – my right one twice. Closer to the surface I started to get pains like I had never experienced before. Tiny strange twinges in my joints grew to the point where I started praying that I would soon die.

'What is happening?'

'I am stopping your blood from boiling – shush,' she said as she hugged me from behind. Her legs changed from fish to feet with increasing speed – each change brought blessed relief.

By the time we felt the chamber bob to the surface, the two of us were physically spent. Graysea was crying and I held her.

'Are you all right?'

Sobbing, she didn't say anything but nodded her head yes.

'Thank you,' I said, holding her until her crying turned to sniffles.

I wiped the tears from her eyes. She was remarkably beautiful, my giggling angel, and it pained me to see her cry. When she finally had the strength to return my smile, I couldn't resist it – I kissed her.

That, of course, is the position that the captain of the King's school found us in. Graysea got up so fast she banged her head and it rang in the chamber like a bell. My body felt like I had tripped at the opening gun of a marathon and had been trampled by the subsequent five hundred runners. Graysea didn't look like she was moving all that well either until she hit the water and then she ... she flew. I doggie paddled underwater until I broke the surface and saw that we were like a mile from an island. I wasn't sure I was going to make it but my choice was either swimming or drowning, so I started kicking. Graysea saw me struggling and swam up under me. She turned her back and gestured for me to place my hands on her shoulders. I did and she reached up, grabbed both my wrists and dived straight down underwater. We went so fast the water scrunched my face like an astronaut during a rocket launch. After travelling to what felt like forty thousand leagues under the sea, she turned and we broke the surface, clearing the water by at least ten feet. If Graysea was giggling, I couldn't hear it over my screaming. We were on the beach in no time.

As I crawled to the shore I said, 'Warn me next time you do that.'

She tilted her head. 'Do what?'

Standing shivering on solid ground I willed my robe to dry. It did, but also shrank to the size of a halter top. Graysea ran over quickly and made it become a full-sized, dry, warm robe again.

'You shouldn't do that here,' she said with a disapproving look.

'Thanks, I'll remember that.'

The walk to the royal residence was a quick march along the sand. Not that I could feel the sand, my feet were like blocks of ice. None of the Mertain, I noticed, wore shoes. I found out later that if their feet were cold or sore all they had to do was a quick change and everything was back to warm baby softness again. It was a trick the Pookas of the Pinelands hadn't learned. When their animal selves are injured they carried their injuries through the change.

The King had a cool beach house that had a wide porch-like jetty that stuck out over the water. Graysea had told me that the King was old – when I asked how old, she said, 'Old old.'

Me and my frozen feet were escorted to the royal porch where I stood and waited for about a quarter of an hour. Finally I sat on the decking and tried to instruct my robe to cover my feet, but I only succeeded in making it turn pale blue – the same colour as my toes. Talking to this robe was like trying to communicate with a blind Chinese guy. I decided to give up 'cause I didn't want to be left in a miniskirt when the King arrived.

A huge whoosh startled me to my feet as the King vaulted out of the water and landed dry as bone, on his feet, on his porch. It was a very ostentatious entrance but I must admit – impressive. I'm sure if I could do it, I would do it all the time too.

I shouldn't have worried about showing off my legs 'cause this guy's kelp robe looked like a very short Roman toga. He seemed youngish, late twenties or early thirties, but the weird thing about him was that he had absolutely no hair. Not on his head, not on his legs and, disconcertingly, no eyebrows. He paced back and forth, never once actually looking at me.

'Why were you dropped by Tughe Tine?' he asked the sea.

'Your Highness, that is a long story – that I am happy to tell you but right now I think I'm going to either faint or go into hypothermic shock. Can we have this chat inside over a cup of tea?'

He finally looked me straight in the eyes. He was as humourless as his bodyguards. I tried desperately not to stare at the space where his eyebrows should have been.

'Tell me, what are your dealings with the dragon?'

As he spoke my teeth started chattering again. My cold brain started to slip into that state where I just didn't care what happened to me any more – I got lippy. 'Do you know who I am?'

In response the King snarled – I was beyond caring.

'I'm the friggin' Prince of Duir and I deserve better than this. Now, I'm happy to answer any of your questions but only over a cup of tea and with a blanket over my feet.'

The only good thing about the Mertain dungeon was that it was warm. I got a cup of water and a leathery piece of dried fish. The fish smelled like sulphur but then so did the rest of the place. I'm sure that if I lived in that cell on a diet of baked beans, no one would notice.

At that moment in my life, a dungeon was not a good place for me to be. It wasn't just that it was damp and dark and dingy. The main problem was that there was nothing for me to do, so I was forced to live with my thoughts – and they were far from comforting. War was coming to the Hazellands. I needed to get off this rock to warn everybody about Turlow, but even if I could get out of this cell, I had no idea how to get back to the Tir na Nog mainland.

I had no idea how Dad was. The last thing I had heard was that he was slowly getting worse. Was that still the case, or was his condition rapidly worsening? Or was he dead?

I didn't have to wonder if my travelling companions were dead. I hoped that somehow their end was swift but in my heart I knew it wasn't and it was all my fault. I should have insisted that Brendan stay in Duir and I should have listened to him when he told me not to trust Turlow. If I ever got out of here, I knew I would have to go back to the Real World and try to explain to his mother and daughter about how he had died trying to help me. I dreaded that moment almost as much as having to tell Queen Rhiannon what had happened to her Tuan. The last thing she had said to me was, 'Look after my son.' If there was one thing I didn't do on this trip, that was look after anybody. And I lost Araf – first Fergal and now Araf – there is just so much a heart can take. Not hearing Araf not speaking was deafening in its silence.

I tried not to think about how they died. I tried to push it out of my mind but with nothing else to distract me in my prison's gloom, the imagined images of their agonising death overwhelmed me until I was curled up into a foetal ball, openly weeping on the dungeon floor.

That was the position that the King of the Mertain found me in. I heard the sound of a throat clearing and looked up to see his face in the barred window of the door. 'This is how a Prince of Oak acts.'

I didn't stand but I did sit up. I wiped my cheeks with my knees. 'You don't know what I have lost.'

'No loss would make me act like that,' he said.

'No,' I said, looking fully at him for the first time. 'No, this would never happen to you 'cause you have lost it all anyway. You may have followed Moran out of the Pinelands and escaped the dependency of hazel but you have lost what it means to be human – no, you have lost what it means to be Pooka.'

The King's eyes grew wide in surprise. 'How do you know of Moran and the hazel?'

I stood, reached into my collar and pulled out my athrú medallion. 'I know these things 'cause I am barush.'

*   *   *

Well, what a difference one little word and a necklace can make. Guards were called and I was taken to a royal guest suite where I was fed and bathed. I even had my back scrubbed and my face shaved by mermaids. It's not often you can say that and yes, it's as nice as it sounds. After a short nap I was escorted *inside* the King's abode and sure enough, there was a blanket and a cup of tea waiting.

'My apologies, Prince Conor, for my previous abrupt manner; I am unaccustomed to visitors and your arrival, it must be said, was troubling.'

I came real close to saying, 'Just don't do it again,' but instead I apologised for my own behaviour.

'So, Son of Duir, you have a cup of tea and a blanket, will you now tell me what your relationship with my brother is?'

'Your brother?'

'Yes, Moran is my brother.'

I squinted my eyes and tilted my head a bit, then in my mind's eye I used an orange crayon to draw hair and eyebrows on the King. Sure enough he was Red's hairless twin. 'I see it now,' I said. 'Has your brother always been that strange?'

'I believe I have waited long enough for my answers,' he said but then a tiny smile crossed his lips, 'but I shall answer one last question of yours. Yes.'

So I spewed out the whole tale again. It seemed that on this trip to The Land I was doomed to constantly meet people and tell them my entire life story. I was getting pretty good at it. The last bit was hard to tell but I got through it without choking up – just. I finished by saying, 'So as you can see I must get back to the mainland as soon as possible. Can you help me?'

The King sat and stared for a while. I took that as a testament to my superior story-telling ability – he was stunned into silence. Finally he said, 'I can and I will.' For the first time in a long while my spirits rose only to have them dashed by his next sentence. 'As soon as Moran arrives to verify your story.'

'When is Red due?'

'My brother comes and goes as he pleases but he will definitely be here for the blood fete.'

'And when is that?'
'In three years.'

THIRTY-FIVE
THE STREAM

When he finally let me out of his dungeon again, the King explained that he *had to* lock me up 'cause I insulted him in front of his guards. I was surprised that he knew what a 'trumped-up spineless guppy' meant but I guess the tone was pretty clear. He only made me sit in his sulphur pit for a day.

When I was released I was shown to a little beach shack and was told I had the freedom of the island. I went back to the King's royal beach house but the guards there wouldn't let me enter and finally told me that the King was elsewhere. I doggedly sat in front of the house for three days waiting for his return. I waited and thought. Thoughts filled with dead friends, a dying father and a disappointed family and clan. If I had owned a neurology textbook I would have performed a self-lobotomy. I had to get out of there.

There was always food outside my shack in the mornings and in the evenings but I never saw anyone put it there. No one came near me. After two stints in the King's dungeon, not many of the Mertain had the courage to talk to me. There was obviously no ex-con chic culture going on in Mermaid Island.

My only contact was with two kids. They had obviously been told to stay away from the dangerous Faerie. So obviously they didn't. They would hide in bushes until I passed and then dare each other to touch the back of my robe. I remembered being a kid myself and throwing snowballs at cars. The fun wasn't in the throwing – the fun was when the driver got out and chased us. I usually saw the kids hiding but pretended not to until after they touched me, then I would roar and chase after them. I mean, what's the point of being a monster if you can't scare kids?

On this particular day, I just couldn't stare at the King's beach house any more. I went for a walk to clear my mind. It seemed all of my injuries from being swooped on by a dragon had healed. I tested my legs with a jog and it felt pretty good. In the distance I saw the two pint-sized Mertains hiding so I quickly changed direction, doubled back and came up behind them as they were craning their heads out of the bushes trying to see where I had gotten to. I rushed them screaming, 'I want filet-o-fish!' I think one of them wet himself, but you can't really tell with those quick-drying robes of theirs. As I vaulted after them through a bush, I practically ran into Graysea.

'What in the sea are you doing?' she said, crossing her arms.

'I'm scaring the crap out of little kids. What does it look like I'm doing?' I then explained that tormenting these guys was pretty much the only contact I had with any of the Mertain since the King had thrown me into his dungeon – twice.

Graysea took me by the arm and we found the kids. She made us apologise to each other and shake hands. A shame really – I'm sure they were going to miss their dangerous game.

She told me that she had gone back to work at the Grotto of Health and this was the first time she could convince the matron to get some time off.

'I think one of the guards told her that we were kissing.'

'Oh,' I said, 'sorry about that.'

'Are you?' she replied with a shy smile. 'I'm not.'

I spent a lovely day walking the beaches with Graysea. As much as I tried to convince myself that I was fine with my own company, just talking to her made me realise how lonely I had been. She gave me lessons in the care and feeding of my robe. I had mentioned that it had recently been ignoring me and she told me that that was 'cause it hadn't been in the ocean for a long time. We took a swim that wasn't so bad after Graysea taught me how to regulate my robe's warmth and then she coached me in the subtler ways of making it lengthen and even change colour.

Once again I blurted out my life story (conspicuously leaving out any mention of Essa). Graysea was particularly interested in my father's illness and thought the King was being unreasonable by not helping. The day ended with a campfire on the beach before she swam back to work the midnight shift, which matron insisted she be on time for. If I said there was no kissing involved, I'd probably be lying.

The next day the war between me and the mini-Mertains was back with a vengeance. The little twerps obviously realised that détente was dull and began tormenting me by throwing pebbles. I ignored them, even when the pebbles got bigger, until one of them hit me in the head with a rock. Now I was chasing them for real. If I caught them I was going to kill the little dirt-bags. Fortunately for all of us Graysea appeared right before I caught the littler one.

'He started it,' I said to Graysea when she had once again got the three of us around a peace table.

'I did not,' the bigger one said.

'You did too – you threw a rock at my head.'

He put on the most angelic of smiles and turned to Graysea. 'We were just quietly playing and he tried to attack us. We feared for our lives.'

'You little—' I said as Graysea stopped me from grabbing the smiling liar by his neck. 'I hope you find a jellyfish in your trousers the next time you go swimming.'

Graysea patted the little future politician on the head, promising that 'the mean old Faerie' would never bother him again.

'You really shouldn't scare them so,' she said after the boys skipped off cackling to themselves.

I started to protest but instead just said, 'Sorry,' vowing to myself that the next time I saw the brats they'd really be in fear of their lives.

'Come with me,' my dizzy mer-friend said, 'I have a surprise for you – actually two surprises.'

She took me by the hand and led me across the island. It was so good to see Graysea again. You may find this hard to believe but walking hand in hand with a beautiful mermaid is preferable to being hit in the head with rocks.

After about an hour of walking, during which Graysea infuriatingly refused to tell me what her surprises were, we climbed over a bluff of rocks and then down onto a small beach. At the edge of the sand sat a conspicuous pile of branches. Graysea, looking and acting like a magician's lovely assistant, pushed away the brush to reveal Tuan's portable boat.

'Surprise!' she said, jumping up and down.

'That's our boat,' I said as I gave it a closer look. 'Where did you find it?'

'I saw it ages ago drifting all by itself on the far side of Inis Tughe Tine. So I went back to see if it was still there – and it was.'

'Did you find oars?'

'You don't need oars.' She reached into the bow of the boat and took out two metal rings attached to a rope. They were exactly like the ones that Red had on his boat. 'I'll pull you back to the mainland.'

'Are you strong enough?'

'It will be easy – I'll take The Stream.'

'The Stream?'

'There is a sea current that travels around Tir na Nog. I can find The Stream and then it will be easy to fly through the water. I can do it in my sleep.'

'You can swim and sleep?'

'Not my whole brain, silly,' she said, playfully slapping my chest, 'I can only sleep one side of my brain while I swim.'

'You can sleep one side of your brain at a time?'

She leaned in and spoke as if it was a secret. 'Some people think half my brain is asleep most of the time – and they'd be right.'

'So I can get off this island,' I said as the realisation dawned on me. 'I can warn my friends.'

'Yes,' she said, and I joined her jumping up and down.

'When can we go?'

'Now.'

'Thank you, Graysea, they are wonderful surprises.'

Graysea stopped jumping. 'No, that's only one surprise.'

'Really? What's the other?'

She reached into a pocket and handed me a small glass vial that was set into a gold mesh sleeve. Inside was a dark liquid.

'What's this?'

'It is dragon's blood.'

I hadn't realised until that moment just how much hope I had lost. Deep down I had all but given up on saving my father; now this wonderful girl had just handed me the ways and the means of curing him. I lifted her off the ground, spun her in my arms and then kissed her. But as soon as my lips met hers a question flashed in my mind. I pushed her away and held her at arm's length.

'What's the matter?' she asked.

'Where did you get this?'

A coy smile crossed her face. 'I sort of borrowed it.'

'Borrowed it – with permission?'

'Well,' she said, pivoting on one toe, 'not really.'

'You stole it?'

'You could say that.'

'From the King?'

'Well yes; who else?'

'I can't take it.'

This produced a pout that made her look like a ten-year-old. 'Why not?'

'Because you will get into too much trouble.'

'No I won't,' she said casually.

'Oh I think you will.'

'No,' she said, 'I never really get into too much trouble – you see, people think I'm really dumb. So they never stay mad at me.'

'But you have never been in as much trouble as this will get you into.'

'Maybe. But believe it or not, I have thought about this. Moran is due within three years, the King is not going to die of old age before then and your father is sick. I am a healer, remember – he needs this. I may get into trouble, but what I am doing is not wrong.' She placed her hands on her hips in a defiant *so there* type of pose.

I stepped forward and kissed her on the cheek. 'If anybody calls you dumb, tell me and I'll punch him in the nose.'

She placed her hand on my robe and a pocket appeared. She dropped the dragon blood in the pocket and then sealed the vial within the fabric.

We decided to swim the surf, towing the boat, as opposed to risking me being tossed out by the breakers. This was the third time I had swum with Graysea and I still couldn't get used to the way those gills opened up on her neck. To be honest it creeped me out a bit. But boy oh boy, once those gills appeared and her feet finned that chick could swim. I held on to the rings that were attached to the boat and then she grabbed me around the waist from behind and zoom, like being strapped to a jet-ski, we were off. She dived down at a speed I thought was impossible in water and then we soared out of the ocean like dolphins at a SeaWorld show. This happened over and over again. I wasn't sure if we were diving through the air so I could breathe or if she was repeatedly trying to kill me. Once past the surf I had to pry her hands from my waist to make her stop. I floated on the surface – my kelp robe providing buoyancy when I asked for it.

'Did I get carried away?' she asked after she had broken the surface and healed the gills in her neck so she could speak.

'No,' I said, 'my sinuses needed a good flushing.'

'Maybe you should travel in your boat.'

'You think?'

She nodded yes, missing the sarcasm.

'Are you sure you are up to this?'

'It will be easy, honestly. Look, The Stream is just over there.'

I looked to where she was pointing but saw nothing but water. 'I don't see anything.'

'You will when it gets darker. Now would you like me to help you get into your boat?'

I said, 'Yes,' expecting her to hold on to the other side so I could climb in without tipping it, but she had another idea. She gave me a quick kiss then once again grabbed me from behind. The next thing I knew I was plummeting to the bottom of the sea before changing direction and diving straight out of the water. As we were directly over the boat Graysea dropped me and I landed flat on my side on the bottom of the boat. I was very lucky to have not put my foot through the canvas. Then the boat lurched, as my own personal mermaid escort broke the water before me, holding the rings in both hands. She gave a hoot, which was the only sound she could make with a neck-full of gills and then did a lovely flip while blowing me an upside-down kiss. Then we were off.

It was not a smooth ride, being towed from the front means that you bounce on every wave and swell. The afternoon sun was setting and I hunkered down trying to think about anything other than the break-dancing my stomach was doing.

As the sun began to set The Stream came into view. It was a watery road filled with luminous algae that, as the night grew darker, became more incandescent. I could see that we were travelling in the opposite direction to the current and that made me wonder if Graysea was lying about this not being difficult for her, but those fears disappeared when I peeped over the bow. Graysea was just below the surface and completely outlined with the glowing algae. Her arms were outstretched like an Olympic gymnast performing the iron cross. Her tail wasn't even moving. She looked like an angel. Graysea had told me that the Mertain gain power from The Stream and I had just thought she meant it made ocean swimming easier, but here I saw The Stream provided real power, like gold in Truemagic or tree sap in Shadowmagic. Graysea was truly 'flying'.

But just 'cause my mermaid outboard motor was sailing smoothly, that didn't mean I was. I had to tear my eyes away from my miraculous escort and lie down in the boat to make sure I didn't blow chunks.

It was just before dawn when Graysea woke me up by tipping me out of the boat. As soon as her gills disappeared she started to giggle and my anger at my damp awakening evaporated. She was still covered with whatever luminous microorganisms that lived in The Stream and it transformed her into the most beautiful creature I had ever seen.

'You are glowing.'

'I know,' she said, spinning around. 'Do you like it?'

'You are radiant,' I replied, 'in every way.'

She pointed over my shoulder, 'From what you have told me I think this beach is close to your home. I will miss you, Conor.'

'You're not coming ashore?'

'No, matron needs me back at the grotto.'

'You're gonna be in a whole mess of trouble back there. Are you sure you don't want to come with me?'

'No one can stay mad at me, Conor – I am too dumb.'

'Maybe,' I said, 'they can't stay mad at you 'cause you're so wonderful.'

She kissed me and as she did we dropped below the surface. If you're looking to add things to your list of top ten, all-time best experiences I highly recommend kissing a mermaid underwater. She pulled back from me and those (getting less creepy) gills appeared and even though she was underwater I could have sworn there was also a tear in her eye. She turned and disappeared into the gloom of the sea.

THIRTY-SIX
ONA'S BOOK

I swam to the shore, almost drowning when my robe dragged me under. (I was sure I told it to float.) I thought about Graysea. I think she would have come if I pushed her but, to be honest, I really didn't want her with me. I was going into such uncertainty – I didn't want to subject my innocent glowing angel to that kind of danger and chaos. I could almost imagine her standing in the middle of a battlefield saying, 'Why is everyone being so mean to each other?' It was better that she was with matron back in her grotto. I just hoped she didn't catch too much grief for helping me escape and giving me the dragon's blood. I was also glad I didn't have to explain her to Essa.

Of course I couldn't be sure that Essa and Yogi got out of the Alderlands alive. For that matter, I couldn't be sure that any of my loved ones were safe. I started to fret over all the time that I had lost and swam harder. My robe increased its buoyancy and I body-boarded the surf right onto the shore. The sun was newly up as I stood on the beach and rubbed the stinging saltwater out of my eyes with the sleeve of my warm insta-dry robe. I looked around and what I saw almost made my already queasy stomach bring up everything I had ever eaten. I was in the Reedlands.

There was no mistaking the foul vegetation. This was the land that had been created when Cialtie had first taken his Choosing. The last time I had been here Fergal had almost been drawn and quartered by living vines and a band of feral Banshees (the same ones who had destroyed the Heatherlands) had used me and my friends for archery practice.

A shout to my left made me scamper into a mangle of trees, the like I had only ever seen in B-grade horror movies with names like *The Re-return of the Swamp Creature.* The trees didn't provide much cover but I might not have been spotted if I hadn't then instructed my robe to darken so as to blend in with the vegetation. As the troop of soldiers came towards me, my annoyingly disobedient robe went practically fluorescent orange. Then, when I tried to run, I found that some vines had wrapped around my ankles – I couldn't have gotten away even if there had been anywhere to go. As they came closer I noticed that they were Brownies and the one at the front was an old acquaintance of mine. He stepped right up to me wearing a smug smile that only a Brownie mother could love.

'Hi, Frank,' I said. 'Did you get the knife I sent you?'

The soldier's uniform did nothing to make the Brownie prince look any older than the kid I had reprimanded for stealing my shoes so many months before. He pointed to his ankle where a sheath held the green-handled throwing knife to his leg.

'Yeah, I did,' he said and as a thank you, he clocked me in the head with his banta stick.

There are many times when little situations remind me of how much I miss Fergal. I must say that waking from a concussion tied to a post was much more fun with my cousin bound to the one next to me.

At least this place was a cut above my usual stinky dungeon. I was tied to the centre pole of a pretty opulent tent. This was no travelling structure, or if it was, then somebody was doing some serious heavy lifting. There was a full oak-framed bed in the corner, a complete eight-seat dining table set, and an office desk adorned with a collection of peacock quill pens. When the occupant of these posh digs came into the tent I wasn't surprised. I was expecting him. He stood in front of me with his right wrist tucked into his shirt like Napoleon. On his face he wore a smirk that made me want to slap him, but then, all of his expressions make me want to do that.

'Hello, Uncle, I was so worried that we weren't going to get to meet this trip. You know how difficult it is finding time to see *all* of one's relatives.'

I had been practising that line for the entire time I had been waiting for Cialtie to arrive. I hoped that the bravado of it would hide the bowel-clenching fear that was ripping through my body.

'Why are you here and how did you get here?'

'I was hoping to borrow some money for university. You know Dad, he's such a skinflint. Why he won't even pay for—'

A backhand across my face shut me up. While I fought to remain conscious I said, 'I could have sworn uncles are supposed to give you hugs and kisses when they see you.'

'I don't want to hurt you.'

'I don't believe you,' I said. The time for jokes was over. 'In fact I think that is exactly what you want to do. I think that this interrogation is an annoyance. I think what you really want to do is kill the nephew that made you a lefty. Am I right?'

Cialtie took his wrist from his shirt and with his remaining hand scratched the stump that I had created. Then he dragged a chair from across the room and sat down in front of me. 'You think me a monster.'

'No, monsters have no choice, that's just the way they are. I think you are a demon.'

This brought a look of incredulity to my uncle's face. 'You think I have *choice*? You think any of us has choice? You of all people should know that we are all just pawns of Ona's prophecies.'

'Oh don't make me sick. You killed your son, my cousin, my friend. *You*. You did that. Don't you dare try to pass off that responsibility to some old fortune teller.'

'Old fortune teller?' Cialtie laughed. 'You have no idea, have you?' He stood and walked over to his desk. From his pocket he took a key and opened a golden box, from which he took a leather-bound manuscript. He sat down again and placed the book at my feet. 'These are Ona's predictions. She was truly omniscient – we have no choice but to do what she knew must be done.'

'Is that why you killed her, to get that book?'

'No. I had the book before I killed her.'

'You sound proud of yourself.'

'No, not proud, only … resigned. When I had seen only twenty summers, I stole into Ona's room and found this book. As if guided by fate I opened it to the page that foretold my ultimate destiny. When I looked up Ona was standing beside me. She told me that if she were to be allowed to leave that she would tell my father what I had done and he would banish me. Then she took the book and opened it to the page that foretold *her* death. She handed the book to me and lay down on the bed. As I stood over her she handed me a pillow and I smothered her – just as she had written. There was none of your precious *choice*.'

'You could have chosen not to kill her.'

'You can think that if it helps you sleep – I know better.'

'So did Ona tell you to destroy the whole land with your golden circle?'

'No, that was my idea. I thought if I wiped clean the slate of The Land, that finally Tir na Nog would be free of the cage that Ona has put us in.'

I laughed at that. 'So you wanted to free The Land by destroying it? I think if you asked, a few of us would have objected to that.'

'Your precious free will is an illusion. You too are doomed to follow Ona's puppet play whether you know it or not.'

'So you're back in The Land-destroying business again.'

'No, I have learned my lesson. Ona's will is not to be denied. I now only seek to regain the Oak Throne. As long as I am the King of Castle Duir, I will be safe. That is why I must do this.' He reached into a pouch on his belt and took out the gold-rimmed glass vial. I looked down to where Graysea had sealed the vial of dragon's blood into my robe. There was a slit cut into the living fabric. Cialtie undid the stopper and began to tilt.

'No, please,' I begged.

He stopped. 'Turlow told me that you sought dragon's blood, but he told me you failed. Where did you get this?'

'I stole it,' I lied. I didn't want Graysea to be dragged into all of this.

'From where?'

'Duh – from a dragon.'

He looked as though he was going to hit me again but then just said, 'No matter, my spies in Castle Duir have told me that Oisin is much worse. It will not be long.' Then he lifted the corner of the carpet and poured the blood into the dirt below.

I tried to scream, I tried to tell him that I was going to kill him but nothing would come. As if I had been punched in the solar plexus, I had no breath. When finally I could speak, I found I had no strength to do it. You can only lose hope so many times before life is no longer worth fighting for. I dropped my head to my chest and waited for the sword that I knew was going to come, not even caring.

I think I actually dozed off then. I had a vision that I was dead – riding a dragon off into a heavenly sunset filled with red and gold clouds and beams of light like you see in the paintings on the walls of Italian churches. I sputtered awake as hot liquid slipped down my throat and exploded my senses. I opened my eyes to see Cialtie holding a bottle of poteen.

'I thought you had killed me already,' I said with the husky voice of an alcohol-burned throat.

'I have not decided what to do with you yet,' he said, sitting back into his chair. 'I've won you know. The Brownies and the Banshees are loyal to me. The Faeries, without your father, will splinter back into a squabbling mess. The Pookas will all turn again into dogs once I destroy the Tree of Knowledge. That only leaves the Imps and the Elves. The Elves, as usual, will scamper up their trees and wait to see what will happen – and the Imps … well, the Imps fight like farmers.'

'We'll stop you.'

'Or you could help me. You know I'm right, you know I will win. You don't have to like me but you can see that if you stand by my side we can avoid this war. You can save your friends and The Land much heartache.'

'What do you know about heartache? You have to have a heart for that.'

Cialtie stood and returned Ona's book to its box. Without looking around he said, 'When one's entire lifetime is presented to you in an afternoon then one experiences a lifetime of pain – in a day. Oh, nephew, I know heartache.' He turned back to me. 'Think about what I have said,' and then he left.

As much as I wanted not to do as he commanded, thinking is pretty much the only thing you can do when left tied to a pole. I didn't believe it was possible but I felt a little sorry for my uncle. I tried to imagine what life would be like if I knew everything that was going to happen to me and I had to admit it would be a nightmare – especially if my life was like Cialtie's. I also had to admit that he had a point about my family and friends being in trouble – things didn't look good. I wanted to laugh at the clichéd 'Join me and together we can rule the universe' speech but I'd be lying if I wasn't tempted. Don't get me wrong, the idea of spending any time with Cialtie made my stomach churn but the thought of all my loved ones getting massacred in the Hazellands made it churn more. I had seen the young troops that Dahy had put together, I had trained with them and if I was brutally honest – they weren't up to much. They were no match for a well-trained army of Banshees and Brownies. If I was certain my friends were going to be killed, wasn't it my duty to save them? But then I imagined Essa and Dahy's faces as I rode in at Cialtie's side. It wouldn't make any difference – they would never give up. The only difference would be that before they died they would hate me and I was pretty sure that Essa would find a way to haunt me for the rest of my life.

Cialtie knew what he was doing; he had left me alone to think and that was the cruellest cut of all. In the end I came to the conclusion that, preordained or not, Cialtie was a monster I could never join with. I had failed my father, my friends were almost certainly doomed and I would soon die. Cialtie didn't need to torture me – I was doing it to myself. I would like to be able to say that at that moment I welcomed death but the truth is I was afraid. I decided that when my uncle returned that I would accept his offer just so I could survive the day and maybe find a chance to escape later.

'You were not thinking of accepting his offer were you?' I heard a familiar voice say from behind me and then I felt the ropes being cut from my wrists.

'Not me,' I said, as a spark of hope returned to my soul and blood returned to my hands. I silently groaned as I stood and turned to see a very welcome face covered with camouflaging dirt.

'I myself would have accepted,' he said, his white teeth shining in his dark face, 'and then looked for a chance to escape.'

I started to say, 'Actually that's what I was going to do,' but then just decided to say, 'That's why they call you *Master* Spideog.' I bowed and then hugged him.

'I think we should get out of here,' he said, crossing the tent and opening Cialtie's wardrobe.

'What are you looking for?'

'You need to wear something that is a bit darker than that bathrobe.'

'Hold on, let me try something.' I concentrated. This time the robe cooperated and turned a dark bark brown.

'Impressive,' the old archer said while throwing me a pair of my uncle's shoes.

I was still putting on the left shoe when he grabbed me by the collar and I hopped out of the slit he had cut in the back of the tent. There was more moon than we would have liked as we tried to keep the vegetation between us and the roving soldiers. Spideog held a staff but no bow. Seeing him without a bow was like seeing a zebra without stripes. It made me want to ask what had happened to him in the Yewlands but this was no place for a chat.

He led me through the spooky vegetation and then pointed into the gloom. In the distance I made out a horse corral with two guards. We snuck in closer, then Spideog offered me a knife and pointed to the guard on the left. I looked at the deadly weapon.

'Can't I have your stick?' I whispered.

His face showed his displeasure at the breach of silence, then he surprised me by saying, 'No.'

'I can't just stab a man in the back.'

'Conor, we are at war.'

'Why won't you let me use the stick?'

'Because it is mine. Now do you want to get out of here or not?'

I knew by the tone that this was the end of the conversation. I took the knife and as I crept up on the guard I repeated to myself, 'We are at war ... we are at war.' But the closer I got, the less my resolve became. While I was still in the open, the clueless soldier bent down, picked up a rock and batted it into the night with his staff. This was just a kid and then when I got closer still I realised it was a kid I knew. What were the odds? Like he was the only Brownie in all of the Reedlands – it was Frank. I came up behind him and placed the knife onto the front of his neck but I couldn't kill.

'Make a sound, Frank, and I'll slit your throat from ear to ear.'

Frank let loose a tiny childish squeal.

'That would be a sound. Would you like to try me again?'

I took his silence for a 'no'. I instructed him to plant his staff in the ground and take a step forward. I held the knife to his back and picked up his staff.

'You should have said "thank you",' I whispered as I clocked him in the side of his head. He went down with a slow wobble of the knees. I took back the green-handled knife but then had an image in my mind's eye of poor worried Jesse and replaced it in his sock. 'Stay out of trouble, Frank.'

THIRTY-SEVEN
WAR

We rode out on two mares. I wanted to stampede the herd but Spideog thought getting out of there unnoticed was more important than making them round up horses for a couple of hours. We galloped into the night.

Since we couldn't find any saddles, we rode bareback. And since all I was wearing was my stupid kelp robe thing, I really was riding bareback. Last summer Mom had taught me the basic techniques of riding without a saddle but on that occasion I didn't have to hoik up a robe exposing my bare bottom to horsehair and the rest of my lower parts to a winter breeze. Spideog rode in front of me and to be honest, I couldn't blame him. I wouldn't want to be confronted with that view for a prolonged period of time either.

Kidding aside, it was a profoundly uncomfortable ride. Riding bareback is twice the work than in a saddle. I was already exhausted from being knocked out and trussed up, and my legs (as well as my nether regions) were going numb with the cold. Spideog was determined to get far away from Cialtie's camp before I was discovered missing and he wanted to reach the Hazellands as soon as possible to warn of the imminent attack. So we travelled fast and only stopped to rest the horses. I couldn't disagree with his logic but I would have loved to curl up in a pile of leaves for an hour or twenty.

The sky was dark and overcast during our entire escape. A couple of snow squalls made it almost impossible to see our way but then again, it made us also impossible to spot. All the while I practised the Fili mind-calming chant that Fand had once tried to teach me. I decided on and repeated a mantra 'Would you like fries with that burger?' over and over again until my mind and body were almost separate. Spideog said it took a full twenty hours to get out of the Reedlands but I hardly remember anything except the cold.

There were two Banshee guards at the border path leading into the Hazellands. Spideog spotted them before they spotted us. I waited while he snuck up and dispatched them. All that could be heard were two quiet thumps.

In the Hazellands we found our first clean stream. The horses drank greedily and I fell into it face down. My robe had been getting lighter and colder the longer it had been away from water; after the bath it dried and warmed itself and me. I noticed that the slit that Cialtie had cut in the fabric had healed so I decided to give something a try. I slit the robe down the middle from my crotch to the floor and wrapped the dangling pieces of fabric around my legs and then willed the fabric to join together like trousers. It worked – my butt still hung out of the back but I was much warmer for the rest of the trip.

A day into the Hazellands I could go on no longer. Spideog decided we were not being followed. He caught a rabbit and risked a small fire.

'Do you have enough energy to tell me what has happened to you since we parted?'

I had dreaded that question. The Fili chanting had not only helped me endure the cold, it had also stopped me from remembering how badly I had failed and how many friends I had lost.

'Brendan is dead,' I blurted, hoping that if I said it fast it wouldn't hurt so much.

The archer gave a deep sigh that was the only grieving he allowed himself. 'And the rest?' he asked.

'Araf is dead too, along with a Pooka prince who was our guide. Essa left for the Hazellands, I don't know if she made it or not. Turlow betrayed us.'

'I gathered that from what Cialtie said.'

'You heard our whole conversation?'

'Most of it,' he said. 'I had already cut a slit in the back of the tent when your uncle came in. If I had had a bow, he would be dead now.'

'So the yews didn't give you a bow?'

'The yews do not give bows, Conor, the yews give wood for a bow – if they find you worthy.' To answer my question he held out the staff he was holding – it was of course yew wood.

'So the yews told you that you were worthy, eh? I could have told you that.'

'They also told me something else. They say that someone has killed one of them.'

'But I always thought a yew could kill anybody before they could chop one down.'

'That is how it has always been.'

'Then who did it?'

'I do not know, nor do I know what this means, but I do know that it does not bode well.'

I asked Spideog if I could have his knife to cut some roast rabbit and he asked, 'Did I not see you take a knife from that Brownie in the corral?'

'I did but then I gave it back to him,' I replied.

'Why in The Land would you do that?'

So I told him the story about how I had first met Frank and how I had given the worried Jesse the knife that had been thrown at us on Mount Cas.

That sat the old guy up. 'What did you say?'

'You know – the knife with the message that was thrown at Brendan when we were up at the mountain.'

He shook his head. He looked confused and very concerned.

'Oh yeah, I forgot, you were a bit out of it when it happened and you were gone when I found the knife.' So I told him the whole story about finding the message in the sheath of the knife, which then led us to the Pinelands. I wanted to get some rest but he insisted I tell him everything in detail, especially describing the knife.

'It was a gold-tipped throwing knife with a green glass handle with a spiral of gold embedded in it. It was almost identical to the one that Queen Rhiannon gave me.'

Spideog was on his feet now. 'Where did Rhiannon get her knife?'

'Ah …' I said, not knowing what could possibly have gotten the old guy so worked up. 'She said my grandfather Liam gave it to her.'

'We must go now,' Spideog said, kicking out the fire and knocking my half-eaten rabbit into the dirt.

'What? I thought you said we are safe for a bit.'

'You have had your *bit* – we leave now.' He picked up his yew staff and jumped on his horse before I even stood up.

I struggled onto my horse. It took some hard riding but I finally caught up with him. That didn't mean he was answering any questions. Whatever I had said that was making him ride at that breakneck speed was not up for discussion. I mumbled back in to my McMantra, clamped my thighs to my poor frightened, overworked mount and zoomed into the remainder of the afternoon.

As the sun got low in the sky I started recognising landmarks – we were at the outskirts of the Hall of Knowledge. Every bone in my body screamed for rest and every cell of my skin yelled for a bath, but I also dreaded arriving and having to tell the Imps that their prince was dead. I thought about how Essa would take it and then it hit me that I wasn't sure if she had even made it out of the Alderlands. I kicked my poor horse and bent my back into the wind.

At dusk, Spideog dropped in next to me, grabbed my horse's mane and gestured for me not to speak. We dismounted but were spotted by a group of riders in the distance. Spideog looked around for options, cursed under his breath and braced himself for what was to come. We were definitely under-armed. The old guy handed me a throwing blade and held his yew staff in readiness for a fight. I knew that the knife wasn't going to save me from being killed but at least I would be able to take one down with me.

As they drew closer Spideog sighed with relief and then waved. I recognised one of them, a Leprechaun from a training session in the Hall of Knowledge. Fortunately they recognised us as well.

'Did Essa return safely?' I asked, waving away all of the saluting and bowing. This question confused the senior officer.

'I do not think so,' he said.

'She never returned from the Alderlands?'

'Oh yes, ages ago. I thought you meant now.'

'Where is she now?'

'She should be a league east of here.'

'Is Turlow with her?'

Confusion once again crossed the Leprechaun's face. 'We are seeking The Turlow.'

'Explain,' Spideog commanded.

'A pair of Brownie swiftriders arrived this morning, waited outside our embattlements and demanded a parley with The Turlow. Turlow wanted to go alone but Dahy insisted he bring a guard. When they met the swiftriders at the bottom of the windward knoll, the guard was killed and The Turlow was taken.'

Spideog and I exchanged knowing looks. 'Are you in contact with Essa?'

'I have a whistle but it is only to be used in an emergency.'

'This is that emergency, soldier,' Spideog said. 'Blow it.'

Ten minutes later we heard the thundering hooves of a company in full gallop. Essa saw me and dismounted without even slowing her horse. She hugged me while still at a run and almost knocked me over.

'I thought you were dead.'

I allowed myself a momentary return hug before I told her my grim news.

Essa spoke before I could say anything. 'The Brownies have taken Turlow.'

'No, Essa, they haven't.'

'What do you mean they haven't? I saw them.' She looked around. 'Where is Araf?'

Which question should I answer first? Neither was good news. 'Turlow hasn't been taken – he has escaped. The Brownies knew that I was coming and they rode here to warn him.'

Essa threw her shoulders back. 'Warn him of what? Where is Araf? Where are Brendan and Tuan?'

'Dead,' I said bluntly, there was no other way. 'Turlow betrayed us.'

'You lie.' Her eyes blazed.

'No, I don't. Turlow is working with Cialtie. Because of his treachery Araf, Brendan and Tuan are dead. I barely escaped with my life.'

'That's not true.'

'It is true, Princess,' Spideog said.

Essa turned to the archer as if she had only just noticed he was there. 'What do you know, you crazy old hermit! You've spent the last hundred years dusting banta sticks.' Then she turned on me. 'You never liked him. You're jealous, you're making this up.'

'I'm not, Essa. Use your Owith glass if you don't believe me.'

She looked like I had just slapped her in the face. She pressed her hand to her chest on top of the place where her truth-seeking glass hung from a gold chain. 'I will not go about interrogating people with the Owith glass.'

Spideog stepped up to her and took her by the shoulders; for a moment I thought she was going to squirm away and for another second I thought he was going to slap her. 'Use the glass, Princess. We are at war – we must be certain. Use the glass on us, as you should have used it on him.'

She looked at me. For a nanosecond she was just a girl with pleading eyes wishing me to say it wasn't so. She bowed her head and removed the finger-sized crystal from around her neck. As tears welled up in her eyes she asked, 'Did Turlow betray … me?'

'He did, Princess,' Spideog replied.

'He betrayed us all,' I said.

The crystal remained clear. Essa turned and secretly wiped her eyes as she placed the crystal back around her neck. Then she got back on her horse, raised her chin high and shouted to her company, 'Mount up! We must return to the Hall of Knowledge. Prince Conor and Master Spideog bring news and it means – war.'

THIRTY-EIGHT

RIBBONS OF GOLD

My return to the Hall of Knowledge was not the triumphant one I had imagined when I left. News of Araf's death swept through the camp. The usually taciturn Imps jabbered among themselves and often broke down into mournful cries. Yogi ran up to me and asked about Tuan. When I shook my head, he threw his own back and turned into the bear. His cry transformed into a roar. It was frightening and heartbreaking. I reached to comfort him but he growled and swung at me. Even so I tried again and this time he let me hug him. He shrank in my arms and I was left with this strongest of men crying on my shoulder.

'Where's Mom?' I asked Nieve, who was the only one in the head-quarters tent.

'She has returned to Castle Duir.'

'How is my father?'

'Oisin lives but I fear not for long.'

Nieve waited for me to say more; when I didn't, she asked a one word question, 'Brendan?'

Oh gods, I thought, *I had forgotten that there was something going on between those two.* 'I'm sorry,' I said.

She dropped her chin and allowed herself one deep sigh then said, 'Dahy has called for a war council in half an hour. You should freshen up.' Before she left she held my face in her hands and then kissed my forehead. 'I am very glad you are safe,' she said.

There was hot water, so I washed up a bit and found some clothes. By the time I got to the meeting everyone was there. Dahy looked up and said, 'I'm glad you could make it, Prince Conor.' I couldn't figure out if he was being sarcastic or not so I just bowed and found a place to sit.

'I believe the attack will come as soon as Cialtie's forces arrive. This is good. It means that tomorrow's battle will only be half of the day.'

'Cialtie's attacking tomorrow?' I blurted.

'If we are lucky tomorrow's attack will not be until the afternoon or late morning at the worst.'

'When did we find that out?'

'We, meaning everyone here, found out fifteen minutes ago when they arrived at the war council – on time,' Dahy said, laying to rest my doubt over whether his greeting had been sarcastic or not. 'We must assume the attack is imminent. With your escape, Cialtie knows that surprise is no longer on his side. He will attack swiftly before we can call for reinforcements. Our Pooka hawk scout has just confirmed my suspicion. The Brownie and Banshee army is less than a day's march away.'

A day, I said to myself, *I was hoping to join the contingent that rode to Castle Duir for reinforcements.* I was hoping to see Dad before it was too late. Now, looking around the faces in the room, I knew I couldn't leave. Tomorrow we make a stand and the only thing that I could hope for was to survive the day.

'As you all must have heard by now The Turlow has betrayed us,' Dahy said without emotion. I looked to Essa. Other than her jaw clenching, she too showed nothing. 'That means the enemy knows our strengths and our weaknesses. We can put this to good use. We have erected stone ramparts on three sides of the Hall but the western ridge above the valley, as you know, is undefended. This is where the main attack will come. Turlow will be certain that there is no way to defend the hill from a frontal assault – tonight we will prove him wrong.'

I turned to Yogi, who was next to me. 'What is he talking about?' I asked but the Pooka shushed me.

'Archers, go with Master Spideog to the battlements – the rest of you grab a shovel and come with me.'

Any thought of spending my last night resting and reminiscing about the shortness of my life were dashed when I got to the hill. This was going to be a big job. Using swords, long strips of turf were carefully cut from the ground and then five shallow trenches were dug the length of the entire hill.

Five impromptu gold forges were set up on the summit. Leprechaun goldsmiths minted and hammered long strips of thick gold ribbons that were then laid into the trenches. Essa, Nieve and a handful of Imp and Leprechaun sorceresses spent most of the night kneeling and incanting their mumbo-jumbo over the gold. Then the turf was carefully replaced.

It was only a couple of hours before dawn by the time we were finished. I saw Essa almost swoon when she placed a spell over the last of the strips of gold. I ran to her and placed her arm around my neck and walked her back to her tent. She was almost unconscious when I laid her down, but before I could go she said, 'Stay.' I held her as she instantly dropped off into a heavy sleep. I was glad she asked me to stay; if I was to die tomorrow she was the one with whom I wanted to spend my last hours.

As I held Essa I slid seamlessly into a dream. Her tent faded away and we were lying in front of the fireplace back in my house in the Real World. I knew at once that this was just a dream and not a prediction. I never had the courage to ask Essa how old she was but I wouldn't be surprised to find that she had like fifty years on her. Although that makes you a youngster around here, I'm sure she wouldn't appreciate a couple of decades worth of wrinkles just for a tour of my old high school in Scranton, Pennsylvania. Shame, I'd love to show her around where I grew up. I have no idea what she would make of the Real World – it would be fun to find out.

Saying that, as I watched the fire dance in the fireplace of my old living room, I realised that I would never in reality see that sight again. I would never go back to my home. I lived in The Land now and if I made it through tomorrow's battle, I knew I would only be taking one last trip to the Real World. That would be to tell Brendan's mother and daughter how he had died. They probably wouldn't believe me but it's the least I could do.

Still in my dream, I was grabbed from above by the talons of a dragon. He zoomed me into the sky as the sun was setting and flew me to Castle Duir. Ah, the more accustomed I became with dreaming, the more my dreams became just like everyone else's. There in my subconscious I acted out my heart's desire. The dragon dropped me into my father's room where he was sitting up, drinking a cup of tea (there seemed to be no ceilings in my dreams), and standing next to his bed were Tuan and Brendan, all fit and smiling. I reached for my fallen companions ...

I awoke with the euphoria that for a microsecond follows a dream into wakefulness – before the realities of life crush it. My father and my friends were gone, and soon I would engage in a hopeless battle. I turned to Essa but she too was gone. It took all of my will to get out of that bed.

I expected everyone to be a hive of busyness but they weren't – they were just sitting around waiting. Some were writing letters, others were polishing their swords or fussing with their bows. Morale was definitely not good.

Spideog spotted me having breakfast in the canteen. 'You must speak to them.'

'Speak to who?'

'Your troops.'

'There not my troops, they're Dahy's troops.'

'Dahy is their general,' the old archer said, 'but you are their prince.'

'Look, I told you before I don't feel very comfortable with all of this royal stuff.'

Spideog scoffed, 'Since when is *your* comfort an issue? You are what you are – and what you are is the royal heir to the Throne of Duir. These men and women need to know what they are fighting for and you must tell them.'

'I don't even know what we are fighting for.'

'Well, you had better figure it out fast, Conor. Dahy is massing the troops now.'

Dahy was finishing up explaining the battle plan when I finally emerged from the canteen. It had occurred to me that none of these guys knew anything about the Real World and I thought about stealing a choice speech from history.

The first thing that came to mind was, 'We have nothing to fear but fear itself.' That might have been appropriate for Americans safe in their homes during the Great Depression but these guys did have something to fear – screaming Banshees.

I toyed with 'We shall fight them on the beaches,' but the beaches were miles away. And 'Ich bin ein Tir na Nogier,' would most certainly go way over their heads.

So as I walked to the front of the eager faces of the troops ... my troops, I still didn't know what I was going to say.

'Friends, Tir na Nogians, countrymen, lend me your ears.' I instinctively looked around for someone to get the joke but the only two who could, Brendan and Dad, were not there. I paused and looked at the eager faces waiting for me to orate some great wisdom but all I could think of were the people that weren't there.

'I have only been here a short while,' I said quietly.

Someone shouted, 'Speak up.'

I cleared my throat. 'I have only been here a short while but during that time I have lost much: my cousin, my friends, and as I speak my father lies dying in Castle Duir.' I looked at the soldiers, they were all silently nodding. 'I know I'm not the only one. You Imps and Pookas have lost your princes and we all know of the hardships that you Leprechauns suffered when Cialtie held the Oak Throne. It would be easy to say this battle was about revenge.' A few cheers popped up in the crowd but I waved them quiet. 'But my father once told me that revenge was a poisonous emotion. He said, if we must fight, we must fight because it is right.

'This battle didn't start today. Decades ago the same people who attack us now trashed the Hazellands. They wrecked the Hall of Knowledge and they destroyed everything in it. You know, I once had a teacher in high school – he was a real jerk but he did say one thing that has always stayed with me. He said, "History is not about what we did, it is about who we are." By destroying the Hall of Knowledge, Cialtie and Turlow are not only trying to kill us, they are also trying to kill what we are as people. My mother, using Shadowmagic, has invented a way to get much of our history back from this place. We must hold the Hall of Knowledge. By holding the Hazellands long enough for reinforcements to come, we will not only be giving ourselves a chance to live tomorrow but we will be saving what we were – and *are* – we give ourselves a chance to be remembered. That is what immortality truly is.

'We stand together at the brains of Tir na Nog. Let's kick some Banshee tail!'

A cheer rose up that was so loud and fast, it shocked me.

Spideog walked up to me and did something he had never done before. He bowed and said, 'My Prince.'

'I did good?' I asked.

He smiled – a rare smile. 'You did good.'

I spent the rest of the day visiting with the troops – basically acting like a prince. I walked around faking being brave and I actually think it helped calm people. Maybe that's what bravery is – pretending not to be scared. Many soldiers told me stories of their homes and their families that made me realise just how little I truly knew of Tir na Nog. It made me determined to save as much of it as I could.

Essa was doing pretty much the same thing. I was watching Essa help a man write a letter when Spideog caught me staring at her. 'Can I ask you a personal question, Conor?'

'Sure,' I said.

'I thought you and her …' the old archer nodded his head towards Essa, 'I thought you two were … you know … wooing.'

'Oh Master, that was a long time ago.'

Spideog looked confused and said, 'I thought you only first arrived in The Land last summer?'

'I did,' I said and laughed. 'I guess you and I have a different definition of "a long time ago".'

'So what happened between you two – *so long ago*?'

'Well, she tried to kill me.'

He turned and took a long look at Essa, then looked me in the eyes and said, 'If I were you, I wouldn't let a little thing like that put me off.'

It was well into the afternoon when I found myself with Dahy standing on the makeshift battlements.

'Have you ever fought against Banshees before?' I asked the old warrior.

The question made him look older. 'I have fought with them – never against them.'

'So what about that Banshee sixth sense? If they can tell when they are going to win a battle, doesn't that mean we have already lost?'

Dahy gave me a look like I had just cursed in church. 'I spoke with the troops about this before you came out this morning. The Banshees have a very good sense of how a battle is going but they cannot predict the future. Just because they are good at knowing which way the wind blows doesn't mean that winds cannot change. They are not the mystics they think they are. They drop their trousers to crap just like the rest of us.'

'But if they attack, doesn't that mean the wind is blowing their way?'

Dahy laughed. 'There is a tornado blowing our way, son. Any fool can see that. I have sent wolves to Castle Duir and to the Pinelands. I wanted to send the bird but I needed her for reconnaissance.' He looked to the sky but it was empty. 'Our only hope is to hold out until we get reinforcements. When we do, the Banshees will turn tail. That sense of theirs also tells them when they are going to lose.'

A screech above us forced our eyes to the sky as a streak of black came towards us. I stepped instinctively back but Dahy just reached into his satchel and took out a silk robe. The hawk landed between us and as it raised its head it continued to grow into a black-haired woman. Dahy handed her the robe.

She looked at me and then, like a bird, sharply turned her head to the general. 'They are here,' she said.

THIRTY-NINE
THERE WILL BE BLOOD

J ust as Dahy had predicted, Cialtie's army, using Turlow's intelli-
gence, ignored the stone ramparts, swept wide behind the Hall
and prepared to attack what yesterday had been the unprotected
hill. Cialtie's forces took their time setting up. If their sixth sense was
warning them about the buried gold barrier, then they weren't showing
it. We stood in a row, two deep, banta sticks in hand, waiting for the
attack.

The previous night there had been a pretty heated debate about
whether we should be defending with swords or sticks. Spideog said we
were at war and should be using swords like warriors, but I said no.
These people were not monsters or robots – they were men and women
whose only crime was to have their minds corrupted by evil men.
Spideog pointed out that they would not give us the same courtesy.
Before I could reply Essa said something that finished the argument.

'What would we win,' she asked, 'if after we defeat our enemy, we
then become just like them?'

At that moment I wanted to kiss Essa square on the mouth – but
then again I could say that about most moments.

The battle began with a mortar attack. The enemy cheered as they
sent conch shells sailing overhead. Except for the one that Essa batted
back like a major league baseball player, half a dozen shells landed on

the ground with smoke rising out of them. We backed away expecting the worst but they did nothing. Finally brave souls picked them up and threw them back. Our enemy's cheering stopped and for a while they looked confused. Orders barked from the back of their ranks refocused the troops and they strapped short shields to their arms, drew their swords and waited for the order to charge.

The silence, as the old expression goes, was deafening. I looked to my left and saw Yogi morph into a bear and growl. I looked to my right; Essa nodded and spun her banta stick. There wasn't a smiling face to be seen. How I wished Fergal was there with me.

I didn't hear the order to charge but I sure saw the results. A couple of hundred screaming Banshees and howling Brownies charged up the hill under the shadow of a flock of arrows launched from the rear. The attackers must have seen the arrows explode into flame as they crossed the gold barrier. They probably expected it. What they didn't expect was what came next. As the first line of Banshees crossed the point where we had buried the ribbons of gold, their swords and shields vanished in a puff of smoke. Their forward momentum carried them straight into our waiting sticks. It was like hunting in a zoo. Baffled and surprised Banshees ran straight at us as we mercilessly clubbed them and then dropped back so as to let the next line step up and have a full swing. Banshees, then Brownies, dropped like bowling pins and piled up on one another. Others collided and tripped over confused retreating soldiers who were running in every direction. It was horrible. The sound of it was sickening and the look on their faces just before we hit them was pathetic. I thank the gods we weren't using swords. I don't think even the hardest of us could have withstood that guilt.

When they finally retreated, what remained was a long pile of moaning Banshee and Brownie bodies lying twisted in a heap three deep.

Since we had no provisions to take prisoners, a detail of soldiers was chosen to untangle and roll the unconscious aggressors back down the hill. Among them were Nieve and her little cabal of sorceresses. They stuck most of the enemy in the leg with one of my aunt's special paralysing pins – when they woke up, they found it difficult to use that leg for a day or so. It would make a little bit of a difference but not much. Cialtie's forces were still substantially larger than ours.

It was too late for my uncle to mount another attack. Since he knew he had the upper hand and we had little chance for reinforcements by tomorrow, they simply backed out of archery range and made camp.

'Well, it looks like we won round one,' I said to Spideog.

'War is scored with the dead, Conor,' the old warrior said. 'This battle has yet to begin.'

I continued with my morale-man job, dispensing pep talks as deemed necessary for a while, and then went to headquarters to check if I was needed or maybe get a little nap in. I caught my Aunt Nieve by surprise and she quickly turned away and wiped her eyes.

'Are you OK?' I asked.

She tried to put on a brave face but at the last second she told the truth. Her voice wobbled as she said, 'No,' and sat down.

That was an answer I wasn't ready for. Of all people Nieve was the last person I would have expected to crack under pressure. I sat on the arm of her chair and put my hand on her shoulder.

'How did he die?' she asked, not looking at me.

That question hit me like a slap. How should I answer that? How did Brendan die? If I was truthful I would have told her that one of her spells made him powerless to move while he was burned alive, but instead I said, 'It was instant, and painless, he wouldn't have even known what hit him.'

That seemed to do the job. She wiped her face, stood up and said, 'Right, we have a battle to prepare for, yes?'

'Actually I was hoping to have a kip. Do you think that's OK?'

'Of course,' she said as we gave each other a proper hug. 'You may be our Prince but you're still just a Faerie.'

I nodded and left for my tent. I understood what she meant but it still didn't sound right.

I willed myself to not dream but that didn't work. Once again in dreamland I zoomed to my father's side. I have to admit that even though I would never abandon my comrades, I'd be lying if at that moment flying away to Castle Duir wasn't what I truly wished I could do.

It was well after midnight when I awoke. I walked to the battlements and found Spideog with a very short Imp sorceress. The sorceress mumbled over an arrow and then handed it to the old archer, who notched it into the biggest bow I had ever seen. He let it fly and I lost it in the night sky. I started to look away but Spideog said, 'Keep watching.'

As the lost arrow began to descend, it started to glow then it exploded on top of a tent, showering it in flames. Screaming and cursing could be heard wafting up from the enemy camp.

'You havin' fun?' I asked.

'We are not sleeping tonight,' Spideog said. 'There is no reason why they should.'

We spent the rest of the night lobbing arrows into Cialtie's camp. By morning Essa, Yogi, Dahy and Nieve had all joined us and we giggled like schoolchildren every time Spideog let an arrow fly. Some of Spideog's archery students tried their hand with the big bow but none of them was as good as the Master. It was amazing how many tents he hit even though he couldn't see them until they went up in flames.

With the troops assembled at the ramparts, Dahy asked me if I wanted to address them again. I told him I had already done my bit and maybe he should do it. He didn't disagree.

'Today will be different from yesterday,' Dahy said, raising his gruff voice. 'Today, we use swords – today, there will be blood. But the first victim of your sword should not be your enemy, it should be the little voice inside you that is saying that this battle is already lost. You must find that voice and kill it – because all is not lost. I would not have us here if it was. I have trained you and I know what you can do – and this – together – we can do. Today there will be swords – today there will be blood – let us make sure that the blood that runs is not ours. Let us make sure that those who would take away who we are will pay for their arrogance. Today there will be blood and today we shall endure.'

The crowd went wild. I patted my old master on the back and said, 'Awesome, dude.'

Spideog turned to Dahy and said, 'I thought it was a bit flowery,' then he smiled and the two old rivals shook each other's hand.

'Are you ready to go into battle with me again – old friend?' Dahy said.

'Who are you calling old,' Spideog replied. 'By the by, remind me that I have to tell you something when this is all over.'

Dahy was just about to ask what, when someone cried, 'Incoming!' and the battle began.

The sky blackened with arrows. We all ducked behind the battlements and watched in horror as soldiers who were caught out in the open scrambled for cover. Then I saw a conch shell hit the ground about twenty-five feet behind me. This one, unlike the ones yesterday, wasn't smoking. I peeped over the battlements and seeing that there were no arrows on the way, I dashed over intending to throw it back. I was no more than an arm's length away when I heard an ear-piercing sound and was instantly doubled up in pain. All around me men dropped to the ground pulling their knees up to their chest. I'm sure that like me they were howling in pain but nothing could be heard other than the screaming sound that was coming from the shell. I knew we had to get rid of it but every time I tried to straighten my legs, the pain, which was already unbearable, doubled. I had started dragging myself forward with my fingers in the dirt when I saw Essa, obviously in pain but on her feet, stagger over to the shell and then smash it with her banta stick. The sound and pain went as suddenly as they had come. Essa poked through the rubble of the shell and picked up a small gold amulet that was buzzing with a tinny sound. Then using her teeth and fingers she bit and twisted it until it stopped.

Dahy, who I am embarrassed to say was on his feet much faster than me, walked over and took the amulet from Essa. 'It's a *gleem*,' he said.

Gleem, where had I heard that before? That was the thing that Cialtie had used on Dad to win the boat race. It inflicted the pain of childbirth.

'Well, that settles it,' I said. 'I'm not *ever* getting pregnant.'

Someone shouted, 'INCOMING!' and we ran back to the ramparts for cover. Spideog kept his nose over the wall and then popped up to shoot a second shell out of the air like a Kentucky skeet shooter.

Essa ducked next to me. 'Didn't that gleem thing hurt?' I asked her.

'Of course it hurt but it was nothing I couldn't take.' She rolled her eyes and shook her head. 'Men.'

Cialtie's first attack was small – designed to force us to show our strengths and weaknesses – it was also designed to fail. On strictly a tactical standpoint I guess it was sensible but using any other yardstick, especially a moral one, it was despicable. It was a suicide mission – that is if the attackers in the first wave volunteered. If they were ordered to go, then it was a death sentence and we were the executioners. About seventy Brownies dashed directly at the ramparts. The first thing they discovered was that Dahy and the Leprechauns had, for months, been hammering every flat rock or piece of shale that they could find into the ground in front of the stone defences. Running on it at any speed was almost impossible – it was a minefield for ankle twisting.

Many Brownies tripped and many more were mowed down by Spideog and his archers. Only four Brownies reached the wall and when they did they seemed not to know what to do. Several of their attacking comrades had been carrying siege ladders but they had been stopped by arrows. As our archers bore down on the four, Dahy ordered them not to fire.

'Brownies,' Dahy called down to them, 'you have fought bravely but you have no chance to scale these walls. I offer you safe passage if you go back now.'

As I watched, I prayed that they would take his offer. They looked like lost cold orphans shivering in a big city alley. If they defiantly started to climb we would have no choice but to kill them. I can't tell you how quickly I was getting tired of this war stuff. They huddled up and then accepted. With their heads held high, they marched back over the ankle-twisting stone field. About halfway across, a huge volley of arrows from Cialtie's camp dropped all of them as one. It was my uncle's way of showing the rest of his army how he felt about surrender.

Dahy made no comment, nor showed any emotion in regards to the slaughter, he just nodded like this was business as usual. 'Cialtie and

Turlow have learned all that they need to know,' the general said. 'The next attack will be all of them.'

I stepped off my post in hopes of getting to the wash tent so I could splash some water on my face and maybe wash away some of the horror that I had just seen – some of the horror that I had just been part of. I used a shortcut that brought me around the back of the tent and there I found Spideog sitting with his back to a low ruined wall, his knees up and his face in his hands. I hesitated before I disturbed him. I hoped that when he removed his hands that his eyes were not awash with tears. If Spideog broke under this pressure, what chance had the rest of us for surviving unscathed? But surviving unscathed was probably impossible anyway.

'Are you OK?' I asked, crouching down to his level.

He looked up. His eyes were clear but filled with a millennium's worth of sadness. 'May the gods damn your uncle.'

'Yeah,' I agreed, 'and they will have to get in line. There are a few of us around here who would like to damn him and do a bit more.'

'Those Brownies ...' Spideog paused – on his face he wore the sorrow of a man searching through old, painful memories. 'Those Brownies fought like the Fili. During that war, Maeve threw her Fili at us like they were toy soldiers that could later just be glued back together.' He shook his head and looked down. 'How do they do it? How do these madmen get their people to follow them with such suicidal abandon?'

'I don't know, Master,' I said. 'I don't think we will ever know but isn't that what makes us better than them?'

He looked up, smiled at me, then stood, instantly regaining his innate heroic stance. 'You have your grandmother's eyes, you know.'

'You must tell me about her sometime.'

'I will, when this is all over.' He laughed to himself as he turned. 'I might even do better than that.'

He jogged back to his post without giving me a chance to ask him what he meant.

* * *

Back on the battlements the sun rose to its zenith in a crystal-clear blue winter sky. The heat was welcome as it allowed us to believe that the sweat that was dripping down our backs was caused by the sun and not our jangling nerves.

In Cialtie's camp there could be heard orders being barked and bugle-sounding things being played as the army of Banshees and Brownies readied for their main offensive. Essa dropped in next to me.

'Dahy thinks that the attack will be soon,' she said. 'Are you ready?'

'Born ready,' I said automatically. As I scanned the horizon I felt Essa reach down and entwine her fingers in mine. I looked at her, she was fierce and scared and oh so achingly beautiful – all at the same time. She leaned in and kissed me. I placed my hands gently on her shoulders and pushed her back.

'We are not going to die,' I said.

She turned away, looking out over the field and then I felt her tense up like the strings of a tennis racket. She pointed to the edge of the rise. I followed the line of her finger and saw hundreds of screaming soldiers charge into view.

'Tell that to them,' she said as she drew her sword.

FORTY

THE ISLES

What must have been a thousand Brownies and Banshees swarmed onto the stone plain. They looked like those red army ants that you see in old Tarzan movies. I was half expecting the fallen to end up as stone-white skeletons.

As soon as they got into range, our arrows flew. The fallen were not even considered by their comrades – if the arrows didn't kill them then the trampling surely must have. The same fate awaited those that tripped on the stone field. Just behind the first wave were a line of siege ladders carried by teams of three. The ladders had shields strapped to the front so as to protect the carriers from all but the sharpest archers who aimed for their heads and legs. Spideog assigned his best bowmen for that task and they had a reasonably high measure of success. Still, any ladder bearer that was hit was instantly replaced by another. The ladders clambered closer.

All the while volleys of arrows came at us from the back of the enemy's advance. Dahy's ramparts were designed well, giving cover as well as enough gaps for the archers to continue shooting even while arrows were flying in. One gleem arrived during the first part of the attack but was swiftly taken care of by the special gleem-team that Nieve had equipped with gold earplugs.

The enemy soldiers that reached the ramparts huddled together under their shields in an arrow-proof phalanx. The ones that did this too close to the walls had boulders thrown at them by teams of very brawny Leprechaun miners. The huge rocks smashed into the shields then the archers finished them off.

I'd like to be able to say that I was appalled by all of this bloodshed but as those ladders drew closer and with the realisation that this screaming horde was hell bent on killing me, it caused a bloodlust to explode in my brain. Some men never get over this experience and sell themselves as mercenaries for the rest of their lives in order to feel that savage passion again. As for me I have no want to repeat the experience but I would be lying if I said it was unpleasant. In fact it was damn exciting. Never have I felt so alive. It was kill or be killed and every fallen enemy soldier was one that I knew I wouldn't have to face with my sword and I cheered with the rest of my comrades as each went down.

When the ladders reached the ramparts I finally got to use my sword. It was a good blade but heavier and nowhere near as finely balanced as the Sword of Duir. I missed the Lawnmower. I had a fleeting image of the last time I saw it, sticking out of the underbelly of Dragon Red. A ladder hit below my gap in the wall. I tried to reach down and push it but it was just out of reach. Leprechaun boulder tossers were engaged elsewhere so I waited for the first of the Brownies to climb the ladder. He reached the top in no time and we engaged in a pointless just out-of-reach sword-fight where we clinked sword tips but were too far away from each other to make serious contact. My father's sword-fighting instructions sprang into my head. 'When an attack ceases to make sense,' he once said to me, right before he tripped me over a low wire he had earlier set up in the garden, 'look around – something else might be happening.' I continued to swing but looked under the ladder and saw another Brownie with a crossbow taking aim at my nose. I ducked back just in time to avoid a bolt in the brain.

A gleem came over the wall far to my right. The gleem-team got to it quickly but not in time to prevent a couple of Banshees from clearing the ramparts. They fought and another five were allowed to reach the top before they were thrown back over. Ladders had now reached almost every part of the rampart wall. All of the ladders seemed to me to be too low. It made them difficult for us to repel by pushing them over but it also made it extremely difficult for the enemy to breach the top of the walls. It didn't make sense. I used my father's advice again and scanned the length of the battlements. That's when I noticed that under every ladder was a team of two soldiers crouched down fiddling with something at the base of the wall.

I shouted to Dahy, 'SOMETHING IS HAPPENING UNDER THE LADDERS.'

As he looked, a horn was blown and all the attackers dropped from their ladders and ran away from the wall.

'RETREAT!' Dahy shouted. 'EVERYONE OFF THE BATTLEMENTS!'

Having been a student of the Master I didn't have to hear a Dahy order twice. I flew off my post and into the midst of the Hall of Knowledge. A few of my comrades were not so lucky. The explosions blew a dozen holes in our defences. The Leprechauns and Imps who were on the wall were thrown twenty feet in the air.

'BACK TO THE AISLES,' Dahy ordered. 'BACK TO THE AISLES.'

Our secondary defence was what Dahy had called 'The Aisles'. We had knocked down some of what was left of the Hall's walls and reinforced others. The idea was to force any advancing army into narrow channels – aisles, allowing us to battle one or two abreast as opposed to a huge wave of marauders. Archers were positioned so as to shoot anyone that tried to come over the top.

The air hadn't even cleared when the Banshees, covered with the white dust of the explosions, came screaming out of the smoke. Dahy had said that there would be blood; well, this was the time he was talking about. I don't know how many I killed. All I know is that they weren't very well trained. They had strength and the energy that adrenalin brings but they all swung madly and allowed me to parry their wild swings to the outside and stab them in the chest, or the shoulder if they were wearing a breast protector. May the gods forgive me but what else could I do?

Even though I was killing many, I gave ground with almost every clash and I was getting tired. An Imp finally grabbed me from behind, pulled me back into the Hall and took my place at the front of the aisle.

I found Dahy barking orders outside of the library. On my left a bunch of Banshees broke through and Yogi, as a bear, roared into them, throwing two into the air and shocking the others into a retreat, while Dahy ordered swordsmen back into that aisle. This battle was not going well and it was just about to get a whole lot worse.

A troop of Banshees had snuck around to the site of the first attack. They guessed that if they each carried a bough of a tree that the gold strips might not register the branches as weapons and would let them through. They guessed right. Because of our small numbers we had only defended the hill with a handful of soldiers. The Banshees attacked with the branches and at the same time catapulted a bag of swords over a wall from the side. The Banshees quickly overpowered the guards on the hill and armed themselves. Our defences were dangerously thinned as soldiers were ordered to defend the Tree of Knowledge on two fronts.

I think at this point Dahy would have surrendered but no one was offering. This was it – it was a fight to the death and the realisation hit me that the death would be ours.

That's when time began to slow for me, not a good sign. My gift is only a help when I am personally in a fight. Here, watching this failing battle, my gift was a curse, just as it was when I watched Fergal die. I saw my comrades fall in slow motion. I saw every wound, every spurt of blood as if I was watching some bad war movie. It also gave me time to assess the entire battlefield and what I saw told me it was all over. We were moments away from being overrun.

The aisle on the left broke. Banshees and Brownies poured out. Dahy called forward the soldiers that had been guarding the Tree of Knowledge. A mêlée of hand-to-hand combat opened in the yard.

I looked for Essa. If this was to be the end I wanted to be at her side. In the confusion I couldn't see her but I heard her when she yelled, 'THE SKY!'

I looked up as the entire firmament turned into flame. A huge fire-ball rolled over and through the holes in the shattered battlements. Fire leapt in and set alight the attackers at the entrances of the aisles. Flames rolled over the top of the defences forcing us to hit the ground as hairs curled on the top of our heads. Then, swooping through the smoke flew a huge green dragon. It circled and came in to land almost exactly where I was standing. As I dived for cover I saw that the dragon had a rider. I got to my feet just in time to see him jump off as the dragon skidded into a stone wall. The dragon rider hit the ground in a graceful roll and popped up on his feet, banta stick in hand. It was – Araf!

I didn't question how or why. I just got to my feet and shouted, 'IMPS AND LEPRECHAUNS, TO ME. THE DRAGON IS ON OUR SIDE. EVERYONE, TO ME.' Araf blew his whistle. To their credit our force spent no time in dazed wonder when they saw their prince arrive miraculously from the grave astride a dragon, they went right into battle mode and cheered as they went back on the offensive.

The attackers that were still standing retreated as fast as their legs would carry them. If that Banshee sixth sense is true then it pretty quickly told them to *get the hell out of there.*

Another explosion of fire lit up the southern end of the battlefield as a crimson-coloured dragon – one that I recognised as Red – swooped over our position. Its rider, with that unmistakable American accent, shouted, 'YEE HA.'

Dragon Red landed on the top of the headquarters building just long enough for Brendan to slide off.

'Hey, O'Neil,' the policeman/dragon-rider shouted over the sound of Red launching himself back in to the sky, 'it's good to see you're not dead.'

'Same to you, Copper,' I shouted. I was just about to ask Araf what the heck was going on when we heard a sound of a battle horn coming from the courtyard.

Someone shouted, 'THEY ARE ATTACKING THE TREE!'

By the time I got to the entranceway it was almost over. A dozen Brownies were lying dead on the ground with arrows sticking out of the centres of their chests. Spideog was still firing even though he had a crossbow bolt in his thigh and another in his shoulder. There were four remaining Brownies; two of them had axes and were trying to get to the Tree of Knowledge. Spideog went for the axe bearers when he should have gone for the one in the back. I saw that Brownie cock his arm and then I saw the dagger leave his hand. A split second later two arrows hit the knife thrower – one in the throat from Spideog and another in the chest from Brendan on the roof – but they weren't in time to stop the throw. The knife was well off the mark but as I watched, it curved in midair and honed in on the ancient archer's heart. It hit him square in the chest. He dropped his bow, then crumpled first onto his knees and then onto his back.

Brendan dispatched the other attackers from the roof and then out of habit shouted, 'OFFICER DOWN.' He slid down a buttress and arrived at Spideog's side almost as quickly as I did. I lifted the archer's head; he coughed and blood poured from his mouth.

'Is the Tree safe?' he asked.

'Yes, Master.'

'Good.' He coughed again, closing his eyes in pain. 'Conor, don't let Essa go. If you don't tell her how you feel, you will regret it for the rest of your life – trust me, I know.' He coughed again and wiped his mouth with the back of his hand. When he saw the blood on his fingers he said, 'Oh dear, could you find Dahy for me?'

Brendan took the archer's head. I turned, there were several soldiers watching dumbfounded. 'Get Dahy,' I ordered and they scattered in several directions.

Brendan was weeping openly. Spideog smiled and said to him, 'If the yews allow it, I want you to have my bow.'

Brendan tried to speak but nothing came out.

Dahy crashed to his knees next to us. He took Spideog's hand and said, 'Hey, old man.'

'Who are you calling old?' Spideog smiled, his eyes still closed.

Dahy looked up and barked, 'Someone get a healer.'

Dahy's old comrade in arms shook his head. The meaning was obvious – a healer would do no good. Then he opened his eyes and said, 'She lives, Dahy.'

'Who lives, old friend?' Dahy asked.

Pain and coughing racked Spideog's body, blood poured freely from the side of his mouth. I didn't think he would open his eyes again but then he reached up and grabbed Dahy on the side of the arm. 'Macha … Macha lives.' Then his hand dropped and he breathed his last.

The folds of his tunic had obscured the knife in Spideog's chest. As Brendan laid him down the material fell away and the green knife handle came into view. Dahy pulled it from the torso and examined it closely. 'Where did this come from?'

A sinking feeling like a punch in the stomach almost made me retch. I walked over to the dead Brownie that had thrown the knife. I knelt down and rolled his body over – it was Demne, the eldest son of the Brownie King. It was Frank.

By the time I looked up Essa, Araf and Tuan were in the courtyard. My head was spinning. Overwhelmingly conflicting emotions mixed with confusion made me almost catatonic. I had just won a battle but had been partly responsible for the death of Master Spideog. But then – here were my friends brought back from the dead.

The sound of flapping and screaming in the sky snapped me back to full attention. High, high above us flew a dragon; below him hung a writhing, screaming man. When Red was directly above our heads he opened his talons and let the man go. The screaming ended when the freefalling body hit the side of the headquarters roof. The snapping of his neck was plain to hear. He bounced and landed on the ground face down, not far away from Essa. The Princess used her foot to flip him over. It was Turlow. Essa stared at him with a clenched jaw as her eyes watered up.

'I wanted to do that,' she said.

FORTY-ONE

THE GREEN DRAGON

I looked back up and saw Dragon Red flying away and remembered. I remembered what the last months had all been about. I started shouting, 'NO, RED, RED COME BACK.'

I looked to Brendan. 'Where is he going?'

I didn't wait for an answer, I was getting frantic. 'RE-E-E-ED!' Then I spun on Araf. 'You were riding a green dragon – where is the green dragon? Where?'

Araf grabbed me by the shoulders, he was uncharacteristically smiling. I looked to Brendan and Tuan; despite the recent tragedies, they were smiling too.

'I need dragon's blood!'

'Calm down, Conor,' Araf said. 'The green dragon is here.'

I spun around, searching the courtyard for any sign of a dragon. They were all still smiling like idiots. I was just about to slap them when Tuan placed his hands together into a two-handed fist, then crouched down like a man about to drop to his knees in prayer. When he began to straighten up he didn't just stop at his own height. His clothes tore away as palm-sized green scales loudly clinked into place on his chest and back. He continued to grow as his face extended and spines grew out of his receding hair. As he reached full size he blocked the sun and extended his wings, sending a cloud of dust and leaves swirling around the courtyard, forcing us to shield our eyes.

'*No,*' I said incredulously.

'Oh yes,' Brendan said, patting me on the back.

I stepped up to Dragon Tuan and he lowered his head. I looked into his eyes, thinking that I would recognise my old travelling companion but his eyes were green and yellow with slits for pupils.

'Is that you in there, Councillor Tuan?'

He threw his head violently back and blew a massive plume of fire into the air. Brendan grabbed me by the arm and pulled me back. 'Don't make him laugh, he's having trouble controlling the fire-breathing stuff.'

Tuan folded back his wings and lowered his body to the ground. Brendan took a running start and hopped on his back like a cowboy in a movie. Then he held out his hand and said, 'You comin'?'

'Where?'

'To Castle Duir. Tuan wants to donate some blood.'

I took a running start. I was so excited that I almost sailed straight over the back of Tuan.

Then Nieve ran into the courtyard and shouted, 'Brendan, you are alive.'

'I am indeed, gorgeous,' the cop replied from dragonback. 'I'm off to Castle Duir to save your brother. Come with us.'

Honest to the gods she hopped up and down like a schoolgirl at a boy-band concert and ran two steps towards us before she stopped and dropped her head.

'I cannot. I must tend the wounded.'

Brendan turned to me and said, 'Can you give me a minute?'

I nodded and he slid off Tuan's back and gave my aunt a right proper, back-dipping, snog.

Dahy approached me holding the knife. He looked shell-shocked. 'Where did you get this?' he asked quietly. It was almost as if he was afraid to hear the answer.

'It was thrown out of the window from the house of the Oracle, on Mount Cas. Araf was there, he can tell you all about it.' He nodded thoughtfully and backed off as Brendan dramatically remounted.

Tuan extended his school-bus-sized wings and began to flap. The muscles in his back tightened and rocked me up and down as I searched for something to hold on to. I grabbed Brendan around the waist. He didn't seem to mind.

Detective Fallon turned to me wearing a huge ear-to-ear grin. 'Have you ever been on the rollercoaster at that amusement park in Elysburg, Pennsylvania?'

'Yeah,' I screamed back as the wind roared around us. 'It was very scary.'

'Well, hold on, O'Neil, 'cause this is a whole lot worse.'

As I held on for dear life, Brendan filled me in on what had happened.

'That damn paralysing pin that the *late* Turlow stuck in Araf, Tuan and me was apparently placed high enough on our necks so that we couldn't speak but our eyes and ears still worked. Tuan managed to do that Pooka transforming thing with the unparalysed part of his head. The top of his head changed into like a dozen different animals. Every time he grew feathers or fur or even scales, he managed to push out the pin just a little bit further, until it popped out completely. He saved us.' Tuan, who had been listening, shook his head up and down.

'Nice one, Councillor,' I shouted.

'We were just outside the back door of The Digs,' continued Brendan, 'when the fireball hit. We dived into the swampy bit behind the house to protect ourselves from the heat and by the time we popped out again, you were already being carried off into the wild blue yonder. Tuan used hawk eyes and said he saw you fall into the ocean. How'd you survive that one?'

'Mermaids,' I shouted over the sound of the swirling wind and laughed out loud at the ridiculousness of it.

Brendan laughed with me. 'A couple of months ago I'd have locked you up in the loony bin for saying stuff like that.'

'And now?'

'Now' – the cop thought for a second – 'now my response is – yeah, that sounds about right.'

'So what happened when Red came back?'

'Well, he was surprised to see us alive, 'cause Turlow had told him we were dead. Also he had a problem.'

'What was that?'

'You stuck your sword in him in a spot that he couldn't reach and he was afraid to change back to Red with it sticking out of him. Oh, that reminds me, I've got your sword.' He patted the sword hanging on his belt. I peeped down and instantly recognised the Lawnmower's pommel.

'I hope it hurt him like hell,' I said.

'I think it did. Tuan agreed to pull it out if he consented to listen to us before he tried to kill us again. It didn't take us long to convince him that The Turlow had duped us all. He was livid and zoomed off to try to find him, but he came back a week later having had no success.

'While he was gone we found his house – or I guess I should call it his lair – and waited for him there. Tuan discovered all of these manuscripts in Pooka lingo and sat in the corner and read them the whole time – he hardly talked to us. When Red returned, Tuan and Red got talking shop. I tried to get Red to give me some blood and a lift off the island, but they were so into talking about changeling stuff that they acted like Araf and I weren't even there. When I got mad at them for ignoring us, Red switched to dragon, grabbed Tuan and flew away. The two of them disappeared for another week. When Red came back there was a green dragon with him.

'Apparently in order to become a dragon you have to study how to change into every animal there is and Tuan had done that already. Oh, and that problem that he had about not being able to hold a form – well, that's gone.' Brendan patted the dragon's neck and looked over the side. 'I hope.'

I shivered in the cold air as the sun began to set in an explosion of reds and golds. 'You know I had a dream about this. But I never …' I chuckled to myself. 'I never dreamt it would happen. I only hope we are in time.'

The guards on the ramparts of Castle Duir shot arrows at us as we approached so we had to fly away and land in the field in front of the castle. By the time a whole battalion of soldiers came at us on horseback, Tuan was Tuan again. The captain recognised me – and recognised Brendan as that madman from the Real World – and once we convinced them that there was no dragon attack, he gave us horses and we galloped to the main gates.

The three of us burst into Dad's candlelit room. Mom and Fand and a handful of sorceresses were there. Dad, still encased in amber, looked like he was dead.

Mom flew into my arms and hugged her head to my chest.

'Is he gone?' I asked. 'Am I too late?'

She held my face in her hands; her eyes were swimming in tears. 'It's not long now – I'm glad you are here.'

'He's not dead?' I said excitedly. I looked to Fand. 'He's not dead?'

'No,' the Fili answered.

I grabbed my mother by the shoulders. 'Mom it's not eel's blood. It's not red eel blood.'

She looked at me confused. It had been so long since Mom and I had discovered that old manuscript that she had almost forgotten about it. She had given up hope.

'*Tughe tine* – we thought it meant *red eel*; it doesn't, it means *fire worm*. Fire worm,' I said again louder, trying to make it sink in. '*Dragon!*'

I turned to Tuan and motioned for him to change.

'Here?' he said, looking around. 'Will I fit?'

'We'll find out. You better stick your nose out of the window.'

He did as he was told and clasped his hands together and crouched down facing the window.

OK, maybe it wasn't a good idea to have him change in Dad's room, especially without warning anybody. Dragon Tuan was a lot bigger than I realised. His back pushed up against the ceiling as plaster cracked and rolled down his sides. Sorceresses were pushed into corners and furniture splintered against the walls. Dad's bed was pushed at a forty-five-degree angle but remained unharmed. Deirdre and Fand, backs pressed against the wall, stared open-mouthed. I had to shake Mom to get her attention.

'Dragon's blood, Mom. The mermaids use it to become young again. It will reset Dad. It should save his life.'

Finally Mom said, 'How do we do it?'

'Red told me that just a couple of drops in the mouth should do the trick,' Brendan said.

Mom found a crystal glass as I drew the Sword of Duir and cut a nick into Tuan's wing. We were lucky that his head was out the window 'cause the pain caused him to cough a small fireball that, if it was in here, would have been enough to fricassee us all.

Fand placed her hands on the sides of Dad's head and incanted. The hard amber shell softened and then dripped like honey off of his face and head. She reached into his mouth and removed the gold disc. Brendan quickly held out his hand and the Fili gave it to him. Dad looked bad and he didn't look like he was breathing. Fand placed her ear to his mouth and nose. When she came up she held her thumb and index finger just a quarter of an inch apart indicating that he was still breathing if only a tiny bit. Mom took her yew wand, dipped it into the dragon's blood and then dripped three drops into Oisin's mouth.

The effects took hold almost immediately. First it was just the colour of his lips but then the wrinkles on his face vanished like someone under the bed was pulling his skin from behind. As Tuan changed back, giving everyone in the chamber some elbow room, Fand moved quickly and incanted over the rest of Dad's shell and it dripped away. We watched as life and vigour radiated down his neck and all over his body. By the time the shell exposed his right arm there was no difference between his wrist and his runehand. Mom picked up his hand, looked at it from both sides and then gasped as Dad's fingers entwined with her own. Dad opened his eyes and then amazingly propped himself up on his elbows. He looked like he could have been my fraternal twin.

'Was I dreaming,' he said, his voice betraying no hint of illness, 'or was there just a dragon in my room?'

FORTY-TWO

FRIENDS AND ENEMIES

'Did I wake you?'

'Oh my, no,' she replied faster than I had anticipated. 'Your father did that two days ago. I would have preferred to sleep for at least another moon. I am an old woman you know.'

I had no idea what she looked like two days previously, but by this conversation new shoots and small, almost fluorescent leaves covered all of her boughs. She may be the oldest thing in The Land but to me, she looked brand new.

'I'm sorry, Mother Oak,' I said.

'Oh now, don't listen to me, with all of the excitement in Duir I probably would have scolded you if you had not awoken me. But my, my, your father was a rude awakening. I have never seen a man with such energy. It was hard to keep up with his so many thoughts.'

'Yeah, I'm sorry about him too. He's been pretty embarrassing lately.'

'From what I can tell, it seems that it is a father's responsibility to embarrass his offspring.'

'Maybe so but he is taking it to a whole new level.'

Dad had jumped out of his deathbed with the energy of a five-year-old who had just eaten an entire bag of Halloween candy. What really spooked me was that he looked my age – some said he even looked younger. After lots of hugging and kissing and jumping and staring into mirrors – and way too much loud whooping – he insisted I tell him everything that had happened since he had been paperweight-ed. When I finally finished the whole adventure, he ordered new clothes (he had been listening to my story wrapped only in a sheet, like some Roman emperor) and horses. We eventually convinced him that travelling in the pitch dark would be a bad idea, so he ordered a crack-of-dawn departure for the Hall of Knowledge. I really could have used a lie-in and a day off but Dad had lost the meaning of 'lie-in' along with his grey hair. I tried to convince Tuan to give me a lift but he made it clear that he was not an air taxi service.

We rode to the Hazellands in record time. (There was none of that stopping and resting stuff.) We were greeted by Dahy and Queen Rhiannon. The Pookas had arrived with reinforcements only a day after I had left. Red/Moran had made peace with the Queen and had flown around long enough to make sure that Cialtie and his army had really retreated back into the Reed and Alderlands. Then he flew back to his island.

Dad, despite his newly imposed adolescence, acted mostly kingly. He visited the wounded and held meetings about future defences and the allocation of the kingdom's resources, but at other times he acted annoyingly juvenile, usually by challenging me to arm wrestles or grabbing Mom and dragging her kissing and giggling into any nearby tent.

'I am sure he will calm down soon,' Mother Oak said, reading my thoughts. 'I have never grown young, but I have certainly grown old – it must be an exciting thing for him.'

'I know. It's just a bit – freaky.'

'But enough about your father, Prince of Hazel and Oak, how went your winter?'

How went my winter? Gods, now there was a question.

'Busy,' I said with a sarcastic laugh. 'You know, the first time I came to The Land I was just trying to stay alive. This time I spent the whole time trying to keep my father alive. For once I would love to spend some time here having … fun.'

'Oh my my,' Mother Oak said and I could feel her sad smile. 'Oh, I have heard that grumble before. *Responsibility* is what you complain about. As far as I can tell, as you get older, *responsibility* is what replaces fun.'

'That sounds like a bad deal to me.'

'To me as well, but I can tell you this. The ones that do not shoulder their responsibilities may stay young but – they never stay happy.'

'So what,' I said, 'I should grow up, do my duty, and stop cracking jokes.'

'I am not here to tell you any such thing,' she said forcefully. 'Who am I to give advice? I do nothing but stick in the ground and bathe in the sunlight all day. If you are looking for advice there are countless better than me. But it seems to me that you do not need advice. You did what *needed* to be done. You saved your father from death and the Pookas from extinction. You reunited Moran and Rhiannon, and were victorious against Cialtie and Turlow's forces in the face of overwhelming odds. I have known men centuries older than you who have grown less. No one need counsel you on responsibility.'

'You know, Mother Oak, I think if I burned down a house you would probably compliment me on what nice ashes I made.'

'As long as the house was not made of oak,' she said and in my mind I felt her wooden smile.

Maybe it wasn't just hollow praise, maybe I had grown up a bit. I wasn't sure I liked it. What had been bothering me most lately was the pain of Spideog's loss. Not that it hurt too much but that it hurt too little. I knew war and death had become too commonplace for me, but even after all I had been through, I should have had tears for Spideog.

'Do not worry that you have yet to grieve for the archer,' Mother Oak said, interrupting my thoughts. 'The tears will come soon, or perhaps not for a year, but they *will* come. Grief makes its own appointments.'

I hugged her and hoped that she was right.

'Conor,' she said before I left, 'although I never understand them, I think it would be a shame if you no longer told your jokes.'

I whistled for my horse, gave Mother Oak one last hug and dropped directly into the saddle.

I rode quickly back to Castle Duir. All this talk of responsibility made me realise I had one more thing to do.

* * *

The cold thin air bounced off the warm woollen cap that Mom insisted I wear. At first she forbade me to go on this trip. Like almost everyone, she was dead set against me making this journey. When I put my foot down she actually threatened to have me locked in the dungeon. When I finally convinced her and everyone else that I would probably be OK, considering my travelling companion was a fire-breathing dragon, she insisted that at least I wear long underwear and the woollen cap. The cap I must admit was nice and toasty – the underwear itched a bit.

I patted Dragon Tuan on his green scaly back and shouted, 'You sure you're not lost?'

In reply he banked sharply to the left and bucked. I grabbed tight onto the makeshift dragon reins that the stable master and I had quickly invented earlier that day.

'OK, OK,' I shouted. 'You lose all sense of humour when you're in reptilian form.'

I looked down at the passing Tir na Nogian topography below. Winter was in its last clutches. Every once in a while brave crocuses or a tree defiantly popped a dab of colour into the dying season's grey and brown landscape. It wouldn't be long before it was shorts and tee-shirt weather. I was looking forward to that.

I breathed deeply and collected my thoughts. It was good to be alone for a moment – without Dad around. Since his re-adolescence, every time he saw me he challenged me to a sword-fight or, worse, a wrestling match. A couple of days ago, as he was pinning me with my arm twisted up my back, I asked him if we could talk without violence. I finally impressed on him that I would like it if he acted more like my father and less like an annoying younger brother. He promised he would be more fatherly and then punched me hard in the arm – this was going to take time.

Dahy vehemently didn't want me to go. The old master wasn't big on giving succour to enemies. He also thought this trip was a waste of resources. Dahy was gung ho about putting together an attack force to storm the Oracle on Mount Cas but Dad ordered him to calm down. Dahy insisted that Macha, Dad's mother, was alive, but Dad said finding an old knife didn't prove anything – no matter what some crazy old archer said. (Dad and Spideog had never seen eye to eye.) Dahy didn't

like it but he accepted the orders from the teenage-looking King. In
fact everyone seemed to think that a king that looked like he wasn't
even old enough to drink was just fine.

Essa and I started getting on very well indeed. I took Spideog's
dying advice and told her how I felt. I said if she promised not to try to
kill me again that I would like to have a go at a relationship. She didn't
say yes but then again she didn't say no either and we had been pretty
snuggly ever since. She even said that she wanted to take a trip to see
the Real World with me when we send Brendan back home.

I looked up to the heavens and said a silent thanks to Spideog. If
anybody saw my eyes at that point I would have told them they were
watering because of the cold air, but the truth was the tears Mother
Oak had promised would someday come – came. I finally felt the loss
of that strange but sweet old archer.

I took out my white flag when I saw alder trees below. Our first pass
over Fearn Keep was high, out of crossbow range. As we circled lower
the Brownies showed uncharacteristic restraint and didn't fire at us.
Tuan banked sharply to the right and dropped altitude.

'Hey,' I shouted at him, 'I almost fell off back there.'

Tuan wasn't the best flyer in the sky but I wasn't going to tell him
that. He was still a bit touchy about the ribbing he had been getting
after he accidentally landed on two Leprechauns, breaking one of their
arms.

We landed far enough away from the main entrance so as to not
freak everybody out and so that if Tuan landed on his face, people
wouldn't see. There have been smoother landings. I jumped off when
we started tipping and Tuan hit the ground rolling.

When he finally righted himself, I patted his side and said, 'How are
the ballet lessons going?'

He turned and gave me the dragon equivalent of a dirty look – and
when you are stared at by someone who can breathe fire, that's pretty
scary. Tuan stayed in his dragon form until a Brownie battalion arrived.
Once they knew we were here on a diplomatic mission and not to eat
ice cream and Brownies, Tuan became Tuan again.

'There's a saying that pilots use in the Real World that goes, "Any landing you walk away from is a good landing."'

Tuan delivered another dirty look – this one, less scary. 'You want to walk home?'

Tuan transformed into bodyguard bear and in his arms he carried the reason we had come. At the main gate I declared who I was to the sergeant at arms and asked for an audience with King Bwika. When he told us that we would have to wait in the guest wing, I informed him that we were to see the Brownie King now or we were going home. He came back ten minutes later and informed us that we were, 'in luck', and the King would see us immediately.

We were still made to wait a short time outside the throne room but were then escorted on a long walk between two rows of hastily dressed Brownie honour guard. They did not look kindly on me or my bear. I am sure they had all heard by now that he was one of the dragons that incinerated many of their comrades. I felt like an away-team supporter in a crowd of home-team football fans. King Bwika sat on a dais in his Alder Throne. I approached and bowed my low bow.

Before I could start my practised royal protocol speech, the King said, 'You have a cheek coming here.'

'This visit is neither diplomatic nor is it some sort of victory lap; I come on a sorry task.' I threw back the blanket that covered Tuan's burden and then carefully took the shrouded body into my own arms. 'I have come to return to you the body of your son.' I stepped up on the dais and laid Frank at his father's feet.

Bwika was speechless as I backed away down the steps.

'Did you kill him, Faerie?' came an angry voice from behind the throne that made me and the King jump. I hadn't recognised the voice but when he stepped into the light I of course knew the face.

'No, Jesse,' I replied.

'My name is Codna.'

'Of course, Prince Codna,' I said, bowing. 'I did not kill him. If I had arrived earlier and had recognised your brother I would have done all that I could to prevent it. But I was too late.'

'Who did kill him?' the King asked.

'If it is vengeance you seek, Your Highness, then you should know that the one that killed your son was also killed by him.'

'Who?'

'Spideog, Your Highness.'

'My son killed Spideog – the warrior archer?'

'He did.'

King Bwika sat higher in his seat. 'Then he did indeed die a noble death.'

'He certainly was brave,' I said, 'but I don't think I can call anything about this war *noble*. I knew your son, Your Highness, and even though we had our differences, I liked him. I am very sorry for your loss and I am here to try to make sure that no other fathers lose their sons. What can I do to persuade you to stop this aggression against Cull and Duir?'

The Brownie King sat back in his chair and said, 'Give us what is our due. Give us Castle Duir and the mines beneath.'

'You know I can't do that.'

'Your audience is ended, Son of Duir. Returning my son to me has saved your life today but in the future you will no longer be welcome in the Alderlands.'

I had also rehearsed a royal-style exit speech but since he was no longer being nice I just said, 'I want my horses.'

'What?'

'I left my horses at Fearn Point. I assume that you now have them.'

The King came as close to standing as his hulking frame would allow. 'Are you accusing …'

'The horses are in our corral,' Jesse said, 'I will take you to them.'

The King turned to his son. 'You most certainly will not.'

'Prince Conor has been good to me in the past, Father. He brought Demne back to us and now I am going to give him his horses.'

I don't think I ever really knew the definition of flabbergasted until I saw the look on King Bwika's face. Jesse turned and walked out between the honour guard gauntlet and we followed. I'm sure that all three of us expected a crossbow bolt in our backs at any time. I know I did.

Jesse didn't say anything until we reached the gates of the corral. When he turned, his face and collar were drenched with silent tears.

As soon as we looked at each other he flew in to my arms and buried his face into my chest.

'I'm so sorry, Codna,' I said while stroking his hair. I know it was silly and he was probably older than me but he felt like the little brother I never had.

His crying jag didn't last long and when he finally straightened up and wiped his eyes he said, 'You can still call me Jesse if you want.'

I smiled at him and he tried hard to return it. 'I wish things were different,' he said.

'Yeah, Jesse, me too.'

Cloud, Acorn and Araf and Turlow's horses had, by this time, made it over to where we were standing. Jesse ordered the stable boy to fetch two saddles but Tuan said, 'Just one,' and then changed himself into a horse.

'You keep The Turlow's mount,' I said to Jesse. 'His name is Fluffy. He's a good horse and he deserves a better master than his last one.'

'Will I ever see you again, Conor?'

'I hope so,' I said.

'And if I do, will we still be friends?'

'Ah, Jesse, wouldn't this place be so much better if it was run by smart people like us?' I said, flashing a Fergal-esque smile. 'Others can make us enemies, Jesse, but no one can unmake us friends.' I patted him on the shoulder. 'Be safe, my Brownie friend.'

As I rode away I felt worse with every step. Poor Jesse, stuck alone in that castle without his brother and with a stupid misguided father. I toyed with the idea of turning around and taking him with me but I was certain that that would only end in more tears.

FORTY-THREE

GET A ROOM

'Why don't you two get a room?'

'We have a room,' Dad said while coming up for air after kissing Mom. 'As a matter of fact, we have a whole castle.'

'Well, why didn't you do all of this *in* your room?' I asked.

'We did,' Mom replied with a smile I wasn't all that comfortable with. 'Sorry if we embarrass you, I'm sure your father will calm down in a couple of years.'

I looked over to Brendan for support, but he and Nieve were lip-locked as well.

'Oh for crying out loud,' I protested.

'Conor,' my aunt said, 'I do not know when I will see Brendan again.'

'You've decided to stay in the Real World?' I asked.

Brendan shook his head. 'I still don't know, Conor.'

'So what, you're going to go back to being a cop?'

'I was a good cop.'

'Oh yeah?' I sneered. 'The last bit of detective-ing you did was to accuse me of killing him,' I said, pointing to Dad.

'Well, I knew there was something squirrely about your family and I was right about that.'

Dad untangled himself from Mom and walked over to Brendan. 'You are forever welcome in Duir. The job of armoury master is vacant at the moment.'

'Brendan, Master-at-Arms of Duir,' Nieve said, 'I like the sound of that.'

'I do too,' Brendan replied, looking at his feet, 'but my first responsibility is to my daughter. Until I see her, I have no idea what to do.'

We all turned when we heard horse's hooves coming from the corridor. Essa and Fand appeared at the archway followed by Tuan leading Essa's horse.

'I thought you were going to be my horse on this expedition,' I said to Tuan.

'Your mother did not think that was a good idea,' the Pooka said.

'Well then come as a dragon – we can be on television and freak the whole world out.'

'I don't think so,' Tuan said but he smiled and his ears fuzzed up for a moment as if he liked the idea. 'Be careful in the Real World, my friend.'

Fand walked up to Brendan and said, 'I am very pleased to have met you, pool-eece-man. It does my heart good to see that at least one of the exiled ones is so well. May the blessings of the Fili live with you – Druid.' Brendan bowed and Fand placed her hands on his head. 'And give my regards to your tree-hugging mother.'

Brendan smiled. 'I will, Your Highness. I can't wait to tell her that I know the Queen of the Druids.'

'Are you sure you are up to this?' my mother asked Essa.

Essa nodded. She had volunteered to act as our sorceress for this journey to return Brendan to the Real World. I was going too.

'So how old are you anyway?' I asked Essa. 'Just in case you fall off your horse, will you dust-it?'

'It will not kill me, is all you need to know and Tuan has volunteered some dragon blood in case I do.'

'Thanks, Tuan. I really don't want to date a wrinkly old grey one.' Essa actually laughed at that – I was loosening that girl up.

There was one last round of smooching. Essa mounted up and asked if everyone was ready to go, but before we could reply I heard someone in the corridor screeching my name. We all looked as Graysea came bounding around the corner. She spotted me, shrieked and ran directly into my arms.

'Oh Conor, I have missed you so!'

I tried to say something but couldn't as she planted her lips onto mine. When I finally was able to remove myself from that kiss of life she said, 'Did you miss me?'

I didn't answer; I didn't get the chance. The last thing I saw was Essa's banta stick heading towards my right temple – after that everything went black.

SONS OF
MACHA

For Tim and Sarah (Mel) Lenahan.
The only ones I still show off for.

ONE

SPECIAL AGENT MURANO

He wasn't a Scranton cop. I could tell that as soon as he walked in. The pressed suit and the newly cut hair made me suspicious but the Italian shoes were a dead giveaway.

'Conor O'Neil?' he said in a low voice that made me think he had been practising it in a mirror.

'Hay-na,' I replied using the local vernacular. His confused look confirmed that he was an out-of-towner. Not that I minded; the local police had been none too gentle with me. Understandable, considering they were certain that I killed my father, bombed their police station, hospitalised about two dozen of their fellow officers and kidnapped their favourite detective. So when a Scranton cop elbowed me in the ribs when no one was looking it was forgivable but not pleasant. This new guy was a relief. He looked like he played by the book – hell, he looked like he wrote the book.

'My name is Special Agent Andrew Murano.'

'You're a Fed?'

He flashed his identification card emblazoned with a big 'FBI' across it.

'Wow, what did I do to deserve the Eliot Ness treatment?'

'Kidnapping is a federal crime.'

'Well then you can go home, I didn't kidnap anybody.'

'That's not what Detective Fallon tells us,' the FBI man said, opening a folder on the table between us.

'Well Detective Fallon can kiss my …'

'You claim,' Murano interrupted, 'that you accidentally took Detective Fallon to a magical land where you rode dragons together.'

I winced. 'Well, when you say it like that, it sounds a *bit* far fetched.'

'No, not at all, Mr O'Neil. Do go on.'

I really didn't want to. Telling a story as crazy as mine is kind of fun the first time around but after a while it loses its appeal. I've often heard that women hate it when men mentally undress them with their eyes – well, I had the opposite problem. Everyone I told my story to mentally dressed me *in* a straitjacket. But I recounted my tale once again, 'cause Brendan told me to tell the truth.

Brendan and I had arrived from Tir na Nog into the Real World not far from Brendan's house. The portal connecting The Land to the Real World deposited us inside a small patch of trees exactly at the spot where Brendan's mother said mystical ley-lines converged. Brendan had always considered that just another one of his mother's hippy-trippy crazy ideas, but he was learning that many of her crazy ideas were turning out to be true. Detective Fallon and I were the only ones who made the trip. Essa was supposed to join us but she was still mad at me for the Graysea thing.

Brendan's mother Nora was one of those older women who looked great even into her seventies. You could see by her face that she had all of her marbles (and then some) and her physique showed that she was still strong. Good thing too, 'cause the shock that Brendan and I gave her when we showed up to the front door on horseback would probably have killed a lesser senior citizen.

When his mother asked him where he had been, Brendan started by saying, 'You're not going to believe this.' But only a couple of minutes into the story it was plain to see that she did. She had believed in Filis and Faeries and Brownies and Tir na Nog all of her life and tears came to her eyes as Brendan told her that the Queen of the Druids recognised him as one of their own.

Brendan's daughter Ruby was at school. He wanted to go and get her but Nora convinced him that that was a bad idea. He was apparently a very famous missing person. There had even been a TV show recreating Mom and Nieve's attack on the police station and Brendan's picture had been on every TV, newspaper and Internet screen in the country. Showing up in a third-grade classroom, we decided, might cause a bit of a commotion.

We were sitting down to a nice cup of tea in the kitchen when Brendan saw something outside the window and said, 'Oh my gods.' He jumped up and took a big carving knife out of a wooden block on the counter and said 'Take it!'

I did.

'Now drop it.'

I didn't have a clue what was going on. 'What?'

'I said drop it.'

He was so frantic I did what I was told.

Then he said, 'Tell the truth – it'll keep you out of a serious jail until I can figure things out.'

Before I even had time to say, 'Huh?' a zillion screaming cops barrelled in the front and back doors with guns drawn. Brendan hit me in the stomach, spun me around and dropped me to the ground with my arm twisted behind my back. 'I've got him,' he shouted. 'He's disarmed!'

I was cuffed, dragged to my feet by my hair, slammed against the wall and then tossed head first into a police wagon. All the while I kept hearing cops asking Brendan how *he* was. I saw Brendan's mother on her porch as they were closing the doors of the van.

'It was very nice to meet you, Mrs Fallon,' I said.

Brendan was right. Telling the truth got me a room in a secure mental hospital where my daily interrogators alternated between cops who wanted to kill me and shrinks who wanted to understand me. I couldn't decide which I liked better. Special Agent Murano was my first change in a couple of days.

I took a deep breath and told the story of how my dad was not dead. That he was alive and well in Tir na Nog, the mythical Irish Land of

Eternal Youth, where I assisted him regaining the throne by helping
him attach his missing hand and then chopping off my uncle's hand.

Then I narrated the story of how, when I got back home, Detective
Fallon arrested me for my father's murder and how my mother and
aunt busted me out of jail and how they took me back to The Land and
how Detective Fallon got transported with us by accident and then we
had to search all over The Land and had to fight a battle and ride a
dragon so I could use its blood to save my father's life. And now we
are back again so Brendan can see his daughter and tell his mother
that he is a Druid. I left out the mermaid stuff 'cause that just sounded
kooky.

When I finished I had a long hard look at Special Agent Murano to
see if I could figure out which group he was going to join. The group
that thought I was crazy or the group that thought I was pretending to
be crazy. Agent Andy was difficult to read. He clicked off his tape
recorder and tilted his head towards the armed guard that was standing by the door.

'Would you object, Conor, if we had a little conversation in private?'

'Why?'

Agent Murano leaned in so close I could smell his heavy cologne. 'I
have a lot of experience with unusual events,' he said in a conspiratorial
whisper. 'Let's just say I would prefer to talk about your situation without prying eyes.' Then he winked at me.

'What, are you like an X-File guy?'

He smiled. 'When we are alone.'

'OK,' I said.

The FBI man dismissed the guard and then lowered the Venetian
blinds that were in front of what I assumed was a two-way mirror.

I started to get excited. When you tell a story as crazy as mine, to as
many people as I had and none of them believe you – you start to
doubt your sanity. Could it be that I had finally met someone who truly
believed me?

'Have you met people from The Land before?'

The agent shushed me, took off his jacket and covered the security
camera that was mounted on the corner of the wall.

'So you have a file on Tir na Nog, right?'

Once again he raised his finger in front of his lips, picked the inter-com off the table and unplugged it. Then after looking around to see that no one or nothing could overhear us, he covertly gestured for me to come close. I stood and looked around myself. It was very cloak and dagger. I just got within striking distance of him when – that is exactly what he did – he struck. He slammed the intercom into my stomach just below my ribs. Whether he had been trained or had lots of practice in using office equipment to cause pain, I don't know, but he was certainly good at it. Every molecule of air flew out of my body and the agonising spasms in my solar plexus made it so I was having a hard time replacing any of them. I was on the ground, doing a convincing impression of a fish out of water, when he bent down and slammed the intercom into my right shin.

I once heard that the only good thing about pain is that you can only experience it in one place – let me tell you now: that's not true. Getting slammed in the shin just meant that I hurt from my chest to my toes. Then he slammed the damn thing into my head and I hurt all over. I tried to ask why but my breathing still wasn't working and then I had a thought that terrified me so much I didn't even care about the pain.

'Did Cialtie send you?' I said as loud as I could.

Apparently it wasn't very loud at all because Agent Murano leaned over and said: 'What did you say?'

'Were you sent by my Uncle Cialtie to kill me?'

He grabbed me by my hair and dragged me back into a chair where he handcuffed my hands behind my back.

'Still with the Faerieland stories. Do you want me to kick the crap out of you again?'

'No,' I answered honestly.

'Then enough with the dragons and the Pixies.'

'There are no Pixies in Tir na Nog.'

That line earned me a backhand across the face that made my vision swim for a second. 'What do you want?'

'I want you to knock it off with the insanity talk. The last four federal crimes I have investigated in this state have all gotten off with insanity pleas. My nickname in the office is The Shrink. I refuse to lose another case to the nuthouse.'

Relief washed over me; he was not an assassin hired by my uncle, he was a plain old ordinary Real World jerk. I smiled.

'What, O'Neil, is so funny?'

'The Shrink,' I said laughing.

Murano flew into a rage, he re-hit me in the stomach and over-turned the chair I was cuffed to, my head bounced off the floor and I thought I was going to throw up. I really didn't want to get hit again but I couldn't help it, I was still laughing.

'OK, OK,' I said, my face pressed against the linoleum. 'What do you want me to do?'

The agent picked me off the floor – the cuffs cut in to my wrists. He put his face inches from mine. For a horrible second I thought he was going to kiss me. 'You are going to confess to being a terrorist.'

'What?'

'You're going to admit that you are a terrorist. You don't have to name names. You can claim that you never met your masters but you kidnapped Detective Fallon because you hate your country.'

'You're crazy.'

'Maybe I am,' Murano said, 'but I'm going to make sure you are *not* crazy.'

'So let me get this straight – you are punching a man who is tied to a chair and I'm the terrorist?'

The crazy G-man tipped my chair over once again. This time I think I did black out for a short time. The next thing I remember there was drool on the floor and I finally had a pain in my head that hurt enough to block out all of the other pains in my body.

'OK, OK, I said, 'I'll say anything you want. Let's just try and keep my grey matter inside my skull.'

You know all that talk about how advanced interrogation tech-niques are no good because a tortured prisoner will tell you anything? Well, it's all true. I talked about how Tir na Nog was really a code word for a bunch of anarchists that wanted to overthrow the United States of America and then the world. When I started to get too outlandish, Agent Murano shook his head until eventually I just let him write my confession. We started getting along so well I even persuaded him to get me a burger and a shake. Don't get me wrong, I still loathed the man. Anyone who would use their power to beat a shackled insane person (I know I'm not really insane but he didn't know that) is just below snakes – and that's giving snakes a bad name. I was slurping at the last of my shake when Murano came in holding my 'confession'.

I hesitated before signing. I had been called a lot of nasty things in my day. Once I had even been called 'unfunny' (can you believe that?). But 'terrorist' was not something I wanted people saying about me. I imagined that in prison hierarchy, a terrorist would be just a tiny step above a guy who cooks puppies for supper.

'I don't think I can sign this,' I said.

'You want we go through all this again, O'Neil?' Agent Murano said, rubbing his knuckles.

'Well the way I figure it, either I get a beating from you today or I get one every day from my white supremacist flag-loving cellmate. Sorry, Andy, but I'm sticking with the fire-breathing dragon story.'

'Sign it,' the FBI man said as he stepped menacingly towards me.

'No.'

'SIGN IT!'

'Sign what?' Brendan said as he entered the room. The so-called kidnap victim was flanked by a local cop in uniform and an old, grey-haired lady that I at first thought was his mother. Brendan picked up my confession and scanned it. I kept staring at the wrinkled face of the old lady – something about her intrigued me.

'So you're a terrorist now?' Brendan said to me.

'Special Agent Murano thinks so.'

'Did he coerce you?'

'I'd say he counselled me,' I replied. 'Agent Andy is like a shrink.'

Murano bristled and pulled Fallon into the corner. I'm sure the special agent meant to whisper but he was worked up and not doing it very well. I could hear every word.

'What do you care if I rough him up a bit? According to the report he had you locked up in a closet for a couple of months.'

'It wasn't that bad.'

'Come on,' Murano said, 'you probably want to take a few pops yourself.'

'I'm not sure his attorney would approve,' Fallon said, pointing to the old woman.

'No,' the grey-haired woman said, 'I'd be fine with that.'

At the sound of her voice all the hairs on the back of my neck stood straight out.

'No you are not,' Fallon said to her. 'You were about to tell your client not to sign anything.'

'My what?'

'Your client, Mr O'Neil?' Brendan said pointing to me. 'You were about to tell him not to say or sign anything.'

'Oh yes, I was.' A look of confusion crossed her face – it was maddeningly familiar. 'Yes, what Brendan said – do. Or don't do.'

The old woman tilted her head down and with inordinate interest began inspecting the bulb on the desk lamp.

'She was also about to say that she would like some time alone with her client.' Brendan stared at the woman again. 'Wasn't she?'

The woman straightened up and hurriedly said, 'Yes, I'd like to be alone with Master On-el.'

'O'Neil,' Brendan corrected.

'Yes, Prin— Mr O'Neil.'

Agent Murano finally took notice of the woman. 'Can I see some identification please?'

'Some what?'

'Identification.'

The old woman looked like she didn't know what he was talking about. She looked over to Brendan and said, 'Can we get on with this?'

'Yeah,' Brendan said with a sigh, 'go for it.'

The woman reached up to her ears and pulled off the marble-sized gold earrings that were hanging from her lobes. She held the two shiny spheres in her palm and incanted under her breath. The gold balls glowed then rose from her palm and encircled each other like tiny binary stars.

The uniformed cop stepped in to get a better look but Murano backed up and said, 'What the—' He didn't get to finish before the two balls shot through the air and exploded into the chests of the two officers. They were thrown against the wall in a shower of light. When I could see again it looked like they weren't getting up any time soon.

Brendan went through the FBI man's pockets for the handcuff key while the old woman checked on the health of the cop.

''Bout time you got here,' I said to Brendan. 'That Fed is a nutcase. It was only a matter of time before he dropped a starving rodent down my trousers.'

I stood up and went over to where the old woman was holding the policeman's head. I leaned in and took a close-up look at the old woman.

'Essa?'

She smiled – it wrinkled up her whole face. 'Miss me?'

TWO

RUBY

'Essa, you're so …'

'I'm so what?' she said in a tone that sent warning bells exploding in my brain. 'How do I look, Conor? Tell me.'

'Well, you look …'

'If you say "wrinkled" I'm going to chain you back to that chair. For you, I got off my horse and set foot on the ground in the Real World. Because you and Brendan don't know how to hide, I am what an eighty-year-old woman looks like in this gods forsaken land. So once again, how do I look?'

'I was just about to say that you don't look a day over seventy.'

'Can we get out of here please,' Brendan said, 'I've just assaulted a federal agent. I'd like to be gone before that appears on my permanent record.'

Essa opened her briefcase and took out a jar of Vaseline.

'Are we going to slide out of here?'

Essa didn't even bother with a dirty look.

'Oak tree sap,' Brendan said. 'It was my mother's idea to put it in a Vaseline jar to get it past security.'

Essa smeared the sap in a circle on the windowless wall. Then she placed her hand on the sticky circle and incanted. When she removed her hand a gold handprint glowed in the brown circle. She straightened up, groaned and rubbed her back.

'Ready to leave?'

'I sure am, grandma.' That got me a dirty look.

She shouted a single word that sounded like a sneeze and the circle silently blew out of the wall. Daylight poured in among the dust and I could see parked cars through what moments earlier had been a wall.

Brendan crouched down and pointed. 'We have to get past that gate. My car is parked on the other side.'

I walked over to the unconscious Agent Murano. He was starting to come round and if I was honest, I'd have to admit that I was toying with the idea of kicking him in the ribs so he would have something to remember me by. That's when I saw it. Brendan had emptied the FBI man's pockets looking for the handcuff key. In a pile on the floor, was scattered change and car keys attached to a keychain that said Porsche.

'I've got a better idea.'

In the parking lot I pressed the fob attached to the keychain and lights on Agent Andy's white sports car blinked. It was almost like his car was saying 'Steal me.' The car, like the special agent's shoes, was meticulously cleaned and waxed. It wasn't new but he tried to make it look like it was – right up to the new-car smell air freshener. It was obvious that my torturer loved this vehicle and I was looking forward to smashing it through the front gate. I didn't get a chance. Brendan wouldn't let me behind the wheel. He pointed out that he'd been trained in high-speed driving and I had only been driving for a year. I wouldn't have gotten to smash it into the gate anyway because it was open. We zoomed past a surprised (and soon-to-be unemployed) guard without even a scratch.

It was a tight fit in the car. I got stuffed in to the back and we broke all Pennsylvania speeding laws. After my incarceration I needed some air, so I reached into the front and pulled the latch for the convertible top. The wind took the roof and ripped it right off the car.

'Oops,' I said with a smile worthy of Fergal.

'Yeeha!' Essa whooped.

I laughed and shouted over the sound of the rushing wind, 'Where did you learn to do that?'

'Isn't that what you and Fergal used to do when you were excited?' Essa said, her grey hair swirling around the car.

'It is – well remembered.'

Brendan was tearing around the back country road at an alarming speed. I would have thought that Essa would be terrified but she loved it.

'This is like being on dragon-back,' she shouted. 'Can everybody go around in contraptions like this?'

'If they go this fast they get in trouble from the police,' Brendan answered.

'But it's OK because you are police – right?'

'Not any more,' Brendan said, 'I handed in my badge the instant the FBI man hit the wall.'

Brendan slowed a little bit as we turned onto the narrow roads that led to his house. At last we skidded around a corner and saw Brendan's mother and daughter waiting for us at the exact place where Brendan and I had arrived from Tir na Nog a week earlier.

It was the first time I had ever seen Brendan's daughter. She stood there in a purple tie-dye tee-shirt, a small pack on her back, a white stick in her hand and classic full-sized Ray-Ban sunglasses that took over her whole face.

Essa quickly busied herself opening the portal. Brendan's mother, Nora, said, 'It is very nice to see you again, Conor. Are you OK?'

'I'm fine, Mrs Fallon.'

I crouched down and addressed Ruby. 'And you must be Brendan's little Gem?'

Ruby straightened up and said, 'Only Daddy can call me Gem.'

'Oh, sorry. It is very nice to meet you, Miss Fallon.'

She shot her hand straight out in front of her. 'It is nice to meet you, Mr O'Neil.'

We shook. 'Call me Conor, Mr O'Neil is my dad. Can I call you Ruby?'

'You can call me Miss Fallon.'

'That's my Gem,' Brendan said smiling.

'Well, Miss Fallon, I like your shades.'

Ruby adjusted the huge sunglasses. 'If they're good enough for Ray Charles,' she said, 'then they're good enough for me.'

'Indubitably,' I agreed.

The sound of distant sirens pulled my attention away from the undersized child in the oversized sunglasses. Essa had started the portal to Tir na Nog – there was an outline hanging in the air but it didn't look like anything I wanted to step into.

'Pick up the pace, old lady,' I said. 'We'll soon have company.'

'You want to do this, Duir Boy?' she grumbled. 'Stepping through an unstable portal is almost as dangerous as calling me "old lady".'

'Seriously,' Brendan said. There was concern in his voice. 'How long?'

'It could be soon if you would allow me to concentrate.'

Brendan and I left her alone. The noise of the approaching sirens meant the cops were almost there.

'We've got a problem,' Brendan said.

'You think?'

'Essa wields our only non-lethal weapon and she's busy opening the magic thingy.'

'You missing your bow and arrows?'

'If the cops get here before she finishes they'll shoot you.'

'Me?' I said. 'What about you? How about when they get here, I tell them that this is all your fault, 'cause now that I think about it – it is.'

'I've got an idea of how to slow them down,' Brendan said, 'if Ruby is game.'

For the record I thought it was a dreadful idea. And it certainly made it so I can never return to the Real World. When the two cop cars screeched to a halt in the gravel road, Brendan and his mother stood in front of me frantically waving their hands. Three policemen and Special Agent Murano all got out – guns drawn.

'Don't shoot,' Brendan shouted. 'He's got my daughter.'

What the cops saw was me holding a knife to little Ruby's throat. Actually it was the nail file from Brendan's Swiss army knife but hopefully none of the cops' eyesight was good enough to notice that.

'Stand back coppers,' I said in my best Jimmy Cagney voice, 'or I'll let the girl have it.'

That was Ruby's cue to let loose what her father called one of her 'migraine screams'. Despite the name, I was unprepared for the ear bleeding, high-pitched volume of the screech. I almost dropped the knife and I'm sure that every dog in a five-mile radius ran underneath a sofa.

'Ow,' I said.

Brendan turned around and whispered, 'Told you so.'

'Take it easy, O'Neil,' one of the policemen shouted.

'I don't want to talk to you. I want to talk to The Shrink.'

'OK, O'Neil, we'll get you a psychologist,' the cop replied. 'It's just going to take a little time.'

'I don't want to talk to a psychologist, I want to talk to THE SHRINK aka Agent Andy. Didn't you guys know? That's what they call him at FBI central.'

'Don't hurt the girl, O'Neil,' Murano shouted.

Ruby let loose another one of her sonic screams that made us all tilt our head a bit until it was over. I was surprised that the lenses in her Ray-Bans didn't shatter.

'This is your fault, Shrink,' I shouted. 'I was a mild-mannered fantasist before you tied me to a chair and tortured me. You turned me into a child killer.' I gave Ruby a shake for effect and she bit my arm. It really hurt. I lowered the knife and I saw the cops levelling their guns.

Brendan stepped in front fast and said, 'Don't shoot,' while I repositioned the nail file. I whispered to Ruby, 'What you bite me for?'

She whispered, 'I'm trying to make it look good.'

'Well, ow,' I said and then got back to work on the FBI man. 'So is attacking a shackled man in the FBI interrogation book?'

'I never …'

'Don't make me do it,' I shouted. 'You know what you did. You tortured me and wrote out a fake confession.'

I was stalling for time but I also wanted Murano to feel a little bit guilty about all this. I'm sure in his mind he now felt exonerated about how he treated me. After all, I wasn't being very chivalrous – I had a knife to the throat of a young blind girl – but I hoped that someone would investigate his actions and get him busted to airport bathroom security.

'Almost there,' Essa shouted.

'Thank the gods,' I said.

'O'Neil,' Murano said, 'what is the old woman doing?'

The familiar ring of an active portal reached my ears as Essa said, 'Who you calling old?'

Mom, Dad and Nieve burst through the portal on horseback. Mom threw two of her Shadowmagic exploding light bombs at the two cops on the left and Dad and Nieve threw what looked like small knives at the other cop and the FBI man. The knives swerved directly into the chests of the cop and Agent Murano.

While Mom's victims were blown off their feet, the cop and the FBI man just looked at the knives sticking out of their chests and fell over backwards.

'Hi, son,' Dad said casually as he rode over to Murano.

'You didn't have to kill them!' Brendan shouted as he ran to the FBI man and reached for the knife sticking out of his chest.

Dad stopped him. 'It's not a knife.'

'I can … I can't move,' the Fed said.

'It's a knife handle but no blade,' Dad explained, 'instead of a blade it has one of Nieve's paralysing pins in it. Pull it out.' Brendan pulled the knife blade out of the FBI man's chest and looked at the gold pin.

'Cool,' Brendan said and handed it to me.

Murano sat up and felt his chest. 'I can mo—'

I stuck the pin/knife back in his chest and he fell over like a stuffed teddy bear.

Nieve rode over and while hanging dangerously low to the side of her saddle, gave Brendan a long kiss. When it seemed like it would never stop, Brendan's mother gave a discreet cough. Brendan looked up to see his mother staring at him with her arms crossed.

'Oh yeah. Um, Mom, Gem, this is my … friend, Nieve. Nieve, this is my mother Nora and my daughter Ruby.'

Nieve replied, 'It is very nice to meet you, I've heard so much about you both.'

'We'll have plenty of time for niceties once we are back in The Land,' Mom said, riding by. 'Let us leave this place.'

Brendan turned to his mother and daughter. 'Are you sure you want to do this? You might not ever get to come back.'

'We have already discussed this,' Nora said. 'What you did today was right and I am proud of you but your actions mean you can no longer stay here.'

'We want to be with you, Daddy,' Ruby said taking her father's hand. His mother took the other and the three of them walked through the portal.

Mom was next. I asked her to relay a message to Tuan for me when she got back to Tir na Nog then I cuffed the cop with his own handcuffs and hog-tied the FBI man with his belt. I took back the paralysing throwing pins and made sure that Murano could see both the portal and his car. The Fed was obviously very shook up and when he finally could find his voice he asked, 'Who are you people?'

'We're Faeries from Pixieland and you, Agent Andy, are a jerk, but you were right about one thing – I'm not crazy. I really did ride a dragon and to prove it to you ...' I grabbed his hair and turned his head towards the portal. Tuan in all of his dragon splendour popped his head through and Agent Andy gasped.

'I was thinking about having him eat you,' I said as I walked over and gave Tuan a rub on the snout, 'but then I had a better idea.'

I whispered into Tuan's earhole and stepped back. He gave a shrug that meant, 'If that's what you want', and puffed a perfect little ball of fire directly at Agent Murano's precious Porsche. The car exploded and as the radiator ruptured it gave out a little squeal like a dying mouse. The look on Murano's face almost made this whole debacle seem worthwhile.

THREE
MACHA

Ruby stood in the centre of the Hall of Spells. She tilted her head and spun, dragging her stick on the tiles that represented all of the major runes. 'We're not in Scranton any more.'

'How can you tell that?' I asked.

'I'm blind, not stupid.'

'Ruby!' her father and grandmother shouted simultaneously.

The young girl shrugged, turned to me and said sorry, but it didn't seem like her heart was in it. I laughed.

'Don't encourage her,' Brendan said. 'We are working on Ruby's rudeness.'

'Well,' I said, 'it sounds like frankness to me. If I need an honest opinion I will know who to ask.'

'See?' Ruby said to her father.

'Ruby's opinions tend to be too honest.'

I looked up to see Mom and Dad standing waiting for our discussion to end. I cleared my throat and pointed to Brendan's mother and daughter.

'Nora and Ruby, may I present to you Lord Oisin of Duir and Princess Deirdre of Cull – my mom and dad.'

Nora bowed then whispered to Ruby who bowed too. As she did, Ruby's huge sunglasses dropped from her face. Her eyes were dark blue and seemingly unharmed but scars were still visible high on her cheeks where the shards of glass had entered her face and ruined her optic nerve.

Mom stepped up and took Brendan's mother by the shoulders. 'It is I who should be bowing to you,' she said with a nod of the head. 'You risked your lives today in aid of my son.'

'I would hardly say our lives were at risk, Your Highness,' Nora said.

'You went toe to toe with the FBI and the Scranton cops,' Dad piped in, 'I'd say you were risking something. Welcome to Castle Duir. This is our home and for as long as we live here, it is your home as well.'

I leaned in to Nora and whispered, 'And people live a long time around here.'

'Daddy promised me a huge bedroom,' Ruby announced. 'I'd like to see it now.'

'Ruby,' Nora and Brendan again admonished in unison, but Mom, Dad and Nieve just laughed.

'Of course,' Mom said. 'You must be tired. Let me show you to your rooms.'

As Mom and Nieve escorted the Fallons to the west wing, I looked about for Essa and Tuan but they had left.

'I think she is off with Tuan getting a dragon blood youth tonic,' Dad said.

'Who?' I said nonchalantly.

'Who?' Dad scoffed. 'Essa, the princess that you are looking for.'

'Who said I was looking for Essa?'

'Oh, my mistake,' Dad said sarcastically, 'maybe you were looking for Graysea? By the way, how are the princess and the mermaid getting along?'

'You're enjoying this, aren't you Dad?'

'Oh yes,' Dad said over his shoulder as he ran to catch up with Mom.

Dad came into my room as I was practising my knife throwing. He gingerly pulled the dagger from the wall and inspected the woodwork. 'Don't do that.'

'Mom and Aein told me that you used to do it.'

'Yes and I got in trouble with my father for it too. I'll get you a dart board or something. Just go easy on the walls. It probably took an elf fifty years to carve this little section.'

'OK,' I said, 'sorry.'

Dad laid the knife across his palm, feeling its balance. 'You're not using one of Dahy's gold-tipped specials?'

'No, it's too easy. Also I don't like seeing the way the knife swerves in the air. It … it reminds me of how Spideog died.'

'Oh, of course,' he said, handing me back the knife, 'I was sorry to hear about that. You really liked him, didn't you?'

'Yeah, I did. You didn't though, did you?'

'Oh, I wouldn't say I didn't like Spideog, it was just … well, now that I think about it, I really didn't know him very well. You have to realise that I was Dahy's student from a young age so I just took my master's side. I never really knew what those two guys were feuding over until you told me. It makes sense now. Dad never talked about my mother much. Most of the things I know about her are from what Dahy told me.'

'Don't you remember Macha at all?'

'Oh, I have a memory of smiling eyes, but maybe it's just a false memory that my child mind conjured up while looking at her portrait.'

'Is there a picture of her in the castle?'

'Sure – in the north wing.'

'Can we go see it?'

'Now?'

'Why not?'

We walked through the castle together. Jeez, I thought the bowing and scraping was bad with me but for Dad it was just short of grovelling. He didn't try to discourage it. It was the way I was dealing with it too. You just can't spend all day saying 'Stop that.'

Even though Dad looked like my fraternal twin he was starting to regain the grown-up manner that I remembered. When he first regained his youth by drinking Tuan's dragon blood he acted exactly as he looked – like a teenager. He still drags Mom giggling into private corners of the castle but he doesn't do it *all* the time and he has stopped challenging me to wrestling matches.

'So how's the kinging going?' I asked as we walked.

'To be honest, it's a lot of paperwork,' he said. 'All of the kingdoms are kicking up a fuss about the volatility in Duir and especially how unreliable the gold stipends have been. Mom's been a huge help. She has been holding them off while I was … resting – but now everybody is looking for stability. I'd like a little stability myself but I think pretty soon my brother is going to do some serious destabilising.'

'He told me he wants the throne.'

'Not surprising. Once a guy like Cialtie gets a taste of power – it's hard to let it go.'

'I don't think it's that,' I said. 'I mean it's not just that. He told me that if he became king he would be safe.'

'I wonder where he got that idea.'

'Ona's book.'

That stopped Dad in his tracks. 'What book?'

'Cialtie showed me a book that he found in Ona's bedroom the day he killed her.'

'He told you that?'

'Yeah, but he wasn't bragging. He really believes that he can do nothing except what she wrote in that book.'

Dad started walking again. 'And she wrote that he would be safe if he was king?' When he spoke it was more like it was to himself than me. 'If he had just told me that, maybe I would have renounced the throne … but I did renounce the throne. He had the throne. Why did he insist on trying to blow things up?'

'He told me that he wanted to free The Land of Ona's prophetic chains.'

Dad snorted with derision. 'Freeing The Land by destroying it – typical Cialtie.'

We rounded a corner and entered the north wing's portrait gallery. Pictures lined the walls stretching into what seemed like infinity. That's the funky thing about living in a huge castle. You think you have explored every nook and cranny and then you come across an amazing place you have never seen before.

'Wow,' I said, 'Who are all these people?'

'These are portraits of all of the major and minor rune holders in The Land, and all holders of a yew wand.' Dad pointed far into the distance. 'Your grandmother is over here with the House of Nuin.'

As we walked I asked, 'Can I get one of these?'

'I'd love to have a picture of you if you would ever hold still long enough to sit for one, but I can't hang it in the north hall until you have taken your choosing. I don't have a portrait yet either. Tell you what, after your choosing we should get our pictures painted together.'

'OK,' I said, but didn't relish the idea of having to have to sit still for hours while Dad bestowed his pearls of wisdom.

I spotted the portrait of Macha before Dad pointed it out to me. She had amber hair like Nieve and Dad's long face but her eyes weren't dark like her children's. Her eyes were clear blue – like mine. She was portrayed sitting astride a black horse holding the reins with one hand and her yew wand in the other. Behind her was a hawthorn in full bloom.

'She's definitely your mother,' I said.

'Yes,' he said dreamily like he was lost in the picture.

'You once told me she went on a sorceress' quest and never returned.'

'That is what my father told me but I had a talk with Dahy recently and he says one day – she just vanished.'

'You talked to Dahy about her?'

'How could I not? That's all he wants to speak about since you came back from Mount Cas with that knife.'

I smiled at the memory of the helpful message that had been hidden inside the gold-tipped knife and thrown at us on that mountain pass. 'He thinks Macha is up there with the Oracle?'

'He does,' Dad said.

'But you don't?'

'Actually I'm starting to think that Dahy and Spideog are right. Well, maybe not right but that knife of yours and the message you found with it raises enough doubts in my head to make me think we should find out for sure.'

'Wait,' I said, 'we're gonna storm the Oracle's Yew House?'

He didn't answer at first. He just kept looking at the picture of his mother and then, as if he was making the decision right there on the spot, he said, 'Yes.'

'How? That guy is seriously bad ass. He took out Spideog with a flick of the wrist. And I have no doubt he could drop half of that mountain on your head if he wanted to.'

'Dahy thinks it can be done. There is planning to do. I'll keep you posted.'

Dad ruffled my hair in a way that he knew really annoyed me and rushed off for a meeting with some runelord who I'm sure had a good reason why he needed more gold in his stipend. I was left alone under the dark stare of yet another grandparent I never knew. As much as I didn't want to face the Oracle guy on Mount Cas again – I sure wanted to meet my grandmother. Well, if anybody could come up with a working plan of attack, it was Dahy.

I arrived back in my chamber to find Ruby waiting for me. She sat almost swallowed by an overstuffed chair, her feet sticking straight out, her stick folded across her lap. I don't know if it's the huge sunglasses or just her general demeanour but every time I saw this kid I got the distinct feeling that I was in trouble.

'Where have you been?'

I was a bit shocked by the abruptness of the question and when I didn't answer right away, Ruby said, 'You were probably smooching with your mermaid girlfriend.'

'I was not,' I said and sounded to myself like I was ten years old. 'I was in a meeting with the king.' I thought that sounded better than 'I was with my daddy.'

She seemed to find that acceptable.

'How do you know about Graysea?'

'My father brought her to me to have a look at my eyes. She cooed and ooed and cried and kissed me. She's not very clever, is she?'

'Graysea has other talents,' I said.

'Yeah right. Well, she said she couldn't fix my eyes. That I had waited too long.'

'Oh, I'm … I'm sorry.'

'It's nothing I haven't heard before,' Ruby said dismissively as she stood. 'Now, I would like my pony.'

'I beg your pardon?'

'My pony. Father said I would have a pony when I came to Tir na Nog. When I asked him about it he said he had to talk to you. Since he hasn't yet, I am. I'd like my pony please.'

'I ... I don't know where I'd get a pony at this time of day.'

'I would assume,' Ruby said as she opened the door for me, 'that we will find one in the stables.' She motioned me out of my room like it was hers. I started to protest but then just decided that getting her a pony was probably the path of least resistance.

'I feel sorry for your future husband,' I said.

'Funny, that's what Father says.'

Ruby grabbed my arm and then swung her stick back and forth as she walked so fast I thought we were going to break into a jog.

'You know, Ruby,' I said, 'I'm not sure if I can get you a pony.'

'Why not?' she asked without slowing down in the slightest.

'I don't think they're just going to give me one.'

'Your father is the king – right?'

'Yes but ...'

'And you are a prince?'

'Well, yeah.'

'So just ask for a pony. What is your problem?'

The stable master saw us coming and greeted me at the entrance. He was an old one. It had gotten to the point where I could spot one from a mile away. 'I am Pilib,' he said without bowing or even offering to shake my hand.

'Hi, I'm Conor.'

'I know,' he said. 'You have your grandmother's eyes.'

'Oh, did you know Macha?'

'Of course, she held the Capall yew wand. She had the supremacy over horses. When she lived in Duir she was only ever truly happy when she was here.'

As he spoke Pilib's eyes glossed over lost in the memory. I remembered Spideog telling me that my grandmother loved him and Dahy at the same time. I wondered if I should add the stable master to that list.

Ruby hit me in the shin with her stick. 'Ask him.'

'Ah … Master Pilib, I was wondering if I could have a pony.'

'Certainly. Am I safe to assume that it is for this little lady?'

'I'm not a lady, I'm a young girl.'

I looked down at Ruby, astonished. 'You speak Ancient Gaelic?'

'Grandma taught me some words.'

'OK,' I said turning back to Pilib. 'Can we get this young girl a young-girl-sized pony?'

'Right this way, Prince Conor.'

The stables were quite an operation here at Castle Duir. He led us past what must have been a hundred stalls and then outside to a paddock that contained four ponies.

'Spirited or docile?' Pilib asked.

I toyed with the idea of answering, 'Super spirited.' That would teach her a lesson for putting me through this but I had to remember that no matter how bossy she was – the kid was blind. 'Docile please.'

Pilib placed his fingers in his mouth and emitted a series of whistles. The ponies looked up and then at each other as if saying, 'Who, me?' The smallest of the ponies slowly walked over to us. She was glossy black, just like Ruby's sunglasses. I picked Ruby up and placed her feet on the bottom wooden rail of the corral so she could reach over. The stable master whistled again, this time quietly without the fingers in the mouth and then pointed to the young girl. The pony walked slowly up to Ruby as I guided her hand to the animal's snout.

'This is Feochadán,' Pilib said.

I remembered a story my father used to tell me when I was young about a sheep that got covered with *feochadán*. As Ruby tentatively stroked her pony's nose I said, 'It means thistle.'

A huge smile crossed Ruby's face. It was the first smile I had ever seen on that face and it changed her from a bossy tyrant to the young girl that she was. 'Thistle, that's a lovely name for a pony. Hello Thistle.'

That pony looked up and I could have sworn it recognised its new name. A stable hand showed up with a saddle.

'Oh no, I'm not teaching her to ride.'

'On the day a young girl receives her first pony,' Pilib said, 'surely she must ride it. I wouldn't worry, Feochadán is very easy to ride. Shall I get Acorn for you, Your Highness?'

Acorn, I thought, I did so want to see Acorn and it was a beautiful spring day. Well, I could see no harm in having a quick wander around Castle Duir.

Ruby allowed herself to be hoisted onto Thistle without any of her usual *I can do it myself* fuss. Acorn was brought to me and even though he tried to hide it, I could tell he was pleased to see me. I mounted up and we left through the stable exit. True to Pilib's word, Thistle was the calmest mount I had ever seen. Ruby showed no signs of being scared. She sat on her pony like she had been doing it all of her life.

Outside the castle walls the sun from a cloudless sky stopped the cool spring breeze from being too cold.

'I would like to talk to a tree,' Ruby said.

'You want to talk to a tree?'

'Yes, now. Father said I would have a big bedroom, a pony and I would get to talk to a tree. I'd like to talk to a tree now.'

'Wouldn't you like to just ride for a bit and save some of the other stuff for later?'

'No.'

The best tree to have a conversation with is, of course, Mother Oak but Glen Duir is almost a day away at a hard ride. With Thistle it would probably take a month. Well, Duir doesn't mean oak for nothing. Castle Duir was certainly surrounded by oaks – so I just started for the nearest treeline.

When I got to the edge of the oak forest I had some misgivings. These trees didn't have the same welcoming feel that Mother Oak has – but then what tree does? I dismounted and walked up to a huge snarly barked oak and wrapped my arms around it. Instantly I knew I was in big trouble.

FOUR

THE OAK

This was different from any tree I had ever communicated with. When I touched it I knew instantly that I wouldn't be able to let go until it released me. The world disappeared. All of my senses were lost except for the touch of where I was held to the bark. This tree didn't talk, it probed my mind. What it found it brought to the fore and what it found was stuff that I had buried for a reason.

I was in grade school and all of the kids were bullying Jimmy Murphy. Jimmy was overweight and crap at sports. I just stood there. I should have done something but I just stood there. I liked Jimmy but I just couldn't be seen being his friend. Then the memory I had long tried to forget. He came to me for help and I pushed him over. Aw Jimmy, I'm so sorry.

Then my mind conjured up the image of a Banshee growing up with his family. I saw his entire life, right up to the moment when I stabbed him at the edge of the Reedlands. He was the first man I had ever killed. As my sword pierced his chest I could see everyone he had ever known and loved watching me with eyes filled with hate. I tried to protest, I tried to say that I didn't mean to kill him. That he was trying to kill me. But the words wouldn't come. My mind was not my own. I felt a pain rise in my chest.

That Banshee was replaced by another. This one I knew. This one I loved. I was lying on my sleeping roll the night before we snuck into Castle Duir. Don't make me watch this, I tried to scream. I tried to pull away but my hands, like they were latched onto a high-voltage wire, wouldn't let go. I remember that night. He came to talk to me but I was too tired and I sent him away, but as this memory progressed, instead of sending him away, I sat up and said, 'What's on your mind, cuz?'

He told me about his plans to kill Cialtie. I told him he was nuts and talked him out of it. After Cialtie was kicked out of Castle Duir – Fergal lived. We talked and drank. He met a lovely girl and I was his best man at the wedding. At the wedding reception he stood and tapped his wineglass with a spoon. He turned to me and said, 'I'd like to propose a toast to the man who saved my life ...' The memories abruptly ran in reverse and then the scene in the camp played as it really happened. I fobbed Fergal off and then I watched as the next day Cialtie humiliated and killed him. Then I saw it again ... and again ... and again. The pain in my chest intensified. My head felt like it was going to explode. I watched again as the sword pierced his chest. I watched but this time the man who was wielding the sword – was me.

I screamed.

I was lost. Down so dark a well that I couldn't see the top. The walls of the well weren't made of stone or dirt, they were made of ... me. I was lost deep in my own mind. Deeper even than after the shock of killing the Banshee at the edge of the Fililands. But it was safe down there. Up there was The Tree. The Tree that grew its roots into my memories and plucked out of them everything I had ever regretted and feared. I was safe down here. I had to shut down; I couldn't let him into the brain cells that contained the faces of the scores of Banshees and Brownies I had killed during the battle of the Hall of Knowledge. I wouldn't survive that. Protests, like *I had no choice* and *We were at war*, cut no mustard with the oak. I couldn't let him in there – I was safe in my well. I wasn't ever coming up. I was safe in my well I was never coming up. I was ...

The walls of my well, the walls of my self, my refuge, started to shake. A far-off voice called my name but they would never find me. I was deep, deep in my …

The voice became louder but still it was tiny, tinny, miles away. I could never be harmed … would never let him …

The walls of my sub-subconscious shook more. The voice … I heard the voice. It was … it was … Ruby. I laughed. You'll never find me down here, Ruby. I'm safe. Safe from the forest of trees … I'm safe. But then I heard her scream. It was that high-pitched piercing scream that she does. The one her father calls The Migraine Scream. I forced myself to think. Where are you, Ruby? It doesn't matter I am here and I … I am safe. But where are you Ruby? You were with me. I took you riding. You are alone and blind in the Forest of Duir. But I'm safe here. But little Ruby you are not. I must … safe. Safe here. Safe. No. Save. Save her. I must save her.

I reached to the walls of the well. No. I forced myself to think. Not a well – the walls of my mind. I placed my back against a corner of my brain and I climbed. I climbed. I climbed to the sound of that scream. I still couldn't see anything but the further I went, the closer the sound became. It got so loud it hurt.

I opened my eyes to see Ruby taking another big breath in preparation for another scream. I reached up to stop her but my arm was blocked by a white bed sheet. As she screamed again I freed my hand and caught her by the arm.

'Ruby,' I said.

She stopped, smiled and then started hopping around. 'You see,' she almost sang, 'it worked. It worked. I told you it would work.'

I was very confused. I was indoors and in a clean bed. All around me people were rushing into the room. Presumably to see what all the screaming was about. I looked to my left and saw Dad chuckling.

'Dad? What happened?'

'I've been waiting three days to ask *you* that,' he answered.

'Why was Ruby screaming?'

'I have no idea,' he said. 'She has been waiting by your side for most of the three days that you've been in this coma. Just a minute ago she said to me, "Can I try something?" I said yes and she started scream-ing.'

'And it worked!' Ruby said returning to my bed and bouncing her arms off the mattress. 'Daddy always said my scream could wake the dead and it can. It can, it can. It can. I'm going to tell Daddy.' And she was off.

'Where am I?'

'You're in one of Fand's healing rooms.'

'How did I get here?'

Dad pulled up a chair. 'That's an interesting story. Three days ago, the sergeant at arms was shocked to find a seven-year-old blind girl screaming at the Great Gates of Duir. She told him that you were in trouble and he sent a detail out to investigate. They found you curled up on the ground at the edge of the oak perimeter. Ruby says you went out there to talk to a tree – but you're not that stupid – are you?'

'Well,' I said, 'Ruby wanted to talk to a tree. I, of course, would have liked to have introduced her to Mother Oak but she was too far away …'

'So you just went out and wrapped your arms around any old oak?' Dad was almost shouting. 'What is wrong with you?'

'What's wrong with me? What's wrong with that tree? It was like it grew roots into my head.'

'Didn't anybody ever tell you about the Oaks of Duir?'

'No. No one did and whose fault is that – do you think?'

That stopped Dad's anger. 'Oh, well, I guess I should have told you.'

'You think?'

'Yeah, sorry.'

'So what did that tree do to me?'

'Oaks are dangerous trees, son. If you even brush past one it can snare you. We seem to have no defence against them. They can access our memories and then manipulate our emotions. That's one of the things that makes Mother Oak so wonderful. She searches out the best in people and reminds you that you are a good person but not all oaks are so affirmative. In fact, almost none are. For the most part, oaks are nasty pieces of wood. I liked to think of them as the junkyard dogs of Castle Duir.'

'Gosh, and I thought yews were the dangerous ones.'

'Yews can snare you without touching them but yews aren't nasty. Yews are the judges of The Land – oaks are the criminals.'

'But yews can kill you, right?' I asked.

'True,' said Dad, 'but oaks can drive you mad. Speaking of which – are you OK?'

'I think so, the worst part was …'

'You don't have to tell me. I assure you that whatever the oak stirred up in your mind is nowhere near as bad as he made it seem.'

'Yeah, it was awful, all of the stuff that filled my head but the oak was right about one thing. I did let Fergal down.'

'We all dropped the ball on that one, son. We should have seen it coming but never forget – the one who stuck the sword in Fergal was Cialtie.'

Fand entered and told us that there was a host of people wanting to visit with me. Dad picked up a vial from the bedside table.

'Your mother told me to give you this as soon as you awoke and seemed OK.'

'I'm fine Dad, I don't need any medicine.'

'So you want me to go back to your mother and say that you are defying her?'

I looked at him and frowned. 'You wouldn't do that – would you?'

'Hey, this is your mother we're talking about. You're on your own here, pal.'

I took the vial of liquid. 'OK, I'll take it,' I said, 'but I would really like to …' That's the thing about medicines in Tir na Nog – you don't have to wonder if they are working. There was no possible way I could have even finished that sentence and whatever I thought I wanted to do was instantly of no concern to me. I was back down in my well but this time it was only about six inches deep and lined with satin. Dad said I passed out with a huge smile on my face.

*   *   *

I woke to a question. 'Are you nuts?'

'No, I'm OK; the oak tree didn't drive me mad,' I said before I opened my eyes.

'Oh, that's a huge relief,' the voice said with an uncaring tone that I didn't like. I opened my eyes to see a very angry Brendan looming over me. I instantly sat up and backed into the headboard – he looked like he was going to hit me. 'What were you thinking?'

'I … I …'

'Nora and I didn't know where Ruby was and then you plop her on a horse and take her out to the most dangerous forest in The Land – where you abandon her – on a horse.'

Second most dangerous forest, and it was a pony, I said – to myself, because I knew if I said that to Brendan, there would have been some police brutality.

'You're right, I'm sorry,' I said, 'I wasn't thinking.'

'You're damn right you weren't thinking. She could have been killed, or driven insane. What possessed you to do it?'

'Ruby showed up in my room and said that you promised her a pony but were being slow about it.'

'So you just went and got her a pony?'

'Well,' I shrugged, 'she's kinda hard to say no to.'

Brendan relaxed and sat down. 'Yeah, I can't argue with that, but you've got to remember that even though she acts like she's forty-two she's only twelve.'

'I know, and I'm really sorry. I promise it won't happen again and I won't take her anywhere without you knowing about it.'

He patted me on the head like I was a schoolboy. 'You are forgiven, Mr O'Neil. So,' he said, changing the subject, 'how are you?'

'I'm fine. Dad said I was out of it for three days.'

'The oak roughed you up a bit, eh?'

'The specifics of what happened are fading now. All I remember is that he made me remember every bad thing I had ever done and I couldn't stop it. It was horrible.'

'As bad as being arrested for your dad's murder?'

'I don't want to bruise your ego, Detective Fallon, but compared to the oak – you're a pushover.'

A commotion outside the door made us both turn. A woman was screaming and guards were shouting.

'O gods,' Brendan said, 'I might be a pushover but my mother is not. If she gets in here she's going to tear your head off.'

The door opened and a very fierce looking Nora stomped towards me in a way that reminded me of an attacking Banshee. I looked to my left and saw there was a vial of that medicine on my bedside table. I grabbed it and downed it in one. Nora started screaming. I heard it but really didn't care as I snuggled blissfully down into the satin bed of my unconsciousness.

When you take one of Mom/Fand's potions you really do go out. No dreams, no visions, no nothing. I had no idea how long I had been asleep. It could have been days or minutes. When I woke up I opened one eye and had a look around. Sitting at my bedside, reading a book, was Essa.

She was back to her beautiful young-looking self. I just watched as she brushed a wisp of hair away from her forehead with a gesture that I knew oh so well.

'Hey, old lady,' I said and then braced myself. Essa had been plenty mad at me for so much of the time that I knew her that I was never sure if our meeting was going to be pleasant or not. But then she smiled and my body relaxed and my heart pounded.

'Hi, I … was worried about you.'

I looked around the room to see if anybody else was there. 'You talkin' to me?'

She laughed. 'Yes I am. Are you OK?'

I sat up. 'I am now.' There was an awkward silence where we just stared at each, other until I broke it with, 'You look good without the wrinkles and the grey hair.'

'Why, thank you,' she said with a nod of her head.

'What's it like drinking Tuan's blood?'

'Gross but kind of – wonderful. I haven't felt this good in years. I have tons of energy.'

'Maybe I should order a green dragon cocktail for myself?'

'Maybe we should get my father to whip up some Tuan blood wine?'

We both laughed. It was nice – normal. Could it be that I was forgiven? I wondered. Could Essa and I ever be – normal?

The question was cut short by the sound of bare feet slapping against the stone floor. I was smothered in kisses even before I could see whose lips were administering them. Not that I had to look, there's only one mermaid in all of The Land that greets me like that.

'Oh Conor,' *kiss, kiss,* 'I have been so worried about you,' *kiss, kiss, kiss.*

'Hi Graysea,' I garbled between smooches, 'have you met Essa?'

The introduction had the desired effect of getting Graysea to let up on my face.

'I remember Essa,' Graysea said in a tone I had never heard from her before. 'The first time I saw her she hit you in the head with a stick.'

I expected Essa to storm off, hopefully without hitting me in the head, but instead she stood her ground. 'What are you still doing here?'

Oh my, I thought to myself, this has the potential to turn into a serious cat fight – or a cat and fish fight and they usually don't turn out very well for the fish. I know it was cowardly of me – I reached for the bedside table but, damn it, there wasn't any of that knock-out medicine there.

'Where else should I be but by my beloved Conor's side?'

To be perfectly honest I wasn't the only reason she was still here – Graysea had nowhere else to go. When the Mertain King found out that she had stolen his dragon's blood to give to me, he banished her.

Essa was close to snarling when she said, 'I can think of several places I would rather you to be.'

'Essa,' I said as gingerly as I could, 'Graysea helped me escape from a very difficult situation.'

'Oh, did she?' the Princess said. 'And what other situations did she help you in or out of?'

'I don't understand you,' my mermaid said with her usual tilt of the head. 'Why are you here? Shouldn't you be mourning the loss of your fiancé?'

I instantly popped up on my knees on the mattress between them. Essa had stepped back in what I recognised as a preparation to spring.

I really didn't want to be in the middle of this and suspected that any second I was going to get the worst of it.

'Everyone out,' came a command from the doorway. Dad was standing there in his drill suit. He wore that kingly face that made the two women snap to attention and then quickly leave. Neither said goodbye to me as they never really took their eyes off each other for the entire exit.

'Thank you,' I said when the Princess and the mermaid were out of earshot.

'Don't thank me too soon,' Dad said, throwing me the clothes that he had been carrying. 'Your mother and Fand have given you a clean bill of health, so come with me – it's time for some training.'

'Training for what?'

'We're going to launch an assault on the Oracle of Mount Cas.'

I thought about the prospect of going into battle again and then thought about the skirmish that Dad had just saved me from. War didn't seem that bad at all.

FIVE

GRAYSEA AND ESSA

I was back in Dahy's boot camp. This time it was worse than the first time. The first time I knew I didn't know anything. This time I thought I knew everything and Dahy proved to me that I once again knew nothing. We were learning a new technique. The master didn't have a name for it so I called it ninja school – 'cause that's what it felt like. None of us were allowed to execute any of our showy spins or flip manoeuvres. Every movement had to be minimal. All over the armoury, where we practised, were wooden dowels balanced upright with feathers perched on top. Every time one of us disturbed a feather, or worse, knocked over a dowel, Dahy would shoot us in the legs with a crossbow bolt that had a woollen ball stuck on the end. If you think that doesn't sound like it would hurt – then think again.

Araf was really good at it. It wasn't until I saw him in a room full of feathers did I realise just how economical a fighting style he had. Except for his figure of eight propeller-like stick move, Araf hardly had to change his technique at all. Essa was lucky she didn't have to learn this stuff. Without all of her flipping and twirling she would have been very unhappy. And when Essa is unhappy – everyone is unhappy.

Gerard, Essa's father, forbade her to go into the Oracle's house. She wasn't about to let her father boss her around like that but when Gerard threatened to withdraw all of Castle Duir's wine shipments – Oisin took Essa off active duty. She was furious and Dad had to remind her that he was, like, a king. She stormed off kicking anything, and anyone, in her path. In short, Essa was to be avoided, but I was doing that already.

Even though our practice was deadly serious it was also fun. Dad joined us and so did Mom and Aunt Nieve. The ladies had a hard time casting spells without all of that dramatic wicked-witch arm waving. Dad, who already had, like, a hundred years' worth of Dahy tutelage, just seemed to do whatever the master told him to do without any effort at all. One time I pushed Dad over, just to see if Dahy would shoot the king with his crossbow. He didn't, he shot me.

Brendan trained with us but he wasn't going either. He wanted to come, just like he wanted to ask the yew trees if he could use Spideog's bow, but he had a responsibility to his daughter Ruby not to put himself in harm's way.

'And actually,' he confided to me one day at lunch, 'I'm in no hurry to see that Oracle guy again. If I recall he kicked our butts good with just a flick of the wrist.'

I pointed that out to Dahy but he said he had a plan. So by day we continued to practise our non-feather-disturbing fighting techniques and by night I rubbed healing salve into the black and blue bruises on my legs that Dahy gave me with his crossbow.

The banging on my bedroom door would have busted any Real World door off its hinges but Duir doors are made of hardy stuff.

'Conor,' the voice on the other side bellowed, 'I want to talk to you.' I knew who it was right away – everyone in the castle was talking about it. New wine is news around here but when it's delivered by the master winemaker himself – that's big news.

I opened the door and there stood the largest of all of the larger-than-life characters in Tir na Nog. Gerard stepped into the doorway, blocking out all of the light beyond. In his hand he held a metal bucket with a piece of cloth over the top – it didn't look like a weapon but I kept my eye on it.

He strode further into the room, forcing me to back up, and said, 'If I didn't know better I would think that you have been hiding from me.'

'I ... maybe I have been,' I confessed.

'Why would you do that?'

'I guess you haven't spoken to Essa yet?'

Gerard frowned and placed his bucket on the floor. 'Oh, I have spoken to my daughter all right. She is mighty mad at you and this – what did she call her – "fishy floozy" of yours.'

'That's why I've been avoiding you,' I said.

'Let me get this straight, you think that because my daughter is angry with you, that I will be too.'

'Aren't you?'

He came at me with his arms outstretched. I had a brief flashback of the bear attack in the Pookalands. He wrapped his arms around me and gave me one of his laughing hugs that lifted me off the ground. 'Oh my boy,' he said, and I relaxed even though my ribs were threatening to crack. 'If Essa is mad at you, then you already have more enemies than any one man can stand.' He let go of me and I tested my diaphragm to see if I could still breathe. 'Good gods and monsters, if I had to be angry at everyone that my *little darling* was irritated with – I would not have any friends or customers at all.'

'So you're not here to give me the "don't you dare hurt my daughter" speech?'

Gerard laughed, picked up his bucket and moved over to the table on the other side of the room. 'Oh, I don't give that speech. I usually just try to discourage Essa's beaus for their own safety.'

We laughed at that as he whipped the cloth off his bucket like a TV magician. 'I've brought you a gift.' Buried deep in snow, with only their necks sticking out, were four bottles. I grabbed one, releasing it from its icy bed.

'Beer!' I shouted.

'I remembered that last time you were in Castle Muhn you said you wanted beer that is "lighter, fizzier and colder" – well, try this.' He reached over and placed his hand on the neck of the bottle and mumbled. The cork began to spin and then rise until it shot out of the bottle with a satisfying pop.

I took a quick gulp to catch the foam from overflowing onto the floor. Gerard scrutinised my face for any hint of criticism. 'Well?' he asked as I wiped my mouth with my sleeve.

'I think you should give up on this wine stuff and become a full-time brewer.'

Gerard beamed like a child who had just received a stick-on star on his homework.

'Did I hear someone shouting beer?' It was Brendan at the door.

'Brendan,' I said. 'Come in and meet Essa's father, Lord Gerard of Muhn.'

'Oh,' Brendan said, a bit surprised while improvising a bow. 'How do you do? I'm a big fan of your wine.'

'Well, come in and try my beer,' Gerard said without standing.

Brendan hesitated and said, 'Actually I was just passing with my mother.' Brendan reached into the hallway and took his mother's hand and guided her into the room. 'Lord Gerard, may I introduce Nora Fallon.'

I hadn't seen Brendan's mother since she arrived in the Hall of Spells. She was dressed in a green felt-ish tunic with gold embroidery and leather trousers – pretty much what everyone around here wears and it suited her to a T.

Gerard jumped to his feet, and bowed. 'Of course I have heard about both of you. Welcome home, Druids. Please join us in a drink.'

Nora bowed. 'Thank you, my lord, but no. I have to tend to my granddaughter.' Brendan started to go with her when Nora said to her son, 'No, please stay. I know how much you are missing beer.' She bowed once again to us and left.

'Your mother,' Gerard said after seating Brendan and uncorking a beer for him, 'is … old.'

'Yes, try not to point that out to her when you meet her next. She's getting a bit tired of that.'

'But according to my daughter a couple of drops of blood from that remarkable Pooka friend of yours would change that – would it not?'

'Tuan has offered my mother some dragon blood but she says she feels great and likes herself the way she is.'

'Well, it sounds as if your mother knows her own mind. I like that in a woman.' Gerard slapped Brendan on the shoulder, changing the subject. 'My daughter speaks highly of you, Druid.'

'Well, she hasn't hit me yet,' the cop said.

Gerard laughed, 'It's a shame you are not going on our little expedition but I understand about parental responsibilities.'

'Wait,' I said. 'Are you coming?'

'Oh yes,' Gerard said, 'Oisin has summoned me – I am an integral part of the plan.'

'Look it's a three and a half day ride to the base of Mount Cas,' I said. 'There is no reason to leave at dawn. We can leave at, like, ten and still be there way before it's dark on the fourth day.'

'Son, we leave at dawn – that's how it is.'

'Who says? Where is it etched in stone that all expeditions must leave at dawn?'

Finally Dad gave me one of his patented withering stares that, although he looked like my annoying younger cousin, still worked.

'Yes sir. See you in the morning.'

'Before the morning,' he called after me.

So here I was, yawning while dragging my pack on the ground behind me, trying to get some kind of enthusiasm for the adventure ahead.

Believe it or not, I was early. The only ones in the stable before me were Gerard and four brawny soldiers. I watched and yawned as they hoisted a huge wine barrel on to Gerard's cart.

'Are we planning to get sloshed on this trip?'

'I wish,' Gerard said. 'There is no wine in that barrel.'

'What's in there?'

'Salt water.'

I was about to ask why we needed a barrel of salt water when I was blinded by a pair of hands covering my eyes from behind. 'Guess who?' said the unmistakable voice.

'Is it a person or a fish?' I asked.

'Both.'

I turned to see the ever bubbly Graysea standing behind me. She kissed me on both cheeks and said, 'Good morning.'

'Good morning to you too – how nice of you to see me off.'

'Oh, I'm not seeing you off. I'm going with you.'

'Graysea, this is a very dangerous mission. I really don't think you should come.'

'Think again, son,' Dad said while arriving around the corner with his mount.

I walked Dad out of earshot. 'Why is Graysea coming with us?'

'Because we are going up against a tough customer and I want a healer with us, and I have never seen anything like that Mertain healing power of hers.'

'Yes, Dad, but she's …' I tried to remember what matron had said about Graysea. 'She's a sensitive fishy.'

'I think you underestimate your mermaid, son. Graysea saved your butt out there in the ocean and defied her king. She can handle a three-day hike.'

'Don't you want me with you?' Graysea asked when I got back to her.

'No, I … I'm just worried about you.'

'It'll be fun.'

'Graysea, we are going into battle.'

She put on her serious face but then smiled that room-lighting smile of hers. 'Well, it will be fun until we get there.'

I just couldn't resist the infectious joy of that girl's smile. 'You're right,' I agreed, 'welcome along.'

Who knew what we were going into? At least until then I would have some pleasant company along the way. And luckily Essa wasn't coming so I wouldn't be caught in the middle of a week-long oestrogen nightmare.

Araf showed up and I grunted at him – I've discovered that wordless communication is best with the taciturn Imp. Mom, Nieve and Dahy all dramatically feigned surprise at me being ready before them. I saddled up Acorn (I was tempted to take Cloud but she was Brendan's horse now) and then helped Gerard hitch up the wagon to his monsta-horses.

Actually it was nice being early and not having everybody scowling at me to hurry. I was mounted up, waking up and starting to feel good about this expedition when my spirits were dashed by the arrival of the last two of the party – Tuan and Essa.

I cantered Acorn over to Dad. 'I thought you forbade Essa from coming?' I said in a harsh whisper.

'Gerard had forbidden her to enter the Oracle's house on Mount Cas so she and Tuan are performing a different task.'

'You did this on purpose.'

'What, son, do you accuse me of doing on purpose?'

'You know perfectly well what you did. You invited Graysea and Essa on this trip so you could watch me suffer.'

Dad, who had been wearing the slightest of smirks, became gravely serious. 'Essa is a very important part of Dahy's plan and as I said before, Graysea is the finest healer I have ever seen. The world does not revolve around you, son. I would never ask anyone to join an undertaking as perilous as this just to annoy you.' He kicked his horse away but as he did he said, 'That's just an added bonus.'

We took the main road out and travelled three abreast. On my left was Graysea and on my right was Essa. No one said a word. I was even afraid to shift in my saddle lest the noise break the agonisingly painful silence. Dad looked around and didn't even try to stifle his chuckle. This was going to be a long, long trip. I thought, maybe if I'm lucky I'll die a horrible death on Mount Cas. At least then I'll be saved from a trip home with these two.

SIX
THE YEW HOUSE

We travelled like that for a day and a half. No one said a word. Anybody who knows me understands that I'm uneasy with uncomfortable silences. This was pure torment. I thought my head was going to explode. On the first night I ate and went straight to bed. I was hoping I could get to sleep quickly so I would have someone in dreamland to talk to, but sleep wouldn't come. I was sharing a tent with Araf and still wasn't asleep by the time he came to bed. I was so desperate for conversation I said, 'Say something.'

'What would you like me to say?' he answered, without the puzzlement in his voice that he should have had.

'I don't care – anything. You can tell me about crop rotation if you want.'

'Really?' he said, with more excitement than I have ever heard from him before.

'Yes, anything.'

So off he went babbling on about plants and seeds and hoeing and dirt and bugs. He was so wrapped up in his subject I'm sure he didn't notice me nodding off with a smile on my face. Anything was better than the silence I had been enduring sandwiched between the icy glares of those two women.

*   *   *

I got a reprieve the next day when Essa dropped back to have a planning chat with Tuan.

Graysea startled me when she spoke. 'Do you still care for her?'

'Who?' I said lamely.

'Conor, I'm stupid but not that stupid.'

'You're not stupid,' I said, 'you're the cleverest mermaid I know.'

'And how many mermaids do you know?'

'Well, that's not the point.'

'No it's not,' she said. 'The point, which you seem to be avoiding, is whether or not you still have feelings for Essa.'

'Well, that's complicated.'

'And you think I am too stupid to understand. Is that it?'

'No,' I said looking around hoping that a pack of wolves would attack and get me out of this conversation. 'Essa and I have a history.'

'You still haven't answered the question,' she said and then mercifully continued so I didn't have to. 'I just don't understand. When you were on the island with me she was engaged to that Turlow fella – right?'

'Yes.'

'So she is mad at you for being with me when she was engaged to somebody else. That doesn't seem fair.'

'Well, ah …'

'And she hits you all the time.'

'Well, I don't know about all the time … but often.'

'And is it true that last summer she tried to kill you?'

'She … she didn't try to kill me,' I stammered, 'she was just part of a plot to have me killed.'

Graysea shook her head and sighed. 'And people think I'm stupid.' She kicked her horse and sped ahead.

Gosh, I thought, when you add it all up like that she had a point. Araf had silently sidled up next to me. I turned to him and said, 'What do you think, big guy?'

'About what?'

'About my women problems?'

'I think,' the Imp said, 'I was more comfortable with questions about crop rotation.'

* * *

I got another reprieve that night when they both ignored me. Essa finally came up to me after dinner. A firefly sat on her shoulder illuminating one side of her face.

'Your little mackerel is lounging in her barrel.'

'She is not a mackerel, she's a Mertain. She is a healer from the Grotto of Health on the Mertain islands. And she is not lounging. She is recharging – preparing herself so she can help any of us in case we are injured.'

Essa was taken aback by my tone. She stood.

'Maybe you would prefer to join her in her bath tub.'

'Maybe I would. At least she's not mad at me all the time and she never hits me with sticks.'

Essa looked at me like she had never seen me before. I stood and faced her. 'Anyway, I haven't seen you for an hour or so – are you sure you haven't gotten engaged to someone in that time?'

Essa looked like she had been slapped. 'You promised you would never mention that.'

'No I didn't. *You* told me not to mention it. I never got a chance to promise. Well, maybe I'm tired of being bossed around by you.'

It didn't take long for the surprised Essa to kick back. 'Fine,' she hissed. 'I hope you and your fish will be happy together.' She stomped away, leaving her firefly to flutter around confused, and then she turned. I took a step back expecting a blow. 'Now that I think of it, you and your fish are perfect together – because you're an eel.'

I tried riding with Araf the next day but he insisted on continuing his dissertation on agriculture so I dropped to the rear to have a long over-due catch-up with Tuan. Araf didn't even notice I was gone.

'Councillor Tuan,' I said, 'I'm surprised you're still in Duir. Don't get me wrong, it's great having you around, but shouldn't you be in the Pinelands impressing girls with your super-Pooka act?'

'Girls,' Tuan sighed, 'are the reason I am here.'

'Oh?' I said with my inflection going up.

'My mother wants me to marry.'

'Oh,' I said with my tone going down.

'Yes, Mother wants me to marry a mousy woman from the council.'

'When you say mousy, Tuan, do you mean she's small or that she changes into a mouse?'

'Both.'

'And you're not into rodents?'

'It's not that ...'

'What is it then?'

Tuan looked around to make sure no one could overhear. 'There's this girl in Castle Duir.'

'Oh, do tell.'

'This mustn't get back to my mother.'

'I'll be as quiet as the mouse you're cheating on.'

Tuan snarled at me then straightened up in his saddle and said, 'Never mind.'

'No, no, I'm sorry T. I promise I won't make jokes. Who is she?'

'I better not say.'

'Aw come on, what's the big secret?'

'She is an Imp.'

'Oh, and Mom's not into mixed marriages?'

'Mother thinks that Pooka power as strong as mine shouldn't be diluted.'

'So she's hooking you up with a mouse?'

Tuan shrugged.

'Why don't you just tell your mother to get stuffed?' I said. 'You do realise you're a dragon?'

Tuan laughed. 'Being one of the most powerful creatures in The Land has little sway with my mother.'

'Yeah, big guy,' I said, nodding. 'I guess I can relate to that.'

We made good time and got to the base of Mount Cas on the evening of the third day. As we set up a base camp, I expected Dad to make some comment like, 'Aren't you glad we left at dawn?' but all he gave me was that look that said it all. Where do parents learn that all-encompassing look? Is there some sort of instructional video you get when you have your first kid? Does it come with a mirror to practise in?

Gerard brought out a couple of bottles of dark red wine. It was fabulous. I wasn't worried about the upcoming confrontation until I tasted it. When Gerard brings out the special stuff then you know there's going to be hard times ahead.

That night I dreamt about the Oracle. He leaned forward into the light. As his wispy grey hair blew in a breeze, his wrinkled eyes smiled at me. Then with the tiniest flick of the wrist, he sent me sailing off the side of Mount Cas. I screamed all the way down until the moment I hit the ground. I sat bolt upright in my tent and stared into the darkness, willing my breath to calm and my heartbeat to return to normal. Was that just a nightmare, I wondered – or a prophecy?

We set out long before dawn. Every campaign seemed to be getting earlier and earlier. Soon we would be leaving before we even went to bed. Essa, Tuan, Gerard and Graysea stayed behind in base camp. The last time I climbed Mount Cas it took us three days but that was in the winter. This day was dry and sunny and we set a ridiculous pace. We hiked way into the cold night and found a place to camp on the opposite side of the mountain from where the Yew House stood. We didn't know if the Oracle had enough power over the mountain to cause avalanches, but didn't want to chance it.

Mom sat next to me over what was laughingly called dinner. 'Are you OK?' she asked.

'Other than the fact that my legs feel like jelly after that climb and I have to sleep on cold hard stone on the edge of a cliff the night before I re-tangle with the nastiest sorcerer I have ever seen – yeah, I'm fine.'

'I was talking about your girlfriend problems.'

'Oh, well I don't think I have a problem any more 'cause after this trip I probably won't have any girlfriends.'

'Well, that would suit me fine. Then I would have you all to myself.'

She put her arm around me and gave me a hug that made me feel like I was five. I placed my head on her shoulder and closed my eyes. I was awfully tired. I don't know if it was Shadowmagic or just Mom magic but the next thing I noticed I was in my sleeping roll and Dahy was shaking me awake and offering me a cup of breakfast tea.

If yesterday my legs felt like jelly, today they felt like lead. Dad, in front, set a stride that some would call a sprint. We only slowed down on the parts of the trail that were visible from the Yew House above, then we would press against the rock face and slink along in single file so as not to be seen.

It was nightfall when we reached the wide shelf where, months before, Araf and I had almost fallen off the side when caught in an ice slide. If we had been spotted during our ascent, we figured that the Brownie guards would be there to meet us as they had done the last time. Since they didn't, we decided to camp the night there and meet the Oracle guy in the morning. We didn't risk a fire but Nieve got some water hot using gold wire she incanted over and then dropped into the kettle. Dad hadn't spoken all day and looked kinda off. I made him a cup of tea and then pointed to the stone wall next to him. 'Excuse me sir, is this seat taken?' I asked.

He was lost in thought but then finally said, 'No,' without even noticing any irony in the question.

'You OK, Dad?'

He noticed me then and said, 'Yeah, yeah, I'm fine.'

'You know I'm old enough that you don't have to play Strong Dad for me. You're obviously distracted. What's on your mind?'

'It's nothing. I'm just mulling over tomorrow.'

'Or maybe you're nervous about meeting a mother that you hardly even remember?'

Dad looked shocked – then smiled. 'How did you get so smart?'

'I actually have experience in meeting a mother for the first time in adulthood, remember?'

'Yeah, I guess you do. Any advice?'

'Yes, I do,' I said, sipping my tea. 'Get some rest, 'cause it's nothing you can prepare for.'

*   *   *

The next morning as we walked to the front porch of the Yew House, Dahy threw something off the side of the mountain. There was no one outside the house so we opened the door and let ourselves in. We obviously caught everyone napping. A Brownie saw us in the hallway and yelped like a puppy that had accidentally been trodden on. He scurried away and it wasn't long before there was a wall of armed Brownies between us and the end of the hallway.

I recognised the tall Brownie in front as the one that, months earlier, I had pinned to a wall by the neck. I knew that these guys weren't as tough as they looked.

'You are not welcome here,' tall guy said.

'We are not looking for a welcome. We are looking for Macha,' Dahy said.

They all flinched in surprise at the mention of her name. If I had any doubts that my grandmother was there they left me then.

Tall guy repeated himself. 'You are not welcome here.' This time he emphasised his words by levelling a crossbow at us. Or I should say started to level a crossbow at us, because he never got it even close to level. As soon as the weapon started to rise, Mom and Nieve performed some kind of magic. There was a flash of light and the Brownies went down like bowling pins.

'Strike,' I said, and Dad gave me a smile.

We walked the length of that dark stone cold corridor until we reached the yew door with the Eioho Rune carved into the finish.

'Ready?' Dahy asked and in response we fanned out into our rehearsed positions.

The room beyond was exactly as it had been the last time I was there. Light shining from round discs set into the ceiling refused to bounce off the pitch-black floors. On a dais in the centre of the room, bathed in shadows, sat the Oracle on his Yew Throne. You couldn't see his face, only the outline of his hair and robe as both fluttered in the wind that whistled through the room.

We stepped through the doorway, spread out and awaited Dahy's command.

I stood at the back and tried to be as inconspicuous as possible. I wasn't interested in having my conversation with him pick up where it had last left off.

'Where is Macha?' Dahy demanded.

Oracle guy leaned in, letting the light hit his face for the first time. It was as effective as any lighting trick done in a Hollywood horror movie and I'm sure he did it for its impact. The next time I had to scare the crap out of someone I decided I would hire this guy to do my special effects.

'The last time I spoke to a Lord of Duir, he had manners,' he said, looking at Dahy, but then he turned to my father and said, 'and the last time I spoke to a Lord of Duir, he spoke for himself.'

'I have had reports of the reception you offered my son at his last visit,' Dad said, 'the time for manners was then.'

The Oracle cast an eye in my direction. *I wish you'd leave me out of this, Dad*, I thought to myself.

'As for my general's question,' Dad continued, 'I shall repeat it. Where is my mother?'

The Oracle started to smile and then sat back into the shadows and laughed. One of those bad-guy laughs that irritates everyone except the laugher. We waited.

'I never thought I would see the day when the Lord of Duir would climb up my mountain only to say, 'I want my mommy.' He laughed again. I'm glad it was dark in there 'cause I smiled too.

'Conor, welcome back,' he said, wiping the smile from my face, 'I see you have brought your Imp with you. But where are the archer and the Druid? Oh dear, did I kill them?'

'No,' I said trying hard not to let my voice wobble. 'Not that you didn't try.'

'Impudent as ever,' he said in a tone that almost had some warmth in it. 'Someday that will get you killed.'

'I would advise you not to threaten my son.' Dad obviously had heard something different in his tone than I had.

'Or what? Your Shadowwitch will cover me with sap?' Oracle looked to Mom and Nieve. 'Which one of you is the Daughter of Hazel that practises the forbidden lore?'

Mom stepped forward but didn't say a word.

'So who are you?' the Oracle asked pointing to Nieve.

'I am Nieve of Duir and I too want my mommy.'

That should have been funny, but the way my aunt said it made it sound menacing. Saying that, Oracle guy laughed – apparently he doesn't menace easily.

'Well, now that we are all introduced,' the Oracle said rising, 'it is time for you to go. Apologise to my Brownies on your way out.'

Dahy is not the kind of guy who lets emotions get in the way of his tactics but on this day, the arrogance of the Oracle and the anticipation of seeing Macha again got the best of him and he jumped the gun. He raised his banta and stepped towards the dais. All I remember of the next ten seconds was: G-forces, wind and pain. By the time I came back to my senses I saw that I, like everyone in my party, was pinned to the wall by a force of wind that made our faces scrunch up like astronauts during take-off. When I finally could force my head to move, I saw I was three feet off the ground.

Oracle guy was standing in front of his dais with his arms outstretched as dust and leaves swirled around him under the light from the ceiling discs. If before I thought that this plan was maybe a mistake, now, seeing Oracle guy looking so all-powerful, I wondered if this was actually a fatal mistake.

'What arrogance,' he said; his voice, carried on the wind, was so loud it made my head vibrate against the stone. 'To imagine that sticks and swords – and even Shadowmagic are enough to defeat ME!'

SEVEN

DIDDO

I tried to speak and then yell but the wind seemed to push my
words back in to my head. I wasn't party to the entire plan for this
campaign but I was pretty sure that getting pinned to a wall
wasn't part of it. I could only hope that we got back on schedule before
Oracle guy killed us.

The pressure of the wind was so intense that I was starting to have
trouble breathing. Now that would be one for the books – being suffo-
cated because of too much air. I looked to my left. Not because I wanted
to, it was just that I could no longer keep my head straight. As my
cheek pressed painfully against the stone wall I saw Mom moving her
hand into her pouch. I don't know how she did it, I couldn't move a
thing. Her hand came out with one of those gold and amber balls that
she had invented. It was a hybrid weapon made from Real and
Shadowmagic. I had never seen it fail to kick the crap out of anybody
she had lobbed it at. Ever so slowly she brought her hand to her lips
and incanted directly onto the ball. The gold and amber glowed and
then despite the force of the wind it started towards the Oracle – but
not for long. I heard him laugh through the howl as Mom's bomb came
back at her and silently exploded as it reached her chest. Normally I
would have had to turn my head or cover my face at the brightness of
it but all I could do was close my eyes. When the flash blindness finally

receded to small black dots I saw that Mom was out cold. At least, I hoped she was just unconscious. For all I could tell she might have been dead.

The horror of that thought hit me at the same time as all the noise stopped. Blessed quiet filled the room as the wind and pressure ceased and I slid down the wall onto my feet. Mom crumpled to the ground. As I ran to her I heard Dahy's voice shouting the word that I had taught him, 'Ninja!' My training kicked in and I slowed to a crawl. Mom looked like she was still breathing so I slowly turned to see that the rest of my team had already gently flowed into action. Oracle guy looked very confused. He waved his arms and flicked his wrists but in the windless chamber he seemed powerless.

I breathed a small sigh of relief, making sure I created no air current. We had all been working on the assumption that Oracle guy's powers came from wind. It seemed not to be such a stretch after seeing how the Mertain harvested power from ocean currents. Days before, Tuan in the form of a crow had carried a parcel of stuff that Mom, Essa, Nieve and Fand had come up with. I know it sounds silly but it was like magic expanding cavity filler. As a test they had set off a teaspoon of it in Castle Duir. It filled the room with an amber coloured substance with the consistency of light pumice. It kept going into the hallway and for a minute Mom was worried that it was going to take over the entire floor. There were people back at the castle who were still trying to dig out the room.

Tuan had reconnoitred the mountain and discovered two large holes at about the height of the Yew Throne Room. We figured that if we plugged those holes, the wind in the chamber would stop and Oracle guy would be powerless. The Shadowmagic baton Dahy threw off the mountain just before we entered the Yew House was Essa's signal to ride Dragon Tuan up to the summit, detonate the parcels and draught-proof the throne room. If Dahy hadn't jumped the gun maybe we could have done all this without so much pain.

Once the wind stopped, subduing Oracle guy was easier than any of us expected. He was still trying to figure out what had happened to his powers when Nieve came up behind him and pinned him with one of her paralysing specials. As soon as he was incapacitated Dad and Nieve went to Mom. Nieve placed her hands on both sides of Mom's head. She was like that for a long time before she said, 'I think she will be fine, but I would like to get her to your mermaid as quickly as we can.' I didn't like hearing Nieve using words like 'I think'. I sat and held Mom's hand, not knowing what else to do.

Dahy made us all jump when he shouted into the darkness, 'MACHA.' Just the sound of that one word spoke the decades of loss the old warrior felt. Dad rose and stood beside him.

A form in a black hooded cloak seemed to appear out of the darkness as it stepped into the light. It made the hairs stand up on the back of my neck. I was half expecting the hood to drop back to reveal the face of The Grim Reaper. As if we were still in our ninja mode none of us even breathed. The reaper raised her hands and pushed back the hood. Amber hair, just like Nieve's, fell across her face. As she pushed it away I saw her eyes. They weren't dark brown like Dad's and his sister's but pale blue – like mine. Then I remembered something that Spideog had said to me: 'You have your grandmother's eyes, you know.'

No one said a word. Like a bunch of zombies, we all stood and stared at each other until I just couldn't stand it any more.

'Are you my grandmother?' I asked.

She smiled at me then. It was strange. Not the grandmotherly smile that I had ever imagined. She was far too young looking and beautiful for that. 'Yes, I am,' she said. 'I see you received my message.' She looked to my father.

Dad stood stock still as she walked up to him, placed her hands on both sides of his face and tenderly kissed him on the forehead. 'I thought, my son, I had lost you to the Real World and when I heard Conor's tale of your strange illness, I thought I had lost you again. But here you are and looking fit and well.'

Dad was at a loss for words. They stared at each other and as every agonisingly long second passed, my father seemed to lose a year. When he finally spoke he sounded like a five-year-old. 'Where have you been?'

Tears welled up in Macha's eyes. 'Here my son, locked in this dreadful place.'

Nieve stepped into the light and quietly said, 'Hello Mother.'

Macha looked to her daughter and then took her hand. 'You have become a proper sorceress, my child.'

Nieve could only nod yes.

Macha hugged her and then turned to Dahy. 'General, can you take me away from here?'

'I can, my Queen,' Dahy said dropping to one knee.

My grandmother walked over to him, knelt down and placed her hand on his cheek. 'Not your queen, Diddo, only me, Macha.'

'Did you just call Dahy Diddo?' I blurted.

Dahy stood and gave me a look that made me think he was going to snap me in half. And considering that Dahy *can* snap me in half, it was a pretty scary look.

'Hey,' I said, raising my hands in a gesture of surrender, 'I'm sorry to break this tearful reunion, but we have an injured Shadowwitch here and I for one would sorely like to get the hell off this mountain. What do you say, guys?'

Dahy kicked into leader mode, with a little more chest-puffing gusto than normal. If I didn't know better, I would have said he was showing off. 'How many others are in the house?' he asked Macha.

'There are seven Brownies that live here,' she replied, 'but I think one is away from the mountain.'

'Well, we took out six on the way in. Conor and Nieve, go see if the ones in the hallway are still down.'

Nieve and I opened the door and peeped around the corner. The pile of Brownies were still there but they were moaning and moving. Nieve dashed up and quickly poked all of them in the butt with one of her pins while I picked up the weapons.

The tall Brownie opened his eyes fully and then a look of panic crossed his face. 'I cannot move my legs! What have you done to me?'

'Relax,' I said, trying to pat him on the shoulder but he took a swipe at me when I got close. 'Seriously, chill. You just got pinned by one of my aunt's specials. You'll be fine in a couple of hours.' He sat up and then pushed himself along the floor until he had his back to the wall. I felt sorry for him.

'Where is Lugh?'

'Lugh?'

'Yes, the master of this house is Lugh. Lord of All. Where is he?'

As if to answer the Brownie's question my party came into the hall-way. Dad was carrying Mom and Araf had 'The Lord of All' hoisted over his shoulder like a bag of manure. Most of the Brownies, now conscious, watched with open mouths as their master was carried to the front door.

'Did you kill him?' the tall Brownie asked.

'No,' I said, 'but we are taking him back to Castle Duir. You're free now. Go back to the Brownielands, he no longer has a hold on you.'

He smiled at me then. One of those smiles that lets you know that the smile-ee knows something you don't. 'As long as he lives,' he said, 'we will never be free. We will await Lord Lugh's return. It will not be long.'

I left them with a canteen of water and they left me with a feeling of … doom.

Outside, Dragon Tuan began to ferry all of us off the mountain. Early on in his dragon life, Tuan made it perfectly clear that he was not going to be an air taxi service for the House of Duir so this was a favour I really appreciated. I had no desire to ever see this mountain again and getting off it as fast as I could was a top priority.

Dad and the unconscious Mom went first, then Araf and the uncon-scious Lugh, followed by Dahy and Nieve. As my grandmother and I waited for Tuan to return she said, 'I worried about you trying to get blood from a fire worm, I worried that I led you on an impossible task – never in my life did I imagine that you could enslave a dragon.'

As I started to reply, Dragon Tuan flapped up onto the shelf. We had to cover our faces to protect our eyes from the swirling dust. 'Oh, I wish he was my slave,' I shouted over the noise, 'then I wouldn't have to walk as much as I do.'

I took Macha by the arm and led her over to the green lizard. 'Grandma, I would like you to meet my friend, Councillor Tuan.' Tuan rocked his head back and blew a puff of fire that finished with a perfect smoke ring.

Macha bravely walked right up to him and patted him on the snout like he was a horse. Tuan dropped to one knee and lowered his head as Grandma said, 'I am honoured to meet you, Councillor.'

The flight down was the scariest ride I had ever had with a dragon – and that included when Dragon Red tried to kill me. Tuan was so tired from all the upping and downing that he pretty much just dive-bombed off the mountain. I screamed like a little girl all the way down but Grandma didn't make a peep even during the G-force-inducing last second level-out. When Tuan became Tuan again I promised I would punch him for that – immediately after I threw up.

I was expecting Macha to be open-mouthed like everyone else who witnesses Tuan's transformation for the first time but when I looked at her, she had her eyes closed and her arms outstretched. I heard a snort from Acorn – looking not like the bold stallion that often gives me a hard time but more like a colt approaching his mother. That's when I noticed that all the horses were doing the same thing. They slowly approached Macha with their heads down and then shivered with delight as my grandmother caressed each one of them. It was remarkable to watch. It was like she was part of them but also above them, like a horse god. Macha the Horse Enchantress – the yews had given her the power over horses, and there in front of us was the proof. She hugged each horse in turn. The look on her face was like a mother returning to her children after a long time away.

Mom was awake, sitting with her back against a rock, with a blanket on her lap and drinking willow tea when I found her. She gave me one of those forced smiles that let me know she was OK.

'Hey Mom, it's good to see you with your eyes open. You gave me a scare. How do you feel?'

'Good, considering. Your Graysea is a remarkable healer. I'm starting to see what you see in her. I don't think she is as witless as she would have us believe.'

'That depends on which side of her brain she is using.'

'Seriously?'

I nodded and she laughed but stopped right away and held her chest in pain.

'I think you need another session. I'll see if she's up for it.'

I found Graysea and asked her if she could gill-up for Mom again. She said she was on her way to do just that now that she had seen that everyone else was OK. Out of the corner of my eye I saw Gerard's big fist hand me a glass.

'Is that wine?'

'It's something a bit stronger,' the big man replied.

'Good,' I said, knocking whatever it was back in one. The whole world wobbled like I was about to do a flashback on a bad sitcom.

When I could risk moving again without falling over, Gerard said, 'More?'

'Yes please,' I replied holding out my glass.

'You wouldn't have any of your wine with you, Gerard?' Macha asked, coming over to the fire. Behind her stood all of the horses, like groupies awaiting the beckon of a prima donna rock star.

'You know I do.' Gerard poured her a glass and she took a sip with her eyes closed like it was a chalice filled with the elixir of youth.

'Oh, it has been so long,' she sighed.

'It has indeed,' Gerard said. 'You look good for a dead woman.'

Macha smiled at him but he didn't return it. 'I'm surprised to find you here, winemaker. Thank you for coming to save me.'

'Spend no thanks on me, my Queen, I came because of Dahy. I would follow that man to the gates of hell if he wished it and I will defend him from all harm.'

'Well then let us both make sure no harm befalls him,' Macha said, still smiling but not as much.

'Let's,' Gerard said. 'More wine?'

'No,' she said, placing her hand over the top of her glass. 'I have been long away from your wine for too long. Like your company, too much of it would be overly intoxicating, but thank you.' She handed me her empty glass and walked away.

'So you two have met?' I asked Gerard.

'Oh yes,' he replied. 'We have met.'

Tuan offered to fly Mom home. She must have still felt pretty banged up 'cause she accepted. Oracle guy was given something that put him into a coma, and then stuffed in the barrel that just yesterday had held Graysea's saltwater bath. For good measure he also had a paralysing pin stuck in his neck. I wanted to feel sorry for him but I once had travelled on a wagon in a barrel and I'm sure that it was much more comfortable to do it unconscious. Still I made sure he had a few pillows in there with him.

As Gerard hammered the barrel lid closed I said, 'Well, Lugh is lugh-ed up tight.'

'What did you say?' Dad asked, and I also noticed that everyone else had stopped in their tracks.

'It was a joke. You know, locked up tight?'

'But what did you call him?'

'Lugh, the Brownies said Oracle guy's name is Lugh.'

Gerard stepped back like the barrel was about to bite him. All eyes shot to Macha.

'Is this true?' Dad asked.

She looked surprised. 'I thought you knew.'

Nieve stepped up to Macha. She had a look on her face I'm pretty sure I had never seen before. She looked – frightened. 'Are you saying that the one who had kept you prisoner for all of these years is Lugh of the Samildanack?'

'Yes,' Macha replied.

Gerard actually stumbled into me when he heard this. I steadied him and said, 'What does this mean?'

'It means,' he said, looking at the mallet in his hand, 'that in that barrel, I have just sealed – a god.'

EIGHT

LUGH

Macha rode in front on the way home. Not because she was a queen, but because we quickly figured out that if she wasn't in front then all of the horses would keep trying to look around to see where she was. Dahy rode with her and the two of them chatted the entire time like teenagers on the telephone. Dad and Nieve rode wordlessly behind. If Macha had any guilt in leaving them motherless for so long, she showed no sign of now trying to make up for it. I couldn't see their faces but their body language in the saddle made them look like unhappy children forced to ride a pony at a birthday party.

I was behind them with Araf – tantamount to riding alone – and behind me rode my girls, Essa and Graysea. I didn't hear them share even one syllable and I wasn't about to turn around to see if they were OK. The tension permeated the entire group to the point where Gerard, riding in the cart at the rear, was singing dirges as opposed to his usual ditties.

It wasn't just the imminent outbreak of a cat fight that was upsetting the group, it was like the whole party was spooked. And the thing that was spooking everybody was the guy locked in the barrel on Gerard's cart. I needed more details on this 'Lugh being a god' thing but Mom and Nieve were not in a talkative mood and Gerard didn't like talking to me when Essa was around, in case she thought he was taking sides. (Even a father can be afraid of a child like Essa.) And I could never get Dahy away from Macha.

At night I tried to entice Grandma into talking about Lugh and her imprisonment but she said that it was far too horrid to speak of. She went to bed early every night with a horse standing guard outside her tent.

I was reduced to spending my days staring at the scenery – not a bad thing. Spring had fully sprung and summer was once again upon The Land. The vibrancy, the … aliveness permeated everything, and – if they were like me – everyone. The feeling – no, not the feeling – the knowledge that you can live for ever came from days like these.

News of Queen Macha's return preceded us. An hour before our arrival at Castle Duir a rumble and a cloud of dust could be seen in the distance. Dahy and Dad sped to the front and were about to throw us all into battle stations when Macha said, 'There is no need for concern. It is just my children.'

Sensing the Horse Enchantress's approach, the horses in Castle Duir's stables had become anxious. The master of the stables, having heard that Macha was soon to arrive, left open all the stable doors and let the horses run to meet their mistress.

Macha dismounted and walked ahead of us as the sound of thundering hooves intensified. What a scary and magnificent sight: Macha standing alone in an open field, her hands held out as a stampede of galloping horses came directly at her. As they got nearer they squeezed together so as to be close to the Horse Enchantress as they passed. I thought for sure they were going to trample her but at the last second they parted. They swarmed past her like a flock of birds – her hands brushing the charging beasts. They swung around for another pass. They did this three times and I'm sure they would have done it all day if Macha hadn't put a stop to it. She raised her yew wand and the horses swung in front of her and then stopped as if at attention. From the middle of the herd came a huge silver stallion. I recognised him. The stable master had told me that his name was Echo because he was the spitting image of the horse that sired him – King Finn's horse. When I once asked if I could ride him I was told that he was wild – unrideable. Yet here he was, head down, offering himself to the Horse Enchantress. Macha patted him on the snout and Echo quivered. Then, fast as a tree monkey, she mounted him and galloped towards Castle Duir. The herd whinnied and followed – leaving us behind.

We didn't even have to kick our horses to catch up; Acorn leapt to join the herd whether I liked it or not. I galloped up next to Dad and Nieve. 'I'll say this about Grandma,' I shouted into the dust-filled air, 'she knows how to make an entrance.'

Mom had not been idle with the days that travelling dragonback had given her. She had prepared a special airtight cell and had a Leprechaun smith make a pair of silver gloves/handcuffs that would hopefully render Lugh unable to whip up a breeze or any magic. While Dad and Nieve secured the prisoner, I went in search of answers.

I found Fand in the Shadowmagic laboratory she set up with Mom. She was stirring something in a small pot.

'If that's a super delicate Shadowpotion you're working on,' I said, 'I can come back later.'

'It's tea,' Fand replied reaching under the counter and producing two cups. 'Would you like some?'

'Oh, yes, thank you.'

She stirred the pot with a gold stick and when she removed it all of the used tea leaves had stuck to it. She mumbled something and the leaves all fell into a rubbish bin. Then she poured us both a cup.

'What brings you down here, Prince Conor?'

'I want to know who Lugh is.'

That query made Fand lean back and sigh. She took a sip of tea before she answered. 'Maybe that is the wrong question,' she said. 'Maybe you should be asking: what is Lugh? A question that many have been asking for a long time. Or maybe the most important question is: who is the man we have locked up in the windless cell? I'm not certain he is Lugh.'

'Gerard said he was a god.'

'A god. One man's god is another man's false idol. What is a god?'

'I don't want to interrupt you mid-flow, Fand, but do you think maybe you could answer one of my questions with something other than another question?'

Fand laughed; it was not something I had ever heard her do before. It was sweet. 'Sorry Conor, it is just that this appearance of Lugh, or whoever he is, has raised many questions.'

'OK,' I said, 'let's forget about this Oracle guy we have locked up. What are the old stories about Lugh?'

'Well, that depends on who you are talking to. Among most of the houses of Tir na Nog, Lugh is thought of simply as Banbha's consort.'

Banbha, there was that name again. Whenever there are dark tales of the early days of The Land, Banbha is the name that usually comes up. 'Banbha was one of the three original sisters that founded Tir na Nog right?'

Fand nodded.

'So Lugh was Banbha's husband.'

'This was long before customs such as marriage came about but that is essentially the idea.'

'So why did Gerard call him a god?'

'Well, as you know, many in The Land worship one or all of the sisters as gods. Leprechauns pray to Ériu for gold and most Imps venerate Fódla.'

'I've seen Araf make a blessing gesture when hears Fódla's name.'

'Yes, I imagine he does,' she said. 'But others in The Land revere Lugh as much more than a consort. There are many, especially the Brownies, who look at him as a deity.'

'Why?'

'Most in The Land believe that the first land of Tir na Nog was Duir – the Oaklands – and this was found or created by Ériu who then sent for her sisters who in turn created other lands.'

'I know this much,' I said. 'Fódla created Ur – the Heatherlands – and Banbha created Iodhadh – the Yewlands.'

'That is what the Faeries believe, but lore reads differently. Most Brownies believe that the Yewlands were first and that Lugh was already there when Banbha found it. They say Banbha was the first sister and that Ériu and Fódla betrayed and banished her. What happened to Banbha no one knows but when she vanished – so did Lugh.'

'Yeah, but the Brownies will believe anything if it gets them closer to Duir's gold.'

'It is not only the Brownies that believe that Lugh was The First – my mother believed it too.'

Fand's mother was Maeve. As the inventor of Shadowmagic, she had decimated a forest to steal sap, the blood of trees, to fuel a war against my grandfather and the House of Duir. At almost her moment of triumph she blew herself up along with many of the Fili, with a giant Shadowspell that went terribly wrong.

'No offence, Fand, but your mother had a lot of wrong ideas.'

'I will not argue with you on that point, Conor, but she once told me that she learned these tales from an Elf.'

'So the Elves are in the Lugh-is-a-god camp too?'

'Who can tell what the Elves think. I've never had a conversation with an Elf that was not about trees or wine. They do know the yews though. They are the only ones that can pass through the Yewlands unmolested by the trees.'

'I've been to this Oracle guy's house. You know it's made from yew wood.'

Fand thought and then poured us both some more tea. 'As I said, Conor, this man raises many more questions than he answers.'

When I got back to my room Ruby was waiting for me. She was sitting in my big leather chair.

'How did you get in here?'

It was like a scene from a spy movie.

'I walked in. I'm blind, not lame.'

'Well, you can walk right out again. Last time you came here I almost got killed by a tree and then again by your father and now that I think of it, I'm pretty sure your grandmother wants to kill me too.'

'Yeah,' she said with no intention of leaving, 'sorry about that.'

'Are you?'

'Of course I am. It was very nice of you to take me riding and I'm sorry you got hurt and I'm sorry you got in trouble.'

I took a hard look at her with her huge sunglasses and her feet sticking straight out from my chair and I reminded myself that even though she acted like she was forty-two, she was still only twelve. 'OK,' I said, 'and I'm sorry you had to fend for yourself outside the wall. Let's not do that again. OK?'

'Deal,' she said, sticking her hand out, not quite towards me, to shake.

'Deal,' I said, shaking. 'So what are you doing in my room?'

'I need something Daddy and Grandma can't give me.'

'Hold on, isn't this how we got into trouble last time?'

'Relax, O'Neil,' she said, and I had to laugh. She sounded so much like her father. 'I just need some advice.'

'About what?'

'I want to be a sorceress. How do I do it?'

'Oh, I don't really know.'

'Who does?'

'Well, my mother is a sorceress.'

'OK,' she said, sliding off the chair and striding to the door. I just stood there befuddled until she turned around and said, 'Are you coming or what?'

Now I promised myself the last time Ruby got me into trouble that I wouldn't allow myself to be bossed around by someone a third of my weight, but I had planned to check in on Mom later anyway, and I really wouldn't mind knowing how she had become a sorceress myself.

'Fine,' I said, taking her by the hand. 'We'll see if she's busy.'

While Dad was ill, Mom had set up the room next to the master bedroom as her queenly office. As we drew closer I saw that the door was ajar and stuck my nose through the crack.

Mom was down on all fours behind her desk, I could only see her feet sticking out. I heard what sounded like hammering and then wood splintering.

I walked over and said, 'Are we doing a little remodelling?' It wasn't Mom. Macha popped up so quick that I jumped and almost fell over Ruby.

'Ow,' Ruby squealed. 'Watch it. There's a blind kid here you know.'

Macha initially looked like I had just caught her with a hand in the cookie jar, but when she noticed Ruby she became very interested. She walked around the desk, took Ruby's sunglasses off, then placed her hands on both sides of her head and tilted her face up so she could look closely into Ruby's sightless eyes.

'Hey, who are you?' Ruby demanded.

I wasn't quite sure what to do. Macha was being awfully rough with Ruby, but then she was my grandmother and what do I know about how to treat kids? Still, it was plain to see that Ruby didn't like it. When I saw Ruby cock her blind stick back ready for a strike, I grabbed her wrist and got between the two of them. I never saw Ruby hit anybody with her stick but I'd bet money that she was good at it. Macha looked angrily at me.

'Sorry Macha,' I said trying to explain myself, 'but she can't see, you know.'

'I do know,' Macha said. 'I have been waiting for you, little girl.'

'Is my mother here?' I asked.

'No,' Macha answered absently, never taking her eyes off Ruby.

'Are you waiting for her?'

Macha didn't even answer that. I walked over and looked behind the desk. There was a dagger on the floor and the skirting board had been prised away from the wall.

'What were you doing behind the desk?' When she didn't answer me I said, 'Does Deirdre know you are here?'

That seemed to get her attention. She started to answer then looked to Ruby then back to me like she was trying to make up her mind about something. 'Oh well,' she said reaching into a fold on the side of her dress. 'I was hoping that I could be around for longer but it seems that now is the time.' Out of a pocket she produced a lace fan that she snapped open like a Spanish lady at the opera. With a flick of her wrist the door to Mom's room slammed closed in a way that looked a lot like the magic that Oracle guy used on the mountain. I started to ask her how she had done that but I only got as far as, 'How …' before her fan flicked in my direction and I sailed across the room and into the wall. By the time I came to my senses she was sitting on my chest painfully holding my nose. I opened my mouth to gasp for air and when I did I felt and tasted some kind of liquid hitting the back of my throat. She then pushed my mouth closed and jumped on my chest – it was swallow or drown. It tasted awful and I coughed and rolled onto my side as Macha jumped off me.

Ruby let loose one of her migraine-inducing screams. Macha was on her in an instant, covering her mouth, snatching her stick and throwing it across the room. I got up to help her but Macha shouted at me, 'Stay where you are!' And I did. Unlike one of my aunt's paralysing pins it wasn't like I couldn't move, it was like my body just didn't want to move.

'What have you done to me?' I said, desperately trying to move my legs.

'That fluid I placed in your mouth was horse … well you are better off not knowing what part of a horse it was but now that you have ingested it, I have control of your body. Sit,' she commanded and I dropped hard on my butt. 'See?'

'What do you want?'

Ruby squirmed and then Macha pulled her hand away in pain. Ruby had obviously bitten her. As she started to scream again Macha gave her a hard slap. Shock and then tears came to the poor kid's face. She went instantly from the woman-child that bosses me around to an all-too-fragile twelve-year old.

'What I want,' Macha said, looking at her bitten hand, 'is this child to be silent.' She reached into her pocket and produced a handkerchief. 'Come over here, Conor, and gag her.'

I almost laughed. There was no way I was going to do that but even as the smirk hit my face my body stood up, took the handkerchief from my puppet-master grandmother and pulled it across the child's mouth.

Macha said, 'Make sure it's tight,' and, despite every cell in my brain telling me to stop, I pulled it tighter before I tied it in the back. A muffled cry of pain came from Ruby and the only thing I could do was say 'Sorry.'

Macha went back down onto the floor and recommenced ripping up the skirting boards. I looked to the door and felt that with

Macha's attention elsewhere I could pick up Ruby and make a break for the door, but when I tried Macha said, 'Don't even think about leaving.'

'What are you doing?' I tried to ask and was surprised to find I could.

Macha didn't stand up but from the floor said, 'Do you know whose room this is?'

'Yes, it's my mother's.'

'Do you know whose room this was before your mother?'

'No.'

There was another sound of splintering and wrenching of wood. I heard Macha exclaim, 'Ah ha,' followed by the sound of scraping. Macha then reappeared from behind the desk in a plume of dust and loudly dropped on it – a leather-bound manuscript. 'This room was once Ona's lair.'

Holy cow, I said to myself. A manuscript chock full of Ona's predictions. As if her prophecies hadn't caused enough problems – here were a stack more.

'Where are they keeping Lord Lugh?'

I didn't want to answer her but found myself saying, 'The guest chambers, one floor down.'

'Come. Bring the girl and make sure you are not seen.'

My possession was the strangest thing. I was still able to do ordinary things as long as they didn't seem to contradict the will of Macha. Before we left the room I picked up Ruby's sunglasses and put them on her face. I pushed her hair back and told her everything would be OK just before I gruffly dragged her by the arm. I stuck my head through a crack in the door and saw a guard on his usual patrol. I tried to shout to him but instead I unwillingly ducked back inside the room and waited for him to pass. When he had gone I led us past my room and down the servants' staircase.

The floor had been cleared of all guests except Lugh. There were two guards posted outside the door and another two walking a patrol. Macha waited for one of the patrol guards to come past and blew him hard into the wall with her fan. I was surprised his head didn't crack open.

Macha pointed to the unconscious guard and said, 'Take his sword and kill the other one.'

'No,' I said. I was proud of myself when that came out. All the way down the steps I had been incanting a Fili meditation chant and was beginning to think I was getting control again.

Macha spun on me, 'I said ... take his sword and kill the other guard.'

I felt a strange nauseous pressure building in my stomach and chest. 'I ... I will not ... not kill one of my ... my own guards.'

'Kneel, Conor,' Macha commanded and I dropped to my knees. 'You will ...'

With all of my will power I struck at her. I wanted to get her in the head and hopefully knock her out against the wall but she hissed, 'Stop,' just as I began to move and I only succeeded in slapping Ona's manuscript out of her hand.

'You cannot breathe,' she said to me and instantly the breath that I had been taking at that second stopped in my throat. My lungs and diaphragm seemed to still be working but nothing could get past my throat. She rolled me on my back and said, 'You will kill that guard or I will have you strangle the little girl. Do you understand?'

I nodded, clutching my throat, I couldn't even gasp. Tears flooded from under Ruby's Ray-Bans as she whimpered, lost in this confusing darkness.

'Good,' Macha said, 'then breathe.'

Precious air filled my lungs as I propped myself up on all fours.

'Now hand me the manuscript and kill that guard.'

I did as she commanded and handed her Ona's book from the floor, then went to the fallen guard. As I reached for his sword I said, 'Please Grandma, don't make me do this.'

'Fine,' she said, 'take the stick. Just get it done.'

I walked the length of the hall past the two guards at the door and met the second patrolling guard around the corner. He was an Imp and was surprised to see me.

'Prince Conor,' he said, 'I ... I don't think you are supposed to be here.'

'Relax, I'm the Prince of Hazel and Oak,' I said and then pointed behind him saying, 'and he's the King of Duir.'

The guard looked around and I clocked him high in the neck with the banta. I caught him before his head hit the stone floor. I wished I had a willow tea bag to put in his pocket for when he woke up.

I was just about to walk back to the guest room/cell when the two guards sailed past me in the air and smashed into the wall in front of me. Two more victims of my grandmother's hurricane fan. Since Macha was out of vision I felt I could make a run for it but just as I took my first steps to leave Macha said, 'Conor,' and I could do nothing but follow that voice. Macha was at the door holding Ruby in front of her by both shoulders.

'Search the guards for keys,' she said and I obeyed.

I tried not to give the keys to her but was unsuccessful in operating my hand. I did manage to get a question out. 'Why are you doing this?'

'Why am I following Lugh's plan? Because dear boy, he is a god and not to would be a sin.'

'But you also helped Cialtie, didn't you? Why help him?'

Macha turned the key in the lock. We walked in and then opened the inner doors that had been newly constructed to prevent any wind from entering the room when the outer door was opened. Lugh was chained to the bed. A muslin cloth across his mouth stopped him from even whistling and his hands were shackled in silver gloves. Macha pointed to him.

'I did not want to take sides when it came to my children,' Macha said, 'but Lugh insisted on helping – his son.'

NINE

ONA'S BOOK

Cialtie is not Finn's son, he's Lugh's son. He's Dad's half-brother. I imagine news like that would shock some people but as soon she said it I thought, *that makes sense.* Sure Dad and Uncle Cialtie looked alike, but I could never get over how differently their minds worked. Now that I had met Lugh and then heard this news – it all started to make sense.

Lugh, still under the influence of one of my mother's specials, was awake but looked pretty out of it. Grandma ordered me to unlock his custom-made silver gloves and chains. Macha then stood over him and fanned his face like a trainer between rounds in a boxing match. The more the wind hit his face the clearer his eyes became until he reached out and grabbed her fan. Macha backed away as Lugh ripped the sheets from the bed. In one hand he fluttered the fan towards his chest. Even to me, uneducated in the ways of wind magic, it looked like he was building up energy. In his other hand he swirled the sheet around his head. He then turned to the window that only days before had been bricked up and let loose a scream. A blast of air blew the bricks and the window right out into the night.

'Open the doors,' Lugh commanded.

Macha looked to me and said, 'Well? Open them.'

I opened the inner and outer doors and a breeze flew through the room. Lugh stood on the bed feeding on the air. The colour returned to his cheeks and lips; it almost looked like he grew muscles and a couple of inches. He took in a huge gasp of air, then turned and vomited out of the blown-out window. He turned back to us, wiping his mouth on his sleeve and smiling.

'Excuse me, my love, I had to purge the poisons that that Shadowwitch had filled my body with.'

Macha let go of Ruby and ran into Lugh's arms. As they embraced, Ruby made a pitiful attempt to find her way out of the room. Macha saw her as Lugh's embrace spun her around. 'Stop her,' she said and I did.

'I'm sorry Ruby,' I whispered, 'she has control of me but I'll find a way to get us out of this. I promise.' She buried her face in my stomach and hugged me. I hugged her back, glad that I could at least do that but desperately wishing I could do more.

I looked up to see Macha kissing Lugh. If there was any part of me that wasn't sure that these two were in love and in league with each other, it was dispelled then. Anybody that kisses someone immediately after seeing him puke … well … that's true love.

'How long have I been here?' Lugh asked.

'Not even a day, my love.'

'And so soon you have found the girl, Ona's writings and the bows?'

'The girl came to me as I was searching for the book. As for the bows – they are in the armoury. Not far from here in the north wing.'

'What do you want with Ruby?' I said.

Lugh looked shocked and turned to Macha. 'I thought you had him under your control.'

'His body and will are mine, my love, but that impudent tongue is harder to subdue.'

Lugh laughed. 'Well, he is your grandson. Would you prefer if I killed him?'

I felt Ruby's shoulders begin to shake, or maybe it was me.

'There is no need, my lord, he knows no more than they will deduce when we are gone.'

'He is a loose end and you know how I hate loose ends, but I understand your sentimentality, I will do it.'

'No,' she said, and for a moment I thought she was about to fight for me until she said, 'Let me. Sleep.'

I felt my knees buckle but then I heard her speak again and my body stopped its race to unconsciousness just long enough to hear my own grandmother say, 'Sleep and *never* awaken.'

Sleep and never awaken. That refrain followed me down into the well of unconsciousness. *Sleep and never awaken.* Unlike the well of despair the oak tree had dragged me into, this well had no sides, no bottom, no top. No nothing. Calling it a well was wrong. I wasn't falling, because falling would imply I fell from somewhere and there was no longer a somewhere to fall from. As I existed in a void so lacking anything, my mind tried to grasp onto thoughts. Thoughts of a world where senses actually sensed things. Things, tangibles, objects began to be impossible for me to even imagine. As I fell … no, drifted … even words to represent anything were slipping away from me. I forced myself to at least remember where I was.

I remembered going to an old cemetery once when I was a kid and seeing names on gravestones where underneath it said 'Sleeping', and I remembered thinking, *they're not sleeping – they're dead.* But now I was doomed to an eternal sleep and I thought maybe those stonemasons got it right. But I didn't think that for long because my thoughts were fleeting. Or maybe my thoughts were long thoughts and just seemed fleeting because I had thought them for a long, long time. Never is a long time to not awaken. What is time when the last hour on the clock – is for ever?

It was only a matter of time in that un-land of timelessness before I would go mad. Either that or sail into nothingness. *Madness or nothingness, here's a choice you don't get every day*, said the man existing in a realm with no days.

Vivid memories filled my thoughts. I was a child. I was sick. My mother sang to me in a language so old I couldn't understand it but I felt it healing me. My mother placed a cool compress on my brow. I could feel her smile but not see it. Then it came to me that this couldn't be a memory. My mother was never there when I was a child. These memories were false and I was losing it. I was slipping into a world made only of my own making. Madness – that's what my mind had chosen – an eternity of madness. I wanted to shout and wondered if I could. I almost felt my lungs expand, I …

I shot up in bed and screamed, 'NO!' The cold compress fell onto my lap. Mom had her arms around me in a second.

'It's all right, Conor,' my mother said, patting my hair. 'You're safe, you're with me, it's Deirdre.'

I reached up and felt her hand – the first sensation I had actually felt in … I don't know how long. I looked and she was there. I touched her face and she felt real.

'Mother?' I asked and was surprised at the sound of my own voice. It was deep. I felt my chin and the stubble there brought me forward in time – I was not a boy – I was a man. 'Where am I?'

'You're safe, my son, you're with me in your own room.'

I looked around and saw the knife-marked wood panelling and said, 'In Duir?'

'Yes.'

I pushed myself higher in the bed. The world around me solidified as the dream world I had been lost in receded. 'How long have I been gone?'

'You have been asleep for two days. We could not wake you.'

'Two days?'

'Yes I have been worried about you. How do you feel?'

'Only two days? I feel like I have been gone for … ever.' I smiled then as that blessed relief hit me. The relief that comes with the realisation that the nightmare was only a dream and its burdens were only an illusion. But as the problems of the dream realm faded into smoke, the waking world crashed down on me. 'Ruby!' I swung my legs out of the bed. 'Where is she?'

'Easy, Conor,' Mom said placing her hand on my shoulders, 'She's missing. We have scoured the castle and the grounds but she is gone.'

'They have her.'

'Who?'

'Macha and Lugh.'

I dropped back into bed and for the first time looked in to my mother's eyes. She had that haggard look that moms get when their children are sick. I never saw it when I was young but it was instantly recognisable now. I reached up and touched the side of her face. 'I'm OK, Mom. I think. Macha forced some sort of essence of horse down my throat and I was like a zombie.' When she looked confused I said, 'It was like she had control over me and I had to do what she told me to do. The last thing she commanded me to do was, "Sleep and never awaken." I thought she had killed me.'

Mom thought for a bit. 'That would make sense. Her power over you only lasted for as long as the horse essence was in your system.'

'You're saying the reason I woke up was that … I, like, sobered up from the spell?'

'Basically.'

So I filled Mom in on how I caught Macha searching her room and finding Ona's book of prophecies and then how they said they wanted the book, the girl and the bows.

'The bows on the wall of the armoury – the ones left by the dead Fili – are they the bows they were talking about?'

'Yes,' she said, 'they are gone.'

'All of them?'

She nodded.

The door opened and when Brendan stuck his face in the room and saw me awake, he ran up to the bed.

'Where is she?'

He had the same look on his face that I had seen on my mother's just moments before, except he looked a lot worse. Brendan wore the frantic face of a parent who had lost a child and I could tell just by looking at him that he had been playing worst-case scenarios over and over in his head for the last two days. 'I don't know where she is. Macha and Lugh took her.'

'Why?'

'I don't know,' I said. 'I do know that it was not a whim. From the way they were talking, it seemed that kidnapping Ruby and stealing the yew bows was part of a plan.'

Brendan sat on the bed and hung his head. 'But it doesn't make sense.'

'I know,' I said, placing my hand on his shoulder, but he shook it off. This was Detective Fallon and he wasn't looking for sympathy.

'Taking my Ruby makes no sense, but taking the bows makes no sense either. I once asked Master Spideog if I could use his bow and he said I could not. I thought he meant I wasn't allowed but he said I couldn't because I wouldn't be strong enough to pull the string back. I scoffed, so he handed over his bow with that all knowing look on his face and – he was right. I couldn't even bend the bow an inch. Spideog explained to me that a yew bow changes its tension in tune with the archer that owns it. The wood is flexible when the string is drawn back and then stiffens when the arrow is being released. Only the person who has been judged by a yew, and given that piece of wood, can operate that bow. Those bows should be useless to all except their owners.'

'Lugh has proved himself to be a master of yew wood so who knows what his plans for the bows are,' Mom said. 'One thing is clear: it seems that we have all been unwitting players in Macha and Lugh's puppet play. And we have lost an important clue – the book of Ona's writings that Macha found in my office.'

A memory flashed in my mind. A memory of something that seemed like years ago but as I smiled, I knew it was just from a couple of days earlier. I reached for my pocket and then realised I was in bedclothes. 'Where are my clothes?'

Mom pointed to a chair in the corner of the room. I ran to them and found in a pocket what I was looking for.

'When I was under Macha's control I had a moment when I almost broke free. I slapped Ona's book from her hand, but then she regained control and made me pick it up for her.' I held out a small ripped piece of paper. 'But as I was giving it back, I ripped a corner from a page.'

Mom removed an amber stone that was clipped onto the collar of her robe. It was one of her Shadowmagic book clips. She attached it to the sliver of paper I had given her and almost instantly a ghost of a book appeared in her hand. It was a shimmering translucent replica of the one I had seen Macha remove from under Mom's desk.

'Is that a book full of predictions from that prophet Ona you guys keep talking about?' Brendan asked.

'Yes,' Mom said, 'I believe it is.'

'So with this maybe we can learn why they took my little girl?'

'Perhaps,' Mom said, holding the Shadowbook like it was about to explode, 'but are you sure you wish to learn whatever else this contains?'

'I don't care. I want my daughter back.'

'As do I, Brendan,' Mom said, but learning one's future is not a soothing thing. It has sent many over the brink of madness. In others, like Cialtie, foreknowledge is the fruit that eventually distils into evil.

'I will read it,' said a woman as she entered through the door. She was beautiful, tall with a huge mane of dark brown hair tied back into a ponytail; her cheekbones were high and rosy with youth. She stormed in like she owned the place but I had never seen her before.

'I had thought my future was already written and almost ended,' she said in a voice so pure that I almost wanted to hear her sing. 'I now have a new lease of life and I shall use it for the sole purpose of saving Ruby. The only fear I have of that book is that it will not tell me where the child is.'

Brendan stood up and faced the woman, then crouched down a bit to look directly in her eyes and said, 'Mom?'

TEN

NORA

L ater in the council room it was decided that Fand should read
Macha's manuscript. Everyone agreed that knowledge of the
future was a dangerous thing. Fand would tell us if she found
anything relevant that could help us find Ruby and then, using her Fili
mind juju, she would forget the rest.

'You can do that?' I asked

'No problem-o,' she replied using the phrase I had taught her.

'Wow, can you teach me? I've done a couple of stupid things in my
day that I'd like to forget.' Fand smiled but never took her eyes from the
book.

'Only a couple?' Essa piped in.

Dad held his hands up and shot both Essa and me a look that said,
not now kids. 'Let's keep focused people. If Fand can find out why my
mother took the girl then maybe we can figure out where she is.
Deirdre, could you perform a Shadowcasting?'

'I will try,' Mom said, 'but Shadowcasting is not a reliable locator. It
is good at predicting events but as a tracking spell it is often lacking.'

'Surely she is either on Mount Cas or in the Reedlands,' Nora said.
It still unnerved me a bit when Brendan's mother spoke. Her voice was
completely different and she was so young looking.

When Nora heard that her granddaughter had been kidnapped she
immediately went to Tuan and took him up on his offer of dragon's

blood to make her young again. She said she needed to be strong if she was going to fight to get her Ruby back. It was going to take me a while before I got used to equating the wise deliberate old lady, whom I had originally met, with this jumpy, young and, I'm a bit embarrassed to say, fanciable woman before me.

'The Reedlands is not a place to enter blindly,' Dahy said.

'I can vouch for that,' I said. 'I almost died the two times I went there and you know what they say: the third time's the charm.'

'And I believe,' Dahy continued, 'that our assault on Mount Cas was easy because it was part of Lugh's plan. If he were to oppose us he could defend his Yew House easily – with disastrous results for us.'

'We can't just sit here!' Nora banged the table then closed her eyes to compose herself. 'I apologise, with this body comes the hormones of the young.'

'No apologies are necessary,' Dad said. 'Deirdre, how long will it take to set up a Shadowcasting?'

'Two days,' she said, reaching across and taking Nora's hand. 'That is the very soonest I could be ready.'

'Then I'm going to the Yewlands,' Brendan said.

'What?' was pretty much the reply from everyone there.

'If we are going to war, I want a bow. A yew bow. Spideog said I could have his if the yews allowed it. I'm going to ask the yews for his bow.'

'Brendan, love,' Nieve said, 'it takes decades of study to prepare for a judgement by a yew.'

Brendan stood. 'I have studied with the greatest archer in The Land. He has deemed me worthy and my quest is to save my daughter. I dare them to find me unworthy.'

I expected someone to object but that statement shut everyone up.

'I'll take you,' I said.

'Conor,' Mom said, 'you cannot enter Ioho. The yews will kill you.'

'Oh, don't worry, Mom. I ain't going in there again. I'll just take him to the edge and wait. I know the way.'

'I will accompany them,' Araf said, and as usual everybody jumped a bit.

'Great,' I said, 'I'll have somebody to talk to while I wait.'

'I'm going too,' Nora said. Before anybody could say that that was a bad idea she explained: 'This new body has too much energy for me to be sitting at home and waiting. I'll travel with my son.'

Later that night I stuck my nose into Dad's study. He was busy doing kingy stuff: allotting the stipends to all of the different kingdoms. He looked up and said, 'Do you want me to give more gold to the Vinelands and maybe Essa will start talking to you again?'

'I don't think you have that kind of money, Dad.'

'You looking for advice on your love life?'

'You got any?'

'Sure,' he said. 'Go ask your mother.'

He dropped his pen and got serious. 'Do you think Brendan's mother will be OK with you outside of the castle walls?'

'Well, back in the Real World when, like, a thousand cops invaded her home, she hardly even batted an eyelid. She's coping with all of the turmoil around here pretty well and Brendan says she's a good rider. So I think she'll be fine. And anyway, if she is anything like her son – she'll come whether I let her or not.'

'All right then. I've had scouts patrolling for quite a while now and it's been library-quiet out that way but still – be careful, OK?'

'Hey Dad, it's me. What kind of trouble can I get into?'

The look from Dad said it all.

'Dad? I want to tell you something but I don't know how to, other than to just say it.'

'Shoot.'

'Before Macha left she told me that Lugh was Cialtie's father.'

Dad leaned forward and did that thing he always did when he was deep in thought. He reached up with his left hand and attempted to take off his reading glasses, except he didn't have glasses on. Since his dragon blood rebirth he didn't need them any more. He smiled self-consciously then covered his mouth with his hand. That's the other thing he does when he's deliberating or stressed. It's like he's stopping himself from saying anything stupid before he has thoroughly thought things out. Finally he leaned back and said, 'Good.'

'Good?'

'Conor, it is an awful thing to hate one's brother. Now I only have to hate half of him.'

We left at, you guessed it, dawn. Even when my parents weren't going on the trip, I had to get up before the sun. I didn't try to talk Brendan into leaving later. He was not in the kind of mood where you could joke. Not that I blamed him. The way my luck with women is going these days I will probably never have kids, but I imagine having your child kidnapped is enough to literally drive you crazy. I was impressed with how well Brendan was holding up. He was acting with a swift and deliberate purpose that was hard to keep up with but on the whole he was pretty together. Saying that, he reminded me of the cartoon character that after falling off a cliff only needs one pebble to hit him in the head before he crumbles into tiny pieces. I didn't want to be that pebble.

Nora I could no longer read. She seemed to be all over the place. She was a good rider. The stable master, hearing that she was new to The Land, gave her a gentle mare that she instantly returned like he was a used-car dealer who had tried to sell her a lemon. He shrugged and gave her a frisky stallion named Blackberry. Nora handled him but it took some time. Periodically Blackberry would try it on with his novice rider and bolt or try to rear onto his hind legs, but Nora was up to the challenge and finally got him to calm down. When I felt it was safe enough I rode next to her.

'You've got your hands full with that one,' I said, pointing to her horse.

'I've raised a son,' she said with a nod towards Brendan. 'You just have to set some boundaries and then they're OK.'

'Yes, but baby Brendan couldn't throw you and break your neck.'

'You would be surprised as to what kind of trouble baby Brendan could get into,' Nora replied looking over to her son, who smiled with the forced smile of a man who just couldn't come up with a real one. We slowed a bit to leave him with his thoughts.

'I wish there was more I could do to assure him … and you … that Ruby will be all right.'

'You can't assure that, Conor,' Nora said, 'that's the problem.'

'No, I guess I can't. But she just has to be.'

'Amen to that.'

Blackberry snorted then threw his head back while almost sidestepping into me. Nora tightened the reins and pulled him back into line like an old pro.

'How are you doing?' I asked.

'Ol' Blackberry and I will be OK,' she said patting his neck, 'we just need to get to know each other.'

'No I mean how are *you* doing?'

She laughed a sad laugh. 'Well my body is raging with hormones and wild energy – it's like I went through puberty in a day. And then there is the anger – they took my little Ruby. I want to kill them with a baseball bat – you know?'

I nodded yes – 'cause I did too.

'And then there's this place. Just because I believed in Tir na Nog all of my life doesn't mean I *always* believed it. When you have faith in things that everyone else thinks are crazy, you often have doubts. But here I am. And it's more than just seeing Tir na Nog or smelling it or touching it … I feel it … inside. I feel …'

I waited for her to find the word. When she failed I offered it to her. 'Immortal?'

'Yes,' she said.

We rode in silence for a while. This route was almost identical to the first trip I had ever taken in The Land, except that this time there was no one firing arrows at the back of my head. This was the same place where I first felt what Nora was feeling now. This was where I first learned that beech trees were gossipy and where I caught my first sight of the white plumes of the mountain ash. Riding, with my mother behind me, this was where the vitalising energy of The Land transformed me. It was here where I, too, learned how it felt to live for ever.

We followed the path. It was mid-morning when we came to water.

'River Lugar,' Araf said as he dismounted and then washed his face in the water in a way that seemed more like an ablution.

'Lugar?' Nora said. 'That sounds too much like Lugh for my liking.'

'I was taught that the river was named after him,' Araf said.

'If only the man were as easy to find as the river,' Brendan said.

We followed the river path until we came to the Duir boathouse. Inside were half a dozen small riverboats. Dad said we could take the royal barge with its gold-plated rudder that would propel us if we incanted to it in Ogham. Back at the castle I made Araf learn the mumbo jumbo. Having Dad teach me words in an ancient language was too much like my schooldays.

Just because we were being propelled by magic didn't mean that we were breaking any speedboat records. The ride was less like a high-speed chase from a spy movie and more like that old science experiment where you put a sliver of soap on the back of a bit of balsa wood. But as the old saying goes, beggars who don't want to row can't be choosers – or something like that.

There was plenty of light left in the day but we had been warned by everyone that if you have to disturb a yew, then it should be done in the morning. I wanted to know why. 'Do they get grumpy in the afternoons?' – No one was sure but as a matter of statistics more people survived a yew judging in the morning than in the afternoon. If I were a yew it would probably be the other way around. Gerard had told me that there was one of his luxury camping huts just before the last bend in the river before the Yewlands. I pointed it out to Araf and he beached the barge. After wrapping the rope from the boat around the base of a holly bush we all filed past and touched the tree to say thanks. Nora watched us and then did the same. A small squeal came out of her that at first I thought was a cry of pain but then I saw her face – she was elated.

'You OK?' I asked.

'That tree just said, "You're welcome."'

'Not all of them are so nice,' I warned. 'Trust me on that.'

Dinner was a stew prepared by the chef from Castle Duir that we only had to heat in the fireplace of Gerard's hut. It was the closest thing The Land has to compare with a TV dinner. Actually if any of the Real World's TV dinners were this good there wouldn't be any restaurants. Nora ate like she had never seen food before. I worried that she might just eat her spoon.

She caught us all staring and apologised. 'I haven't had an appetite like this in fifty years.' And then continued eating like there was no tomorrow.

Brendan was outside and the only one of us not chowing down.

'You nervous, Detective?' I asked.

'I'd be lying if I said no.'

'Are you ready for this?'

'I'd better be.'

'No,' I said, 'I mean, have you prepared?'

'Spideog, and others, told me that a judgement for an archer is different than for a sorceress. Sorceresses must prepare for their specialty but an archer need only be a good archer and Clathandian.'

'Clathandian? What does that mean?'

'There is no good English word for it. Even Nieve's gold ear thingy doesn't come up with a translation. The best I could get would be pure of spirit.'

'And is your spirit pure?'

'I once asked Spideog how I could tell if I was in the state of Clathandian and he said, "That is for the yew to decide."'

'That's a drag. It would be nice if you could have, like, a breathalyser test before you risked your neck in there.'

Brendan laughed, the first laugh I had heard from him since Ruby was taken. 'There's a project for your mother – a Clathandian breathalyser. She'd make a fortune.'

But Brendan's good humour didn't last long and his attention drifted away to his daughter and his task ahead. Before I left him alone I said, 'Try and eat something, my friend. I think you might need your strength tomorrow.'

Back inside, Nora, who had eaten probably half of the stew, was asking Araf if she could finish off his leftovers.

'Your nice new body is going to get a bit big around the middle if you keep that up,' I said.

'You know, Conor, I have been given a new life and I think this time around, I'm not going to care.' She smiled the same smile I saw on an older version of the same woman when she saw her son return to her; but then a shadow crossed the face. The smile vanished, replaced by a look of guilt – guilt for even allowing a smile. 'First we find Ruby,' she said.

'You mentioned before that you had believed in Tir na Nog. How did you even know about it? How did you know you were Hawathiee?'

'Hawathiee? What does that mean?'

Oh sorry, Hawathiee means ... of The Land. It's like in the Real World when we say human.'

'Oh, my father told me that his father and his father's father, going back to before there were calendars or even letters to write on them, told him that we came from a race that was banished from paradise for going against the laws of nature. He, and my mother too, believed that my ancestors arrived in the Real World in a barbarous age when Ireland was a vast forest. The newly banished arrivals were humbled by their experience and chose not to subjugate the barbarians of that island. Instead they chose to teach them.'

'Druids,' I said.

'That is what my parents called themselves and their most important rule for me was to keep the faith. Their grandparents had come over to America during the Irish Famine. Keeping the faith was hard in the new world but just as I was about to lose mine to the modern world, I found a man whose parents had handed down to him the same family lore. We were made for each other. I had a friend who once said that rooms were brighter when we were in one together. He was my soulmate.'

'Brendan's father?'

'Yes,' she said with a sigh, 'I lost him to war. He didn't want to leave me but back then they made young men go to war. I was left alone to raise a son on my own. We did well until Brendan became a teen. Then he started to think that what I believed was crazy. I didn't have his father to help me and I feared that I was going to be the first in all of that time to break the chain. To have a son who lost the faith.' She looked out the doorway to her son pacing in the twilight. 'But here I am. If not for you and all of the chaos you have inflicted on my son and my family – my heritage would have been lost.' She reached across and placed her hand on my cheek.

'You're welcome,' I said.

She gave me another one of those forced little laughs. The only kind of laugh I was going to get until Ruby was found.

I heard Araf douse the fire. I shouted out the door. 'Hey copper, you sleepin' tonight?'

'Yeah, I'll be in in a little while,' Brendan called back.

I curled up in one of Gerard's bunks – oh so much better than sleeping on hard ground – and was asleep before I heard him come in.

I awoke feeling great. I made another mental note in the imaginary book *Things to Do When Life Calms Down Around Here*. I promised myself that I would get a map from Essa's dad and take a trip where I only slept in Gerard huts every night. Then I wondered if things ever did calm down around here. I washed in the River Lugar and shared a breakfast with Araf. The other two were too nervous to eat. Brendan sat waiting in the boat, his legs jittering, while Araf and I closed up the hut.

The river bent ahead and if I remembered rightly, as soon as we took it, we would be in view of the two guardian yews that stood on top of the boulders on either side of the river.

The yews were as scary and magnificent as I remembered. A cold sweat dripped down my back as I recalled the first time I had been here, as part of a desperate escape from my uncle's dungeon. Then we travelled silently through the Yewlands hoping the deadly trees would take no notice. And they didn't. I had no desire or intention of repeating that gambit and I worried for my friend who would soon be entering that forest and asking one of those trees to judge his worth – knowing that the price of failure was death.

I saw a small sandy bank on the left and told Araf to steer to it. He was just about to turn the rudder when I saw him bring his hand up fast to his neck like he was swatting a mosquito. He then stared at me wide eyed and fell over the side of the boat.

I was so shocked I didn't do anything for a second, but when I saw him bobbing face down in the water I started to take off the Lawnmower – the Sword of Duir – and dive in after him. As I was fiddling with the buckle, a sharp pain in my neck made me turn. That's when every muscle in my body turned to jelly. I crumpled into the bottom of the barge, but before the world went black I had a chance to see in what direction the boat was heading. It was sailing straight and true into – the Yewlands.

ELEVEN

JUDGEMENT

The stinging in my neck was the first thing I noticed when I awoke. I reached to the source of the pain and removed a gold dart that I only had a couple of seconds to inspect before it dissolved into smoke and ash between my fingers. I was alone in the barge. I knew where I was. The green light filtering through the canopy confirmed I was deep in the Yewlands. I popped my nose up over the side of the barge like a soldier sticking his head out from a foxhole. My travelling companions were nowhere to be seen. Where were they? What had happened? What should I do? I definitely should get out of the Yewlands but what about Brendan and Nora? And Araf? If he fell face down in the water with the same thing that got me in the neck then … he must have drowned. What the hell happened?

Think, Conor. I had to assume that the barge wasn't too far into the Yewlands so if I could get it turned around without disturbing the yews, then I could get back and find Araf, or at least his body. If Brendan and Nora survived then that's the only place I could think that they would know to go.

I crawled to the stern of the barge and then kicked myself, remembering that I hadn't paid attention when my father was teaching Araf the magic words in Ogham that made the rudder propel the boat. Dad had said I should learn the ancient vocabulary too, but as usual I didn't listen. Gods I hate it when he's right.

I could see the entrance to the Yewlands off in the distance. I maybe could have swum that far if the current was with me, but against it I didn't think I could make it. I knew instinctively I couldn't walk along the banks of the river without the yews noticing me. I was literally up you-know-what creek without a paddle. My only other option was to push the barge back into the river and hope the current would eventually take me through the Yewlands without notice. What I would do on the other side was something I would have to deal with when, and if, I got there. This was the least worst of all my options. I hated the thought of abandoning my friends but I really had no way of getting to them even if I had a clue where they were – which I didn't.

All my deliberations were for naught, 'cause when I placed one foot on land to push off the barge, every muscle in my body froze up. No, that's not right, my muscles were fine, I could feel them trying to work. It was my bones. I felt like I was being pushed and pulled from the inside. I tried to yell but as soon as noise began to fly out of my mouth my jaw slammed shut making an audible clack of my molars, which thankfully didn't crack. With one leg still in the barge and the other on the shore, I stiffened up like a guy in a body-cast from some old black and white comedy movie. I stood like this for a minute, only able to grunt and move my eyeballs and then was mercifully released. I instantly tried to push the barge out but as soon as I tried I was turned into a human board again. Whatever was holding me made me wait for several minutes before I was once again released. This time I dove into the river. My thinking (I admit there really wasn't much thinking) was that if I could get some distance between me and whoever my puppet master was, I could get away. What happened was that I froze up again – this time in water with a heavy sword around my waist. I dropped like a stone. I hit the riverbed and said loud in my head, *OK, I get it. I'll go where you want me to.* I didn't know if that message went anywhere but I hoped that it went somewhere soon. I had about twenty seconds of air left in me.

In fact, I had forty seconds' worth. Just as I thought my lungs were going to erupt blowing my head clean off, I was released and scrambled to the surface gasping and spluttering. I waded to the bank and asked the air, 'Now what?'

What was a telekinetic game of hot and cold. Every time I went in a direction that my unseen force didn't want me to go I froze up, usually falling over. I then had to change direction until I found the way it wanted me to go. This went on for quite a while. I was walking deep into the yew forest. Not good. I racked my brains trying to remember if I had ever heard a story about someone accidentally wandering into the Yewlands and making it out alive. I hadn't, 'cause I suspected it had never happened. Finally I decided I wasn't going to play this stupid game any more if it just meant I was prolonging my ultimate demise, so I sat down and refused to move. That's when my possessor actually took control of my walking. Unkind invisible hands manipulated individual bones in my body forcing one foot in front of the other, and pressing so much strain on my knees and hips that I finally screamed and agreed to continue my guided walk on my own steam.

Eventually the powers that drove me only had to give my wrist a tweak to keep me in the right direction. All the while I kept a look out for Brendan and Nora. I hadn't seen what had happened to them. They might have fallen in the water like Araf but if they were in here I worried most about Nora. She was unprepared for this – but then again, so was I. I decided to worry about myself for a while.

After what seemed like hours I came to a point where my spirit guide would only let me walk into a tree. Ahead was a yew that to me looked exactly like the zillions of ones I had been forced to walk past. I took a deep breath and said to myself *this is it*. After all I had been through, I was going to be killed alone in the forest by a tree. I pondered the philosophical implications of this. If a man falls over in a forest without making any noise is he really dead? I thought about that for a nanosecond and decided the answer was – yes. I felt a Fergalish smile light my face and wished my old cuz was here with me to share the joke.

I placed my hand on the bark and said, 'What do you want?'

You would think a tree that was older than most dinosaur fossils would be beyond shocking, but I think I puzzled this one. A voice came into my head that was surprisingly pleasant.

You never know with trees. Some of them just reach into your brain and take what they want to know. Others can't do that and wait for you to speak or at least think purposefully. With the reputation the yews had and the psychic push and pull I had just been through, I was expecting an unpleasant experience. Instead, my mind was filled with a voice (or a feeling of a voice) that was neither male nor female – or maybe it was both.

'*What do I want?*'

'Yeah, what do you what? You just pushed and pulled me like a hundred miles and now here I am so what the hell do you want?'

'*It is we that should be asking that question of you,*' the tree said, using 'we' like it was the 'royal we'.

'Yeah,' I said, 'well, I asked first.'

That was the last thing I got to say for a while. If I can presume to know anything about yew tree behaviour I would have to guess that he/she got tired of this banter and just decided to go straight to the source. Pain and deafening white noise erupted from inside my head. I dropped to my knees, presumably screaming but I couldn't hear anything over the internal commotion. I started to reach for my head but then stopped 'cause I was afraid that I wouldn't find any top to my skull. I had a mental image of my brain being exposed and tree branches spinning around in my grey matter like it was soup.

'*You are terrified,*' the tree said, '*yet you jest.*'

'You discovered my secret,' I said through gritted teeth.

'*I do not understand you. Explain.*'

'Get it over with.'

I remembered seeing an old gory horror movie where people's heads exploded and their insides splattered all over the room. I was now sure I was seconds away from decorating the yew forest in the same way. When I didn't answer the tree, the pressure got worse, something I would have thought was impossible. I remembered the look on Spideog's face when he realised he would have to go back to the Yewlands to be re-judged. The yews had subsequently found him again worthy but at the time he was sure he was going to die. The pain I experienced was so intense that I knew that if I somehow survived, I would choose death rather than go through this again.

'*You wish I should begin the judgement?*' the androgynous voice of the tree shouted in my head.

'Whatever.'

The bush turned the egg beater in my head up to the frappe setting.

'*Once again,*' the tree said, '*you are speaking in contrast to your true feelings.*'

'OK, you want my true feelings? I don't want to be here. I didn't mean to come into the Yewlands, I'm not prepared for a judgement and I don't want to die. And while I'm at it could you loosen the vice on my head?'

Surprisingly he/she did and as soon as I could think properly I said, 'I was unconscious when I entered the Yewlands. Has any of your kind seen my companions?'

'*We are yew. We are not here to answer your questions.*'

'But the woman that was with me, she is unprepared for judgement. Her son was with me too but at least he was trained by Master Spideog.'

'*You speak of the archer?*'

'Yes, his name is Brendan. Have you seen him?'

'*The archer you call Brendan spoke of Spideog's death. Is this true?*'

'It is,' I said, 'I witnessed it.'

'*Let us see,*' the tree said and the pain returned with a vengeance. My brain, like a crappy video movie, fast-forwarded my memories. Stopping, then zooming ahead until once again I was forced to watch Spideog fall. Then the pain in my head subsided, only to be replaced by an ache in my chest.

'*He was killed by your knife,*' said the voice of the tree in my head, but only the male voice. In my defence the female voice said, '*But not by his hand.*'

What followed was a debate in a language (or maybe even a different plane) that I couldn't begin to fathom. As best I could figure out it was a domestic squabble. Where before the voices of the tree were speaking as one, now the male and female were backing and forthing. As it got faster and seemingly more heated I wondered what would happen if they didn't come to a conclusion. Can a tree get a divorce from itself? I wondered if there were yew trees all over the forest where the male and female parts hadn't spoken to each other for centuries.

Finally the squabble ended. *'We shall judge you now.'*

'What happened to the others?'

'You will be judged.'

'I don't want to be judged, I'm not ready to be judged. I want to know what happened to my friends.'

'If you will not be judged then you must eat of the fruit.'

A bough laden with red berries drifted before my face as I felt the bones in my arm and hand reach for the poisonous fruit.

'Who died and made you god?'

The push on my arm stopped as the male voice said with a sneer, *'We are before the gods. We have been makers of gods.'*

'I hope you didn't make Lugh.'

'What do you know of Lugh?' the tree demanded but didn't wait for an answer. Once again the pain dropped me to my knees as my encounters with the Oracle of Mount Cas were replayed for me and the timber sticking into my brain.

When it was done I felt the female tree ask, *'Why would Macha take the child?'*

'I don't know.'

'You will be judged,' they both said.

'I'm not ready.'

'No matter,' the yew replied, *'we must know what you know.'*

This wasn't like the memories that flash before your eyes when you think you are going to die. I've been that close to death enough times since arriving at The Land to know what that is like. No, this remembering was like re-experiencing my life over again. Not just the sights and sounds and smells but also the emotions. The warmth of my father's embrace, the sting of bullying at school, the pain of constantly moving home and the abandonment of friends. The loneliness of being the new kid. The excitement of that first kiss, puberty – oh gods, not again. The attack in my living room that changed my life for ever. The terror of Cialtie. The discovery of my mother – her first approving smile. The other smile – Fergal's smile and then no ... Fergal's death. I knelt, paralysed, re-living my life and all the way through, stabbing like knives and caressing like velvet, were my emotions. My loves, my hates, my losses. Essa, Araf, Tuan, Spideog, Frank, Jesse, Brendan, Ruuuuuby.

When it ended I was in shock. Like when I killed my first person (an event I just replayed seconds ago) I was unable to think. I was unable to … be. I was emotionally spent, not even able to weep.

'*What can we give you?*' the tree spoke into my throbbing head.

I hardly heard the question. I fell prostrate on the ground. 'I don't ever want to go through that again,' I moaned.

'*Very well,*' the tree replied, '*from this day forth, you, Conor of Duir, have safe passage through Ioho.*'

I rolled over on my back and looked up at the branches and needles blocking out the sky. I tried to imagine ever coming here again and knew I never would. At least not alone. 'And any of my travelling companions?'

'*And all that travel with you,*' the tree said without hesitation.

I rolled over and propped myself up on all fours. Then, making sure I didn't touch the tree, I tried to stand. I was wobbly but intact. I felt the tug of the yew and placed my hands once again on its rough bark.

'*You have given us much to contemplate, Prince of Hazel and Oak. We would like to give you a gift but you are unworthy of a wand or bow.*' The female voice then spoke. '*We have seen that you often fight with banta. Accept this with our blessing. May it serve you well.*' The familiar sound that I now know is moisture being sucked from wood, followed by a crack, preceded a large branch falling from the tree. I picked up the staff and cracked off the smaller branches that were withering even as I looked at it. It wouldn't take much work at all to make this into a proper banta stick. I guess I was supposed to say thank you but instead I placed my hand again on the trunk and asked, 'Where are my companions?' But the tree ignored me. I could feel a deep internal conversation that made me feel like I was a long-forgotten annoyance.

I tried to remember which direction I had come but couldn't. That was a lifetime ago. I tried touching another tree to at least get directions, but it seemed that free passage also meant screw you. I was ignored. I wondered what would happen if I decided to carve my initials in one of these trees – would it ignore me then? I almost took out the Lawnmower and put that thought to the test but decided against it. I had just survived a yew judging unprepared – pushing my luck might be foolish. I closed my eyes, spun around and then started walking in the direction I was facing. It was as good a way to go as any.

Even though every cell in my body told me to be quiet, I shouted out, 'BRENDAN, NORA,' but eventually stopped. Not only because it felt so wrong to be making noise in here, but also because I'm sure if they heard me they would be too afraid to answer. Getting out of this forest was the only plan of action I could think of.

The day stretched on. The heat seemed to somehow radiate down from the closed green canopy. The air smelled of moss and didn't move. I had a mental image of filling a balloon with this air and when I got out, watching it sink. Late in the day I heard water and then made it to the river. I began to walk back the way I had come. I must have been upriver from where the boat was beached, either that or somebody had stolen it, 'cause I didn't once see it on my travels. All the while the yews ignored me. It was a strange feeling. Almost like being in a forest back in the Real World.

The sun was low with twilight threatening when I reached the sentinel yews at the entrance of the Yewlands. I had a choice of walking around deep into the forest or climbing the root-covered boulder on the riverside. As much as that tree scared me, I decided to test my freedom of the Yewlands and scrabbled up onto the arthritic roots of that ancient tree. The yew knew I was there. I could feel him/her but I wasn't stopped or interfered with. At the top of the boulder I was rewarded with the sight of Araf and Nora sitting next to a small fire. I shouted to them and received an enthusiastic wave back.

I had so many questions for them but I never got to ask them. As I climbed down I was startled by what I thought was a large yellow insect. It buzzed past my ear and as I watched it fly by it looped in mid-air and came back at me. As it came towards my face I raised my hand to swat it. At first I thought it was a bee or wasp that had stung me but when I looked at the back of my hand I saw it was another gold amulet. I withdrew it from the flesh of my hand; it was shaped like a small tornado. I recognised it immediately. It was almost identical to the one my mother had once given me, except hers didn't have a pin on the end. It was a *rothlú* amulet, and as soon as I recognised it it kicked in. After that, everything was pain.

TWELVE

THE HERMIT OF THUNDER BAY

Pain. Imagine each cell in your body being removed then scrubbed with a wire brush before it was popped back into place. That's the feeling you get from a *rothlú* spell. I never thought I would be nostalgic about pain, but I remembered the last time I had this all-over body ache – my cousin was stealing my shoes. This time there was no tug on my foot to wake me. I opened my eyes the tiniest of cracks. I had no idea where I was but if it was daytime and out of doors, then the light was certainly going to be painful. Luckily when I opened my eyes I was greeted with gloom and deep shadows. I decided to give moving a try and discovered it wasn't a good idea. I dropped my head back onto whatever I was on and slipped back into unconsciousness.

It was just as gloomy when I awoke again but this time, moving was only excruciating as opposed to being beyond the threshold of consciousness. I seemed to be lying on a pile of fresh straw in what I first thought was a dungeon. I crawled over to the only source of light. It was a candle infused with sparkling gold dust, Leprechaun-made – so I knew at least I wouldn't be without light for a couple of years. Next to the candle was a shot glass with something that smelled mighty powerful. All of my instincts told me to leave it alone, but when I thought about it (which was difficult with the fife and drum band playing inside my head) I figured that if whoever got me here wanted me dead, I'd already be in the ground. I held my nose and knocked it back. My toes actually curled and my head tilted to a forty-five-degree angle. A full sweat broke out on my forehead and, even though there was no one there, I said the immortal words, 'Haba yazza.' When my vision cleared and the impulse to vomit passed, I felt much better.

I was in a cave. I guessed that was better than a dungeon. I grabbed the candle and, careful not to let it blow out, I explored the perimeter looking for an exit. After two trips around, I sat down, confused. There was no way out. I went around again – this time slowly looking for a hidden door or a crack or anything but there was nothing. I must have been dropped in from above, but the walls were so smooth there was no way of climbing or seeing what was up there. That's when a memory hit me that filled me with panic. What if there is no way out? I remembered my father warning me that a *rothlú* spell could transport someone to the edge of a cliff. What if it stuck me in the middle of a cave that has no exit? What if I'm doomed to sit and thirst to death in a dark cave?

In all of my days and through all of my troubles I never had an actual panic attack. I was building to a good one but then thought, no, not a dark cave – a cave with a candle in it, a clean bed and a shot of hooch. Somebody brought me here, somebody wants me here. I relaxed, sat on my straw bed and thought. I had been stabbed twice with gold amulet darts. One knocked me out and the other brought me here. Somebody wanted me to drift into the Yewlands and whoever it was wanted me here. But who? I never heard of anybody using amulet darts but now that I thought on it – it was a pretty cool idea. And the *rothlú* that had got me in my hand honed in on me like one of Dahy's knives. All of this information didn't help me figure out who my captor was. Part of me, the same part that previously started to panic, feared that it was Cialtie but somehow this didn't seem like his style.

With nothing better to do, I picked up the candle and climbed onto the rock in the centre of the cave. I was holding the candle up, hoping to see if there was a way out from above when I lost my footing. It was a tiny stumble, I didn't fall but I jostled the flame enough to blow it out.

You just can't imagine how dark cave-dark is, until you're forced to endure it. The black seemed so opaque it felt like I could cut it. I dropped the candle and then carefully climbed down. Then on all fours I crawled until I found my pile of straw and sat. I sat staring into the sense-depriving darkness and started hallucinating shades of blackness. Imagine seeing wind – that was the kind of tricks my brain was playing with that total absence of light. I finally had to close my eyes. Strangely the darkness behind my eyelids was much more bearable.

I dozed again and in my dream, a small hand took my own hand in hers and led me out of the cave. Even though we were outside and I could feel the breeze and sunshine on my face I still couldn't see.

'Is this what it's like for you, Ruby?'

She didn't say anything but I sensed her nodding her head yes. She led me down a grassy hill and asked very politely of a tree if I could have a stick. Together we walked with our sticks sweeping before us as we listened and sensed and smelled our way through a day that – even though I couldn't see – felt glorious.

'See,' she said, 'It's not so bad.'

Light. Blinding light entered the dream, bleaching out the mental image of Ruby and the pastoral scene. Painful blinding light burned into my eyes. I had to cover my face with my arm.

Where the dream ended and the reality began is open for debate. The blinding light focused itself into a doorway of light and in that doorway formed the shape of a man. It wasn't until I pushed myself up into a sitting position and felt the straw underneath my hands that I knew for certain that this was real.

The silhouette in the doorway said, 'Come,' then turned and walked away.

The Lawnmower was still around my waist, so I drew it and walked towards the light.

My captor sat on a cave shelf looking out over a vista of endless sea. If I hadn't heard the voice I would have thought that he was a she. Long brown hair fell to the middle of his back. His clothes were animal skins – not the nicely tailored stuff my Mom often wears, but home-made pelts that wouldn't have looked out of place in a B grade caveman vs. dinosaur movie. He didn't turn around.

'Put away your sword, Prince of Hazel and Oak,' he said in a croaky voice that made me think he didn't use it very often.

'First I want some answers,' I said.

In reply, he threw a speck of gold out in front of him. It hovered in the air and then like a bullet zoomed in and hit me in the hand. I dropped the Lawnmower with a clang. When I tried to pick it up, I found that my right hand was numb and I couldn't move my fingers.

When I reached for the sword with my left hand, he said, 'Do you really wish to lose the use of that hand as well?'

He had turned around, and in his hand was another tiny amulet ready to make it so I would need assistance if I ever wanted to zip up my fly. The long hair down his back was matched by an even longer beard. Even though he looked like a children's picture book version of a comic troll, his eyes told me that he meant business. I let go of the sword and stood. He turned back to his view.

'What have you done to my hand?'

'Sensation in your hand will return in a few moments. I have no desire to harm you, Conor. Come sit next to me and enjoy the vista.'

I've learned the hard way since arriving in The Land that when you're outgunned and outmanoeuvred the best thing to do is just say OK. So I said, 'OK,' and sat. We dangled our legs over the ledge and looked out at a crystal blue sea edged by green rolling hills more manicured than any golf course. On a dock were two simple wooden sailboats. The place was postcard beautiful.

'Where are we?' I asked, trying to sound more conversational and less confrontational.

'This is Ba Toirniúil.'

Ba Toirniúil means Thunder Bay. I had heard of this place. This is where immortals come when they no longer wish to live. This is where you go when you want to sail away into old age.

'Whose boats are they?' I asked.

When he didn't answer, I figured this was going to be one of those I-ask-the-questions-around-here type situations but then he said, 'I make them for whomever needs them.'

'Wait a minute ... are you the Hermit of Thunder Bay?'

He kept looking out to sea but I could see a small smile. 'I suppose I am a hermit and I do live here in Thunder Bay. You have heard of me?'

'I heard one of my guards say that his companion looked like the Hermit of Thunder Bay when he hadn't shaved.'

He thought about this for a long while before he said, 'So I'm famous in Duir for not shaving?'

'Apparently so,' I said.

After another long pause he whispered, almost to himself, 'I suppose it is better than being entirely forgotten.'

I didn't like the tone in his voice and decided that this line of conversation might bring us to morose musings that I wanted to avoid. So I said, 'Should I call you Hermy? Or do you have a real name?'

He actually looked at me then. It's unsettling when a guy as crazy looking as this one gives you a look like *you're* the crazy one. 'Hermy? Why would you call me Hermy?'

'Everyone needs a name.'

The long pause kicked in again. I was starting to realise that chats with Hermy were about waiting a lot. Eventually he said, 'A name is not something I require. One only needs a name if one is going to converse. I have not spoken to anyone but you, Conor of Duir, since ... well, since long before you were born.'

'But you're talking to me now.'

Wait ... 'Yes, it appears I am.'

'Were you the one who knocked me out so I would drift into the Yewlands?'

... 'Yes.'

'And did you throw that homing *rothlú* that brought me here?'

... 'Yes.'

'Why?' He didn't answer, or was taking his usual sweet time so I pressed him. 'Why, Hermy?'

'My mother instructed me.'

'Your mother?' I said looking around. 'I thought the idea of being a hermit is that you live alone. You're a hermit who lives with his mother?'

Hermy laughed at that. It was a sweet little chuckle, like he had only just remembered how to do it. 'No, my mother is long dead.'

'Oh, sorry.'

'You should be. Your family holds the guilt of her murder.'

That reply made my stomach do a little flip-flop. Had he brought a son of Duir here to avenge his mother's death? I looked down at the hundred foot drop and scooted over – out of shoving range.

'Someone in my family killed your mother?'

Hermy nodded once.

'Let me guess – Cialtie?'

Showing no emotion, Hermy nodded again.

Cialtie murdered his mother and this long-dead mother is leaving him instructions. I rattled that riddle around in my noggin and in less than the time it took for Hermy to say, 'Hello,' I came up with the answer.

'You're Ona's son?'

… 'I am,' he said.

'So why did Ona want me to enter the Yewlands?'

In reply he stood and walked over to a corner of his cave, picked up a long banta stick and handed it to me before re-sitting.

The wood was smooth and sticky, with the smell of fresh beeswax polish. 'Is this the branch the yew gave me?'

… 'It is.'

'You finished it for me?'

… 'I did.'

'Thanks,' I said. 'Why does … did your mother want me to have this?'

… 'You of all people, Son of the One-Handed Prince, should know that Ona's will comes without explanation.'

'I'm no longer the Son of the One-Handed Prince,' I said quickly.

… 'My point exactly,' he said, standing. 'Excuse my manners but it has been very long since I have had a guest. Would you like tea?'

'Thank you,' I said and watched him start a small fire with a fire coin then fill a kettle from a rain barrel.

'If you haven't talked to anybody in so long, how did you know I was the Son of the One-Handed Prince?'

My host placed a frying pan on the fire next to the kettle and then reached into a jar and pulled out a dripping handful of some seaweedy

type stuff and threw it sizzling into the pan. 'Would you like some ...'
he stood frozen, looking up to the ceiling, then finally said, 'I do not
think I ever heard a word for what this is.'

I looked at whatever it was steaming in the pan and decided that it
was probably better that it remained unnamed.

'I have heard about your many exploits, Conor, from the beeches.
Beech trees do love to gossip.'

'I've heard that. So what did Ona say about me, exactly?'

I had to wait until Hermy finished making tea out of some sort of
moss. When he handed it to me I was relieved to find that my fingers
worked fine. It tasted exactly like tea made from moss.

'She never mentioned you specifically.'

'Wait, I thought you said Ona told you that I was to get a yew staff?'

... 'No, Ona knew someone was to receive a yew staff – I just guessed
it was you.'

'You sent me into the Yewlands on a guess?'

In reply he shrugged.

'And what if the yews had killed me?'

'That would have been – unfortunate.'

'Yeah, especially for me.'

He nodded in agreement like it was the first time it occurred to him.
He stirred the dinner and then slid a portion into each of two wooden
bowls. 'Would you like some ...'

'Shall we call it gloop?'

He sighed in that exasperated way that made me realise he was
getting to know me. 'If we must.'

After tasting it, I decided that gloop was the perfect name for this
stuff. It's rare to get a dull meal in The Land but Hermy succeeded in
cooking one.

'Do you know what happened to my friends?'

'The archer and the woman both survived their judgement. If that
is what you wish to know. The archer exited the Yewlands not long after
you. He held wood suitable for a bow.'

I hadn't realised how much subconscious tension I had been holding in my shoulders until they relaxed with that news. 'I must get to
them – they will be worried about me.'

'There is no need for them to worry, Conor. I will not harm you.'

'They don't know that.'

'That your disappearance may cause your companions to fret is the least of your worries.'

'So tell me, oh great bearded one who seems to know everything, if my friends are the least of my worries what is the worst of my worries?'

If Hermy noticed my annoyance it didn't make him hurry up with his reply but when he did, he sure got my attention.

'I would say your biggest worry should be – the blind child.'

'What do you know about Ruby?'

This time the pregnant pause before his answer was unacceptable. I didn't care if this guy had gadgets on him that could make me as limp as a Salvador Dali painting, I grabbed him by the arm and spun him to face me. 'Tell me.'

'Ruby,' he said, 'is that her name?'

'What do you know?'

'I, Conor, only know what my mother has written.'

'And what did your mother say?'

'Ona never spoke of these things, all of her prophecies were written.' I stood. 'Don't screw with me, Hermy. What did your mother write?'

I had to take deep breaths while waiting for him to answer; otherwise, I think I would have stabbed him.

'She said, "The blind child will need help from the bearer of the yew staff."'

It took me a moment to realise he was talking about me. 'Where is she?'

'... According to the poplar trees your grandmother, Lugh and Cialtie are holding her in Castle Onn in the Gorselands.'

'I have to get to Duir and put a rescue party together.' I paced around the room looking for an exit. 'How do I get out of here?'

Without looking at me, Hermy made a gesture with his right hand and another one of those damn flying amulets flew out and boomeranged into my neck. This time my whole body went limp and I crumpled to the ground, not even able to move my eyeballs. The hermit rolled me over on my back. His long beard swept over my face but I couldn't feel it. He placed my new yew staff in my hand and said, 'Ona did not write about a rescue party. She only mentioned you. I'm sorry if the paralysing amulet is uncomfortable but in the long run it speeds up the recovery from the *rothlú*. You will thank me later.'

He pulled a chain from round his neck and then from the hundreds of amulets hanging from it, he picked a tiny gold twin tornado. He looped it onto a chain and hung it around my neck. 'If you find her, this will bring you home.' Then he pulled a single twister from his collection, placed it in my palm and closed my fingers around it.

'I have been thinking,' he said, 'and I do not like the name Hermy. If I must have a name then let it be the one I owned when I lived in Castle Duir. Call me Eth.' Then he held my closed fist next to his mouth and incanted, '*Rothlú.*'

THIRTEEN

CAPTAIN JESSE

E th? Eth? I knew that name and I had almost figured out where
I had heard it when my brain was disassembled and scattered
halfway across the land. By the time it got reassembled, that
thought and any other was replaced by pain and unconsciousness.

Eth was right about one thing: this *rothlú* spell didn't seem to hurt
as much as usual. When I finally came to I had specific pains in my
legs, wrists and neck but not the usual all-over pain that comes from
being magically disappeared and reappeared somewhere else. It wasn't
until I attempted to sit up that I realised why I had pains in my wrists,
neck and legs. I was hog-tied. I didn't like waking up in bondage the
first time it happened. Now that it seemed to be occurring with regularity, I really, really didn't like it.

I was in a tent. Not an opulent dwelling that took a dozen servants to
hump around and erect, like Cialtie had. No, this was a thin silken thing,
designed to be light and small to carry. I rolled over – not easy with my
legs tied bent and attached to a cord around my neck. I quickly learned
that my binder knew what he was doing. I tried a couple of times to test
my bonds but soon realised that every time I struggled, the rope tightened around my neck. So I decided to think rather than squirm.

Through the flap of the tent I saw a campfire. The smoke coming
from the fire rose to a screen dome where it disappeared. This was a

fire that belonged to someone who didn't want anyone else to know he
or she was here. Outside, the sound of approaching horses had my
captors on their feet. I could see the shoes and dark leggings – my
captors were Brownies.

I couldn't quite hear all the conversation but my guard's diction was
as good as his knotsmanship. 'Yes sir, I found him just lying unconscious in the middle of the field,' he said but then added a coda to that
sentence that sent a chill down my spine. He finished by saying, 'Your
Highness.'

On no, I thought, and began to struggle even if it was going to strangle me. The last time I had seen the Brownie King I had delivered to
him the body of his dead son. He promised that the next time he saw
me he would kill me. I rolled over and pushed up against the side of
the tent almost knocking it over. I heard the footsteps as they entered
but the noose around my neck was now so tight I could no longer turn
my head. I heard a voice exclaim, 'You!' Then I heard the unmistakable
sound of a knife being pulled from its sheath. I was wheezing, gasping
for breath as the rope cut into my neck but that was the least of my
problems. I closed my eyes and waited for the pain of the knife entering my back.

The knife cut through the rope in a spot that released everything.
My legs dropped straight and my hands were freed. I immediately
worked on loosening the rope around my neck and rolled on my back
gasping for breath. My vision was blurry; I had been seconds away
from passing out. I was expecting a view of Bwika, the hulking King of
the Brownies, but as my vision cleared I was rewarded by the smiling
face of his son Codna.

'Conor?' he said in a voice that changed an octave in the middle of
a word. 'What are you doing here?'

'Choking,' I replied.

I tried sitting up as the prince motioned for the guard to leave us
alone. Then he closed the tent flap, plopped down next to me and
clumsily wrapped his arms around me. 'I'm so glad to see you,' he said.

I was a bit surprised by the attack hug but I returned it. 'Hey Jesse,'
I said, using the nickname I had given him the first time we had met.
'How you doing?'

Jesse looked over his shoulder to make sure no one was listening and then whispered, 'Awful.'

I lowered my tone with him. 'Is your dad outside?'

He looked confused. 'No.'

'Oh, I heard the guard "yes sir"-ing and saying "Your Highness."'

Jesse looked embarrassed and then smiled, 'He was talking about me. This is my troop. I'm the captain.'

'You are?'

'After I stood up to my father in the throne room,' Jesse said. 'Remember? It was over giving you your horse back.'

'Oh I remember,' I replied.

'Well, after that, Dad said I had *bivka*.'

'I have no idea what bivka is but you were pretty awesome that day.'

Jesse blushed. I almost expected him to say, 'Aw shucks.'

'When I came back with The Turlow's horse, you know, the one you gave me, everybody assumed I stole it. Dad was so impressed with my transformation, he gave me a small troop to lead. They were the bottom of the barrel but I didn't know that. I had watched Demne,' Jesse stopped at the mention of his dead brother and swallowed hard. 'You know Frank?'

I nodded. Of course I remembered Frank.

'Well I had watched a lot of his training in the Torkc Guards and I just did the same drills his combat master had put him through. My men loved it. Last month we had war games in the Alderlands and my troop won. Dad promoted me to commander.'

'Congratulations,' I said, slapping him on the arm. 'That's wonderful.'

Jesse rubbed his arm where I had hit him. 'No it's not. I'm just pretending to be a leader. I go watch other commanders and just do what they do. Well, I change it so no one will notice, but I really have no idea what I'm doing. I just put on a gruff voice and make sure nobody sees me …' He turned and looked away, covering his face.

'Hey, guy, it's OK.'

'But it's terrifying, Conor. I think any minute everybody is going to figure out that I'm faking it.'

I had to cover my mouth to stop from laughing. 'Oh Jesse, we're all faking it. Before the battle at the Hall of Knowledge last winter I figured out that bravery was just pretending not to be scared. You're not doing anything every other commander hasn't done. You learn by watching what others do, then you change it to suit you. It sounds to me like you're pretty good at it.'

'Really?' he said, wiping his nose. 'You're not just saying that?'

'If I had a Brownie troop that needed commanding – you would be the guy I would pick.'

'Wow, really?' he said, unconsciously sitting up straighter.

I nodded.

'I'm so glad to see you, Conor. Say, what are you doing out here alone anyway?'

So I told him the whole story about the raid on Yew House on Mount Cas and how my grandmother and Lugh had kidnapped Ruby. Maybe I shouldn't have. He was technically the enemy, but then I remembered what I had said to him so long ago in the Brownielands. 'Others can make us enemies but no one can unmake us friends.' Then I told him how the Hermit of Thunder Bay had puppeteered me into the situation I was in now.

'You went into battle with Lugh? Weren't you scared?'

'I pretended not to be.'

Jesse nodded and smiled like a schoolboy remembering a lesson.

'So I have to get to Castle Onn – the hermit told me that's where they are holding Ruby. Do you know where it is?'

'I've never been there,' Jesse said, 'but that's where I'm going.'

Jesse went on to explain that his father had sent him to represent the Brownies at a meeting called by Cialtie. Apparently the new Turlow was going to attend, and there were rumours that Lugh was again abroad in The Land and that he would be there. Cialtie had promised he would reveal a secret weapon or something that would ensure that Duir would soon be liberated.

'Liberated from its gold you mean,' I said sarcastically.

Jesse laughed. 'That's what my father thinks.'

'Jesse, do you really think that if you win this war Cialtie will just hand over Castle Duir to the Brownies?'

'My father does.'

'Yeah, but do you?'

Jesse thought for a time. It's never an easy thing for a son to judge his father. Finally he looked up and said, 'No, I do not.'

'Can you tell your father that?'

'I could, but he wouldn't listen. What should I do, Conor?'

'Aw, Jesse, I have no idea. He's not only your father, he's also your king. You kinda have to do what he says.'

'Even if he's wrong?'

I shrugged. A wilful father I had experience with, but a wilful *and stupid* father – would be awful.

'The more pressing problem,' I said, 'is what are you going to do with me?'

'What do you mean?'

'Well, I'm your prisoner, aren't I?'

Jesse thought for a second. 'I suppose you are,' he said, then giggled. 'Maybe I should take your shoes.'

I started laughing too until Jesse shushed me and said, 'Wait here.'

Jesse's voice when addressing his scout was so different to the child-like tone he used with me. I couldn't quite make out what was being said until the scout said, 'Right away, sir'. Then I heard him gallop off.

Jesse came back into the tent with water and an apple. I drank deeply then devoured the apple.

'OK,' Jesse said, 'I quizzed my scout and he hadn't recognised you, so I told him you were one of Cialtie's scouts that had been waylaid. I told him not to mention it to anyone for fear of embarrassing Cialtie. Then I sent everyone back to the main troop.' He threw clothes at me. 'Here, quickly, put these on.'

This wasn't the meek weepy Jesse I knew – this was Captain Prince Codna of the Alderlands. His voice shocked me, so I just did what he said. I was bigger than the average Brownie but luckily Brownie clothes are pretty stretchy. Jesse held out a hooded cloak and I put it on. It was tight but if I didn't move around too much it was OK. Jesse walked behind me and tied a triangular cloth across my face like a cowboy train robber's bandana, and then he fixed a translucent piece of black muslin across my eyes. Finally he walked in front of me and lifted the hood over my head.

'This is the uniform of the Brownies Shadowguard. Castle Onn is a half day's ride. You can get to the outskirts of the castle if you run fast.'

We didn't have a lot of time. Our plans were much more hurried than I liked.

'Are you sure you want to do this?' I asked. 'If this plan falls apart then you are going to be in a whole heap of trouble.'

'I can't defy my father, but I can't let Cialtie kidnap a young girl.'

I placed my hand on Jesse's shoulders. As I looked at him it was like looking into an illusion. I saw the young sweet kid I had always known at the same time as I saw the steely commander. 'You're a brave man, Captain Codna.'

'As long as that's what people believe.' He tried to smile but just missed it.

I turned to leave.

'Oh, and Conor – you can't wear those shoes.'

I was never a runner before I got to The Land. I always figured that if the creator of the universe wanted human beings to jog he wouldn't have allowed us to invent the Ferrari. But there was no sports car handy so I was hoofing it as fast as I could, hoping I could get to the place where Jesse and I had agreed to meet before his troop got there. He said he would try to delay them as much as possible but still they were on horseback and I was running. And I wasn't in my Nikes. If I didn't know better, I would have accused that Brownie of orchestrating this whole thing just so he could finally get his hands on my sneakers.

So I was trying to keep up a decent speed in these stupid Brownie slippers. They had stretchy sides so the fact that they were too small wasn't too bad but the leather soles were so thin, I might as well have been barefoot. Every time I stepped on a sharp rock or a pointy twig, I shouted, 'Slek,' which is a very rude Brownie curse word that Jesse's late brother Frank had taught me. I thought it only appropriate. I tried to separate my mind and body the way the Fili had taught me but every time I stubbed my toe, my mind and body came together and my mind told me that I was running too much. This Brownie outfit didn't help either. I tried to remember if I had ever seen an Olympic marathon runner wearing woollen leggings and came up with nothing. Gosh, I wonder why not?

Through my discomfort, I remembered Dad telling me about the mantra that inspired him to win the boat race against his brother. He told me he kept saying, 'Rowing beats Cialtie,' over and over again in his head. I started saying that but then changed my chant to, 'Running saves Ruby.'

My new yew banta staff was heavy in my hand. I said to myself, *I wish this damn stick was lighter* – and it was. That broke my concentration and I thought out loud, 'I wish this stick was heavier.' Even though I had asked for it I was unprepared for the sudden weight in my right hand. I tipped over at full speed and crashed painfully onto the ground. I sat up and when the cartoon tweeting birds that were flying around my head finally disappeared I said, 'Cool,' and then 'Ow,' but maybe not in that order. I started back at a jog and as I picked up speed I willed my stick to go light again and thought, *I need to look into the stuff this stick can do but not now. Now – running saves Ruby. Running saves Ruby. Running ...*

My mindless-running-chanting universe was disturbed by a feeling of vulnerability. I looked around and found I was no longer in a forest. Jesse had told me that before you get to Castle Onn there is an expanse of treeless fields that borders the Hollylands. We had agreed to meet at the treeline. I looked behind me and saw that I had run past that. I circled back, hoping no one had seen me, and finally came to rest under a cherry tree. It was too early in the season for fruit and the tree constantly apologised for that, regardless of how many times I told him it was all right. I was sweating from head to toe and desperately wanted to peel off some of these hot clothes just for a second but was afraid that if I did, that would be the moment when Jesse and the Brownies arrived.

With the tree still pestering me if there was anything he could do, I asked if he minded if I climbed. Delighted that he could be of any service the cherry gladly agreed. I picked up my yew staff from the ground. It was regular yew weight again and I mentally asked it to lose its weight. As it grew lighter I flippantly asked the wood to become lighter than air. The stick shot up and out of my fingers then fell to the ground. I stared at it thinking then smiling. I picked it up again and this time held on tight with both hands.

Lighter than air, I said in my head and I instantly shot twenty feet in to the air until I let go screaming. I hit the ground hard and then was hit in the kidneys by my falling stick. After determining that none of my bones was broken I said, 'Wow,' and tried again. This time when I spoke to the wood I said, *just a little bit lighter than air*. The stick rose and I felt the pull on my outstretched arms. *A tiny bit lighter*, I said as my full weight was slowly pulled off the ground. I found I could regulate this anti-gravity effect. I could only go up and down but I figured if I gave myself enough time I could also get it to hover. But time I didn't have, so I just used my new-found floating stick to propel me to the top of the cherry tree where under the cover of leaves I stripped off some of the sticky wool and let the breeze cool me down while I scratched.

The cherry tree told me of Jesse's Brownie troop's approach. It was something I asked him to do and the tree was delighted he could be of further assistance. Cherries are helpful to the point of annoyance. They are also not very inquisitive. The tree seemed to not notice that I flew into its top branches. I re-donned my damp, smelly Brownie-wear, covered my face and eyes with the Brownie ninja gear and waited until Jesse and his charges were almost below me. I then instructed my staff to go light-ish and jumped.

The effect was just as I had hoped. It looked like a slow motion scene from a bad action movie. I arrived from that dizzying height on my feet and then placed my hands on my hips. Jesse had told me that Shadowguards never speak. Good thing 'cause I almost said, 'Ta da!'

Jesse's troop was stunned and impressed. After their initial shock they gave a Brownie salute that I returned. The most shocked of the entire group was Jesse. I could tell he was dying to ask me how I had just jumped out of a four-storey-high tree but finally he just said, 'Now that my Shadowguard is here, it is time to meet with Cialtie and Lord Lugh.'

FOURTEEN
IVY LODGE

The Ivy Lodge half lived up to its name. It was more of a castle than a lodge, but as for the ivy – it sure had a lot of that. From the outside it looked fine, majestic even, like the main building of some venerable old university. But once you got inside it was terrifyingly apparent that this place was going to come crashing down any second. It seemed that the ivy was the only thing holding it up.

The origins of Ivy Lodge lived in that timeline between history and legend. Apparently Mom and Dad weren't the first to take a Choosing simultaneously. It had been done before, a long time ago. Supposedly these two lovers from an ancient time had a love so strong they couldn't be apart from each other – even for an instant. Against all advice they performed the Rite of Choosing hand-in-hand. For their daring and effort they each received a major rune. The woman was given Gort – the man Tinne. They became the King and Queen of Holly and Ivy. Together they built Ivy Lodge in the new Hollylands far to the north. When the castle was completed they held a midwinter celebration that was ill-attended due to distance and bad weather. After that they never held another party, they never left the castle grounds or each other's side. They received visitors with courtesy but never warmth. They had no children. Then one day, reports came back that the castle was deserted. The holly trees and the ivy, no longer tied to runes, spread across The Land and King Holly and Queen Ivy were never seen again.

The Hollylands we had just passed through were as wild as the inside of the Lodge. It felt cold up here, even though it was approaching high summer. The cool air still didn't stop a trickle of sweat from sliding down my back, but that had less to do with the temperature than the anticipation of waltzing into a lion's den.

Inside the Lodge was crawling with Banshees, which removed all doubt, if there was any, that this was Cialtie's party. I drew some pretty serious stares with my hoodie, bandana-ed face and gauze-covered eyes but I must have been intimidating enough to stop anyone from saying, 'Who are you supposed to be?'

We were ushered into a small room that contained a couple of chairs and a table with a pitcher of water and a bowl of apples. Cialtie obviously wasn't maxing out his hospitality budget. Saying that, as soon as Jesse and I were alone I lifted my bandana and wolfed down an apple. Considering where I was, I wondered if this was to be my last meal. I laughed at that thought and then thought some more and realised it wasn't funny.

'Are you all right?' I whispered to Jesse.

Without looking at me he replied, 'I'm pretending to be fine.'

I smiled under my mask and tried to do the same.

After half an hour we were instructed by our Banshee party-planner that the meeting was about to begin. We were escorted through corridors where periodic cracks in the walls allowed vein-like ivy to push in and attach pale green leaves to the stonework. At the entrance to the main hall, a Banshee honour guard informed us that I could only enter if I unmasked and disarmed.

'I am Prince Codna, Emissary and son of King Bwika of the Alderlands, this is my Shadowguard. We both enter unmolested or I return to my father now.'

Wow, Jesse really had this faking brave stuff down.

The guard didn't protest. When we got inside it was obvious from all of the bodyguards present that he had gotten a similar response from everybody. Bad guys, it seems, like their henchmen.

I was very glad of my mask and eye gauze. Even though I was expecting to see my uncle, I'm pretty sure my heart-pounding terror combined with my overwhelming desire to attack him would have shown on my face. He was flanked by two Banshees: one a male archer and the other a sorceress wearing a thin leather belt that held her wand against her hip.

To his left were Grandma and her boyfriend Lugh. In a normal family, a grandson would be delighted to see his grandmother but normal my family was not. I hadn't expected to see her but I was hoping Ruby would be with them. She had to be nearby – the question was how to find her.

To Cialtie's right was a group of three Banshees, all dressed up in Banshee finery.

There were no chairs. We took our place standing in an empty space between two pillars.

'Mother, Father,' Cialtie said addressing Macha and Lugh, 'may I introduce Prince Codna of the Brownielands.'

Jesse bowed formally. 'Lord Lugh, it is an honour to finally see you. I am, as are all of the Brownie clan, at your service.' He straightened up and then bowed again to my grandmother. 'Lady Macha, The Land rejoices at the news of your reappearance. I am your humble servant.'

As Jesse instructed me, I only slightly bowed my head. I was supposed to act like I wasn't there.

Then Cialtie gestured to his right. 'And may I introduce you to the newly ascended Turlow.'

The new Banshee chief looked small and uncomfortable between his two beefy bodyguards. He bowed and mumbled, 'My lord and lady.'

'Our generals have already had several meetings about our upcoming siege of Castle Duir,' Cialtie said.

Had they? I wanted to turn to Jesse and ask him but remembered I wasn't supposed to be there.

'Both Banshees and Brownies have expressed doubts about the success of such an attack, especially after your defeat at the Hall of Knowledge.'

I noticed Cialtie said 'Your defeat' like he had nothing to do with it. If I was the new Turlow or Jesse I would have pointed out that attacking the Hazellands was Cialtie's idea, but these guys were too green to stand up to my uncle.

'Your hesitations are not without merit, my friends, but worry no longer. As I have promised, we will soon have a new ally, one that will ensure our victory as foretold by Ona.'

Once again I was glad for the mask that covered my face. A new ally? I was expecting a new weapon, maybe, but an ally? Who's left? I thought for a second that maybe it was the Mertain. They were plenty angry at me and Graysea for stealing the dragon blood but Red was furious with Cialtie and the Banshees, he wouldn't allow his brother to fall in with this bunch. That only left the Elves. Dad told me it was hopeless trying to enlist the Elves. He said that when a conflict comes, they disappear into the forest. But if Cialtie could coopt them, then potentially that would mean the trees would be on my uncle's side. At that moment I couldn't imagine what the trees could do to help but I had been surprised by enough plants in The Land to know that making enemies of a tree is a bad idea.

'Following the predictions of Ona has proved a folly for you before, Lord Cialtie,' Jesse said. 'What makes this time different?'

Wow, that snapped me out of my reverie. I take back what I said about Jesse being too green. Cialtie gave the Brownie prince a look that almost made me duck. If my uncle could shoot daggers from his eyes, then Jesse would have been a pegboard. Bringing up Cialtie's unsuccessful tenure as Lord of Duir was either stupid or brave. I previously would have said that Jesse was being stupid but his recent behaviour was changing my opinion of the shoe thief.

After an interminable length of time Cialtie bowed his head as if to say, 'Fair enough,' and composed himself enough to answer. 'It is true that Ona's predictions are often obtuse but tonight you will see for yourself the fruit of our research.' He turned to the Banshee sorceress and said, 'Taline, is all prepared?'

'Yes my lord,' the witch answered.

'Then begin.'

Taline let loose a modulating scream that made all of the non-Banshees in the room wince. From the corners of the chamber servants appeared carrying bowls. Five bowls in all were placed on the floor in a cross pattern. After the servants left, Taline walked to the centre of the receptacles. For a split second I thought I saw a woman walking with her but decided it was a trick of the gauze mask I was wearing. She began to speak in a Banshee dialect I did not understand. Periodically I almost caught a word that sounded like something my father had tried to make me learn as a child. She reached into the bowl in front of her and took out a small glob of sap. Then I heard her use the Ogham word, 'Iodhadh.' My heart pounded in my chest. She was using Shadowmagic and the sap she was using was yew.

I remembered overhearing my mother and Fand speculating about the kind of raw Shadowmagic power that might be attained using yew sap. They had both smiled at the thought of it then stopped themselves as if talking like that was too frightening a prospect.

The Banshee sorceress fanned her hands over the bowls to her right and left – pale Shadowflames sparked to life. Like Mom's Shadowflames, these gave off neither heat nor light but unlike Mom's Shadowmagic, these seemed to suck the light from the room. All around there were candelabras and chandeliers. None of the candles had gone out but it was noticeably darker in there – and colder. Maybe it just seemed colder because of the shiver that was running down my spine as I started to realise what I was witnessing.

When Taline closed her hand around the sap and placed her fist into the Shadowfire and incanted, 'Duir' – I was then sure she was doing something I thought only my mother and Fand could do. This was a Shadowcasting.

The Banshee sorceress rolled her head and warbled as if in a trance then opened her hand and dropped a translucent rune onto the floor. Emblazoned on its surface was the major rune of Duir. While continuing to moan and writhe she picked more sap from the bowl and began the long process of creating a shadow of all the major runes in Tir na Nog. 'Fearn, Saille, Nuin, Tinne, Quert, Muhn, Ur, Nion, Gort, Getal, Straif, Ruis, Ailm, Onn, Eadth, Iodhadh, Beith, Luis', and finally my mother's rune – 'Cull.'

When the formation of the Shadowrunes was complete, the sorceress then placed them in a grid on the floor in front of her and ignited them with Shadowflame. Then began the process of sorting the runes into the proper order for casting. This took longer than when Mom did it. The Banshee didn't really know what she was doing. She looked like some old biddy wondering where to put the next piece in her jigsaw puzzle. That scared me most of all. It felt like I was watching a monkey spinning dials in a nuclear power plant.

All the while she moaned and rocked. The Shadowfire travelled up her hands and then engulfed both of her arms to the shoulder. She tore off her cloak and threw it into the corner where it continued to burn with a pale blue Shadowfire. I was tempted to go over and stamp it out. I wondered if that would even work.

This was taking a long time. I looked around the room. The Turlow and his guards, who had never seen anything like this before, looked on with a mixture of repulsion and anticipation. Jesse was successfully standing expressionless but I knew he was terrified. Lugh and Grandma held maniacal expressions but maybe that was just the way I will always see them now. Cialtie seemed to be getting impatient and then proved it by shouting, 'When will you be ready?'

The sorceress held up a finger as if to say, 'Wait a minute,' but then her loss of concentration allowed the Shadowfire to rocket up her arms and engulf her whole body. She screamed for just a second as if she was being burned. Shadowfire doesn't burn but I imagine if I instantly became covered with that stuff that I'd freak out a lot worse than her. She composed herself and using the palms of her hands she pushed the Shadowfire away from her face and let the rest of her body burn. She may not have been a competent Shadowwitch but no one could accuse her of being undramatic.

At the edges of the Shadowflame that surrounded her I began to see bits of a form: a leg, a hand. Just as I had decided that it must be a trick of the light, I saw the translucent face of a woman whisper into the sorceress's ear. She obviously heard it because she stopped, listened and then changed the pattern of her Shadowcasting runes. The runes were now forming the shape of a star. It was very different from the periodic-table-like pattern my mother used. The ghostlike face continued to appear and instruct the sorceress until finally she rocked her head back and breathed deeply. Then from the bowl of yew sap she took a glob and prepared to make another rune. As she held it over the

Shadowfire and incanted, the face that had only appeared at the edges of the fire began to take form. No longer a reflection of the fire, the face grew more substantial. She still was not real, still translucent, but she was no longer a trick of the Shadowlight. A whole woman appeared before us. I had seen visions in Shadowfire before but this wasn't like that. This was a real rooting-tooting, I'm-about-to-pee-myself ghost.

The ghost, although insubstantial, had some power. She ran her hands over the sorceress and extinguished the Shadowfire on her head and shoulders, until only her hands once again were afire. Then she spoke into the witch's ear. This time I almost heard something. The Banshee turned to Cialtie and said, 'Now.'

Lugh and Macha smiled and left. As we waited, the ghost continued to instruct the sorceress. I shot a quick glance to Jesse and then regretted it. His eyes mirrored the wrongness that we were both feeling about whatever was happening in this place but he, unlike me, had no mask to hide it from Cialtie. But the wrongness had just begun.

I heard her before I saw Lugh roughly drag her in to the room. Little Ruby, not the obstreperous and defiant self-confident woman-child I had known but a scared and frightened blind girl who was alone and mistreated far from home. It took all of my will not to run to her. I remembered the last time I had to stand by and watch someone I love being mistreated by Cialtie. That time I had waited too long and Fergal died. This time I swore to myself I would not let that happen again. But what could I do?

My hand reached slowly up to my neck. If I had to I could rush Ruby and activate the twin *rothlú* amulet that the hermit had placed around my neck. I might make it, but if I did that would leave Jesse with questions he couldn't answer. Questions that would get him killed. I had to wait and watch.

Lugh pushed Ruby to the centre of the flaming Shadowfire bowls. She had lost her sunglasses. Her hair covered half her face and was knotted and wild. Her visionless eyes darted frantically around the room. I so desperately wanted to shout to her to let her know that I was here and she was not alone.

Lugh drew a dagger from his belt and placed it at Ruby's throat. I grabbed the *rothlú* amulet and yanked it. The silver chain broke and clattered loudly to the floor in the pin-dropping quiet chamber. I wondered if I could get to Ruby before Lugh cut. Just when I decided that I had to risk it, Jesse spoke.

'Are you planning to kill that child?'

At first I didn't even know it was Jesse, the voice was so forceful.

Macha answered. 'Ona's prophecy calls for the blood of the blind child.'

'What does it say – exactly?' Jesse almost shouted. 'Does it demand her death?'

My grandmother was obviously not used to being spoken to like this. She replied with only an indignant glare.

Jesse, bless him, was undaunted. He spoke like the prince that he was. Only he and I knew just how badly he was shaking under his cloak. 'If the spell calls for blood, take some blood, but I will not stand by and watch an unnecessary murder of the child.'

I didn't know if it was the right thing to do or not, but I took that to be an order from my prince and stepped forward towards Lugh with my staff held ready to strike. This also got me that bit closer to Ruby if things got really sticky.

During all of this, the ghost impatiently circled around the centre of the room.

'How dare you reproach me,' Lugh said and lifted his hand in a gesture that I knew all too well. I braced myself for the inevitable gale that was about to smash me into the next state.

'Father,' Cialtie shouted. It was maybe the first time I had ever been glad to hear that voice. 'The Brownie is right. There is no need to kill the child. She still may be of use to us.'

Lugh still didn't take the knife away from Ruby's throat. 'Once we have the Shadowwitch we won't need this child.'

'You are probably right, Father, but why chance it? You of all people should know how swiftly winds can change.'

'Very well,' Lugh said and removed the dagger from Ruby's neck. I relaxed then and stepped back into the room. That's when Lugh grabbed the girl's hand and in a flash ran the edge of the blade across Ruby's palm. Ruby screamed and tried to pull away but Lugh held her wrist firm. Blood dripped from her hand as she stopped squirming and fainted dead away. The Banshee sorceress picked up a bowl and let the blood drip into it. The blood continued to drip as Lugh held Ruby's pale lifeless body by her hair. I had to get her out of here. The sorceress held up a finger indicating that she had enough blood. One of the servants was called and Lugh handed Ruby over like she was a rag doll left after play.

'Make sure her wound is dressed,' a voice said, saying what I would have said if I could. It was the new Turlow. The Banshee servant bowed her head yes. I had assumed this Turlow was just a Cialtie lackey; maybe there was hope for him.

Lugh and Macha backed into their original positions as the ghost sat cross-legged across from the Banshee witch. Who was this ghost? Lugh said something about a Shadowwitch? I was pondering this when the Banshee finally opened her hand and revealed the last rune. It was less substantial than the others and was clearer than the blueish Shadowrunes that were scattered around the floor. It looked like it was made of the same stuff as the ghost. Then, proving that it was, the ghost picked it up. That's when I came very close to giving myself away. An audible gasp left my bandana-covered mouth. Luckily only Jesse seemed to notice. He gave me a hard disapproving stare. The reason for my surprise was the rune. It was identical to the one my mother made when she undertook the Rite of Choosing using Shadowmagic as opposed to real magic. Mom for the first time ever used tree sap to fuel the changing as opposed to gold. The rune she received for her efforts was transparent and contained a rune that no one had ever seen before. No one knew its meaning and there had never been anything like it – until now.

The ghost held this new Shadowrune on the palms of her hands. Taline pushed all of the remaining runes into a pile underneath the hands and ignited them with Shadowflame. The ghost threw back her head in a silent scream – could the Shadowfire be burning her? Taline then poured Ruby's blood from the bowl into the cupped hands and onto the rune. Smoke immediately poured up from the hands but then dissipated – there was no scent. Then the changes began in the ghost. First there was red. The major arteries began to form like those see-through pages in a biology book. Then the major organs darkened at the same time as the skeleton. Finally flesh began to appear as the sound of a faraway whine grew into a full-blown scream of agony.

When it was done a naked woman lay still, kneeling with her head in her lap like she was praying. Black hair fell in front of her face. My grandmother stepped forward and took the cloak off her back and laid it over the former ghost's shoulders. Then she shushed the Banshee sorceress away and knelt across from the prostrate woman. She reached over, pushed back her hair and then placed her hands on each side of the woman's face and lifted it to hers. I was amazed that the woman's black eyes were open. My grandmother leaned in and stared directly into the woman's eyes and said, 'Welcome back, Maeve.'

FIFTEEN

MAEVE

Maeve – the first Shadowwitch, the inventor of Shadowmagic, the mad Druid who had decimated half of her people's rowan forest in a maniacal quest for power. The leader who swore an oath to overthrow the House of Duir. The Fili Queen who attempted to harness a power so strong that it destroyed her and her army. She was back, and so was her army.

Outside, hundreds of soldiers suddenly appeared, naked and screaming. Cialtie, it seemed, had anticipated this. Banshees were ready, passing out cloaks and boots. Then they led the dazed Fili into the Lodge where they found their old yew bows hanging. Even though the bows were all almost identical, the proper owner walked straight up to his own weapon and picked it out like it was a son or daughter.

Maeve and her Fili army were back and in league with Cialtie, the Banshees and the Brownies. Cialtie was right. This was the ally that ensured his victory.

I took off my masks when it was just me and Jesse in his tent. 'I have to find Ruby and get back to Duir,' I said, 'but I don't know how to do it without getting you into trouble. Any ideas?'

But Jesse wasn't ready for a chat about planning. He was still way too freaked out. 'Did you see what they did?' he asked, wide-eyed and pale.

'I sure did.'

'Whatever happened in there … it can't be … it can't be right.'

'No, it was very wrong and I'm freaked out too.'

Jesse continued to look off into nothing. I tried to snap him out of it. 'Hey,' I said playfully punching him on the arm, 'you were awesome in there.'

'I was?'

'Hell yes. The way you stood up to Lugh. That was, like, the bravest thing I've ever seen.'

'What?' he said, finally looking at me. 'Really? Gosh I almost forgot I did that. I did do that, didn't I?'

'You sure did.'

Jesse smiled. 'I was terrified.'

'Well, you pretended not to be very well. It was – princely.'

He looked like he'd been slapped. 'Gosh, I think that's the nicest thing anyone has ever said to me.'

Jesse then burst into tears and gave me a hug. That may not be princely behaviour in anybody else's book but it was just fine in mine.

A Banshee guard outside the tent announced himself and asked loudly if he could speak with Prince Codna. I only had time to turn away and throw up my hood before he entered the tent. Jesse nodded to the messenger and wiped his eyes.

'I have been sent to ask if you or any of the Brownies have seen the girl,' the Banshee said, standing to attention.

'What girl?' Jesse asked.

'The blind girl, Your Highness. She has powers of which we were previously unaware. She has killed two guards and escaped.'

I almost turned then. Surely this was some kind of joke.

'I find that hard to believe,' Jesse said.

'It is true, sir. She is gone and all that is left of two of my most trusted guards are their clothes.'

'This is indeed very strange,' he said in his faux-prince voice. 'I shall assign some Brownies to help you with the search.'

The guard saluted and left.

Jesse picked up my bandana and eye gauze mask and handed them to me. 'Go find her, Conor, and get her back home.'

'But what about you? Won't it be suspicious if your Shadowguard disappears?'

'Don't worry about me. I'm sure I can find a new Shadowguard.'

I put on my mask and stood. Before I left Jesse took my hand and said, 'I remember what you once said, Conor. No one can unmake us friends.'

Outside the tent was a disorganised mess. Soldiers were running all over the place looking into tents and under bushes. If Ruby was wandering around out here I had no chance of finding her first. Saying that, how could she have escaped? The messenger said she had killed two guards. Now that certainly wasn't true. Maybe she had help. Maybe Mom or Araf had organised a breakout.

I decided to risk going in to the Lodge to see if I could have a look at where she had been held. I had to risk talking to a couple of Banshee guards. I was worried that maybe speaking would give away that I was a fake Shadowguard, but I didn't seem to arouse any suspicion.

Ruby's holding cell made me want to cry. There was just a straw mat and a bucket for her to use as a toilet. On the floor was a half-eaten apple. How could anybody do this to a young girl? By the door, a pile of soldier's uniforms lay on top of two pairs of shoes. I picked up one of the cloaks and dust fell from the inside of the sleeves.

OK, I said to myself, *let's assume she hasn't been rescued, or worse kidnapped by somebody else – let's assume she really did escape on her own. Where could she have gone?* I imagined I was a young girl groping along these stone walls. I followed a wall out of the room and into the corridor. The roof was broken here and the wall was covered with pale ivy. I got down on my hands and knees and discovered that some of the stems were broken. Could Ruby have done that as she was feeling along the wall? Further along I found what almost looked like an ivy bush. I looked inside and found an opening in the wall behind it. Vines had grown up from below in what must have been an old dumb waiter shaft. There was still a rope hanging down. At the bottom of the shaft was daylight. There was no way I could fit in there, but Ruby could. As I was poking my head back in, I saw a clump of matted hair hanging from a thorny vine. It was black, just like Ruby's. 'Aren't you a clever girl,' I said to myself.

I ran outside and around the Lodge until I found where that shaft let out. There was a half-ruined stone outbuilding that probably had been some sort of cooking place or maybe a laundry. In the dirt I found the imprint of a very Worldly sneaker print. She had definitely been there. I rubbed out her footprint and looked into the holly forest beyond.

A Banshee saw me climbing from the outbuilding. 'Found anything?'

'No,' I replied. 'Have you searched the holly forest yet?'

'Twice,' he said. 'She's not out there.'

'Maybe she climbed a tree.'

'Not those trees, mate. Anytime you get near them they scratch the hell out of you.'

To prove his words he held out his arm. It was covered with deep scratches. He continued around the castle searching in a way a person does when he knows there's no point but has to keep going because his superior officer ordered him to.

I looked at the holly forest before me. *You gotta be out there somewhere, my little gem.* The hollies here weren't like trees, they were more like gigantic bushes. Most were about two storeys high; palm-sized leaves covered them from top to bottom and those leaves were hard and spiked on all sides. There was no way to get to the trunk of these trees without some serious hacking, or permission. I walked up to the nearest plant. I had never spoken to a holly before. I tentatively reached towards it. My last experience with talking to a strange oak made me think twice before bounding up and hugging a tree. I pinched a leaf between my index finger and thumb and gave it a dainty shake like the kind you'd get from a germ-phobic posh lady.

'Hello there, Mr Holly,' I said as politely as I could. I braced myself for an attack but could only hear, no not hear, feel – I could feel a tiny voice, but it was just out of reach like I was trying to listen to a conversation through a hotel wall. I got the impression that if I were able to reach through the leaves and touch some wood that I might be able to converse with this plant. I remembered the welted-up scratches on the soldier's arm but if these trees could help me find Ruby that would be a small price. I scrunched up my eyes and pushed my hand past the wall of leaves and felt around for a branch. The moment I touched it the leaves closed around my arm and spiked leaves penetrated my skin. The pain was excruciating but I was prepared for it and didn't try to pull away. It was the pulling away that had scratched that soldier up so much. Mr Holly's voice was strong in my mind now and the first thing I realised was that it was Ms Holly.

'*Who be you?*' she asked as I grimaced in pain.

The question led me to surmise that hollies couldn't just reach into my head and take out any information like some of the other trees in The Land. I didn't answer. I wanted to keep my identity a secret. I had no idea if Hollies gossiped or not.

She was in my brain enough to ask, '*You are Faerie?*'

'Yes ma'am.'

'*I want you to tell me,*' she demanded.

'I am Faerie,' I said. 'I'm looking for a young girl.'

'*What do you want with this child?*'

'I want to help her, she's lost.'

'*Others today have said this to us but in their blood they harboured malice.*'

I looked down at my wrist, beads of blood oozed out of a ring of tiny pinpricks caused by the sharp leaves.

'You can read blood?'

'*Your blood* [actually it felt more like she said sap] *reveals to us the truth in what you say.*'

'Then know this, ma'am,' I said. 'This young girl is lost and alone. She has been mistreated by these people. I'm here to take her home to her family. Do you know where she is?'

The tree didn't speak for a while. I got a faint impression that she was talking to someone else.

'*The girl is with us. She is very afraid and says she can no longer see.*'

'Will you lead me to her?'

She released my wrist but I remained in contact with the branch. '*Walk north touching my sisters. We will lead you to her.*'

At did as I was told. While trying to look casual, I touched the leaves of every holly I passed. In my head I received instant messages that subtly changed my direction until I found a large tree that somehow I knew she was under. I looked around; I could hear distant shouting but no one was about.

I pinched a leaf between my fingers and asked, 'Is the girl here?'

The tree replied by saying, *'Give me your blood.'*

I tried to reach through the wall of leaves like I did before but the tree instructed me just to prick my thumb on one of the leaf's spines.

As soon as I did the tree asked, *'Do you mean to harm this child?'*

My heart began to race in my chest. I had found her. 'No ma'am,' I said. 'I've come to rescue her.'

'How do you propose to do that? The child cannot travel: she is hurt and exhausted.'

'I have an amulet that will return us home to her father and grand-mother.'

I felt the tree believe me and then heard the creaking sound of living wood moving. A gap opened in the dome of leaves that covered the holly from top to bottom and I entered. I thought she wasn't there at first. I looked all around the base of the trunk and didn't find her. Then I looked up. She was about six feet above me, asleep, cradled in a basket of branches provided by the holly.

I felt tears come to my eyes. I placed my hand on the trunk and said, 'Thank you.'

It was tight in there but the holly pushed apart branches as I climbed. She was still asleep when I reached her. She was pale, dirty and her hair was a tangled mess but still I thought she was the most beautiful thing I had ever seen. I gently pushed her hair away from her face. She opened her eyes and – screamed. She screamed one of those world famous Ruby migraine-inducing screams. I placed my hand across her mouth; I don't know how but the sound was still amazingly loud.

'Shhhhh, Ruby, it's me,' I shout-whispered.

She couldn't hear me over the internal sound she was making with her scream so she bit me. I quickly pulled my palm back and fell back-wards about five feet and got stuck upside-down in the branches. Ruby then started banging on my ankle with something really hard.

'Ruby,' I shouted, not caring who heard me; every living creature within a twenty-five-mile radius must have heard that scream. 'Ruby, damn it, stop. It's me, Conor.'

'Conor, Conor O'Neil?'

'Yes, now shut up.'

The holly tried to help me untangle myself but only succeeded in dropping me another five feet onto my head. Ruby climbed down. When I took her in my arms she broke down into uncontrollable quaking sobs.

'Shhhh, it's all right,' I said, but it wasn't.

Outside the tree I heard soldiers shouting, 'In there. That one.'

There are men surrounding me, the holly pulsed into my brain.

I reached to my neck for the *rothlú* charm and then panicked when it wasn't there. I then remembered I had taken it off inside the Lodge. I frantically searched for the pocket I knew was somewhere in this borrowed set of clothes.

Outside I heard a voice say. 'Hack it down.'

The tree's voice in my head barked, *'Quickly, Faerie.'*

I found the amulet at the same time as I saw a sword slice through the holly's wall of leaves. At the same time I felt the tree's pain and terror.

I didn't have time to thank or apologise to the tree. I only had time to say, 'This is gonna hurt, Ruby,' and then I said, '*Rothlú.*'

I can't tell you how disappointed I was when I felt wet grass pressing against the side of my face. I really thought I was going to wake up between clean sheets in my nice warm bed in Castle Duir. Instead, I was once again face down in a field somewhere. This had been my third *rothlú* spell (or was it four? I didn't even know any more) in two days. Brains were not meant to be scrambled on a regular basis. I tried to think where I was and how I got there. It was definitely a *rothlú* so it must be important, but at that moment I couldn't think and all I wanted to do was go back to sleep in the dirt or if that wasn't possible, then die. At least I wouldn't hurt any more.

Then a scream brought me back to the present. At the sound of Ruby's screech my brain cells finally organised themselves enough so I remembered what I was doing. I was saving Ruby. The hairy hermit told me that the *rothlú* would get me home but it obviously hadn't – I was face down in grass and Ruby was once again in trouble. Forcing myself to ignore the all-over body pain, I jumped to my feet. Ruby stopped screaming and began jumping. She wrapped her arms around my legs.

I pushed her back. 'What's wrong? Are you all right? Where are we?'

Ruby continued to jump. 'You're awake!'

I placed my hands on her shoulder, and tried to make her hold still. It didn't work and it hurt. I felt like I had just been worked over in an alley by a loan shark.

'Ruby, why are you screaming?'

She looked at me like I'd just asked a stupid question. 'You wouldn't wake up so I did one of my waking the dead screams. And it worked.'

'So you're OK?'

'Yes, yes,' she said, grabbing my hand and pulling me.

I took a few steps and then had to stop. I turned away and thought I was going to be sick. She grabbed my hand again.

'Come on, come on, you have to meet someone. She is sooooooo nice.'

I quickly straightened up and finally had a look around. I let Ruby lead me to her new friend as a smile crossed my face. I reached out and placed my hands on that venerable old bark and said, 'Hello, Mother Oak.'

SIXTEEN

THE WORRY STONE

The moment I touched her I received that blessed loving calm that comes every time I'm with Mother Oak, and through her I could also feel the joy and unconditional love coming from Ruby, who was touching the oak's trunk as well. But the calm didn't last. I was surprised and then scared by what I could only describe as panic rising up in Mother Oak. I tried to pull my hand away but was frozen to the spot just like when I was attacked by the oak outside of Castle Duir. I groaned and dropped to my knees as the tree's will probed my mind for information.

'Why are you being so mean to him?' I heard Ruby yell and it stopped.

I fell backwards hard on my butt and caught my breath. Ruby continued to talk to her and I listened to that one side of the conversation.

'Yes ... I guess so ... Promise ... OK.'

Ruby walked over to me and said, 'She said she was surprised and did a bad thing. She wants to talk to you and promises to be nice.'

I didn't get up right away. I really had been sucker punched by the old woman. An attack from Mother Oak was the last thing I expected and after *rothlú*-ing around for a couple of days, I just wanted to curl up and drool for a while. But this was Mother Oak. I had to at least find out what made her act that way. I didn't even stand, I just scooted backwards and sat against her trunk and tentatively placed my hands on her bark.

Back was the old Mother Oak. *'Oh my, I am so sorry Conor. I try never to intrude on anyone's private thoughts but I saw something at the fore of your mind and it scared me so I just had to learn more. I am afraid I forgot myself. Please forgive me.'*

She really was terribly sorry. There was no hiding emotion when you are talking to the Grand Lady of Glen Duir. Of course she was forgiven and I stood, hugged her once and then climbed a little, allowing her to build a place for me to sit in her branches.

As I settled in, I also felt through Mother Oak the emotional presence of Ruby. 'Is everything all right?'

'Yes dear,' the tree reassured.

'I'm fine, Ruby,' I said. 'It was just a misunderstanding.'

'I was wondering, my child, if I may have a chat with Conor on my own for a moment.'

'Oh, like grown-up stuff.'

I felt Mother Oak smile. *'Yes. One thing I certainly am is grown-up.'*

'OK,' Ruby said and then she was out of my head.

'Again I am sorry for my rudeness before, but I saw in your mind that Maeve is alive. Can this truly be so? The child spoke of horrible things that Banshees did to her and she spoke of ghosts.'

'All true, I'm afraid. Cialtie has somehow brought Maeve and her Fili army back.'

'Oh, my, my. I had hoped that the past would stay past. I do not know if I can sprout through another season if such turmoil again grows in The Land.'

The old oak creaked and I could almost feel the weight of her boughs pressing down on my shoulders.

'Don't worry ma'am. My mom and dad will figure out something,' I said, hoping it was true. 'I have to go now and warn everyone.'

'Yes, yes of course, Conor,' the tree said as if I roused her from deep thought. *'And you must get that dear girl back to her father and grandmother. Ask her to come back to me.'*

'Hey Ruby,' I shouted. 'Mother Oak wants to speak to you and then we have to go.'

I climbed down and was going to leave them alone but the tree asked me to stay. Ruby wrapped her arms around the trunk. The two of them didn't speak for a while – they just felt. Love flowed between them like a two-way street.

'You have been through so much my little sprout. But you are with Conor now and he will take good care of you. Can I tell you a secret?'

Ruby nodded her head. 'Yes.'

'Conor is the finest young man I have ever met.'

'Really?' I said.

'Shush, I was speaking to Ruby. Goodbye you two. Take care of each other. I'm afraid there are going to be dark times ahead. Just remember that I have been in this glen for oh so very a long time and the one thing I know is – after winter there has always been spring.'

I had never walked back to the castle from Glen Duir but I knew it was going to take more than a day. 'You up for a long hike?'

Ruby took my hand and said, 'Sure.'

Mother Oak had given her a stick that she had trimmed and she set off sweeping it before her.

'Don't you feel bad after that *rothlú* spell that brought us here?'

'My tummy was a little funny when I first got here but I'm OK now.'

'Well, I feel like crap.'

'You said a dirty word.'

'Sorry.'

'I won't tell.'

'Thanks.'

We trudged along for the rest of the day. Ruby hummed some song, most of the time while I grunted along. The sun got lower and Ruby started to get tired. There was no point in stopping. We had no food and no way to make a fire so I gave her a piggyback. She quickly fell asleep. It's amazing how rapidly the young girl on my back began to feel like a proverbial eight-hundred-pound gorilla. As the sun was setting I had to quit.

'I'm cold.'

I gave her my Brownie cloak. 'I'm afraid I don't have a fire coin, Ruby.'

'That's OK,' she said. 'Go ask a tree for two sticks.'

'Why?'

'To rub together.'

'Oh,' I laughed. 'I'm afraid rubbing sticks together will only get us splinters. I have to rest, Ruby. Just for an hour.'

I lay down and she snuggled up on my chest.

'Will that Lugh man find us here?'

I don't even remember if I stayed awake long enough to answer. The next thing I do remember, Ruby was prying open one of my eyelids and frantically whispering, 'Wake up. Someone's coming.'

The two of us ran out of the clearing and hid behind some oaks, making sure not to touch them. It was a small party of riders. In front, one of the riders hung over his saddle with his head down. In his hand he was dangling a vial that glowed with a yellow light. He was a scout and was obviously following our trail. I thought about climbing the tree in front of us but I was too afraid of getting comatised like the last time I talked to a strange oak. Running was no good either. The forest wasn't thick enough to slow down a rider. I had nowhere to run and nowhere to hide. I drew the Lawnmower and waited. I still could only make out their silhouettes. The scout spotted where we had bedded down, and then looked directly to the tree we were hiding behind.

I stepped out and said, 'Who goes there?'

The scout dismounted and pushed back his hood. Hair cascaded over the scout's shoulders like a cheesy shampoo commercial. It was only when she placed the light next to her face that everything instantly became all right again in The Land.

'Conor,' she yipped. She ran and crashed into me, giving me a bone-crunching hug.

'Hi, Essa. Miss me?'

*　*　*

A fire was built and food was brought. Essa sent a message back to Castle Duir that we had been found and Tuan was flying in to pick us up air-ambulance style.

Ruby started jabbering on about her abduction like it was some sort of fun adventure. I'm sure that if I had experienced a similar trauma at her age I would have become a curled-up snivelling wreck, but Ruby was obviously made of sterner stuff.

As she was recounting her story I remembered something. A Banshee had said she had killed two guards.

'Ruby, how did you escape? Weren't you being guarded?'

Ruby crinkled up her nose at the thought of it. 'The guards were mean. One of them saw me rubbing my worry stone and he told me to give it to him. I said no because Grandma had given it to me, so he grabbed it. Then I was alone. I just crawled along the wall until I found that way out.'

'Ruby, what's a worry stone?'

She reached into her pocket and pulled out a smooth pebble-sized piece of green marble with a dent in it. She held it in her hand and rubbed her thumb on the indentation. 'I found it on the floor as I was crawling out.'

'Can I see it?' Essa asked. 'I promise to give it back.'

As Ruby handed it over, a thought formed in my mind. I reached out to stop Essa from touching the stone but I was too slow.

When Essa touched the pebble, she didn't scream. It was more like she had all of the wind knocked out of her. She dropped her head down and then after catching her breath, she looked at the back of her hands. They were spidery, wrinkled and covered with spots. When she looked up, the firelight showed the eighty-year-old woman who I had first seen at the police station in the Real World.

'Oh, not again!' Essa said in her old woman voice.

'What's happening?' Ruby asked.

'Your worry stone, Ruby, it's from Ireland; when Essa touched it she became the age she would be in the Real World.'

'Damn it, damn it, damn it.'

'She said a naughty word.'

'Yes, Ruby, I think she did.'

* * *

I was expecting Ruby to love the ride home on dragon-back but I could tell it scared her. She held on white-knuckled and shook almost the whole way. Of course, that didn't stop her, when she got back, from bragging about how fun it was.

The return of the prodigal son was nothing compared to Ruby's return. I don't think I had ever seen anybody so happy to see anybody as the residents of Castle Duir were with the rearrival of Ruby. Most of the people there had never seen her, but the gloom that had been hanging over the place since her kidnap broke with an exuberance that was almost like a festival. While Ruby got all the attention I just stood by and said, 'Don't worry about me. I'm fine.'

Brendan unaged, like, ten years instantly when he saw her. I came close to trying to separate them, he was hugging his daughter so hard, but Ruby didn't seem to mind. Nora, who had been mad at me ever since I left her granddaughter alone in the Forest of Duir, kissed my cheek and said, 'I have no words to tell you how grateful I am.'

'Aw shucks, ma'am,' I said. 'It was nothin''

Graysea was very glad to see me. I got smothered with kisses and then she insisted on finning-up and giving me a thorough mermaid medical work-up. I told her I was fine, just tired, and asked her to have a look at Ruby's hand. She healed the cut in seconds.

'I like her better than Essa,' Ruby said after her treatment.

'You have seen Essa already?' Graysea asked curtly.

'Well, yeah,' I said, 'she was the one who found us in the forest. I wouldn't worry about her, she's … well, she's not looking her best.'

Essa was still on her way back to Castle Duir. Tuan had offered her some dragon blood in the forest but I told her I had a plan and it might be a good idea if she stayed like that. She agreed, but wouldn't take a dragon lift back to Duir. I think her exact words were, 'I'll hit the next person who treats me like an old woman.'

Essa was summed up best by Ruby who said, 'She's scary.'

*   *   *

After a night's sleep that I had to insist upon, I sat down with Mom, Dad, Nieve, Fand and Dahy. I felt like I was reporting to the Spanish Inquisition. I told them the whole story of what had happened on my way to the Yewlands. When I got to Hermy, Dad interrupted.

'What did you say his name was?'

'Sorry, I made up Hermy. Let me think. Oh yeah, just as I was *rothlú*-ing away he said his name was Eth.'

Dad was on his feet. 'Eth? What else did he say?'

'He said he was Ona's son.'

Dad covered his mouth with his left hand. I can tell when he's emotional because he never uses his right hand – the one that was missing for so long. As I watched him and waited for him to speak, it came to me where I had heard that name before. Eth was Dad's best friend. He was the one who was with Dad on the day of the boat race. When Dad woke up in the infirmary he had blamed Eth for the loss of his hand and Eth left – never to be seen again.

'I have to go to Thunder Bay at once.'

'Hold on, Dad,' I said. 'There is other stuff I have to tell you and I think there is somewhere I have to go first.'

Mom gave Dad one of those one-second looks that conveyed an entire paragraph of information. It instantly said, 'I know you're upset, but calm down, we have to think about this.' It also said, 'I love you.' It's amazing what women can do with just a look and a tiny finger movement.

I continued recanting my adventure. When I got to Cialtie and his witch's Shadowcasting, it was my mother's turn to get upset. When I told her about how Ruby's blood was used to darken the shadow of her rune she reached to her neck and pulled her rune from under her top. It was dark red, almost black.

'It suddenly went dark two days ago,' Mom said.

'Yeah, that would be about right.'

And then I upset everybody by telling them that Maeve was back. Of all people, it was Fand who was still calm enough to make light of my story. She said, 'Conor, you are many things but you are never dull.'

'And I'm not even done yet. The reason Ruby was able to escape from the Ivy Lodge was because she killed her two guards.'

I'm not sure who said 'What?' but I'm pretty sure it was everybody.

I reached into my pocket and took out Ruby's marble worry stone. Mom went to reach for it but I stopped her. 'Don't touch it, Mom, that little thing will kill you.'

'What is it?'

'It's a stone from a place on the west coast of Ireland called Connemara. They call it Connemara marble. Nora said she bought it on a trip over there. She says that she was aware of major ley-lines while she was in Connemara. Ages ago, Spideog showed me a stone axe that he had brought back from the Real World but it was only a wooden handle. He said the stone vanished in the portal during his journey back to The Land.'

'That is correct,' Mom said. 'Stone will not pass between the worlds.'

'Well, this did,' I said picking up the worry stone. 'And I'm pretty sure if anyone in The Land touches it, it's exactly like when they touch the ground in the Real World. They become their actual Real World age.'

'That is an interesting theory,' Dahy said.

'It's more than a theory, Master D,' I said as I walked to the door. I opened it and the eighty-year-old Essa came in.

'Oh my dear,' Fand said. 'Did you …'

'Yes, I touched the damn rock,' Essa said, already tired of having to explain her looks.

'Why haven't you spoken to Tuan and changed back?'

''Cause Essa is going to help me with something. We're going to go on a trip.'

'A trip,' Dad said. 'To where?'

'I thought we'd go and get some more of this stuff.'

SEVENTEEN

CONNEMARA

'Tell me again why we didn't bring horses?' Essa said as she looked around at the nothingness in all directions.

Essa, Brendan and I had arrived at the Fairy Fingers about ten minutes earlier. Mom, Nieve and Fand had communed with Nora, who was becoming a bit of an insta-sorceress, and they searched for ley-lines on the west coast of Ireland. It was not surprising to learn that for travelling back and forth between the Real World and Tir na Nog, Ireland was ley-line central. The problem was there were so many magic spots in the Emerald Isle that it was hard to find the right one. Especially when the most recent map Mom had of Ireland looked like it was printed on woolly mammoth skin. It was concluded that a stone circle called the Fairy Fingers would be the nearest place to Connemara. Fand said Cullen, or should I say Cucullen, built it to mark his favourite portal spot. She added, 'He was always building crap like that.' I loved how Fand incorporated 'crap' into her daily language ever since I taught it to her.

The Fairy Fingers had a sign pointing to it from the road but no other signs around gave us any help as to what direction civilisation lay. Assuming that the time of day was the same here as in The Land (a big assumption) we decided to walk in the opposite direction to the sun and trudge west. That way if we didn't find any people, at least the sea would stop us from walking for ever.

'Because,' I said answering Essa, 'people in the modern Real World don't ride horses. It would draw attention to us.'

Sometimes I think the gods just spend all of their time messing with my life 'cause at that moment we heard the unmistakable clip-clop of horses' hooves followed by two riders cantering up the middle of the road behind us. Essa gave me one of her most reproachful stares. I turned to Brendan for support.

'Tell her that's just a fluke. People don't ride horses around here.'

'As much as I enjoy watching Conor make a fool out of himself, he's right,' Brendan said, 'people don't ride horses any more.'

Apparently the gods don't just screw with me, they mess with Brendan as well 'cause immediately after saying that, four more riders cantered up behind us. Brendan and I just stared at each other open-mouthed as Essa shook her head.

'Are you certain that you two are from here?' Essa asked.

'We're not from here,' Brendan said, 'we're from a different part of the Real World but still – this isn't the middle of nowhere – this is Ireland. I'm certain they have the internal combustion engine here.'

'Could Mom have sent us back in time?'

'If I had to choose between Deirdre sending us back in time or you two being idiots …' Essa stared at us and then said, 'Do I really have to finish that sentence?'

Several more groups of horses rode past. I really started to think that we were in the past until I saw one of the riders wearing a pair of Nikes. One thing I'm certain of is that Nikes were definitely around at the same time as cars. The question is – where were the cars and why was everybody riding?

A pony and cart came up behind us with an old man holding the reins. 'Get out of the way, you idiots,' he shouted.

He had plenty of room but we moved further over to the side of the road.

As he went, by I asked, 'Why is everybody on horseback?'

'Because they're not so stupid as to be walking like you.'

Obviously this was not the runner up in the Connemara Miss Congeniality contest. Brendan and I smiled at each other and let him past but Essa said, 'Excuse me, can we get a lift in your cart?'

His reply would have made a sailor blush.

'He said a dirty word,' Brendan said, doing an imitation of his daughter.

'I believe you are right, Detective Fallon.'

Brendan and I thought it was funny. Old lady Essa, though, seemed to have outgrown her sense of humour. She reached into her pocket, took out a gold sphere and then blew on it in the direction of the cart. The old man keeled over in his seat and the horse veered off towards the side of the road and stopped. Brendan and my smiles vanished as we ran to the old guy. He was out cold.

'What did you do to him?' Brendan asked.

Essa slowly sauntered up to the old guy and placed her hands on both sides of his head. 'He will be fine. He's just asleep. Throw him in the back.'

Brendan and I looked at each other.

'You can either throw him in the back and cover him with some of that burlap or we can stand around staring at each other until someone comes along and starts asking questions.'

When Essa talks like that there really is no other choice than to do what she says. I picked up the old guy under his shoulders and Brendan got his feet.

As we were carrying him, Brendan said, 'In all of my time as a cop I always wondered how so many nice people ended up leading a life of crime. I'm starting to understand now.'

Essa took the reins and Brendan and I sat on the back of the cart with our legs dangling over the end. It was painfully slow. Riders continually passed us. One shouted, 'Nice pony.' To which I replied, 'Nice horsey.' We eventually passed houses with cars outside but still we didn't see anyone driving. I wanted to ask why everybody was on horses but when you cart-jack an octogenarian it's best to keep a low profile.

After what seemed like days, with every person who rode by looking at us like we were under a microscope, we came to a large plastic road sign that read, 'ROAD CLOSED FOR PONY FESTIVAL.'

It was getting to be around lunchtime and the town was hopping. In all directions there were ponies and horses in stables, attached to pony-carts and with riders. Stalls were set up selling saddles, bridles and all sorts of horsey things. An old-fashioned blacksmith was firing up a forge and performing a horse-shoeing demonstration. And underfoot everywhere was horse crap. All of the festival goers were wearing rubber wellington boots – I on the other hand still had on those flimsy Brownies slippers. I had a look around town to see if there was a proper shoe store but it didn't look like this was a place where I could get a new pair of Nikes.

'You know what?' Brendan said with a smile worthy of Fergal. 'I'd really like a Guinness.'

'A what?' Essa said.

'I'll show you,' Brendan said, pointing to a pub.

Essa parked the cart and the sleeping old man as far back in the parking lot as she could.

The pub smelled of horse manure, decades of stale beer and peat fire smoke. I instantly felt like I could spend some serious time in there. Essa and I found a low table and Brendan went up to the bar to ask where he could change his dollars into local currency. Standing next to him a tall American offered to swap him enough for a few pints and sandwiches. The American, wearing a new tweed flat cap, even helped him carry the food over to the table.

'So y'awl from Scranton too?' the tall American asked in a Dixie accent. He didn't wait for an answer and sat down without an invite.

'Santa's Car,' he said, hoisting his pint for a toast. 'I learned that today.'

'Sláinte Mhaith?' I said.

'Yeah, that's it. A local told me it was Gaelic for "Here's mud in your eye".'

'I'm not sure if that's the literal translation.'

'No? No matter, I've got so much Guinness in me I won't remember tomorrow. I'm Alexander Hawthorn-Twait. Now don't get all excited about the fancy name. My granddaddy was a Texas horse thief who went straight and gave himself a fancy title. I'm just a normal millionaire grandson of a horse thief. Friends call me Al. So where'd yooaall say you were from?'

'I'm a Scrantonian too,' I said.

'And how about you ma'am?

'I am from Munn.'

The American lit up. 'Well my, my, I'd never have thought I'd find me someone from my neck of the woods out here in the middle of nowhere. But I don't know a Munn, Kentucky?'

Essa was speaking English using one of my Aunt Nieve's magic spells. The result was that she sounded to the listener like she was speaking in the accent that they were most familiar with. I didn't hear it because to me it sounded as if Essa was speaking ancient Gaelic.

Before Essa could say anything I reached over, patted her hand and said, 'Essa has a habit of mimicking people's accents. Don't you dear?' I turned back to our guest and secretly twirled my finger around my ear.

'Oh, OK,' he said, 'well, you tell your mother I think that's charming.'

'I am not his mother,' Essa said.

Brendan actually spit out his mouthful of Guinness.

'I beg your pardon.'

Brendan continued to laugh and like a yawn I caught it too. We both giggled like schoolboys as Essa got angrier.

'What's so funny?' Al asked, confused.

'Brendan pointed to me and said, 'She's his girlfriend.'

'I am not.'

Maybe it was the Guinness we had drunk, or the look on Essa's face, or maybe just the niceness of being back in the Real World again but Brendan and I lost it. We were laughing so hard we couldn't speak.

Al looked uncomfortable. 'I think you boys are pulling my leg.'

Essa heard that and actually looked under the table and Brendan laughed so hard he fell off his chair.

'You folks are very strange.' Al stood up to leave.

I wanted to say something, apologise; I knew we were being rude but I just couldn't get any words out. Al stomped off and Brendan and I continued like that until Essa's deadly stares calmed us down.

I raised a toast, 'To Santa's Car.'

Essa finally took a sip of her Guinness. When she placed her glass back on the table she sported a white Guinness moustache.

'Well, watcha think?' Brendan asked.

'Can I have something that isn't black?'

* * *

Brendan figured that we had made too much of a spectacle of ourselves in the pub to then ask questions about where we could get marble, so he left us to nurse our pints and went to ask around town. Essa and I sat in silence. Al went back to drinking at the bar, periodically giving us strange looks.

Finally Essa said, 'I would really like to get back to The Land soon so I can no longer be mistaken for your grandmother.'

'You do make a lovely grandma.'

'Would hitting you in here draw attention to us?' she said.

'Yes.'

'You're lucky then.'

We didn't have enough money to buy anything else so we took tiny sips of our drinks and politely declined every time a barmaid came by and asked us if we wanted anything else. I got the distinct impression that we weren't spending enough money in there.

I got up to use *the loo*. While I was in there I heard a commotion in the pub. As soon as I opened the men's room door I saw a chair flying through the air and heard Essa screaming, 'Get your hands off of me.'

A policeman shouted, 'She's got something in her hand. She's got a gun!'

Everyone was on their feet. I saw Essa's hand being held over her head as her golden ball was prised out of her fingers. There were three cops around her. I knew I couldn't help her in this crowded pub, so, while everyone was looking at her being cuffed, I dropped my chin and began to walk out the door. On the bar I spotted Al's new tweed cap. I swiped it and put it on low so it covered my eyes.

Outside an ambulance was trying to revive the old man. He was still asleep. I could tell that 'cause he was snoring and it was loud. The snoring must have been what made someone look underneath the burlap.

I wandered around town, periodically stopping to admire a pony or peruse a saddle stall. Basically I just tried to look anonymous while keeping an eye out for Brendan. Luckily I spotted him as he was making his way back into the pub. I spun him around and told him to keep walking and act normal.

'What's the matter with you, O'Neil?'

'Essa's been arrested.'

'What?'

'Yeah, three of your guys got her in the pub while I was in the men's room. Somebody found the old guy in the back of the cart. He got taken away in an ambulance.'

'I would have thought Essa would blow the place up before she allowed herself to be arrested.'

'She was about to but they wrestled that gold ball thing out of her hand before she could do anything. Now she's just a crazy eighty-year-old woman with an attitude problem.'

Brendan thought for a moment and despite our situation, smiled. 'I bet she said some naughty words too.'

'Yeah, I imagine she did,' I said matching his smile.

'So what now, another jail break?'

'I've never tried one without any magic backup,' I said.

'We have to reunite Essa with her magic ball,' Brendan said. 'Not only is it our only weapon – it's how we get back to Tir na Nog.'

That hadn't occurred to me. 'Oh yeah. Any ideas?'

'Well, it's risky, but I could see if the local police will extend a little professional courtesy.'

The police station was in the next town over. Brendan had exchanged all of his money so we had enough for a cab but the one cab driver in town was busy 'fleecing rich Yanks', so we took the bus.

The police station was attached to a veterinary practice. Brendan initially told me to wait outside while he went in but I refused. I didn't want to be waiting outside for hours wondering what the hell had gone wrong. My initial idea was to steal a sheep and then mistakenly take it in to the cop station instead of the vet's. That way I would be inside to see what happened. That drew one of those looks from Brendan that stifles all further discussion. Finally we came up with the simpler plan of me going in first and reporting a lost wallet. Sure, it made more sense, but it just didn't have the panache of my sheep idea.

I suspect that in this tiny Irish town a lost wallet would have been the highlight of the day, but on this particular one they had a bona fide crazy criminal locked up in their cell. (Well, it wasn't a cell, it was just a windowless office, but for now it was a cell.) The garda (what they call cops there) hardly listened to me and handed me a pen and a lost property form. While I was dawdling over my paperwork, Brendan came in.

Actually what I should say is Detective Fallon of the Scranton Fraternal Order of Police stormed in. He didn't pause to introduce himself. He strode up to the counter, flashed his badge and ID and said, 'I want to speak to your superior officer.'

The old policeman was taken aback. 'Ah, he's unavailable at this time.'

A younger cop came from the back.

'Where is he?' Brendan demanded.

'I think he's castrating a cat.'

Well, that would explain the police station being next to a veterinarian's office, I thought.

'I can get him,' the younger cop said. 'Who should I say wants him?'

Brendan flashed his badge and ID again but the young cop insisted on looking at it carefully.

'Detective Brendan Fallon of the Scranton, Pennsylvania PD. Is that correct?'

'Yes,' Brendan replied brusquely.

'I'll be back in a moment,' the young cop said.

'Would this be concerning the woman we arrested today?' the older cop asked.

'I would prefer to speak to your superior,' Brendan said.

'I'm not sure you do,' he said, but before Brendan could ask him why, the young cop appeared in the doorway with his hands behind his back. He stepped up to Brendan and then brought out what I thought was a gun. He pulled a trigger and two darts attached to wires exploded out of the front of the thing. The darts hit Brendan in the chest and he started dancing around like a puppet on a string.

The taser stopped humming and Brendan slid to the ground.

'What the hell are you doing?' the old cop shouted.

The young cop pulled the electric darts out of Brendan's chest, 'Jeez, did you see that? This thing really works.'

'I can see that it works,' the old guy said. 'But what the hell did you do it for?'

The young cop rolled Brendan onto his side and reached for his handcuffs. 'This fella's a fugitive. Remember I was telling you about that America's Most Wanted programme I watch on the teli? This guy is wanted by the FBI. He blew up a police station and kidnapped a G-man, or a young girl ... I can't remember, but this is him.'

Brendan was coming to as the cop secured the cuffs. I backed out of the room and mumbled, 'I'll come back when you're less ... busy.' I pulled my stolen cap over my eyes and left. The two cops hardly noticed me.

I got outside and said the only thing I could think of. 'Oh crap.'

EIGHTEEN
CONNEMARA MAEVE

I got a room in Mrs McDunna's Bed and Breakfast. It was not as cheap as I would have liked, but then again, I didn't have any money so she wasn't going to get paid anyway. I spent my first night hidden in my room in case the cops figured out that I was the third member of the international crime syndicate they were arresting.

Mrs McDunna's Irish breakfast was gorgeous. Since the next prospect I had of eating again was this time the next day, I ate an entire loaf of her home-made soda bread. It was lovely but sat in my stomach like a rock. She asked me what I was going to do that day. I panicked and said I was going to buy a pony. So half an hour later I left to pretend to buy one.

The town was nice, but it only took an hour to see every nook and cranny of it. I cased out the police/vet office. There was a door in the back. I snuck up and tried it but it was locked. I knew I should have taken classes in burglary when I was growing up.

By late afternoon I was starving. As I was passing a tea shop with a couple of tables outside, I saw an old lady get up to leave. I quickly dropped into her empty chair and ate the sandwich crusts she had left behind. I checked the tea pot and poured a lukewarm half cup of black tea into her old cup and washed down my salvaged scraps.

'You seem to have gotten younger since sitting here.'

I looked up and a pretty young waitress was staring at me with her arms crossed.

'And I changed sex as well.' I put down my cup. 'This is really amazing tea.'

She was trying to be stern but that got her. She laughed and uncrossed her arms. 'So what's your story?'

'I lost my wallet,' I said. 'I'm waiting for money from my bank but they seem to be sending it via camel train.'

'So you've no money?'

'Not until tomorrow at the earliest,' I lied.

'Well, we're closing up here.'

'Oh, of course,' I said, standing.

She sighed and shook her head. 'Sit,' she said, taking away the old woman's plates. 'I'll bring you a proper cup of tea.'

She did, as well as some scones that stopped me from wanting to eat my shoes.

I waited for her as she locked the front door. 'Thanks for that,' I said.

'Don't mention it. I've always been a soft touch for vagabonds.'

'Well, on behalf of vagabonds and deadbeats everywhere, I salute you.'

She stood stock still and then just stared at me. Her scrutiny was intense. I felt like I was being scanned by a tree. 'What is your name?'

'Conor.'

'What aren't you telling me, Conor?'

That question made the scones do a little flip in my tummy. 'I haven't really told you anything.'

'No,' she said elongating the o like she was figuring something out. 'You haven't, have you? I think you should take me to dinner.'

'Actually, I did tell you one thing. I have no money, remember?'

'OK, I'll take you to dinner and you can pay me back when your money shows up.'

Part of me wanted to turn her down. She had a look about her that reminded me of a CIA interrogator in a spy movie. But the part of me that eats said, 'Great idea.'

* * *

'So is this a traditional Irish dish?' I said, pointing to my chicken vinda-loo.

'Yes – curry is very Irish, right after cockles, mussels and stew.'

I took a big sip of beer to calm the fire on my tongue. 'Well, thank you ... You know, I don't even know your name.'

'It's Maeve, and I should be thanking you. You're paying for this – eventually.'

'Maeve, oh my. That's a name with some history behind it. Is it a family name?'

'No. My ma always said she named me that because I was born a troublemaker.'

'Are you still a troublemaker?'

'What do you think?'

'Well, you do seem to have a penchant for having dinner with strange men.'

'Strange,' she said, rewearing that X-ray look of hers. 'Yes, "strange" is the right word when explaining you. Where are you from?'

'Scranton.'

She stared again. 'Where are you reeeeely from?'

'Scraaaaaaanton.'

'I can tell when you're lying.'

'I'd show you my driver's licence ...'

'But you lost your wallet. Convenient.'

'OK,' I said, 'how about this. I live in the mystical Land of Tir na Nog, on top of a gold mine, and I'm here on a secret mission to get magical stones to stop the impending attack of my evil uncle and your namesake Queen Maeve.'

My confession didn't make my date smile as fast as I thought it would but finally the corners of her mouth turned upwards. 'And what do you do in this magical land?'

'Oh, I'm a prince, of course. I'm surprised you had to ask.'

'I see. So, Prince Conor, if you live on a gold mine why are you so broke?'

'Oh I have gold with me; I just can't find any place to change it into money.'

'Can I see your gold?'

'I don't carry it around. It's ... well, it's heavy.'

She finally broke in to a full-blown laugh. 'You know I almost felt like I believed you, but you went too far with the prince thing.'

'You don't think I'm princely?' I said with mock indignation.

'I'm afraid not.'

'Good, all that bowing and yes Your Highness stuff really annoys me.'

'I can imagine how trying that must be.'

I offered to walk Maeve home but she said since she paid for the date she got to walk *me* home. Outside my B&B she asked, 'Is there a princess in your world?'

There was something about this woman that made me want to tell her the truth. 'Yes, but she's eighty years old, and I'm also kinda seeing a mermaid.'

She smiled and kissed me on the cheek. 'You can find me at the tea shop when your money arrives.' As she walked away she said over her shoulder, 'Good night, Prince Conor.'

I had had a wonderful night and that was the problem. I felt guilty. I shouldn't have been out having fun while my friends were in jail and I was no closer to figuring out how to help them or get back to The Land. I spent half the night staring at the ceiling trying to figure out what to do and awoke no closer to a solution.

After another soda-bread-filled breakfast, I spent most of the next day watching the comings and goings of the vet office/police station. My only hope was that these people were stupid enough to leave this place unguarded so I could just walk in and break out my pals. But I guess that the rule – prisoners must be guarded – had made it even to the west coast of Ireland.

Since I didn't have any money to pay her back, I had meant to stay away from Maeve's tea house but by about four in the afternoon loneliness and, if I'm honest, hunger forced me to swallow my pride and see her. I confessed that I still had no money. When I started to go she commanded me to sit and brought me sandwiches and tea.

'I'll add it to your bill.'

She then invited me to a pub that night to meet her friends. When I said no she said, 'Tonight is my treat.' I said I'd try and went back to the B&B.

I had no intention of going. Along with feeling guilty for taking advantage of the poor girl, I also thought meeting a bunch of people seemed like a bad idea. After all, I was spending my days casing out a police station trying to plan a jail break. I'm pretty sure that when you are about to commit a huge felony, one should keep a low profile. But the bored lonely guy talked the rational soon-to-be felon out of it and I showed up at the pub. It was busy in there. At the corner of the bar were a water jug and some glasses so I helped myself to a glass of water so I wouldn't look too out of place. There were lots of young people around but Maeve wasn't there. I guess I had waited too long to make up my mind. I was about to leave when she walked in.

'Oh, I hope you haven't been waiting all this time.' She was a bit flushed like she had been running.

'No, I just got here.'

'Oh good, sorry I'm late. My father had a guest over for dinner and I had to eat with them.'

'I'm sorry to pull you away.'

'Don't be. The guy was such a drip. You'd think an FBI man would be interesting, wouldn't you?'

I started choking on my water but managed to calm down quickly enough to ask, 'Your father's guest is an American FBI agent?'

'Yes, can you imagine?'

'And what does your father do?'

'He's a policeman.'

It took all of my will to keep a calm exterior. 'And do you remember the FBI man's name?'

'I'm not sure I do. I didn't like him much … It was an Italian name.'

'Was it Agent Murano?'

'Yes. How did you know that?'

'Ah … I … think I met him today. You know, walking around town.'

'Is he here because of you?'

My heart pounded in my chest. I looked around to see where the nearest exit was. 'Me?'

'Yes. Do you think the FBI is here to investigate your lost wallet?' She laughed and asked me what I would like to drink.

'I ... actually, Maeve, I have been waiting a long time and I don't feel very well. I really have to go.'

I knew I wouldn't be able to sustain small talk so I unceremoniously left. As I was walking away I heard her shout after me, 'Conor,' but I kept going. I needed to think.

Back in the B&B I really didn't feel well. This was a serious mess. I wondered how the hell I could get out of it. I went through all sorts of scenarios, including putting my finger in my pocket and pretending I had a gun. I finally settled on watching tomorrow until there was only one person in the station and then attacking with a banta stick. This worried me. We were in the real world and hitting people with sticks could kill them, but I had to get Essa and Brendan out of there before they were moved to a bigger city – or worse, extradited back to the USA. With a plan, of sorts, I placed my head on the pillow and managed sleep. I used to complain how my nights were dreamless in the Real World but it didn't bother me this night.

I heard the bedroom door as it closed. By then it was too late. I opened my eyes to the sight of an Irish policeman aiming a taser at my forehead.

'My daughter told me you were staying here.'

'Honest, sir,' I said, staring cross-eyed at the needles of the taser, 'I didn't even kiss her.'

He backed up and sat in a chair. I sat up in bed.

'Where did you come from?'

'Scranton, Pennsylvania.'

The policeman looked casually at the weapon in his hand. 'I had never actually seen one of these things fire before your friend got it in the chest the other day. He said it was very painful.'

'I really am from Scranton.'

'I didn't ask you where you were from, I asked where you came from. My chief and your FBI have already checked and Detective Fallon didn't enter Ireland on his passport. So how did you get here and where did you come from?'

I dropped back into the bed and spread my arms wide. 'Shoot,' I said.

'Come again?'

'Shoot me. If I tell you the truth you won't believe me. In fact, if I tell my story around here you'll probably think I was making fun of you. So shoot me and get it over with.'

'Before I shoot you, Mr O'Neil … You are Conor O'Neil, yes?'

'Yeah,' I said. Denying it at this point would have been stupid.

'I may believe more than you think. Have you noticed what language we are speaking?'

I hadn't, not really. Because my father is a tyrannical linguist, it's normal for me to just drop into the language that is being spoken to me. Connemara is a gaeltacht, which means that a lot of people around here speak modern Irish. I had impressed a few of the locals by simply chatting to them in their language. But as I thought back on the nice chat me and the armed policeman were having, I realised we weren't speaking Irish, we were talking in ancient Gaelic. 'Where did you learn this language?'

'My parents taught it to me. I also have read all of your father's published work on pronunciation. I've always wondered where he got his insight. But I am not here to answer your questions. You are here to answer mine. How did you get here and from where?'

'Could I pee first?'

NINETEEN
MÍCHEÁL

'How about I shoot you with this, you'll definitely pee yourself then.'

'OK, OK, I came from Tir na Nog. Detective Fallon, Essa and I arrived two days ago by way of ley-lines that intersect at the Fairy Fingers.'

The cop lowered his gun. 'Mick O'Hara said the last thing he remembered was passing the Fairy Fingers.'

'Is that the old guy we stole the cart from?'

'It is.'

'Yeah, sorry about that. Is he OK?'

The policeman laughed. 'He's fine. I don't recommend apologising to him in person. Not unless you want your ears ripped off.'

'I really could use that pee now.'

'One more question and maybe I'll let you relieve yourself. Are you from the House of Luis?'

OK, speaking ancient Gaelic is one thing but using Ogham made it almost unnecessary for me to walk to the bathroom for that pee. 'What do you know of Luis?'

The cop looked me hard in the eyes; it felt like the look a poker opponent has when he is deciding to bluff or not. 'I want to know if I'm speaking to a Fili.'

'What do you know of the Fili?'

'Are you Fili?' he said raising his taser again.

'No.'

He stood and walked menacingly towards me. 'What is your house?'

'Duir,' I said with a pride that surprised me.

'Well, I wouldn't want it be said that the first Faerie I met wet himself.' The policeman pocketed his gun and gestured towards the door. I got up and threw on a pair of trousers. As I reached the door he said, 'If you try to escape I'll find you, and if that happens I'll have to hand you over to Special Agent Murano. We wouldn't want that, would we?'

There was a window in the bathroom and I could have escaped that way if I wanted to, but he was right. Where would I go? The only plan I had come up with was to either single-handedly attack a police station or wait at the Fairy Fingers until someone came from The Land to see what happened to us. Now that I was busted by this guy I couldn't do the former and I didn't have time to wait around for the latter. Besides, this cop intrigued me. Where did he learn all of this stuff? And maybe, just maybe, he was an ally. When he said 'we' was that just a manner of speech or did he mean 'we'? If he was an ally, I could really use one right now.

The cop was in the hallway when I returned. 'You have a name?'

'Mícheál.'

'So what now, Officer Mícheál?'

'Well now, I've persuaded Mrs McDunna to cook me breakfast. Would you care to join me?'

We talked quietly but it didn't matter. I'm sure there were very few people around that could decipher a language that no one had spoken for several millennia.

'Why haven't you turned me over to the FBI?' was my first question.

'Partly because Murano is an idiot.'

'He's a sadistic idiot,' I added.

'That does not surprise me. My daughter took an instant dislike to him. She is usually a very good judge of character.'

'She likes me.'

That drew a stern look. 'Don't push it, O'Neil.'

'Sorry.'

'Now, tell me what you are doing here.'

'If I do,' I said, 'and you don't like what you hear, are you going to arrest me?'

'That depends whether I like what I hear or not.'

'My father is the Lord of Duir.'

'Your father is Finn?'

I was shocked again at his knowledge of The Land. I needed to be careful what I said to this guy. 'No, that was my grandfather but he is dead. My father, the one that the FBI and everyone in Scranton thinks I killed, is the new King of Duir.'

Mícheál took all of this in his stride. He wasn't incredulous at all. In fact, he increasingly looked eager for more news. 'This still doesn't explain why you are here.'

'The Land is at war. I came here to get something that will help us in the upcoming battle.'

'What?'

'Before I answer, can I ask you a question?'

'I suppose you deserve some questions answered.' He nodded yes.

'Why did you call your daughter Maeve?'

'When she was born she cried all the time for the first month of her life, it was maddening. There was nothing we could do to appease her. Every hour of the day when she wasn't eating or sleeping she was shrieking. My wife said if she was going to be this much trouble we might as well name her after the biggest troublemaker of all.'

I thought back to the conversation I had had with Nora and said, 'You're a Druid, aren't you?'

Mícheál snickered at that. 'Druids are misguided hippies who go barefoot and wear woolly robes.'

'But you're not that kind of Druid, are you?'

His false smile vanished. 'No.'

'You know where your ancestors came from and you know why they had to leave.'

'I have been told that we were banished because we followed a sorceress that had the same name as my daughter.'

Here was the moment of truth – this was the moment where I had to decide whose side he was on. It wasn't a hard decision; without his help I was sunk. 'Queen Maeve is back and if you don't help us she will destroy every tree in Tir na Nog to fuel her lust for power.'

The garda sat back in his chair and placed his hand to his cheek like he had been slapped. Finally he said, 'Many of us thought this day would come and we have debated what to do.'

'There are more of you?'

'Yes.'

'What I need to know, Mícheál, is what will *you* do?'

It didn't take long for him to decide. He leaned in and said, 'What do you need?'

I told him about the marble. He suggested I stay out of sight all day in case Murano were to accidentally spot me.

'I've been here too long,' Mícheál, said standing. 'Meet me after dark outside the tea shop. I'll take you to The Grove.'

Before he left I grabbed his arm and said, 'You couldn't lend me some money could ya, I'd kill for a toothbrush.'

Maeve was the one to show up after dark at the tea shop. She was riding a motorscooter.

'Da says you lost your marbles.'

'In a manner of speaking.'

'He also says you're never going to pay me back for that dinner.'

'That, I'm afraid, is true.'

'I sure can pick 'em. Hop on.'

We drove to an old barn on the outskirts of town. Inside were about fifty men and women. The Grove turned out to be not a place but the collective noun for a group of Druids. Imagine a room full of bearded men and wild-haired women in hooded robes, and then throw out that image. The Grove was made up of normal-looking butcher, banker, baker types. The only thing they had in common was a story handed down from mother to son and father to daughter for scores of generations. A story that said their ancestors were expelled from The Land of Immortals. There must now in the Real World have been over a hundred thousand descendants of the original Fili; this group were the last ones, the only ones to keep the faith. The only ones to have never broken the chain.

My arrival silenced what seemed to have been a heated debate.

Maeve was the first to break the silence. 'Are you really a prince?'

'I'm afraid I am.'

Someone in the crowd said, 'A Prince of Oak?'

'Hazel and Oak, yes.'

A young man dressed in motorcycle leathers came to the fore, 'My name is Cullum. How do we know you are what you say?'

'It's a fair question, Cullum. I can offer no proof until after you help me. If at the Fairy Fingers I and my companions vanish in a puff of smoke, then you will know what I have told you is true. If nothing happens then you will know you have been made a fool of by an idiot. What have you got to lose?'

'If I help you break your friends out of jail, I have a lot to lose.'

I started to answer but the policeman held up a hand and stopped me.

'But I am willing to help because I believe he is what he claims to be. We have been waiting for an event like this for ... for ever. Can we now pass it by for lack of faith?'

Cullum spoke again. 'Mícheál tells us you are at war again with Maeve.'

'This is true.'

'Some among us harbour a hope of someday returning to Tir na Nog. Maybe our best bet is to allow Maeve to win.'

'Maybe you're right. I don't know Queen Maeve, but I know her daughter Fand, who is my friend, and I know my uncle Cialtie. I know this war is not ours but has been thrust upon us by others. And I know that we are right.'

'Can you take us back with you?' Cullum asked.

'No, he cannot!' another voice shouted out. 'He is not The One!'

What followed was pandemonium as they all started arguing in a dialect that I couldn't quite grasp. 'Hey, hey,' I shouted, quieting them down. 'There is no use arguing. Essa is our sorceress, only she could answer that.'

'Time is short,' Mícheál said. 'Conor's companions are to be transported to Dublin tomorrow.'

That was the first time I had heard that news and it shocked me.

'I have already had the Mulhern boys, who work at the quarry,
bring bags of marble offcuts to the Fairy Fingers. I won't go against the
wishes of The Grove, but I for one think we should help Conor and his
friends. When our ancestors came to this place they found a simple
time. Still, they didn't subjugate, they were men and women of peace
and teaching. I believe Conor when he says that he and his are not the
instigators of this war. Maeve and her war was what got us into this
mess – I feel it in my bones that backing Maeve again is not the way
to get us out.'

I was asked to wait outside while they deliberated. Maeve said, 'I
vote with Conor,' and came outside to keep me company.

'Could you do me a favour?' I asked.

'If I can.'

'Could you make sure Mrs McDunna gets paid, and those boys who
got the marble from the quarry.'

Maeve placed her hands on her hips. 'You want me to pay all of your
bills on the money I make serving cups of tea? Not forgetting that you
owe me money too.'

'I don't want you to pay it with your salary – I was hoping you could
pay it with this.' I pulled a bar of metal the size of a chocolate bar out
of my backpack and handed it to her. She was so surprised by the
weight, she almost dropped it.

'Is this gold?'

'Yup.'

'And what, you found this at the end of a rainbow?'

'Don't be silly – but I did get it from a Leprechaun.'

'What am I supposed to do with it?'

'Change it for money.'

'Where?'

'I don't know. If I had figured that out, I wouldn't have been hitting
you up for meals this whole time.'

She shook her head no and handed it back to me.

'Take it, please,' I said. 'I really do live on a mountain of the stuff.'

A woman came out and said a decision had been made. Inside the Druids were standing almost at attention. Cullum and Mícheál stepped forward together.

'We have decided to help,' Cullum said.

The plan was a simple one. Mícheál was to start his shift at midnight. When the other cop left, I'd come in, we'd let Essa and Brendan out and then Essa would knock out Mícheál so he wouldn't get into trouble.

I waited outside until the other cop, the one that tasered Brendan the other day, left and then I just walked in the front door. It was easy – too easy. I was just inside the station and walking up to the counter when I heard the door open behind me and a familiar, if not pleasant, voice said, 'Conor O'Neil.'

I turned to see Special Agent Andrew Murano wearing one of those grins. You know like when a power-hungry fast-food manager catches a teen employee stealing a chicken nugget.

'Oh, crap.'

'An American I met over here told me a young Scrantonian stole his cap. I was almost back to my room when I saw a cap-wearing young man skulking around in the dark.'

'Well, aren't you quite the detective,' I said, more casually than I felt. This was not good.

'Officer,' Agent Andy said in his over-practised FBI voice, 'arrest that man, he's in cahoots with the other two.'

I turned and looked Mícheál in the eye. For a moment we communicated wordlessly and he seemed to be saying, 'Do it.' So I slugged him. Not hard but I made contact. I even threw in a grunt to make it sound more vicious than it was. The cop went down behind the counter with a loud moan. I picked up a stapler and brandished it towards the G-man. Murano instinctively reached for his gun but he didn't have one. The Irish wouldn't let him bring one into the country. Mícheál moaned loudly, which made me glance at him. He was pointing to something under the counter. I quickly reached to where he was indicating as Murano was saying something predictable like, 'Give it up' or

'There's nowhere to run', but he stopped mid-sentence when I levelled the taser at his chest.

I could see he was trying to be cool but underneath he was soiling his underwear. 'You don't even know how to use that thing,' he said.

'I bet I do.'

'I'll catch you eventually, O'Neil. There is no place for you to go.'

I dropped my weapon for a second. 'Nowhere to go? You were there last time. Surely you remember me stepping through the portal to Faerieland?'

'I don't remember anything after you attacked me.'

'Oh come on, Agent Andy. I can understand you telling that to your superiors back at the Bureau. I've told people about Faeries and Leprechauns and they tend to look at you funny after you do – but this is me. Surely you remember your car getting trashed by the dragon?'

The FBI man looked very uncomfortable. 'I told you, I only remember you attacking me.'

'Aw Andy, it's one thing to lie to your boss but you're just lying to yourself. Now be a nice G-man and lie down on your stomach with your hands behind your back.'

'No.'

'Andy, I've been told this taser thing hurts. Let me just tie you up nicely and we'll be on our way.'

'You'll have to shoot me first.'

Anybody else I would have argued with, but as far as Agent Andy was concerned – I didn't have to be told twice. The electrodes hit his chest and he danced around like an astronaut walking on the sun. I know it's wrong to enjoy seeing a fellow human being suffer, but – you can't be right all of the time.

TWENTY

ETH

Brendan and Essa were simultaneously happy to see me and furious at me for leaving them to stew in jail for so long. We locked the FBI man in a closet. Essa used the same sleeping spell on him that she used on the old cart driver. Mícheál made us tie him up and put him to sleep too, so as to allay suspicion.

'Thank you Conor, Prince of Hazel and Oak,' Mícheál said before Essa knocked him out.

'I should be the one thanking you, Mícheál, Son of Rowan.'

The title obviously pleased him. 'Eh, this is nothing; what you have done for me is far greater.'

'And what have I done for you?'

'You've shown me that I and my parents and their parents and their parents' parents weren't deluded superstitious fools.'

Essa took out her gold ball and began to incant.

'Can I ask one favour?'

'Sure, Mícheál, anything.'

'Will you return and let us know who won?'

'I will – if I survive – that's a promise.'

* * *

We stole the cop car. After assaulting a garda and an FBI agent, what's another felony among friends? A dozen of the Druids were waiting for us at the Fairy Fingers.

'We want to come with you,' Cullum said speaking for the group.

'I've spoken to Essa about that and she doesn't have the power to do it. I'll speak to my mother and Fand, the Queen of the Fili, and let you know if it is possible when I come back.'

Cullum obviously didn't like that answer but he accepted it. The crowd began to murmur and then step backwards as a humming amber circle appeared in the air in front of Essa.

'Are you really coming back?' Maeve asked.

'I promised your father I would.'

'All is ready,' Essa announced.

'Good,' Maeve said. 'I'll buy you dinner.'

'By then you'll be able to afford it.'

There were six bags of broken marble. We took two bags each. Before I went through Maeve kissed me hard on the lips and then we walked into the portal.

We arrived back in the Hall of Spells. Essa walked up to me and dropped one of the bags full of rocks directly on my foot. 'Who was she?'

While hopping on one foot, I tried to mumble out a reply but she stormed off saying, 'I'm too old for this.' Then she shouted, 'Where is the dragon?'

A guard strode up to me and bowed. Now, as I have said many times, I don't like the bowing and Your Highnessing but right then I welcomed it.

'Oh boy,' I said to him, 'I could just kill a cup of tea.'

'Your father has instructed me to bring you to the Oak Room as soon as you arrive.'

'Tell you what, get me a cup of tea first and you will have the gratitude of the Prince of Oak.'

'Your father ordered me to bring you – right away.'

I guess the gratitude of a king out-trumps a prince.

*   *   *

Dad opened his arms to greet me. I ducked underneath and dove for the bowl of fruit on the table.

'Hungry?'

I swallowed down a mouthful of apple before I spoke. 'Being broke in the Real World is a drag.'

'Oh yes, son – that it is. Why do you think I taught languages to students who didn't care? In the Real World, if you don't work you don't eat. Are you OK? Did you get the marble?'

My answers were unintelligible with my mouth full. Dad, instead of trying to fight me, walked to the door and ordered me a meal.

'Now could we talk a bit before dinner arrives?'

I slowed down on the fruit and said, 'Yeah, sorry. I'm fine and yes we have six big bags of broken marble.'

'Good. The first thing we have to do is make sure it works. You'll need to find a volunteer willing to insta-age who won't turn to dust.'

'Forget Essa, people in the Real World thought she was my grandmother.'

'I imagine she didn't like that.'

'It doesn't take much imagination.'

'I'm putting you in charge of charting and laying the marble,' Dad said.

'Charting?'

'Of course.' Dad walked over to a table that had a map of the castle and its grounds. There were grids on all of the approaching slopes. 'Record and number every piece of marble and log its placement.'

'Why? Why don't we just sprinkle the stuff around? It'll take ten minutes.'

'Conor, these aren't just rocks, they're land mines. When this war is over we have to find every one and lock them away. In three hundred years, when you are Lord of Duir, you don't want to step on one of these things while you're walking the dog.'

'When I'm Lord of Duir I'm gonna get somebody else to walk my dog.'

Dad gave me his 'this is serious time, not joke time' look.

'OK, OK, I see your point. I'll start in the morning, unless it is morning. What time is it anyway?'

My dinner arrived and Dad sat with me while I filled him in on my adventures in Ireland.

'It's a lovely place, isn't it?' he said.

'Yeah, I wish I could have relaxed more,' I said. 'As usual I was too busy trying to stay out of jail. You know what else? I missed trees.'

'The older guys in The Land talk about going to Ireland in their youth and it being nothing but trees.'

'What happened to them all?'

'Modern man and their houses and their war ships. What is one tree when you have so many? When everyone thinks like that – well, then in time the land becomes as bald as an old admiral's head.' Dad thought for a while. Finally he said, 'It is the fate of Tir na Nog if Maeve is allowed to succeed.'

I finished my meal and could hardly keep my eyes open.

'Three more things, son.'

I did my best impression of a bored adolescent.

'There's a council meeting an hour after dawn tomorrow – be there.'

'OK,' I said with a moan.

'Secondly, you must take your Choosing.'

'Fine.'

'Seriously, there is a war coming. If something happens to me …'

'I said fine. Dad, I hate it when you talk like this.'

'I don't care what you hate. I'm a king and you are a prince. If I die without you holding a Duir Rune then Cialtie has a "legitimate" claim to the Oak Throne.'

'OK, after I get a couple of hours' sleep, I'll go to your crack-of-dawn meeting, then I'll mine the castle – and *then* I'll take my Choosing.'

'It's not that easy – you must prepare.'

'All right, all right,' I said stumbling to my feet. 'I'll do anything you want. Just let me go to bed.'

Dad smiled and kissed me on the forehead. 'Goodnight, my son.'

As I got to the door I made the mistake of saying, 'You said "three things"?'

'Yeah.' Dad sighed. 'You gotta tell your mermaid girlfriend that she can't just barge into my office any time she wants.'

'Firstly, she's not my girlfriend.'

Dad gave me a 'you're kidding me right?' look.

'OK, well she's … OK, I don't know what she is. But what do you mean "barge" into your office?'

'Every day, sometimes twice a day, she barges in and asks if there is any news about you. It's exasperating.'

I started laughing. 'Didn't you point out that you are, like – the king?'

'I did – several times. She doesn't take a hint. Even when the hint is "Don't come in here again." She says, "Even a king must be worried about his son."'

'Don't you have guards?'

'Yes! She gets past them too. She's amazing and annoying. Maybe I should stick her on my brother. She'd probably drive him so crazy he'd hang himself. Please tell her to stop.'

'I'll try.'

'There is no try, only do or not do,' Dad said joining his laughter with mine. 'Do … please.'

I was so tired I don't even remember walking back to my room. I think I actually started dreaming as I walked. When I first came to The Land, my dreams were so clear. I had never dreamt in the Real World, so when I awoke I actually had premonitions of what was to come but now as I got used to dreaming my dreams were getting like everyone else's. Just the crazy jumbled up fast-forward video of recent events. I dreamt of Ireland and The Grove of Druid. I dreamt of stealing hats from rich Americans, of dining with Maeve and tasering FBI men, but my favourite image was the one right before I woke up. Graysea talking so much that Cialtie was holding his head and screaming.

Graysea was waiting outside my door when I got up. She did the usual smother-with-kisses greeting and then came with me to breakfast. I filled her in on all of my exploits in the Real World. I left out any mention of Maeve; I still didn't have enough strength for that.

I excused myself but Graysea continued to follow me.

'I'm going to a high council meeting, Graysea, I don't think you can come.'

'Don't be silly. Your father loves me.'

'Well … be that as it may. This is a war council and I don't think you should be there.'

'If this is about a war then I'm more needed than ever.'

I reminded myself to apologise for laughing at Dad. This mermaid was not for turning.

I was late as usual. Dahy was talking about wall fortifications. I had obviously missed something as everybody gave me that look again. Everyone was there. Mom, Dad, Dahy, Nieve, Brendan, Gerard, Araf, Tuan, Fand, and even Lorcan the Leprechaun had been dragged out of his mine and made to don a general's cap again.

Essa was back to her beautiful young-looking self. I mouthed, 'You look great', but she only dagger-stared at Graysea. Dad took one look at Graysea and then at me. I shrugged, which said, *I couldn't stop her*. He nodded, which said, *I told you so*.

The big shock was the thin guy sitting next to Dad. His hair and face looked newly cut and shaved and he wore clothes a bit too big for him. He caught me looking at him and wiggled a few fingers at me for a wave.

'Hermy?' I said. 'I mean Eth?'

Dahy, who hates being interrupted, said, 'If you had been here at the beginning of this meeting, Prince Conor, then you would have been party to introductions.'

Dad came to my rescue. 'I had the prince up late last night; his tardiness is partly my fault. Yes, Conor, while you were away Tuan graciously offered me a lift to Thunder Bay. I reunited with my old friend Eth and he agreed to return with me.'

Eth looked as though he was going to speak. We waited and when he didn't Dahy continued with his assessment of arrow resupply on the parapets. Dahy was mid-sentence when Eth finally spoke. 'This is an exciting time for me.'

Eth sounded anything but excited. He spoke without emotion – or much volume. I'm pretty sure most people in the room didn't even hear what he said.

'It is good to be among people again. Overwhelming … but good … I think.'

Everyone leaned in and strained to hear what the hermit had to say.

'For the first time since the Race of the Twins of Macha, I have no idea what is in store for all of us.'

We all waited, not knowing if this was just another pregnant pause or if he was done.

Finally I asked, 'Your mother said nothing about this upcoming war?'

'There are only two prophecies left.'

We all waited. I was just about to say, 'And they are?' when Fand piped up.

'Eth is correct. I have studied the book of Ona's prophecies that Macha stole when she kidnapped Ruby. Every event has come to pass except two. One we know. It reads: "The elder son will die at the hand of the Lord of Duir." Cialtie has told Conor that this is the reason he wants the Oak Throne. If he is the king then there will be no king to kill him.'

Everyone looked to Dad, who betrayed no emotion.

'The other foresight seems to be about the upcoming war. It says: "Trees are the salvation of the Faeries." Fand looked to Eth. 'Are they the two prophecies of which you speak?'

'Essentially, yes.'

'Do you know what the latter means? Which trees and how can they help us?'

Eth opened his mouth but it took ages for anything to come out. 'As I am sure you are aware, my mother's pronouncements are all too often only transparent after the event. I do not know what that means. But when these two events come to pass then the era of my mother's visions will be at an end. Then maybe all of our lives will be our own again.'

Dad placed his hand on his old friend's shoulder. Eth looked close to tears. Cialtie's life wasn't the only one that had been ruined by Ona. I wonder if in her visions she saw what a curse her gift was to be for her son.

Dahy went back to droning on about armoury supplies. I was just wondering how I could position my head so as to nod off without anybody noticing when Graysea interrupted: 'There is going to be a war?'

Everyone silently moaned but only Essa had the courage to say what we all thought, 'That is what we have been speaking about for the last hour.' She uncharacteristically didn't add, 'You stupid trout.'

We all waited for Graysea to slink down in her seat, but the Mertain girl was not the slinking kind. 'If we are going to be at war, then why are we talking about weapons when the first thing we should be doing is preparing the infirmary. This castle is woefully unprepared for a rash of casualties. Many more Fili- and Imp-healers must be recruited now, and as for supplies ... I don't even know where to begin.'

Dad looked at Mom and then to Fand, they both nodded. I smiled at Dad.

'Thank you, Graysea,' Dad said, 'for pointing out our inadequacies. Would you care to assume supervision of the infirmary?'

'Yes, my lord. I will draw up an inventory and report to you as soon as it's done.'

'I'm sure there is someone else you can report to.'

'No,' she chirped, 'I like reporting to you.'

Dahy stood to resume his droning on but Dad mercifully stopped him. 'Master Dahy, I'm sure we can do the rest without everyone here. You all have a thousand things to do. Dismissed.'

Outside the room I was about to tell Graysea that I had to get to work when she said, 'I'd love to chat, Conor, but I'm too busy to just hang about.'

Looks like Dad found the answer to the Graysea problem. Just keep her busy.

I called Dahy's platoon together and asked all the soldiers younger than twenty-five to help me. We took over the Hall of Spells and laid out all of the pieces of marble. One soldier, who had been overeager to help, had lied about his age. He touched a piece of marble and instantly became a wrinkled old man. It was a stupid thing for him to do but at least no one got hurt and it saved me from having to find a volunteer to see if the marble worked. I sent him to Graysea's infirmary where I had heard she already had a supply of dragon blood on ice. I'm sure

Tuan appreciated not being stuck with a needle every time somebody needed a face lift.

I got a bunch of paper from Nieve. Paper, being made from trees, is a rare commodity in The Land. We laid out all of the pieces of marble on the paper and then drew outlines of them with charcoal. Then we numbered the pieces and their outlines. When this was over I wanted every one of those rocks back. I got Ruby to help. She was great at outlining – she said it was like being back in school. I met Dad later that evening and showed him what I had done. He said I should write down instructions on the last piece of paper.

When I asked why, he said, 'In case we're not around later to tell anybody what this is.' That was sobering.

TWENTY-ONE
MASTER EIRNIN

There wasn't enough marble to lay land mines around the perimeter of the entire castle so we decided to lay most of the marble in the North Glen. This was the same place that Maeve had assembled her army during the last Fili war. It was there she cast the Shadowmagic spell that went wrong and vanquished her and her army. Mom and her sorceress pals had a feeling Maeve would try to repeat the same spell – this time getting it right. Dad didn't want to give her a chance to do it from the same place.

What was left of the marble we decided to use to mine both sides of the road up to the main gate and the stable entrance. They were the weakest parts of the outer wall. This would force an aggressor to attack the main gate almost in single file. As far as the south and west battlements – well, they were up to us.

The next morning Dad called a general assembly in the courtyard to warn everyone to stay out of the glen and not stray from the main road up to the castle. My team and I spent the entire day pushing marble pieces into the ground and lightly covering them with grass cuttings. It would have only taken a couple of hours but we had to carefully log where every piece was placed for later mine removal. Finally, Dahy posted soldiers to warn anyone that this was a bad place to take a stroll with your grandmother.

I wasn't the only busy one around. Daily groups of Imps, Faeries and Pookas arrived at the castle to swell the ranks of the army, help build fortifications, smith swords and axes, make arrows and bows, cook food in makeshift kitchens, and prepare the infirmary. Essa and Dahy were drilling the soldiers and when they weren't, they were neck deep in the logistics of preparing for a siege. Nieve, Mom and Fand were like the three witches in *Macbeth*; they spent most of their time working on magical defences in their Shadowmagic laboratory, a lab that really did have a bubbling cauldron in the corner.

Everybody was pulling double duty. Lorcan was preparing the new recruits by night and spending the days inspecting the outer walls. He was worried that the mortar in the east wall, the one that had been rebuilt after the Battle of the Twins of Macha, hadn't had long enough to set. The three witches made up some sort of Shadowmagic goo that Lorcan's workmen and women were using to repoint the stonework.

Brendan took archery practice. Without any formal announcement Detective Fallon took Spideog's place and became the Duir Master-at-Arms. When he wasn't eating, sleeping or quality-timing with Ruby, he was in the armoury.

Araf tutored the soldiers in hand-to-hand combat. We all hoped it wouldn't come to that. At night he skirted around the castle and uprooted all the flowers that he had planted and repotted them safe in a greenhouse inside the east wall.

Graysea was really in her element. I don't think anyone had ever thought her smart enough to put her in a position of authority – what a mistake that was. She shouldered her new responsibility with the tenacity of a shark. She enlisted healers, knocked down walls and had a team of weavers working day and night making bandages. She turned the little room of healing into a full-blown hospital that included a salt-water swimming pool in the corner. Any time I stopped by to have a quick word she always told me she was too busy to talk. She looked awfully flustered but happy.

Pooka hawks came back with twice daily reports of Brownie and Banshee armies mustering for a march. No one other than me had seen Maeve and her Fili army. At one meeting Lorcan asked if I was sure I saw her but Mom had only to show her blood-blackened rune and all doubts were put to rest.

Dad wanted me to start preparing for The Choosing but since I was the only person who could walk among the yew without being judged or forced to eat poison berries, I was drafted to enter the Yewlands to ask the oldest of the trees if they knew what Ona meant when she said, 'Trees are the salvation of the Faeries.' Nora volunteered herself to join me.

'You wanna get judged again?' I joked.

'Oh, I have no intention of chatting with a yew ever again,' Nora said. 'It's just I have been cooped up in this castle worrying about my granddaughter … I've got this young body – I need to ride. I need to stretch my legs.'

Since we didn't need to get to the yews at any specific time we decided that we would try to get there in a day. We left before dawn. (That was my idea, would you believe?) I don't know if it was Nora's new body or that she was unburdened from the worry of her grand-daughter's safety, but Nora was lightning in the saddle. I remembered thinking last time that she was a pretty good equestrian – this trip she was on fire. Her horse Blackberry seemed to obey her every whim and kept Acorn galloping a lot faster and longer than he or I liked. The sun was still pretty high in the sky when we got to the River Lugar boat-house.

I had left the royal barge in the Yewlands. I thought we were going to have to row but then found a small boat with a gold rudder. This time I had bothered to learn the incantation and we sailed towards the Yewlands oar-free.

Nora took a seat in the back of the skiff and laid her head back, closed her eyes and held her face to the sun.

'Is this the tonic you were looking for?'

She didn't open her eyes but smiled as a breeze took her hair. 'It's nice to be out of that castle.'

'Aw come on, it's a nice castle.'

'That it is, Prince Conor. No offence to your little house, it's me that needed out. I now see why you young people are moving all the time. Your bodies (and now mine) just don't know how to sit still.'

'So you're not a fan of your new young frame?'

Nora laughed – a good laugh, not like the stilted things she uttered when her granddaughter was in peril. 'Oh, I wouldn't say that, Conor. I wouldn't say that.'

We travelled in silence. As Nora sunned herself, I worked on my new yew staff. I carefully carved a notch all around the diameter about three quarters of the way up and then around that tied a leather loop. My thinking was that if I ever needed to lighten the staff so much as to lift me in the air, I could secure my grip with the strap. I had visions of me being thirty feet in the air and then accidentally letting go of the stick. I knew that would hurt without ever needing to experience it. I was tempted to give my new adaptation a try but decided I'd probably just end up in the water.

I pulled over at Gerard's hut just before the entrance to the Yewlands and dropped Nora off.

'Sure you don't want to have a meal before you go in there?' Nora asked.

'No, but brew up some willow tea for when I get back. Yews give me a headache. I shouldn't be long.'

And I wasn't. I found the royal barge where I had left it and beached my little boat alongside. I got out and tried to speak to some trees – tried being the operative word. Just because I had the freedom of the Yewlands didn't mean that they would speak with me. I went from tree to tree and got nothing until I took out a knife and threatened one tree that I was going to carve 'Conor & Essa & Graysea' inside a heart on its bark. That did the trick and I felt that familiar bone-crunching feeling as the tree made me drop the knife and fall to my knees.

'Hey, hey,' I said, 'I was just trying to get your attention.'

The male and female twin voice of the yew echoed in my head. '*Freedom of the Yewlands does not allow you to disturb our solemnity.*'

'I didn't mean to disturb you. I just have a question.'

'*We are not hazels, we are not here to bestow knowledge.*'

The tree made me stand and then spun me around. Just before it pushed me away I said, 'I know who has been killing yews.'

The tree acted faster than I expected. '*Who?*' it said with a voice so loud in my head I was glad I asked Nora to have that willow tea ready.

'Maeve.'

'*Maeve is gone.*'

'She's back. She's been around in a Shadowghost form but now she and her army are back. I suspect she was the one that has been killing trees. In her ghost form she would have been hard to detect.'

'*Where is she?*'

'I don't know but I do know that she will soon attack Duir. My mother thinks that with yew sap she might succeed where before she failed.'

'*Do you have more news?*'

'No, but I have a question.'

'*Ask.*'

So I told the tree about Ona's prediction about trees being the salvation of the Faeries. I waited as I felt the trees confer in the entire forest. The reply didn't take long.

'*The yews have no knowledge of what you ask.*'

'Who would?' I asked, but I had been released, and the yew once again ignored me. I wanted to ask again but then I laughed as I imagined the yew saying '*What part of "no knowledge" do you not understand?*'

I tied my little boat to the barge and then incanted the Ogham Dad had taught me and sailed back upstream to Nora.

Nora not only had tea ready but also soup and bread. We didn't have time for me to sit and eat so I carried the food into the barge and let Nora navigate for a while.

'What did the yew say?' she asked when we had gotten under way.

'They don't know.'

'Are you OK?'

'Yes, I'm just sore.'

'I have more tea in a flask if you're interested.' Nora poured me some more willow tea. 'I remember how I felt after tangling with a yew,' the young grandmother said.

'Oh yeah, I forgot. You got judged by a yew without any preparation and you came away worthy.'

'You sound surprised?'

'No offence Nora, but that's not usually how it works. Did the yews give you anything?'

Nora sat like Mona Lisa for a while and said, 'That would be telling.'

Nora rode back to Castle Duir like the wind and I followed like a leaf caught in her vortex. We got home just after midnight. I was shattered but Nora was exhilarated. She offered to stable and brush Acorn for me and I didn't say no.

The next day Dad ruined a good lie-in.

'I always thought being a prince meant that I could sleep late and do anything I wanted.'

'That's what "commoners" think when they dream about being royal,' Dad said. 'You know what royal people dream about?'

I didn't answer – it was too early for riddles.

'They dream about being commoners.'

We ate in silence. Well, Dad was silent; I produced a continuous low growl hoping that he would leave and let me go back to bed. He just sat there smiling like he had a surprise for me. Finally I cracked.

'What?'

'I don't think I'd have a breakfast that big if I were you.'

There are few things that can make me stop chewing but a sentence like that from my father is one of them. 'Why?'

'It's just that I've heard rumours that the first day at The Hive can be pretty rough.'

'The Hive?'

'Yes, you'll be spending the next couple of days with Master Eirnin.'

I tried to remember where I had seen the name Eirnin and then picked up the jar of honey on the table and read the name. 'You're sending me to the royal beekeeper?'

'You know how the US Secret Service not only guards the president but they also are in charge of catching money forgers?'

'No.'

'Well,' Dad went on, 'they are. Many people around here have more than one job.'

'Oh, can I be Court Jester?'

'You don't need any help from me to be a fool, son. As I was saying … Master Eirnin is not only the royal beekeeper, he is also in charge of preparing candidates for The Choosing.'

'Dad, there's a war coming. There are a million things that I should be doing.'

'Like sleeping late?'

'That is such a Dad thing to say.'

'I agree there are a million things you should be doing but the first thing on that list is The Choosing. You know why it's important. This is not open for discussion.'

'How old do I have to be before I am no longer bossed around by my dad?'

'You are old enough now that you no longer have to do what a father tells you to do.'

He stood and walked towards the door but before he went through he stopped and said, 'But you will never be too old to do the bidding of your King. Be in the stable in ten … and I wouldn't wear your good Nikes if I were you.'

I didn't like the smile on his face. It was the same look that he had when he invited Essa and Graysea on the Mount Cas trip. I didn't have to worry about not wearing my Nikes, Jesse had mine. When this all calmed down and I went back to Ireland like I promised, I was going to get to some big city and swap a bar of gold for a couple of pairs of cool shoes.

Master Eirnin was waiting for me in the stables. He was an Imp, unsurprisingly. He didn't look very tall but he was on horseback so it was hard to tell. His cloth robe was stained and bulged in the middle. He looked jolly. 'You're late,' he said.

'Funny, that's what everyone says.'

This produced no response other than, 'Come.' He turned and walked his mount out of the stables. I hurried to find Acorn.

Master Eirnin came back and asked, 'What are you doing?'

'I'm saddling my horse.'

'Prince Conor, if I had wanted you to saddle your horse I would have said, "Saddle your horse." Now come.'

'On foot?'

He turned again. This time he took a coil of rope from his saddle-bag. 'Would you prefer I tie this around your neck like a dog?'

'No sir.'

'Come.'

So I jogged next to the Master Beekeeper. He was not jolly.

'What did you have for breakfast?'

'What?'

The Imp pulled his reins to the right and reared his horse. It stopped directly in my way and I hit the horse and almost fell over. 'When I say come, I want you to come. When I ask you a question I expect an answer. Not another question. This is my final warning.'

He was wearing a floppy cap and I wondered if there was literally a bee in the beekeeper's bonnet. He started again and said, 'Come.'

I came.

'What did you have for breakfast?'

'I had tea, apple slices, eh … If I had known there was going to be a test …'

Snap; the crack of a whip made it to my ears a nanosecond before my mind registered the searing pain on my back.

'Hey!'

'Focus, prince. I asked about your breakfast. Not about what you think.'

'That doesn't mean …' I looked up and he was raising the whip again so I said quickly, 'OK, apple, tea, two eggs, oatmeal and bread.'

'And what did you have the previous morning?'

'Well, I really didn't have a normal breakfast …'

Crack. This time I lost my footing and went down. The whip cracked on my upper arm and it stung like I had been stabbed. 'What the hell are you doing?'

Master Eirnin walked his horse back and loomed over me. 'You only have two days to prepare, young prince. There is very little time to teach you.'

'Teach me what? That you're a sadist? I got that.'

'I am attempting to teach you to focus, Conor. If you fail to concentrate with me you will experience pain. If you lose your concentration in the Chamber of Runes – you will die.'

TWENTY-TWO
THE HIVE

I jogged behind Master Eirnin as he asked me all manner of mundane questions. Many of which I had no answer for, like 'Name the lineage of your mother's line back five generations.' I knew Mom and her father Liam but after that, nothing. That didn't stop the lash. Eirnin was a whip now, ask questions later kind of Imp.

Eirnin lived in a large conical brick house called The Hive. It did indeed contain a hive. Bumblebees half the size of my fist flew in and out of the many vents in the walls. These bees knew who was boss. They swerved for Master Eirnin but they acted like I wasn't even there. During my next two days at The Hive, I spent most of my time ducking insects big enough to carry off puppies. It was a shock when one bounced off your face as you turned but it was worse if one stung you. Luckily it only happened twice: once when I stepped on one in my bare feet and another time when I accidentally caught one under my armpit. Both times I felt like Julius Caesar just after he turned his back on Brutus. The one under my armpit actually hurt the most but the one on my foot made walking a chore. All this, though, was ahead of me as the beekeeper led me into the training room.

The air was stiflingly thick with the overpowering smell of honey. In the middle of the room was what looked like a long narrow Olympic-sized swimming pool. Instead of water, the pool seemed to be filled with a white mould. Eirnin picked up a rake and skimmed the mould from the top of the pool. Then with his bare hand he scraped the mould off the rake into a bucket and walked outside. By now I knew that if I didn't follow him, it hurt. Outside he dumped the mould on top of a compost heap.

'Oh, I get it,' I said back inside as he handed me the rake. 'This is one of those kung fu master things where after I do your cleaning, I learn something. This is like a metaphor – as I clean your mould, you mould my mind?'

Eirnin was immune to my charms. As he walked away he shook his head and said, 'If you were not Oisin's son I would be tempted to release you now and let you die.'

Underneath the mould was honey. I spent the entire morning skimming the mould off and piling it in the garden. It wasn't as disgusting as it sounds. The mould was pretty innocuous and the fresh air was a relief after spending time in the thick air of the training room. By lunch I was staring at a brick trench filled with golden honey. Eirnin returned and inspected my work. He inspected every edge to make sure no mould remained and found none.

'Come,' he said.

I was tempted to say, 'Aren't you going to give me a gold star?' but then remembered the lash and stepped lively into his wake.

On the other side of The Hive the master had set out a table with bread, dried fruit and meats and, of course, honey.

'Was yesterday's lunch as lavish as this?' he asked.

'Yesterday, I had a salad with …'

'Relax, young prince,' he said with a wave of his hand, 'that was not a test. I am only making conversation. Rest your mind for a bit, Conor; you will need all of your mental strength for this afternoon.'

Eirnin piled some special dark honey from a jar onto a slab of bread. After breathing honey fumes all morning I really was in no mood to eat the stuff but the Marquis de Beekeeper was a hard man to deny. He said it would make my brain work better and, since around here slow brains mean skin welts, I ate.

After lunch I followed the master back into the training room.

'Remove your clothing.'

'You speak English?'

Eirnin removed his whip from his belt and I started, reluctantly and nervously, to take off my clothes. When I got down to my underwear he said, 'That will be enough. I will answer your last query, Conor, for I know this must be confusing but after that you do my bidding or feel the lash.'

'Yes sir.'

'In order to implement your training I have met many times with your father about your upbringing. I have also endured your Aunt Nieve's hot gold ear and tongue treatment so I may speak to you in the language of your schooling.'

'Gosh. Well, that explains why you're so cranky.' I instantly regretted saying that and expected my all too exposed flesh to get a whuppin' but he ignored me – with maybe just the tiniest of smiles. There is no long-term defence against my charm.

Eirnin pointed to the pool of honey. 'Get in.'

'In there?'

This time the whip cracked and I jumped in before it hit me. Jumping into a pool of honey is not like jumping into a pool of water. I hit the surface expecting to go through but it was almost as bone-jarring as if I had hit concrete. The entire surface wobbled as I bounced back up. Then I started to sink but at an angle. That meant my feet wouldn't be under me when my head went below water … I mean honey. I tried to move my legs but – I was in honey. I looked to Master Eirnin – he was nowhere to be seen. My panic increased proportionately with every inch I sank. I was seconds away from screaming when I thought *maybe this too is a test. Surely he won't let me drown?* I mastered my panic as the honey reached level with my chin. My face fully submerged and I was thinking *maybe I could panic now* when I felt rope hit my hands. Eirnin hoisted me out and I hung there until my feet were directly below me.

'Why did you not call for me?'

'I thought it was a test.'

'Next time you are about to drown, feel free to call out.'

He slowly lowered me so I could stand, shoulder-deep in the honey. 'Now what?'

'Now you walk.'

And I did. For the rest of the day I did walking laps in a swimming pool filled with honey. What was it like? It was like walking in a pool of honey. It was hot, sticky and unbelievably slow going. As it got close to nightfall, the beekeeper had me walking sideways and then backwards. After rinsing in a nearby ice-cold spring, I was sent off to bed. I went back to my room and asked Aein to bring me some supper but I didn't eat it. My head hit the pillow and I went out like a used match.

The last place I wanted to go the next day was back to The Hive but a prince has to do what a king tells him to. Eirnin didn't even speak to me when I arrived. He just pointed to the pool and I slowly dropped into the honey so as to not lose my footing. This day began with mundane questions. He asked me to name all of my school teachers. Hesitation was met with the crack of a lash. Most of these didn't actually make contact but the memory of the pain from the ones that did made the sound as effective as the real thing. Let's just say, I hope nobody actually eats that honey. Dad showed up late in the morning wearing a smirk and drilled me on German, French and Greek verb conjugation. It was just like when I was a kid and I could see how much he was enjoying my torment.

Essa's dad showed up with lunch.

'I imagine,' Gerard said, 'you would like something that did not have honey on it.'

'Amen to that, Mr Winemaker. What brings you to Duir?'

'Oh I don't know, Conor, maybe the impending war.'

'Oh yeah. You know, I had almost forgotten about that with all of this hiking in honey stuff.'

'Then you are doing it right. I have been through Master Eirnin's tutelage. I know it feels pointless at the moment but what you are learning is to blend mind and body into one. You will be thankful when you step into the First Muirbhrúcht.'

'That's what I thought I would be doing here. I thought Eirnin would be telling what it would be like to walk The Choosing but he hasn't said a thing. I saw Dad and Mom do it and it looked awfully difficult. So what's it like?'

Gerard leaned back in his chair and laughed. 'Conor, my Choosing was long, long ago. You want to know what it was like? I'll tell you. It is like ... walking in honey.'

'Really?'

'No, not really, but that is as close as you are going to get without actually entering the Hall of Choosing. Everyone says the First Muirbhrúcht is the hardest and in a way it is. You must be prepared for the shock of it. Like walking in honey, it will be like hitting a brick wall at first. You must slide into it. But unlike the pool here you will simultaneously be buffeted from all sides. Keeping your balance will require perfect concentration but your concentration will be tested by memories. Not actual memories – they will come during the Second Muirbhrúcht – but emotional memories. It is very disconcerting to have emotions without the underpinning memories. Many find it too much to bear. Fortunately you can quit after the First Muirbhrúcht and live.'

'But not after that?'

'That is correct. Once you enter the second archway only success allows you to survive.'

'But the Second Muirbhrúcht is easier?'

'That is what others say but I found it harder. Just remember: whatever the Chamber throws at you, you must keep walking, you must keep your balance and you must hold on to your rune.'

'What about the Third Muirbhrúcht?'

'Ah well,' the big man said. 'The third one is different for everyone. It is not difficult. In fact, it is the opposite, it is quite a relief. You see, if you make it that far – you receive a gift.'

'A gift?

'Yes. Some receive an insight into their lives. A blacksmith may realise how better to forge steel, a dancer will leave The Choosing knowing a new step. Others get a glimpse of their future.'

'What did you get?'

'Oh my, I've never told anyone that.'

'Sorry, I didn't mean to pry.'

'No. I think I'd like to tell you, Conor.'

And he did. I felt honoured. When he was through I asked, 'You didn't bring any beer with you, by any chance?'

'There is far too much work ahead of you for beer drinking.' He stood to leave and then opened his arms to administer his famous rib-crushing hug. I stood and accepted it. As he lifted me off the ground he said, 'I'll have a cold one waiting for you in your chamber tonight when this is done.'

'Thanks, Gerard.'

As he walked away he stopped and said, 'Essa is very mad at you.'

'What did she say?'

'Nothing. That's how I know. I would look out if I were you.'

The rest of the day was more of the same with Master Eirnin making me walk while quizzing me and trying to make my concentration slip. Focusing had always been a problem for me at school. Maybe they should fill swimming pools with honey and give the teachers whips. OK, that's a bad idea but at this time in my life – with that life being on the line – the technique worked. I really did think I was ready.

Eirnin didn't, but he had no choice but to graduate me. 'Your father has told me that the Pooka hawk scouts have spotted Banshee troops marching towards Duir. You are needed at the castle.'

I got out of the pool and rinsed off. When I was clean and dressed I reported one last time to the Master Beekeeper.

'I listened to what Gerard told you at lunch, young prince. I have little to add. Your task is to keep focused and your goal is to reach past the Third Muirbhrúcht with your rune still in your fist. That may sound simple but the Chamber makes even that simple task very diffi-cult. I hope to see you again, Prince of Hazel and Oak.'

'Won't you be at my Choosing?'

'No, I have seen too many of my pupils fail. I can no longer watch Choosings.'

With that cheery statement ringing in my ears I limped back to the castle. My first stop was to see Graysea in the hope that she had enough time to unswell the bee stings on my foot and armpit. If I hadn't just walked in there myself, I would have sworn I was in a different place than Castle Duir. The Room of Healing was now a proper blinding white infirmary with fully stacked shelves of bandages, sheets and medicine bottles. Cots were lined up in rows like airplanes on an aircraft carrier. Graysea was taking an inventory of a pile of things on the far wall but dropped everything when she saw me limping.

'Are you injured?'

'No … well … yes. It's a bee sting.' I sat on a cot, took off my Brownie slipper and showed her my double-sized foot.

'That is a bee sting?'

'They were big bees. I also got stung under my arm.'

Graysea sat down behind me and pulled my shirt over my head. 'You smell like honey.' She was reaching around to feel where the sting was when, of course, Essa walked in. Graysea didn't see her and started her healing fish transformation. I was hit with the pain of the stings for a second and then experienced that wonderful relief that only mermaid healing can provide. I had to close my eyes. When I opened them – Essa was gone.

'Damn.'

'Does something else hurt?'

'Oh, no, Graysea, thank you, I feel much better now.'

She kissed me on the cheek. 'I have so much to do. I imagine you do too.'

'Yes. Sleep.'

She slapped me on the arm. 'You're so silly.'

This time I managed to eat my supper before passing out.

I awoke to find Dad standing over me with a steaming cup of tea. I sat up in bed and groaned. Every muscle in my body was sore.

'I'm going to go back to the Real World,' I said, 'and open a gym with a honey pool. It's a hell of an all-body work-out.'

'That's why I brought you willow tea. Normally I would have given you a couple of days to recover but we don't have that kind of time.'

'How far away is Cialtie's army?'

'They're not here yet but they are coming. It's nothing for you to worry about today. Today is the day of your Choosing.'

744   JOHN LENAHAN

'Dad, I know you're gung ho about me doing this but really with Cialtie on the march and me feeling like five miles of bad road, can't my Choosing wait?'

'No. Cialtie on the march is the reason why we can't wait. If something happens to me, you have to be holding a Duir Rune or my brother has a "legitimate" claim to the Oak Throne.'

'That's not the way Ona's prediction goes ...'

Dad put up his hand to stop me. 'You of all people should know that Ona's predictions are a curse and certainly are nothing to act upon. I loved that old woman but I often wish she had never been born. Her damn predictions are almost as much to blame for my brother as he is. We fight Cialtie not because of anything Ona has said. We stop him because he must be stopped. Get dressed, Prince of Hazel and Oak.'

I walked down the long staircase by myself. When I arrived at the Chamber of Runes, I had to momentarily shield my eyes from the supernova-like glow coming from the thousands of Leprechaun candles that covered almost every surface. When my pupils had finally contracted to a suitable diameter, I saw that almost everybody was there.

Mom and Dad were flanked by Nieve, Fand, Dahy, Gerard. Brendan and Araf were standing holding up a ceremonial robe. I waved hi to everybody and then turned my back to let my mates help me don what I hoped was not going to be my funeral shroud.

'If you don't make it,' Brendan said in my ear, 'can I have your room?'

'Araf,' I said, 'shouldn't you be doing a Choosing too?'

'I thought I would see if you survive before I tried it,' the Imp replied.

These guys were my mates. Making jokes was exactly what I needed.

As I walked to Mom I stopped and quietly asked Gerard, 'Essa?'

He just shook his head.

Well, that cinched it. I had suspected that I had blown it with the princess and now that she hadn't shown up here, I was sure of it.

Mom placed a blank wooden rune in my hand and then tilted my head down with both of her hands and kissed me on the forehead. She didn't say anything, and that scared me too.

Dad lifted the rune in my right hand and placed a nugget of gold underneath it. He placed his hands on my shoulders. 'For once in your life – concentrate.'

I turned and faced the first archway. It looked perfectly clear just like any other hallway I had ever walked down. I turned. 'Are you sure this thing's plugged in?'

I got nothing – not even a snicker. So what else is new? I stepped into the First Muirbhrúcht.

TWENTY-THREE
THE CHOOSING

There is an old expression in The Land: 'The First Muirbhrúcht is the hardest.' That's what people say in Tir na Nog when they start some mundane task like baking a cake or cleaning out a moat. It's like when Real Worlders say: 'Every journey begins with a first step.' Well, let me tell ya: the First Muirbhrúcht is not like baking a cake.

I had once seen Dad thoughtlessly run at a Muirbhrúcht and bounce back like a pinball off a bumper so I entered it slowly expecting the barrier to be a bit like jumping into Master Eirnin's honey pool. What I wasn't prepared for was the turbulence. I had seen people walk in the Chamber of Runes and you don't walk that slowly for nothing, but I expected the resistance to come from the front. In reality it came from all directions. Like the honey pool, the surrounding air – or whatever was in it – was hard to push against but forces pushed different parts of you in different directions – and they were fierce. I thought I was going to get my ears ripped off. Saying that, losing my ears wouldn't have been that bad a thing 'cause it sounded like my head was in a washing machine. That must be where they got the name from. *Muirbhrúcht* means tidal wave and it sounded like my head was under one.

I wasn't three steps in when I started laughing. At first I thought it was just the usual little nervous giggling bout I get when I'm in mortal danger or in an uncomfortable situation, like when Fergal and I thought we were going to be killed by Big Hair and his Banshee tribe – but when I tried to stop, I found that I couldn't and I didn't know why. No matter what horrible things I imagined: squashed puppies with their eyes bulging out, Essa snogging The Turlow, tofu burgers, I still couldn't stop laughing. The strange thing was, I wasn't laughing *at* anything. I just had an overwhelming need to laugh but nothing in my head said anything funny. I threw my head back and howled with laughter, for a nanosecond I stopped my forward momentum. Immediately the ear-ripping turbulence intensified by a factor of 100. Let me tell you, even though I was laughing there was nothing funny about that. I instinctively knew that the increased pressure was because I had stopped moving and pushed into the non-gooey ectoplasm that passed for air in there. I continued to move. The turbulence subsided and so did my giggles.

When the sorrow hit me I remembered what I had been told. The First Muirbhrúcht bombards the Chooser with emotions. Getting past these emotional attacks was not easy. In life when emotions hit it is almost always the result of a thought but here in the First Muirbhrúcht the emotions were pure feeling. No manner of cheery thought could dispel the soul-crushing sorrow. I am tempted to call it grief but it wasn't that. Grief is the cause of sorrow – this feeling had no cause. There was no poisonous thought I could divert or mask with levity. I simply wanted to die – to sit and stop everything because what was wrong with my life at that moment went beyond my mind. My entire being was simply agony and nothing anywhere, in any world, could fix it. Through all of this I kept my feet moving and my fingers wrapped around my rune. I don't know how. I'm sure I couldn't have withstood one second longer. Fortunately sorrow was replaced by rage and I welcomed it. Even though I could feel the veins in my temples popping and my jaw clamping down until I thought my face would snap – I welcomed the rage. I wanted to kill someone and that was a lot better than wanting to die. I toyed with putting a thought with the emotion and it wasn't hard to imagine my Uncle Cialtie. I thought of what he did to Fergal. How he killed his mother and how he lied to his own son and then shamed him before ultimately killing him. And then like a snowball tumbling down a hill gaining size as it went, I added Fergal's death to all of the other deaths he was responsible for: Frank, Spideog, everyone who died in the attack on the Hall of Knowledge, all who died in the Battle of the Twins of Macha, the genocide of the village of More, the destruction of the Hazellands. By the time my mind had conjured up all of those atrocities, I wasn't sure if the rage I felt came from The Choosing or from my own mind.

The last emotion was contentment. It was a little gift that the First Muirbhrúcht gave me right at the end. In some respects this was the most dangerous emotion of all. After all that went before, I felt like sitting down and just enjoying the feeling. I think I would have, but the habit of putting one foot in front of the other that had been whipped into me by Master Eirnin came in handy.

Then I popped out of the First Muirbhrúcht.

The silence was almost the best part. I wanted to turn around and shout 'I did it!', but I had been instructed not to turn except on the way out or if I wanted to give up. Apparently you can turn around after the First Muirbhrúcht and live – but Oisin didn't raise no quitter. I wanted to rest a while but I had been warned not to do that also. Apparently taking too long of a break saps your energy. I didn't have all that much zip to begin with, so I gritted my teeth and entered the Second Muirbhrúcht.

If the First Muirbhrúcht is the hardest then the second one is the prettiest. I was faintly aware of lights and colours sparkling in the air while in the First Muirbhrúcht – when I entered the second one, colour was all I saw. What, minutes before, had been crystal clear air was now alive with pulsating light. It was like the luminescent algae in the ocean that the Mertain call 'The Stream', except here it wasn't one colour, it was thousands.

The electric rainbow air made me hesitate but what made me stop in my tracks was the huge vision of my mother's face that loomed in front of me. Master Eirnin's training kicked in. I could almost feel the sting of his whip on my back and I automatically willed my feet to keep moving. Even though I was looking straight ahead, in the vision, I was looking *up* at my mother's face. This was the kind of paradox that usually happens in dreams but this was no dream. This was a memory, my memory. I not only saw the huge face looking down on me but I felt the loving arms that cradled the tiny me. I grew up with no memory of my mother but obviously they were in there. You might imagine that this would be emotionally overpowering but I reacted to this memory with the emotions of an infant. Babies are binary. They are either happy or sad, wet or dry, hungry or satiated. I was happy and it was such a simple happiness that I slowed. Immediately the pressure of the Muirbhrúcht forced the training back into my head and I continued forward.

The next memory was the other side of that coin – it was simple unhappiness. I was crying because she was crying. My mother was crying. I felt myself being taken from her arms. I tried to reach for her but I was so young my arms would not obey. When she was out of view I felt and tasted a salty tear hitting my face; when I looked up, Dad's face was as miserable as my mother's had been.

More childhood memories floated into view. Just like no one else can hear a tree talk, even though it's perfectly loud in your head, I'm sure no one else could see these visions but to me they played in the air like a Shadowcasting. These were memories that I had almost forgotten and they were captivating. The desire to just sit on the floor and watch, cross-legged, was overwhelming and if not for Master Eirnin I would have done just that and died. I took back everything I ever said about the old beekeeper and his lash.

I remembered living in Ireland and then moving to England. I replayed a childhood event that always puzzled me. I saw myself maybe seven years old and coming home from school and telling Dad that a rider on a black horse had spoken to me. We were packed and in a hotel before midnight. Two days later we were on a boat to America.

I got to watch puberty and adolescence again which made me want to close my eyes and press fast-forward – and I found that I kind of could. I slowed things down when I came to Sally. Sally hadn't fared very well in my recent memories and it was nice to relive how wonderful we had been in the beginning. I had had girlfriends before her, but she was a real relationship. She taught me … no that's wrong … together we learned how to be close and how to trust. I was mad at her for her choices at the end but now I saw she didn't have the full picture – I never gave her a chance.

Nieve's spear flew at me again and I felt the tingling glow of my mother's protective force-field. And then I sped through the memories of my life since I discovered I was the Prince of Hazel and Oak: escaping from Cialtie, meeting my mother, meeting Fergal. I willed that scene to slow down and it did. My smile matched the ear-to-ear smile my cousin wore and I realised that the debilitating sorrow that I felt in the First Muirbhrúcht was the missing of Fergal. I re-saw that first sight I had of Essa with the light shining up on her face from that glowing ball. I swallowed hard as I walked, just as I had at her father's party.

I relived joining up with the Army of the Red Hand and how with Dad we stopped my uncle from destroying The Land. I remembered how proud I was of Dad and how I regained the feeling I had when I was a little kid – that he could do anything.

I got to travel back to the Hazellands with my mother again. How wonderful it was to get to actually know a mother that I had only ever fantasised about. That warm motherly love that I imagined and missed didn't even come close to the real thing.

Like an anchor against the madness, Araf was a solid presence all through the visions.

I had to laugh when I remembered how angry Brendan was when the cop was accidentally dragged to The Land. He came around fast. I don't know what I would have done if he hadn't been there to help me save my father.

I saw the bravery of Tuan, the treachery of The Turlow, the magnificence and terror of Red's transformation into a dragon. And then came Graysea. She really is the sweetest creature in any land. OK, she's a bit ditzy, but she is beautiful and talented and funny and would literally give anything to make me happy. But I realised that even though I am oh so fond of her, when I saw her she didn't make my heart skip like Essa. Maybe that was the gift of The Choosing. I knew now that I had to make Essa know that she is the only one for me.

After saving Dad with his dragon blood rebirth, all the most recent events sailed past. As I saw the scene of me entering the Chamber of Runes, I popped out. I took one deep breath and entered the Third Muirbhrúcht.

As Gerard warned me – this was a piece of cake. The resistance was still in the air but the pressure was gone. This was more like the honey pool than the previous two and I found myself sighing at the relief of it. A shower of sparks like from a grinding wheel issued from my closed fist but it didn't hurt and I hardly noticed it. I thought about what Gerard said had happened to him when he was here. Gerard had been hoping for some tip on how to make super wine but instead he received a vision of a young girl. He spent years looking for her but never found her until he had a child of his own. His gift from The Choosing was the promise of Essa.

I wouldn't mind a promise of Essa myself. I then had a panicky thought about seeing what our child would look like and then had another panic attack about receiving any vision of the future. Visions of the future were how The Land had gotten into this mess. Ona's predictions had ruined countless lives. I wasn't sure I wanted to know where the river of my life was to flow.

My gift was not a glimpse into my future. At least I think it wasn't. In front of me I saw the Druids I had met in Connemara, Ireland – the group calling themselves The Grove. They stood there waiting. The vision was as clear as it was completely unfathomable. I tried to ask them what they wanted but nothing would come out of my mouth. Then, at the last second, Ruby came up beside me and they all freaked.

The pressure of the air evaporated and I stumbled forward into the antechamber at the back of the Chamber of Runes. I had done it, I had walked my Choosing. In front of me was the oaken table – I opened my hand and let my new rune fall to the tabletop.

My rune didn't stay on the table for long. Before I even got a chance to look at it, an explosion shook the Chamber. I was thrown into the table, knocking it over as plaster and centuries of dust fell from the ceiling. I turned. This was supposed to be a proud moment, like a graduation. I had imagined my family and friends smiling and applauding – instead I saw them rushing out of the room. As she disappeared around the corner and up the staircase I saw that one of them was Essa – she had come. Another explosion rocked the room, the battle had begun.

I ran to join my comrades forgetting that Muirbhrúchts must be entered slowly and just like my father before me, I hit the backside of the barrier and bounced off it like it was a vertical trampoline. My body and head were thrown to the back wall and for a moment I saw stars. Then I pulled my wits about me, walked up to the archway, took a deep breath and began to slowly step in. I hesitated just in time to remember the rune. I picked it up, put it in my pocket and slid slowly past the barrier. Walking back through the Muirbhrúcht has all of the resistance without the mind games. It was still one of the most physically exhausting things I have ever done but at least my brains weren't being haunted by ghosts of Christmases past.

I dropped into a Fili mind chant. It was a version of the same chant Dad had used on the day he had lost his hand. His chant was 'Rowing beats Cialtie.' Mine was, 'Climbing stops Cialtie.'

'Climbing stops Cialtie.' I worried about my friends but then pushed that thought from my mind and chanted. 'Climbing stops Cialtie.' I wondered what kind of weapon could have caused such a violent tremor this deep inside the castle … 'Climbing stops Cialtie.' I should have spent this time trying to figure out what my Choosing gift meant. What did the grove of Irish Druids have to do with me? But instead I chanted, 'Climbing stops Cialtie.' I was so lost in my mantra that I didn't even know I had made it through the Muirbhrúchts until I fell out into the Chamber on my hands and knees.

The Chamber was eerily silent. All around Leprechaun candles lay on their sides, burning where they had fallen. Several were scorching the base of the oak table and I crawled over and blew them out. It would be ironic to win a battle and lose the castle to a candle fire. I was completely drained. There was nothing I would have liked better than to have a beer and a nap but the time for leisure was not now and if my uncle got his way it would not be ever. I stood, took a deep breath and began the long sprint up the staircase to defend Duir.

TWENTY-FOUR

WAR

The staircase back up from the Chamber of Runes has got to be the longest flight of stairs in any world. I had read reports of others, after walking The Choosing, being carried up those stairs on a stretcher. I initially tried to take them two at a time but after five minutes I was panting like a Himalayan mountain climber without oxygen.

Another explosion rocked the castle. I slipped and then bumped down half a dozen steps on my backside. Burning candles dropped on me from above, attempting to make me look like an illustration from a Jack Be Nimble rhyming book. I breathed a sigh of relief while I extinguished myself. If I had taken a full-blown tumble down these stairs ... well, let's just say when you look up broken neck in a Tir na Nogian dictionary you see a picture of a guy lying at the bottom of *these* stairs.

Regardless of how tired I was, I got up and kept climbing. I really needed to get out of here before this castle shook again. Barring falling all the way down and breaking every bone in my body, I was worried that if this place got hit again there might be a cave-in and I would have to change my name to Rubble. It was now pitch dark in many places and there was no handrail. I really must institute a Castle Duir Department of Health and Safety.

My legs shook every time I put weight on them. Every step became a little mountain. Without realising it I was moving on all fours with my hands in front of me like a dog. *Climbing stops Cialtie … Climbing stops Cialtie …* The chant popped into my head instinctively.

It was so dark at the top of the stairs I banged my head into the door. I almost swooned when I stood but managed to fall forward, blinking into the light of the east wing corridor. I was expecting the guard to help me up but even he wasn't there. All hell really must be breaking loose if the Chamber guard had to leave his post.

I ran into the courtyard. All the activity was up on the battlements. I looked at the long flight of stairs up and knew that my legs wouldn't make it. I wished I could fly and then remembered that I almost could. I wrapped my fingers around my staff, slipped my other hand into the new leather strap and then willed my staff to lighten. I shot straight up into the air and found myself directly in the path of a huge boulder that had been propelled by a catapult. I panicked and commanded my staff to become heavy. It became so heavy so quickly that my hands went straight down, almost pulling my arms out of their sockets. Screaming, I commanded my staff to lighten again and this time I really did dislocate my shoulder. The boulder at least missed me and sailed over my head into the section of the castle that I had just come from.

A guard spotted me writhing on the grass in pain. I recognised him. He was one of the guards that I had assigned to guard Brendan when he first came to The Land.

'Frick?' I asked.

'Frack,' he replied with a smile.

My arm was completely unusable. I told him that I had dislocated my shoulder and without asking, he picked me up and then slammed my upper arm into a wall. I blacked out. When I came to, the arm hurt like hell but it at least worked again.

'What is the situation?' I grunted.

'The Banshees have a catapult with an amazing range. They are alternately throwing boulders and some sort of explosive. Brendan has your mother and aunt conjuring up magic arrows. I cannot tarry any longer; I have been ordered to get gold from the infirmary.'

'I'll help.'

Frack ran ahead and I tried to keep up. He made it to the infirmary long before I did. Initially it looked like mayhem in there but I soon saw that my mermaid was coping with the injuries admirably. A guard told me that Graysea had just saved his best friend's life when he was sure he was a goner. It seemed that Graysea had cleared all of her critical patients from triage and was now working on the less injured. Frack was having trouble getting her attention; she kept telling him she was too busy to speak to anyone. I jumped in and pulled her away from an injured woman before she could fish up.

'Graysea, we need the gold my mother has stored here.'

She had that glow of a woman on a mission but I could also see the fatigue in her eyes.

'I don't have time ...'

I didn't let go of her as she tried to go back to the injured woman. 'Listen. I need that gold. Brendan may have a way to stop other people from being injured by the catapult.'

That got her attention and she led me over to her store room and pointed to four small crates. I tried to lift one but my shoulder rebelled and I dropped the box screaming.

'Oh my, what has happened to you?'

'I dislocated it,' I said holding my shoulder.

Graysea slumped down next to me and placed her hand on my shoulder. I saw those gills slit open on her neck as I felt her fin press against my legs. I noticed the wince of pain on her face as my pain vanished. When she un-fished again she sighed, and I saw on her face the effort her healing was costing her.

'Thanks,' I said, and meant it. 'But you have to slow down, Graysea. This battle has only just begun. You can't heal everybody. You have to let the other healers do normal first aid. If you go all fishy on every injured person that comes in here – you won't make it.'

'But it's so hard to watch people suffer,' she said.

'I know but most will get better. You have to save yourself for the real life-threatening stuff. You're already exhausted.' I had a look around. Things here seem to be under control. 'Let the Imp-healers take over for a while – you should have a swim and recharge.'

An Imp came over to help us up. She said, 'Listen to him; we'll be fine for a while.'

Graysea reluctantly agreed and I led her over to her little swimming pool.

'I gotta go, thanks for the shoulder fix.' I kissed her and she flipped over the side of her pool. I watched as her face went under the water then a fin popped up like a dolphin.

I picked up two of the crates and tried to follow Frack but two crates of gold were one too many for me. A Leprechaun repair team ran past and I commandeered one of them to carry a crate. When their commander saw me struggling he decided that one crate was one too many for me and gave me another of his men. The two of them jogged behind me like they were carrying feather pillows.

I reached Brendan and his archery team just as the Banshees had launched another projectile.

'It's one of the bombs,' Brendan shouted.

The archers lifted their bows. The arrows were gold-tipped. Over in a corner I saw Mom and Nieve incanting over more arrowheads. Next to them were Leprechauns with a melting pot atop a blazing fire. The pot was streaked with overflowing molten gold.

It was way too frantic to ask what was going on so I just stood back and watched. The bomb that was shot from the catapult was as big as the boulder that had almost creamed me but it was rounder – more obviously manmade. Whoever did the aiming was having a good day 'cause it was coming right for us.

'Wait … wait,' Brendan was shouting. 'Wait for it to break its arc … Now!'

Brendan's archers were well trained. All but one arrow hit the bomb. I was expecting the arrows to make the thing blow up but when they hit they just bounced off. I turned to run but no one followed me; instead everyone just stared. That's when I noticed that the bomb wasn't falling. The arrows had hit just as it should have started on the downward trajectory of its arc, but instead the ball kept climbing.

I looked over to Brendan and said, 'What?'

He was smiling. 'The arrows make anything they hit lighter. It's one of your mom's spells. She said she got the idea from your yew staff.'

The bomb sailed well over the castle.

'So it's really my idea.'

'Yeah, right,' Brendan said. 'Deirdre and Nieve have arrows that can make stuff heavier too. If we alternate, then whoever is aiming that thing won't know what to do.'

'You learn this at cop school?'

'Nope, I'm making it up as I go along. I know it's hard to believe but in the police academy they didn't teach how to defend a castle from a siege.'

'Doesn't sound like a very good academy.'

'At the moment, Mr O'Neil, I would have to agree.'

A call went up and we all turned. The Banshees' catapult had let loose another one. This time it was a really big rock. Brendan ordered the heavy arrows and they fired as soon as the boulder was in range. The rock took a nosedive like a major league pitcher's slide and half buried itself in the muddy earth just past the treeline.

'You survived The Choosing, I see,' a familiar voice behind me said.

I turned to see Essa all decked out in her battle leathers. I felt guilty thinking how fantastic she looked but then realised that I think she looks great in everything she wears. 'You're speaking to me?'

'We're at war, Conor. There are thousands of people out there who are trying to kill you. You don't need to add me onto that list too.'

'Who says no good comes from war?'

'I'll get back to hating you when this is over,' she said.

'Right. What have you been doing?'

'I just came from a war council with Dahy and your father.'

'What's our next move?'

'Nothing really. Fortifications are good but we can't really plan anything until Cialtie shows his hand.'

'Any guesses?'

'Lots,' Essa said. 'Mostly it comes down to Maeve's Shadowmagic. Your mom and Fand are working on that.'

So we just wait and play Scrabble until something happens?'

'Scrabble?'

'Oh, it's a game with wooden tiles with letters on them.'

'You play games with runes?'

'No … well, I guess …' I was saved a long explanation by the cry of a Pooka who was stationed on the wall to my left. He pointed to a dive-bombing hawk that was rocketing out of the sky. The bird extended its wings at the last second and landed on the Pooka's arm. He then gently placed the bird on the ground where it transformed into a naked woman. Another Pooka threw a robe over her as she cocked her head quickly over her shoulder just like a bird. The bird/scout tried to speak but failed on her first attempt. Often Pookas, after a change, take a moment to get their heads back into non-animal mode. She dropped her head to compose herself; when she looked back up her jerky movements were gone.

'They are coming,' she said.

The Pooka/hawk informed us that a division of Banshee and Brownie foot soldiers were making their way through the oaks and seemed to be converging on the north face of the castle. Dahy sent troops to all of the other battlements and ordered scouts to check the other approaches to make sure that this was not some sort of diversion.

Dad stood next to me on the battlements as I waited for the first of our attackers to appear.

'We'll see now if your Irish stone minefield works.'

'I guess.'

He placed his hand on my shoulder. 'Gosh, I almost forgot. How was The Choosing? I'm so sorry we all had to leave you in there.'

'That's OK, Dad. War is pretty much as good an excuse as any.'

Dad didn't laugh like I had hoped he would. 'I guess,' he said turning away, 'but damn it, how much more of my life can my brother screw up? This has got to stop.' He paused and I could tell he was thinking about what it was going to take to stop my uncle. Then he shook his head as if to drive away the mood. 'So can you tell me what you saw in the Third Muirbhrúcht?'

'Well …'

'Hey,' Dad said quickly, 'you don't have to tell me.'

'No it's not that. It's just I don't really know what it meant.'

'Oh, that's not unusual, son. Ona once said that the visions of the Third Muirbhrúcht are like when you are trying to remember someone's name. You try and try but you can't remember it – so you give up. Then it comes to you.'

'I saw the Druids I had met in Ireland – the descendants of the banished Fili. They seemed to want something from me but I don't know what.'

'Well, maybe when this is all over we can go back together and find out. We'll probably need a holiday.'

It was nice pretending for that second that we were a normal father and son planning a summer holiday and not two soldiers about to spin the coin on our futures with the fortunes of war.

'I'd like that, Dad.'

A sentry shouted, 'Invaders north!'

We ran to the parapet as a row of Brownies stepped out of the tree-line and set up long-range crossbows in the dirt. Unlike handheld crossbows, these were the mortars of the arrow-shooting family. The strings had to be set while the archer was sitting, using his feet to steady the bow. Two hands were needed to pull back the bow strings, then they were aimed using a monopod. These guys were well trained and successfully got off almost a shot a minute. The arrows were big and had some sort of enchantment in them. As they approached their target they split into twenty or so smaller arrows, producing in the sky the same effect as an entire platoon of synchronised archers.

Still, we were behind a stone wall and it was just a matter of ducking to avoid getting struck. However, we soon found out that the shafts of the arrows were covered in poisonous thorns. Dahy quickly set up an arrow-sweeping team but it meant you had to watch your step. These things were everywhere.

Brendan set his best archers to the task of taking out the crossbows but they were pretty far away. Until we could come up with a plan it looked like we would have to live with incoming fire for a while.

Under the cover of the arrow artillery, about two hundred Banshees and Brownies advanced out of the forest. They walked behind siege ladders that had shields attached to them.

When Dahy saw the small size of the force he said, 'Damn him.' There was no disguising the revulsion on his face. 'Cialtie is doing it again. How can he send so many to slaughter just to test our defences?'

As he had done on the attack of the Hall of Knowledge, Cialtie sent a small group on a suicide mission, just to see what kind of defences we had. I wanted to shout at them to go back but I knew it would do no good. I remembered what Cialtie did to the survivors of his last suicide wave. As they marched back to their own lines, Cialtie mowed them down like blades of grass.

Brendan's elite archery team aimed arrows at the feet of the advancing soldiers. They were remarkably accurate. Don't get me wrong, most of them missed, but they hit about one in ten. Not bad going considering the size of the targets. I didn't feel bad for the ones that got hit – they were, in fact, the lucky ones. They wouldn't have to walk into my minefield.

Often the shields would drop when someone went down and I saw with a heavy heart that most of the attackers were Brownies. I scoured the field to see if Jesse was in the group. What lies had Cialtie told the Brownies to make them do such a foolish thing? How stupid could King Bwika be if he thought that an alliance with my uncle would be good for his people?

As they came closer the ladder-bearers got smarter and hunkered down behind their shields. Brendan stopped firing and we just watched as they approached the line were I had buried the Connemara marble. Some of the advancing soldiers noticed the lack of arrow fire and boldly stuck their heads above their shields so as to see what was going on. They looked nervous. They knew something was going to happen. A good soldier always knows that whenever war gets easy – that's the time to worry.

I was worried.

TWENTY-FIVE
DUMB IDEA

They were behind their shield/ladders so I didn't see it happen. Half of the ladders just fell as if there had never been anyone carrying them. Almost all the rest of the shield/ladder teams had fatalities. The ones that survived were in shock after experiencing galloping old age.

A group of three newly made octogenarians dropped their shields and tried to hobble back to their own lines where they were reminded that retreat was not an option. Their own men filled them with arrows. The remaining men, some looking ancient, regrouped under a handful of shield/ladders. An archer shot one of them before Brendan could stop him. We did nothing as the old men found the base of the walls and set up their siege ladders. It was pathetic to watch the terrified and exhausted soldiers struggling up the ladders with swords drawn. No one lifted a bow or a blade to stop them.

A guy who looked like he was over a hundred crested the wall to my right, sword drawn. As I went to him he jabbed the blade at me, but I casually parried it to the right and grabbed his wrist with both of my hands. I shook the sword free of his grasp as he swung pathetic punches with his other hand. He was panting and out of breath as I pulled him from his ladder and onto the parapet.

'It's OK,' I said to him, 'we won't hurt you.'

The fall to the ground had obviously pained him. I wondered if he had broken his hip or something. I felt awful, like I had started a fight in an old folks' home. When he finally rolled onto his back he had tears in his eyes. 'What happened to me?' he said.

When Cialtie realised that instead of fighting the attackers we were actually saving them, he ordered a resumption of the crossbow fire. In the end we saved about half who tried to scale the walls. A couple who were young and unaffected by the marble spell put up a fight but most, like any old man after climbing a fifty-foot ladder, appreciated the help.

Araf and I locked up our prisoners of war. I wondered if Tuan had enough blood in him to help all of the new Grey Ones that we would have after this thing was over. No, not this thing – this war. We were at war. I was at war – again – and it made me sick to my stomach. I watched in horror as people marched and died, as comrades took arrows and attackers fell screaming. I had been here before. I had been in battle and I knew that this was just the beginning. That it would get worse and worse until it was just me and someone else, toe to toe, swords drawn. Me and a stranger with whom I had no quarrel would be locked into the dance called kill or be killed. But the part I dreaded most was what would happen to me. What I would become when it was just me or him. That was the time when the primordial part of my brain would flood with those Neanderthal endorphins that would fool me into thinking I was enjoying this. Like some stupid junkie who thinks heroin is his friend, I would revel in the event. I had experienced that battle lust before and it had scared me, revolted me, but at the same time I had never felt so alive. I was afraid to experience that again. Right there and then I swore I wouldn't.

Dragon Tuan kept glancing over his shoulder and giving me that look.

'Keep your eyes on the road … or the air,' I shouted to him. 'I know what I'm doing.'

The Pooka turned his huge reptilian head back towards the open skies but not before he gave a smoky snort that I interpreted as, 'Do you?'

The brimstone smoke made me tear up. As I rubbed my eyes I wondered, *Do I know what I'm doing?* I hadn't told anybody other than Tuan about this escapade. My dragon pal had wanted nothing to do with it until I blackmailed him. I wasn't proud of myself but it did tickle me that probably the most powerful creature in all of The Land could be so easily manipulated by threatening to tell his mom he had an Imp girlfriend.

I definitely hadn't told my mom where I was going. I didn't even have to wonder what her response would be. Hey, I knew what everyone's opinion of what I was about to do would be. They'd all say I was crazy and I'd be lying if I said a pretty big part of me didn't agree with them.

I shivered in my dragon saddle. Tuan had warned me that I would need a coat but as usual I hadn't listened. It was so warm at ground level I couldn't imagine that we would be flying high enough so as to see my breath. What else was I unprepared for?

It was easy to imagine how badly Dad was going to flip out when he heard about this. Tuan wasn't even supposed to be in dragon form let alone flying over enemy lines. I think maybe that was one of the reasons Tuan had agreed to help me – he was miffed that Dad had grounded him. Dad had said that they would be expecting us to use Dragon Tuan as a weapon and he was sure they had an anti-dragon defence waiting. Dad ordered Tuan to stay at ground level for his own safety but my Pooka buddy thought that maybe he should have had a say in this decision. Saying that, if Cialtie did have anti-dragon cannons, Tuan wanted to be out of range and that's why we were flying so high.

We were almost to the drop zone. I looked over the side of my magical mount and saw the tiny campfires below just beginning to be lit. They were pinpricks of light and I wondered if this is what the paratroopers on D-day felt like. But then I thought, *at least those guys jumped as a team – I am going in there all by myself with no real plan and no real parachute*. I came close to not going through with it, but then in my mind's eye I saw the bleeding and bloated corpses of my friends and family. Before I could chicken out I just pulled my feet out of the stirrups and slid off into the twilight sky.

I always thought that I would never have enough courage for skydiving, and now here I was jumping off a dragon without a parachute. I hoped my yew staff was up to the demands that I was about to put on it and, for that matter, I hoped I had enough command over the staff so as not to become a strain. I had tied some ropes around my waist and then attached them to the staff in case the G-forces were too much for my hands. After all, skydivers don't hang by their hands from parachutes.

As The Land began to get closer below me I decided it was time to order my yew staff to slow my descent. I was sure I told it to slow down just the tiniest bit, but as usual the stick read that as *slow down a lot* and I was almost cut in half by the force on my waist. I now see why skydivers use harnesses around their backsides and not rope tied around their waists. I instantly had the wind knocked out of me and worried I had ruptured some vital internal organ. I lost grip on the staff and went back into free-fall. When I finally got my senses back I was a lot closer to the ground than I wanted to be. I once again asked for a tiny slowdown and got it. I inched up the magical anti-gravity and, bit by bit, I was just about under control when I hit the ground. I rolled like a good paratrooper and then tried to stand. My midsection felt like I had just gone twelve rounds with a welterweight boxing champion but worse than that, I was exactly opposite to where I wanted to be.

The Brownies had bivouacked on the edge of the yew forest. Luckily I had fallen inside of the guarded perimeter which meant the sentries were looking the wrong way when I descended from the sky. However, I was on the wrong side of the camp. Since I had been given freedom of the Yewlands, I hoped I would touch down close enough to the forest so I could scamper into the yews if there was trouble. Only an idiot would follow me into Ioho but considering where I was, there would be no briar patch for this Brer Rabbit to escape into. I had worn a Brownie-like cloak, so I pulled the hood over my head and started walking for the centre of camp. There were a lot of Brownies here. It made me wonder if anybody was left in the Alderlands but it gave me confidence. If it had just been a small troop someone might have wondered who I was, but since almost the entire Brownie nation was here I didn't expect anyone to say, 'I never saw you at the Brownie prom.'

Now that I was in the thick of this huge camp I started to wonder *what was I thinking?* My plan seemed like a good idea back at Castle Duir when I was all fired up, but here I started to realise how thin and downright stupid it was – not to mention dangerous. My idea was to find Jesse and then get him to let me in to see his father so I could talk some sense into him. Now I knew why I hadn't told anybody about this plan. I knew they would try to talk me out of it or forbid it, and now that I was here I realised that they were right. I repeat – what was I thinking?

I reached into my robe and fumbled for my ropes to attach to my yew staff. Tuan said he would fly around as a bat or something looking for a signal and would pick me up in the sky. I felt bad about chickening out on my noble quest but I remembered my Shakespeare: 'The better part of valour is discretion.' Dad had once told me that the great thing about Shakespeare is you can always find a quote to help you justify anything. I remembered saying, 'Don't you mean Shookspeare?' He looked at me confused. 'You know, 'cause he's dead.'

I let out a snorting laugh at the memory. Hey, if I don't laugh at my jokes – who will? I heard a whispering voice ask, 'Conor?'

Twilight was almost finished. Out of the darkness, Jesse walked up to me and pushed back my hood, then quickly pulled it back up again. Of all the things that could have given me away, it had to be my laugh.

'What are you doing here?' he hissed.

'It was such a lovely night for a stroll I ...'

He grabbed my arm and dragged me over to a more secluded spot. 'If you are discovered here it will be your death – and now maybe mine too. You are here to spy? How many of you are there?'

'No,' I said louder than I meant to and then quietly added, 'no, I came to talk to you and your father.'

'Why?'

'I wanted to try to talk you out of attacking Duir.'

'And what magical rhetoric did you have in mind that would turn all of these soldiers into farmhands?' This was a much more forceful and confident Jesse than I had known from just last winter.

'I … I just was going to say that – you can't trust Cialtie.'

Jesse turned away, mad, then spun and planted his face inches from mine. 'Are you *that* stupid? You thought if you showed up and said "pretty please" we would all go home?'

'No,' I said, 'well, yes. I'm sorry Jesse, I saw so many Brownies die today – I just had to do something to stop it. As soon as I got here I realised what a dumb idea this was. I was just about to fly out when you heard me.'

The old childlike Jesse flickered in the Brownie's eyes. 'You can fly?'

'Well, up and down.'

'What good would that do?'

'Tuan's out there ready to pick me up.'

Jesse quickly backed up and looked to the sky. 'Your battle dragon is above us now?' He said that louder than he should have and others began to notice.

I tried to quiet him down. 'He's not a battle dragon and he's only here as a taxi service.'

'A what?'

'To give me a ride. This was … *is* a peace mission. I promise.'

Jesse calmed down. 'I believe you, Conor, but coming here was madness.'

'Well, I'm famous for my wit and good looks, not my smarts.'

Jesse forced a pained smile. 'If we win this war you don't think Cialtie will give the Brownies Duir?'

'You know he won't, Jesse.'

Jesse nodded.

'And what will your father do when he realises that Cialtie has tricked him?'

Jesse turned his back on me and then in the dark I heard him say with a sigh, 'He will declare war on the Banshees.'

'And how will that turn out?'

Jesse didn't answer so I answered for him. 'Win or lose, there can be no good in this.'

He turned back. The only light came from a distant campfire that flickered and danced on Jesse's face. It created an illusion – one second I saw the confident young commander that he had become and the next

I saw the frightened young boy. His eyes gleamed with boyish water but the soldier refused to allow a tear to fall. 'What should I do, Conor?'

I never got to answer. Not that I had an answer. Torkc guards appeared like magic out of the darkness. I got broadsided by an uncharacteristically brawny Brownie and went down like a quarter-back on a broken play. The wind was knocked out of me for the second time in half an hour. I was still seeing stars when I was dragged to my feet. Then somebody clocked me in the head with something and I saw galaxies.

I awoke sitting on a wooden floor with my hands tied to a wooden pillar in the middle of a very large and very nice tent. As my eyes focused I saw a dais and at the top was the Alder Throne. This was King Bwika's tent. It didn't surprise me that the old jerk made his subjects cart around his quarter-ton throne. Those who are insecure in their power never leave their trappings of power behind. My father, on the other hand, only sat on the Oak Throne when he absolutely had to.

To my left and right there were guards. 'Hey guys,' I said, 'I'm not planning on making any trouble. Would you mind untying me?'

I didn't even get a smirk for my effort. 'No prob, I'm fine like this really.'

But despite what I said, I wasn't fine. In fact, I was in deep do-do. Bwika had me dead to rights. He now had me as a bargaining chip, a hostage. My mom and dad would now be forced to decide what was more important to them – their kingdom or their son. They would choose the kingdom – at least I hoped they would. I couldn't blame them after raising a son as stupid as me. And what if Bwika told Cialtie? I'm pretty sure my uncle would send me home a piece at a time. I could see him sending Mom and Dad an ear-gram with his list of demands. After that, my nickname could be Van Gogh.

I heard a bunch of people enter the tent from behind. Jesse appeared in my peripheral vision flanked by three guards. He wasn't tied up or anything but he didn't look like he was free to go. I almost said hello to him but decided he was in enough trouble without me adding to it. When he caught my eye there was no smile.

We were left waiting like this for a long while before Bwika waddled in flanked by his snazzily dressed honour guard. I know I should have been worried about other things but I asked the guard nearest me, 'How do you get your shirts ironed so neatly way out here?'

Bwika stopped in front of his dais and said, 'Prince Codna, inform the prisoner that he is to speak only when spoken to.'

Jesse looked to his dad then to me and said, 'Prince Conor, you are to speak only when …'

'No,' shouted Bwika. 'Like this.' The king turned, strode up and backhanded me across the face.

The blow cracked something in my jaw and my vision went white around the edges. I thought I was definitely going to pass out and then wished I had. Every part of me from the neck up screamed in pain.

By the time I was seeing things without little birdies flying around, Bwika was sitting on his throne.

'Who else is with you, spy?' Bwika asked.

'I didn't come here to spy, Your Highness.'

Bwika whistled and the rope around my chest tightened. All of the air was forced out of my lungs and I thought I was going to suffocate. Another whistle came from the king and I once again could breathe.

'Don't think about lying again, Faerie. Did you come to corrupt my son?'

'I admire your son, Your Highness. I imagine he is incorruptible.'

'Don't bandy words with me, Faerie. Why are you here?'

'I came to warn you,' I said.

'About what?'

'I came to warn you about Cialtie – he is not to be trusted.'

The king said nothing.

'My uncle started this war so he can take Duir for himself. He needs to retake the Oak Throne in order to fulfil Ona's prophecies. He will never let you or the Brownies have it.'

Bwika stared at me for long enough to make me wonder if maybe I had gotten through to him. Then he laughed. That cocky laugh that reaffirmed what I always thought about the Brownie monarch – he was an idiot.

I hung my head and whispered to Mom and Dad like it was a prayer, 'I'm so sorry for the trouble I'm about to cost you.' I had been so stupid and now I had given my enemies the upper hand in this battle. What would Dad have to concede to get me back? If he didn't give up his kingdom he would have to give up part of his heart. I was so sorry I was about to put him through this.

'You are a spy, Faerie,' Bwika said, 'and I sentence you to death by the sword.'

Death? Oh, crap. I hadn't thought of that.

TWENTY-SIX

KING BWIKA

The king pointed to the chief of his honour guard, who drew his sword and came at me.

'Father,' Jesse said, 'you should listen to what Prince Conor has to say.'

Bwika was on his feet. 'In this room,' he shouted, 'I am addressed as Your Highness.'

I wouldn't have wanted to be Jesse at that moment but the king's outburst was enough to halt the progress of my decapitator.

'I have tried speaking to the king and it hasn't worked,' Jesse said. 'Now I am appealing to my father. Listen to Conor, Father, he makes sense.'

'You dare defy me in the room of the Alder Throne.'

'The room of the Alder Throne is back in the Alderlands, Father – where we should be. We don't belong here. Can you actually say you like it here?'

Bwika was turning red with rage. 'This land should be ours.'

'But do you like it here? Would you really rather live here than in the Alderlands?'

'The gold his father sits on belongs to us. They disrespect the Brownies – they have even stopped our stipend.'

'Now hold on,' I said, 'Duir only stopped your stipend of gold after you declared war on us.'

I shouldn't have spoken. Jesse had been getting through to him but then idiot Duir boy had to open his big mouth. Bwika exploded like a thermometer in a heat wave. I didn't even understand him for about a minute. There were some Brownie swear words in there, and my ancestors were mentioned, but he was so manic that a translation would have been impossible. Let's just say he was very, very angry. When Jesse tried to calm him down, Bwika barked something at his guards that made all of us look at each other to see if anyone understood it.

Bwika repeated himself. 'GAG HIM.'

The guard started to walk towards me.

'Not him – Codna.'

Jesse looked shocked and then hurt as the guard tied a handkerchief across his mouth. When Jesse tried to remove it the guard tied his hands behind his back as well. I looked to my Brownie friend. Despite what a brave soldier he had become, the wounded son had a tear sliding down his cheek.

'Now,' Bwika said, pointing to me, 'kill him.'

The honour guard, still shaken by the unrest in the room, hesitated, but not for as long as I would have liked. He hoiked up his sword and came at me. From his posture I had the awful feeling that he was going to attempt to split my head straight down the middle – not the way I had imagined I would go. My idea of a good death was in bed from old age. I took in a long breath, revelling in the enjoyment of just that simple act. Life slowed down for me as it always does when I'm in mortal peril. I was glad of it this time 'cause I couldn't think of any way out of this mess. I had time to compose my final words. I toyed with some sort of death curse or something noble like, 'I only regret that I have but one life to give for Duir.' That would play well but then I figured Dad would probably rumble me and everyone would think I was a jerk for plagiarising my final words. I decided on cheeky, my default for covering when I was actually scared out of my wits.

'Don't I even get a chance to duel one of you guys to the death?' I said, squeezing my eyes shut. And then … nothing.

When I opened my eyes to see what was taking so long, everybody was looking at me. I glanced to the gagged Jesse and saw him nodding at me with wide eyes. I got the message – *Yes* – but *yes* what? I had been in so much terror that I hadn't even remembered what I said. My executioner looked at me waiting and then looked to Bwika.

'Kill him,' Bwika said.

'Wait, wait,' I said retracing my mental steps, 'I challenge you to a duel to the death.' Then as an unsure question I added, 'As is my right?' I looked to Jesse, who again nodded yes.

Bwika forced his bulk off his throne and then walked down the dais until he was inches away from my face. He was still awfully red. 'Who do you challenge?' he asked.

'Ah … you … Your Highness.'

Bwika straightened and then laughed. He walked past me and shouted, 'Bring him.'

News had obviously swept through the camp that I was here. Bwika ordered light, and a ring of torch-bearing Brownies stood in a semicircle making and lighting the fighting area. In the middle of the makeshift arena stood a hulking Brownie. Seriously, this guy was like an extra for a barbarian vs. caveman movie. I didn't know they actually made Brownies that big. He, of course, was topless except for strange leather shoulder pads and wore a short leather skirt. It was the kind of outfit that people couldn't help but make fun of but with this guy, if they did, they only did it once. He held a shiny, sharp blade. Stuck in the ground in front of him was a dull old sword. I pulled it out and ran my finger down it. You could shave a balloon with the edge on this thing without popping it.

'Sporting,' I said. 'Can I have my own sword?'

'The Sword of Duir,' Bwika said, 'is back with its rightful owner. Me.'

I started to say, 'What do you mean back, it was never yours.' But instead I said, 'It looks good on you. Why don't *you* use it then? I thought I was fighting you, not Steroid Boy here.'

I don't think Steroid Boy knew what steroids were but I could tell he didn't like the nickname.

'A king may choose his champion.'

'I'm a prince, you know, can I call home and get one too? Why don't you fight me, Your Highness? Tell you what, I'll fight you with my banta against your sword.'

Bwika smiled but it was forced.

'No, I imagine you're too slow even for a fight like that.'

Steroid Boy wasn't waiting for '1, 2, 3 start'. He raised his sword and came at me with the kind of ferocity that you usually get when someone insults one's king or mother. I parried the swing above my head and let his blade slide past my shoulder. His right side was wide open and I caught him on the arm with a counter-attack. My sword didn't even break his skin.

'Thanks so much for this sword. I might as well be fighting with a tent pole.'

Steroid Boy was fast and strong but luckily he had no finesse. Don't get me wrong, fast and strong were enough to get me very dead but if this guy had had any training, I would have been watching this scene from above while grooming my wings. I ducked and rolled and succeeded on coming up on the other side so I could look Bwika in the eyes.

'It's the weight, isn't it? You've gotten too fat even to fight against a guy with only a stick.'

I did another duck and dive. This time Steroid Boy's blade came so close to my nose I wasn't sure if I had been nicked or not. I really had to start paying attention to the fight, but I thought maybe I was getting through to the monarch.

'You know, maybe if you cut the cakes out of your diet you could lose a stone or two and you could get back to fighting weight.'

I parried a forearm swipe and tried to lock swords with my attacker – big mistake. He threw me off and onto my back like I was a schoolgirl – and I've known a few tough schoolgirls. I was winded and the big guy wasn't waiting for me to get up. I was just deciding which way to roll when Bwika shouted, 'Stop!'

Steroid Boy halted like he was on a leash. I slowly got to my feet, panting.

'Give him his stick,' the king ordered.

I threw away my useless sword.

Bwika stepped up and drew the Sword of Duir. 'I shall enjoy killing you with your own blade.'

'The Lawnmower would never hurt me.'

'The what?'

'The Lawnmower, that's the name of the sword you stole from me.'

'What is a lawnmower?'

'It's a machine in the Real World that keeps grass short.'

'What is wrong with sheep?' the king asked as my stick was thrown to me.

I caught my banta then immediately flipped it under my armpits and commanded it to lift me up and away from there. I didn't want or need this fight. I was doing the noble thing – running away. OK maybe I have a different definition of noble but I knew that this was a no-win situation. If I lost I died and if I won then somebody here would kill me for killing their king. Running away may not be dignified but it was smart. Bwika took a menacing step towards me and I again commanded my stick to lift me out of there – nothing. I pulled the staff out from under my arms and had a look.

'Hey, this isn't my banta stick.' Bwika took a couple of steps closer and I held the stick in front of me in a defensive position.

'That seems to be a fine alder wood banta stick – what is your problem?'

'My problem is that one of your henchmen is a thief.'

Bwika gave me a look that reminded me that calling a Brownie thief was not an insult. Then he ran at me swinging steel.

Like all big guys he surprised me with how fast he moved. He may have been old, stupid and overweight but you don't get to be King of the Brownies without knowing how to handle yourself in a fight. I used the stick to deflect his sword, being careful to give a little, so he wouldn't cut the wood. I remembered the stick vs. sword fight I had with Essa so long ago and wished I had paid more attention. He was backing me into a crowd of Brownies. I had a feeling that if I landed in with them it would hurt as much as the blade so I took a wide swipe at Bwika's head and rolled over so my back was Brownie-free.

I back-pedalled as Bwika swung. I succeeded in getting a few body hits in with my stick but they hardly seemed to faze the big guy. I knew I didn't have a chance up close with the Lawnmower. My only hope was that he would tire out as I kept losing ground. I blocked one forearm swipe too well and he took about half a foot off the top of my stick. It wasn't that bad though, he had cut it at an angle and I now had a pointy end to my weapon.

Then he made what could have been a fatal mistake. He tried one of those Zorro-like forehand/backhanded swipes and when he finished his whole body was wide open. I instinctively jabbed the sharp end of my stick towards his throat but pulled back just before contact. I could have done it then. I could have killed him but as I said, regicide was not the idea here. The idea was to get out alive. I locked eyes with Bwika hoping he would acknowledge that I just gave him his life but there was no such recognition on his face. The only thing on his face was growing rage. I used that and waited for his next attack. It was wild, I dodged it and while the sword was out of position I jammed the sharp end of my stick into the king's foot. Then I turned and ran.

The Brownies had grouped, not into a circle like with most fights but in a semi-circle. I made an assumption – one that my life depended on – that the reason they didn't want to place their backs to that part of the night was because that part creeped them out. And the creepiest place in all The Land is the yew forest. Bwika chased after me but I don't think he could have caught me even without the limp I had just given him. Other Brownies closed in. It was dark, I had no idea where the edge of the forest was, or even if it was the right kind of forest, but if trees didn't start looming soon I was done for.

A quick Brownie came from my right and tried to tackle me. With a move that would have made an All-American fullback proud, I straight-armed him. He hit the ground and enjoyed a dirt sandwich just as I saw the skeletal outlines of yews form out of the darkness.

A Brownie came at me from the left. I pointed ahead and shouted, 'Yews', and it worked. He pulled up so fast he lost his footing and ate a bit of earth himself. All the other Brownie soldiers stopped too. I found out later that the Brownies have a children's poem that teaches them about the dispositions of different trees. The first line goes, 'When you meet a yew – that's the end of you.'

All of the Brownie soldiers held back but I guess Bwika was no poetry fan. When I cleared the first tree I looked back and saw the beefy monarch loping at full speed, red-faced, sword outstretched and he was coming right for me.

'Bwika, NO!' I shouted but the king was not in his right mind. He got within two footfalls of the first yew and stopped like he was a bird hitting a window. I ran to the tree and placed my hands on the sinuous bark. 'Stop, leave him, he didn't mean to come here. He was chasing me. He didn't come here to be judged.'

I ran to Bwika and tried to pull him away. He groaned from the pain of my pull fighting against the yew tree's bone hold. When I tried a second time to move him the trees pushed me back by my sternum. It felt like I had been kicked in the chest.

To Bwika's credit he knew what was happening and he knew the danger he was in but he didn't whimper or beg – just the opposite. He tried to turn to me; when he found that impossible he shouted, 'I don't need help from you, Faerie.'

I ran around the tree so I could see the king's face. Once more I touched the yew. 'You said I have freedom of the Yewlands, King Bwika is with me.'

The tree broke his/her silence. '*This Brownie is not your companion, he was attempting to kill you. Your minds are open to us, Faerie – do not attempt to lie.*'

'He's not prepared for the Choosing, he didn't mean to enter the Yewlands. He shouldn't have to die because of an accident.'

'*Falling from a cliff is an accident,*' the tree said with its twin male and female voice, '*yet often there is death.*'

'But you can stop this,' I pleaded. 'Let him go.'

'*The Brownie has entered the Yewlands, he shall be judged.*'

'I told you, Faerie, I need no succour from you,' Bwika grunted. 'I'm not afraid of being judged by a damn tree.'

There was nothing I could do. I may have the freedom of the Yewlands but that sure doesn't mean I have any sway over them. I thought, *You're on your own, Brownie king, but if I were you I wouldn't start a trial by swearing at my judge.*

'When I want your advice I'll ask for it,' Bwika said. That's when I realised we were linked in mind through the tree. I should have let go. A yew trial should be a private thing but, like seeing a car wreck, I just couldn't look away.

Bwika's life flashed before my eyes. His was not a privileged royal upbringing. Unlike most princes he came from humble stock and rose through the Brownie military. Through sheer hard work, physical strength and cunning Bwika gained the highest of military positions in the Alderlands – Chief of the Torkc Guards. It was there he saw his chance and he sowed seeds of discontent into the king's son and finally influenced him into challenging his father to a duel. The prize – the throne. Bwika secretly coached both father and son and, as the fight's referee, poisoned both combatants' blades. When it was over the Brownielands had no king and no heir. Bwika ascended to the throne until a rune holder could be found. Two years later he came to Duir, took his Choosing and received the Alder Rune.

My anxiety lessened. If the Chamber of Runes found him worthy of a major rune then maybe so will the yews. But then I remembered something that Spideog had said to me, 'Many a Runelord had been found wanting by the yews.'

Next was the birth of his sons: two in quick succession by two different women. He banished both mothers as soon as they dared to even suggest a course of parenting different to the father. Both children were raised by a succession of nannies who were fired with regularity. Demne, the one I called Frank, was so desperate for his father's approval that he volunteered for a suicide mission to destroy the Tree of Knowledge. Bwika, in his hubris, let him do it and we all know how that ended. Jesse's upbringing was even more painful to watch. Every time I saw him through his father's eyes he was a cowering slip of a thing. Bwika only recently had come to show any interest in him, now that he had come into his own.

When the tree started to ask Bwika about this war and why he supported Cialtie and Maeve – the Yew Killer – I couldn't take it any more. I let go of the tree and dropped to my knees with the kind of emotional exhaustion that can make even opening your eyes seem like a chore.

When I did look up I saw Jesse. He alone had ventured close to the yew forest. He was watching his father looking up, kneeling, straining at the base of the yew.

'Don't come any closer, Jesse,' I warned.

'What are they doing to him?' he asked. There were tears in his eyes.

'He's being judged.'

'Will they kill him?'

I wanted to give him hope. He looked like he needed hope but I had been listening in and I knew Bwika's chances were not good. 'Maybe.'

A groaning defiant scream made me turn. Bwika was on his feet; his hands were shaking, reaching for the now low hanging yew berries. It was over. He had been judged and found unworthy. The tree was forcing him to eat its poisonous fruit.

Jesse screamed, 'No', and ran to his father. I screamed the same thing and ran to intercept him but was way too late. Jesse's hand touched his father's shoulder and then he too froze solid. Bwika stuffed a handful of berries into his face; the juice of them flowed down his chin like blood. He had one last effort of will in him and he used it to look at his son and smile, then he collapsed face first into the tree's trunk.

I ran to Jesse; he was immobile with his hand outstretched. Moments before, that hand had rested on the shoulder of his father. His eyes were swimming in the tears of a child. I came up behind him and reached around his waist trying to drag him back into the camp. I couldn't budge him an inch. I gave up and buried my face into his back.

'Jesse, do you know what you have done? You're going to be judged.'

TWENTY-SEVEN
PRINCE CODNA

The tree pulled Jesse's hands to its trunk. I ran around and touched the tree myself.

'He really is a friend of mine. I demand he be given the freedom of the Yewlands. I came to see him. He must not be judged.'

The yew didn't answer, he/she ignored me.

'HE IS MY FRIEND!'

A movie of Jesse's life entered my mind as I fell to my knees pleading for the tree to stop. His earliest memories were of nannies who, while outwardly raising him with iron discipline, secretly tried to give him some of the nurturing that every child needs. He was never as fast or as strong as his brother and his father set the tone for the way everyone looked at him. All considered him a weedy child, a sissy. Only his brother gave him the kind of love and defence that he needed. I saw that without his brother, Jesse may not have made it in that tough Brownie world. It made me sad that Frank was dead. Jesse finally, just in the last year, had started coming into himself. His confidence and stature both grew. Now his father began to take pride in him, but Jesse's newfound prowess was despite his father's influence not because of it.

The tree pushed me away as it spoke privately with its defendant. Out in the open field the Brownie soldiers were slowly moving closer. I motioned for them to stop and they did. I waited, my heart pounding, for any movement of the branches that bore the yew's poisonous berries. After what was probably only five minutes but seemed like hours, Jesse stood up, said, 'Thank you', and then stepped away from the tree.

'Are you OK?'

Jesse didn't reply for the longest time and then nodded yes.

'Jesse, you passed the judgement.'

'Yes,' he said still staring at the yew.

'Did you receive a gift?'

'I did,' he said.

'What did you get?'

'The yew asked me what I wanted,' he said, finally looking at me. 'I asked for the body of my father.'

I saw him start to stagger. I quickly ran to him and put my arms around his waist. He dropped his head on my shoulder and burst into tears. It didn't last long. He pushed me away, keeping his back to the rest of the Brownies, and composed himself.

'This is no way for a captain of the Torkc Guards to behave,' he said.

'Don't you mean – this is no way for the King of the Brownies to behave?'

He looked at me incredulously.

'Aren't you the next in line to the throne?' I asked.

'I … I guess I am … until a major rune is chosen.'

'Which I'm sure will be chosen by you.'

Jesse stood for a minute taking this all in, then a tiny smile crossed his face as he wiped the tears from his eyes. 'Then this is definitely no way for the King of the Brownies to behave.'

'I think, Your Highness, this is absolutely the right way for a king to behave.'

We carried Bwika out of the forest. Now I know what they mean by dead weight. When we had staggered clear of the yews, Steroid Boy came towards us and drew on me. I dropped Bwika's legs to defend myself.

'Prince Conor is under my protection,' Jesse said.

'But Captain Codna,' Steroid Boy began.

'I think, soldier, the title you should be using is – Your Highness.'

Steroid Boy was obviously not the brightest bulb in the marquee. He looked to the dead king and then to the son. Finally he twigged. 'Yes, Your Highness.'

'Make yourself useful, big boy,' I said, 'relieve the king of the king.'

This confused Steroid Boy even further until he said, 'Oh, of course.' He picked up the late King Bwika. I was pleased to see that even he struggled a bit with the weight of him.

What looked like half of the Brownie nation was waiting for us in the field in front of the camp. Jesse walked up to one of the soldiers and took from him a torch. Then he placed his fingers in his mouth and produced a whistle that made me stick my finger in my ear hole to make sure it wasn't bleeding. The crowd started to part in the back as Jesse's horse cantered his way to his master. I smiled to see that the obedient steed was The Turlow's old horse that I had given him. Jesse handed me his torch and then performed an impressive running mount on the bareback horse. I returned the torch. From atop his mount and in the dramatic flickering light of the flame, King Codna addressed his people.

'King Bwika is dead. He died under the branches of the yews,' he shouted, then waited for the murmur to die down. 'My father was a great king ...'

I waited and wondered if he was going to follow that statement with, 'But not a good father.'

Instead he said, 'But he was not infallible. He grew up in an age that believed the Alderlands were a place of banishment. Understand, he loved the Brownielands, and Alder Keep, but he believed that our rightful home was there on top of Duir Hill.'

Jesse turned his horse and pointed to Duir, then turned back to his people. He looked more regal with every passing second.

'I do not know what happened in the first age. I have no magic that can show me what the Ancients did or did not do to our ancestors. But I do know one thing. If they envisioned the Alderlands to be an abyss, a prison we Brownies were supposed to escape from, then they were oh so very wrong. If the Ancients gave us the Alderlands as banishment then they were not as all-knowing as the great stories have said.

Because as you all know, when they threw away the Alderlands they threw away Paradise.'

This was good stirring stuff but it was also a tiny bit heretical. I looked around to see what the reaction would be. I didn't have to wait long.

A voice from the back started it: 'Codna, Codna.' It didn't take long before the chant was taken up by everyone in the field. 'Codna, Codna, Codna, Codna.'

Jesse held up his hand and silenced the crowd. 'Prince Conor came here on a mission of peace. He came with information that makes me believe that Cialtie never had any intention of giving us Duir if we win this war.'

A loud murmur rumbled through the crowd. It raised the emotional temperature in the field. Jesse silenced it with two words.

'No matter … I for one miss my home. I don't like it here and I don't think that even all the gold in the mines of Duir are worth the lives of the good Brownies that we will lose in this quarrel. For what will we win? A home we don't like? And what will happen if we have all the wealth in the land? I'll tell you what would happen – there would be nothing left to steal. What fun would that be?'

A Fergalish smile overtook my face. Jesse looked to me for affirmation and I bowed my lowest bow.

'I want to go home,' King Codna shouted. 'Are you with me?'

There was no doubting the answer. The Brownies went wild.

When we got back to his tent and we were finally alone, Jesse asked, 'Was that all right?'

'All right?' I said, 'All right? What are you talking about? That was awesome.'

'Oh gods, Conor, how can I be king?'

'Just like that, Jesse,' I said. 'I've never seen anything more kingly in my life.'

He smiled and held his hand out for me to shake. It was still trembling.

'Screw that,' I said and gave him a big hug.

Jesse gave me back the Lawnmower and sent someone out to retrieve my yew staff. Outside, the Brownie camp was wasting no time packing up to go home. Jesse gave me a sitting harness that Brownies use to sit in trees and I tied that to my staff.

'Long live King Codna,' I said.

'Maybe I should call myself King Jesse,' then he crumpled his face and said, 'maybe not. Goodbye Conor, I shall always remember what you said, "No one can unmake us friends."'

'And now I hope no one can ever make us enemies again.' I bowed once more to the new king and commanded my yew staff to lift me into the night. When I had well cleared the treetops I fired one of my mother's Shadowmagic flares and waited comfortably in my new harness.

It only took a couple of minutes for Tuan to show up. He had been flying around as a bat waiting for me so he had lost his saddle. It took me three attempts at landing on his back before I held on long enough to get my balance and crawl into a decent riding position.

Tuan gave me evil looks all the way home. He's good at it in his dragon face. When we landed in the courtyard of Castle Duir, the dragon turned into Tuan again and instantly gave me an earful.

'What took you so long? I was flapping around in the dark for hours.'

'Sorry. Eh ... could you put some clothes on?'

'I almost went into the Brownie camp all flames-a-flaming.'

'I'm really sorry but it got complicated. I'm glad you didn't fly in. Bwika's dead and the Brownies are going back to the Alderlands.'

'What? How did you do that?'

'I'll tell you when there is less of you to see. Will you get dressed please?'

For the sake of modesty, Tuan turned into his wolfhound and went in search of one of his several clothes stashes as I made my way to a bed. I always find this waking in bondage thing exhausting. I just wanted sleep.

An honour guard intercepted me before I even got under a roof and I was unceremoniously escorted to the War Room. I felt like a prisoner.

'You guys know I'm a prince, right?' They all said they did but that didn't stop them from insisting I go with them. I toyed with the idea of testing whether I was, in fact, free to go to my room but I just didn't have the strength for those kinds of games. Saying that, I was pretty sure I was in big trouble with my friends and family for escaping on Tuan-back – I wasn't sure I had the strength for this meeting either.

Behind me I heard Tuan. I turned to see him with his own soldiers. 'I would advise you to take your hand off my arm,' he said with a very animal-like growl, 'unless you want to be holding on to the arm of a bear.' The guard let go quickly.

Essa was in the hallway outside the meeting room. She ran at me and I immediately put my arms up to defend myself – this was Essa after all – but she wrapped her arms around my neck and said, 'Thank the gods you're all right.'

'Maybe I should go for a late night walk more often.'

Essa pushed back. 'You weren't walking. You were flying with Tuan.'

'Oh you know about that?'

'Everyone knows about that,' Essa said. 'Your mother performed an emergency Shadowcasting to find out where you were. The casting said you were in the Yewlands. Your father mobilised an entire platoon to figure out a way to get you.'

'Oh, so maybe they're a little mad at me?'

Essa's face went through four seasons of emotions. She laughed, then her eyes welled up, then she looked like she was going to hit me before she re-hugged me and said, 'I thought I would never see you again.'

'Hey, I ain't going anywhere,' I said, smoothing her hair. 'You're stuck with me for a long time.'

She looked up at me; her face was inches from mine. 'How long?'

'For ever,' I said. 'That is if my mother doesn't kill me in the next ten minutes.'

A cough from behind broke our embrace. It was Dahy. 'The king demands your presence.' He looked embarrassed at interrupting us.

'I thought you would be mad at me too.'

'I'm furious,' the old general said, 'but kissing a sweetheart in a time of war is an important thing.'

'Well, Dahy! I never realised what an old softie you are.'

'Careful, Conor,' he said as he motioned me through the door.

Everybody was there: Mom, Dad, Dahy, Lorcan, Nieve, Fand, Brendan, Nora, Gerard, Eth, two Runelords I didn't know and half a dozen other uniformed types and they all looked awfully mad at me. Dad had that look I had only seen a couple of times before. It was where he was so mad that he actually couldn't get the first syllables out of his mouth. Mom, whom I didn't have as much experience reading, had a face like I had *never* seen before.

I decided to head off what was coming. 'Bwika's dead,' I said calmly. 'Codna is king and the Brownies are no longer at war with us. They are on their way back to the Alderlands now.

If Dad found it difficult speaking before, he found it impossible now. It was a nice moment. Mom stepped up. 'Could you tell us this news again, Conor, and extrapolate a bit.'

So I did. I told them the whole tale leaving out only what I had used on Tuan to blackmail him into giving me a lift.

When I finished Dad said, 'You could have been taken hostage. You could have compromised us all.'

'I know it was stupid. I promise I won't do it again, but right now I need to put my head down. Can I go to bed now, Mommy and Daddy?'

I stood up and had one of those head rushes I get when I stand up too fast on the same day that I've been knocked unconscious. Essa jumped up and gave me a hand. We were almost at the door when Graysea burst in.

'You're safe,' she gushed, taking my arm away from Essa. She placed her hand on my neck and announced, 'He is exhausted. I am taking him straight to bed.'

Essa looked miffed and took my other arm. For a second I thought she was going to start pulling and I was going to be drawn and quartered by competing women.

Nieve behind me said, 'Now to our Shadow defences.'

Essa had to stay for that meeting. She let go of my arm and said to Graysea, 'Take good care of him.'

I thought that maybe I should stay too, but then I figured I had just cut the size of the attacking force by half – that was enough for a day. War would have to be planned without me.

Graysea walked me back to my room and lay down in my bed with me. When I started to protest she shushed me and then sprouted gills in her neck and a fin. I had bruises and rope burns and contusions that were so all over I hadn't even noticed how bad I felt until my mermaid doctor melted them all away.

'I thought I told you to stop doing that for everybody.'

'You were right; I was overextending myself in the infirmary. I am now only healing in the urgent cases. But you, dear sweet Conor,' she kissed me on the cheek as she got up and walked to the door, 'are not everybody. Sleep.'

Sleep came instantly. I had one of those strange movie dreams where I was a private detective. I was waiting in my 1920s decorated office when in came a beautiful client. It was Maeve, the girl from the tea shop in Connemara. She wore red lipstick and a low-cut red dress that had a slit that showed off her shapely right leg as she walked. She said she wanted to find her real mother and I agreed when she paid me in advance – with a pair of Nikes.

I put on the sneakers; they didn't go with my grey suit and fedora but hey, this was my dream. I wandered through countless speakeasies and police stations until, finally, I told Connemara Maeve I had found her mother. Together we drove up a long gated driveway of a Hollywood house that looked like it belonged to a movie star. The door opened and my Irish client came face to face with her mother – it was Maeve. The other Maeve, the outlawed Queen of the Druids, the tree killer that almost destroyed all of The Land with her corruption of Shadowmagic – the Maeve that was brought back from some abyss by the spilled blood of Ruby. She looked at the Irish girl and said, 'Who are you?'

I turned to my glamorous client but she no longer wore makeup and was dressed in her modest tea-shop waitress's uniform. 'Tell her,' she said.

I opened my eyes with a start. On either side of my bed stood two burly soldiers in green-stained leather armour. At the foot of my bed a wild-haired woman, also in green leathers, stood staring at me with eyes that had almost no colour at all. I sat up in bed my heart pounding.

'I was just dreaming about you,' I said.

TWENTY-EIGHT

FAND

'Y ou were in the Hollylands when I regained form.'

How the hell did she know that? I thought. *I was hooded.*

Like Maeve was reading my mind she said, 'I sensed your presence from the hallway. Who are you?'

This was a freaky moment. I had been in a deep sleep and then woke up only to be confronted with the very scary long-lost legendary Shadowwitch and her two eyeless henchmen. Then the realisation hit me that this was one of those dreams within a dream and I relaxed.

'Buzz off lady; I got more sleeping to do.'

I was about to snuggle down under my covers again when Maeve kind of went see-through and walked towards me. She didn't stop at the bed. When she came to the footboard she just kept coming and walked right through it like it wasn't there. She stood translucent in the middle of my bed like she was waist deep in a swimming pool. Dream or no dream, I instinctively backed up; she didn't look like a healthy thing to touch. I pulled my legs back and then she solidified again. When she did, the bed around her just exploded. The sheets and the mattress ripped apart and the wood frame of the bed cracked in two, sending wood splintering across the room. I ended up on the floor at the Fili Queen's feet and said, 'OK, maybe this isn't a dream.'

'I ask again, Faerie, who are you?'

Considering she had trashed my bed by just touching it, I thought that maybe answering her was a good idea. 'I'm Conor, nice to meet you.'

'You are Conor, Son of Oisin?'

'That's me.'

'Where is your father?'

I didn't have to answer because at that moment, one of the west-wing guards burst into the room with his sword drawn. 'Stand away from the prince,' he said.

It wasn't until then that I noticed that Maeve's henchmen were unarmed. One of them faced the guard who repeated his command, 'Back away from the prince.'

The henchman reached towards the confused guard who must have been wondering, *What is this unarmed nut doing?* The guard finally reared back and swung. It was a long wide swing. He did it that way to allow the unarmed man time to get out of the way but he just stood there. A second before the guard's sword hit him, the Fili became ghost-like and the blade sliced through him like he wasn't there. The guard, who had been preparing for impact, fell forward, off balance, and exposed his back. Maeve's man reached his hand into the guard's side and then solidified. The guard screamed but only for a second. There was a crack of bones and a horrible squelching noise. I could only imagine that what had just happened to my bed was what was happening inside that poor guard's body. The guard went limp. It looked as if the Fili was holding him up, then as if to confirm that thought, he went spooky and the guard fell to the floor.

Another guard came through the door and the other Fili dispatched him in exactly the same manner. The floor was now covered with more blood than I had ever seen. And I have seen a lot of blood.

Maeve loomed over me. My feet slid on the bed sheet under my heels as I tried to push myself back into the wall. 'I tire of asking you questions twice, Faerie. Where is your father?'

'I am here.' Dad was standing at my door. Two of his honour guard entered the room before him.

'Don't attack,' I called from the floor, 'they can kill with a touch.'

Dad stepped into the room. 'What do you want, Maeve?'

The ghost queen smiled but not in anything resembling a heartwarming way. 'I want from you what I wanted from your father – Duir.'

'Duir is not mine to give. Tenure of the Oak Throne is chosen by the Chamber of Runes.'

Maeve threw her head back and laughed one of those laughs that only bad guys and bad actors can do. 'The clan of Duir builds a magic room that always magically seems to give the clan of Duir their magic Rune. Magically convenient, do you not think?'

'And you think you deserve the Oak Throne? Why?'

Maeve walked right up to Dad. His guard went to step in between them but Dad stopped him. When they were nose to nose Maeve flickered into her ghost form. It only took a second but in that time she reached into the chest of Dad's bodyguard. He gasped as she solidified and he screamed as her hand came out holding his beating heart.

'Power,' she said. 'Duir is mine because this time, you cannot stop me.'

She dropped the heart to the ground and then looked at her hand. It was covered with blood but then she flickered translucent, and the blood fell to the floor – her hand was clean. No one tried to attack or stop her. It was an impressive display of power and ruthlessness.

'You cannot stop us. I have an army with this power. And your son cannot stop me by corrupting the Brownie prince. We don't need the Brownies.' I was now on my feet. She looked at me and said, 'We will deal with Prince Codna in time.'

She reached into a pouch that hung from her waist and took out a piece of marble. 'And I will not be stopped by pieces of the Real World.' She threw the rock to Dad's other guard. I started to shout, 'Don't touch that!' but didn't have time. He instinctively caught the piece of Connemara marble and instantly was reduced to dust.

'What has happened to you?' Dad hissed. 'You are not even Hawathiee.'

'You are right, son of Finn. I am better than Hawathiee and I shall rule you all. But I am not without a heart.'

I found that statement hard to believe after what she had just done to our guard's heart.

'I shall give you until sunrise tomorrow to leave. After that …'

She didn't say anything else but she didn't have to. They went see-through and turned to leave. Maeve walked through the door but the bodyguards went through the wall. One of them bumped into my yew banta stick and was surprised that it blocked his way just as if he had been solid. The stick then fell to the ground and he stepped over it.

Dad shouted to the guards outside in the hall, 'Let them pass unmolested.'

After they left I tried to speak but I couldn't breathe. I ran out of the room and vomited in the hallway. Dad came out and held my shoulders. After everything in my stomach had come up I still retched. When I finally finished I stood shaking like I was standing outside in the snow. A guard held out his canteen and I rinsed out my mouth. The hallway was crowded by then. I looked to Dad and said, 'What are we going to do?'

An Imp-healer came running down the corridor calling my name. 'Prince Conor, come quick.'

I looked up confused, tired.

The woman slid to a stop in front of me and said, 'It's Matron Graysea.'

There was a circle of people in the infirmary around Graysea's lifeless form. Blood had pooled on one side of her kelp robe. A nurse was applying a pressure bandage to her injured side. I knelt down and asked if I could see the wound. It was not as bad as the ones I had seen in my room but it was the same thing. I could spot bits of broken ribs oozing out with the blood before the bandage was replaced.

'What happened?' I asked.

'That woman and those men walked through the walls into the infirmary then started pushing over tables. Graysea went to yell at them – you know like she does – and the woman slid her hand right through her side.'

'Get her in water,' I said.

Araf was already in the infirmary and he lifted her up as the nurse kept pressure on the wound. Araf went into the pool holding her in his arms. When he dipped her head under the water gills appeared on her neck and her feet melded into one fin.

'This is a good sign,' one of the Imp-healers said.

Still she didn't wake up.

'Conor, is she OK?' came a voice behind me. It was Essa.

I remembered all of the names Essa had called Graysea and I almost shouted, 'What do you care?' but before I lost it, I recognised that my anger was not with Essa. 'I don't know.'

She nodded. 'I hate to pull you and Araf away but the king wants you both at the war council.'

The Imp-healer said, 'Go. We will look after her. I will notify you of any change.'

'I'll be there presently,' Araf said as he stepped dripping out of the pool.

The war council was waiting for my report but when I sat I was too choked up to start. Dad broke the silence as someone brought me a cup of tea that soothed my stomach and steadied my nerves.

'Maeve was here,' Dad said. 'She has a power over her corporeal being. She is impervious to a sword, can walk through solid walls and can reach inside and ... she can kill with a touch. Her soldiers can too.'

Everyone looked to me and I nodded in agreement.

'Are you saying,' Dahy asked, 'that she and her army are invincible?'

Dad looked to everyone in the room. They all wanted him to say it wasn't so but he couldn't. 'I am,' he said, 'I see no way to stop her.'

'My lord?' Lorcan said.

Dad's eyes stared at the table. His shoulders were hunched over like that statue of Atlas, except the world that was pressing down on Dad was invisible. Finally he looked up and pushed his shoulders back. 'We must evacuate Castle Duir.'

'Where will we all go?' Mom said with uncharacteristic panic in her voice.

'Faerie and Leprechaun are always welcome in the Heatherlands,' Araf said as he entered the room wearing a robe from the infirmary.

'And Cull,' Gerard said.

'And the Pinelands,' Tuan echoed.

Dad nodded, acknowledging his allies. 'Lorcan, we cannot give Maeve unfettered access to the gold. We can't leave her with that much power. Can you seal the mines?'

Lorcan looked like he had been slapped. 'You mean destroy them?' Dad nodded yes.

Lorcan looked around like he wanted someone to slap him on the back and say, 'Just kidding.' Finally he said, 'Yes, my lord.'

'No,' said a soft voice at the end of the table. Fand was looking straight at Dad. Her usual delicate expression was gone and in its place was the countenance of a determined queen. 'No. I will not run. I will not allow my mother to simply take Duir. I will not allow my mother to ruin more lives. After her last atrocity the Fili nation was almost destroyed. Most were killed and the rest banished with only a handful of us left to bear her shame. I have lived most of my life in shame. I will not watch her do it again. Tomorrow I will face her. Tomorrow I will stop her – or die.'

'And I will stand with you.' It was Nora.

'Mother, no,' Brendan said.

'Son, my father and his father and his father before that told of the folly of Queen Maeve. We were told that the reason we were banished from Paradise was because none of the Druids had the guts to stand up to her. I will not be banished again. Take Ruby and get far from here, but Maeve is entering Duir over my dead body.'

Ever since I had heard Dad say that there was no way to stop Maeve, something was tugging at the corner of my mind. Even while Fand and Nora were proposing to fight to the death, my concentration was being pulled by something. The recent events had been so traumatic I couldn't put my finger on it but some little part of my brain was telling me that I must remember. Then … pop … it came to me.

'We can fight them,' I said. Everyone looked. 'When one of Maeve's thugs left my room he knocked over my yew banta stick – while he was in ghost form. If we can convince the yews to give us enough wood – I think yew arrows will stop them. At least we can go down swinging.'

'Yew arrows will work?' Dad asked.

'I'm pretty sure. The soldier was surprised when he couldn't walk through it.'

'Son, I know you are tired but can you convince the yews to help us?'

'I can try – but with those trees it's anybody's guess.'

'Tuan,' Dad said, 'I realise I have been treating you like a glorified flying carpet, but will you help us?'

'Of course, Lord Oisin. But tell me – do you have a flying carpet?'

'So let me get this straight,' I said. 'Are we staying and fighting?'

I looked around the room. Fand was defiantly determined to stand up to her mother. Everyone else was looking to everyone else. Dad stood. 'Get the wood, son.'

'Bet you didn't expect to see me so soon,' I said to the yew. If the tree found my salutation amusing he/she hid it well. 'Maeve is back,' I said. 'She is about to attack Duir. I … we need yew wood to stop her. Will you help?'

'*We do not concern ourselves with the landly doings of the Hawathiee.*'

'Then concern yourself with the safety of your own. Maeve is a tree killer. She decimated the rowans when she was queen and I am certain she is responsible for the recent killings of the yew.'

'What proof do you have of that?' said an actual voice, not an inside-my-head tree voice. I turned and saw an elf leaning against the adjacent tree.

Elves in The Land dress like you would think an Elf would dress – dark green tights and a leather tunic tied tightly around the waist. They are always thin – not Brownie thin but I've never seen a fat one. And do they have pointy ears? I hear you ask. Don't be silly. Saying that, I hadn't met many Elves during my time in The Land, except for the one I talked to at Gerard's party; all the other sightings were fleeting glimpses in distant trees. Elves keep to themselves.

Just the other day I asked Dad what side the Elves would take in the upcoming war and he said exactly what Cialtie had said. 'At the first sign of trouble Elves climb their trees and hide.'

'Hi,' I said to the Elf. 'Were you eavesdropping?'

'What proof do you have that Maeve killed yews?'

'Maeve was brought back to life with yew sap. Whether she got it herself or got someone else to get it for her – she is responsible.'

'How do you know this?'

'I was there when she was ... reborn.'

Another real voice, this time from the tree behind me said, 'Show us.'

I turned in time to see another Elf with his hand on a yew trunk before the painful yew brain scan began.

I fell to my knees as the scene of Maeve's rebirth played in my head. The vision was dark, just like it had been when I watched it through the gauze mask I was wearing. It was not only painful to watch because of what the yews were doing to my head, it was also hard to see Ruby again being treated so badly.

When the mind-video of Maeve solidifying had finished, a different voice asked, 'Why do you need yew wood?'

I didn't know who had spoken but when I looked up every yew within my vision had an Elf at its trunk.

'I can't believe I'm saying this, but – have a look at what happened to me first thing this morning.' I squeezed my eyes in anticipation of the pain. I watched again the horror movie that was my morning. It was just as bad the second time around.

'We must confer,' the yew said. I started to listen to the conversations that seemed to be happening all over the yew forest – male/female yews and also Elves – but soon the noise and information got too much. I remembered what happened to me when a pine tree gave me information overload and backed my hand off the tree. I rolled onto the grass and placed my head down just for a second. I was asleep in a minute.

I was in that barn in Connemara, Ireland. The Druids – The Grove – were around me wearing robes. 'Awake,' they were chanting, 'awake.'

When I opened my eyes I was being shaken by an Elf saying the same thing. I sat up quickly, not knowing how long I had slept. 'Will you help us?'

The Elf turned his back on me and placed his palms skyward.

All trees make a sound when they are donating wood. It's an eerie sound as the tree sucks the moisture out of the wood before cracking off a branch. I had heard it many times when I had begged for firewood but I ... in fact, no one ... has ever heard an entire forest donating wood at the same time. The sound of cracks began to domino around the entire forest as every yew dropped branches to the ground. It sent chills down my back.

'Thank you,' I said to the Elf.

He shook his head, grabbed my wrist and pushed my palm onto the yew. 'Thank Ioho.'

I felt the contact not only with the tree I was touching but it almost felt like I was in contact with the entire forest, which I suppose I was. 'Duir thanks you.'

'*Your request was just and your adversary is ours,*' the trees spoke. '*May you succeed in your undertaking, Hawathiee.*'

'Prince Conor,' the Elf said, 'I am Bran. It is the way of the Elf to stay out of conflicts. When other Hawathiee ask us, "Whose side are you on?" it has been our custom to say, "We side with the trees." This time it seems that Duir and the trees are on the same side. We will help you.'

'Do you speak for all the Elves, Bran?'

The Elf thought about that for a bit. 'I speak *with* all the Elves.'

'Good enough for me. Let's get to work and get some ghost-proof arrows to Castle Duir.'

We bundled up the branches and Elves packed them on their backs and legged it to Castle Duir. I warned them about the marble mines and told them to go around to the west side where there was a small entrance. I was going to be back to the castle before them and promised to warn the guards of their approach.

Eth had given me some gold wire and a half a dozen *rothlú* charms. We bundled some of the bigger branches with that and then shouted, '*Rothlú.*' The bundles vanished – presumably to reappear at home. I asked Bran if he could coordinate from here and he said he could. For a pacifist Elf type he got military pretty quick. We hung bunches of yew wood off dragon Tuan until he gave me a look that I interpreted as, 'Put one more stick on my back and I'm making charcoal.' And we headed back to Duir.

I wasn't going to be there long, though. The Chamber of Runes had given me a gift and I had just figured it out.

TWENTY-NINE
THE GROVE

'Does it always rain like this here?' Ruby asked me with a jiggly voice as we galloped down the road from the Fairy Fingers.

'This is Ireland,' I said as the horizontal rain dripped off my nose and onto her head, 'so to answer your question – yes.'

'That must be why it's so green here.'

I laughed. 'I never thought about it but I guess you're right. And how do you know it's green? Can you, like, smell it?'

'It's called the Emerald Island, bozo. I can read braille, you know?'

'Do you think if I got into one of those automobile contraptions without touching the ground, that I would still end up looking like your grandmother?' Essa shouted over her shoulder.

'What do you suggest, we steal one?' I shouted back.

'Yes.'

'Last time we were here you stole a horse and cart, and ended up in jail. Remember?'

'This time,' she said, 'I'll add a snoring cure to the spell.'

'The town's not far. If you're nice I'll see about getting you a towel.'

I kicked my horse and got a sense that she didn't like it. I hadn't brought Acorn in case things got hairy and I had to leave my mount behind. I didn't even know this horse's name so Ruby dubbed it Connie. Short for where we were going.

I looked behind to make sure that the young woman we had brought with us, Anula, was keeping up. She looked scared and unhappy but she kept the pace.

Tuan and I had made it back to Castle Duir from the Yewlands – just. Towards the end of the flight every wing stroke bobbed us up and down in a way that gave me the impression that if Tuan stopped flapping, we would drop like a stone. I asked him if he wanted me to dump the load of yew wood but I only got a dirty look in reply. When we finally arrived, Tuan near collapsed. I wanted to throw up but didn't have time.

I got Mom, Dad, Nora, and Brendan together and told them about the vision I had in the Chamber of Runes. Then I told them what I thought it meant.

'I won't take Ruby unless you want me to,' I said to Brendan and Nora, 'but if she comes it will make my mission a whole lot easier, and she can stay there until this war is over. They are good people – they're Druids – they will take care of her.'

I had never seen two people more torn. They wanted to have their girl by their side but they also wanted her safe. They wanted to go with her to the Real World but they knew if they didn't defend their newly adopted home that there would be no place for them to go back to. In the end they agreed. That's why Ruby, her babysitter Anula, Essa and I were hammering down an Irish back road in the pouring rain.

It was getting late in the day. I didn't dare go to the police station to see Mícheál in case one of his fellow officers recognised me. Now that the pony show was over, three galloping horses were conspicuous enough. I pulled my hood down over my eyes and prayed that Agent Murano wasn't still around.

I walked dripping into the tea shop just as Maeve was closing up. She didn't look all that surprised to see me. She just smiled and said, 'I have been thinking about you all day.' She hugged me and as she did

she saw Ruby come through the door. I felt her stiffen and say, 'Oh my
…' She pulled away from me. Her whole front was wet from my rain.
She dropped to one knee. I'm not sure if it was to get onto Ruby's level
or if she went weak at the knees.

'Is she … blind?' Maeve asked with a hushed reverence.

'Hey lady,' Ruby said, 'I'm right here. You can ask me yourself, you
know?'

Then Ruby turned to me and said, 'Is she another one of your idiot
girlfriends?'

Mícheál organised a meeting of 'The Grove' outside town in the same
barn as before. He said it wasn't hard to get everyone together; they had
all been on high alert since the last time we Tir na Nogians showed up.
Still, it was almost midnight before everyone arrived. I felt sorry for
Essa. Anula, Ruby and I were young enough to walk around but poor
Essa was stuck sitting on her horse for hours. If she had to, she could
have gotten down, but becoming an old woman was something she
was not willing to do again. 'Three times was quite enough,' she said.
So while we sat around drinking cups of tea she sat high above us like
some princess, which – when you think about it – she was.

Ruby's appearance had freaked out Maeve. When I asked her why,
she clammed up, saying I had to speak to her father, but her reaction
fortified my suspicion. I had interpreted my vision properly.

At the barn I kept Ruby hidden for optimal effect. When everyone
was there, I was called into the main room. This time they were decked
out in long-hooded Druidy-type robes but the effect was ruined when
I noticed most of them wearing modern sneakers. I wanted to ask
them where I could get a nice pair of Nikes around here but then
reminded myself to concentrate. This was an important occasion and
I wanted to begin with the solemnity that it deserved – but as usual
instead my opening salutation was more Scranton Conor than the
Prince of Hazel and Oak.

'Hi everybody. Ah … the last time I was here one of you asked if you
could come back with us and then another said that I wasn't "The One".
That would be "The One" with a capital O.'

'That is correct, Conor,' Mícheál said. 'Since you have been here there has been much debate among The Grove. We do believe you are from The Land but you do not fulfil what was foretold.'

'Yeah, I get it. I'm not "The One".' I stepped around the corner and led Ruby by the hand into the main room. 'How about her?'

You know that look when everyone yells 'Surprise!' and the birthday person jumps and then opens her mouth wide right before she almost faints? Well this was like that but in reverse. Everybody freaked and two people actually did go down – just like I had seen in the Chamber of Runes.

'Hey, hey, listen up everybody,' I said, 'I don't have much time. Would any of you like to take a trip to Tir na Nog? We got apples there you just wouldn't believe.'

It was an hour before dawn when I rode through the portal back into the Hall of Spells. Nieve and Nora were there waiting.

'You are very wet,' Nieve said.

'Really? I hadn't noticed,' I replied as I dismounted into a growing puddle.

'Is she safe?' Nora asked, like the nervous grandmother that she was.

'Yes, Nora. She is with Mícheál. He is a good man. He helped me the last time I was there. He wanted to come but he saw that looking after the Blind Child Who Was Foretold was more important.'

'Oh, I hope they don't spoil her.'

'I wouldn't worry about that, Grandma. Ruby has a way of bringing people who know her down to earth.'

Nora nodded and relaxed, but I was pretty sure I wouldn't get a smile out of her until she saw her little Gem again.

Just then, the first of the two dozen Irish Druids came through the glowing circle. Tea shop Maeve was one of the first and I introduced her to Nora so she could tell her about her father.

Initially a lot more of The Grove wanted to come after seeing the Blind Child but then I warned them that we were walking into a war – possibly an unwinnable war. Dropping everything and travelling to a mystical land is a tough decision. Jumping into possibly certain death is even harder. I was impressed that I got twenty-four.

Brendan tore himself away from arrow-making when he heard I was back. I assured him that his daughter was safe and in good hands and he brought me up to speed on the defences. 'We have made about three hundred yew arrows. They are not all actually straight and I wouldn't bet on my chances of a bull's-eye at any distance but at close range they'll work. We also have quite a.few yew bantas and a couple dozen pointed sticks.'

'Pointed sticks? Is that in case of vampire, Fili?'

Brendan smiled and shook his head. 'Is there any occasion where you aren't a wise ass?'

I went to visit Graysea in the infirmary. She had finally come out of her underwater coma and had changed back and forth from fish to female a couple of times. With each change she lost more of her injury. She could probably have fixed up someone else with a similar wound without too much trouble but apparently healing herself was harder. She tried to get out of bed when I came in but the Imp-healer threatened to sit on her if she tried to get up one more time.

'She talks mean,' Graysea said quietly after the healer was out of earshot, 'but she really is nice underneath. She reminds me of matron back in the grotto.'

'I wish matron was here to help you,' I said. 'You still look a bit pale.'

Graysea turned way and pinched her cheeks then turned back with a forced smile. 'Better?'

'Much,' I said. Out of the corner of my eye I saw the Imp-healer motioning me with her head that I should leave.

'Conor, I must talk to you … but … I'm very tired. Can we talk soon?'

'Of course,' I said, kissing her on her forehead. 'We'll talk tomorrow. You get some rest.'

I walked away with the sound of my own voice echoing 'tomorrow' in my mind and wondered if for any of us there would be a tomorrow.

I slept for an hour. What a mistake that was. I had one of those dreams that was so crazy I woke up more exhausted than when I went to sleep. I was at a square dance. All of my comrades in arms were on one side of the room: Brendan, Nora, Araf, Nieve, Essa, Dahy, Mom and Dad. Lined up on the other side were: Cialtie, The new Turlow, Macha, Oracle Lugh, Maeve and Cialtie's Banshee sorceress. We started off with a frantic square dance that culminated with us once again facing each other across the room. Then the square dance caller cried, 'Do-si-do!' and we came towards each other again but this time Cialtie and his side all grew fangs and pulled daggers. I found myself sitting up awake with sweat streaming down my back and a scream just south of my larynx. It was still an hour before dawn. Believe it or not I got out of bed without any prompting. When the day may be your last – getting up at dawn isn't such a bad idea after all.

Dad was up on the parapet looking out at the night sky as it was losing its daily fight with the sun. I climbed up next to him and handed him an apple.

He took a bite and then shook his head. 'We shouldn't be here,' he said dreamily to the night.

'Where should we be?' I asked.

'We should be … we should be tucked up in a cosy bed and then when we finally wake up we should be having a huge cooked breakfast next to a roaring fire. Instead we're chomping an apple on a cold wall. You know Conor, my biggest worry shouldn't be war, my biggest worry should be whether or not there is enough wine in the castle cellars.'

'Didn't your mother warn you there would be days like these?'

Dad laughed. I was glad to see he still could. 'My mother is one of the people out there making this day the way it is.'

'Oh yeah, I forgot that.'

We stood some more in silence until I broke it. 'Gods, I hate waiting.'

'Really. I like waiting. I use the time to think. Not daydreaming, mind you, but really thinking.' He looked at me and it seemed he looked older – like he used to look – and I felt younger, like I was looking up. 'Didn't I ever teach you to use waiting time to think critically?'

'Every time we had to wait in line and I said I was bored, you made me conjugate Latin verbs. Now that I think of it, maybe that's why I hate waiting so much.'

'Ire,' Dad said.

'Ire, eo, is, it, imus, itis, eunt,' I instantly responded.

Dad had said the Latin verb *go* and I involuntarily responded by conjugating it – the English equivalent of saying: I go, you go, he goes she goes …

'It seemed our waiting time was not wasted.'

'Yeah, Dad. My Latin will come in handy when we get attacked by Julius Caesar.'

'Mihi vera placet quod tu es callidissimus, nate,' Dad said. Loosely translated that is: *I am very proud of you, my son*.

Since Latin was the language of the day, I replied, 'Et tu, pater.'

Mom came up on the wall and took one look at the two of us with our watered-up eyes and said, 'Aw, you two are just a bunch of softies.'

'He started it,' I said.

She hugged us both and watered up a bit herself. Dahy crested the stairs and said, 'Are you ready for today, Your Highness?'

Dad and I simultaneously replied, 'Born ready.'

'How about you, my love?' Dad asked.

'As long as I am with my boys I can do anything,' Mom said.

By this time the sky was lightening and the wall was filling up.

'Lorcan,' I called. 'You ready?'

'Lorcan the Leprechaun is ready, my lord,' he shouted in reply.

'Brendan?'

'Detective Fallon of the Scranton PD is ready and able, Mr O'Neil.'

'Nieve?'

'I am with you, nephew of Oak.'

'Gerard?'

'The beer is free when this is over.'

'Tuan?'

The Pooka lifted his chin and as he did his head transformed into the head of a wolfhound. He barked once.

'Araf?'

The Imp didn't reply – but he did nod.

Essa by this time was at my side and I quietly asked, 'You ready for this?'

'As long as I'm with you, Conor.'

We all turned as Fand came up the stairs. Nora was at her side. It struck me that she had yet to see her mother. I could only imagine the conflicting emotions that must have been going through her mind.

'Are you ready, Your Highness?' I said to her.

She looked to the sky that was now almost fully light and said in that quiet composed voice of hers, 'If the sun in the sky is willing to face this day – then so am I.'

'Well, that's everybody, Mr King,' I said to Dad.

Dad slapped me on the back and said, 'You will make a wonderful Lord of Duir someday.'

'Thanks, Dad, but I've been meaning to speak to you about …'

I didn't get to finish that thought for just then, directly below us, the Fili ghost army solidified one row at a time. Each row appeared chanting until the whole army culminated in a cacophony that halted with the appearance of Maeve. The Fili Queen looked down at her cupped hands and they erupted with Shadowfire. She then tossed the fire in the air where it sparked like a firework. Each of the sparks found the hidden Connemara marble in the field. Then Maeve threw her hands forward and all of the marble came out of the ground and splatted into the castle wall.

I turned to Fand and said, 'I'll say one thing for your mom – she knows how to make an entrance.'

As soon as I said it I felt bad. For Fand this was not the time for levity. But then a strange, almost spooky, smile infected just the tiniest corner of her mouth. She never took her eyes off of her mother but she said, 'Yes, Conor, she does.'

THIRTY
THE SHADOWRUNE

Let me tell you, walking right up, practically unarmed, to an army of people who had the power to casually rip major organs out of your chest was one of the most terrifying things I have ever done. Intellectually I had decided that I would do it, but it wasn't until I started actually moving towards them that the terror gripped me. It took every fibre of my being to stop myself from wrapping my arms around Dad's leg screaming, 'Please don't make me go.' I was really scared and I know I wasn't the only one. If we made it out of this alive I promised myself I would buy everyone new underwear. If they were anything like me, they were going to need it.

'Hello Mother.'

'Hello Fand.'

I don't know what I was expecting. I had never walked up to a murdering queen and her bloodthirsty army before but I was expecting something different than English afternoon-tea etiquette.

Maeve raised her hand and lifted it towards her daughter. Dahy tensed up and looked like he was going to give one of those pointed sticks a try. Fand raised one finger and calmed everyone. Maeve continued forward and gently placed her hand on the side of her daughter's face. Fand closed her eyes. Then Maeve went into ghost form and her hand entered Fand's head. Fand's eyes shot open and the two queens stared at each other with a burning intensity. I placed my hand on the pointed stick secured in my belt. If Maeve's palm came out with Fand's brain on it I was going to kill her no matter what happened to me.

Her hand came out brainless.

'You have become a Shadowwitch, daughter.'

'I have,' Fand replied.

'Then come and join us.'

'No, Mother.'

Maeve looked confused. 'You would oppose me?'

'With my life,' Fand said.

'As will I,' Nora said.

Maeve turned sharply to Nora. 'Who dares interrupt a conversation between the Queen of the Fili and her daughter?'

'I am your daughter too,' Nora said. 'I am the daughter of the daughter of the daughter's daughter who had to pay the ultimate price for your arrogance. I am the Fili that was banished from this land when you chose power over harmony. We are the Fili,' she said, pointing to the two dozen very brave Druids from Connemara who were standing behind us in the field. 'We are the Druids who have endured disease and hunger and old age and death for your sins. So do not presume it is not in my right to talk in front of the queen – for I am Fili and as far as I'm concerned you forfeited your crown eons ago. My queen is Fand.'

Maeve was taken aback but her honour guard were incensed and made a move towards Nora for speaking in such a way to their queen. Fand stood between them and Maeve called them off. Let's just say it was tense out there.

'You are a Shadowwitch, you know the kind of power we wield. You cannot stop me.'

'I do not know the power you wield, Mother. I have learned Shadowmagic not for power but for peace. I learned Shadowmancy not to emulate you but to understand you and ultimately avoid your fate. I have no idea of the power you wield, for I have never killed a tree.'

Maeve baulked at her daughter. 'How can you be a Shadowwitch without sap?'

'Oh, I use sap.'

'How do you get it?'

'I ask for it. Have you become so brutal, Mother, so power mad that you have forgotten how just to say "please"?'

Maeve was at least listening but her entourage was getting anxious – I could feel it in the air. Before another word could be said, a call came from the battlements behind us. From out of the oak forest on horseback came Macha, Lugh, The Turlow and Cialtie. Behind them followed what looked like the entire Banshee nation in full battle armour. They filled every visible space.

Maeve looked to her daughter and said: 'It is too late for talk, you cannot stop us.'

'We can stop you, Mother, with this.' Fand took an arrow out of her belt and handed it to Maeve who received it on the face-up palms of both her hands.

'Don't be foolish, daughter, have you not seen what we can do?' Maeve then faded into her ghost form. The arrow remained on her hands. Her face was the picture of confusion. She grabbed the arrow with one translucent hand and then felt the sharp tip with the other. When it pricked her spirit-skin, fear crossed her face and she dropped the arrow.

'Go back from where you came, Mother.'

'But I thought, Fand, it was you who called me forth.'

'I did not call you.'

'Then who?' Maeve asked, truly confused. 'We were lost in a void and then we … were … We found ourselves on a shadow island. A Shadowwitch of great power must have called us. I thought it was you.'

'When did this happen?' Mom asked. She walked up to Maeve and the old queen stepped back.

Maeve placed her hand out as if she was sensing the air in front of my mother. 'You have power. I can feel it. What do you conceal?'

Mom reached to her neck and pulled out from under her tunic her Shadowrune. When it was made during the unorthodox Choosing in the Chamber of Runes it was so clear it looked to me almost like a hologram of a rune. Now it looked old and cracked as if it was made out of ancient dried blood. Maeve instinctively reached for it but Mom pulled it back.

'Where did you get that?' Maeve asked.

'Last summer I performed The Choosing with oak sap and the Chamber rewarded me with this.'

Maeve was really shocked. 'Even I would not dare to do such a thing. You *created* that day. From your Choosing an island … a shadow island *became*. We who last saw the sun on this field during our battle with Finn found ourselves alive once more – with form but not substance.'

'How did you get here?' Mom asked.

'We simply walked under the waves to the mainland. We need neither food nor air.'

'This rune was clear for almost a year,' Mom said, 'and then this summer, on the night you stole the blood of a child, it darkened.'

Maeve thought, then nodded. 'We have a bond, Shadowwitch. What is your name?'

'Deirdre.'

'Daughter of Liam of the Hall of Knowledge?'

'I am his daughter,' Mom said, 'but Liam and the Hall are no more. All was destroyed – by your allies.'

'And the Tree of Knowledge?'

'What care you of a tree?' Fand spat.

'The Great Hazel is a very special tree.'

'They are all special, Mother. The day you forgot that is the day you forgot how to be Hawathicc. Do you even remember why you fight? Has power corrupted you so that you use it only to gain more? Is power enough reason to lose me? Is your power enough reason to condemn the Fili to suffer, to grow old and die?'

Cialtie and his Banshee sorceress rode closer. He shouted, 'Enough talk, Maeve.'

'Your comrade Cialtie,' I said, 'tried to destroy all of The Land and everything in it. Has he told you that?'

The old queen looked sharply to me in a way that made me regret speaking then she looked to her daughter for affirmation. Fand nodded yes.

'I do not wish to kill you, daughter.'

'I have lived too long with your name,' Fand said. 'If I fail to stop you today I will kill myself for the shame of being your progeny.'

I imagine that even if I were to stab Maeve with my pointy stick it wouldn't hurt her as much as did her daughter's words.

Macha on horseback stepped forward with Lugh at her side. 'Enough, Maeve! Let this begin.'

'Macha kidnapped a Fili child so as to bleed her for you,' Nora said, 'and when she was through she wanted to kill her. Is this the kind of future you want for The Land?'

'And you know Lugh,' Dad piped in. 'Do you really think he will let you rule? Do you think any of them will?'

Maeve looked to all of us. If I was a betting man I would have bet that we were getting through to her. She looked down thoughtfully at her hands and then as fast as any viper she lashed out. Her hand in ghost form shot into Mom's chest. Mom screamed and arched her whole body back in pain and terror.

We were all frozen with shock but that didn't last long. When we all stepped forward to intervene, Maeve hissed, 'One step closer and you shall see her heart.'

That's the kind of threat that can stop you in your tracks. Maeve reached her other hand into Mom's chest and when she pulled it out, her fist contained Mom's Shadowrune. You could see it through her translucent fingers. She pulled sharply and it broke free of the leather necklace it hung from.

'Your opinion, daughter, is something I have never valued. Your intellect and thoughts have not ever been worthy of my notice.' Maeve, still with her hand in my mother's chest, held the rune up to the sunlight. 'And now I see – too late – how wrong I have been. You have become a better Fili Queen than I could ever be. Goodbye, my daughter … try to forgive me.' She placed the rune between her back teeth and then bit down hard. The Shadowrune erupted with amber light that made us all cover our eyes. When we could see again, we saw Maeve and her Fili army fading into their ghost form and then they kept on fading. Before anyone could speak – they were gone.

We all stared at the place where they had been with a 'What the heck happened here' expression on our faces – everyone except Cialtie. I could come up with a lot of nasty names for my uncle but 'slow' isn't one of them. He was looking around like a dog deciding whether or not to steal a hot dog from a picnic table. He was reassessing his rapidly changing power base. So I did the same.

OK, we had gotten rid of Maeve and her ghost army – this was a very good thing – but Cialtie still had a kick-ass Banshee army. Just us against them was a battle that could go either way, especially if Cialtie and his gang decided to take us out before we could get back behind castle walls.

'Maeve,' I shouted.

Dahy jumped and said, 'Where?'

Despite the tenseness of the moment, that made me laugh. 'No, not that Maeve – Connemara Maeve.'

'Yes, Conor,' came the waitress's voice from behind me.

'I think you should slowly walk the rest of The Grove back to the castle.'

'OK,' she said, in a voice I could tell was trying to be braver than she felt.

'Have your people stay where they are, Oisin,' Cialtie said, 'or my archers will fell them where they stand.'

'We are here under the protection of a parley, brother. Even you would not break that faith.'

'With all of the things you have accused me of,' Cialtie said, 'breaking a parley seems insignificant. Anyway, your parley was with Maeve, not me.'

'Uh oh,' I thought, but apparently I said it out loud. I got unanimous dirty looks from everyone on my side and a sickeningly sweet smile from my uncle.

'I have archers trained on this position,' Dahy said.

'Arrows do not worry a Lord of Wind,' Lugh said and then to demonstrate he flicked his hand and a wind tussled all of our hair.

I stifled a fart joke. This was definitely the wrong time for that.

'I see we have a new Turlow,' Dad said, bowing one of those little bows a king gives to another king. 'Now that you have lost your ghost army and the Brownies, are you sure you want to continue this conflict without allies? I will hold no ill will if you withdraw now.'

You got to hand it to Dad for a gutsy move but the new Turlow didn't look like he had enough backbone to dump Cialtie with the guy sitting right next to him.

'We Banshee have nothing to fear from the Faerie.'

'The day I lose my fear is the day I think I would be most afraid,' Dad said.

'Hey, Turlow,' I said. 'You know it's not just Faeries around here. We got Imps and Pooka, and Fili. There's even a mermaid back in there. And oh, I bet these guys will surprise you.' I pointed to the treeline and from every visible oak an Elf dropped down on a rope. The Elves, I learned, could climb oaks without the trees making them relive every horrible minute of their lives. I waved and they shot back up like their ropes were some kind of slow acting bungee. 'Those guys are, like, invisible when they are in the trees. I'd worry about getting out of here through that forest.'

'You have persuaded the Elves to enter this conflict?' The Turlow said, amazed.

'Yup,' I said, 'and I definitely would stay out of the Yewlands for a while if I were you. Boy, are those trees mad.'

'This matters not,' Cialtie said. 'We are not leaving. We are taking Castle Duir and you have made it easy for us to do it. My army is on the field, brother, your archers are useless and there are less than three score of you. Lay down your arms and I will be merciful.'

This wasn't good. As I looked to Cialtie and The Turlow and Lugh and Macha all glaring down on us from horseback like we were ants under a magnifying glass, the elation of Maeve's heart-ripping ghost army vanishing was starting to wane. We really were in a bad spot here. The Irish Druids weren't even armed. It was really just, me, Mom, Dad, Dahy, Essa and Araf. Brendan was up on the battlements with archers who were useless because of Lugh. We were so truly stuffed that even I couldn't come up with a smile, but amazingly and uncharacteristically – Dad did.

A tiny smile that was just noticeable enough to unnerve his opponent and hearten me appeared on the corners of his mouth. 'Are you sure, brother, you want to start this now?'

Cialtie's mouth turned at the corners as well. For as opposite as these two men were, the mirrored smile reminded me that they were still siblings. 'This day, my little brother, is long overdue.'

Dad nodded one of those slow thoughtful nods and took a deep breath. The scene reminded me of a showdown at the end of an old black and white western movie. 'Then I would like to introduce you to someone.'

Cialtie's smile vanished as he looked around for some kind of trick.

'This is Nora Fallon,' Dad said, pointing to his left.

Cialtie's smile returned. I half expected him to say, 'So what?'

Dad then addressed Macha. 'Mother, this is the grandmother of the little girl you kidnapped. Lugh, you may remember her son Brendan. Before we begin, she has something to say to all of you.'

Dad looked to Nora and nodded. She held her hands out in front of her, took a deep breath and shouted the immortal magic word, 'YEEEEHAAAA!'

THIRTY-ONE

NORA

W hile I was begging the yews for arrows and then flitting to the Real World, Dad, Dahy and the rest of the war council were coming up with a plan – a plan they forgot to tell me about. I thought the idea was fight Maeve and die, but Dad formulated a strategy in case Fand succeeded in convincing her mother to give up the ghost. I guess that's why they pay him the big bucks.

Nora never did tell me what gift she received from the yews but she obviously told Dad. When the yews asked me what gift I desired, I didn't know what to say but Nora knew exactly what she wanted. She wanted the same power as the woman who had stolen her grandchild. She wanted power that could trump Macha's power. The yews gave Nora power over horses. They gave her power that superseded Macha's horsemanship. When Nora held out her arms and yeehaa-ed, Cialtie, Lugh, The Turlow and especially Macha were thrown from their rear-ing horses. All of them as you would imagine were shocked but Macha – the queen of all things equestrian – was absolutely dumbfounded. I'm pretty sure it had been a thousand years since a horse had diso-beyed her.

Dahy had always taught us, 'When you're in a brawl, punch the biggest guy first.' Now that Maeve was gone, the new biggest guy was

Lugh. With him still on the chessboard we had no archery cover and without arrows, we were sunk.

Lugh went off the back of his horse just like the others but unlike his companions he didn't hit the ground. As instinctively as you and I would reach out to grab a banister when we stumbled on a flight of stairs, Lugh conjured up a wind that caught him and sat him down on the ground feet first.

Dahy stepped up and threw a dagger directly at his head. The mountain oracle flicked his hand and Dahy's knife was blown off to the right. But this was a Dahy blade and it swung back on its target. I held my breath as it came at him from behind but just as the blade was about to stab the self-proclaimed god in the back of the neck, Lugh threw up his hand again. It was like he had eyes in the back of his head. The knife, though, wouldn't give up. Dahy must have incanted some serious knife homing voodoo into the thing 'cause it kept coming back like a stupid growling puppy that didn't know when to give up. Finally Lugh grew annoyed at swatting away at the knife like it was a persistent mosquito. With an increasingly aggravated look on his face, he finally held his hand in front of the approaching blade. The knife's homing magic was neutralised by the wind coming from his hand and the blade hovered just before the oracle's face.

'I think, Dahy,' Lugh said, 'I think I am going to kill you with your own blade.' Lugh reached through the wind tunnel he had created and grabbed the handle of the hovering knife. That was the last anybody saw of him. Dahy had made the handle of the knife out of Connemara marble. The moment the oracle touched it, he got old real fast and the dust he instantly became blew away in the last breeze he ever made. Then lots of things happened all at once.

The first thing was the arrows. As soon as Brendan saw Lugh dust it, he let the arrows fly. Since I had no idea what the game plan was, I decided to make sure I got the Connemara Druids back to the safety of the castle walls. From above it might have looked like I was running away but the reason these people were here was me. I didn't want perforated Irishmen and Irishwomen on my conscience.

A huge Banshee battle scream rose from the army. I had to cover my ears but as I looked to the Irish Druids they were all pointing and smiling. I looked back and saw the Banshees in full retreat. Then I heard more screaming – this time less Banshee-like. I looked to the north side of the castle and saw Jesse riding in front of the entire Brownie army as they charged at the now retreating Banshees.

The reason why Banshees are such good warriors is that they have that sixth sense that tells them when they are going to win. Conversely when they are going to lose, they know that too. King Jesse and the Brownies joining the side of the good guys was too much for them – they scampered.

A Banshee scream from Cialtie's sorceress made me turn. She was throwing sparks and fire from her fingertips but Nieve and Mom were repelling it until it backfired on the sorceress and she was blown off her feet. Dahy walked up to Macha who smiled seductively at him. He unceremoniously clocked her in the head with his banta stick.

Dad drew his sword and came for Cialtie. For a guy who had just lost two armies, a ghost army and a god, he didn't look as worried as he should have been. As Dad approached he just stood there with his hands at his sides. If it was me I think I would have stabbed him right then and there but Cialtie knew his brother. Dad placed the edge of the blade at Cialtie's chest. There was still so much noise around I didn't hear what Cialtie said. I watched his lips move and I saw the shock on my father's face. Then I saw him mouth '*Rothlú*', and he was gone.

Essa ran up and hugged me. 'Are you all right?'

'Yes,' I said incredulously. 'It looks like we all are. This is the strangest war I have ever been …' I didn't get to finish that statement due to the huge wet kiss that she planted on my lips. I guess now that the war between Duir and the Banshees was over, so was the war between Essa and me. In both conflicts – peace felt good.

Jesse galloped up to us and performed an impressive moving dismount from his horse Fluffy. I bowed my lowest bow and he did the same.

'King Codna,' I said.

'Prince Conor,' he replied and then ran and gave me a very un-royal-like hug.

'Thanks for coming back, Jesse.'

'It wasn't me – it was them,' Jesse said, pointing to his troops who were still chasing Banshees out of the field. 'With each step home, the angrier my people became. After a night at camp my commanders came to me and said they wanted Cialtie and his Banshees to pay for deceiving them.'

'Duir thanks you all,' I said, bowing again.

'Aw, any excuse to see my old friend Conor.'

What minutes before had been a battlefield began to resemble a family outdoor barbecue. Brendan came down and was snogging Nieve. I saw Dahy carrying Macha into the castle fireman style. I know it's not right for a grandson to think like this but after what she did to Ruby, I hoped they put her into that smelly dungeon that I was in the first time I got here.

Mom and Nora were on either side of Fand helping her back to the castle. Fand had been as strong as a steel girder during her spar with her mother but now that it was over she looked frail. Dad stood staring off into the distance. I came around his side and searched his eyes trying to figure out what he was looking at. He wasn't looking at anything. He was lost in thought.

'You OK, Dad?'

'Yes,' he said long and slow. Then he looked at me and smiled. 'Yes. Why shouldn't I be? We won. Or actually we averted a war, which is even better.'

'You are a victor in peace, Father.'

'A victor in peace,' Dad repeated. 'I like that. If only I could resolve all of my conflicts without bloodshed.'

I stepped over to where Dahy's blade was still sitting in the ground. The handle was roughly hewn out of marble and the blade was completely covered with gold. I picked it up. 'Good idea. Whose was it?'

'Dahy's,' Dad said. 'When it comes to killing bad guys – Dahy knows his business. Be careful with that. Actually, can I leave you with the job of making sure all of the Connemara marble is locked safely away?'

'Yes, Your Highness,' I said with a mocking bow.

Dad laughed. 'I give you one chore and you get stroppy.' When I straightened up he placed his hands on my shoulders and then brought me in for a hug. 'I'm so glad you're safe, son.'

'Me too ... I don't mean I'm glad I'm safe, I mean I'm glad you're safe too.'

'I understood,' he said loosening his clinch. 'Oh, and I need the Lawnmower back for a little while.'

'OK,' I said, undoing the buckle on the belt that the Sword of Duir hung from. I handed it to Dad. 'You need it for some official kinging thing?'

'Yeah,' he said. 'Something like that.'

The Connemara Druids were all milling around in a bit of a daze. I asked them if they would help me move the marble inside and they all agreed – happy to have a job to do. In no time we had all the pieces of the Real World locked up in one of the dungeon vaults.

Later I had a meeting with Brendan and Nora. They wanted to go back to the Real World right away but Essa had sorceress stuff to do with Mom and Nieve. There had been protective snap spells placed all over the castle and they needed to be removed before one of us hurt ourselves. So we promised to go to the Real World in the morning to retrieve Ruby.

Araf found me right before sundown and said Graysea wanted to see me. He had a look on his face that made me worried.

'Is she OK?'

'She is fine, she ... she wants to talk to you.'

'OK,' I said as he walked away. For as long as I have known that big guy I still have a hard time reading his thoughts.

I walked to the infirmary a bit slower than I could have. To be honest I was a little bit dreading seeing Graysea. Don't get me wrong, I still think she is one of the most beautiful and the sweetest women in all of The Land, but I was in love with Essa. From the moment I saw her – 'till the day I die – it's Essa and it was unfair to Graysea not to tell her that. It was just that it's never a good time to tell Graysea anything. She did that smothering me with kisses thing when she saw me and she had those lovely puppy dog eyes – it was just ... hard to break her heart. And now that she was injured, I felt like I was kicking her when she was down. But I had to tell her.

I found her out of her tank and in a hospital bed. She looked so much better than the last time I had seen her. She had colour in her cheeks and her face lit up with a healthy smile when she saw me. She started to get out of bed but her Imp-healer grumbled, 'Graysea', and she meekly obeyed and sank back into her pillows.

'How is my Mertain wounded warrior?' I said kissing her on the cheek. She didn't answer and when I looked at her again her expression was disquieting. 'Graysea, are you OK?'

'Oh, yes,' she said, forcing a smile. I gave her a stern look and she said, 'No really, I'm fine, Conor. I found out that it takes me a lot longer to heal myself than others. My prison guard,' she said pointing to the Imp-healer, 'says I'll be up and around in a couple of days.'

I relaxed. 'That is very good to hear. So why the long face?'

'Well,' she said, looking down at her hands, 'you know I am very fond of you?'

Wait a minute, I thought, *that's what I was going to say.*

'You know I'm very fond of you,' she repeated, 'but I think that maybe we ...'

'Hold on – are you breaking up with me?'

Graysea's angelic face started to crumble into tears. 'Oh, my poor sweet Conor. I don't know what to say. I just don't think it's fair of me to lead you on any more.'

'You are. You're breaking up with me. Why?' I said indignantly. I know it makes no sense. I should have been relieved. Hell, I had gone in there to break up with her but the male ego isn't a logical thing. 'Is there someone else?'

She once again concentrated on her hands and then nodded yes without looking up.

'Who?'

'I didn't mean for anything to happen.'

'Who?'

She lifted her gaze and pointed over my shoulder. I turned to see Araf duck back behind the doorframe like a naughty schoolboy.

'Araf! You're dumping me for Araf?'

'I'm sorry, Conor. I healed a small cut he had and then we started talking. It's just I need someone who talks to me.'

'And he does?'

'I'm so sorry, Conor.'

I looked back and the Imp was once again peeping around the corner. 'Araf,' I shouted and he ducked back around again. 'You come back here,' I said as I stormed towards the door.

'Don't hurt him,' Graysea called from her bed.

When I got to the doorway Araf was already halfway down the hall speeding like he was in an Olympic walking race. The sight of Araf, the toughest guy I know, running away from me, added to Graysea saying, 'Don't hurt him', made me smile and that smile popped the stupid male ego bubble that was growing in my head. I ran after Araf and as I did I started laughing. He looked behind and started running. As I have mentioned before, for a big guy Araf can move awfully fast. I finally had to call to some guards to stop him, 'In the name of the prince.'

'Honest to the gods, Conor,' Araf said, panting, 'nothing has happened.'

I forced a stern countenance onto my face; it wasn't easy.

'We just started talking and then we talked some more. But nothing has happened. I haven't even kissed her.'

I just stared. It was fun watching Araf ramble.

'I'll leave Duir immediately.'

I had to grit my teeth to stop from cracking up. 'You haven't kissed her?' I asked.

'No … Your Highness.'

When he said that, I had to turn away. I'm pretty sure he thought I did it 'cause I was mad. When I composed myself I turned back and said, 'I think it's about time you did.'

'I beg your pardon?' Araf looked very confused. 'About time I did what?'

'Kiss her, you idiot.' I placed my hands on his broad shoulders as a Fergal-like ear to ear smile erupted on my face. 'You are two of my favouritest people in all of The Land. I couldn't be happier. I'm delighted for you both.'

He tried to say something but nothing came out.

'Now that's the Araf I know and love.'

He hugged me, almost breaking my back, and then ran off to the infirmary for that first kiss. With a sigh I remembered my first mermaid kiss – it's worth running for.

Speaking of kisses, now that she didn't want to kill me, I thought it might be a good moment to spend a little time with Essa but Mom and Nieve had her working late. I had a meal with the Connemara Druids but didn't have the strength to hang out with them. They were so enthusiastic. The older ones were getting that immortality buzz where they kept saying how they hadn't felt this good in ages and all the rest were going on and on about how good the apples were. I know I was just like them but I was really tired after all the almost dying stuff, so I snuck away to my room.

My head told me it was too early to go to bed but my body vetoed that thought as soon as I hit the mattress. It wasn't until I was horizontal that I realised just how stressful a couple of days I had had. I closed my eyes for a long peaceful sleep. But as so often happens in The Land – dreamland was not restful.

The entire night was a swordfight. I watched the Lawnmower face a thinner blade but the whole time I couldn't see who was fighting. It was just sword vs. sword. Even though there didn't seem to be anyone holding the blades the intensity was just the same as if it was a life and death battle. I squinted, trying to see who the fighters were. It wasn't until the earthquake hit that the fighters came in to focus and I saw where I was. The earthquake struck again and I opened my eyes.

The source of my dreamquake was Mom. She was shaking me with a voice and a facial expression that shot me instantly awake.

'What's wrong, Mom?' I asked but I didn't have to. My dream had told me all I needed to know.

'He's gone,' she said.

THIRTY-TWO
THE TWINS OF MACHA

The sunrise was beautiful from dragon-back but I hardly noticed. All I could think about was Dad. It was madness that he had gone off to fight Cialtie by himself. He had apparently slipped out not long after the non-battle. He wrote a note and gave it to a guard instructing him not to give it to Mom until morning. The note said what he intended to do, duel his brother, but it didn't say where. I knew. My dream filled in that missing piece.

This had to be a trap. What possessed Dad to just walk into a fight with his brother, I couldn't imagine. Cialtie couldn't be trusted – Dad of all people knows that.

My flight wasn't a long one but my mind was spinning back in time to cold winter mornings when I was a kid and Dad would make me cinnamon toast and hot chocolate. I remembered him biting into his toast, smiling and saying, 'They didn't have cinnamon when I was a boy.' I promised myself that when I went back to the Real World to get Ruby I would get Dad some cinnamon.

I frowned, remembering my behaviour as he forced me to learn dead languages. I felt goose bumps as I remembered him lifting the Sword of Duir high over the walls of Castle Duir. I started remembering the things he had said to me but I didn't recall them all. For instance, I didn't recollect him saying, 'Don't fly Dragon Tuan over

Cialtie or his army, I'm sure by now he has come up with some sort of anti-dragon weapon.' As usual Dad was right.

I don't know what hit us but Tuan folded his wings, dropped his head and went into a kamikaze nose dive. I kicked and shouted at him but he was out cold. I wrapped the reins around my yew staff and tried to slow the monster's fall. I could hear my yew staff threatening to crack but it was working. I was actually slowing our descent – still the ground was coming at us faster than I would have liked. Finally it was the reins that couldn't take the strain. They snapped and my stick kicked up and slammed into my chin. That is all I remember.

'You are awake, oh my, I was worried about you.'

I hadn't opened my eyes but the person who was talking to me didn't need to see me to know my brain was working again. *Mother Oak?* I thought.

'You have been in a fall, young Conor. I was worried you would never wake up.'

I tried to move and found that I couldn't. My first thought was that I had hurt my spine but as I opened my eyes I saw that I was tied to a tree – to Mother Oak. I was sitting on the ground with my back to her trunk. A rope, entwined with fine gold wire, went across my chest and under my armpits. It made it hard to breathe. I reached up to see if I could push the rope down and maybe shimmy out but pain shot through my body when I tried to move my left arm. Little white dots swam in front of my vision as I almost blacked out. My left arm was definitely broken and I think my left leg too. I tried to push down on the rope with my right hand but the rope seemed to know I was trying to escape and tightened until I couldn't breathe. I gave up and the rope actually cut me a little slack.

Can you get me out of this? I thought to Mother Oak.

'Oh my poor sweet prince, if only I could.'

My uncle tied me here didn't he?

'Yes,' came the tree's answer in my brain and I could feel the contempt she had for Cialtie. It was the first time I had ever felt anything but sweetness from the family tree.

Do you know where Tuan is?

'The Pooka is on the other side of the glen where you crashed. I do not know his health but he is breathing.'

That's good. Is my father here?

'No, should Oisin be here?'

He came to fight Cialtie.

'Oh my, my, this is such an awful thing. The sons of Macha fighting.' Then Mother Oak did what I can only describe as the tree equivalent of a sigh. 'But dear me, I would not be completely honest if I said I am surprised.'

I tried to reach to my sock for my throwing knife but that was gone.

'Your uncle took your knife, young one. He leaned you against my trunk and then simply threw the rope that holds you. It seemed to tie itself. I think it is Brownie-made.'

Did you speak to him?

'No, he knows better than to talk to me. I'd give him a piece of my mind, I would.'

Despite my pain and my dire situation, I had to smile at the old tree's feistiness.

'He is here,' Mother Oak almost whispered in my head.

Who?

'Nephew,' came the slimy salutation that answered my question.

'Where is Tuan?'

Cialtie shook his head. 'What happened to, "Hello Uncle, it is good to see you again"? When the young forget their manners it is the beginning of the end of civilisation. But, if you must know, your Pooka flying horse woke up in considerable pain and I put him out of his misery.'

'What did you do to him?'

'Relax,' Cialtie said, 'I simply placed a sleeping coin under his head. I won't kill him unless I have to. It would be handy having a dragon for a pet.'

'Tuan will never be your pet.'

'OK,' Cialtie sighed. 'I'll kill him then – but not yet. There is a queue and you will be happy to know that you are in it. But first in the queue is your father. Where is he?'

'I was about to ask you that.'

'Oh, I see. I told your daddy that I was going to chop down Mother Tree here if he didn't face me. Let me guess, he didn't tell you he was coming and when you found what he was up to, you hopped on a dragon and beat him here?' Cialtie laughed. 'Oh, that's good. Is anyone else coming?'

I didn't answer.

'That's a maldar rope you're tied with. The Brownies use it for torture.' Cialtie whistled and the rope around my chest tightened. 'I can make you answer.'

The pressure on my chest made it hard to breathe. I replied, 'No', even though I was sure Mom was on her way.

'You are lying,' Cialtie said then he whistled again this time in a lower tone and the rope slackened. 'No matter. Any help leaving Duir on horseback will arrive long after this is done.'

'My father will kill you. You know that's what's going to happen. Ona predicted it. You of all people should know you can't thwart Ona's predictions.'

Cialtie turned on me with such fury that I was sure I had just moved up to the premier spot in his queue. 'Do not presume to lecture me on Ona's prophecies. This is the last prediction; there is none after this. You are right that Ona's predictions cannot be thwarted but there are none to follow this. This prediction can last for ever and all I have to do is rid The Land of the holders of the Duir Runes. With you and your father dead the Banshees will return, and since I will hold the only Duir Rune, the Runelords will be forced to accept me on the Oak Throne. The age of Ona's predictions will last for ever.'

'Let Conor go,' I heard Dad shout as he rode in to the field. 'He has nothing to do with this.'

'Hello brother.' Cialtie spun and drew his sword. 'He has everything to do with this. After I killed you, my plan was to track and kill Conor. It is so much more convenient that he is here. Now get down and let us commence.'

Dad dismounted and slowly drew the Lawnmower.

'I was foolish losing the Sword of Duir,' Cialtie said, 'I so wished to kill you with that blade. You wouldn't lend it to me now, would you?'

In reply Dad adopted an *en garde* position. If this was a fencing match he would have then saluted his opponent, but I had a feeling these guys were going to skip the niceties.

'Do you remember our last swordfight, brother?' Cialtie asked as he turned sideways and extended his sword with his left hand. Thanks to me it was the only one he had. His blade was thinner than the Lawnmower, just like in my dream.

'I do,' Dad said as he advanced on his brother. It wasn't a serious attack, just a preliminary thrust followed by Cialtie's back-handed parry. It was Dad's way of saying, 'Let's get this done.'

'I remember our father,' Cialtie paused and thought, 'or should I say your father, stopped the match before I killed you. Shame – imagine all of the trouble we could have avoided.'

'Is that why you killed him?' Dad said, attacking with a downward sweep that his brother easily deflected to the left.

'Are you still annoyed I killed your father? You just killed mine. I say we are even.' Cialtie threw himself at Dad with a ferocious attack that took him by surprise. He parried, back-pedalled and then stumbled but kept his footing. If I was Cialtie I would have followed it up with another attack but my uncle just stopped and laughed. Was he that confident or was it something else? Was he just past caring?

Dad again looked to me and said, 'Let the boy go.'

'No,' Cialtie replied as he wiped his nose with the stump of his right hand. Then he extended the hand-less arm to me. Around his wrist he wore a tight silver band. 'Even if he leaves here alive he is not leaving with his runehand. Isn't that the law in the Real World – an eye for an eye?'

Dad kinda lost it then. Dahy had always warned us about letting emotions cloud our fighting but I have always found that a little bit of old-fashioned rage can come in handy as long as you don't let your defences down. Dad came at his brother with a series of savage sweeping attacks alternating left and right. He even performed a full pirouette that brought with it 360 degrees of force. Cialtie went down blocking that one but quickly rolled. He was on one knee when Dad came at him with a sledge-hammer attack. Cialtie blocked it above his head and their pommels locked.

'Your fight is with me,' Dad grunted

'Everything is about you, isn't it?' Cialtie said. The strain of his defence showed in his voice.

That's when I saw Cialtie extend his arm. He turned his wrist back and forth. Since he had no hand, I at first didn't recognise the gesture but then it hit me. I shouted, 'Dad, watch out, he has a Banshee blade.'

A short blade shot out and hooked on the band that encircled Cialtie's stump. Dad took no time backing off and luckily wasn't there when the blade sliced through the space he had just occupied.

The sons of Macha, panting, once again faced off.

'If you had come to me earlier, Cialtie, we could have worked something out.'

'You don't get it, do you, brother?' Cialtie said. 'I am not fighting you – I am fighting Ona. I have been Ona's puppet since I was born. There is nothing you or anyone could have done. This now is the only chance I have at a life.'

'I feel sorry for you, brother, I really do, but I can't let you win.'

Dad called up to the tree. 'Mother Oak, can I have a banta stick?'

Above I heard the familiar sound of water being drawn from wood. A perfect fighting-stick-sized branch fell just behind Dad. He picked it up and quickly shaved off the dead small twigs that stuck out from the side.

Sword and sword vs. sword and stick – I remembered Dahy putting me through this muscle-aching drill. I also remembered thinking why do I need to learn that – when will this ever happen? As usual Master Dahy was right.

Cialtie didn't seem as confident as he had been before. Dad performed stuff right out of Dahy's drill book. Anything Cialtie tried was countered like Dad knew it was coming. But then Dad let his left hand drop. Cialtie came around with a full swing of his Banshee blade just as Dad brought the stick up to block. The blade stuck into the wood. Dad pulled the blade down and then kicked Cialtie in the wrist. The Banshee blade broke free from the silver cuff and then with another tug Dad snapped the gold wire that rode up my uncle's sleeve. Dad threw the stick, with the Banshee blade still attached, away and it was sword vs. sword again.

'When I took my Choosing,' Dad said, 'this is what I saw.'

'Fascinating,' Cialtie said. 'How did it end?'

Dad launched himself at his brother, shouting, 'Not well!'

I was forced to watch the sons of Macha do battle and with every thrust and parry I strained my muscles against my bonds. I watched as the man who made me sword-fight with him every week before he gave me my pocket money fought for his life. In my mind's eye I saw us sword-fighting in the backyard and sometimes in the living room and I watched him use the same techniques and tricks he taught me.

The good thing was that Dad was in great shape. Not just because of the dragon blood youth tonic but he had also been practising his swordsmanship. When he first became young again he would draw on me almost every time he saw me. When I finally impressed on him how annoying that was, he started sparring with the young castle guards who couldn't really complain about their king. Dad and Dahy still squared off periodically. The result was that Dad was a better swordsman than Cialtie and it was beginning to show. Cialtie was back-pedalling with every parry. Dad manoeuvred his opponent onto a downward slope. That was Dahy's rule number three – find the high ground.

Dad was now battling like a man possessed. Cialtie successfully turned and got the fight onto even ground and once again the swords-men locked pommels.

'You never studied with Dahy, did you, brother?'

'I've always hated that pompous blowhard,' Cialtie said.

'I thought not,' Dad said, disengaging.

That's when Dad started an attack I was very familiar with. He came at his brother with a high downward swipe. Cialtie parried it off to his right – exactly as Dad expected. Then Dad did the move he always called, The Dahy. His sword kept going to the right. Cialtie fell for the fake. His eyes followed the blade when they should have been looking at the arm. Dad clocked him high in the cheek with his elbow and Cialtie went down. He raised his sword while lying on his back but Dad swatted it out of his hand.

If Cialtie was expecting mercy from his brother, he was mistaken. The time for mercy was over. Dad placed both hands on the hilt of the

Lawnmower and came down on Cialtie like he was going to split him in half. Cialtie raised his right arm and the blade slammed into his stump and then notched into the silver cuff that encircled his wrist. Blood shot from his stump as Cialtie let out a painful grunt – then he whistled twice. The rope around my chest tightened with such a force that I screamed. Dad turned to look at me and that was all the distraction Cialtie needed. Life slowed down as I tried to warn Dad but the rope made it so I couldn't even catch a breath. When Dad's eyes turned back at his brother he saw him holding a knife. Before he could even react, Cialtie pushed the blade into Dad's chest.

I had been fighting the pressure on my ribs but when I saw that I shouted, 'NO!' As the air left my lungs the rope took up the slack and blackness crept into my peripheral vision. The last thing I heard, or should I say felt, was Mother Oak in my head saying, *'Oh no, not Oisin.'*

THIRTY-THREE

MOTHER OAK

For the second time today I came to from unconsciousness without opening my eyes. This time I didn't want to see what was out there. *Make it a dream*, I said to myself, *make it a dream. Let me open my eyes and see my father sitting on the edge of my bed brushing the hair out of my eyes.*

But the chest pain that came with every breath proved to me that this was real. I touched the rough bark at my back to see if Mother Oak was still there. She was and she was … she was crying.

I opened my eyes as leaves fell around me and saw Dad face down on the grass. His chest was tilted up at a strange angle because of the knife still sticking out of it. Another pain hit me in the chest and this pain had nothing to do with the Brownie rope. *Daddy.*

'Conor, be sharp,' Mother Oak shouted into my head. '*He comes.*'

Cialtie staggered into my vision. His right sleeve was torn off and wrapped around his bleeding stump. He plopped down on the ground cross-legged in front of me like he was drunk. Then he leaned in and said, 'Tears for your father, good.'

'You bastard,' I said without looking at him – I couldn't.

'I've been a bastard since the day I was born, nephew, but I was genuine when I said your tears were good. He was a man worthy of tears.'

I looked up and saw tears in Cialtie's eyes. It's a rare thing to see a grown man cry but my uncle's crocodile tears didn't induce any sympathy in me. 'Go to hell,' I said to his face.

'Hell is where I have been,' he replied, standing. 'I have been in a living hell every day since I read Ona's prophecies. I have been marching to the rhythm of her maddening tin drum all of my life.'

'Oh shut up,' I shouted. 'I am so tired of your "this isn't my fault" speech. Save it for someone who doesn't know you.'

'I thought you at least would understand.'

'Oh I understand, Cialtie – I understand that you are an idiot as well as a sadistic bastard. You think because something is written it's done. Well, give me a pen and I'll write – Drop Dead. You did what you did. No one made you do anything. You killed your brother, my father – you. Your son ran to you and instead of hugging him – you chose to stab him – you. I was there. There was no one behind you. You killed Fergal – you. So go peddle your sob story somewhere else.'

'I had hoped to avoid this, nephew. I know you don't believe me but I don't want to kill you. I was saddened when I heard you took your Choosing. I was hoping just to take your runehand but now that you hold a Duir Rune I must kill you. Then I will finally be king, finally be safe.'

I laughed then, or at least I think it was a laugh. I was such a mess of emotions; if you were looking at me I don't know what you would have thought I was doing.

'I'm surprised you find that funny,' Cialtie said.

'You really are an idiot,' I said as I reached in to a small pocket on the side of my tunic. Cialtie raised his sword and stepped back but when he saw what was in my hand he stopped dead in his tracks.

You see, almost immediately after I completed my Choosing all hell broke loose and I never had the chance to talk to anybody about what happened. Since everyone assumed I would pick Duir and inherit the Oak Throne, nobody asked to see my new rune. I hadn't even told Dad. I was worried he was going to be disappointed, so I was waiting for a quiet moment alone to tell him but I never had the chance and now I never will.

I held up my new rune for Cialtie to see. On it was engraved the major symbol of – Cull. 'I'm not the new king – you are,' I said. 'I'm the new Lord of the Hazellands.' I thought of what Dad would have said to that. After the disappointment, he would have laughed at the thought of me being the new Dean of the Hall of Knowledge. I tried to laugh, too, but couldn't.

'You chose Cull?' Cialtie said, stepping forward for a closer look.

'Yes.'

'Then … then I am king.'

'Don't expect me to bow.'

'I'm safe. It is … it is over.'

I held out the rune. He sheathed his sword and came towards me to take it. I don't know what possessed me to do what I did. It might have been some sort of subliminal message from Mother Oak but I think it was just me remembering what she had said earlier about giving Cialtie 'a piece of my mind'. All I know is that at that moment I needed Cialtie to talk with the family tree. As he reached for my rune I dropped it, grabbed my uncle's wrist and pushed it against Mother Oak's trunk. Both he and I stuck to the bark like we were steel touching an electromagnet.

I recognised the sensation instantly. It was identical to the attack of the oak tree at the perimeter of Castle Duir. The difference was that this time the attention was not directed at me. This time the guy in the hot seat was Cialtie.

The first thing I saw was the circular tree amulet. I had seen a template of it made in silver but I had never seen the one made of gold, the one that was used to obliterate a town. I had watched Cialtie place it on the stump of a tree he had just chopped down. In the centre he placed a small glass bottle, and stopped inside the bottle was a moth. Then he hopped on his horse and galloped out of there. Mother Oak's vision showed both of us what no one had ever seen – no one who lived, that is. Cialtie's amulet bomb went off and the destruction rippled out from the stump. The eerie thing about it was the sound – except for the crashing stones and the screaming people it was silent, even though it looked just like a shot from one of those ground-zero cameras at atomic blasts. It was hard to watch, no … not just hard, it was almost impossible. Admittedly these images were horrible but I was feeling them at a gut level that … I don't know how to describe it. It was so intense, I wasn't sure I could stand it. I screamed and then I heard Mother Oak in my head say, *'Oh I'm so sorry dear, that was not meant for you.'* Swiftly the overpowering intensity lifted. The vision was still forced on me and it was still tough to watch but I was saved the gut-churning emotional power – Cialtie was not.

The destruction of the village of More was followed by Cialtie's seduction of Mná, the Banshee sorceress who became Fergal's mother. I watched with nausea as Cialtie purred while he lied to the poor girl. He promised her he loved her – he promised her she would be his queen. Then I had to watch as her screams of labour were cut short by Cialtie beheading her.

Next came a string of murders: the cowardly attack on my grandfather's horse as he stepped through the portal to the Real World, Ona being smothered by a pillow, the killing of four striking Leprechaun miners as an example to the others.

Then I saw something that really surprised me. A Banshee carrying Dad's severed runehand through the Choosing. Cialtie had been too cowardly to attempt that himself so he promised the Banshee great riches for the attempt. When he succeeded in getting a Duir Rune he was rewarded only with death.

Hundreds of indecencies ranging from rudeness to inflicting debilitating pain flashed by, each one painting a portrait of a poisonous life. In the end Mother Oak did to Cialtie what the oak at Castle Duir had done to me. She showed him what his life could have been like if instead of killing Fergal he had accepted him. She showed a Cialtie walking along a beach with his boy. She showed him hugs and handmade presents and bedtime stories. She made him feel the joy of parenting, the swell of pride, the unconditional love. Then she showed him the truth. I heard Cialtie moan as he relived the stabbing of his son. I moaned with him as I again watched the blade enter Fergal's chest.

'You could have stopped all of this at any time,' Mother Oak said. *'Shame. Shame on you.'*

Mother Oak let us go. I almost blacked out from the emotional roller-coaster I had just been through. Then a sharp pain shot through my broken arm as the Brownie rope was ripped away from me and the tree. I was free. I tried to stand but found out, by falling, that my leg was definitely broken. I fell on my broken arm and once again my brain threatened unconsciousness. I looked across the field and saw the Sword of Duir lying about twenty-five feet away. I looked to Cialtie – he was down on his knees with his face buried in his hands. I started to crawl; it was agonisingly slow and painful. I didn't dare look behind me. I knew as soon as he saw what I was doing I was a goner. I finally got my hand on the pommel and turned to defend myself. I didn't need to.

What I saw was my uncle throwing the end of the Brownie rope up into Mother Oak where it attached to one of her higher boughs. Then he wrapped the other end around his neck and simply said, 'I'm sorry.' He whistled twice and the rope instantly halved in length, breaking his neck with an audible snap. I watched him twitch for a few seconds then slowly swing in the breeze.

Cialtie was wrong. The age of Ona wasn't meant to last for ever. It was meant to end today. Ona's final prediction finally came true. It was written that Cialtie would be killed by the Lord of Duir. The day Cialtie became king was the day he killed himself. We were finally free of Cialtie and Ona – but at what cost?

I crawled over to Dad and pushed him over onto his back. I pulled the knife out of his chest. It wasn't one of Dahy's knives – it was mine. 'Oh Dad, I'm so sorry,' I said as I dropped my head on his chest. A sob sent so much pain through my body I don't remember much after that.

I remember waking up still in the field and Mom was next to me. That was nice. She asked me what had happened and I told her in a dopey matter-of-fact way like it was some TV show I had seen years ago. It felt a lot like that time I killed that guy in the Fililands – my lights were on but nobody was home.

Next thing I remember I was under bedclothes in the infirmary. It was dark and I wondered where I was. A failed attempt to sit up made me realise that my arm and leg were encased in splints. I wondered what had happened to me. Did I fall out of a tree? I looked to my left and saw Tuan in the bed next to me. I was with Tuan, wasn't I? We crashed … Where were we going? Then the memory of the events in Glen Duir flooded back.

'Dad,' I said aloud.

Grief is a leash. I remembered this feeling after Fergal died. My thoughts would drift to the mundane things, the normal stuff of life: idle chat, food or laughter – then I would remember and the leash would stretch taut like a dog in the yard being pulled back by the neck – a crushing sadness and loss would snap me back into that place where my stomach would hurt and laughter was a foreign language. I knew from experience that the leash would grow longer each day but at that moment I found it hard to imagine life with idle anything.

The Imp-healer, the one that Graysea called the Prison Guard, shot up from her night duty desk and came over to me. She lifted up my head and held a shot glass of liquid to my lips. I didn't protest.

As I drifted off to what I hoped was dreamless sleep she brushed the hair from my eyes and said, 'I'm so sorry, Prince Conor.'

The next time I awoke it was daylight. I saw that Graysea was in the bed next to me. Her beautiful innocent face made me smile before the leash of grief snapped my mind back to reality. I gasped and she turned to me.

'Hi Conor, how are you feeling?' she asked.

Grief and pain are cousins to anger. A tiny demon in my brain wanted to yell at her and say, 'How do you think I feel, you stupid trout', but I remembered this from last time as well and I knew that misdirected anger only made things worse. I forced a comforting smile. 'Like I fell off a flying dragon.'

I sat up and saw that Tuan was in the bed to my right. 'How is the dragon?'

'He'll be OK,' she said. 'He broke a few more things than you, though. Your mom gave him something. He's going to be like that for a while.'

'As long as he's going to be OK. I don't think I could stand another …' I couldn't finish that sentence. My brave face was going to need some work. I turned away.

'Oh, you poor sweet thing,' Graysea said as she hopped over to my bed and hugged me. While I wept on her shoulder I was hardly aware of being transferred into another embrace. When I looked up bleary eyed, Essa was looking down at me.

'Oh Conor, I'm so sorry about your father,' she said.

We wept some more – she loved Oisin too.

There would be more tears later but when I finally got control of myself Araf was there with a pot of willow tea.

'Araf hasn't left your side since you were brought in here, except to get the tea,' Graysea said.

'Yeah,' I said, 'you mean he hasn't left *your* side.'

The two of them blushed.

Essa picked up the Cull Rune that was sitting on my bedside table. 'Your mother tells me that this is yours.'

'I'm afraid so,' I said. 'The Prince of Hazel and Oak is now Lord of the Hazellands.'

'I'm not sure what to say,' she said, and then laughed a little. 'Sorry.'

'No, no, I'm there with you, Essa. This is ridiculous.'

'It is not ridiculous, it is … just right,' Mom said.

'Hi Mom.'

'Hello son.'

We locked eyes and I knew what her look meant. 'Later,' it said clearer than any words. 'Later we will grieve but now I must be strong or else I won't be able to go on.'

I clenched my jaw and nodded to her and she nodded back.

'I always thought there was more hazel in you than oak,' she said.

Mom sat on the edge of Tuan's bed and placed her hands on both sides of his head. The Pooka blinked and then opened his eyes. He looked scared but Mom shushed him and told him everything was all right. The Prison Guard helped him sit up. It looked like it hurt – a lot.

When he was settled I said, 'How's it going, Councillor Tuan?'

Tuan tried to turn but it hurt too much. 'Is that you, Prince Conor?'

'It is.'

'No more dragon rides for you.'

'Fair enough,' I said.

Tuan started to cough and it looked like it hurt. The Imp-healer gave him something to drink that brought the colour back to his face, then she sat on the side of his bed and held his hand.

I stared at both of them. 'You and the Prison Guard?'

They both smiled at each other and Tuan shrugged.

I heard the tapping long before I saw the girl. Ruby came around the corner in high-speed mode, which meant she was thrashing her stick back and forth and people were diving out of her way.

'Where are you?'

'I'm here, Ruby.'

She came up to the side of the bed and then hopped on, making me gasp quite loudly.

'Careful, I broke my leg.'

'Oops, sorry. Why don't you get your mermaid girlfriend to fix it?'

'She won't let me,' Graysea said, pointing to the Prison Guard. 'And I'm not his girlfriend any more.'

'He dumped you for the princess, huh?'

'Ruby,' Brendan admonished as he rounded the corner.

'That was rude of me?' she asked from under her huge sunglasses.

Her dad said, 'Yes.'

'Sorry.'

'That's OK, Ruby.' Then Graysea leaned down and whispered, 'For the record, I dumped him.'

Ruby turned to me with a huge smile on her face and said, 'Ha ha.'

'Ruby,' her dad said again.

'Sorry,' the young girl said, but we all knew she wasn't.

'How was your stay in Connemara?'

She wrinkled her nose. 'It rained a lot and the food wasn't as good as here but Mícheál and his wife were nice. They taught me to play dominoes. But I'm glad to be back with Daddy and Grandma.'

'Well, I'm glad you're back. Shall we go for a pony ride when I get better?'

'No trees, though,' she said.

'No trees.'

Brendan picked her off my bed and she swiped her way out of the room.

'Sorry about Oisin,' Brendan said.

My chest was completely black and blue from the Brownie rope but it didn't hurt near as much as when people mentioned Dad. 'Thanks.'

'Who went to Ireland and got Ruby?'

'Nieve and I.'

'Did you get another Guinness?'

'Na. Considering I'm a wanted fugitive I decided against going to a pub and anyway, Nieve had to stay on a horse.'

'Fair enough.'

On cue Nieve came around the corner. She sat on the edge of my bed and took my hand in both of hers. Her eyes were awash with tears.

'You OK, Auntie?'

'I am not sure I know what *OK* means. I lost two of my brothers, I am the last of my generation and the only family I have left is you. OK is one of those strange words that you have brought from the Real World but if I understand it correctly – I am OK as long as I still have you.'

I couldn't actually make words right then but I vigorously nodded yes and we held each other for a time.

Over my aunt's shoulder I saw Dahy standing at the door. He looked ... worried and old – not his usual confident and commanding presence. I waved and said, 'I'm OK, Dahy.'

'Good,' he said lowering his head again and left.

'So,' Brendan said when the leash of grief loosened a bit, 'what are you going to do now?'

'I don't know,' I said. 'I guess I have to build another dolman.'

THIRTY-FOUR

A WAVE

We buried Dad next to Fergal. Gerard sang a dirge and Mom spoke. She talked about meeting Dad at one of Gerard's parties. She admitted that she first fell in love with him when she saw him dance.

Oisin dancing? We were talking about the same guy? Dad dancing, now that's something I'd pay good money to see. But then, as would happen so often for so long, I was stabbed by the reality that never again would I get the chance to see Dad do anything.

I had been asked if I wanted to speak but I said no, I didn't think I could do it. Mom kept up her stoic face through the whole ceremony. Some may have thought she was being incredibly strong but to me she looked like a violin string about to snap.

When it was over, a bunch of burly Leprechauns lifted a capstone up onto two standing stones just like we had for Fergal. When it was done I picked up a pebble and threw it on top of Dad's dolman, and said, 'Goodbye Dad.'

I chose a pebble and handed it to Mom. She looked at it in her hand for a long time until tears dotted the small stone. 'I only just got him back,' she said. Then she threw the pebble onto her husband's monument and collapsed onto my shoulder weeping.

* * *

Fand and I got Mom into bed. The Fili Queen convinced her to take a dram of poteen and she fell into her first proper sleep since the war ended.

'You could probably use a shot yourself,' I said to Fand. 'How are you holding up?'

'Grief, young Conor, is an emotion in which I am well versed. It is a wave that ebbs up and down – and like a wave over time, it diminishes in intensity until – calm. To answer your question, how would you say it? I'm doin' OK.' She smiled and placed her hand on my cheek. 'And you?'

'I wouldn't say I'm OK,' I said, turning away.

Fand placed her hand on my shoulder and said, 'Grief is a wound like any other. And like other wounds, healing takes time. We are fortunate here in The Land to have a surplus of time. Today, tomorrow seems far away but in some future tomorrow you will find peace. May I give you one piece of advice, Lord Conor?'

'Please,' I said.

'There is only one salve I know of that speeds the healing of this particular wound. That salve is forgiveness.'

I wanted to ask her what she meant but in that Fili ninja mystical way, she was almost out the door before I opened my mouth.

That night I had a strange triple date. Essa and I had dinner with Araf and Graysea, and Brendan and Nieve.

I told Nieve what Fand had said and asked her if she could forgive Cialtie.

'I think of Cialtie when he was my baby brother,' Nieve said. 'When I remember him like that it is easy to forgive him. I refuse to believe that my brother was born bad. I know how Ona's writings can push one into bad actions. I almost killed you, Conor, because of them.'

'Ah, water under the bridge, Auntie,' I said with a Fergalish smile.

She tried to return the smile but the weight of her thoughts thwarted her. 'My baby brothers fought and I have lost them both. My sorrow allows no room for hate.'

Brendan put his arm around her and she leant her head on his shoulder. The subject was changed by, of all people, Araf. 'Graysea and I are taking a trip to Mertain Island. I want to talk to the Mertain King about unbanishing Graysea.'

'Wow, that's a big trip. Don't you think you should learn to swim first?'

Graysea turned to Araf. 'You don't know how to swim?'

Araf hemmed and hawed but no actual words came out of his mouth. He did succeed in giving me a look that made me think I was going to get clubbed with a banta next time we were alone.

Believe it or not, I was up before the sun the next morning. I made a pot of tea and knocked on Macha's door. She answered faster than I expected. She was wearing a dressing gown.

'Did I wake you?' I asked.

'Sleep, Conor, has not been my companion as of late. What is this on the tray?'

I cleared my throat and said, 'Grandma, would you like to have tea with me this morning?'

I don't think she would have been more shocked if I had slapped her. 'Yes … Thank you, please come in.'

Her prison was a comfortable room in the east wing. The windows were barred and she had two guards at the door but it was a far cry from the dungeon I initially wished on her. She made space on a coffee table. When she asked me to sit I saw there was only one chair.

'I suppose they assumed I would not be having guests.'

I walked to the door and asked the guard if I could have his chair. He wanted to get me a fancier one but I assured him that his was OK. I returned and sat across from the woman who bore my father. She had poured two cups already and was tasting hers.

'This is lovely, what is it?'

'It's a Pooka blend. Queen Rhiannon sent it to me.'

She sipped some more and a faraway look washed over her face. 'I have never seen the Pookalands. I suppose now I never will. I cannot imagine I will ever be welcome anywhere again.'

I wanted to reassure her, tell her that she was being silly but I couldn't, she was probably right.

'I can't imagine anyone being kind to me ever again after what I have done. You, Conor, here, and with tea, is a shock.'

'Fand told me I should work on my forgiveness.'

'The apple has fallen far from the tree with that one.'

'Yeah, Fand is great. Saying that, her mother did a noble thing in the end.'

'You think killing one's self is noble?' Macha asked.

'I'm not sure about that but I do know that continuing the way she was going would have been wrong.'

'What is right and what is wrong is in the purview of the victors.'

'I've heard that before and I don't buy it. I think right and wrong is easier than that. I watched Maeve rip out a man's heart. Some things are just plain wrong.'

'Like kidnapping a young girl?'

My instinct was to reply, 'Yes', but I bit my tongue. 'I didn't come here to judge.'

'Why are you here, Conor?'

'I thought you might like to visit your sons' graves.'

I picked up a pebble and threw it on top of Fergal's dolman.

'Is that Cialtie's grave?' Macha asked.

'No, that's Cialtie's son's … your grandson. His name was Fergal.'

There was an awkward moment with neither of us knowing what to say. The uncomfortable silence was broken by a voice behind us.

'Hello Mother.'

Macha turned and was stunned to see her daughter holding a wooden box. Then she dropped her gaze and said, 'Nieve.'

Nieve stepped up to her mother and kissed her on the cheek. Macha tensed up like she was expecting a blow. There was history between these two women that existed long before recent events. 'I too, Mother,' Nieve said, 'am working on my forgiveness.'

Macha said nothing but her eyes filled up.

We walked over to a corner of the courtyard where a hole had been dug. Nieve opened the lid on her box and said, 'This is what is left of Cialtie.'

Cialtie's body had been cremated. Mom thought his ashes should be scattered, but after talking with Fand, Nieve argued that regardless of what we thought of him he did at one time sit on the Oak Throne and should be buried in Castle Duir. Mom acquiesced and we all agreed that maybe we should keep the grave unmarked until tempers cooled down.

Macha reached into the box and then placed a handful of the dust that was once her son into the grave. 'Goodbye, my Cialtie.'

Nieve poured in the rest of the remains and then left after I finished shovelling the dirt back into the hole.

As I walked my grandmother back to the castle, I threw a stone on top of Dad's dolman.

'Why do you do that?' Macha asked.

'It's what they do in Ireland. I do it just as a way of remembering.'

Macha picked up a pebble and said, 'Goodbye, my Oisin.' Then she threw the stone and missed. She placed her hand in front of her mouth trying to hide the flood of emotions but then succumbed to them. She plopped down on the path cross-legged like a little girl.

I didn't know what to do. I sat down across from her and took her hand in mine. When she finally looked at me her face was streaked with tears. I don't think I had ever seen a more wretched face on a woman.

'I have been a failure as a mother.'

Again my immediate instinct was to say, 'No', but that would have been a lie.

'I was a failure as a wife and a queen.' She placed her hand tenderly on my cheek, 'And as a grandmother. I have wasted my life loving the wrong men and now they are all dead because of me.' Then she dropped her chin onto her chest and said in a voice so low I almost didn't hear, 'Except Dahy, and he cannot even look at me.'

'You know Dad said something to me that I am using at the moment. He said, "No matter how dark things become, eventually they do get better."'

She looked me in the eyes and forced a smile. 'You are a good boy, Conor. You and my daughter have been kind to me but I do not believe there will be many more so forgiving … And who can blame them.' She dropped her head again and said, 'The Pookas think that when we die we are reborn. Maybe next time I can be … good.'

'What are you talking about?'

'I would like you to find someone who could escort me to Thunder Bay. I would like to sail off into the great unknown.'

Helping someone kill themselves went against everything the mortal me believed in, but here we were immortals and the only option for death was sailing out to sea. To sail past the vitalising power that was The Land. I didn't know what to say. Luckily, I didn't have to say anything.

'I will take you, Macha,' Dahy said. He was standing off to our left. I suspect he had been watching us ever since I escorted Macha from her room.

Macha's head snapped towards the old master. She quickly stood and brushed her dress flat and wiped her eyes. 'That is very kind of you, Diddo,' she said.

The days passed like Fand warned me they would. Some were good and some were bad. Mom dragged me out for regal duties when some visiting Runelord appeared. It made my heart ache when I instinctively turned to smile with Dad only to find the Oak Throne empty.

Eventually the Runelords ordered a meet to discuss the House of Duir. It was decided that since no one held an Oak Rune that Castle Duir should be queened by Mom. It was not a unanimous vote. Some objected to someone from the House of Cull controlling the gold stipend but most of the Lords realised that without a rune the Leprechauns wouldn't follow anyone except their warrior queen. I was just glad nobody tried to foist the job on me.

After the meeting Mom and I were left alone in the Throne Room. She looked tired and I pointed to the Oak Throne and said, 'Well, my Queen, why don't you have a seat?'

Mom sat down on the dais steps and said, 'No, that is your father's chair. I'm only here stopping this place from crashing into chaos until someone chooses the Duir Rune. I suspect it won't be long. Master Eirnin told me that half of the un-runed Faeries in The Land have booked Choosing classes with him.'

'Rather them than me,' I said and sat next to her. 'Well, I think you're a great queen.' I raised an imaginary glass and toasted, 'May ye reign for ever.'

'Oh gods no, Conor,' she said placing her head on my shoulder and wrapping her arm around mine. 'I do not want this job for ever. I'm only doing this because Oisin would have wanted me to. If I had my choice I would lose myself in the Fililands. I would go someplace where I wasn't reminded of your father at every corner.'

'Dad always said, "Things do get better."'

'He also said he would never leave me and now he has left me twice.' She tried to smile with that line but failed. 'I hope someone chooses an Oak Rune soon – so I can maybe come and join you.'

'Me?' I said. 'Where am I going?'

She stood, placed her hands on her hips and put on her Queen Deirdre face. 'You, young man, have a kingdom to rule.'

I slouched on my step. 'Aw, Mom.'

THIRTY-FIVE

BEGINNINGS

You would think that since marriages around here have the potential to last centuries that the service would be longer than five minutes. Like some ceremony from America's old west, the Tir na Nogian wedding vows are practically, 'Take him? Take her? You're hitched.'

Not that I'm complaining. The faster the ceremony then the sooner we could start with the reception party. And since the reception was being thrown by the father of the bride and The Land's best party thrower, Gerard, then all of that 'Till death do us part,' stuff is something to get through quickly.

Yes, Essa and I got married. Hell, if attempted homicides, Banshee fiancés, Mermaids and even wars couldn't keep us apart then we figured – why fight it any more?

Gerard cracked open the wine that he had been saving since Essa was in the womb and we all had the most amazing vinous experience of our lives.

I wouldn't say it was a typical wedding. My best man, Araf, had a banta stick fight with my beautiful bride and beat her. Tuan got very drunk and started running and barking in his wolfhound mode. When he bit one of the guests, Graysea had to be called in to use her fish power to sober him up before he turned into a sloshed dragon and burned the place down. Jesse's Brownie entourage was caught stealing the Nikes that the Connemara Druids had bought me as a wedding present. I had the Brownies locked in a dungeon.

The only one missing was Dahy. He had escorted Macha to Thunder Bay a week earlier. I had hoped he would be back. When I mentioned it to Brendan he said something that sent a chill down my spine. He said he got the impression that Dahy was going to sail out to sea with her. Gods, I hoped not. I couldn't lose Dahy too.

Gerard caught me before the night ended and asked me if I wanted a beer.

'No thanks,' I said, 'I never thought I would say this but this wine is better than any beer.'

Gerard bowed a low bow and said, 'That is high praise indeed, Lord of the Hazellands.' Then he wrapped his huge arms around me and applied one of his anaconda-like hugs that lifted me off the ground and threatened to permanently damage my respiratory system. He released me but still held me at arm's length. 'I always wanted a son,' he said, his eyes getting misty, 'and you have just lost a father. No man can ever replace Oisin. Your father was a great man, Conor. But know this – I will always be here for you.'

This time it was my turn to mist up and attack *him* with a bear hug.

We let it be known the first order of business in the recovering Hazellands was to start a new junior school. Nora and Nieve shared the major teaching duties and half a dozen families took us up on the offer. Ruby now had classmates to boss around and hopefully that would stop her from getting me into trouble.

I convinced Lorcan to come and supervise the rebuilding of the Hall of Knowledge. If I was going to be in charge of creating a Tir na Nog university then I needed the very best builder/architect for the job. His one condition – I never call him Lorcan the Leprechaun again. I'll keep to that – until he's finished.

Tuan agreed to make his home in the Hazellands too. He is teaching Pooka studies and advanced critter morphing. Brendan is on a monthly commute between running the armoury in Duir and coming to the Hazellands to teach archery and spend time with Ruby. 'Even in Pixieland I can't avoid a long commute to work,' he complains.

Graysea teaches swimming and her first pupil was Araf. Every time I saw him walking back dripping from the pond I would hide so he wouldn't kill me.

Araf and Essa are really in their elements. Araf teaches agriculture and flower arranging as well as supervising The Field. Essa became professor of winemaking and banta-stick fighting.

Dahy had been gone for months when he showed up in the Hazellands. Weeks ago I had given him up as lost at sea.

'I thought you had sailed off and become a Grey One and more,' I said when he showed up in my temporary office in the ruins of the Hall of Knowledge.

'I will not lie to you, Conor, I came very close to doing just that but then I remembered your grandfather Liam and how he so loved this place and I had to help you restore it.'

Dahy wasn't a huggy kind of guy but I hugged him anyway. He even kind of returned it with a little pat on the back. 'Thanks Diddo, I need you.'

When I stepped back there was a scary look on the old master's face. 'Just because you are a Runelord now,' he said, 'doesn't mean you can call me Diddo.'

'Sorry, Master Dahy,' I quickly replied as I backed out of striking distance.

On the morning of the first day of the very first autumn term at the Hall of Knowledge University, Essa met me at the door and said, 'What the hell is that thing hanging around your neck?'

'It's a tie. It's what professors wear when they go to work in the Real World.'

'Well, I think it looks stupid,' she said.

'I always thought so too but today I need all of the psychological support I can get.'

'I have no idea what psychological means but I will always support you, my prince.' She kissed me and then hopped into the house and came back with a box tied with a bow.

'What's this?'

'I asked Nora what you are supposed to give as a gift to a first-day teacher.'

I undid the bow and smiled as I looked down at a beautiful shiny apple.

'Oh, and you get this too.' She kissed me, bade me good luck and pushed me out the door.

I walked into the central courtyard and stood before the new Tree of Knowledge. It was still young but it was lush and well over two storeys high. I placed my hand on the trunk and asked, 'Are you going to wish me luck too?'

Hazels are much too cool to actually converse with the Hawathiee but I could have sworn I felt an approving nod.

When I turned to leave I saw that Nieve had been watching me.

'You're not going to throw a spear at me, are you?'

My aunt walked towards me, took my face in her hands and kissed my forehead. 'No, I was going to do this.' She hooked her arm into mine and walked me to the new classrooms. It was fitting that Nieve was with me. The moment I first set eyes on her was the beginning of all the madness that I now just call life. 'Your father would be very proud, Conor.'

'My father, when he found out what I was teaching, would laugh his butt off.'

Nieve laughed with me. 'He probably would, but he still would have been very proud. I'm actually a little surprised you are teaching a course. I would have thought you would have been too busy.'

'Oh, I am too busy but I refuse to be relegated to ministerial paperwork and manuscript filing. I wanted to teach a course on joke-telling but no one would let me. Even when I pointed out I was the Lord of the Hazellands, they still wouldn't let me.'

We arrived at the classroom door. She brushed some lint off of my shoulder and then reached for my tie. 'What is this around your neck?'

'I'm not even going to explain it to you Auntie, 'cause I'm never going to wear one again. Do you want to come in and watch my first day as a professor?'

'No, Brendan and I are soon leaving for Castle Duir.'

'You know I would love to have you here, Nieve, but I'm glad you are helping Mom.'

She kissed me again, 'Are you all prepared?'

'Oh, if there is one thing Dad prepared me for – it's teaching this class.'

My students all stood and came to attention when I walked into the room. There was half a dozen: four Faeries, one female Imp and, I was glad to see, a nervous looking Banshee. They were all bright-eyed and young. They had taken this course in hopes of soon going on a Real World walk-about.

'Sit, sit,' I said, 'there is none of that bowing stuff in here. In here I am not Lord Anything.' I scratched my name on the blackboard behind me. 'I am Mister Conor O'Neil. You can call me by my first name – Mister.'

I looked for a reaction and got nothin'. Maybe it was a good thing I wasn't teaching joke-telling.

'Right, welcome to my class – Modern Real World Languages. I know you're not going to like it much but I'm going to teach you the way I learned. So,' I took a deep breath and when I spoke I surprised myself at just how much I sounded like my father. 'The language of the day is – Greek.'

AUTHOR'S NOTE

I started to write the story that would become *Shadowmagic* just to see if I could. I'm sure that like a million other would-be novelists out there I probably would have given up after a score of pages if not for my son Finbar. As soon as I began to read him my daily crop of words as a bedtime story his insistence to know what was going to happen next was the reason I persevered. I thank him for that and also for making me so very proud. (Check out the Ogham runes at the front and back of this book – the child that I first read *Shadowmagic* to is now a talented professional graphic artist.)

Shadowmagic would have been a private manuscript known only to me and my nearest and dearest if not for Evo Terra and all at www.podiobooks.com. Evo's amazing website allowed me and hundreds of authors to give voice to their creations and let them run free over the interwebs. The thousands of uplifting emails I received from podiobooks' listeners allowed me to believe that I was actually pretty good at this and helped me keep writing book two and three after my son was too old for bedtime stories.

Then Scott Pack and the wonderful team at The Friday Project believed in me enough to put my name on the spine of a book – for which I am eternally grateful.

Anyone who has ever received an illegible piece of correspondence from me will know that these books could never have happened without a team of great proofreaders. I have few regrets in life but one is that my first proofreader, my late wife Caroline, never got to see *Shadowmagic* in print. She would have been so pleased (and probably shocked).

I met my partner Nadene partly through *Shadowmagic*. She is a wonderful mix of fan and critic – just one of the many reason's I dedicated Hazel and Oak to her.

And then there is Yvonne Light – the uber-hyphenator who took on the ordeal of editing my early drafts and still managed to retain her beautiful smile.

Lastly thank you so much for all of the correspondence I have received at john@shadowmagic.com. One only needs naiveté to write a first novel but it takes confidence to write another. Your emails gave me the belief that I could tell stories worth reading and I thank you for that.